PENGUIN BOOKS

THE THREE MUSKETEERS

ALEXANDRE DUMAS was born in 1802 at Villers-Cotterêts and was only four when his father, a general in the French republican army, died. Dumas received little formal education; as a teenager he became a copying clerk for the local notary, and he developed voracious reading habits. At eighteen he discovered the theater, started an amateur theater group, and began writing plays. A few years later, in Paris, he entered the service of the duc d'Orleans as a secretary and continued writing plays, which eventually brought him his first literary success. In 1839 Dumas turned to writing historical novels, often using collaborators to suggest plots or historical backgrounds, but always transforming their drafts—and the historical record—into something utterly his own. Highly prolific, he was one of the first writers of serial fiction in France, a form that suited his dramatic skills. *The Three Musketeers* was first published in 1844, followed a year later by a sequel, *Twenty Years After*. His many other novels include *The Count of Monte Cristo*, *The Man in the Iron Mask*, and *The Black Tulip*. He died in 1870.

RICHARD PEVEAR, with his wife, Larissa Volokhonsky, translated Leo Tolstoy's *Anna Karenina* (winner of the PEN/Book-of-the-Month Club Translation Prize) as well as the work of Mikhail Bulgakov, Fyodor Dostoevsky, Nikolai Gogol, and Anton Chekhov, from the Russian. He has also translated from the French, Italian, and Greek. Originally from Boston, he now lives in Paris, where he teaches at the American University of Paris.

THE
THREE
MUSKETEERS

by

ALEXANDRE DUMAS

TRANSLATED BY
RICHARD PEVEAR

PENGUIN BOOKS

PENGUIN BOOKS

Published by the Penguin Group

Penguin Group (USA) Inc., 375 Hudson Street, New York, New York 10014, U.S.A.

Penguin Group (Canada), 90 Eglinton Avenue East, Suite 700, Toronto,
Ontario, Canada M4P 2Y3 (a division of Pearson Penguin Canada Inc.)

Penguin Books Ltd, 80 Strand, London WC2R 0RL, England

Penguin Ireland, 25 St Stephen's Green, Dublin 2, Ireland (a division of Penguin Books Ltd)

Penguin Group (Australia), 250 Camberwell Road, Camberwell,
Victoria 3124, Australia (a division of Pearson Australia Group Pty Ltd)

Penguin Books India Pvt Ltd, 11 Community Centre,
Panchsheel Park, New Delhi – 110 017, India

Penguin Group (NZ), 67 Apollo Drive, Rosedale, Auckland 0632,
New Zealand (a division of Pearson New Zealand Ltd)

Penguin Books (South Africa) (Pty) Ltd, 24 Sturdee Avenue,
Rosebank, Johannesburg 2196, South Africa

Penguin Books Ltd, Registered Offices:
80 Strand, London WC2R 0RL, England

First published in the United States of America by Viking Penguin,
a member of Penguin Group (USA) Inc. 2006
Published in Penguin Books 2007
This edition published 2011

1 3 5 7 9 10 8 6 4 2

Translation and introduction copyright © Richard Pevear, 2006
All rights reserved

THE LIBRARY OF CONGRESS HAS CATALOGED THE HARDCOVER EDITION AS FOLLOWS:
Dumas, Alexandre, 1802–1870.
[Trois mousquetaires. English]
The three musketeers / by Alexandre Dumas ; translated
with an introduction by Richard Pevear.
p.   cm.
ISBN 0-670-03779-6 (hc.)
ISBN 978-0-14-310500-8 (pbk.)
ISBN 978-0-14-312084-1 (pbk. movie tie-in)
1. France—History—Louis XIII, 1610–1643—Fiction.   2. Swordsmen—Fiction.
I. Title: 3 musketeers.   II. Pevear, Richard, 1943–   III. Title.
PQ2228.A355   2006
843'.7—dc22   2005058468

Printed in the United States of America
Set in Sabon • Designed by Elke Sigal

Contents

THE THREE MUSKETEERS

Preface

IN WHICH IT IS ESTABLISHED THAT, DESPITE THEIR
NAMES ENDING IN -OS AND -IS, THE HEROES OF THE
STORY WE SHALL HAVE THE HONOR OF TELLING
OUR READERS ARE IN NO WAY MYTHOLOGICAL

About a year ago, while doing research in the Royal Library
for my history of Louis XIV, I chanced upon the *Memoirs of
Monsieur d'Artagnan,* printed—like most works of that period, when authors were anxious to tell the truth without going for a more or less long turn in the Bastille—in Amsterdam, by
Pierre Rouge. The title appealed to me: I took the book home,
with the librarian's permission, of course, and devoured it.

I have no intention of making an analysis of this curious
work here, and will content myself with recommending it to
those of my readers who appreciate period pieces. They will
find portraits in it penciled with a masterly hand, and though
these sketches are most often drawn on barracks doors and the
walls of taverns, they will nonetheless recognize the images of
Louis XIII, Anne d'Autriche, Richelieu, Mazarin, and most
of the courtiers of the time, of as good a likeness as in
M. Anquetil's history.

———✹———

But, as we know, what strikes the capricious mind of the poet
is not always what impresses the mass of readers. Now, while
we admire, as others no doubt will, the details we have pointed
out, the thing that concerned us most was something to which
quite certainly no one before us has paid the least attention.

D'Artagnan tells us that at his first visit to M. de Tréville,
the captain of the king's musketeers, he met in his antechamber three young men serving in the illustrious corps into which
he was requesting the honor of being received, and who were
named Athos, Porthos, and Aramis.

We admit that these three strange names struck us, and it
immediately occurred to us that they were merely pseudonyms

I

by means of which d'Artagnan had disguised possibly illustrious names, if the bearers of these borrowed names had not chosen them for themselves on the day when, out of caprice, discontent, or lack of fortune, they had donned the simple tabard of a musketeer.

From then on we could not rest until we had found, in works of that time, some trace of these extraordinary names which had so strongly aroused our curiosity.

The mere catalogue of the books we read through in order to reach that simple goal would fill a whole installment, which might well be highly instructive, but would surely not be very amusing for our readers. We will content ourselves, therefore, with telling them that at the moment when, discouraged by so many fruitless investigations, we were about to abandon our research, we finally found, with the guidance of our illustrious and learned friend Paulin Paris, a folio manuscript, shelf-marked number 4772 or 4773, we no longer remember very well, with the title:

Memoirs of M. le comte de La Fère, concerning some events
that transpired in France towards the end of the reign of King Louis XIII
and the beginning of the reign of King Louis XIV.

One may imagine how great our joy was when, in leafing through this manuscript, our last hope, we found on the twentieth page the name of Athos, on the twenty-seventh page the name of Porthos, and on the thirty-first the name of Aramis.

The discovery of a completely unknown manuscript, in a period when historical science has been raised to such a high level, seemed almost miraculous to us. Thus we hastened to request permission to have it printed, with the aim of presenting ourselves to the Academy of Inscriptions and Belles-Lettres with other men's baggage, if we should not succeed, as is highly likely, in entering the French Academy with our own. This permission, we must say, was graciously granted; which fact we record here in order to give a public refutation to those malicious persons who claim that we are living under a government which is not especially well disposed towards men of letters.

Today we offer our readers the first part of this precious manuscript, giving it a more suitable title, with the commitment that if, as we have no doubt, this first part obtains the success it merits, we will shortly publish the second.

In the meantime, as a godfather is a second father, we invite the reader to lay the blame on us, and not on the comte de La Fère, for his pleasure or his boredom.

That said, let us go on to our story.

The Three Musketeers

I

The Three Presents
of M. d'Artagnan Sr.

On the first Monday of the month of April 1625, the village of
Meung, where the author of the *Romance of the Rose* was
born, seemed to be in as total an upheaval as if the Huguenots
had come to make a second La Rochelle. Many of the townsmen, seeing women fleeing along the main street, hearing children crying on the doorsills, hastened to put on their
breastplates and, backing up their somewhat uncertain coun-
tenances with a musket or a partisan, headed for the Jolly
Miller Inn, before which jostled a compact group, noisy, full of
curiosity, and growing every minute.

At that time panics were frequent, and few days passed
without one town or another recording some such event in its
archives. There were lords who fought among themselves; there
was the king who made war on the cardinal; there was the
Spaniard who made war on the king. Then, besides these hidden or public, secret or open wars, there were also the robbers,
the beggars, the Huguenots, the wolves, and the lackeys, who
made war on everybody. The townsfolk always took up arms
against the robbers, against the wolves, against the lackeys—
often against the lords and the Huguenots—and sometimes
against the king—but never against the cardinal or the Spaniard.
The result of this acquired habit thus was that, on the first
Monday of the month of April 1625, the townsmen, hearing
noise, and seeing neither the yellow-and-red standard, nor the
livery of the duc de Richelieu, rushed for the Jolly Miller Inn.

Arrived there, each of them could see and identify the
cause of the stir.

A young man . . . —let us draw his portrait with a single
stroke of the pen: picture to yourself Don Quixote at eighteen,
Don Quixote husked, without hauberk and greaves, Don
Quixote dressed in a woolen doublet whose blue color has

been transformed into an elusive nuance of wine lees and celestial azure. A long, brown face; prominent cheekbones, a token of shrewdness; enormously developed jaw muscles, an infallible sign by which to recognize a Gascon, even without a beret, and our young man was wearing a beret, decorated with a sort of feather; eyes open and intelligent; nose hooked but finely drawn; too tall for an adolescent, too small for a grown man, and whom an inexperienced eye would have taken for a farmer's son on a journey, were it not for his long sword, hung from a leather baldric, which slapped against its owner's calves when he was on foot, and against the bristling hide of his mount when he was on horseback.

For our young man had a mount, and this mount was even so remarkable that it was remarked: it was a Béarnais nag, twelve or fourteen years old, yellow of coat, without a hair in its tail, but not without galls on its legs, and which, though it walked with its head lower than its knees, rendering the application of a martingale unnecessary, still made its eight leagues a day. Unfortunately, the qualities of this horse were so well hidden under its strange hide and incongruous bearing that, in a time when everyone was a connoisseur of horses, the appearance of the abovementioned nag in Meung, which it had entered about a quarter of an hour before by the Beaugency gate, caused a sensation the disfavor of which reflected back on its rider.

And this sensation had been all the more painful to the young d'Artagnan (as the Don Quixote of this other Rosinante was called), in that he was unable to conceal the ridiculous side lent to him, good horseman that he was, by such a mount; indeed, he had sighed deeply on accepting the gift of it from M. d'Artagnan Sr. He was not unaware that such a beast was worth at least twenty livres; but in truth the words that had accompanied the gift were beyond price.

"My son," the Gascon gentleman had said, in that pure Béarnais patois of which Henri IV had never managed to rid himself, "my son, this horse was born in your father's house some thirteen years ago, and has remained there ever since, which should bring you to love it. Never sell it, let it die peacefully and honorably of old age, and if you go on campaign with it, handle it as you would an old servant. At court," M. d'Artagnan Sr. went on, "if you should have the honor of going there, an honor to which, moreover, your old nobility entitles you, uphold worthily your gentleman's name, which has been borne worthily by your ancestors for more than five hundred years. For you and yours—by yours I mean your relations and your friends—never bear with anything except from M. le cardinal and the king. It is by his courage, understand me well, it is by his courage alone that a gentleman makes his way nowadays. He who trembles for a second may let the bait escape which, for just that second, fortune held out to him. You are young, you must be brave for two reasons: first, because you are a Gascon, and second, because you are my son. Do not shrink from opportunities and seek out adventures. I have taught you to handle a sword; you have legs of iron, a fist of steel; fight whenever you can; fight all the more because duels are forbidden, and therefore it takes twice the courage to fight. All I can give you, my son, is fifteen écus, my horse, and the advice you have just heard. Your mother will add the recipe for a certain balm, which she got from a Bohemian woman, and which has the miraculous virtue of healing every wound that does not attain the heart. Take your profit from everything, and live happily and long. I have only one more word to add, and it is an example I propose to you—not my own, because as for me, I have never appeared at court and only fought as a volunteer in the wars of religion; I mean to speak of M. de Tréville, who was my neighbor once upon a time, and who had the honor while still a child of playing with our King Louis XIIIth, God keep him! Sometimes their games degenerated into fighting, and in these fights the king was not always the stronger. The blows he received gave him much esteem and friendship for M. de Tréville. Later M. de Tréville fought against others during his first trip to Paris, five times; from the death of the late king to the coming of age of the young one, not counting wars and sieges, seven times; and from that coming of age till today, maybe a hundred times! And so, despite edicts, rulings, and writs, here he is captain of the musketeers, that is, head of a legion of Caesars which the king sets great store by, and which the cardinal fears, he who does not fear much, as everyone knows. What's more, M. de Tréville earns ten thousand écus a year; so he is a very great lord. He began like you. Go to see him with this letter, and rule yourself by him, in order to become like him."

Upon which, M. d'Artagnan Sr. buckled his own sword on his son, kissed him tenderly on both cheeks, and gave him his blessing.

On coming out of the paternal chamber, the young man found his mother, who was waiting for him with the famous recipe, a rather frequent use of which would be necessitated by the advice we have just reported. The farewells on this side were longer and more tender than they had been on the other—not that M. d'Artagnan did not love his son, who was his only progeny, but M. d'Artagnan was a man and would have regarded it as unworthy of a man to let himself give way to his emotion, while Mme d'Artagnan was a woman and, what's more, a mother. She wept abundantly, and, let it be said in praise of M. d'Artagnan Jr., despite the efforts he made to remain firm as a future musketeer should be, nature prevailed, and he shed many tears, only half of which he managed with great difficulty to conceal.

That same day the young man set out, provided with three paternal presents, which consisted, as we have said, of fifteen écus, a horse, and the letter to M. de Tréville. The advice, of course, had been thrown in on top of it all.

With such a vade mecum, d'Artagnan turned out to be, morally as well as physically, an exact copy of Cervantes's hero, to whom we so happily compared him when our duties as historian made it necessary for us to draw his portrait. Don Quixote took windmills for giants and sheep for armies; d'Artagnan took every smile for an insult and every glance for a provocation. As a result of which he kept his fist clenched from Tarbes to Meung, and all in all brought his hand to the pommel of his sword ten times a day; however, the fist never landed on any jaw, and the sword never left its scabbard. Not that the sight of the wretched yellow nag did not spread many smiles across the faces of passersby; but since above the nag clanked a sword of respectable size, and above this sword shone an eye more fierce than proud, the passersby restrained their hilarity, or, if hilarity won out over prudence, they tried at least to laugh on one side only, like antique masques. D'Artagnan thus remained majestic and intact in his susceptibility until that unfortunate town of Meung.

But there, as he was getting off his horse at the gate of the Jolly Miller, without anyone, host, waiter, or groom, coming to hold his stirrup at the mounting block, d'Artagnan caught sight, through a half-open window on the ground floor, of a gentleman of fine proportion and haughty bearing, though with a somewhat sullen look, talking with two persons who appeared to be listening to him with deference. D'Artagnan quite naturally believed, according to his habit, that he was the subject of conversation, and he listened in. This time d'Artagnan was only half mistaken: it was a question not of him, but of his horse. The gentleman was apparently enumerating all its qualities to his listeners, and since, as I have said, the listeners appeared to show great deference to the narrator, they burst out laughing every moment. Now, since a half smile was enough to awaken the young man's irascibility, one can imagine what effect this loud hilarity had on him.

However, d'Artagnan wanted first to take account of the physiognomy of the impertinent fellow who was mocking him. He fixed his proud gaze on the stranger and made him out to be a man of forty to forty-five, with dark and piercing eyes, pale skin, a strongly accentuated nose, a black and perfectly trimmed mustache. He was dressed in a violet doublet and knee breeches, with aiguilettes of the same color, without any ornament other than the usual slashes through which the shirt appeared. These knee breeches and doublet, though new, looked wrinkled, like traveling clothes long shut away in a portmanteau. D'Artagnan made all these observations with the rapidity of the most meticulous observer, and no doubt from an instinctive feeling which told him that this unknown man would have a great influence on his life to come.

Now, since at the moment when d'Artagnan fixed his gaze

on the gentleman in the violet doublet, the gentleman was making one of his most learned and profound demonstrations anent the Béarnais nag, his two listeners burst out laughing, and he himself, contrary to his habit, visibly allowed a pale smile to stray, if one may put it so, over his face. This time there was no more doubt, d'Artagnan had really been insulted. And so, filled with that conviction, he pulled his beret down over his eyes, and, trying to copy some of the courtly airs he had picked up in Gascony from traveling noblemen, stepped forward, one hand on the hilt of his sword and the other resting on his hip. Unfortunately, as he advanced, blinded more and more by anger, instead of the dignified and haughty speech he had prepared to formulate his provocation, he found on the tip of his tongue only words of a crude personality, which he accompanied with a furious gesture.

"Hey! Monsieur," he cried, "Monsieur, hiding there behind that shutter! Yes, you! Tell me a little of what you're laughing at, and we'll laugh together!"

The gentleman slowly shifted his eyes from the mount to the rider, as if it took him some time to understand that such strange reproaches had been addressed to him; then, when he could no longer entertain any doubt, his eyebrows knitted slightly, and after a fairly long pause, with an accent of irony and insolence impossible to describe, he answered d'Artagnan:

"I am not speaking to you, Monsieur."

"But I am speaking to you!" cried the young man, exasperated by this mixture of insolence and good manners, of propriety and disdain.

The unknown man looked at him an instant longer with his slight smile, and, withdrawing from the window, slowly came out of the inn to approach within two steps of d'Artagnan and plant himself facing the horse. His calm countenance and mocking physiognomy redoubled the hilarity of the men he had been talking with, who for their part remained at the window.

D'Artagnan, seeing him come, drew his sword a foot's length from its scabbard.

"This horse is decidedly, or rather was in its youth, a buttercup," the unknown man picked up, continuing the investigations he had begun and addressing his listeners at the window, without seeming to notice the exasperation of d'Artagnan, who was nevertheless standing between him and them. "It is a color well known in botany, but till now extremely rare among horses."

"He laughs at the horse who would not dare laugh at its master!" cried the furious emulator of Tréville.

"I do not laugh often, Monsieur," the unknown man picked up, "as you can see yourself from the look of my face; but I nevertheless intend to keep the privilege of laughing when it pleases me."

"And I," cried d'Artagnan, "I do not want anyone to laugh when it displeases me!"

"Indeed, Monsieur?" the unknown man went on, calmer than ever. "Well, that's perfectly fair!" And turning on his heel, he was about to go back into the inn through the main gate, under which d'Artagnan, on his arrival, had noticed an already saddled horse.

But d'Artagnan was not of a character to let a man go like that who had had the insolence to mock him. He drew his sword all the way out of the scabbard and set off in pursuit, shouting:

"Turn, turn then, Mister scoffer, so that I don't strike you from behind!"

"Strike me?!" said the other, swinging round on his heel and looking at the young man with as much astonishment as scorn. "Come, come, my dear fellow, you're mad!"

Then, in a low voice, as if talking to himself, he went on:

"It's too bad. What a find for His Majesty, who is searching everywhere for brave men to be recruited into his musketeers!"

He had barely finished when d'Artagnan lunged at him with such a furious thrust that, if he had not made a quick leap backwards, he would probably have joked for the last time. The unknown man saw then that things had gone beyond raillery, drew his sword, saluted his adversary, and put himself gravely on guard. But at the same moment, his two listeners, accompanied by the host, fell upon d'Artagnan with great blows of sticks, shovels, and tongs. This made so quick and complete a diversion to the attack that d'Artagnan's adversary, while the former turned to face this hail of blows, sheathed his sword with the same precision, and, from the actor he had failed to be, became a spectator of the combat, a role he fulfilled with his ordinary impassivity, though muttering to himself:

"A plague on these Gascons! Put him back on his orange horse and send him on his way!"

"Not before I've killed you, coward!" cried d'Artagnan, still holding up the best he could and not yielding one step to his three enemies, who were flailing away at him.

"Another gasconade," murmured the gentleman. "On my honor, these Gascons are incorrigible! Keep up the dance, then, since he absolutely insists on it. When he gets tired, he'll say he's had enough."

But the unknown man did not know yet what kind of entity he was dealing with: d'Artagnan was not a man ever to cry mercy. The combat thus went on for several seconds more; finally d'Artagnan, exhausted, dropped his sword, which the blow of a stick broke in two. Another blow, which opened up his forehead, brought him down at almost the same time, all bloody and nearly unconscious.

It was at that moment that people came running from all sides to the scene of the event. Fearing a scandal, the host, with the help of his waiters, carried the wounded man to the kitchen, where he was looked after a little.

As for the gentleman, he had gone back to take his place at the window and looked with a certain impatience at the whole mob, which seemed to cause him sharp vexation by staying there.

"Well, how's that wild man doing?" he asked, turning around at the sound of the opening door and addressing the host, who came to inquire after his health.

"Your Excellency is safe and sound?" asked the host.

"Yes, perfectly safe and sound, my dear innkeeper, and it's I who am asking you what's become of our young man."

"He's better," said the host. "He passed out completely."

"Really?" said the gentleman.

"But before passing out, he gathered all his strength to call you out and challenge you."

"Why, then this strapping lad is the devil in person!" cried the unknown man.

"Oh, no, Your Excellency, he's not the devil," the host picked up, wincing with scorn, "for we searched him while he was passed out, and he has nothing in his pack but a shirt and nothing in his purse but twelve écus, which didn't keep him from saying as he passed out that if such a thing had happened in Paris, you would have repented of it at once, while here you'll repent of it later."

"So," the unknown man said coldly, "he's some prince of the blood in disguise."

"I'm telling you this, sir," the host went on, "so that you'll keep on your guard."

"And he didn't name anyone in his anger?"

"Yes, he did. He slapped his pocket and said: 'We'll see what M. de Tréville will think of this insult to his protégé.'"

"M. de Tréville?" said the unknown man, turning all attention. "He slapped his pocket while pronouncing the name of M. de Tréville? . . . Look here, my good host, while your young man was passed out, I'm sure you didn't do without looking in that pocket as well. What was in it?"

"A letter addressed to M. de Tréville, captain of the musketeers."

"Indeed!"

"It is as I have the honor of telling you, Your Excellency."

The host, who was not endowed with great perspicacity, never noticed the expression his words had given to the unknown man's physiognomy. The latter left the sill of the casement on which he had been leaning, propped on his elbow, and knitted a worried man's brows.

"Devil take it!" he murmured between his teeth. "Could Tréville have sent me this Gascon? He's quite young! But a sword stroke is a sword stroke, whatever the age of the one who gives it, and one is less wary of a boy than of anyone else; a weak obstacle is sometimes enough to thwart a grand design."

And the unknown man fell to thinking for several minutes.

"Look here, host," he said, "won't you rid me of this frenetic? In all conscience, I can't kill him, and yet," he added with a coldly menacing expression, "and yet he's a nuisance to me. Where is he?"

"In my wife's bedroom, being bandaged, on the first floor."

"His rags and sack are with him? He didn't take off his doublet?"

"All that, on the contrary, is down in the kitchen. But since he's a nuisance to you, this young fool . . ."

"To be sure. He's causing a scandal in your inn that honest people are unable to stand. Go to your room, make out my bill, and alert my lackey."

"What! Monsieur is leaving us already?"

"You know very well I am, since I gave you orders to saddle my horse. Have they not been obeyed?"

"They have, and as Your Excellency may have seen, his horse is under the main gate, all fitted out for departure."

"That's good, now do as I just told you."

"Hah!" the host said to himself, "can he be afraid of the little lad?"

But an imperative glance from the unknown man brought him up short. He bowed humbly and left.

"The scamp mustn't catch sight of Milady,"* the stranger went on. "She ought to be passing soon; she's even already late. It will decidedly be better if I get on my horse and go to meet her . . . If only I knew what's in that letter to Tréville!"

And the unknown man, muttering all the while, made his way to the kitchen.

During this time the host, who had no doubt that it was the young man's presence that drove the unknown man from his inn, had gone back up to his wife's room and found d'Artagnan finally master of his wits. Therefore, making him understand that the police might give him a bad time for hav-

---

*We know very well that the term "Milady" is used only when followed by the family name. But we find it thus in the manuscript, and do not want to take it upon ourselves to change it. [Dumas's note]

ing sought a quarrel with a great lord—for, in the host's opin-ion, the unknown man could only be a great lord—he per-suaded him, despite his weakness, to get up and continue on his way. D'Artagnan, half-dazed, without his doublet, and his head all swathed in linen, got up then and, propelled by the host, began going downstairs; but, arriving in the kitchen, the first thing he saw was his provoker, calmly chatting away on the footboard of a heavy carriage harnessed to two big Normandy horses.

His interlocutrice, whose head appeared framed by the carriage door, was a woman of twenty or twenty-two. We have already said with what rapidity of investigation d'Artagnan could take in a whole physiognomy; he thus saw at first glance that the woman was young and beautiful. Now, this beauty struck him all the more in that it was perfectly foreign to the southern lands which d'Artagnan had inhabited up to then. This was a pale and blond person, with long curly hair falling on her shoulders, with large, languishing blue eyes, with rosy lips and hands of alabaster. She was having a very lively chat with the unknown man.

"And so, His Eminence orders me . . ." said the lady.

"To return to England this very instant, and to inform him right away if the duke leaves London."

"And as for my other instructions?" asked the beautiful traveler.

"They're contained in this box, which you are to open only on the other side of the Channel."

"Very good. And you, what are you doing?"

"Me? I'm returning to Paris."

"Without punishing that insolent little boy?" asked the lady.

The unknown man was about to respond, but the moment he opened his mouth, d'Artagnan, who had heard everything, came leaping out of the doorway.

"It's that insolent little boy who punishes others," he cried, "and I hope that this time the one he must punish will not es-cape him as he did the first time."

"Will not escape him?" the unknown man picked up, frowning.

"No, before a woman I presume you won't dare to run away."

"Consider," cried Milady, seeing the gentleman reaching for his sword, "consider that the least delay may ruin everything."

"You're right," cried the gentleman. "You go your way, and I'll go mine."

And nodding to the lady in farewell, he leaped onto his horse, while the coachman vigorously whipped up his team. The two interlocutors thus set out at a gallop, moving off along opposite sides of the road.

"Hey, your expenses!" shouted the host, whose affection for his traveler had changed to a deep contempt, seeing him go off without settling his accounts.

"Pay the rascal," the traveler, still galloping, cried to his lackey, who threw two or three silver pieces at the host's feet and went galloping after his master.

"Ah, you coward! ah, you wretch! ah, you bogus gentleman!" cried d'Artagnan, rushing in turn after the lackey.

But the wounded man was still too weak to withstand such a shock. He had hardly gone ten steps when his ears started ringing, dizziness came over him, a bloody mist passed before his eyes, and he fell down in the middle of the road, still shouting: "Coward! coward! coward!"

"He is quite cowardly, in fact," murmured the host, going up to d'Artagnan, and trying by this flattery to make things up with the poor boy, like the heron of the fable with his last night's snail.

"Yes, quite cowardly," murmured d'Artagnan. "But she, she is quite beautiful!"

"She who?" asked the host.

"Milady," babbled d'Artagnan.

And he passed out a second time.

"It's all the same," said the host. "I've lost two, but I still have this one, whom I'm sure to keep for several days at least. That's already eleven écus to the good."

We know that eleven écus was exactly the sum that was left in d'Artagnan's purse.

The host had reckoned on eleven days of convalescence, at one écu a day, but he had reckoned without his traveler. The next day, at five o'clock in the morning, d'Artagnan got up, went down to the kitchen by himself, asked for wine, oil, and rosemary, among other ingredients, the list of which has not come down to us, and, with his mother's recipe in his hand, made up a balm with which he anointed his numerous wounds, refreshing the compresses himself and not allowing the addition of any medicine. Thanks, no doubt, to the effectiveness of the Bohemian balm, and perhaps also to the absence of any doctor, d'Artagnan was on his feet that same evening and very nearly cured the next morning.

But when he went to pay for that rosemary, that oil, and that wine, the master's only extra expenses, because he had kept to a strict fast, while the yellow horse, on the contrary, at least according to the innkeeper, had eaten three times more than one would reasonably have supposed from its size, d'Artagnan found in his pocket only the threadbare velvet purse along with the eleven écus it contained, but as for the letter to M. de Tréville, it had disappeared.

The young man began searching for the letter with great impatience, turning his pockets inside out twenty times, rummaging in his sack again and again; but when he arrived at the conviction that the letter was not to be found, he went into a third fit of rage, which nearly cost him a new consumption of wine and aromatic oil: for, seeing this headstrong young man becoming heated and threatening to smash everything in the establishment if they did not find his letter, the host had already seized a pike, his wife a broom handle, and his waiters the same sticks that had served them two days before.

"My letter of introduction!" cried d'Artagnan, "my letter of introduction, sangdieu! or I'll skewer you all like buntings!"

Unfortunately, one circumstance kept the young man from carrying out his threat: this was, as we have said, that his sword had been broken in two during his first fight, a fact he had completely forgotten. The result was that, when d'Artagnan actually went to draw, he found himself armed, purely and simply, with a piece of sword some eight or ten inches long, which the host had carefully stuffed back into the scabbard. As for the rest of the blade, the chef had skillfully appropriated it for use as a larding needle.

However, this deception would probably not have stopped our hotheaded young man, if the host had not reflected that the complaint his traveler had addressed to him was perfectly just.

"But," he said, lowering his pike, "where indeed is that letter?"

"Yes, where is that letter?" cried d'Artagnan. "First of all, I warn you, that letter is for M. de Tréville, and it must be found; or if it's not found, he'll know how to find it himself!"

This threat thoroughly intimidated the host. After the king and M. le cardinal, M. de Tréville was the man whose name was perhaps most often repeated by the military, and even by townsmen. True, there was of course Father Joseph; but his name was always uttered only in hushed tones, so great was the terror inspired by the Gray Eminence, as the cardinal's familiar was known.

And so, flinging his pike away, and ordering his wife to do the same with her broom handle and his servants with their sticks, he gave the first example by setting out in search of the lost letter himself.

"Did that letter contain anything valuable?" the host asked, after some useless investigations.

"Sandis! I should say so!" cried the Gascon, who was counting on the letter to make his way at court. "It contained my fortune."

"Savings bonds?" asked the worried host.

"Bonds on His Majesty's private treasury," replied d'Artagnan, who, counting on entering into the king's service thanks to this introduction, believed he could make that somewhat rash reply without lying.

"Devil take it!" said the utterly desperate host.

"But never mind," d'Artagnan went on with his national aplomb, "never mind, the money's nothing—that letter was everything. I'd rather have lost a thousand pistoles than that letter."

He would have risked nothing more if he had said twenty thousand, but a certain youthful modesty held him back.

A ray of light suddenly struck the mind of the host, who was sending himself to the devil for not finding anything.

"The letter isn't lost," he cried.

"Ah!" said d'Artagnan.

"No, it was taken from you."

"Taken? But by whom?"

"By yesterday's gentleman. He went down to the kitchen, where your doublet was. He was alone there. I'll bet it was he who stole it."

"You think so?" replied d'Artagnan, little convinced; for he knew better than anyone the entirely personal import of the letter, and saw nothing in it that could tempt greed. The fact is that none of the servants, none of the travelers present could have gained anything by the possession of that piece of paper.

"So you say," d'Artagnan picked up, "that you suspect that impertinent gentleman?"

"I say to you that I'm sure of it," the host went on. "When I announced to him that Your Lordship was the protégé of M. de Tréville, and that you even had a letter for that illustrious gentleman, he looked terribly worried, asked me where the letter was, and went down at once to the kitchen, where he knew he'd find your doublet."

"Then he's my thief," replied d'Artagnan. "I'll complain to M. de Tréville, and M. de Tréville will complain to the king." And he majestically took two écus from his pocket, gave them to the host, who accompanied him to the door hat in hand, and got back on his yellow horse, which brought him without further incident to the porte Saint-Antoine in Paris, where its owner sold it for three écus—a very good price, considering that d'Artagnan had badly overtaxed it during the last stage. The horse dealer to whom d'Artagnan surrendered it for the abovementioned nine livres did not conceal from the young man that he was paying that exorbitant sum only because of the originality of its color.

D'Artagnan thus entered Paris on foot, carrying his little pack over his arm, and walked on until he found a room suited to the scantiness of his resources. This room was a sort of garret, situated on the rue des Fossoyeurs near the Luxembourg.

Having paid down his key money, d'Artagnan took possession of his lodgings and spent the rest of the day sewing braid to his doublet and hose that his mother had removed from an almost new doublet of M. d'Artagnan Sr. and given him in secret. Then he went to the quai de la Ferraille and had his sword fitted with a new blade; then he went back to the Louvre to find out from the first musketeer he met the whereabouts of the hôtel of M. de Tréville, which was located on the rue du Vieux-Colombier, that is, just in the neighborhood of the room d'Artagnan had taken—a circumstance which to him seemed to augur well for the success of his journey.

After which, content with the way he had conducted himself at Meung, with no remorse for the past, confident in the present, and full of hope for the future, he went to bed and slept the sleep of the brave.

This sleep, still quite provincial, stayed with him till nine o'clock in the morning, at which hour he got up to go to this famous M. de Tréville, the third personage of the realm in his father's estimation.

II

M. de Tréville's Antechamber

M. de Troisvilles, as his family was still known in Gascony, or M. de Tréville, as he had ended by calling himself in Paris, had really begun like d'Artagnan, that is, without a penny to his name, but with that wealth of audacity, wit, and understanding which makes it so that the poorest Gascon squireling often receives more from his hopes of a paternal inheritance than the richest gentleman of Périgord or Berry receives in reality. His dauntless bravery, his still more dauntless luck, in a time when the blows poured down like hail, had raised him to the top of that difficult ladder known as court favor, which he had taken four rungs at a time.

He was the friend of the king, who, as everyone knows,

greatly honored the memory of his father, Henri IV. M. de Tréville's father had served him so loyally in his wars against the League that, for lack of ready cash—something the Béarnais lacked all his life, constantly paying his debts with the one thing he never needed to borrow, that is, with wit—for lack of ready cash, as we have said, he had authorized him, after the surrender of Paris, to take for his coat of arms a golden lion passant upon gules with the motto: *Fidelis et fortis.** That did much for his honor, but little for his prosperity. And so, when the great Henri's illustrious companion died, the only inheritance he left his son was his sword and his motto. Thanks to this double gift, and to the spotless name that accompanied it, M. de Tréville was admitted to the house of the young prince, where he served so well with his sword and was so loyal to his motto that Louis XIII, one of the best blades in the realm, got into the habit of saying, if he had a friend who was fighting a duel, that as seconds he would advise him to take himself first and then Tréville, and perhaps even the other way round.

And so Louis XIII had a real affection for Tréville—a royal affection, an egoistic affection, true, but an affection nonetheless. The fact is that, in those unfortunate times, one tried hard to surround oneself with men of Tréville's temper. Many could take as their motto the epithet "strong," which was the second part of his epigraph, but few gentlemen could lay claim to the epithet "faithful," which formed the first part. Tréville was one of the latter; he was one of those rare organizations, of an obedient intelligence like that of a mastiff, of blind valor, of quick eye, of prompt hand, who had been given eyes only in order to see if the king was displeased with someone, a Besme, a Maurevers, a Poltrot de Méré, a Vitry. Finally, all Tréville had lacked till then was the occasion; but he watched out for it, and firmly promised himself to seize it by its three hairs if it ever came within reach of his hand. And so Louis XIII made

*In heraldry, a golden lion on a red background, walking to the right and looking straight ahead, with three paws on the ground and the right forepaw raised. The Latin motto means "faithful and strong."

Tréville captain of his musketeers, who in their devotion, or rather fanaticism, were for Louis XIII what his regulars were for Henri III and what his Scots Guard was for Louis XI.

On his side, and in this respect, the cardinal was not to be outdone by the king. When he saw the formidable élite Louis XIII had surrounded himself with, this second, or, rather, this first king of France wanted to have a guard of his own. Thus he had his musketeers as Louis XIII had his, and these two rival powers were seen in all the provinces of France, and even in all foreign states, selecting men for their service who were famous for great strokes of the sword. And so Richelieu and Louis XIII often argued, during their evening game of chess, over the merits of their servants. Each boasted of the bearing and courage of his own, and while pronouncing themselves aloud against duels and brawling, they quietly encouraged them to go at it, and felt genuine sorrow or immoderate joy at the defeat or victory of their men. So, at least, it is said in the memoirs of a man who took part in some of those defeats and many of those victories.

Tréville had grasped his master's weak side, and it was to that cleverness that he owed the long and constant favor of a king who has not left behind the reputation of having been very faithful in his friendships. He paraded his musketeers before Cardinal Armand Duplessis with a sardonic air that made His Eminence's gray mustache bristle with wrath. Tréville understood admirably well the warfare of that period, when, if you did not live at the enemy's expense, you lived at the expense of your compatriots: his soldiers formed a legion of daredevils, undisciplined for anyone else but him.

Slovenly, tipsy, scruffy, the king's musketeers, or rather M. de Tréville's, spread themselves about the taverns, the promenades, the gambling halls, shouting loudly and twirling their mustaches, clanking their swords, bumping delightedly into M. le cardinal's guards when they met them, then drawing in the middle of the street with a thousand jests; sometimes killed, but sure then of being mourned and avenged; often killing, but sure then of not rotting in prison, M. de Tréville being there to reclaim them. And so M. de Tréville was praised in all tones, sung in all keys by these men who adored him, and who, gallows birds that they were, trembled before him like schoolboys before their master, obeying at the least word, and ready to get themselves killed in order to wipe out the least reproach.

M. de Tréville had used this powerful lever for the king, first of all, and the king's friends—and then for himself and his friends. Moreover, in none of the memoirs of that time, which has left so many memoirs, do we find that this worthy gentleman had been accused, even by his enemies—and he had as many among quillsmen as among swordsmen—nowhere, as we said, do we find that this worthy gentleman had been accused of profiting from the cooperation of his henchmen. With a rare genius for intrigue, which made him a match for the best intriguers, he remained an honest man. What's more, despite great crippling sword strokes and arduous, exhausting exercises, he had become one of the most gallant men about town, one of the most discriminating of ladies' men, and one of the most refined sweet talkers of his time. The successes of Tréville were spoken of as those of Bassompierre had been spoken of twenty years before—and that is saying a lot. The captain of the musketeers was thus admired, feared, and loved, which constitutes the apogee of human fortunes.

Louis XIV absorbed all the lesser stars of his court in his own vast radiance; but his father, a sun *pluribus impar,** allowed each of his favorites his own personal splendor, each of his courtiers his own individual worth. Besides the king's levee and the cardinal's, they counted in Paris then more than two hundred lesser levees that were somewhat select. Among those two hundred lesser levees, that of Tréville was one of the most frequented.

The courtyard of his hôtel, located on the rue du Vieux-Colombier, resembled a camp, starting from six o'clock in the morning in the summer and eight o'clock in the winter. Fifty or sixty musketeers, who apparently took turns there in order to maintain an imposing number, walked about constantly, armed for war and ready for anything. Up and down the length of one

* "unequal to many."

of its great stairways, on the site of which our civilization could build an entire house, moved a procession of Paris solicitors seeking some sort of favor, provincial gentlemen anxious to enlist, and lackeys decked out in all colors, who came to bring M. de Tréville messages from their masters. In the antechamber, on long circular benches, rested the elite, that is, those who had been summoned. A buzzing went on there from morning till night, while M. de Tréville, in his office adjacent to this antechamber, received visits, listened to complaints, gave his orders, and, like the king on his balcony at the Louvre, had only to go to his window to pass men and arms in review.

On the day d'Artagnan presented himself, the gathering was impressive, above all for a provincial fresh from his province: true, this provincial was a Gascon, and especially at that time d'Artagnan's compatriots had the reputation of not being easily daunted. Indeed, once one had gone through the massive door, studded with long, square-headed nails, one landed in the midst of a troop of swordsmen who passed each other in the courtyard, calling out, quarreling, and playing among themselves. To make one's way through all these turbulent waves, one would have had to be an officer, a great lord, or a pretty woman.

So it was through this crush and disorder that our young man advanced, his heart pounding, holding his long rapier to his lean leg, and keeping one hand on his hat brim, with the half smile of a provincial who wants to put on a bold front. Having gotten past one group, he breathed more freely; but he realized that they were turning to look at him, and for the first time in his life, d'Artagnan, who till that day had had a rather good opinion of himself, felt ridiculous.

When he reached the stairway, things became still worse: there were four musketeers on the first steps, amusing themselves with the following exercise, while ten or twelve of their comrades waited on the landing for their turn to take part in the game.

One of them, standing on a higher step, a drawn sword in his hand, was preventing, or attempting to prevent, the other three from coming up.

These other three were fencing with him, wielding extremely agile blades. D'Artagnan at first took their weapons for fencing foils and thought the tips were blunted, but he soon recognized from certain scratches that each blade was, on the contrary, perfectly pointed and sharpened, and at each of those scratches not only the spectators but the participants themselves laughed like fools.

The one who occupied the upper step at this moment kept his adversaries at bay quite marvelously. A circle formed around them: the condition was that at each hit, the one touched would leave the game, losing his turn for an audience to the one who touched him. In five minutes, three were grazed, one on the wrist, another on the chin, another on the ear, by the defender of the step, who was himself unscathed: which skill, according to the agreed conventions, earned him three turns of preference.

Difficult not as it was but as he wished it to be to astonish him, this pastime astonished our young traveler. In his province, that land where all the same heads become so swiftly heated, he had seen a bit more in the way of preliminaries to a duel, and the gasconade of these four players seemed to him the best of all he had heard of up to then, even in Gascony. He thought he had been transported to that famous country of giants where Gulliver went later and got so frightened; and yet he had not reached the end: there remained the landing and the antechamber.

On the landing they no longer fought, they told stories about women, and in the antechamber stories about the court. On the landing, d'Artagnan blushed; in the antechamber, he shuddered. His lively and roving imagination, which in Gascony had made him devastating to young chambermaids and sometimes even to their young mistresses, had never dreamed, even in the wildest moments, of half of these amorous wonders and a quarter of these gallant feats, spiced with the most well-known names and the least shrouded details. But if his love of good morals was shocked on the landing, his respect for the cardinal was scandalized in the antechamber. There, to his great astonishment, d'Artagnan heard criticized aloud the policy that made Europe tremble and the private life of the cardinal, which so many high and mighty lords had been punished for trying to penetrate: this great man, revered by M. d'Artagnan Sr., was a laughingstock for M. de Tréville's musketeers, who jeered at this bandy legs and hunched back. Some sang ditties on Mme d'Aiguillon, his mistress, and Mme de Combalet, his niece, while others got up parties against the cardinal-duke's pages and guards—all things that seemed monstrous impossibilities to d'Artagnan.

However, when the king's name sometimes suddenly came up unexpectedly in the midst of all these cardinalesque gibes, a sort of gag stopped all these mocking mouths; the men glanced around hesitantly and seemed to fear the indiscretion of M. de Tréville's office wall; but soon some allusion brought the conversation back to His Eminence, and then the laughter picked up again even more, and none of his actions was spared the light.

"These men are all sure to be imprisoned and hanged," d'Artagnan thought in terror, "and I undoubtedly with them, for once I've heard and understood them, I'll be held as their accomplice. What would my good father say, who so strongly enjoined respect for the cardinal upon me, if he knew I was in the society of such pagans?"

And so, as you will have guessed without my saying it, d'Artagnan did not venture to involve himself in the conversation; he only looked all eyes and listened all ears, avidly straining his five senses so as to miss nothing, and despite his trust in the paternal injunctions, he felt himself brought by his tastes and led by his instincts to praise rather than blame the unheard-of things that were going on there.

However, as he was a total stranger to the crowd of M. de Tréville's courtiers, and it was the first time he had been glimpsed in this place, someone came to ask him what he wanted. In reponse to this request, d'Artagnan very modestly gave his name, bolstered himself with the title of compatriot, and entreated the valet who had come to ask him this question to request a moment's audience for him with M. de Tréville, a request which the latter promised in a protective tone to transmit in the proper time and place.

D'Artagnan, slightly recovered from his initial surprise, thus had leisure for a brief study of costumes and physiognomies.

At the center of the most animated group was a tall musketeer, of haughty appearance and of a peculiarity of dress that attracted general attention to him. He was not, for the moment, wearing a uniform tabard, which in any case was not absolutely obligatory in that time of lesser freedom but greater independence, but a sky blue jerkin, a bit faded and frayed, and over this garment a magnificent baldric, embroidered in gold, which glittered like the sparkles that scatter over the water in bright sunlight. A long cloak of crimson velvet fell gracefully from his shoulders, revealing only the front of the splendid baldric, from which hung a gigantic rapier.

This musketeer had just come off guard duty that same moment, complained of having a head cold, and coughed affectedly from time to time. That was why he had taken the cloak, as he said to those around him, and while he spoke from his great height, disdainfully twirling his mustache, everyone enthusiastically admired the embroidered baldric, and d'Artagnan more than anyone.

"What can you do," said the musketeer, "it's the coming fashion; it's an extravagance, I know very well, but it's the fashion. Besides, a man has to use his inheritance for something."

"Ah, Porthos!" cried one of those present, "don't try to make us believe that baldric came to you by paternal generosity: it was given to you by the veiled lady I met you with the other Sunday near the porte Saint-Honoré."

"No, on my honor and faith as a gentleman, I bought it myself, and out of my own pocket," replied the one who had just been called by the name of Porthos.

"Yes," said another musketeer, "just as I bought myself this new purse with what my mistress put in the old one."

"It's true," said Porthos, "and the proof is that I paid twelve pistoles for it."

The admiration increased, though the doubt persisted.

"Isn't that so, Aramis?" said Porthos, turning to another musketeer.

This other musketeer formed a perfect contrast with the one who questioned him and who had just called him by the name of Aramis: he was a young man of twenty-two or twenty-three at most, with a naive and sweet expression, dark and gentle eyes, and cheeks as pink and downy as an autumn peach; his thin mustache traced a perfectly straight line on his upper lip; his hands seemed to fear being lowered, lest their veins swell, and from time to time he pinched the tips of his ears to maintain their tender and transparent rosiness. By habit he spoke little and slowly, bowed frequently, laughed noiselessly, showing his teeth, which were fine and of which, like the rest of his person, he seemed to take the greatest care. He responded with an affirmative nod to his friend's appeal.

This affirmation seemed to settle all doubts concerning the baldric; they continued to admire it, but no longer talked about it; and by one of those quick turnabouts of thought, the conversation suddenly went on to another subject.

"What do you think about the story Chalais's equerry tells?" asked another musketeer, not questioning anyone directly, but on the contrary addressing them all.

"And what story does he tell?" asked Porthos in a self-important tone.

"He says he found Rochefort, the cardinal's tool, in Brussels, disguised as a Capuchin. Thanks to this disguise, the cursed Rochefort played M. de Laigues for the ninny he is."

"A real ninny," said Porthos. "But is it certain?"

"I got it from Aramis," replied the musketeer.

"Really?"

"Ah, you know it very well, Porthos," said Aramis. "I told it to you yesterday, so let's not talk about it anymore."

"Let's not talk about it anymore—that's your opinion," Porthos picked up. "Let's not talk about it anymore! Damn, that's a quick end to it! Why, the cardinal has a man spied on, has his correspondence stolen by a traitor, a brigand, a scoundrel; with the aid of that spy and thanks to that correspondence, he has Chalais's throat cut, under the stupid pretext that he wanted to kill the king and marry Monsieur to the queen! Nobody knew a word of this riddle, you informed us of it yesterday, to everyone's great satisfaction, and while we're still all astounded by this news, you come today and say: 'Let's not talk about it anymore.'"

"Let's talk about it, then, since you want to," Aramis patiently replied.

"This Rochefort," cried Porthos, "would spend a nasty moment with me, if I were poor Chalais's equerry."

"And you would spend a sorry quarter of an hour with the red duke," replied Aramis.

"Ah! the red duke! Bravo, bravo—the red duke!" responded Porthos, clapping his hands and nodding in approval. "The 'red duke' is charming. I'll spread the word, my dear, rest assured. He's a wit, this Aramis! Too bad you didn't follow your vocation, my dear! What a delightful abbé you'd have made!"

"Oh, it's just a momentary delay," replied Aramis. "Some day I'll become one. You know very well, Porthos, that I've continued studying theology for that."

"He'll do it as he says," Porthos picked up, "that is, sooner or later."

"Sooner," said Aramis.

"He's just waiting for one thing to decide on it entirely and take back the cassock that's hanging behind his uniform," said one musketeer.

"And what thing is he waiting for?" asked another.

"He's waiting for the queen to produce an heir to the Crown of France."

"Let's not joke about that, gentlemen," said Porthos. "Thank God, the queen is still of an age to produce one."

"They say that M. de Buckingham is in France," Aramis picked up with a sardonic laugh, which gave to this seemingly simple phrase a rather scandalous significance.

"Aramis, my friend, this time you're wrong," interrupted Porthos, "and your compulsive wit always takes you beyond bounds. If M. de Tréville could hear you, you wouldn't speak so unfittingly."

"Are you reading me a lesson, Porthos?" cried Aramis, in whose gentle eye lightning suddenly seemed to flash.

"My dear, be a musketeer or an abbé. Be one or the other,

but not one and the other," replied Porthos. "Look, Athos told you the other day: you sup from all troughs. Ah, let's not get angry, I beg you, it would be useless, you know very well what's been agreed among you, Athos, and me. You call on Mme d'Aiguillon and pay court to her; you call on Mme de Bois-Tracy, the cousin of Mme de Chevreuse, and you pass for being well advanced in the lady's good graces. Oh, my God, don't confess your happiness, no one's asking you your secrets, we all know your discretion! But since you do possess that virtue, devil take it, use it with regard to Her Majesty! Let anyone concern himself with the king and the cardinal if he likes and as he likes; but the queen is sacred, and if we speak of her, let us speak well."

"Porthos, you're as conceited as Narcissus, let me tell you," responded Aramis. "You know I hate moralizing, except when Athos does it. As for you, my dear, you have too magnificent a baldric to be strong on that subject. I'll become an abbé if it suits me; meanwhile I'm a musketeer: in that quality, I say what I please, and at this moment it pleases me to tell you that you annoy me."

"Aramis!"

"Porthos!"

"Ah! Gentlemen! Gentlemen!" cries came from all around them.

"M. de Tréville awaits M. d'Artagnan," the lackey interrupted, opening the office door.

At that announcement, during which the office door remained open, everyone fell silent, and in the midst of the general silence, the young Gascon crossed the antechamber for a good part of its length and entered the office of the captain of the musketeers, congratulating himself wholeheartedly on escaping the end of this bizarre quarrel just in time.

III

The Audience

M. de Tréville was for the moment in a very bad humor. Nevertheless, he politely greeted the young man, who bowed all the way to the ground, and smiled on receiving his compliments in that Béarnais accent which reminded him at the same time of his youth and of his birthplace, a double memory that makes a man smile at any age. But, going towards the antechamber almost at once, and making a sign to d'Artagnan with his hand, as if asking his permission to finish with the others before beginning with him, he called out three times, raising his voice more each time, so that he ran through all the intermediary tones between the imperative and the irritated:

"Athos! Porthos! Aramis!"

The two musketeers whose acquaintance we have already made, and who answered to the last two of these three names, immediately left the groups they were part of and advanced towards the office, the door of which closed behind them the moment they crossed the threshold. Their bearing, though not entirely calm, still aroused d'Artagnan's admiration by its casualness, which was at once full of dignity and of submission. He saw these men as demigods and their chief as an Olympian Jupiter armed with all his thunderbolts.

When the two musketeers came in; when the door was closed behind them; when the buzzing murmur of the antechamber, to which the summons that had just been made had given fresh nourishment, started up again; when, finally, M. de Tréville, silent and frowning, had paced the whole length of his office three or four times, passing each time before Porthos and Aramis, rigid and mute as if on parade, he suddenly stopped in front of them and, looking them up and down with an irritated glance, shouted:

"Do you know what the king said to me, and that no later than yesterday evening? Do you know, gentlemen?"

"No," replied the two musketeers after a moment of silence. "No, Monsieur, we don't know."

"But I hope you will do us the honor of telling us," Aramis added in his most polite tone and with a most graceful bow.

"He told me he would henceforth recruit his musketeers from M. le cardinal's guards!"

"From M. le cardinal's guards! And why would that be?" Porthos asked sharply.

"Because he saw very well that his local vintage needed fortifying with a dose of good wine."

The two musketeers blushed to the roots of their hair. D'Artagnan did not know what it had to do with him and wished he was a hundred feet underground.

"Yes, yes," M. de Tréville continued, growing animated, "yes, and His Majesty is right, for, on my honor, it's true that the musketeers cut a sad figure at court. Yesterday, playing chess with the king, M. le cardinal told us, with an air of condolence which greatly displeased me, that the day before yesterday those damned musketeers, those daredevils—he stressed these words with an ironic accent that displeased me still more— those true destroyers, he added, looking at me with his tiger-cat's eyes, had stayed late at a tavern on the rue Férou, and that a patrol of his guards had been forced to arrest the trouble-makers. Morbleu! you must know something about it! Arresting musketeers! You two were in on it, don't deny it, you were recognized, and the cardinal named you. But it's all my fault, yes, my fault, since it's I who pick my men. Look here, Aramis, why the devil did you ask me for the tabard when you would have done so well in a cassock? Look here, Porthos, have you got such a handsome gold baldric only to hang a straw sword on it? And Athos! I don't see Athos. Where is he?"

"Monsieur," Aramis responded sadly, "he is ill, very ill."

"Ill, very ill, you say? And with what illness?"

"They're afraid it may be smallpox, Monsieur," answered Porthos, who wanted to add a word of his own to the conversation, "which would be regrettable in that it would quite certainly spoil his looks."

"Smallpox! That's another glorious story you're telling me, Porthos! . . . Sick with smallpox, at his age? . . . Not so! . . . but wounded, no doubt, maybe killed . . . Ah, if I'd only known! . . . Sangdieu! you gentlemen musketeers, I don't mean to have you haunting low places like that, picking quarrels in the street and playing with swords at the crossroads. I don't want you, finally, to give the laugh to M. le cardinal's guards, who are brave men, calm, clever, who never put themselves in danger of being arrested, and besides would not let themselves be arrested, not them! . . . I'm sure of it . . . They'd much rather die on the spot than retreat a single step . . . To run away, to bolt, to flee—that's fit for the king's musketeers!"

Porthos and Aramis were trembling with rage. They would gladly have strangled M. de Tréville, if at the bottom of it all they had not felt that it was the great love he bore them which made him speak to them that way. They stamped the carpet with their feet, bit their lips until they bled, and gripped the hilts of their swords with all their might. Outside, as we have said, the others had heard Athos, Porthos, and Aramis summoned, and had guessed, by the accent of M. de Tréville's voice, that he was in perfect wrath. Ten curious heads were pressed against the tapestry and turned pale with fury, for their ears, glued to the door, did not miss a single syllable of what was said, while their lips repeated the captain's insulting words bit by bit to the whole population of the antechamber. In an instant, from office door to street door, the entire hôtel was in turmoil.

"So the king's musketeers get arrested by M. le cardinal's guards!" M. de Tréville went on, inwardly as furious as his soldiers, but halting at each word and plunging them one by one, so to speak, like so many thrusts of a stiletto, into the breasts of his listeners. "So six of His Eminence's guards arrest six of His Majesty's musketeers! Morbleu! I've made my choice! I'm going straight to the Louvre! I shall turn in my resignation as captain of the king's musketeers and ask for a lieutenancy in the cardinal's guards, and if he refuses me, morbleu, I'll become an abbé!"

At these words, the murmur outside became an explosion: everywhere one heard nothing but oaths and blasphemies. The "morbleus," the "sangdieus," the "forty pockmarked devils" crisscrossed in the air. D'Artagnan looked for a tapestry to hide behind, and felt an immense desire to crawl under the table.

"Well, then, Captain," said Porthos, beside himself, "the truth is that we were six against six, but we were set upon treacherously, and before we had time to draw our swords, two of us had fallen dead, and Athos, grievously wounded, was hardly worth more. For you know Athos. Well, Captain, he tried to get up twice, and he fell back twice. But all the same we didn't surrender. No! We were dragged off by force. On the way, we escaped. As for Athos, they thought he was dead, and they left him quite calmly on the battlefield, thinking he wasn't worth carrying off. That's the story. Devil take it, Captain, you can't win every battle! The great Pompey lost at Pharsalia, and King François I, I've heard tell, was as good a man as any, yet he lost at Pavia."

"And I have the honor of assuring you that I killed one of them with his own sword," said Aramis, "for mine was broken at the first parry . . . Killed or stabbed, Monsieur, whichever you please."

"I didn't know that," M. de Tréville picked up in a slightly softened tone. "M. le cardinal was exaggerating, as I see."

"But, for pity's sake, Monsieur," continued Aramis, who, seeing his captain calm down, dared to venture an entreaty, "for pity's sake, Monsieur, don't say that Athos himself is wounded: he would be in despair if it came to the ears of the king, and as the wound is most grave, seeing that after passing through the shoulder it penetrated the chest, it is to be feared . . ."

At that same instant the portière was raised, and a noble, handsome, but dreadfully pale head appeared under the fringe.

"Athos!" cried the two musketeers.

"Athos!" repeated M. de Tréville himself.

"You sent for me, Monsieur," Athos said to M. de Tréville in a weakened but perfectly calm voice, "you sent for me, as our comrades have told me, and I hasten to respond to your orders. Well, Monsieur, what do you want of me?"

And at those words the musketeer, irreproachably dressed, tightly belted as was his custom, entered the office with a firm stride. M. de Tréville, moved to the bottom of his heart by this show of courage, rushed to him.

"I was just telling these gentlemen," he added, "that I forbid my musketeers to risk their lives unnecessarily, for brave men are very dear to the king, and the king knows that his musketeers are the bravest men on earth. Your hand, Athos."

And without waiting for the newcomer to respond to this show of affection himself, M. de Tréville seized his right hand and pressed it with all his might, not noticing that Athos, for all his self-mastery, let escape a wince of pain and grew paler still, which one would have thought impossible.

The door had been left ajar, such was the sensation made by the arrival of Athos, whose wound, despite the well-kept secret, was known to everyone. A hubbub of satisfaction greeted the captain's last words, and two or three heads, carried away by the enthusiasm, appeared through the openings in the tapestry. M. de Tréville was no doubt on the point of sharply reprimanding this infraction of the rules of etiquette, when he suddenly felt Athos's hand clench in his own, and, turning his eyes to him, saw that he was about to faint. Athos, who had summoned all his forces to struggle against the pain, was finally defeated by it, and fell to the floor like a dead man.

"A surgeon!" cried M. de Tréville. "Mine, the king's, the best! A surgeon, sangdieu! or my brave Athos will depart this life."

At M. de Tréville's cries, everyone rushed into his office, for he never thought of closing the door on anyone, each of them coming to the wounded man's aid. But all this concern would have been useless, if the doctor sent for had not been found right in the hôtel itself. He broke through the crowd, approached the still unconscious Athos, and, as all this noise and movement hampered him greatly, demanded first and most urgently that the musketeer be carried to a neighboring room. M. de Tréville opened a door at once and showed the way to Porthos and Aramis, who carried their comrade in their arms. Behind this group came the surgeon, and behind the surgeon, the door was closed.

Then M. de Tréville's office, ordinarily so respected a place, momentarily became a subsidiary to the antechamber. Everyone held forth, declaimed, spoke out, cursing, swearing, sending the cardinal and his guards to all the devils.

A moment later, Porthos and Aramis reappeared; the surgeon and M. de Tréville alone had stayed by the wounded man.

Finally M. de Tréville reappeared in his turn. The wounded man had recovered consciousness; the surgeon declared that there was nothing in the musketeer's condition that should worry his friends, his weakness having been caused purely and simply by loss of blood.

Then M. de Tréville gave a sign of the hand, and they all withdrew, except for d'Artagnan, who had by no means forgotten that he had an audience and who, with a Gascon's tenacity, had stayed where he was.

When everyone was gone and the door was closed again, M. de Tréville turned and found himself alone with the young man. The event that had just occurred had made him lose the thread of his thoughts somewhat. He asked what the obstinate petitioner wanted of him. D'Artagnan then gave his name, and M. de Tréville, recalling at a single stroke all his memories both present and past, found himself informed of the situation.

"Forgive me," he said with a smile, "forgive me, my dear compatriot, but I had completely forgotten you. No help for it! A captain is nothing but the father of a family, burdened with greater responsibility than the ordinary father of a family. Soldiers are big children; but as I insist that the orders of the king, and above all those of M. le cardinal, be carried out . . ."

D'Artagnan could not conceal a smile. At that smile, M. de Tréville decided that he was by no means dealing with a fool and changed the subject, coming straight to the point.

"I loved your good father very much," he said. "What can I do for his son? Be quick, my time is not my own."

"Monsieur," said d'Artagnan, "in leaving Tarbes and coming here, my intention was to ask you, in memory of that friendship which you have not forgotten, for the tabard of a musketeer; but, after all I've seen in the last two hours, I realize that it would be an enormous favor, and I fear I am not at all worthy of it."

"It is indeed a favor, young man," answered M. de Tréville, "but it may not be so far above you as you believe, or as you seem to believe. However, a decision of His Majesty has provided for this case, and I regret to inform you that no one is made a musketeer without the prior proof of several campaigns, of certain brilliant actions, or two years of service in some other regiment less favored than ours."

D'Artagnan accepted without any reply. He felt all the more eager to put on the uniform of a musketeer, since there were such great difficulties in obtaining it.

"But," Tréville went on, fixing such a piercing gaze on his compatriot that one would have thought he wanted to read to the bottom of his heart, "but, for the sake of your father, my old companion, as I have told you, I would like to do something for you, young man. Our cadets from Béarn are ordinarily not rich, and I doubt that things have changed greatly since I left the province. So you must not have much to live on from the money you brought with you."

D'Artagnan drew himself up with a proud air which meant to say that he asked no alms of anyone.

"Very well, young man, very well," Tréville went on, "I know those airs. I came to Paris with four écus in my pocket, and I'd have fought with anybody who told me I was in no condition to buy the Louvre."

D'Artagnan drew himself up still more. Thanks to the sale of his horse, he was beginning his career with four écus more than M. de Tréville had begun his with.

"So, as I was saying, you must have a need to hold on to what you've got, great as that sum may be; but you must also have a need to perfect yourself in the exercises proper to a gentleman. I will write a letter today to the director of the Royal Academy, and as of tomorrow he will admit you without any payment. Do not refuse this small kindness. Our best born and richest gentlemen sometimes seek it without managing to obtain it. You will learn horsemanship, fencing, and dancing; you will make good acquaintances there; and from time to time you will come back to see me and tell me where you've gotten to and if there's anything I can do for you."

D'Artagnan, stranger as he still was to court manners, found a certain coolness in this reception.

"Alas, Monsieur," he said, "I see how great a loss the letter of introduction my father gave me for you is to me today."

"Indeed," replied M. de Tréville, "I was surprised that you should have undertaken such a long journey without this obligatory viaticum, the only resource known to us Béarnais."

"I had it, Monsieur, and, thank God, in fine form," cried d'Artagnan, "but somebody perfidiously robbed me of it."

And he recounted the whole scene at Meung, depicting the unknown gentleman in the minutest detail, and all of it with a warmth, a truthfulness that charmed M. de Tréville.

"That's a strange thing," the latter said, pondering. "So you mentioned my name aloud?"

"Yes, Monsieur, I undoubtedly committed that imprudence; but what do you want, a name like yours was to serve me as a shield on the way: you may judge how often I took cover behind it!"

Flattery was quite an acceptable thing then, and M. de Tréville loved incense as much as any king or cardinal. So he could not help smiling with visible satisfaction, but his smile soon vanished, and he returned to the adventure in Meung.

"Tell me," he went on, "did this gentleman have a slight scar on his temple?"

"Yes, the kind left by the graze of a bullet."

"Was he a fine-looking man?"

"Yes."

"Tall?"

"Yes."

"Pale-skinned and brown-haired?"

"Yes, yes, that's right. How is it, Monsieur, that you know this man? Ah! if ever I find him again, and I will find him, I swear to you, even in hell . . ."

"He was waiting for a woman?" Tréville went on.

"At least he left after talking for a moment with the woman he was waiting for."

"You wouldn't know what the subject of their conversation was?"

"He gave her a box, told her the box contained her instructions, and advised her not to open it until she got to London."

"The woman was English?"

"He called her 'Milady.'"

"It's he," murmured Tréville, "it's he! I thought he was still in Brussels."

"Oh, Monsieur, if you know this man," cried d'Artagnan, "tell me who he is and where he is, and then I won't hold you to anything else, not even your promise to take me into the musketeers; for before all else I want to avenge myself!"

"Don't even try it, young man," cried Tréville. "On the contrary, if you see him coming down one side of the street, cross to the other! Don't hurl yourself against such a rock: he'll smash you like a glass."

"All the same," said d'Artagnan, "if I ever find him again . . ."

"Meanwhile," Tréville picked up, "don't go looking for him, if I have one piece of advice to give you."

Tréville stopped all at once, struck by a sudden suspicion. The great hatred that the young traveler made such a display of for this man who, unlikely as it was, had robbed him of his father's letter—did this hatred not conceal some perfidy? Had this young man not been sent by His Eminence? Had he not come to set some trap for him? Was this would-be d'Artagnan not an emissary from the cardinal whom they sought to introduce into his house, and whom they had placed close to him in order to betray his confidence and to ruin him afterwards, as had been done a thousand times before? He looked at d'Artagnan still more fixedly this second time than he had the first. He was not much reassured by the sight of that physiognomy sparkling with sly wit and affected humility.

"I know very well he's a Gascon," he thought, "but he can

just as well be a Gascon for the cardinal as for me. Come, let's test him."

"My friend," he said to him slowly, "I would like, as for the son of my old friend—for I take the story of that lost letter to be true—I would like, I say, in order to make up for the coolness you noticed at first in my reception, to reveal to you the secrets of our policy. The king and the cardinal are the best of friends; their apparent disputes are meant only to deceive fools. I do not intend that a compatriot, a fine cavalier, a brave lad, made for advancement, should be the dupe of all this trumpery and run his head into the wall like a ninny, in the wake of so many others who have perished from it. Understand well that I am devoted to these two all-powerful masters, and that my serious efforts will never have any other end than service to the king and to M. le cardinal, one of the most illustrious geniuses France has ever produced. Now, young man, rule yourself by that, and if you have, either from your family, or through relations, or even by instinct, any of those hostile feelings against the cardinal such as we see break out among these gentlemen, say good-bye to me, and let us part. I will help you in a thousand circumstances, but without attaching you to my person. I hope that my frankness, in any case, will make you my friend; for up to the present you are the only young man to whom I have spoken as I am speaking now."

Tréville said to himself: "If the cardinal has sent me this young fox, he will certainly not have failed, he who knows how much I loathe him, to tell his spy that the best way to pay court to me is to tell me the worst muck about him; so, despite my protestations, the cunning accomplice is quite certainly going to answer me that he holds His Eminence in horror."

But it turned out quite differently than Tréville expected. D'Artagnan replied with the greatest simplicity:

"Monsieur, I have come to Paris with exactly the same intentions. My father instructed me to bear with nothing except from the king, M. le cardinal, and you, whom he held to be the three foremost men in France."

D'Artagnan added M. de Tréville to the two others, as we can see, but he thought the addition would not hurt anything.

"I thus have the greatest veneration for M. le cardinal," he went on, "and the most profound respect for his acts. So much the better for me, Monsieur, if you speak to me, as you say, with frankness; for then you do me the honor of valuing this similarity of taste. But if you have felt some mistrust, quite natural in any case, I will feel that I am erring by telling the truth. That is too bad, but you will esteem me nonetheless, and I care more about that than about anything else in the world."

M. de Tréville was utterly astonished. So much penetration, so much frankness, finally, aroused his admiration, but did not entirely remove his doubts: the more superior this young man was to other young people, the more he was to be feared if he was mistaken. Nevertheless, he shook d'Artagnan's hand and said to him:

"You're an honest lad, but at the moment I can do no more than what I offered you earlier. My hôtel will always be open to you. Later on, being able to ask for me at any hour and therefore to seize every opportunity, you will probably obtain what you wish to obtain."

"That is to say, Monsieur," replied d'Artagnan, "that you are waiting until I make myself worthy. Well, don't worry," he added with Gascon familiarity, "you won't have to wait long."

And he began bowing his way out, as if the rest was henceforth up to him.

"But wait a moment," said M. de Tréville, stopping him, "I promised you a letter to the director of the Academy. Are you too proud to accept it, my young gentleman?"

"No, Monsieur," said d'Artagnan, "and I give you my word that what happened to the other will not happen to this one. I'll keep it so well that it will arrive at its destination, I swear to you, and woe to him who tries to take it from me!"

M. de Tréville smiled at this fanfaronade, and leaving his young compatriot in the embrasure of the window where they found themselves and where they had talked together, he sat down at a table and began writing the promised letter of introduction. During this time, d'Artagnan, who had nothing better to do, started beating out a march on the window panes, watching the musketeers who went out one after another, and following them until they disappeared around the corner.

M. de Tréville, after writing the letter, sealed it and, getting up, went over to the young man to give it to him; but at the very moment when d'Artagnan held out his hand to receive it, M. de Tréville was quite astonished to see him give a start, flush with anger, and go rushing out of the office, shouting:

"Ah! sangdieu! he won't escape me this time!"

"But who is it?" asked M. de Tréville.

"He, my thief!" answered d'Artagnan. "Ah! the traitor!" And he disappeared.

"Mad devil!" murmured M. de Tréville. "Unless," he added, "it's a skillful means of slipping away, seeing that his attempt failed."

IV

ATHOS'S SHOULDER, PORTHOS'S BALDRIC, AND ARAMIS'S HANDKERCHIEF

D'Artagnan, furious, had crossed the antechamber in three bounds and was rushing for the stairway, where he counted on going down the steps four at a time, when, carried away by his chase, he ran head first into a musketeer who was coming out of M. de Tréville's by a side door, and, butting him in the shoulder, made him utter a cry, or rather a howl.

"Excuse me," said d'Artagnan, trying to race on, "excuse me, but I'm in a hurry."

But he had hardly gone down the first stair when an iron fist seized him by the sash and halted him.

"You're in a hurry!" cried the musketeer, pale as a shroud. "Under that pretext, you butt into me, say 'Excuse me,' and think that's enough? Not at all, my young man. Do you think, because you heard M. de Tréville speak to us a bit cavalierly today, that you can treat us the way he speaks to us? Think again, friend, you are not M. de Tréville."

"By heaven," replied d'Artagnan, recognizing Athos, who, after the bandaging performed by the doctor, was returning to his apartment, "by heaven, I didn't do it on purpose, and I said 'Excuse me.' So it seems to me that that is enough. I repeat to you, however—and this time, on my honor, it may be too much!—that I am in a hurry. Release me, I beg you, and let me go about my business."

"Monsieur," said Athos, releasing him, "you are not polite. One can see you come from far away."

D'Artagnan had already gone down three or four steps, but Athos's remark pulled him up short.

"Morbleu, Monsieur!" he said, "however far away I come from, it is not for you to give me a lesson in good manners, let me tell you."

"Perhaps," said Athos.

"Ah! if I wasn't in such a hurry," cried d'Artagnan, "and if I wasn't running after someone . . ."

"Monsieur-in-a-hurry, you will find me without having to run, understand?"

"And where is that, if you please?"

"By the Carmes-Deschaux."

"At what time?"

"Around noon."

"Around noon, then. I'll be there."

"Try not to keep me waiting, for at a quarter past noon, I warn you, it is I who will go running after you, and I'll cut your ears off on the run."

"Fine!" d'Artagnan shouted to him. "I'll be there at ten to noon!"

And he set off running as if the devil was after him, still hoping to find his unknown man, whose leisurely pace could not have taken him far.

But at the street door Porthos was talking with a soldier of the guards. Between the two talkers there was just the space of a man. D'Artagnan thought the space was enough for him, and he shot like an arrow between the two of them. But d'Artagnan had not counted on the wind. As he passed through, the wind swelled out Porthos's long cloak, and d'Artagnan dove straight into it. Porthos undoubtedly had reasons for not abandoning this essential part of his clothing, for instead of letting go of the side he was holding, he pulled it to him, so that d'Artagnan was rolled up in the velvet by a rotating movement explained by Porthos's stubborn resistance.

D'Artagnan heard the musketeer curse, wanted to get out from under the cloak that was blinding him, and sought his way through the folds. Above all he was afraid of damaging the magnificent baldric we are acquainted with; but, on timidly opening his eyes, he found his nose pressed between Porthos's shoulders, that is, precisely against the baldric.

Alas! like most things in this world that have nothing to boast of but their appearance, the baldric was gold in front and simple buff behind. Porthos, vainglorious as he was, unable to have an all-gold baldric, at least had one by half: the necessity of the head cold and the urgency of the cloak thus became comprehensible.

"Vertubleu!" cried Porthos, doing his best to rid himself of d'Artagnan, who was scrambling about on his back, "you must be mad to go throwing yourself at people like that!"

"Excuse me," said d'Artagnan, reappearing from under the giant's shoulder, "but I'm in a great hurry, I'm running after someone, and . . ."

"And do you forget your eyes when you run, by any chance?" asked Porthos.

"No," replied d'Artagnan, nettled, "no, and thanks to my eyes I even see what others don't see."

Porthos may or may not have understood, but in any case, giving way to his anger, he said:

"Monsieur, you'll get roughed up, I warn you, if you rub musketeers the wrong way."

"Roughed up, Monsieur!" said d'Artagnan. "That's a harsh word."

"It's the right word for a man accustomed to looking his enemies in the face."

"Ah! Pardieu! I know very well you won't turn your back on them!"

And the young man, delighted with his waggishness, walked away laughing his head off.

Porthos seethed with rage and was about to hurl himself at d'Artagnan.

"Later, later," cried the young man, "when you're no longer wearing your cloak."

"At one o'clock, then, behind the Luxembourg."

"Very well, at one o'clock," replied d'Artagnan, turning the corner.

But neither on the street he had just walked down, nor on the one he now took in at a glance, did he see anyone. Slowly as the unknown man had been walking, he had still gotten away; or perhaps he had gone into some house. D'Artagnan inquired about him from everyone he met, went down as far as the ferry, came back up by the rue de Seine and the Croix-Rouge—nothing, absolutely nothing. However, the chase was profitable to him in this sense, that as the sweat drenched his forehead, his heart cooled down.

Then he began to reflect on the events that had just occurred. They were many and ill-fated. It was barely eleven o'clock in the morning, and the day had already brought him into disgrace with M. de Tréville, who could not fail to find the manner in which d'Artagnan had left him a bit cavalier.

Moreover, he had picked up two fine duels with two men, each of whom was capable of killing three d'Artagnans, with two musketeers finally, that is, with two of those beings whom he esteemed so highly that, in his mind and in his heart, he placed them above all other men.

It was a sad prospect. Sure of being killed by Athos, it is understandable that the young man did not worry much about Porthos. And yet, as hope is the last thing to die in a man's heart, he came to hope that he might survive these two duels, with terrible wounds, of course, and in case of survival, he gave himself the following two reprimands for the future:

"What a birdbrain I was, and what a boor I am! This brave and unfortunate Athos was wounded in just the shoulder I ran into, butting him like a ram. The one thing that surprises me is that he didn't kill me on the spot. He had every right to, and the pain I caused him must have been atrocious. As for Porthos—oh, as for Porthos, my God, that's much funnier!"

And despite himself the young man started to laugh, though still looking out for whether this isolated laughter, and with no cause apparent to those who saw him laugh, might not offend some passerby.

"As for Porthos, that's much funnier, but that doesn't make me less of a scatterbrain. Does one charge into people that way without any warning? No! And does one go looking under their cloaks for what isn't there? He'd certainly have forgiven me; he'd have forgiven me if I hadn't gone and mentioned that cursed baldric to him—in veiled terms, it's true; yes, prettily veiled! Ah! cursed Gascon that I am, I'd make jokes in the frying pan! Come, d'Artagnan my friend," he continued, talking to himself with all the amenity he thought was his due, "if you come through, which is unlikely, it's a question in future of being of the most perfect politeness. Henceforth you must be admired, you must be held up as a model. To be considerate and polite is not to be a coward. Rather look at Aramis: Aramis is all gentleness, he is grace personified. Well, then, did anyone ever dare say that Aramis was a coward? No, certainly not, and henceforth I intend to model myself on him in every point. Ah! here he is!"

D'Artagnan, while walking along and soliloquizing, had come within a few steps of the hôtel d'Aiguillon, and in front of this hôtel he caught sight of Aramis talking gaily with three gentlemen of the king's guards. Aramis, for his part, also caught sight of d'Artagnan, but as he had by no means forgotten that it was before this young man that M. de Tréville had flown into such a temper that morning, and that a witness to the upbraiding the musketeers had received was in no way agreeable to him, he pretended not to see him.

D'Artagnan was not so foolish as to fail to perceive that he was one too many; but he was not yet so broken to the ways of society as to gallantly get himself out of such a false situation as is generally that of a man who comes to mix with people he hardly knows and in a conversation that does not concern him. He was thus racking his brains for a means of making his retreat with the least possible awkwardness, when he noticed that Aramis had dropped his handkerchief and, no doubt inadvertently, had placed his foot on it. It seemed to him that the moment had come to make up for his impropriety: he bent down and, with the most graceful air he could muster, drew the handkerchief from under the musketeer's foot, for all the efforts the latter made to keep it there, and said as he handed it to him:

"I believe, Monsieur, that this is a handkerchief you would be sorry to lose."

The handkerchief was indeed richly embroidered and bore a coronet and a coat of arms at one of its corners. Aramis blushed exceedingly and tore rather than took the handkerchief from the Gascon's hands.

"Aha!" cried one of the guards. "Will you still say, discreet Aramis, that you're on bad terms with Mme de Bois-Tracy, when the gracious lady is kind enough to lend you her handkerchiefs?"

Aramis shot d'Artagnan one of those glances which make a man understand that he has just acquired a mortal enemy. Then, resuming his suave air, he said: "You're mistaken, gentlemen, this handkerchief isn't mine, and I don't know what whim made Monsieur give it to me rather than to one of you. The proof of what I'm saying is that my own is here in my pocket."

With those words he pulled out his own handkerchief, a very elegant one as well, and of fine cambric, though cambric was costly at that time, but a handkerchief without embroidery, without a coat of arms, and ornamented with a single initial, that of its owner.

This time d'Artagnan did not breathe a word; he had realized his blunder; but Aramis's friends would not be convinced by his denials, and one of them, turning to Aramis with affected seriousness, said:

"If it were as you claim, I would be forced, my dear Aramis, to demand it back from you; for, as you know, Bois-Tracy is among my intimates, and I do not want anyone to make a trophy of his wife's belongings."

"Your demand is ill put," replied Aramis, "and while I recognize the fundamental fairness of your objection, I refuse on account of the form."

"The fact is," d'Artagnan ventured timidly, "that I didn't see the handkerchief come from M. Aramis's pocket. He had his foot on it, that's all, and I thought, since he had his foot on it, that the handkerchief was his."

"And you were mistaken, my dear Monsieur," Aramis replied coldly, little sensible of the amends.

Then, turning to the guard who had declared himself a friend of Bois-Tracy, he continued:

"Besides, it occurs to me, my dear intimate of Bois-Tracy, that I am no less loving a friend of his than you may be yourself; so that, strictly speaking, this handkerchief could just as well have come from your pocket as from mine."

"No, on my honor!" cried His Majesty's guard.

"You will swear on your honor and I on my word, which means that one of us will obviously be lying. Wait, let's do better, Montaran, let's each take a half."

"Of the handkerchief?"

"Yes."

"Perfect," cried the other two guards, "the judgment of Solomon. Decidedly, Aramis, you are filled with wisdom."

The young men burst out laughing, and, as we might well expect, the affair had no further consequences. A moment later, the conversation came to an end, and the three guards and the musketeer, after cordially shaking hands, went off, the three guards one way and Aramis the other.

"Now's the moment to make peace with this gallant man," d'Artagnan said to himself, having stood aside during the whole last part of this conversation. And, with that good sentiment, he went up to Aramis, who was going away without paying any further attention to him, and said:

"Monsieur, you will excuse me, I hope."

"Ah! Monsieur," Aramis interrupted, "allow me to observe to you that in this circumstance you have by no means acted as befits a gallant man."

"What, Monsieur!" cried d'Artagnan. "Do you suppose . . ."

"I suppose, Monsieur, that you are not a fool, and that you know very well, though you come from Gascony, that one does not step on pocket handkerchiefs without a reason. Devil take it! Paris isn't paved with cambric."

"Monsieur, you are wrong in trying to humiliate me," said d'Artagnan, whose quarrelsome nature was beginning to speak louder than his peaceable resolutions. "I'm from Gascony, it's true, and since you know that, I needn't tell you that Gascons are not very forbearing; so that, when they've excused themselves once, even for some stupidity, they are convinced that they've already done half more than they ought."

"Monsieur, what I said to you," replied Aramis, "was not said in order to pick a quarrel with you. Thank God, I'm not a swordslinger, and being only an interim musketeer, I never fight unless I'm forced to, and always with great reluctance; but this time the matter is serious, for a lady has been compromised by you."

"By us, that is," cried d'Artagnan.

"Why did you have the tactlessness to give me back the handkerchief?"

"Why did you have the tactlessness to drop it?"

"I said, and I repeat, Monsieur, that this handkerchief did not come from my pocket."

"Well, then, you've lied twice, Monsieur, for I myself saw it fall!"

"Ah! so you take it in that tone, Monsieur le Gascon! Well, then, I'll teach you how to live."

"And I will send you back to your mass, Monsieur l'Abbé! Draw, if you please, here and now."

"No, if you please, my fine friend; no, not here, at least. Don't you see that we're in front of the hôtel d'Aiguillon, which is full of the cardinal's creatures? Who will tell me that it wasn't His Eminence who charged you to fetch my head? Now, I'm ridiculously attached to my head, seeing that it seems to go rather well with my shoulders. I'll kill you, rest assured, but kill you quite calmly, in a closed and covered place, where you won't be able to boast of your death to anyone."

"I gladly accept, but don't be too sure of it, and take your handkerchief, whether it belongs to you or not; you may have occasion to use it."

"Monsieur is a Gascon?" asked Aramis.

"Yes. Monsieur is not putting off the meeting out of prudence?"

"Prudence, Monsieur, is a rather useless virtue for musketeers, I know, but indispensable to men of the Church, and as I am a musketeer only provisionally, I intend to remain prudent. At two o'clock I shall have the honor of awaiting you at the hôtel of M. de Tréville. There I shall point out the suitable places to you."

The two young men bowed to each other, then Aramis went off up the street that leads to the Luxembourg, while d'Artagnan, seeing that time was passing, took the road to the Carmes-Deschaux, saying to himself:

"Decidedly, I won't survive; but if I'm killed, at least I'll be killed by a musketeer."

V

THE KING'S MUSKETEERS AND THE CARDINAL'S GUARDS

D'Artagnan knew no one in Paris. So he went to meet Athos without bringing a second, resolved to content himself with those chosen by his adversary. Besides, it was his definite intention to make the brave musketeer all suitable apologies, but without weakness, fearing that the result of the duel would be what is always the most regrettable result in an affair of this kind, when a young and vigorous man fights against a wounded and weakened adversary: vanquished, he doubles the triumph of his antagonist; victorious, he is accused of treachery and easy audacity.

Moreover, either we have poorly introduced the character of our adventure seeker, or our reader must already have noticed that he was by no means an ordinary man. And so, while repeating to himself that his death was inevitable, he was not at all resigned to dying meekly, as another man less courageous and less reasonable than he would have been in his place. He hoped, thanks to the honest excuses he had saved up for him, to make a friend of Athos, whose lordly air and austere appearance pleased him greatly. He flattered himself that he might frighten Porthos with the adventure of the baldric, which, if he was not killed at once, he could tell to everyone, a story which, skillfully brought to full effect, should cover Porthos with ridicule. Finally, as for the sly Aramis, he was not much afraid of him, and, supposing that he got to him, he undertook to dispatch him well and good, or at least to strike him on the face, as Caesar recommended doing to Pompey's soldiers, thus spoiling forever that beauty he was so proud of.

Furthermore, there was in d'Artagnan that unshakable supply of resolution which his father's advice had deposited in his heart, advice the substance of which was: "Suffer nothing from anyone except the king, the cardinal, and M. de Tréville." Thus he rather flew than walked to the convent of the Carmes Déchaussés, or Deschaux, as they said at that time, a sort of windowless building bordered by barren fields, a subsidiary of the Pré-aux-clercs, and which commonly served for the encounters of men who had no time to lose.

When d'Artagnan came in view of the little wasteland that lay at the foot of the monastery, Athos had been waiting for only five minutes, and it was striking noon. He was thus as punctual as the Samaritaine, and the most rigorous casuist with regard to duels had nothing to say.

Athos, who was still suffering cruelly from his wound, though it had been newly bandaged by M. de Tréville's surgeon, was sitting on a post and awaiting his adversary with that peaceful countenance and dignified air which never left him. At the sight of d'Artagnan, he stood up and politely took a few steps towards him. The latter, for his part, approached his adversary not otherwise than with his hat in his hand and its plume dragging on the ground.

"Monsieur," said Athos, "I have informed two of my friends

who will serve me as seconds, but these two friends have not yet arrived. I'm surprised that they are late: it is not their habit."

"I myself have no seconds, Monsieur," said d'Artagnan, "for, having come to Paris only yesterday, I know no one here as yet except M. de Tréville, to whom I was recommended by my father, who has the honor to be something of a friend of his."

Athos reflected for a moment.

"You know only M. de Tréville?" he asked.

"Yes, Monsieur, I know only him."

"Ah, but that . . ." Athos went on, speaking half to himself and half to d'Artagnan, "but if I kill you, I'll look like a child eater!"

"Not so much, Monsieur," replied d'Artagnan with a bow that was not lacking in dignity, "not so much, since you do me the honor of drawing with a wound that must be a great hindrance to you."

"A great hindrance, on my word, and you caused me the devil's own pain, I must say; but I'll use my left hand, as is my habit in such circumstances. Don't think I'm doing you a kindness; I draw just as well with both hands; and there will even be a disadvantage for you: a left-handed man is very troublesome for people who are not forewarned. I regret not having informed you of this circumstance earlier."

"Truly, Monsieur," said d'Artagnan, inclining once more, "you are of a courtesy for which I could not be more grateful."

"You embarrass me," replied Athos with his gentlemanly air. "Let's speak of something else, I beg you, unless you find it disagreeable. Ah, sangbleu, you really hurt me! My shoulder's on fire!"

"If you would permit . . ." d'Artagnan said timidly.

"What, Monsieur?"

"I have a miraculous balm for wounds, a balm that comes to me from my mother, and which I have tried myself."

"Well, then?"

"Well, then! I'm sure that in less than three days this balm will cure you, and at the end of three days, when you're cured, well, then, Monsieur, it will still be a great honor for me to be your man."

D'Artagnan spoke these words with a simplicity that did honor to his courtesy without damaging his courage in any way.

"Pardieu, Monsieur," said Athos, "there's a proposition that pleases me—not that I accept it, but it smells of its gentleman a league away. It was thus that valiant knights spoke and acted in the time of Charlemagne, upon whom every cavalier must seek to model himself. Unfortunately, we are no longer in the time of the great emperor. We are in the time of M. le cardinal, and three days from now it will be known, however well the secret is kept, it will be known that we are going to fight, and our combat will be opposed. Ah! but will those meanderers never come?"

"If you're in a hurry, Monsieur," d'Artagnan said to Athos with the same simplicity with which, a moment before, he had suggested putting off the duel for three days, "if you're in a hurry, and you'd prefer to dispatch me at once, please go ahead."

"There's another word that pleases me," said Athos, nodding gracefully to d'Artagnan. "It hardly speaks for a witless man, and certainly speaks for a man of courage. Monsieur, I like men of your temper, and I see that, if we don't kill each other, I will afterwards take real pleasure in your conversation. Let us wait for these gentlemen, I beg you. I have plenty of time, and it will be more correct. Ah, here's one of them, I believe."

Indeed, at the end of the rue de Vaugirard the gigantic Porthos began to appear.

"What!" cried d'Artagnan. "Your first witness is M. Porthos?"

"Yes, do you object?"

"No, not at all."

"And here is the second."

D'Artagnan turned to where Athos was pointing and recognized Aramis.

"What!" he cried with still more astonishment than the first time. "Your second witness is M. Aramis?"

"You are doubtless unaware that one of us is never seen without the others, and that we are known among the musketeers and the guards, at court and in town, as Athos, Porthos, and Aramis, or the three inseparables. However, as you come from Dax or Pau . . ."

"Tarbes," said d'Artagnan.

". . . your ignorance of that detail is permissible," said Athos.

"By heaven," said d'Artagnan, "you are well named, gentlemen, and my adventure, if it causes some stir, will prove at least that your union is not based on contrasts."

Meanwhile, Porthos had come up and greeted Athos with a wave of the hand; then, turning to d'Artagnan, he stopped in utter amazement.

Let us mention in passing that he had changed his baldric and taken off his cloak.

"Aha!" he said, "what's this?"

"This is the gentleman I am to fight with," said Athos, indicating d'Artagnan with his hand and greeting him with the same gesture.

"I am to fight with him, too," said Porthos.

"But not until one o'clock," said d'Artagnan.

"And I, too, am to fight with the gentleman," said Aramis, arriving on the scene in his turn.

"But not until two o'clock," d'Artagnan said with the same calm.

"But what are you fighting about, Athos?"

"By heaven, I don't quite know, he hurt my shoulder. And you, Porthos?"

"By heaven, I'm fighting because I'm fighting," Porthos replied, blushing.

Athos, who missed nothing, saw a slight smile pass over the Gascon's lips.

"We had a discussion about clothes," said the young man.

"And you, Aramis?" asked Athos.

"Me? I'm fighting for reasons of theology," replied Aramis, making a sign to d'Artagnan that he begged him to keep the cause of his duel secret.

Athos saw a second smile pass over d'Artagnan's lips.

"Indeed," said Athos.

"Yes, a point in St. Augustine on which we disagree," said the Gascon.

"He's decidedly a witty man," murmured Athos.

"And now that you're all together, gentlemen," said d'Artagnan, "allow me to make you my apologies."

At the word "apologies," a cloud darkened Athos's brow, a haughty smile flitted over Porthos's lips, and Aramis responded with a negative gesture.

"You misunderstand me, gentlemen," said d'Artagnan, raising his head, on which a ray of sunlight played at that moment, gilding its fine and bold features. "I apologize to you in case I cannot pay my debt to all three of you, for M. Athos has the right to kill me first, which takes away much of the value of your claim, M. Porthos, and renders yours virtually null, M. Aramis. And now, gentlemen, I repeat to you my apologies, but only for that, and—on guard!"

At these words, with the most gallant gesture one could ever see, d'Artagnan drew his sword.

The blood had risen to d'Artagnan's head, and at that moment he would have drawn his sword against all the musketeers in the realm as he had just done against Athos, Porthos, and Aramis.

It was a quarter past noon. The sun was at its zenith, and the place chosen as the theater for the duel was exposed to its full ardor.

"It's very hot," said Athos, drawing his sword in his turn, "but I'm unable to take off my doublet; for just now I felt my wound bleeding again, and I'm afraid I may hamper the gentleman by showing him blood that he has not drawn from me himself."

"That's true, Monsieur," said d'Artagnan, "and whether drawn by another or by myself, I assure you that I will always greatly regret to see the blood of so brave a gentleman. I will therefore fight in my doublet like you."

"Come, come," said Porthos, "enough of such compliments. Remember we're waiting our turn."

"Speak for yourself, Porthos, if you want to make such unseemly remarks," interrupted Aramis. "As for me, I find what they are saying to each other very well said and entirely worthy of two gentlemen."

"Whenever you like, Monsieur," said Athos, putting himself on guard.

"I was awaiting your orders," said d'Artagnan, crossing his blade.

But the two rapiers had barely rung on touching when a squadron of His Eminence's guards, commanded by M. de Jussac, appeared around the corner of the convent.

"The cardinal's guards!" Porthos and Aramis cried out together. "Put up your swords, gentlemen! Put up your swords!"

But it was too late. The two combatants had been seen in a posture that left no doubt of their intentions.

"Ho, there!" cried Jussac, advancing towards them and making a sign to his men to do as much. "Ho, there, musketeers! So you're fighting here? And the edicts? What about them?"

"You are very generous, gentlemen of the guards," said Athos, full of rancor, for Jussac had been one of the aggressors the night before. "If we saw you fighting, I promise you, we'd keep from interfering. Leave us alone, then, and you'll enjoy yourselves without going to any trouble."

"Gentlemen," said Jussac, "with great regret I must inform you that the thing is impossible. Duty above all. Put up your swords, if you please, and follow us."

"Monsieur," said Aramis, parodying Jussac, "it would be a great pleasure for us to obey your gracious invitation, if it depended on us; but unfortunately the thing is impossible: M. de Tréville has forbidden it. Go your ways, then; that's the best thing you can do."

This mockery exasperated Jussac.

"We shall charge you then," he said, "if you disobey."

"There are five of them," Athos said in a low voice, "and only three of us. We'll be beaten again, and we'd better die here, for I declare I will not reappear in defeat before the captain."

Then Porthos and Aramis instantly closed ranks with him, while Jussac lined up his soldiers.

That single moment sufficed for d'Artagnan to choose sides: this was one of those events that determine a man's life; it was a choice between the king and the cardinal; once made, it had to be persevered in. To fight, that is, to disobey the law, that is, to risk one's head, that is, to make at one stroke an enemy of a minister more powerful than the king himself: that was what the young man foresaw, and, be it said in his praise, he did not hesitate a second. Turning to Athos and his friends, he said:

"Gentlemen, if I may, I shall revise your words somewhat. You said there were only three of you, but it seems to me that we are four."

"But you're not one of us," said Porthos.

"That's true," replied d'Artagnan, "I don't have the clothes, but I have the soul. My heart is a musketeer's; I feel it very well, Monsieur, and that leads me on."

"Get out of the way, young man," cried Jussac, who had undoubtedly guessed d'Artagnan's intentions by his gestures and the expression of his face. "You can leave; we give our consent. Save your skin; go quickly."

D'Artagnan did not budge.

"You're decidedly a fine lad," said Athos, shaking the young man's hand.

"Well, make your choice!" cried Jussac.

"Come on," said Porthos and Aramis, "let's do something."

"Monsieur is full of generosity," said Athos.

But all three were thinking of d'Artagnan's youth and were fearful of his inexperience.

"There will be just three of us, one wounded, plus a boy," said Athos, "and all the same they'll say we were four men."

"Yes, but to back out!" said Porthos.

"It's difficult," replied Athos.

D'Artagnan understood their indecision.

"Gentlemen, try me anyway," he said, "and I swear to you on my honor that I will not leave here if we're defeated."

"What's your name, my brave lad?" asked Athos.

"D'Artagnan, sir."

"Well, then! Athos, Porthos, Aramis, and d'Artagnan, forward!" cried Athos.

"Well, gentlemen, have you decided to decide?" Jussac cried for the third time.

"We have, gentlemen," said Athos.

"And what is your choice?" asked Jussac.

"We shall have the honor of charging you," replied Aramis, raising his hat with one hand and drawing his sword with the other.

"Ah! so you resist!" cried Jussac.

"Sangdieu! does that surprise you?"

And the nine combatants rushed at each other with a fury that did not exclude a certain method.

Athos took a certain Cahusac, a favorite of the cardinal; Porthos had Biscarat, and Aramis was faced with two adversaries.

As for d'Artagnan, he found himself up against Jussac himself.

The young Gascon's heart beat as though it would burst his chest—not from fear, thank God! there was not a shadow of it in him, but from emulation. He fought like an enraged tiger, circling ten times around his adversary, and twenty times changing his guard and his ground. Jussac was, as they said then, partial to the blade, and had a great deal of experience; however, he had all the trouble in the world defending himself against an adversary who, leaping and agile, deviated from the received rules every moment, attacking from all sides at once, and all the while parrying like a man who has the greatest respect for his own epidermis.

This struggle finally ended by exasperating Jussac. Furious at being kept in check by someone he had considered a mere boy, he became excited and started making mistakes. D'Artagnan, who, though lacking in practice, had a profound theory, redoubled his agility. Jussac, wishing to end it, aimed a terrible blow at his adversary, lunging full length; but the latter parried in prime, and while Jussac was straightening up, slipped under his blade like a snake and ran him through. Jussac collapsed in a heap.

D'Artagnan then cast a quick and worried glance over the battlefield.

Aramis had already killed one of his adversaries, but the other was pressing him hotly. However, Aramis was in a good position and could still defend himself.

Biscarat and Porthos had just scored a double hit: Porthos had received a sword stroke through the arm, and Biscarat through the thigh. But as neither wound was serious, they went at it all the more fiercely.

Athos, wounded anew by Cahusac, turned visibly pale, but did not yield an inch: he only changed sword hands and now fought with his left.

D'Artagnan, according to the laws of dueling of that time, could help someone. While he was trying to see which of his companions needed his aid, he caught a glance from Athos. That glance was of a sublime eloquence. Athos would have died rather than call for help, but he could look, and with his look ask for assistance. D'Artagnan guessed it, made a terrible leap, and landed beside Cahusac, crying:

"Face me, Monsieur le garde, I'm going to kill you!"

Cahusac turned; it was just in time. Athos, whose extreme courage was all that sustained him, dropped to one knee.

"Sangdieu!" he cried to d'Artagnan, "don't kill him, young man, I beg you; I have an old matter to settle with him, when I'm healed and fit again. Just disarm him, wrench his sword away. That's it. Good! Very good!"

This exclamation was torn from Athos by Cahusac's sword, which landed twenty paces from him. D'Artagnan and Cahusac both rushed, the one to pick it up again, the other to take it away; but d'Artagnan, the more nimble, got there first and placed his foot on it.

Cahusac ran to the guard Aramis had killed, took his rapier, and was returning to d'Artagnan; but on his way he met Athos, who had caught his breath during the moment's pause that d'Artagnan had procured him, and who, for fear d'Artagnan might kill his enemy for him, wanted to take up the fight again.

D'Artagnan understood that it would be offensive to

Athos not to let him do so. Indeed, a few seconds later Cahusac fell, his throat run through by the stroke of a sword.

At the same moment, Aramis pressed his sword to the chest of his fallen adversary and forced him to beg for mercy.

There remained Porthos and Biscarat. Porthos produced a thousand fanfaronades, asking Biscarat what time it might be, and complimenting him on the company his brother had just obtained in the regiment of Navarre. But his mockery gained him nothing. Biscarat was one of those men of iron who only fall when dead.

However, it had to end. The watch might come and seize all the combatants, wounded or not, royalists or cardinalists. Athos, Aramis, and d'Artagnan surrounded Biscarat and called on him to surrender. Though alone against them all, and with a sword stroke through the thigh, Biscarat wanted to hold out; but Jussac, who had raised himself on one elbow, called on him to surrender. Biscarat was a Gascon like d'Artagnan; he turned a deaf ear and contented himself with laughing, and between two parries, finding time to point out a place on the ground with the tip of his sword, he said, parodying a verse from the Bible:

"Here dies Biscarat, alone of those who are with him."

"But you've got four men against you; end it, I order you."

"Ah! if you order it, that's another thing," said Biscarat. "Since you're my commander, I must obey."

And, leaping back, he broke his sword over his knee, so as not to surrender it, threw the pieces over the convent wall, and crossed his arms, whistling a cardinalist tune.

Bravery is always respected, even in an enemy. The musketeers saluted Biscarat with their swords and put them back in their scabbards. D'Artagnan did the same; then, aided by Biscarat, the only one left standing, he carried Jussac, Cahusac, and the one of Aramis's adversaries who was merely wounded, under the porch of the convent. The fourth, as we have said, was dead. Then they rang the bell, and, taking four of the five swords, went off drunk with joy to the hôtel of M. de Tréville.

They were seen arm in arm, taking up the whole width of the street, and accosting every musketeer they met, so that in the end they formed a triumphal march. D'Artagnan's heart was drunk to overflowing; he walked between Athos and Porthos, clutching them tenderly.

"If I'm not yet a musketeer," he said to his new friends, as they went through the door to the hôtel of M. de Tréville, "at least I've been accepted as an apprentice, haven't I?"

VI

His Majesty King Louis the Thirteenth

The affair caused a big stir. M. de Tréville scolded his musketeers a great deal aloud, and congratulated them quietly; but, as there was no time to lose in warning the king, M. de Tréville hastened to the Louvre. It was already too late, the king was locked in with the cardinal, and M. de Tréville was told that the king was working and could not receive at the moment. That evening, M. de Tréville went to the king's games. The king was winning, and as he was quite miserly, he was in excellent humor. And so, catching sight of M. de Tréville from afar, he said:

"Come here, Monsieur le capitaine, come and let me scold you. Do you know that His Eminence came to complain to me about your musketeers, and with such emotion that His Eminence is sick from it this evening? Ah, but what daredevils, what gallows birds your musketeers are!"

"No, Sire," replied Tréville, who saw at first glance how things would turn out, "no, on the contrary, they're good creatures, gentle as lambs, and have only one desire, I guarantee it: it is that their swords never leave the scabbard except in Your Majesty's service. But, what can you do? M. le cardinal's guards are constantly picking quarrels with them, and for the very honor of the corps, the poor young men are obliged to defend themselves."

"Listen to M. de Tréville," said the king, "listen to him! You'd think he was talking about a religious community! Truly, my dear captain, I'd like to take your commission and give it to Mlle de Chemerault, to whom I've promised an abbey. But don't think I'll take you at your word. I'm known as Louis the Just, M. de Tréville, and we shall see, we shall soon see."

"Ah! it's because I trust in that justice, Sire, that I patiently and calmly await Your Majesty's good pleasure."

"Wait, then, Monsieur, wait," said the king. "I won't make you wait long."

Indeed, the luck turned, and as the king began losing what he had won, he was not sorry to play—allow us this gambler's expression, of which, we admit, we do not know the origin— he was not sorry to play Charlemagne. The king thus stood up after a moment, and pocketing the money that was in front of him, the major part of which represented his winnings, said:

"La Vieuville, take my place, I must speak with M. de Tréville about an important matter. Ah! . . . I had eighty louis in front of me; put down the same amount, so that those who have lost won't have any reason to complain. Justice before all."

Then, turning to M. de Tréville and walking with him toward the embrasure of a window, he went on:

"Well, Monsieur, so you say it was the guards of the Most Eminent who picked a quarrel with your musketeers?"

"Yes, Sire, as always."

"And how did the thing come about, eh? For you know, my dear captain, a judge must hear both sides."

"Ah, my God, in the simplest and most natural way possible! Three of my best soldiers, whom Your Majesty knows by name and whose devotion you have more than once appreciated, and who, I may affirm it to the king, take his service greatly to heart—three of my best soldiers, I say, MM. Athos, Porthos, and Aramis, went for an outing with a young lad from Gascony whom I had introduced to them that same morning. The outing was to be in Saint-Germain, I believe, and they had agreed to meet at the Carmes-Deschaux, where they were disturbed by M. de Jussac, MM. Cahusac and Biscarat, and two other guards, who surely did not come there in so numerous a company without bad intentions against the edicts."

"Aha! you've just made me think of it," said the king. "No doubt they came to fight themselves."

"I do not accuse them, Sire, but I let Your Majesty consider what five armed men could be up to in such a deserted place as the environs of the Carmelite convent."

"Yes, you're right, Tréville, you're right."

"So, when they saw my musketeers, they changed their minds and forgot their private hatred of the corps; for Your Majesty is not unaware that the musketeers, who are the king's and only the king's, are the natural enemies of the guards, who are M. le cardinal's men."

"Yes, Tréville, yes," the king said melancholically, "and it's very sad, believe me, to see two parties like this in France, two heads to the royalty; but that will all end, Tréville, that will all end. So you say the guards picked a quarrel with the musketeers?"

"I say it's possible that things went that way, but I can't swear to it, Sire. You know how difficult it is to learn the truth, and unless one is gifted with that admirable instinct which gave the name 'Just' to Louis XIII . . ."

"And right you are, Tréville; but they weren't alone, your musketeers, didn't they have a boy with them?"

"Yes, Sire, and a wounded man, so that three of the king's musketeers, one of them wounded, and a boy not only held their own against five of M. le cardinal's most terrible guards, but brought four of them down."

"Why, that's a victory!" the king cried, beaming. "A total victory!"

"Yes, Sire, as total as at the pont de Cé."

"Four men, one of them wounded, and one a boy, you say?"

"Barely a young man, who even bore himself so perfectly on this occasion that I will take the liberty of recommending him to Your Majesty."

"What's his name?"

"D'Artagnan, Sire. He's the son of one of my oldest friends; the son of a man who was in the partisan wars with the king, your father, of glorious memory."

"And you say he bore himself well, this young man? Tell me about it, Tréville; you know how I love stories of war and combat."

And King Louis XIII put one hand on his hip and with the other proudly twirled his mustache.

"Sire," Tréville picked up, "as I told you, M. d'Artagnan is almost a boy, and as he does not have the honor of being a musketeer, he was in civilian dress. M. le cardinal's guards, perceiving his extreme youth and, what's more, that he was a stranger to the corps, invited him to withdraw before they attacked."

"So you see, Tréville," the king interrupted, "it was they who attacked."

"That's right, Sire, there's no further doubt. So they called on him to withdraw, but he replied that he was a musketeer at heart and all for His Majesty, and that he would remain with the gentlemen musketeers."

"Brave young man!" murmured the king.

"Indeed, he did remain with them; and Your Majesty has so firm a champion in him that it was he who gave Jussac that terrible stroke of the sword which so greatly angers M. le cardinal."

"It was he who wounded Jussac?" cried the king. "He, a mere boy? That's impossible, Tréville!"

"It is as I have the honor of telling Your Majesty."

"Jussac? One of the best blades in the realm?"

"Well, then, Sire, he has met his master."

"I want to see this young man, Tréville. I want to see him, and if something can be done, well, then we shall take care of it."

"When would Your Majesty deign to receive him?"

"Tomorrow at noon, Tréville."

"Shall I bring him alone?"

"No, bring me all four of them. I want to thank them all at the same time. Devoted men are rare, Tréville, and devotion must be rewarded."

"At noon, Sire, we shall be at the Louvre."

"Ah! by the back stairs, Tréville, by the back stairs. There's no use in the cardinal's knowing . . ."

"Yes, Sire."

"You understand, Tréville, an edict is an edict; fighting is forbidden, when all's said."

"But this encounter, Sire, lies completely outside the ordinary conditions of a duel: it was a brawl, and the proof is that there were five of the cardinal's guards against my three musketeers and M. d'Artagnan."

"That's right," said the king, "but never mind, Tréville, still come by the back stairs."

Tréville smiled. But since it was already a great deal for him to have made this child revolt against his master, he bowed respectfully to the king, and with his permission took leave of him.

That same evening, the three musketeers were informed of the honor that had been accorded them. As they had known the king for a long time, they were not too excited; but d'Artagnan, with his Gascon imagination, saw in it his approaching good fortune, and spent the night in golden dreams. By eight o'clock in the morning, he was at Athos's place.

D'Artagnan found the musketeer dressed and ready to go out. As their meeting with the king was only at noon, he had made plans with Porthos and Aramis to go and play tennis at a sporting house near the Luxembourg stables. Athos invited d'Artagnan to go with them, and despite his ignorance of the game, which he had never played, he accepted, not knowing what else to do with his time from barely nine in the morning till noon.

The two musketeers had already arrived and were batting the ball around. Athos, who was very good at all physical exercises, went with d'Artagnan to the other side and challenged them. But with the first movement he made, though he was playing with his left hand, he understood that his wound was still too recent to allow him such exercise. D'Artagnan thus remained alone, and as he declared that he was too clumsy to keep up a regulation game, they simply went on hitting balls back and forth without counting points. But one of these balls, sped by the herculean fist of Porthos, came so close to d'Artagnan's face that he thought if, instead of passing by, it had gone right into it, his audience would probably have been ruined, seeing that it would have been quite impossible for him to present himself to the king. Now, since his whole future, in his Gascon imagination, depended on that audience, he politely saluted Porthos and Aramis, declaring that he would not take up the game again until he could hold his own, and went to take a seat in the gallery close to the rope.

Unfortunately for d'Artagnan, among the spectators there happened to be one of His Eminence's guards, who, still all fired up by the defeat of his companions only the day before, had promised himself to seize the first occasion to avenge it. He now thought the occasion had come, and turning to his neighbor, said:

"It's not surprising that this young man is afraid of a ball, no doubt he's an apprentice musketeer."

D'Artagnan whipped around as if stung by a serpent and stared fixedly at the guard who had just made this insolent remark.

"Pardieu!" the latter picked up, insolently twirling his mustache, "look at me as much as you like, my little sir, I said what I said."

"And since what you said is too clear for your words to need any explanation," d'Artagnan replied in a low voice, "I will ask you to come with me."

"And when might that be?" the guard asked with the same mocking air.

"At once, if you please."

"And I suppose you know who I am?"

"I have no idea, and it doesn't worry me in the least."

"You're wrong there, for if you knew my name, you might be in less of a hurry."

"What is your name?"

"Bernajoux, at your service."

"Well, then, M. Bernajoux," d'Artagnan said calmly, "I'll be waiting for you at the door."

"Go on, Monsieur, I'm right behind you."

"Don't be in too much of a hurry, Monsieur; they shouldn't

see us leaving together. You understand that, for what we're about to do, too big a crowd would be a hindrance."

"Very well," replied the guard, surprised that his name had no effect on the young man.

Indeed, Bernajoux's name was known to everyone, with the sole exception of d'Artagnan, perhaps, for he was one of those who figured most often in the daily brawls that all the edicts of king and cardinal had been unable to curb.

Porthos and Aramis were so caught up in their game, and Athos was watching them with such attention, that they did not even see their young companion leave. He stopped at the door, as he had said to His Eminence's guard. A moment later, the man came down in his turn. As d'Artagnan had no time to lose, seeing that the audience with the king was fixed for noon, he cast a glance around him, and seeing that the street was deserted, said to his adversary:

"By heaven, it's a lucky thing for you, though your name is Bernajoux, that you only have to do with an apprentice musketeer. Don't worry, however, I'll do my best. On guard!"

"But," the man thus provoked by d'Artagnan said, "it seems to me the place is rather ill chosen. We'd be better off behind the abbey of Saint-Germain or in the Pré-aux-clercs."

"What you say is quite sensible," replied d'Artagnan. "Unfortunately, I have little time, because I have an appointment at noon. On guard then, Monsieur, on guard!"

Bernajoux was not a man to have such a compliment repeated to him twice. At the same instant his sword flashed in his hand, and he fell upon his adversary, whom, owing to his extreme youth, he hoped to intimidate.

But d'Artagnan had served his apprenticeship the day before, and, freshly graduated from his victory, filled with his future favor, he was resolved not to yield a step: the two blades thus found themselves engaged to the hilt, and as d'Artagnan firmly stood his ground, it was his adversary who stepped back. But d'Artagnan seized the moment when, in that movement, Bernajoux's blade deviated from the line, disengaged, lunged, and wounded his adversary in the shoulder. D'Artagnan at once took a step back in his turn and raised his sword, but Bernajoux cried to him that it was nothing and, lunging blindly at him, impaled himself. However, as he did not fall, as he did not declare himself defeated, but only backed away towards the hôtel of M. de La Trémouille, where one of his relations was in service, d'Artagnan, unaware of the gravity of the last wound his adversary had received, pressed him hotly, and would no doubt have finished him off with a third stroke, when, the rumor in the street having reached the tennis court, two of the guard's friends, who had heard him exchange a few words with d'Artagnan and had seen him leave after those words, rushed sword in hand out of the sporting house and fell upon the victor. But Athos, Porthos, and Aramis appeared at once in their turn, and just as the two guards were attacking their young friend, forced them to turn around. At that moment, Bernajoux fell; and as the guards were only two against four, they started shouting: "To us, hôtel de La Trémouille!" At those shouts, everything that was in the hôtel came out and hurled itself upon the four companions, who for their part began shouting: "To us, musketeers!"

This cry was ordinarily heeded, for the musketeers were known enemies of His Eminence, and they were loved for the hatred they bore the cardinal. And so the guards from other companies than those belonging to the red duke, as Aramis had called him, generally took the side of the king's musketeers in these sorts of quarrels. Of three guards from the company of M. des Essarts, who were passing by, two went to the aid of the four companions, while the third ran to the hôtel of M. de Tréville, crying: "To us, musketeers, to us!" As usual, the hôtel of M. de Tréville was filled with the bearers of that arm, who went running to help their comrades. The melée became general, but the musketeers were the stronger. The cardinal's guards and M. de La Trémouille's people withdrew into the hôtel, where they shut the doors just in time to keep their enemies from bursting in along with them. As for the wounded man, he had been carried off at the start and, as we have said, was in a very bad state.

The excitement was at its peak among the musketeers and

their allies, and they were debating whether to punish the insolence of M. de La Trémouille's servants for making a sortie
against the king's musketeers by setting fire to his hôtel. The
proposition had been made and greeted with enthusiasm,
when fortunately the clock struck eleven. D'Artagnan and his
companions remembered their audience, and as they would
have been sorry to see such a fine coup brought off without
them, they began to calm things down. Men contented themselves with throwing a few cobblestones at the doors, but the
doors held. Then they wearied of it. Besides, those who had to
be regarded as the leaders of the enterprise had just left the
group and set off for the hôtel of M. de Tréville, who was waiting for them, already informed of the escapade.

"Quick, to the Louvre," he said, "to the Louvre without a
moment's loss, and let's try to see the king before the cardinal
alerts him. We'll tell him the thing was a follow-up of yesterday's affair, and the two will go by together."

M. de Tréville, accompanied by the four young men, set
out for the Louvre. But, to the great amazement of the captain
of the musketeers, it was announced to him that the king had
gone stag hunting in the forest of Saint-Germain. M. de
Tréville made them repeat this news twice, and each time his
companions saw his face darken.

"Had His Majesty already planned this hunt as of yesterday?" he asked.

"No, Your Excellency," replied the valet, "the king's master of hounds came this morning to announce that they had
rounded up a stag for him last night. He replied at first that he
would not go, but then was unable to resist the pleasure that
the hunt promised and left after dinner."

"And did the king see the cardinal?" asked M. de Tréville.

"In all probability," replied the valet, "for I saw His
Eminence's horses being hitched up this morning, and when I
asked where he was going, I was told: 'To Saint-Germain.'"

"We've been forestalled," said M. de Tréville. "Gentlemen,
I will see the king this evening; but as for you, I don't advise
you to risk it."

The advice was too reasonable and above all came from a

man who knew the king too well for the four young men to try struggling against it. M. de Tréville invited them to go each to his own home and wait for his news.

On going into his hôtel, M. de Tréville reflected that he ought to steal a march by making the first complaint. He sent one of his servants to M. de La Trémouille with a letter in which he begged him to expel M. le cardinal's guards from his house and to reprimand his people for having the audacity to make a sortie against the musketeers. But M. de La Trémouille, already informed by his equerry, who, as we know, was Bernajoux's relation, replied to him that it was neither for M. de Tréville nor for his musketeers to complain, but, quite the contrary, for him whose people had been attacked by the musketeers and whose hôtel they had wanted to burn. Now, as the debate between these two lords could have lasted a long time, each of them naturally holding stubbornly to his opinion, M. de Tréville devised an expedient aimed at ending it all: this was to go to see M. de La Trémouille himself.

So he went at once to his hôtel and had himself announced. The two lords greeted each other politely, for, if there was no friendship between them, there was at least respect. They were both men of courage and of honor; and as M. de La Trémouille, a Protestant, and rarely in the king's presence, was of no party, he generally brought no prejudice to his social relations. This time, nevertheless, his welcome, though polite, was colder than usual.

"Monsieur," said M. de Tréville, "each of us believes he has a complaint against the other, and I have come to you myself so that together we can bring this affair to light."

"Gladly," replied M. de La Trémouille. "But I warn you that I am well informed, and the fault lies entirely with your musketeers."

"Monsieur, you are too just and reasonable a man," said M. de Tréville, "not to accept the proposition I am going to make."

"Make it, Monsieur, I'm listening."

"How is M. Bernajoux, your equerry's relation?"

"Why, very bad, Monsieur. Besides the wound he received in the arm, which is not especially dangerous, he acquired another that went through the lung, about which the doctor has very poor things to say."

"But has the wounded man remained conscious?"

"Perfectly."

"Can he speak?"

"With difficulty, but he can."

"Well, then, Monsieur, let us go to him; let us make him swear by the name of God, before whom he is perhaps about to be summoned, to tell the truth. I will take him as judge of his own case, Monsieur, and what he says, I will believe."

M. de La Trémouille reflected a moment; then, as it was difficult to make a more reasonable proposition, he accepted.

They both went down to the room where the wounded man lay. The latter, on seeing these two noble lords coming to visit him, attempted to raise himself on his bed, but he was too weak, and, exhausted by the effort, fell back almost unconscious.

M. de La Trémouille went up to him and held smelling salts to his nose, which brought him back to life. Then M. de Tréville, not wanting anyone to be able to say he had influenced the sick man, invited M. de La Trémouille to question him himself.

It happened as M. de Tréville had foreseen. Hovering between life and death as Bernajoux was, he never even thought for a moment of concealing the truth, and told the two lords everything exactly as it had happened.

That was all M. de Tréville wanted. He wished Bernajoux a quick recovery, took leave of M. de La Trémouille, went back to his hôtel, and immediately notified the four friends that he was expecting them for dinner.

M. de Tréville received the very best company—all anti-cardinalist to boot. It is understandable, then, that the conversation throughout dinner turned to the two defeats His Eminence's guards had just suffered. Now, since d'Artagnan had been the hero of both days, it was upon him that most of

the congratulations fell, and Athos, Porthos, and Aramis relin-
quished them to him not only as good comrades, but as men
who had had their own turn often enough to let him have his.

Towards six o'clock, M. de Tréville announced that he had
to go to the Louvre; but as the hour of the audience granted by
His Majesty was past, instead of requesting entry by the back
stairway, he placed himself with the four young men in the antechamber. The king had not yet come back from the hunt. Our
young men had waited no more than half an hour, mingling
with the crowd of courtiers, when all the doors were opened
and His Majesty was announced.

At that announcement, d'Artagnan felt himself shudder to
the marrow of his bones. The moment that was to follow
would, in all probability, determine the rest of his life. And so
his eyes were fixed with anxiety on the door through which the
king would enter.

Louis XIII came marching in first. He was in hunting dress,
still all dusty, wearing high boots and holding a crop in his
hand. At first glance, d'Artagnan judged that the king was in a
stormy mood.

This disposition, visible as it was in His Majesty, did not
keep the courtiers from lining up as he passed: in royal ante-
chambers it is better to be seen by an irate eye than not to be
seen at all. The three musketeers did not hesitate, then, and
took a step forward, while d'Artagnan, on the contrary, stayed
hidden behind them. But though the king knew Athos,
Porthos, and Aramis, he passed in front of them without looking at them, without speaking to them, and as if he had never
seen them. As for M. de Tréville, when the king's eyes rested a
moment on him, he endured that gaze with such firmness that
it was the king who looked away; after which, grumbling all
the while, the king went to his apartments.

"Things are going badly," Athos said, smiling. "We won't
be made knights of the order this time."

"Wait here for ten minutes," said M. de Tréville, "and if
you don't see me come out after ten minutes, go back to my
hôtel, for it will be useless for you to wait for me any longer."

The four young men waited ten minutes, fifteen minutes,

twenty minutes; and seeing that M. de Tréville did not reappear, they left, greatly worried about what was going to happen.

M. de Tréville had boldly entered the king's room and had found His Majesty in a very foul humor, sitting in an armchair and tapping his boots with the handle of his crop. But this had not prevented him from asking with great composure for news of his health.

"Bad, Monsieur, bad," replied the king. "I'm bored."

This was indeed the worst ailment of Louis XIII, who often took one of his courtiers, drew him over to a window, and said: "Monsieur So-and-So, let's be bored together."

"How's that? Your Majesty is bored?" said M. de Tréville. "Then you didn't take pleasure in the hunt today?"

"Fine pleasure, Monsieur! Everything's degenerating, by my soul, and I don't know whether the game no longer leaves a trail or the dogs no longer have noses. We let loose a ten-point stag, we pursue him for six hours, and when he's ready to be taken, when Saint-Simon is already putting the horn to his lips to blow the mort—bang! the whole pack changes direction and takes off after a brocket. It's evident that I shall be obliged to give up hunting as I've given up hawking. Ah! I'm a very unhappy king, M. de Tréville! I had only one gyrfalcon, and it died the day before yesterday."

"Indeed, Sire, I understand your despair, and the misfortune is a great one; but it seems to me you still have a good number of falcons, sparrow hawks, and tiercels."

"And not a man to train them. Falconers are disappearing; I'm the only one left who knows the art of venery. After me all will be said and done, and they'll hunt with pits, snares, and traps. If only I still had time to instruct some pupils! But no, there is M. le cardinal, who doesn't give me a moment's rest, who talks to me about Spain, talks to me about Austria, talks to me about England! Ah! speaking of M. le cardinal, M. de Tréville, I am displeased with you."

M. de Tréville was waiting for the king at this turning. He knew the king from long experience; he had understood that all his laments were only a preface, a sort of warm-up to encourage himself, and that he had finally got where he wanted to go.

"And in what am I so unfortunate as to have displeased Your Majesty?" asked M. de Tréville, feigning the deepest astonishment.

"Is this how you fulfill your responsibilities, Monsieur?" the king went on, without responding directly to M. de Tréville's question. "Is it for this that I named you captain of my musketeers, that they should murder a man, stir up a whole quarter, and try to burn down Paris without your saying a word? However," the king went on, "I am no doubt being hasty in accusing you. No doubt the troublemakers are in prison, and you have come to inform me that justice has been done."

"On the contrary, Sire," M. de Tréville replied calmly, "I have come to ask you for justice."

"Against whom?" cried the king.

"Against slanderers," said M. de Tréville.

"Ah! here's something new!" the king picked up. "Are you going to tell me that your three damned musketeers, Athos, Porthos, and Aramis, and your lad from Béarn, didn't throw themselves like madmen on poor Bernajoux and mistreat him so badly that he's probably on his way out of this world as I speak? Are you going to say that after that they didn't lay siege to the hôtel of the duc de La Trémouille, and that they didn't intend to burn it? Which would perhaps have been no great misfortune in time of war, seeing that it's a nest of Huguenots, but which, in time of peace, is a regrettable example. Tell me, are you going to deny all that?"

"And who told you this fine tale, Sire?" M. de Tréville asked calmly.

"Who told me this fine tale, Monsieur? Who else could it be, if not he who wakes while I sleep, who works while I amuse myself, who runs everything inside and outside the realm, in France as well as in Europe?"

"His Majesty is doubtless referring to God," said M. de Tréville, "for I know of no one but God who could be so far above His Majesty."

"No, Monsieur, I am referring to the sole support of the state, to my only servant, to my only friend—M. le cardinal."

"His Eminence is not His Holiness, Sire."

"What do you mean by that, Monsieur?"

"That only the pope is infallible, and that this infallibility does not extend to cardinals."

"You mean to say he's deceiving me, you mean to say he's betraying me? You're accusing him, then. Come, tell me, admit frankly that you're accusing him."

"No, Sire. But I say that he is deceived himself; I say that he has been ill informed; I say that he was in haste to accuse Your Majesty's musketeers, towards whom he is unjust, and that he has not drawn his information from the best sources."

"The accusation comes from M. de La Trémouille, from the duke himself. What do you say to that?"

"I might say, Sire, that he is too interested in the question to be an impartial witness; but beyond that, Sire, I know the duke to be a loyal gentleman, and I will defer to him, but on one condition, Sire."

"Which is?"

"That Your Majesty have him come, question him, but yourself, one to one, without witnesses, and that I see Your Majesty again as soon as you have received the duke."

"Why, yes!" said the king. "And you will defer to what M. de La Trémouille says?"

"Yes, Sire."

"You will accept his judgment?"

"Unquestionably."

"And you will submit to the reparations he demands?"

"Completely."

"La Chesnaye!" cried the king. "La Chesnaye!"

The trusted valet of Louis XIII, who always stood by the door, came in.

"La Chesnaye," said the king, "send someone this instant to summon M. de La Trémouille to me. I wish to speak to him this evening."

"Your Majesty gives me his word that he will see no one between M. de La Trémouille and myself?"

"No one, as I'm a gentleman."

"Till tomorrow, then, Sire."

"Till tomorrow, Monsieur."

"At what hour, if it please Your Majesty?"

"At whatever hour you like."

"But if I come too early in the morning, I fear I shall awaken Your Majesty."

"Awaken me? Do I ever sleep? I no longer sleep, Monsieur; I dream sometimes, that's all. Come as early in the morning as you like, at seven o'clock; but woe to you if your musketeers are guilty!"

"If my musketeers are guilty, Sire, the guilty ones will be handed over to Your Majesty, who will deal with them as he sees fit. Does Your Majesty require anything else? Speak, I am ready to obey."

"No, Monsieur, no, and it's not without reason that they call me Louis the Just. Till tomorrow, then, Monsieur, till tomorrow."

"God keep Your Majesty till then!"

Little as the king slept, M. de Tréville slept still worse. That same evening he sent notice to his three musketeers and their companion to be at his place at half-past six in the morning. He brought them with him without affirming anything, without promising them anything, and not concealing from them that their favor and even his own depended on a throw of the dice.

Coming to the foot of the back stairs, he had them wait. If the king was still angry with them, they could go away without being seen; if the king consented to receive them, they would only have to be called.

On entering the king's private antechamber, M. de Tréville found La Chesnaye, who informed him that they had not found M. de La Trémouille the evening before at his hôtel, that he had come back too late to present himself at the Louvre, that he had only just arrived, and that he was even now with the king.

This circumstance pleased M. de Tréville greatly. He was thus certain that no foreign suggestion would slip between M. de La Trémouille's deposition and himself.

Indeed, ten minutes had barely passed when the door to

the study opened and M. de Tréville saw M. de La Trémouille come out. The duke came up to him and said:

"M. de Tréville, His Majesty just sent to summon me in order to learn how things went yesterday morning at my hôtel. I told him the truth, that is to say, that the fault was with my people, and that I was ready to make you my apologies. Since I find you here, kindly receive them, and always hold me as one of your friends."

"Monsieur le duc," said M. de Tréville, "I was so fully confident of your loyalty that I wanted no other defender before His Majesty than yourself. I see that I was not mistaken, and I thank you that there is still in France a man of whom one can say without being deceived what I said of you."

"Very well, very well," said the king, who had listened to these compliments between the two doors. "Only tell him, Tréville, since he claims to be one of your friends, that I would also like to be one of his, but he neglects me, that it's three years now since I've seen him, and that I never see him except when I send for him. Tell him all that on my behalf, for these are things that a king cannot say himself."

"Thank you, Sire, thank you," said the duke, "but Your Majesty is well aware that it is not those—I am by no means saying this of M. de Tréville—it is not those he sees every hour of the day who are most devoted to him."

"Ah! so you heard what I said! So much the better, Duke, so much the better," said the king, going to the door. "Ah! it's you, M. de Tréville! Where are your musketeers? I told you the day before yesterday to bring them to me. Why haven't you done so?"

"They're downstairs, Sire, and with your leave La Chesnaye will go and tell them to come up."

"Yes, yes, let them come at once; it's nearly eight o'clock, and at nine I expect a visit. Go, M. le duc, and above all come back. This way, Tréville."

The duke bowed and left. Just as he opened the door, the three musketeers and d'Artagnan, escorted by La Chesnaye, appeared at the head of the stairs.

"Come, my brave lads," said the king, "come, I must scold you."

The musketeers approached bowing; d'Artagnan followed behind them.

"What the devil!" the king went on. "Seven of His Eminence's guards put out of action by you four in two days! It's too much, gentlemen, too much. At that rate, His Eminence will be forced to replace his company in three weeks, and I to apply the edicts in all their rigor. One now and then is another thing, but seven in two days—I repeat, it's too much, much too much."

"And so, Sire, Your Majesty can see that they have come to you all contrite and repentant to make you their apologies."

"All contrite and repentant! Hm!" said the king. "I don't trust their hypocritical faces, above all that Gascon-looking one. Come here, Monsieur."

D'Artagnan, who understood that the compliment was addressed to him, approached, putting on the most desperate air.

"Well, now, what did you mean by telling me he was a young man? He's a boy, M. de Tréville, a mere boy! And it was he who gave that mighty stroke to Jussac?"

"And those two fine strokes to Bernajoux."

"Really!"

"Not to mention," said Athos, "that if he hadn't taken me out of Cahusac's hands, I would most certainly not have the honor of making my most humble bow before Your Majesty at this moment."

"Why, he's a veritable demon then, this Béarnais—eh, M. de Tréville? Ventre-saint-gris! as the king my father used to say. In that trade, you have to pierce many a doublet and break many a blade. Now, Gascons are always poor, are they not?"

"Sire, I must say that they have yet to find gold mines in their mountains, though the Lord owes them that miracle in reward for the way they upheld the claims of the king your father."

"Which is to say that it was the Gascons who made me king myself, isn't that so, Tréville, since I'm my father's son? Well, then, when the time is right, I don't say no. La Chesnaye, go rummage through all my pockets, see if you can find forty pistoles; and if you find them, bring them to me. And now, young man, tell me, hand on heart, how did it go?"

D'Artagnan recounted the adventure of the day before in all its details: how, having been unable to sleep on account of the joy he felt at seeing His Majesty, he had come to his friends three hours before the time of the audience, how they had gone together to the sporting house, and how, for the fear he had shown of being hit in the face by a ball, he had been mocked by Bernajoux, who had nearly paid for that mockery with the loss of his life, and M. de La Trémouille, who had no part in it, with the loss of his hôtel.

"That's exactly it," murmured the king, "yes, that's just how the duke told it to me. Poor cardinal! Seven men in two days, and some of his most prized! But enough of that, gentlemen, you hear, enough! You've taken your revenge for the rue Férou, and even more; you should be satisfied."

"If Your Majesty is," said Tréville, "then we are."

"Yes, I am," added the king, taking a fistful of gold from La Chesnaye's hand and putting it into d'Artagnan's. "Here," he said, "is proof of my satisfaction."

At that time, the notions of pride current in our day had not yet come into fashion. A gentleman received the king's money from hand to hand, and was not humiliated in the least. So d'Artagnan put the forty pistoles into his pocket without any fuss, and, on the contrary, thanked His Majesty greatly.

"There," said the king, looking at his clock, "there, and now that it's half past eight, you may retire; for, as I told you, I'm expecting someone at nine. Thank you for your devotion, gentlemen. I may count on it, may I not?"

"Oh, Sire!" the four companions cried with one voice, "we would get ourselves cut to pieces for Your Majesty."

"Very well, very well; but stay whole—that's better still, and you'll be more useful to me. Tréville," the king added in a low voice while the others were leaving, "since you have no vacancy in the musketeers, and, besides, we decided that to enter that corps one has to make a novitiate, place this young man in the guards company of M. des Essarts, your brother-in-law. Ah, pardieu, Tréville, I rejoice at the grimace the cardinal is going to make! He'll be furious, but I don't care; I am within my rights."

And the king waved to Tréville, who left and went to rejoin his musketeers, whom he found dividing up the forty pistoles with d'Artagnan.

And the cardinal, as His Majesty had said, was indeed furious, so furious that for eight days he stayed away from the king's games, which did not prevent the king from putting on the most charming airs in the world with him, and asking him in the most caressing voice each time they met:

"Well, now, Monsieur le cardinal, how are those men of yours, poor Bernajoux and poor Jussac, getting on?"

VII

THE MUSKETEERS AT HOME

Once outside the Louvre, d'Artagnan consulted his friends on what use he should make of his share of the forty pistoles. Athos advised him to order a good meal at the Pomme de Pin, Porthos to hire a lackey, and Aramis to take a suitable mistress.

The meal was executed that same day, and the lackey served at table. The meal had been ordered by Athos, and the lackey furnished by Porthos. He was a Picard whom the vainglorious musketeer had hired that same day and for this occasion on the Pont de la Tournelle, while he was spitting into the water to make rings.

Porthos had held that this occupation was proof of a reflective and contemplative organization, and had brought him along without further recommendation. The grand bearing of this gentleman, in whose service he believed himself engaged, had seduced Planchet—for that was the Picard's name. He was slightly disappointed when he saw that the place had already been taken by a colleague named Mousqueton, and when Porthos pointed out to him that his household, though large, could not include two servants, and that he was to enter d'Artagnan's service. However, when he assisted at the dinner given by his master, and saw the latter take a fistful of gold from his pocket in order to pay, he thought his fortune was made and thanked heaven that he had fallen into the possession of such a Croesus. He persevered in this opinion until after the feast, from the leftovers of which he rewarded himself for much abstinence. But when he went to make up his master's bed in the evening, Planchet's pipe dreams vanished. The bed was the only one in the apartment, which consisted of an antechamber and a bedroom. Planchet slept in the antechamber on a blanket taken from d'Artagnan's bed, which d'Artagnan henceforth did without.

Athos, for his part, had a valet whom he had trained for his service in a rather special manner, and who was named Grimaud. He was extremely taciturn, this worthy lord. We are speaking of Athos, of course. For five or six years he had lived in the most profound intimacy with his companions Porthos and Aramis, the latter recalled having seen him smile often, but they had never heard him laugh. His utterances were brief and expressive, always saying what they meant to say and nothing more: no embellishments, no embroideries, no arabesques. His conversation was a fact without accessories.

Though Athos was barely thirty years old and was extremely handsome of body and mind, no one knew him to have a mistress. He never spoke of women. But he did not prevent people from speaking of them in front of him, though it was easy to see that this sort of conversation, which he mixed into only with bitter comments and misanthropic observations, was perfectly disagreeable to him. His reserve, his unsociability, and his silence made him almost an old man. Thus, in order not to depart from his habits, he had accustomed Grimaud to obeying him at a simple gesture or a simple movement of the lips. He never spoke to him except in ultimate circumstances.

Sometimes Grimaud, who feared his master like fire, though he had great affection for his person and great veneration for his genius, believed he had perfectly understood what he wanted, rushed to carry out the order received, and did precisely the contrary. Then Athos would shrug his shoulders and, without getting angry, give Grimaud a thrashing.

Porthos, as we have seen, had a character totally opposite to that of Athos: he not only talked a great deal, he also talked loudly; moreover, it mattered little to him—we must do him justice—whether anyone listened or not; he talked for the pleasure of talking and for the pleasure of hearing himself; he talked about everything except the sciences, pleading on that side the inveterate hatred which he had borne for scholars since childhood. He had less of a grand air than Athos, and his feeling of inferiority in that regard, at the beginning of their relations, had often made him unfair towards that gentleman, whom he attempted to surpass by his splendid outfits. But, with his simple musketeer's tabard, and merely by the way he threw back his head and advanced his foot, Athos instantly took the place that was his due and relegated the showy Porthos to second rank. Porthos consoled himself for that by filling M. de Tréville's antechamber and the guards corps at the Louvre with the noise of his successes, which Athos never spoke of, and for the moment, after passing from the nobility of the robe to the nobility of the sword, from the "judgess" to the baroness, it was a question for Porthos of nothing less than a foreign princess who wished him enormously well.

An old proverb says: "Like master, like man." Let us go on, then, from Athos's man to Porthos's man, from Grimaud to Mousqueton.

Mousqueton was a Norman whose master had changed his name from the pacific name of Boniface to the infinitely more sonorous and bellicose Mousqueton. He had entered Porthos's service on condition that he would be housed and clothed only, but in magnificent fashion; he required just two hours a day to devote himself to an industry that was sufficient to provide for his other needs. Porthos had accepted the deal; the thing suited him perfectly. He had doublets made for Mousqueton out of his old clothes and spare cloaks, and, thanks to a highly intelligent tailor, who made these rags like new by turning them inside out, and whose wife was suspected of wishing to bring Porthos down from his aristocratic habits, Mousqueton cut a very fine figure behind his master.

As for Aramis, whose character we believe we have sufficiently introduced, a character moreover which, like that of his companions, we will be able to follow in its development, his lackey was named Bazin. Thanks to his master's hope of one day entering into orders, he always went dressed in black, as a churchman's servant should do. He came from Berry, was thirty-five or forty years old, gentle, peaceable, plump, occupied with reading pious works in the moments of leisure his master left him, and in a pinch could prepare a dinner for two, of few dishes, but excellent. Deaf, dumb, and blind to boot, and of the staunchest loyalty.

Now that we know both the masters and the valets, at least superficially, let us go on to the dwellings they occupied.

Athos lived on the rue Férou, two steps from the Luxembourg. His apartment consisted of two small rooms, very decently furnished, in a rooming house whose still young and truly still beautiful hostess uselessly made soft eyes at him. Some fragments of a great past splendor shone here and there on the walls of these modest lodgings: there was a sword, for example, richly damascened, of the sort fashionable in the period of François I, and of which the hilt alone, encrusted with precious stones, might have been worth two hundred pistoles, and yet, in his moments of greatest distress, Athos had never agreed to pawn or sell it. Porthos had long had his heart set on this sword. He would have given ten years of his life to own it.

One day when he had a rendezvous with a duchess, he even tried to borrow it from Athos. Athos, without saying a word, emptied his pockets, collected all his jewels—purses, aiguillettes, and gold chains—and offered it all to Porthos; but, as for the sword, it was sealed in its place and would never leave it until its master himself left his lodgings. Besides his sword, he also had a portrait of a lord from the time of Henri III, dressed with the greatest elegance and wearing the Order of the Holy Spirit, and this portrait bore a certain resemblance to Athos in its lineaments, a certain family resemblance, which indicated that this great lord, a chevalier of the king's orders, was his ancestor.

Finally, a casket of magnificent goldsmith's work, with the same coat of arms as the sword and the portrait, made a chimneypiece that clashed frightfully with the rest of the trimmings. Athos always carried the key to this casket with him. But one day he had opened it in front of Porthos, and Porthos had been able to assure himself that it contained only letters and papers: love letters and family papers, no doubt.

Porthos lived in an apartment of vast size and sumptuous appearance on the rue du Vieux-Colombier. Each time he passed with some friend in front of his windows, at one of which Mousqueton always stood in full livery, Porthos would raise his head and his hand, and say: "There's my abode!" But he was never found at home, he never invited anyone to come up, and no one had any idea of what this sumptuous appearance enclosed by way of real riches.

As for Aramis, he lived in small quarters consisting of a boudoir, a dining room, and a bedroom, which bedroom, located on the ground floor like the rest of the apartment, gave onto a small garden, cool, green, shady, and impenetrable to neighboring eyes.

And as for d'Artagnan, we already know how he was lodged, and we have already made the acquaintance of his lackey, Master Planchet.

D'Artagnan, who was of a very curious nature, as people with a genius for intrigue generally are, made every effort to find out who Athos, Porthos, and Aramis really were; for, under these noms de guerre, each of the young men concealed his name as a gentleman, Athos above all, who smelled of a great lord a league away. He thus turned to Porthos for information about Athos and Aramis, and to Aramis for the truth about Porthos.

Unfortunately, Porthos himself knew nothing about his silent comrade's life except what had come to light. It was said that he had known great misfortunes in his amorous affairs, and that a terrible betrayal had poisoned the gallant man's life forever. What was this betrayal? No one knew.

As for Porthos, apart from his real name, which M. de

Tréville alone knew, along with those of his two comrades, his life was easily learned. Vain and indiscreet, he could be seen through like a crystal. The only thing that could have thrown off the investigator would have been to believe all the good he said of himself.

As for Aramis, while he had an air of having no secrets, this was a lad all steeped in mysteries, responding little to questions put to him about others, and eluding those put to him about himself. One day, d'Artagnan, after having interrogated him for a long time about Porthos, and having learned the rumor then going around about the musketeer's success with a princess, also wanted to know about his interlocutor's amorous adventures.

"And you, my dear companion," he said to him, "you who talk about other men's baronesses, duchesses, and princesses?"

"Excuse me," Aramis interrupted, "I talked about them because Porthos talks about them himself, because he has cried out all these pretty things in front of me. But believe me, my dear M. d'Artagnan, if I had them from another source, or he had told them to me in confidence, he could have had no confessor more discreet than I."

"I don't doubt it," d'Artagnan picked up, "but actually it seems to me that you yourself are rather familiar with coats of arms—witness a certain embroidered handkerchief to which I owe the honor of your acquaintance."

This time Aramis did not become angry, but put on his most modest air and replied affectionately:

"My dear, don't forget that I wish to be in the Church, and I flee all worldly circumstances. That handkerchief you saw was never entrusted to me, it had been forgotten at my place by one of my friends. I had to take it so as not to compromise them, he and the lady he loves. As for me, I do not have and do not wish to have a mistress, following in this the highly judicious example of Athos, who has one no more than I do."

"But, devil take it, you're not an abbé, you're a musketeer!"

"An interim musketeer, my dear, as the cardinal says, a musketeer against my will, but a man of the Church at heart, believe me. Athos and Porthos dragged me into it to keep me occupied: at the moment of my ordination, I had a small difficulty with . . . But that hardly interests you, and I'm taking up your precious time."

"Not at all, it interests me very much," cried d'Artagnan, "and for the moment I have absolutely nothing to do."

"Yes, but I have my breviary to recite," replied Aramis, "then some verses to compose at Mme d'Aiguillon's request; then I have to go to the rue Saint-Honoré to buy rouge for Mme de Chevreuse. So you see, my dear friend, if you are not in a hurry, I certainly am."

And Aramis affectionately held out his hand to his friend and took leave of him.

D'Artagnan, for all the pains he took, could find out nothing more about his three new friends. He chose therefore to believe for the present all that he had been told about their past, hoping for more certain and extensive revelations in the future. Meanwhile, he considered Athos an Achilles, Porthos an Ajax, and Aramis a Joseph.

Besides, the life of the four young men was merry. Athos gambled, and always unluckily. However, he never borrowed a sou from his friends, though his purse was constantly at their service, and when he gambled on credit, he always woke up his creditor at six o'clock the next morning to pay him his debt from the day before.

Porthos had his impulses: on those days, if he won, he went around insolent and splendid; if he lost, he disappeared for several days, after which he reappeared looking pale and drawn, but with money in his pockets.

As for Aramis, he never gambled. He was quite the worst musketeer and the most miserable guest you could ever see. He always had to work. Sometimes, in the middle of a dinner, when everyone, carried away by the wine and the heat of conversation, thought they would remain at the table for a good two or three hours more, Aramis would look at his watch, get up with a gracious smile, and take leave of the company—to go, he said, and consult a casuist with whom he had a rendezvous. Other times he would return to his lodgings to write a thesis, and begged his friends not to distract him.

However, Athos would smile that charming, melancholy smile that suited his noble face so well, and Porthos would drink an oath that Aramis would never become a village priest.

Planchet, d'Artagnan's valet, bore good fortune nobly. He received thirty sous a day, and for a month returned to his lodgings gay as a chaffinch and feeling affable towards his master. When the wind of adversity began to blow on the household of the rue des Fossoyeurs, that is to say, when the forty pistoles of King Louis XIII were eaten up, or almost, he began to complain in a way that Athos found nauseating, Porthos indecent, and Aramis ridiculous. Athos then advised d'Artagnan to dismiss the rascal, Porthos wanted him cudgeled first, and Aramis maintained that a master should only heed the compliments he was paid.

"That's easy enough for you to say," d'Artagnan picked up, "for you, Athos, who live mutely with Grimaud, who forbid him to speak, and who, consequently, never have any bad words from him; for you, Porthos, who live in a magnificent manner and are a god to your valet Mousqueton; for you, Aramis, who are always distracted by your theological studies, inspiring a deep respect in your servant Bazin, a gentle and religious man; but I, who am without substance and resources, I who am not a musketeer nor even a guard, what can I do to inspire affection, terror, or respect in Planchet?"

"It's a grave matter," replied the three friends. "It's an internal affair. It's the same with valets as with women: you have to put them straight away on the footing you want them to remain on. Reflect, then."

D'Artagnan reflected and decided to thrash him for a start, which was done with the conscientiousness that d'Artagnan put into everything; then, after thrashing him well, he forbade him to leave his service without his permission. "For," he added, "the future cannot fail me; I inevitably await better times. So your fortune is made if you stay with me, and I am too kind a master to make you miss your fortune by granting you the leave you are asking me for."

This way of acting gave the musketeers a great deal of respect for d'Artagnan's diplomacy. Planchet was also struck with admiration and said nothing more about quitting.

The lives of the four young men became a common one. D'Artagnan, who had no habits, since he had come from his province and fallen into the midst of a world that was entirely new to him, soon took up the habits of his friends.

They got up towards eight o'clock in the winter, towards six o'clock in the summer, and went to take their orders and the air of events at M. de Tréville's. D'Artagnan, though he was not a musketeer, did the service of one with a touching punctuality: he was always on guard duty, because he always kept company with the one of his three friends, who mounted guard himself. He was known in the hôtel of the musketeers, and everyone held him to be a good comrade. M. de Tréville, who had appraised him at first glance, and who bore a genuine affection for him, constantly recommended him to the king.

For their part, the three musketeers loved their young friend greatly. The friendship that united the four men, and the need to see each other three or four times a day, either for a duel, or for business, or for pleasure, kept them constantly running after one another like shadows; and one could always come upon the inseparables if one searched between the Luxembourg and the place Saint-Sulpice, or between the rue du Vieux-Colombier and the Luxembourg.

Meanwhile M. de Tréville's promises were taking their course. One fine day, the king commanded M. le chevalier des Essarts to take d'Artagnan as a cadet in his guards company. D'Artagnan sighed as he put on the uniform, which he would have exchanged at the price of ten years of his existence against the tabard of a musketeer. But M. de Tréville promised him that favor after a two-year novitiate, a novitiate which, moreover, could be shortened, if the occasion presented itself for d'Artagnan to render some service to the king or to perform some brilliant action. D'Artagnan withdrew on that promise, and the next day began his service.

Then it was the turn of Athos, Porthos, and Aramis to mount guard with d'Artagnan when he was on duty. The company of M. le chevalier des Essarts thus acquired four men instead of one on the day it acquired d'Artagnan.

VIII

A COURT INTRIGUE

However, the forty pistoles of King Louis XIII, like all things in this world, having had a beginning, also had an end, and since that end our four companions had fallen into tight straits. At first Athos had supported the association for a time out of his own pocket. Porthos had succeeded him, and, thanks to one of those disappearances to which they were accustomed, had met the needs of all for another fortnight. Finally had come the turn of Aramis, who had complied with good grace, and managed, as he said, to get hold of a few pistoles by selling his theology books.

Then, as usual, they had recourse to M. de Tréville, who gave them some advances on their pay; but on these advances three musketeers who already had many accounts in arrears, and a guard who as yet had none, could not go far.

Finally, when they saw that they would soon run out entirely, they gathered eight or ten pistoles in a last effort, and Porthos gambled on them. Unfortunately, his luck was bad: he lost it all, plus twenty-five pistoles on credit.

Then tight straits became real distress. The hungry men were seen, followed by their valets, roaming the quais and guards' quarters, gleaning from their outside friends all the dinners they could find; for, according to Aramis, in prosperity one should sow meals right and left, in order to harvest some in adversity.

Athos was invited four times and each time brought along his friends with their lackeys. Porthos had six occasions and let his friends enjoy them equally. Aramis had eight. He was a man, as we have already been able to perceive, of little noise and much work.

As for d'Artagnan, who still knew no one in the capital, he found only a breakfast of chocolate with a priest from his part of the country, and a dinner with a cornet of the guards. He led his army to the priest, where they devoured two months' worth of his provisions, and to the cornet, who worked wonders; but, as Planchet said, you only eat once, even when you eat a lot.

D'Artagnan thus found himself rather humiliated to have only a meal and a half, for the breakfast with the priest could count as only half a meal, to offer his companions in exchange for the feasts procured by Athos, Porthos, and Aramis. He felt himself a burden to the society, forgetting in his quite youthful good faith that he had fed that society for a month, and his worried mind began working actively. He reflected that this coalition of four brave, enterprising, and active young men should have some other end than swaggering promenades, fencing lessons, and more or less witty gibes.

Indeed, four men like them, four men devoted to each other from their money to their lives, four men always supporting each other, never retreating, performing singly or together the resolutions they had made in common; four arms threatening the four points of the compass or all turning to a single point, must inevitably, be it surreptitiously, be it openly, be it by mines, by entrenchments, by guile, or by force, open a way to the end they wanted to reach, however well defended or far off it might be. The only thing that surprised d'Artagnan was that his companions had never thought of it.

He was thinking of it, and even seriously, racking his brain to find a direction for this single force multiplied four times, with which he had no doubt that, as with the lever sought by Archimedes, they would be able to lift the world—when someone knocked softly on his door. D'Artagnan woke Planchet and ordered him to go and open it.

This phrase—d'Artagnan woke Planchet—should not lead the reader to conclude that it was night or that day had not yet come. No, it had just struck four! Two hours earlier, Planchet had come to ask his master for dinner, and in reply had received the proverb: "He who sleeps, eats." And so Planchet ate by sleeping.

A man was ushered in, of rather simple bearing and with the air of a bourgeois.

Planchet would have liked to listen to the conversation for dessert, but the bourgeois declared to d'Artagnan that, as what he had to tell him was important and confidential, he wished to be alone with him.

D'Artagnan dismissed Planchet and invited his visitor to sit down.

There was a moment of silence during which the two men looked at each other as if to make a preliminary acquaintance, after which d'Artagnan nodded as a sign that he was listening.

"I have heard M. d'Artagnan spoken of as a brave young man," said the bourgeois, "and that reputation which he justly enjoys made me decide to entrust him with a secret."

"Speak, Monsieur, speak," said d'Artagnan, who instinctively scented something advantageous.

The bourgeois paused again and then went on:

"My wife is a seamstress to the queen, Monsieur, and is lacking neither in wisdom nor in beauty. It will soon be three years since she was married to me, though she had only a little fortune, because M. de La Porte, the queen's cloak bearer, is her godfather and protector . . ."

"Well, then, Monsieur?" asked d'Artagnan.

"Well, then," the bourgeois picked up, "well, then, Monsieur, my wife was abducted yesterday morning as she was coming out of her workroom."

"And by whom was your wife abducted?"

"I know nothing for certain, Monsieur, but there is someone I suspect."

"And who is this person you suspect?"

"A man who has been pursuing her for a long time."

"Devil take it!"

"But let me tell you, Monsieur," the bourgeois went on, "I myself am convinced that there is less love than politics in all this."

"Less love than politics," d'Artagnan picked up with a very thoughtful air, "and what do you suspect?"

"I don't know if I should tell you what I suspect . . ."

"Monsieur, I will point out to you that I am demanding absolutely nothing from you. It is you who have come to me. It is you who have told me that you have a secret to entrust to me. Do as you please, then, you still have time to back out."

"No, Monsieur, no; you seem to be an honest young man, and I will trust you. I believe, then, that my wife has been apprehended not on account of her love affairs, but on account of those of a woman higher than she."

"Aha! might it be on account of the love affairs of Mme de Bois-Tracy?" said d'Artagnan, who wished to have the air, vis-à-vis his bourgeois, of being in the know about the doings at court.

"Higher, Monsieur, higher."

"Of Mme d'Aiguillon?"

"Still higher."

"Of Mme de Chevreuse?"

"Higher, much higher!"

"Of the . . ." d'Artagnan stopped.

"Yes, Monsieur," the frightened bourgeois replied, so softly that he could barely be heard.

"And with whom?"

"Who can it be, if not the duke of . . ."

"The duke of . . ."

"Yes, Monsieur!" replied the bourgeois, giving a still lower intonation to his voice.

"But how do you know all that?"

"Ah! how do I know?"

"Yes, how do you know? No half trust, or . . . you understand."

"I know it from my wife, Monsieur, from my wife herself."

"Who knows it from whom?"

"From M. de La Porte. Didn't I tell you that she is the goddaughter of M. de La Porte, the queen's trusted man? Well, M. de La Porte placed her near Her Majesty so that our poor queen would have at least someone to trust, abandoned as she is by the king, spied on as she is by the cardinal, betrayed as she is by everyone."

"Aha! something's taking shape here," said d'Artagnan.

"Now, my wife came four days ago, Monsieur. One of her conditions was that she should visit me twice a week, for, as I have had the honor of telling you, my wife loves me very much. So my wife came and confided to me that the queen was in great fear at that moment."

"Really?"

"Yes, M. le cardinal, as it seems, is pursuing her and persecuting her more than ever. He cannot forgive her the story of the saraband. You know the story of the saraband?"

"Pardieu, as if I didn't!" replied d'Artagnan, who knew nothing at all about it, but wanted to have the air of being in the know.

"So that now it is no longer a matter of hatred, but of vengeance."

"Really?"

"And the queen thinks . . ."

"Well, what does the queen think?"

"She thinks someone has written to the duke of Buckingham in her name."

"In the queen's name?"

"Yes, to make him come to Paris, and once he has come to Paris, to draw him into some trap."

"Devil take it! But what, my dear Monsieur, does your wife have to do with all this?"

"Her devotion to the queen is known, and they want to distance her from Her Majesty, or intimidate her in order to find out Her Majesty's secrets, or seduce her in order to use her as a spy."

"That's probable," said d'Artagnan. "But do you know the man who abducted her?"

"I've told you that I think I know him."

"His name?"

"I don't know that; I know only that he is a creature of the cardinal, his tool."

"But have you seen him?"

"Yes, my wife showed him to me one day."

"Does he have any signs one could recognize him by?"

"Oh, certainly! He's a lord of haughty bearing, black hair, dark skin, a piercing eye, white teeth, and a scar on his temple."

"A scar on his temple!" cried d'Artagnan. "And along with that, white teeth, a piercing eye, dark skin, black hair, and a haughty bearing! It's my man from Meung!"

"Your man, you say?"

"Yes, yes, but that doesn't change anything. No, I'm wrong; that simplifies a great deal. On the contrary: if your man is mine, I'll have two vengeances at one stroke, that's all. But where can the man be found?"

"I don't know."

"You have no information about where he lives?"

"None. One day as I was taking my wife back to the Louvre, he came out as she was going in, and she pointed him out to me."

"Devil take it! Devil take it!" murmured d'Artagnan. "This is all very vague. Who told you about your wife's abduction?"

"M. de La Porte."

"Did he give you any details?"

"He had none."

"And you've learned nothing from any other quarter?"

"Yes, I have. I received . . ."

"What?"

"But perhaps I am committing a great imprudence?"

"You're starting on that again? However, I'll observe to you that this time it's a bit late to back out."

"I am not backing out, mordieu!" cried the bourgeois, swearing in order to work himself up. "Besides, on Bonacieux's honor . . ."

"Your name is Bonacieux?" interrupted d'Artagnan.

"Yes, it is."

"So you were saying: on Bonacieux's honor! Forgive me for interrupting you, but it seemed to me that the name was not unknown to me."

"That's possible, Monsieur. I am your landlord."

"Aha!" said d'Artagnan, half rising and bowing to him, "you are my landlord?"

"Yes, Monsieur, yes. And as it's three months now that

you've been with me, and, no doubt distracted by your great occupations, you have forgotten to pay me my rent—as, I say, I have not pestered you once, I thought you might show consideration for my delicate position."

"But of course, my dear M. Bonacieux!" d'Artagnan picked up. "Believe me, I'm filled with gratitude for such fair dealing, and, as I've said, if I can help you somehow . . ."

"I believe you, Monsieur, I believe you, and as I was about to tell you, on Bonacieux's honor, I trust you."

"Then finish what you've begun telling me."

The bourgeois drew a paper from his pocket and handed it to d'Artagnan.

"A letter!" cried the young man.

D'Artagnan opened it, and as the light was beginning to fade, he went over to the window. The bourgeois followed him.

" 'Do not look for your wife,' " d'Artagnan read. " 'She will be returned to you when there is no more need for her. If you take a single step to find her, you are lost.' "

"That's straightforward enough," d'Artagnan went on. "But, after all, it's just a threat."

"Yes, but this threat frightens me. I, Monsieur, am no swordsman at all, and I'm afraid of the Bastille."

"Hm!" said d'Artagnan. "But I care no more for the Bastille than you do. If it's only a question of swordplay, it's not much."

"However, Monsieur, I've been counting on you in this matter."

"Oh?"

"Seeing you constantly surrounded by superb-looking musketeers, and recognizing that these musketeers were those of M. de Tréville, and consequently the cardinal's enemies, I've been thinking that you and your friends, while rendering justice to our poor queen, would be delighted to do His Eminence a bad turn."

"Unquestionably."

"And then I've been thinking that, owing me three months rent, which I have never mentioned to you . . ."

"Yes, yes, you've already given me that reason, and I find it excellent."

"Counting, what's more, on never mentioning your future rent, as long as you do me the honor of staying with me . . ."

"Very good."

"And added to that, if need be, counting on offering you fifty pistoles, if, against all probability, you find yourself in tight straits at the moment."

"Wonderful! So you're a rich man, my dear M. Bonacieux?"

"I'm comfortably off, Monsieur, that's the word. I've put together something like two or three thousand écus of income in the mercery trade, and above all by investing certain sums in the last voyage of the famous navigator Jean Mocquet, so that, you can understand, Monsieur . . . Ah! but . . ." cried the bourgeois.

"What?" asked d'Artagnan.

"What's this I see?"

"Where?"

"In the street, across from your windows, in that doorway: a man wrapped in a cloak."

"It's he!" d'Artagnan and the bourgeois cried out at once, each having recognized his man at the same time.

"Ah! this time," cried d'Artagnan, leaping for his sword, "this time he won't escape me!"

And, drawing his sword from the scabbard, he rushed out of the apartment.

On the stairs he ran into Athos and Porthos, who were coming to see him. They separated, and d'Artagnan passed between them like a shot.

"Ah! but where are you running like that?" the two musketeers called after him.

"The man from Meung!" replied d'Artagnan, and he disappeared.

D'Artagnan had more than once told his friends about his adventure with the unknown man, and of the appearance of the beautiful traveler to whom this man seemed to have entrusted some important missive.

Athos's view had been that d'Artagnan had lost his letter in the scuffle. A gentleman, according to him—and from the portrait d'Artagnan had painted of the unknown man, he could only have been a gentleman—a gentleman would have been incapable of such baseness as stealing a letter.

Porthos had seen nothing in it all but an amorous rendezvous granted by a lady to a cavalier or by a cavalier to a lady, and which had been disturbed by the presence of d'Artagnan and his yellow horse.

Aramis had said that, such things being mysterious, it was better not to go into them.

They understood, then, from the few words d'Artagnan let drop, what the matter was, and as they thought that, after overtaking his man or losing sight of him, d'Artagnan would in any case come back home, they continued on their way.

When they came into d'Artagnan's room, the room was empty: the landlord, fearing the consequences of the encounter that was undoubtedly about to take place between the young guard and the unknown man, had, in consequence of the display of character he himself had just made, judged it prudent to decamp.

IX

D'ARTAGNAN SHOWS HIMSELF

As Athos and Porthos had foreseen, d'Artagnan came back in half an hour. This time, too, he had missed his man, who had disappeared as if by magic. D'Artagnan had run, sword in hand, through all the surrounding streets, but had found nothing resembling the man he was looking for; then he had finally come back to what he perhaps should have started with, which was to knock on the door against which the unknown man had been leaning. He had rapped with the knocker ten or twelve times, but in vain; no one had answered, and the neighbors, who, attracted by the noise, had come running to their doorways or stuck their noses out the window, had assured him that the house, in which, moreover, all the openings were closed up, had been uninhabited for six months.

While d'Artagnan was running through the streets and knocking at doors, Aramis had joined his two companions, so that when he came home, d'Artagnan found the reunion at full strength.

"Well, then?" the three musketeers said at once, on seeing d'Artagnan come in, sweat on his brow and his face distorted with wrath.

"Well, then," he cried, throwing his sword on the bed, "the man must be the devil himself! He disappeared like a phantom, a shade, a ghost."

"Do you believe in apparitions?" Athos asked Porthos.

"Me? I only believe what I've seen, and since I've never seen any apparitions, I don't believe in them."

"The Bible," said Aramis, "makes it a law for us to believe in them: the shade of Samuel appeared to Saul, and that is an article of faith I would be sorry to see put in doubt, Porthos."

"In any case, man or devil, body or shade, illusion or reality, that man was born for my damnation, for his escape has cost us a splendid business, gentlemen, a business in which there were a hundred pistoles to be gained and maybe more."

"How's that?" Porthos and Aramis said at once.

As for Athos, faithful to his system of silence, he contented himself with questioning d'Artagnan with a look.

"Planchet," d'Artagnan said to his servant, who just then stuck his head through the half-open door to try to catch some shreds of the conversation, "go downstairs to the landlord, M. Bonacieux, and tell him to send us a half dozen bottles of Beaugency—it's my favorite wine."

"Ah, well, so you have open credit with your landlord?" asked Porthos.

"Yes," replied d'Artagnan, "starting from today, and don't worry, if his wine is bad, we'll send him out for better."

"One must use, not abuse," Aramis said sententiously.

"I've always said that d'Artagnan had the best head of the four of us," said Athos, who, after coming out with this opinion, to which d'Artagnan responded with a bow, relapsed at once into his customary silence.

"But, look here, what's he got finally?" asked Porthos.

"Yes," said Aramis, "confide it to us, my dear friend, unless the honor of some lady happens to be involved in the confidence, in which case you'd do better to keep it to yourself."

"Don't worry," replied d'Artagnan, "nobody's honor will find fault with what I have to tell you."

And then he told his friends, word for word, what had just gone on between himself and his landlord, and how the man who had abducted the worthy householder's wife was the same with whom he had had a bone to pick at the hôtel of the Jolly Miller.

"It's not a bad business," said Athos, after having tasted the wine as a connoisseur and indicated with a nod of the head that he found it good, "and we could get fifty or sixty pistoles out of the brave man. Now it remains to find out if fifty or sixty pistoles are worth the trouble of risking four heads."

"But mind you," cried d'Artagnan, "there's a woman involved in this business, an abducted woman, a woman who is no doubt being threatened, who is perhaps being tortured, and all that because she's faithful to her mistress!"

"Take care, d'Artagnan, take care," said Aramis, "you're getting a bit too excited, in my opinion, about the fate of Mme Bonacieux. Woman was created for our ruin, and it is from her that all our miseries come."

At this pronouncement from Aramis, Athos frowned and bit his lips.

"It's not at all Mme Bonacieux that worries me," cried d'Artagnan, "it's the queen, whom the king has abandoned, whom the cardinal persecutes, and who has seen the heads of her friends fall one after another."

"Why does she love what we detest most in the world—the Spanish and the English?"

"Spain is her country," replied d'Artagnan, "and it's quite simple why she loves the Spanish, they're children of the same land as she. As for the second reproach you make against her, I've heard it said that she loves not the English, but one Englishman."

"Ah, by heaven," said Athos, "one must admit that that Englishman was quite worthy of being loved! I've never seen grander bearing than his."

"Not to mention that he dresses like no one else," said Porthos. "I was at the Louvre the day he scattered his pearls, and, pardieu, I gathered up two that I sold for ten pistoles apiece. And you, Aramis, do you know him?"

"As well as you do, gentlemen, for I was one of those who arrested him in the garden at Amiens, where I had been introduced by M. de Putange, the queen's equerry. I was in seminary at that time, and the adventure seemed to me cruel for the king."

"Which wouldn't prevent me," said d'Artagnan, "from taking the duke of Buckingham by the hand, if I knew where he was, and bringing him to the queen, if only so as to enrage the cardinal; for our real, only, eternal enemy, gentlemen, is the cardinal, and if we could find the means of playing him some really cruel turn, I confess I'd gladly risk my head on it."

"And," Athos picked up, "the mercer told you, d'Artagnan, that the queen thought someone had made Buckingham come on false notice."

"She's afraid so."

"Wait," said Aramis.

"For what?" asked Porthos.

"Just a minute, I'm trying to remember the circumstances."

"And now I'm convinced," said d'Artagnan, "that the abduction of this woman of the queen's is connected to the events we're speaking of, and maybe to M. de Buckingham's presence in Paris."

"The Gascon's full of ideas," Porthos said with admiration.

"I love to hear him speak," said Athos, "his patter amuses me."

"Gentlemen," Aramis picked up, "listen to this."

"Listen to Aramis," said the three friends.

"Yesterday I happened to be with a learned doctor of theology, whom I consult occasionally to do with my studies . . ."

Athos smiled.

"He lives in a deserted quarter," Aramis went on, "his tastes and his profession demand it. Now, just as I was leaving his place . . ."

Here Aramis stopped.

"Well?" asked his listeners, "just as you were leaving his place?"

Aramis seemed to be struggling with himself, like a man who, in the midst of a lie, finds himself stopped by some unforeseen obstacle. But the eyes of his three companions were fixed on him, their ears waited gaping, there was no way to retreat.

"This doctor has a niece," Aramis went on.

"Ah! he has a niece!" Porthos interrupted.

"A highly respectable lady," said Aramis.

The three friends began to laugh.

"Ah, if you laugh, or if you doubt me," said Aramis, "then you'll learn nothing!"

"We're as believing as Mohammedists and as mute as catafalques," said Athos.

"To continue, then," Aramis went on. "This niece sometimes comes to see her uncle. Now, she happened to be there yesterday at the same time I was, by chance, and I had to show her to her carriage."

"Ah, the doctor's niece has a carriage?" interrupted Porthos, one of whose failings was great verbal incontinence. "A nice acquaintance, my friend."

"Porthos," Aramis picked up, "I've already pointed out to you more than once that you are extremely indiscreet, and that it does you harm with women."

"Gentlemen, gentlemen," cried d'Artagnan, who began to see the point of the game, "this is a serious thing; let's try not to joke if we can help it. Go on, Aramis, go on."

"All of a sudden a tall man, dark-haired, with the manners of a gentleman . . . in fact, just like your man, d'Artagnan . . ."

"The same, perhaps," said the latter.

"It's possible," Aramis continued, ". . . approached me, accompanied by five or six men who followed ten paces behind him, and said to me in the most polite tone: 'Monsieur le duc, and you, Madame,' he went on, turning to the lady who was on my arm . . ."

"The doctor's niece?"

"Be quiet, Porthos," said Athos, "you're insufferable!"

" '. . . kindly get into this carriage, and without offering the slightest resistance, without making the slightest noise.' "

"He took you for Buckingham!" cried d'Artagnan.

"I believe so," replied Aramis.

"But the lady?" asked Porthos.

"He took her for the queen!" said d'Artagnan.

"Precisely," said Aramis.

"The Gascon's a real devil!" cried Athos. "Nothing escapes him!"

"The fact is," said Porthos, "that Aramis is the same size and has something of the same figure as the handsome duke. It seems to me, however, that the uniform of a musketeer . . ."

"I had an enormous cloak," said Aramis.

"In the month of July, devil take it!" said Porthos. "Is the doctor afraid you'll be recognized?"

"I can understand," said Athos, "that the spy was taken in by the figure; but the face . . ."

"I had a big hat," said Aramis.

"Oh, my God!" cried Porthos. "Such precautions in order to study theology!"

"Gentlemen, gentlemen," said d'Artagnan, "don't waste time bantering. Let's divide up and search for the mercer's wife, that's the key to the plot."

"A woman of such inferior condition? Do you really think so, d'Artagnan?" said Porthos, drawing out his lips in disdain.

"She's the goddaughter of La Porte, the queen's trusted valet. Didn't I tell you that, gentlemen? And besides, maybe it was out of calculation that Her Majesty sought support, this time, in such low places. High heads can be seen from far off, and the cardinal has good eyes."

"Well, then," said Porthos, "first come to a price with the mercer—and a good price!"

"There's no point," said d'Artagnan, "for I believe that if

he doesn't pay us, we'll be paid well enough from another quarter."

At that moment, the noise of hurrying footsteps was heard on the stairs, the door opened with a bang, and the unfortunate mercer flew into the room where the council was being held.

"Ah, gentlemen!" he cried. "Save me, in the name of heaven, save me! Four men have come to arrest me! Save me, save me!"

Porthos and Aramis stood up.

"One moment," cried d'Artagnan, making a sign for them to push their half-drawn swords back into their scabbards, "one moment, it's not courage that's needed here, it's prudence."

"All the same," cried Porthos, "we won't let . . ."

"You'll let d'Artagnan do it," said Athos. "He is, I repeat, the best head among us, and I, for my part, declare that I will obey him. Do as you like, d'Artagnan."

At that moment, the four guards appeared at the door of the antechamber, and seeing four musketeers standing with swords at their sides, hesitated to go further.

"Come in, gentlemen, come in," cried d'Artagnan. "You are here in my home, and we are all faithful servants of the king and M. le cardinal."

"In that case, gentlemen, you won't oppose us if we carry out the orders we've received?" asked the one who seemed to be the chief of the squad.

"On the contrary, gentlemen, and we'll even lend you a hand if need be."

"What's he saying?" murmured Porthos.

"You're a ninny!" said Athos. "Keep quiet!"

"But you promised me . . ." the poor mercer said in a whisper.

"We can only save you if we remain free," d'Artagnan replied rapidly and in a whisper, "but if we make as if to defend you, they'll arrest us with you."

"It seems to me, though . . ."

"Come, gentlemen, come," d'Artagnan said aloud. "I have no reason to defend the man. I've seen him for the first time today, and he'll tell you why himself—it was to demand my rent from me. Isn't that true, M. Bonacieux? Answer!"

"It's the pure truth," cried the mercer, "but Monsieur isn't telling you . . ."

"Not a word about me, not a word about my friends, not a word about the queen above all, or you'll lose everyone without saving yourself. Go on, go on, gentlemen, take the man away!"

And d'Artagnan pushed the stunned mercer into the hands of the guards, saying to him:

"You're a knave, my dear sir; you come to ask money from me—me, a musketeer! To prison, gentlemen, I say again, take him away to prison, and keep him under lock and key for as long as you can. That will give me time to pay."

The beagles overflowed with gratitude and went off with their prey.

As they were going downstairs, d'Artagnan slapped the chief on the shoulder.

"Why don't I drink your health and you mine?" he said, filling two glasses with the Beaugency that he owed to M. Bonacieux's liberality.

"It would be an honor for me," said the chief beagle, "and I accept with gratitude."

"So, then, to your health, M. . . . what is your name?"

"Boisrenard."

"M. Boisrenard!"

"And to yours, sir. What is your name, if you please?"

"D'Artagnan."

"To your health, M. d'Artagnan!"

"And above all the rest," cried d'Artagnan, as if carried away by his enthusiasm, "to the health of the king and the cardinal."

The chief beagle would perhaps have doubted d'Artagnan's sincerity if the wine had been bad; but as the wine was good, he was convinced.

"But what the devil sort of villainy have you pulled now?" said Porthos, when the alguazil in chief had rejoined his companions, and the four friends found themselves alone again. "Pah! Four musketeers let a wretch who is calling for help be arrested right in their midst! A gentleman clinks glasses with a writ server!"

"Porthos," said Aramis, "Athos has already informed you that you are a ninny, and I concur with his opinion. D'Artagnan, you're a great man, and when you replace M. de Tréville, I'll ask for your patronage in getting myself an abbey."

"Ah, well, I'm completely lost!" said Porthos. "So you approve of what d'Artagnan has just done?"

"I think it's splendid, parbleu!" said Athos. "I not only approve of what he's just done, but I congratulate him for it."

"And now, gentlemen," said d'Artagnan, without bothering to explain his conduct to Porthos, "all for one and one for all—that's our motto, isn't it?"

"But still . . ." said Porthos.

"Hold out your hand and swear!" Athos and Aramis cried at once.

Defeated by example, grumbling quietly, Porthos held out his hand, and the four friends repeated with one voice the formula dictated by d'Artagnan:

"All for one and one for all."

"Good. Now let's each retire to his own home," said d'Artagnan, as if he had done nothing but give orders all his life, "and watch out, for from this moment on, we're at grips with the cardinal."

X

A SEVENTEENTH-CENTURY MOUSETRAP

The mousetrap was not invented in our day. Once societies, in their formation, had invented any sort of police, the police in turn invented the mousetrap.

As our readers may not yet be familiar with the jargon of the rue de Jérusalem, and this is the first time since we began to write—and we have been at it for fifteen years—that we have used this word applied to this thing, we shall explain to them what a mousetrap is.

When, in whatever house it may be, an individual has been arrested on suspicion of some crime, the arrest is kept secret. Four or five men are set in ambush in the first room, the door is opened to all who knock, it is closed behind them, and they are arrested. In this way, after two or three days, just about all the familiars of the establishment have been taken.

That is what a mousetrap is.

Master Bonacieux's apartment was thus made into a mousetrap, and whoever turned up there was taken and questioned by M. le cardinal's people. It goes without saying that, as a private alley led to the second floor inhabited by d'Artagnan, those who came to his place were exempt from all such visits.

Besides, the three musketeers came there separately. Each of them had set out searching in his own direction, and had found nothing, had discovered nothing. Athos had even gone so far as to question M. de Tréville, a thing which, given the customary silence of the worthy musketeer, had greatly surprised his captain. But M. de Tréville knew nothing, except that the last time he had seen the cardinal, the king, and the queen, the cardinal had had an extremely worried look, the king had been upset, and the reddened eyes of the queen had indicated that she had lain awake or wept. But this last circumstance had not struck him very much, because, ever since her marriage, the queen had lain awake and wept a great deal.

M. de Tréville charged Athos in any case to serve the king and above all the queen, begging him to give the same charge to his comrades.

As for d'Artagnan, he did not budge from home. He had converted his room into an observatory. From the windows he saw people coming to be caught; then, as he had removed some tiles from the floor and dug through the subflooring, and only the simple ceiling separated him from the room below where the interrogations took place, he heard everything that went on between the inquisitors and the accused.

The interrogations, preceded by a thorough search carried out on the arrested person, almost always ran as follows:

"Did Mme Bonacieux give you anything for her husband or for some other person?

"Did M. Bonacieux give you anything for his wife or for some other person?

"Did either of them confide anything to you by word of mouth?"

"If they knew anything," d'Artagnan said to himself, "they wouldn't question that way. Now, what are they trying to find out? Whether the duke of Buckingham is anywhere in Paris, and whether he has had or is going to have another interview with the queen."

D'Artagnan stopped at this idea, which, after all he had heard, was not without probability.

In the meantime, the mousetrap stayed in place, and d'Artagnan's vigilance as well.

The evening of the day after poor Bonacieux's arrest, as Athos was leaving d'Artagnan to report to M. de Tréville, as it had just struck nine, and as Planchet, who had not yet made the bed, was getting to work, someone was heard knocking on the street door. The door opened at once, and closed again; someone had just been caught in the mousetrap.

D'Artagnan rushed for the untiled place, lay down on his stomach, and listened.

Soon cries rang out, then moans that they attempted to stifle. This was no interrogation.

"Devil take it!" d'Artagnan said to himself. "It seems to be a woman! They're searching her, she's resisting—they're forcing her, the scoundrels!"

And d'Artagnan, despite his prudence, had all he could do to keep from interfering in the scene that was taking place below him.

"But I tell you I am the mistress of the house, gentlemen; I tell you I am Mme Bonacieux; I tell you I am attached to the queen!" cried the unfortunate woman.

"Mme Bonacieux!" murmured d'Artagnan. "Can I be so lucky as to have found what everyone is looking for?"

"That's just what we've been waiting for," said the interrogators.

The voice became more and more muffled; a violent movement made the wainscotting echo. The victim was resisting as much as a woman can resist four men.

"Forgive me, gentlemen, for . . ." the voice murmured, after which it produced only inarticulate sounds.

"They've gagged her, they're going to drag her off," cried d'Artagnan, straightening up as if moved by a spring. "My sword—good, it's at my side. Planchet!"

"Monsieur?"

"Run to find Athos, Porthos, and Aramis. One of the three will surely be at home, maybe all three will have come back. Tell them to bring their arms, to come, to come running. Ah! I remember, Athos is with M. de Tréville."

"But where are you going, Monsieur, where are you going?"

"I'm climbing down by the window," cried d'Artagnan, "to get there the sooner. You put the tiles back, sweep the floor, leave by the door, and run where I've told you."

"Oh! Monsieur, Monsieur, you'll get yourself killed!" cried Planchet.

"Quiet, imbecile," said d'Artagnan. And clinging to the windowsill with his hands, he let himself drop from the second floor, which fortunately was not very high, and ended up without a scratch.

Then he went at once to knock on the door.

"It's my turn to get caught in the mousetrap, and too bad for the cats who come up against such a mouse!"

The knocker had barely rung out under the young man's hand, when the tumult ceased, footsteps approached, the door opened a crack, and d'Artagnan, his sword bared, burst into M. Bonacieux's apartment, the door of which, no doubt moved by a spring, closed behind him of itself.

Then those who still lived in the unfortunate house of Bonacieux and the nearest neighbors heard great cries, stamping, the clash of swords, and a prolonged smashing of furniture. A moment later, those who, surprised by this noise, had come to their windows to find out what was causing it, were able to see the door open again and four men dressed in black, not coming out of it, but flying out like frightened crows, leaving on the floor and the table corners the feathers of their wings, that is, tatters of their clothing and shreds of their cloaks.

D'Artagnan emerged the victor without much difficulty, it must be said, for only one of the alguazils was armed, and he only defended himself for the sake of form. It is true that the other three had tried to knock the young man out with chairs, stools, and pottery; but two or three scratches inflicted by the Gascon's blade had frightened them. Ten minutes had sufficed for their defeat, and d'Artagnan was left master of the field.

The neighbors, who had opened their windows with the coolness peculiar to the inhabitants of Paris in those times of riots and brawls, closed them again once they had seen the four men in black run off: instinct told them that for the moment everything was over.

Besides, it was getting late, and, then as now, people went to bed early in the Luxembourg quarter.

D'Artagnan, left alone with Mme Bonacieux, turned to her. The poor woman lay sprawled in an armchair and half in a swoon.

She was a charming woman of twenty-five or twenty-six, with brown hair and blue eyes, a slightly upturned nose, admirable teeth, a marbled complexion of rose and opal. There, however, ended the signs that might make one confuse her for a grande dame. Her hands were white, but without delicacy; her feet did not speak for a woman of quality. Fortunately, d'Artagnan was not yet concerned with such details.

While d'Artagnan was examining Mme Bonacieux, and had come to her feet, as we have said, he saw a fine cambric handkerchief on the floor, which he picked up out of habit, and at the corner of which he recognized the same monogram he had seen on the handkerchief over which he had almost had his throat cut by Aramis.

Since that time, d'Artagnan had been wary of handkerchiefs with coats of arms, so he put the one he had picked up back in Mme Bonacieux's pocket without saying a word.

At that moment, Mme Bonacieux came to her senses. She opened her eyes, looked around in terror, and saw that the apartment was empty and she was alone with her deliverer.

She held out her hands to him at once and smiled. Mme Bonacieux had the most charming smile in the world.

"Ah, Monsieur!" she said. "It is you who have saved me; allow me to thank you."

"Madame," said d'Artagnan, "I have done only what any gentleman would have done in my place. You therefore owe me no thanks."

"But I do, Monsieur, I do, and I hope to prove to you that you have not done a service to an ungrateful woman. But what did these men, whom I took at first for thieves, want of me, and why isn't M. Bonacieux here?"

"Madame, these men were more dangerous than thieves could ever be, for they are agents of M. le cardinal, and as for your husband, M. Bonacieux, he is not here because yesterday they came to take him and convey him to the Bastille."

"My husband in the Bastille!" cried Mme Bonacieux. "Oh, my God! but what did he do? The poor, dear man, he's innocence itself!"

And something like a smile broke through on the still frightened face of the young woman.

"What did he do, Madame?" said d'Artagnan. "I believe his only crime is to have at once the good fortune and the misfortune of being your husband."

"But, Monsieur, you know then . . ."

"I know that you were abducted, Madame."

"And by whom? Do you know that? Oh, if you know, tell me!"

"By a man of forty to forty-five, with black hair, dark skin, and a scar on his left temple."

"That's right, that's right—but his name?"

"Ah, his name? That I don't know."

"And did my husband know I was abducted?"

"He was informed of it in a letter written to him by the abductor himself."

"And did he suspect," Mme Bonacieux asked with embarrassment, "the cause of this event?"

"He attributed it, I believe, to a political cause."

"I doubted that at first, but now I think as he does. So, then, this dear M. Bonacieux never suspected me for a single instant . . . ?"

"Ah, far from it, Madame! He was too confident of your wisdom and above all of your love."

A second almost imperceptible smile brushed the rosy lips of the beautiful young woman.

"But," d'Artagnan went on, "how did you escape?"

"I took advantage of a moment when they left me alone, and as I knew since this morning what to make of my abduction, I climbed down from the window with the help of my sheets; then, as I thought my husband was here, I came running."

"To put yourself under his protection?"

"Oh, no! The poor, dear man, I knew very well he was incapable of defending me; but as he could serve us in another way, I wanted to warn him."

"Of what?"

"Oh, that is not my secret, so I cannot tell it to you."

"Besides," said d'Artagnan, "—forgive me, Madame, if, guard though I am, I urge you to prudence—besides, I think that we are not in a very opportune place for exchanging confidences. The men I put to flight will come back with reinforcements. If they find us here, we're lost. I've sent to inform three of my friends, but who knows if they've been found at home!"

"Yes, yes, you're right," cried Mme Bonacieux in fear. "We must flee, we must escape!"

At these words, she put her arm under d'Artagnan's and pulled him sharply.

"But flee where," said d'Artganan, "escape where?"

"Let's get away from this house first, then we'll see."

And the young woman and the young man, without bothering to shut the door again, went quickly down the rue des Fossoyeurs, turned into the rue des Fossés-Monsieur-le-Prince, and did not stop until the place Saint-Sulpice.

"And now what are we going to do," asked d'Artagnan, "and where do you want me to take you?"

"I'm really at a loss to answer you, I must admit," said Mme Bonacieux. "My intention was to warn M. de La Porte through my husband, so that M. de La Porte could tell us precisely what has gone on at the Louvre over the past three days, and whether it's dangerous for me to appear there."

"But I can go and warn M. de La Porte," said d'Artagnan.

"No doubt, only there's one problem: my husband was known at the Louvre, and they would let him in, while you are not known, and they will shut the door on you."

"Ah!" said d'Artagnan, "but you must have a porter at some gateway of the Louvre who is devoted to you, and who, thanks to some password . . ."

Mme Bonacieux looked fixedly at the young man.

"And if I give you that password," she said, "will you forget it as soon as you've used it?"

"Word of honor, as I'm a gentleman!" said d'Artagnan, with a tone the truthfulness of which was unmistakable.

"Very well, I believe you: you have the look of a brave young man, and besides your devotion may make your fortune."

"I will, without any promises and in all conscience, do all I can to serve the king and to be agreeable to the queen," said d'Artagnan. "Dispose of me, then, as of a friend."

"But where will you put me in the meantime?"

"Don't you have someone from whom M. de La Porte could come and fetch you?"

"No, I don't want to trust myself to anyone."

"Wait," said d'Artagnan, "we're at Athos's door. Yes, that's it."

"Who is Athos?"

"A friend of mine."

"But what if he's at home and sees me?"

"He's not there, and I'll take the key with me after I've installed you in his apartment."

"But if he comes back?"

"He won't come back. Besides, he'll be told that I brought a woman, and that the woman is at his place."

"But you know that will compromise me very badly!"

"What does it matter to you? You're not known, and besides, in our position we can do without certain proprieties!"

"Let's go to your friend's place, then. Where does he live?"

"Rue Férou, two steps away."

"Let's go."

And the two hastened on their way again. As d'Artagnan had foreseen, Athos was not at home. He took the key, which they were accustomed to giving him as a friend of the house, went upstairs, and ushered Mme Bonacieux into the small apartment that we have already described.

"Make yourself at home," he said. "Wait, lock the door from inside and don't open for anyone, unless you hear three knocks like this." And he knocked three times: two taps close together and rather loud, then one lighter tap.

"Very well," said Mme Bonacieux. "Now it's my turn to give you my instructions."

"I'm listening."

"Go to the gateway of the Louvre on the side of the rue de l'Échelle and ask for Germain."

"Very well. And then?"

"He will ask you what you want, and you will answer with these two words: Tours and Brussels. He'll be at your orders at once."

"And what shall I order him to do?"

"To go and find M. de La Porte, the queen's valet."

"And when he has found him and M. de La Porte has come?"

"You will send him to me."

"Very well, but where and how will I see you again?"

"Are you very anxious to see me again?"

"Of course."

"Well, then, leave that up to me, and don't worry."

"I rely on your word."

"You may."

D'Artagnan bowed to Mme Bonacieux, throwing her the most amorous glance it was possible to focus on her charming little person, and as he went downstairs, he heard the door close and the lock turn twice behind him. In two bounds he was at the Louvre: as he entered the gateway on the rue de l'Échelle, it was striking ten. All the events we have just recounted had taken place in half an hour.

Everything went as Mme Bonacieux had foretold. At the agreed password, Germain nodded his head; ten minutes later, La Porte was in the porter's lodge. In two words d'Artagnan laid the facts before him and told him where Mme Bonacieux was. La Porte checked the accuracy of the address twice and set off at a run. However, he had barely gone ten steps when he came back.

"Young man," he said to d'Artagnan, "a piece of advice."

"What?"

"You could be bothered because of what has just happened."

"You think so?"

"Yes. Do you have a friend whose watch runs slow?"

"Eh?"

"Go to see him, so that he can testify that you were with him at half-past nine. In legal circles, that is known as an alibi."

D'Artagnan found the advice prudent. He took to his heels and went to M. de Tréville's hôtel, but instead of going into the reception room with everyone else, he asked to be let in to his office. As d'Artagnan was a habitué of the hôtel, they never made any difficulties about granting his requests, and they went to inform M. de Tréville that his young compatriot had something important to say to him and was seeking a private audience. Five minutes later, M. de Tréville was asking d'Artagnan how he could be of service to him and to what he owed this visit at such a late hour.

"Forgive me, Monsieur!" said d'Artagnan, who had profited from the moment when he had been left alone to set the clock back three-quarters of an hour. "I thought that, as it was only twenty-five past nine, it was still possible to present myself to you."

"Twenty-five past nine!" cried M. de Tréville, looking at the clock. "But that's impossible!"

"But you see, Monsieur," said d'Artagnan, "there's the proof."

"Right enough," said M. de Tréville. "I'd have thought it was later. Now, then, what do you want of me?"

Then d'Artagnan told M. de Tréville a long story about the queen. He disclosed to him the fears he had formed concerning Her Majesty; he told him what he had heard said about the cardinal's plans with respect to Buckingham, and all that with a calm and self-assurance that took in M. de Tréville all the more in that he himself, as we have said, had noticed something new between the cardinal, the king, and the queen.

At the stroke of ten, d'Artagnan left M. de Tréville, who thanked him for his information, charged him to keep at heart his service to the king and queen, and went back to the reception room. But at the foot of the stairs, he remembered that he had forgotten his walking stick. He therefore hurried back upstairs, went into the office again, reset the clock to the right time with the touch of a finger, so that the next day no one would notice it had been tampered with, and, certain now that he had a witness to prove his alibi, went downstairs and soon found himself in the street.

XI

THE PLOT THICKENS

His visit to M. de Tréville over, d'Artagnan, lost in thought, took the longest way home.

What was d'Artagnan thinking about, if he wandered from his path like this, looking up at the stars in the sky, and sometimes sighing, sometimes smiling?

He was thinking of Mme Bonacieux. For an apprentice musketeer, the young woman was almost an amorous ideal. Pretty, mysterious, initiated into almost all the secrets of court, showing such a charming seriousness in her graceful features, she might also be suspected of not being indifferent, which is an irresistible attraction for novice lovers. What's more, d'Artagnan had delivered her from the hands of those demons who had wanted to search her and ill-use her, and that important service had established between them one of those feelings of gratitude that can so easily take on a more tender character.

Dreams advance so quickly on the wings of imagination that d'Artagnan already saw himself approached by a messenger from the young woman, who hands him a note for a rendezvous, or a gold chain, or a diamond. We have said that young cavaliers received without shame from their king; let us add that, in this time of easy morals, they felt no more abashed with regard to their mistresses, and that the latter almost always left them precious and lasting souvenirs, as if trying to conquer the fragility of their feelings by the solidity of their gifts.

One made one's way then by means of women, without blushing at it. Those who were merely beautiful gave their beauty, whence no doubt came the proverb that even the most beautiful girl in the world can only give what she has. Those who were rich gave a portion of their money as well, and one could cite a good number of heroes from that gallant age who would not have won their spurs first, nor their battles afterwards, without the more or less well-stuffed purse that their mistress tied to their saddlebow.

D'Artagnan had nothing. Provincial hesitation—a thin polish, an ephemeral flower, the down on the peach—had evaporated in the wind of the hardly orthodox advice the three musketeers had given their friend. D'Artagnan, following the strange custom of the time, saw himself in Paris as if he was on campaign, and that no more nor less than in Flanders: the Spaniard there, woman here. Everywhere there were enemies to be fought and contributions to be imposed.

But, let it be said, for the moment d'Artagnan was moved by a nobler and more disinterested feeling. The mercer had told him he was rich; the young man had been able to divine that, with a ninny the likes of M. Bonacieux, it must be the woman who held the purse strings. But none of that had in any way influenced the feeling aroused by the sight of Mme Bonacieux, and self-interest had remained virtually a stranger to the nascent love that had resulted from it. We say "virtually," for the idea that a young, beautiful, gracious, witty woman is at the same time rich, takes away nothing from this nascent love and, quite the contrary, corroborates it.

There is in affluence a host of aristocratic attentions and caprices that go well with beauty. Fine white stockings, a silk dress, a lace bodice, a pretty slipper on the foot, a fresh ribbon in the hair, will never make an ugly woman pretty, but will make a pretty woman beautiful, not to mention what the hands gain from it all: hands, women's hands especially, must remain idle to remain beautiful.

Then, too, d'Artagnan—as the reader knows very well, for we have not concealed the state of his fortune—d'Artagnan was not a millionaire. He hoped to become one some day, but the time he set himself for that happy change was rather far off. In the meantime, what despair to see a woman one loves longing for those thousand nothings from which women compose their happiness, and to be unable to give her those thousand nothings. At least, when the woman is rich and the lover is not, what he cannot offer her she can offer herself; and though it is usually with the husband's money that she affords herself this pleasure, it is rarely he who gets the thanks.

Then, too, d'Artagnan, disposed as he was to be the most tender lover, was meanwhile a very devoted friend. In the midst of his amorous designs on the mercer's wife, he did not forget his comrades. The pretty Mme Bonacieux was a woman to take on an outing to the plain of Saint-Denis or the fair of Saint-Germain, in the company of Athos, Porthos, and Aramis, to whom d'Artagnan would be proud to show such a conquest. Then, too, when one has walked for a long time, hunger comes; d'Artagnan had noticed that some time ago. They would have those charming little dinners, where on one side you touch a friend's hand, and on the other a mistress's foot. Finally, in pressing moments, in extreme circumstances, d'Artagnan would be his friends' savior.

And M. Bonacieux, whom d'Artagnan had pushed into the hands of the police, repudiating him aloud when he had promised in a whisper to save him? We must confess to our readers that d'Artagnan gave him no thought at all, or, if he did, it was to tell himself that he was well off where he was, wherever it might be. Love is the most egotistical of passions.

However, our readers may rest reassured: if d'Artagnan forgets his landlord, or pretends to forget him, under the pretext that he does not know where they took him, we will not forget him, and we know where he is. But, for the time being, let us do like the amorous Gascon. We will come back to the worthy mercer later.

D'Artagnan, while reflecting on his future amours, while speaking to the night, while smiling at the stars, was walking up the rue du Cherche-Midi, or Chasse-Midi, as it was called then. As he found himself in Aramis's quarter, the idea came to him to pay his friend a visit, to give him some explanation of the motives behind his sending Planchet with an invitation to proceed at once to the mousetrap. Now, if Aramis had been found at home when Planchet came, he would undoubtedly have run to the rue des Fossoyeurs, and finding no one except perhaps his other two companions, neither he nor they would have known what to make of it. This inconvenience thus deserved an explanation, as d'Artagnan said aloud.

Then, in a whisper, he reflected that this would be an occasion for him to speak about the pretty little Mme Bonacieux, of whom his mind, if not his heart, was already quite filled. Discretion cannot be demanded of a first love. A first love is accompanied by such great joy that the joy must overflow; otherwise, it will choke you.

Paris had been dark for two hours and was beginning to become deserted. It struck eleven on all the clocks of the faubourg Saint-Germain. The weather was mild. D'Artagnan was following a lane along the place where the rue d'Assas now runs, breathing in the fragrant emanations that came on the wind from the rue de Vaugirard, sent from gardens refreshed by the evening dew and the night breeze. In the distance, though muffled by stout shutters, rang out the songs of drinkers in the few taverns scattered over the place. On reaching the end of the lane, d'Artagnan turned left. The house Aramis lived in was located between the rue Cassette and the rue Servandoni.

D'Artagnan had just passed the rue Cassette and had already made out his friend's door, buried under a mass of sycamores and clematis that formed a vast swelling over it, when he spied something like a shadow emerging from the rue Servandoni. This something was wrapped in a cloak, and d'Artagnan thought it was a man at first; but, by the smallness of the waist, the uncertainty of the gait, the timidity of the step, he soon recognized that it was a woman. What's more, this woman, as if she was not at all sure of the house she was looking for, raised her eyes to get her bearings, stopped, turned around, then came back again. D'Artagnan was intrigued.

"What if I go and offer her my services!" he thought. "By the look of it, she's young; perhaps pretty. Oh, yes! But a woman going through the streets at this hour would hardly be out except to meet her lover. Damn! if I went and disturbed their rendezvous, that would be entering into relations through the wrong door."

However, the young woman was still approaching, counting the houses and windows. Nor was that a long or difficult task. There were only three hôtels on that portion of the street, and two windows looking onto the street; one was that of a house parallel to the one Aramis occupied, the other was that of Aramis himself.

"Pardieu!" d'Artagnan said to himself, as the theologian's niece came back to his mind. "Pardieu, it would be funny if this belated dove was looking for our friend's house! But, by my soul, it looks very much that way. Ah, my dear Aramis, this time I mean to get to the heart of it!"

And d'Artagnan, making himself as thin as possible, hid on the darker side of the street, near a stone bench at the back of a niche.

The young woman continued to approach, for besides the lightness of her footfall, which had given her away, she had just let out a little cough, which had revealed the freshest of voices. D'Artagnan thought the cough was a signal.

However, either because someone had responded to that cough with an equivalent signal that had settled the nocturnal seeker's hesitations, or because she had recognized without foreign aid that she had reached the end of her journey, she went resolutely to Aramis's shutter and tapped at three equal intervals with her bent finger.

"That's Aramis's window," murmured d'Artagnan. "Ah! Mister hypocrite! I've caught you at your theology!"

The three knocks had barely been tapped when the inside casement opened and a light appeared through the slats of the shutter.

"Aha!" said the listener not at doors but at windows, "the visit was expected. Now the shutter will be opened and the lady will climb in. Very good!"

But, to d'Artagnan's great astonishment, the shutter remained closed. What's more, the light that had flared up for a moment disappeared, and everything fell back into darkness.

D'Artagnan thought it could not go on that way, and continued watching with all his eyes and listening with all his ears.

He was right: after a few seconds, two sharp knocks rang out from inside.

The young woman in the street responded with a single knock, and the shutter opened slightly.

One can imagine how avidly d'Artagnan watched and listened.

Unfortunately, the light had been taken to another room. But the young man's eyes were accustomed to the dark. Besides, like the eyes of cats, the eyes of Gascons, as we have been assured, have the property of seeing in the dark.

D'Artagnan then saw the woman draw a white object from her pocket, which she unfolded quickly and which took the form of a handkerchief. Having unfolded the object, she pointed out the corner to her interlocutor.

This reminded d'Artagnan of the handkerchief he had found at Mme Bonacieux's feet, which had reminded him of the one he had found at Aramis's feet.

"What the devil could this handkerchief mean?"

Placed where he was, d'Artagnan could not see Aramis's face—we say Aramis, because the young man had no doubt that it was his friend who was carrying on a dialogue from inside with the lady outside. Curiosity won out over prudence, and, profiting from the distraction into which the sight of the handkerchief seemed to have plunged the two characters we have put on stage, he left his hiding place and, swift as lightning, but muffling the sound of his footsteps, went and flattened himself against a corner of the wall, from where his eye could perfectly well plumb the depths of Aramis's apartment.

At that point, d'Artagnan nearly let out a cry of surprise: it was not Aramis who was talking with the visiting lady in the night; it was a woman. Only d'Artagnan could see well enough to recognize her clothing, but not to make out her features.

At the same instant, the woman in the apartment drew a second handkerchief from her pocket and exchanged it for the one she had just been shown. Then a few words were spoken between the two women. Finally, the shutter closed again. The woman who was outside the window turned around and passed within four steps of d'Artagnan, pulling down the hood of her cloak. But this precaution came too late; d'Artagnan had already recognized Mme Bonacieux.

Mme Bonacieux! The suspicion that it was she had already crossed his mind when she drew the handerchief from her pocket. But how probable was it that Mme Bonacieux, who had sent for M. de La Porte so that he could take her back to the Louvre, would be going through the streets of Paris alone after eleven o'clock at night, at the risk of being abducted a second time?

It must then have been on a very important matter. And what is the important matter for a woman of twenty-five? Love.

But was it on her own account or someone else's that she was exposing herself to such dangers? That is what the young man asked himself, the demon of jealousy gnawing his heart no less than if he was an acknowledged lover.

There was, in any case, a very simple means of finding out where Mme Bonacieux was going; this was to follow her. This means was so simple that d'Artagnan employed it quite naturally and by instinct.

But, at the sight of the young man detaching himself from

the wall like a statue from its niche, and at the sound of his footsteps, which she heard coming after her, Mme Bonacieux let out a little cry and fled.

D'Artagnan ran after her. It was not difficult for him to catch up with a woman hampered by her cloak. He thus caught up with her a third of the way down the street she had taken. The poor woman was exhausted, not from fatigue but from terror, and when d'Artagnan placed his hand on her shoulder, she fell to one knee, crying out in a stifled voice:

"Kill me if you want, but you'll find out nothing."

D'Artagnan put his arm around her waist and picked her up; but as he felt by her weight that she was on the point of fainting, he hastened to reassure her with protests of his devotion. These protests were nothing to Mme Bonacieux, for such protests can be made with the worst intentions in the world; but the voice was everything. The young woman thought she recognized the sound of that voice: she reopened her eyes, cast a glance at the man who had frightened her so much, and, recognizing d'Artagnan, gave a cry of joy.

"Oh! It's you, it's you!" she said. "Thank God!"

"Yes, it's I," said d'Artagnan, "whom God has sent to keep watch on you."

"Was that the reason you followed me?" the young woman asked with a smile filled with coquetry. Her slightly bantering character gained the upper hand, and all her fear disappeared the moment she recognized a friend in the one she had taken for an enemy.

"No," said d'Artagnan, "no, I confess, it was chance that placed me in your way. I saw a woman knocking at the window of a friend of mine . . ."

"A friend of yours?" Mme Bonacieux interrupted.

"Of course. Aramis is one of my best friends."

"Aramis? Who is that?"

"Come, now! Do you mean to tell me you don't know Aramis?"

"It's the first time I've heard mention of his name."

"So it's the first time you've come to that house?"

"Of course."

"And you didn't know that a young man lived there?"

"No."

"A musketeer?"

"Not at all."

"So it wasn't him you came looking for?"

"Not in the least. Besides, you saw very well that the person I spoke with was a woman."

"True; but that woman is one of Aramis's friends."

"I know nothing about it."

"Since she's living at his place."

"That's no concern of mine."

"But who is she?"

"Oh, that is not my secret!"

"Dear Mme Bonacieux, you are charming; but at the same time you are the most mysterious woman . . ."

"Do I lose anything by that?"

"No, on the contrary, you are adorable."

"Give me your arm, then."

"Gladly. And now?"

"Now escort me."

"Where to?"

"Where I'm going."

"But where are you going?"

"You'll see, since you're going to leave me at the door."

"Shall I wait for you?"

"It will be useless."

"So you'll come back alone?"

"Maybe yes, maybe no."

"But will the person who accompanies you afterwards be a man or a woman?"

"I don't know yet."

"Well, I will certainly know!"

"How's that?"

"I'll wait for you to come out."

"In that case, good-bye!"

"How's that?"

"I don't need you."

"But you asked for . . ."

"The help of a gentleman, not the surveillance of a spy."

"That's a rather strong word!"

"What do you call someone who follows people against their will?"

"Indiscreet."

"That's too mild a word."

"Come, Madame, I see clearly that one must do everything you want."

"Why deprive yourself of the merit of doing so at once?"

"Is there no way to repent?"

"And do you really repent?"

"That I don't know. But what I do know is that I will promise you to do all you want, if you let me accompany you where you're going."

"And you'll leave me then?"

"Yes."

"You won't spy on me when I come out?"

"No."

"Word of honor?"

"As I'm a gentleman!"

"Take my arm then and let's go."

D'Artagnan offered his arm to Mme Bonacieux, who hung on it, half laughing, half trembling, and together they came to the top of the rue de la Harpe. There the young woman seemed to hesitate, as she had done already on the rue de Vaugirard. However, she seemed to recognize a door by certain signs, and going up to that door, she said:

"And now, Monsieur, my business is here. A thousand thanks for your honorable company, which has spared me all the dangers to which I would have been exposed alone. But the moment has come to keep your word: I have reached my destination."

"And you will have nothing to fear on coming back?"

"I will have only thieves to fear."

"Is that nothing?"

"What could they take from me? I haven't got a penny."

"You're forgetting that beautiful handkerchief embroidered with a coat of arms."

"Which one?"

"The one I found at your feet and put back in your pocket."

"Silence, silence, poor boy!" cried the young woman. "Do you want to ruin me?"

"You see very well that there is still danger for you, since a single word makes you tremble, and you admit that, if that word were heard, you would be lost. Ah! wait, Madame," cried d'Artagnan, seizing her hand and covering her with an ardent gaze, "wait! Be more generous, confide in me; haven't you read in my eyes that there is only devotion and sympathy in my heart?"

"I have," replied Mme Bonacieux, "and so, if you ask me my secrets, I'll tell them to you; but those of others are something else."

"Very well," said d'Artagnan, "I will find them out. Since those secrets may have an influence on your life, those secrets must become mine."

"Beware of doing that," the young woman cried with a seriousness that made d'Artagnan shudder in spite of himself. "Oh! Do not interfere in anything that has to do with me, do not seek to aid me in what I am carrying out; I ask you that in the name of the interest I inspire in you, in the name of the service you have rendered me, which I will not forget as long as I live. Believe rather in what I am saying to you. Do not occupy yourself any further with me, I no longer exist for you, let it be as if you had never seen me."

"Must Aramis do the same, Madame?" d'Artagnan asked, piqued.

"This is the second or third time you've mentioned that name, Monsieur, and yet I've told you that I do not know it."

"You don't know the man on whose shutter you were knocking? Come, Madame, you think me all too credulous!"

"Admit that you have invented this story and created this character in order to make me talk."

"I am inventing nothing, Madame, and creating nothing. I am speaking the exact truth."

"And you say a friend of yours lives in that house?"

"I say it and I repeat it for the third time: that house is inhabited by a friend of mine, and that friend is Aramis."

"This will all be cleared up later," murmured the young woman. "For now, Monsieur, keep quiet."

"If you could see into my open heart," said d'Artagnan, "you would read so much curiosity in it that you would have pity on me, and so much love that you would satisfy my curiosity that same instant. There is nothing to fear from those who love you."

"You are rather quick to speak of love, Monsieur!" said the young woman, shaking her head.

"That is because love has come to me quickly and for the first time, and I am not yet twenty years old."

The young woman looked at him furtively.

"Listen, I'm already on the scent," said d'Artagnan. "Three months ago I nearly had a duel with Aramis over a handkerchief like the one you showed to that woman who was in his house, over a handkerchief marked in the same way, I'm sure of it."

"Monsieur," said the young woman, "I swear you weary me terribly with these questions."

"But you who are so prudent, Madame, just think, if you were arrested with that handkerchief, and the handkerchief was seized, wouldn't you be compromised?"

"Why is that? Aren't the initials mine: C. B., Constance Bonacieux?"

"Or Camille de Bois-Tracy?"

"Silence, Monsieur, once again, silence! Ah! since the risks I am running on my own cannot stop you, think of those you are running yourself!"

"I?"

"Yes, you. There is a risk of prison, there is a risk to your life in knowing me."

"Then I shall never leave you."

"Monsieur," said the young woman, imploring him and clasping her hands, "Monsieur, in the name of heaven, in the name of soldierly honor, in the name of gentlemanly courtesy, go away. Wait, it's striking midnight; that's the hour when I'm expected."

"Madame," the young man said, bowing, "I am unable to refuse someone who asks me in that way. Be content, I am going away."

"But you won't follow me, you won't spy on me?"

"I will go straight home."

"Ah! I just knew you were a brave young man!" cried Mme Bonacieux, holding one hand out to him and placing the other on the knocker of a little door all but lost in the wall.

D'Artagnan seized the hand held out to him and kissed it ardently.

"Ah! I'd much rather I had never seen you," cried d'Artagnan, with that naive coarseness that women often prefer to the affectations of politeness, because it reveals the depths of thought and proves that feeling has won out over reason.

"Well," Mme Bonacieux picked up with an almost caressing voice, and pressing d'Artagnan's hand, which had not abandoned her own, "well, I wouldn't go so far as that: what's lost for today is not lost for the future. Who knows whether, one day when I'm free, I won't satisfy your curiosity?"

"And will you make the same promise to my love?" cried the overjoyed d'Artagnan.

"Oh! in that respect, I don't wish to bind myself; it will depend on the feelings you are able to arouse in me."

"So, for today, Madame . . ."

"For today, Monsieur, I have only come as far as gratitude."

"Ah, you are too charming," d'Artagnan said sadly, "and you take advantage of my love!"

"No, I have the advantage of your generosity, that's all. But, believe me, with certain people, everything comes out right."

"Oh, you make me the happiest of men! Do not forget this evening, do not forget this promise."

"Don't worry, in the right time and place I'll remember everything. Well, go then, go, in heaven's name! They were expecting me at midnight sharp, and I'm late."

"By five minutes."

"Yes, but in certain circumstances, five minutes are five centuries."

"When one is in love."

"Well, who told you I'm not meeting a lover?"

"So it's a man who's waiting for you?" cried d'Artagnan. "A man!"

"Come, the discussion's going to start up again," said Mme Bonacieux with a half smile that was not without a certain shade of impatience.

"No, no, I'm going, I'm off; I believe you, I want to have all the merit of my devotion, even if it should be a stupid devotion. Good-bye, Madame, good-bye!"

And as if he did not have strength enough to separate himself from the hand he was holding except by a jolt, he set off at a run, while Mme Bonacieux knocked three times slowly and evenly, as on the shutter; then, at the corner of the street, he turned around: the door had opened and closed again; the pretty mercer's wife had disappeared.

D'Artagnan continued on his way. He had given his word not to spy on Mme Bonacieux, and if his life had depended on the place she was going to or the person who would accompany her, d'Artagnan would still have gone home, because he had said he would. Five minutes later, he was in the rue des Fossoyeurs.

"Poor Athos," he said, "he won't know what to make of it. He'll have fallen asleep waiting for me, or he'll have returned home, and on going in, will have learned that a woman had been there. A woman at Athos's! After all," d'Artagnan went on, "there certainly was one at Aramis's. This is all very strange, and I'd be curious to know how it's going to end."

"Badly, Monsieur, badly," replied a voice that the young man recognized as Planchet's, for while soliloquizing aloud, as very proccupied people do, he had gone down the alley at the bottom of which was the stairway leading to his room.

"How, badly? What do you mean, imbecile?" asked d'Artagnan. "What's happened?"

"All sorts of troubles."

"Which?"

"First of all, M. Athos has been arrested."

"Arrested? Athos arrested? Why?"

"He was found at your place; they took him for you."

"And who arrested him?"

"The guards summoned by the men in black you chased away."

"Why didn't he give his name? Why didn't he say he had nothing to do with the matter?"

"He was careful not to do that, Monsieur; on the contrary, he came over to me and said: 'It's your master who needs his freedom at the moment, and not me, since he knows everything and I know nothing. They'll think he's arrested, and that will give him time; in three days I'll say who I am, and they'll have to let me go.'"

"Bravo, Athos! Noble heart," murmured d'Artagnan, "that's just like him! And what did the beagles do?"

"Four of them took him away, I don't know where, to the Bastille or the Fort-l'Évêque; two stayed with the men in black, who ransacked the place and took all the papers. Finally, the last two stood guard at the door during the expedition. Then, when it was all over, they went away, leaving the house empty and wide open."

"And Porthos and Aramis?"

"I didn't find them, they never came."

"But they may come at any moment, because you left word for them that I was expecting them?"

"Yes, Monsieur."

"Well, then, don't budge from here. If they come, tell them what has happened to me and that they should wait for me at the Pomme de Pin; it's dangerous here, the house may be watched. I'll meet them there, after I run over to M. de Tréville's to inform him of all this."

"Very good, Monsieur," said Planchet.

"But you'll stay, you won't be afraid?" said d'Artagnan, coming back to enjoin courage on the lackey.

"Rest assured, Monsieur," said Planchet, "you don't know me yet. I'm brave when I set myself to it, you'll see. All I have to do is set myself to it. Besides, I'm a Picard."

"It's agreed, then," said d'Artagnan, "you'll get yourself killed rather than quit your post."

"Yes, Monsieur, and there's nothing I wouldn't do to show Monsieur how attached I am to him."

"Good," d'Artagnan said to himself, "it seems the method I've employed with the lad is decidedly the right one. I'll use it again if I have occasion."

And he headed for the rue du Vieux-Colombier as fast as his legs would carry him, slightly wearied as they were by all the running around that day.

M. de Tréville was not at his hôtel; his company was on guard at the Louvre; he was at the Louvre with his company.

He had to get to M. de Tréville; it was important that he be informed of what was happening. D'Artagnan decided to try entering the Louvre. His uniform as a guard in M. des Essarts's company would serve as his passport.

So he went down the rue des Petits-Augustins, and went back up the quai to cross the Pont Neuf. For a moment he had thought of taking the ferry, but on reaching the riverside, he had mechanically put his hand into his pocket and discovered that he had nothing with which to pay the ferryman.

As he came to the top of the rue Guénégaud, he saw emerging from the rue Dauphine a group composed of two figures whose look struck him.

The two persons who composed the group were: one, a man; the other, a woman.

The woman had the shape of Mme Bonacieux, and the man looked exactly like Aramis.

Furthermore, the woman was wearing the black mantle that d'Artagnan could still see outlined against the shutter on the rue de Vaugirard and the door on the rue de la Harpe.

What's more, the man was wearing the uniform of the musketeers.

The woman's hood was pulled down, the man held his handkerchief to his face; they both, as this double precaution indicated, they both thus had an interest in not being recognized.

They took the bridge. This was d'Artagnan's route, since he was going to the Louvre. D'Artagnan followed them.

D'Artagnan had not gone twenty steps before he was convinced that the woman was Mme Bonacieux and the man was Aramis.

He felt in the same instant all the jealous suspicions that were stirring in his heart.

He had been doubly betrayed, by his friend and by her whom he already loved like a mistress. Mme Bonacieux had sworn to him by all the gods in heaven that she did not know Aramis, and a quarter of an hour after making that oath, he finds her on Aramis's arm.

D'Artagnan did not even reflect that he had known the pretty mercer's wife for only three hours, that she owed him nothing but a bit of thanks for having delivered her from the men in black who wanted to abduct her, and that she had promised him nothing. He saw himself as an offended, betrayed, flouted lover. The blood and wrath mounted to his face; he resolved to clarify everything.

The young woman and the young man had noticed that they were being followed and quickened their pace. D'Artagnan started to run, passed them, then turned on them just as they found themselves in front of the Samaritaine, lit by a street lamp that cast its light on that whole part of the street.

D'Artagnan stood facing them, and they stood facing him.

"What do you want, Monsieur?" asked the musketeer, stepping back and speaking with a foreign accent which proved to d'Artagnan that he had been mistaken in one part of his conjectures.

"It's not Aramis!" he cried.

"No, Monsieur, it is not Aramis, and by your exclamation I see that you have taken me for someone else, and I excuse you."

"You excuse me!" cried d'Artagnan.

"Yes," replied the unknown man. "Let me pass, then, since your business is not with me."

"You're right, Monsieur," said d'Artagnan, "my business is not with you, but with Madame."

"With Madame! You do not know her," said the stranger.

"You are mistaken, Monsieur, I do know her."

"Ah!" cried Mme Bonacieux in a tone of reproach. "Ah,

Monsieur! I had your word as a soldier and your oath as a gentleman; I hoped I could count on them."

"And I, Madame," said d'Artagnan, embarrassed, "I had your promise . . ."

"Take my arm, Madame," said the stranger, "and let us continue on our way."

However, d'Artagnan, stunned, astounded, overwhelmed by all that had happened to him, remained standing with crossed arms in front of the musketeer and Mme Bonacieux.

The musketeer took two steps forward and moved d'Artagnan out of the way with his hand.

D'Artagnan leaped back and drew his sword.

At the same time and swift as lightning, the unknown man drew his.

"In the name of heaven, Milord!" cried Mme Bonacieux, throwing herself between the two combatants and seizing their swords with her bare hands.

"Milord!" cried d'Artagnan, lit up by a sudden idea. "Milord! Pardon me, Monsieur, but might you be . . ."

"Milord the duke of Buckingham," said Mme Bonacieux in a half whisper, "and now you can ruin us all."

"Milord, Madame, a thousand pardons; but I loved her, Milord, and I was jealous. You know what it is to love, Milord. Pardon me, and tell me how I can get myself killed for Your Grace."

"You are a brave young man," said Buckingham, holding a hand out to d'Artagnan, which the latter shook respectfully. "You offer me your services, I accept them. Follow us at twenty paces to the Louvre, and if anyone spies on us, kill him!"

D'Artagnan put his bare sword under his arm, allowed Mme Bonacieux and the duke to go twenty paces ahead, and followed them, ready to carry out to the letter the instructions of the noble and elegant minister of Charles I.

But luckily the young henchman had no occasion to give the duke that proof of his devotion, and the young woman and the handsome musketeer entered the Louvre by the gate on the rue de l'Échelle without any trouble.

As for d'Artagnan, he went at once to the Pomme de Pin, where he found Porthos and Aramis waiting.

But, without giving them any other explanation of the inconvenience he had caused them, he told them that he himself had finished the business for which he had thought briefly that he might need their intervention.

And now, carried away as we are by our story, let us allow our three friends to go to their own homes, while we follow the duke of Buckingham and his guide through the intricacies of the Louvre.

XII

GEORGE VILLIERS, DUKE OF BUCKINGHAM

Mme Bonacieux and the duke entered the Louvre without difficulty. Mme Bonacieux was known to be connected with the queen; the duke was wearing the uniform of M. de Tréville's musketeers, who, as we have said, were on guard duty that night. Besides, Germain was attached to the queen, and if anything happened, Mme Bonacieux would be accused of having brought her lover into the Louvre, that was all. She would take the crime upon herself: true, her reputation would be ruined, but what value does the reputation of a little mercer's wife have in the world?

Once inside the courtyard, the duke and the young woman followed the base of the wall for a distance of some twenty-five steps; having gone that distance, Mme Bonacieux pushed at a small service door, open during the day but ordinarily locked at night. The door yielded; they both went in and found themselves in the dark, but Mme Bonacieux knew all the twists and turns of that part of the Louvre, which was reserved for attendants. She closed the door behind her, took the duke by the hand, felt her way for a few steps, grasped a banister, touched a step with her foot, and began climbing a stairway: the duke counted two floors. Then she turned right, followed a long corridor, went back down one floor, took several more steps, put a key into a lock, opened a door, and pushed the duke into an apartment lit only by a night-light, saying: "Stay here, Milord Duke, someone will come." Then she went out by the same door, which she locked, so that the duke found himself literally a prisoner.

However, isolated as he turned out to be, it must be said that the duke of Buckingham felt not a moment of fear; one of the conspicuous sides of his character was the search for adventure and a love of the romantic. Brave, bold, enterprising, this was not the first time he had risked his life in such endeavors. He had learned that the supposed message from Anne d'Autriche, on the credit of which he had come to Paris, was a trap, and instead of returning to England, he had declared to the queen, abusing the position he had been put in, that he would not leave without seeing her. The queen had positively refused at first, but finally became afraid that the duke, in exasperation, would commit some folly. She had already decided to receive him and beg him to go away at once, when, on the very evening of that decision, Mme Bonacieux, who had been entrusted with finding the duke and bringing him to the Louvre, was abducted. For two days they had no idea what had become of her, and everything remained in suspense. But once she was free, once she was back in touch with La Porte, things had taken their course again, and she had just accomplished the perilous enterprise that, without her arrest, would have been carried out three days earlier.

Buckingham, left alone, went up to a mirror. This musketeer's outfit suited him perfectly.

At thirty-five, as he then was, he rightly passed for the most handsome gentleman and the most elegant cavalier in France and England.

The favorite of two kings, rich by millions, all-powerful in a kingdom that he stirred up at his whim and calmed at his caprice, George Villiers, duke of Buckingham, had undertaken one of those fabulous existences that remain over the course of the centuries as an astonishment to posterity.

And so, sure of himself, convinced of his power, certain that the laws which ruled other men could not touch him, he went straight to the goal he had set himself, even if that goal was so high and so dazzling that it would have been folly for another man merely to conceive of it. It was thus that he had happened to approach the beautiful and proud Anne d'Autriche several times and to make her love him, by dint of bedazzlement.

George Villiers thus stood before the mirror, as we have said, restored the waves to his handsome blond hair, which had been flattened by the weight of his hat, twirled his mustache, and, his heart swelling with joy, proud and happy to have reached the moment he had so long desired, smiled to himself in pride and hope.

At that moment, a door hidden in the tapestry opened, and a woman appeared. Buckingham saw this apparition in the mirror. He gave a cry: it was the queen.

Anne d'Autriche was then twenty-six or twenty-seven; that is, she was in the full radiance of her beauty.

Her step was that of a queen or a goddess; her eyes, which gave off glints of emerald, were perfectly beautiful, and full at once of mildness and of majesty.

Her mouth was small and bright red, and though her lower lip, as with the princes of the house of Austria, protruded slightly beyond the upper, she was eminently gracious in her smile, but also deeply disdainful in her scorn.

Her skin was much mentioned for its velvet softness, her hands and arms were of a surprising beauty, and all the poets of the time sang of them as incomparable.

Finally, her hair, which had been blond in her youth but had turned chestnut, and which she wore curled and very fluffy, and with much powder, admirably framed her face, in which the most rigid censor might have desired only a little less rouge, and the most demanding sculptor only a little more fineness in the nose.

Buckingham remained dazzled for an instant. Anne d'Autriche had never seemed so beautiful to him in the midst of balls, feasts, and carrousels as she seemed to him at this moment, dressed in a simple gown of white satin and accompanied by Doña Estefania, the only one of her Spanish women who had not been driven out by the king's jealousy and the cardinal's persecutions.

Anne d'Autriche took two steps forward; Buckingham threw himself on his knees and, before the queen could stop him, kissed the hem of her gown.

"Duke, you already know that it was not I who wrote to you."

"Oh, yes, Madame, yes, Your Majesty!" cried the duke. "I know I was a fool, a madman, to believe that snow could become animate, that marble could become warm; but, what do you want, when one loves, one easily believes in love; besides, the journey has not been a total loss for me, since I am seeing you."

"Yes," Anne replied, "but you know why and how I am seeing you, Milord. I am seeing you out of pity for you; I am seeing you because, insensitive to all my difficulties, you have stubbornly remained in a city where, by remaining, you risk your life and make me risk my honor; I am seeing you in order to tell you that everything separates us, the depths of the sea, the hostility of kingdoms, the sacredness of vows. It is a sacrilege to fight against these things, Milord. I am seeing you, finally, in order to tell you that we must not see each other again."

"Speak, Madame; speak, queen," said Buckingham. "The softness of your voice covers the hardness of your words. You speak of sacrilege, but the sacrilege is in the separation of hearts that God has formed for each other!"

"Milord," cried the queen, "you forget that I have never told you I loved you."

"But neither have you ever told me that you do not love me; and indeed, to say such words to me would be too great an ingratitude on Your Majesty's part. For, tell me, where will you find a love like mine, a love which neither time, nor absence, nor despair can extinguish, a love that contents itself with a lost ribbon, a stray look, a dropped word?

"It was three years ago, Madame, that I saw you for the first time, and for three years I have loved you like this.

"Do you want me to tell you how you were dressed the first time I saw you? Do you want me to list each ornament of your toilette? Wait, I can still see you: you were sitting on cushions, in Spanish fashion; you had on a green satin gown with gold and silver embroideries; pendant sleeves tied back over your beautiful arms, over these admirable arms, with heavy diamonds; you had a fastened ruff, and a little bonnet on your head the color of your gown, and on the bonnet a heron's feather.

"Oh! wait, wait, I close my eyes and see you as you were then; I open them again and see you as you are now, that is, a hundred times more beautiful still!"

"What madness!" murmured Anne d'Autriche, who did not have it in her to be vexed with the duke for preserving her portrait so well in his heart. "What madness to feed a useless passion with such memories!"

"And what do you wish me to live on? I have nothing but memories. They are my happiness, my treasure, my hope. Each time I see you, it is one more diamond that I shut up in the jewel case of my heart. This is the fourth that you have let drop and I have picked up; for in three years, Madame, I have seen you only four times: that first which I have just mentioned, the second in Mme de Chevreuse's house, the third in the gardens of Amiens."

"Duke," the queen said, blushing, "do not speak of that evening."

"Oh, on the contrary, let us speak of it, Madame, let us speak of it: it is the happiest and most radiant evening of my life. Do you remember what a beautiful night it was? The air was so sweet and fragrant, the sky such a deep blue and all spangled with stars! Ah! that time, Madame, I was able to be alone with you for a moment; that time you were ready to tell me all, the loneliness of your life, the sorrows of your heart. You were leaning on my arm, here, like this. Bending my head towards you, I felt your beautiful hair brush my cheek, and each time I felt it I shivered from head to foot. Oh, queen, queen! Oh, you do not know all the heavenly felicities, all the paradisal joys contained in such a moment! I would give my goods, my fortune, my glory, all the days of life that remain to me for such a moment and for a night like that! For on that night, Madame, on that night you loved me, I swear to you."

"Milord, it is possible, yes, that the influence of the place, the charm of that beautiful night, the fascination of your gaze, that those thousand circumstances, finally, which sometimes come together to ruin a woman, had grouped themselves around me on that fatal evening. But you saw, Milord, how the queen came to rescue the weakening woman: at the first word you dared to speak, at the first boldness to which I had to respond, I called out."

"Oh, yes, yes, that's true! And another love than mine would have succumbed to that test; but my love came out of it more ardent and more eternal. You thought to flee me by returning to Paris, you thought I would not dare abandon the treasure my master had charged me to watch over. Ah! what are all the treasures in the world and all the kings on earth to me! Eight days later, I came back, Madame. This time you had nothing to say to me: I had risked my favor, my life, to see you for a second; I did not even touch your hand, and you pardoned me on seeing me so submissive and repentant."

"Yes, but calumny seized on all these follies in which I had no part, as you know very well, Milord. The king, spurred on by the cardinal, made a terrible scandal: Mme de Vernet was driven out, Putange exiled, Mme de Chevreuse fell into disfavor, and when you wanted to return as ambassador to France, the king himself, you remember, Milord, the king himself opposed it."

"Yes, and France will pay for her king's refusal with a war. I cannot see you again, Madame. Well, then, I want you to hear about me every day!

"What do you think might be the goal of this expedition to the Île de Ré and this league with the Protestants of La Rochelle that I'm planning? The pleasure of seeing you!

"I cannot hope to penetrate all the way to Paris by force of arms, I know that very well; but this war may lead to a peace, that peace will need a negotiator, and that negotiator will be me. They will not dare refuse me then, and I will return to Paris, and I will see you, and I will have a moment of happiness. True, thousands of men will have paid for my happiness with their lives; but what will that matter to me, provided I see you again! All this may well be mad, it may well be absurd; but tell me, what woman has a more loving lover? What queen has ever had a more ardent servant?"

"Milord, Milord, you call things for your defense that accuse you still more. Milord, all these proofs of love that you wish to give me are almost crimes."

"Because you do not love me, Madame: if you loved me, you would see it all differently; if you loved me—oh! but if you loved me, the happiness would be too much, and I would go mad. Ah! Mme de Chevreuse, of whom you just spoke, Mme de Chevreuse was less cruel than you. Holland loved her, and she returned his love."

"Mme de Chevreuse was not a queen," murmured Anne d'Autriche, conquered despite herself by so deep a love.

"Would you love me, then, if you were not one yourself, Madame, tell me, would you love me then? I may believe, then, that it is the dignity of your rank alone that makes you so cruel towards me; I may believe, then, that if you had been Mme de Chevreuse, poor Buckingham would have been able to hope? Thank you for those gentle words, O my beautiful Majesty, thank you a thousand times."

"Ah! Milord, you have misunderstood, you have misinterpreted me. I did not mean to say . . ."

"Silence! Silence!" said the duke. "If I am happy by an error, do not have the cruelty to take it from me. As you have said yourself, I have been drawn into a trap, and it will perhaps cost me my life, for, you know, it's strange, for some time now I have had presentiments that I am going to die." And the duke smiled a sad and at the same time charming smile.

"Oh, my God!" cried Anne d'Autriche, with an accent of fright that proved how much greater an interest she took in the duke than she was willing to say.

"I do not say that to frighten you, Madame, not at all; what I've said is even ridiculous, and, believe me, I never concern myself with such dreams. But those words you just spoke, that hope you have almost given me, would have paid for all, even my life."

"Well!" said Anne d'Autriche, "I also have my presentiments, Duke, I also have my dreams. I dreamed that I saw you lying wounded in a pool of blood."

"In the left side, wasn't it, with a knife?" interrupted Buckingham.

"Yes, that's right, Milord, that's right, in the left side with a knife. Who could have told you I dreamed that? I confided it only to God, and in my prayers alone."

"I want nothing more, and you do love me, Madame, that's good."

"I love you?"

"Yes, you do. Would God send the same dreams to you as to me if you did not love me? Would we have the same presentiments if our two existences did not meet in the heart? You love me, O queen, and you will weep for me?"

"Oh, my God! my God!" cried Anne d'Autriche, "it's more than I can bear. Listen, Duke, in the name of heaven, go away now, withdraw. I don't know whether I love you or not, but what I do know is that I will never be unfaithful. Take pity on me, then, and go away. Oh! if you are struck down in France, if you die in France, if I could suppose that your love for me were the cause of your death, I would never be consoled, I would go mad from it. Go away, then, go away, I beg you."

"Oh, how beautiful you are like this! Oh, how I love you!" said Buckingham.

"Go away, go away, I beg you, and come back later; come back as an ambassador, come back as a minister, come back surrounded by guards who will defend you, with servants who will watch over you, and then I will no longer fear for your days, and I will be happy to see you again."

"Oh, is it really true what you are saying to me?"

"Yes . . ."

"Well, then, give me a pledge of your indulgence, an object of yours to remind me that I am not dreaming; something you have worn and that I can wear in my turn, a ring, a necklace, a chain."

"And you will go away, you will go away if I give you what you ask?"

"Yes."

"That same instant?"

"Yes."

"You will leave France, you will go back to England?"

"Yes, I swear it!"

"Wait, then."

And Anne d'Autriche went to her apartment and returned almost at once, holding in her hand a little rosewood box with her initial, all inlaid with gold.

"Here, Milord, here," she said, "keep this in memory of me."

Buckingham took the box and fell to his knees a second time.

"You promised me to go away," said the queen.

"And I will keep my word. Your hand, your hand, Madame, and I will go."

Anne d'Autriche held out her hand, closing her eyes and leaning with the other hand on Estefania, for she felt her strength was about to fail.

Buckingham pressed his lips to that beautiful hand with passion, then stood up and said:

"Within six months, if I am not dead, I will have seen you again, Madame, though I have to overturn the whole world to do it."

And, faithful to the promise he had made, he rushed from the apartment.

In the corridor he met Mme Bonacieux, who was waiting for him, and who, with the same precautions and the same luck, brought him out of the Louvre.

XIII

MONSIEUR BONACIEUX

There was in all this, as the reader may have noticed, a character about whom, despite his precarious position, we seem to have worried very little. This character was M. Bonacieux, a respectable martyr of the political and amorous intrigues that became so easily entangled in that at once so chivalric and so gallant age.

Fortunately—the reader may or may not remember it—fortunately we have promised not to lose sight of him.

The men-at-arms who had arrested him took him straight to the Bastille, where he passed all atremble before a squad of soldiers loading their muskets.

From there he was ushered into a half-subterranean gallery, where he was made the butt of the grossest insults and the most savage treatment on the part of those who had brought him. The beagles saw they were not dealing with a gentleman and treated him as a veritable boor.

After about half an hour, a court clerk came to put an end to his tortures, but not to his worries, by giving orders to take M. Bonacieux to the interrogation room. Ordinarily prisoners were interrogated in their cells, but with M. Bonacieux they did not stand on such ceremony.

Two guards took charge of the mercer, made him cross a courtyard, made him enter a corridor where there were three sentries, opened a door, and pushed him into a low room in which the only furnishings were a table, a chair, and a commissary. The commissary was sitting on the chair and was busy writing at the table.

The two guards brought the prisoner before the table and, at a sign from the commissary, withdrew out of earshot.

The commissary, who until then had kept his head bent over his papers, raised it to see whom he had to deal with. This commissary was a repulsive-looking man, with a pointed nose, prominent yellow cheeks, small but lively and inquisitive eyes, and a physiognomy that had something both of the weasel and the fox. His head, supported on a long and mobile neck, emerged from his large black robe with a swinging movement something like that of a tortoise sticking its head out of its shell.

He began by asking M. Bonacieux his last name and first names, his age, his profession, and his address.

The accused replied that he was Jacque-Michel Bonacieux,

that he was fifty-one years old, a retired mercer, and lived at 11 rue des Fossoyeurs.

Then the commissary, instead of continuing to interrogate him, made him a long speech on how dangerous it was for an obscure bourgeois to mix in public affairs.

He complicated this exordium with an exposition in which he told of the power and deeds of M. le cardinal, that incomparable minister, that vanquisher of past ministers, that example for ministers to come: deeds and power that no one could oppose with impunity.

After this second part of his speech, fixing his hawklike gaze on poor Bonacieux, he invited him to reflect on the gravity of his situation.

The mercer's reflections were ready-made: he consigned to the devil the moment when M. de La Porte had had the idea of marrying him to his goddaughter, and above all the moment when this goddaughter had been received as a seamstress in the queen's household.

The essence of Master Bonacieux's character was profound egotism mixed with base avarice, the whole seasoned by an extreme cowardice. The love his young wife had inspired in him, being quite a secondary sentiment, could not struggle against the primal sentiments we have just enumerated.

Bonacieux reflected indeed on what had just been said to him.

"But, Monsieur le commissaire," he said timidly, "believe me, I know and value more than anyone the merit of the incomparable Eminence by which we have the honor to be governed."

"Really?" asked the commissary with a doubtful look. "But if that is indeed the case, how is it that you are in the Bastille?"

"How it is that I am here, or, rather, why I am here," replied M. Bonacieux, "it is perfectly impossible for me to tell you, seeing that I do not know myself; but quite certainly it is not for having displeased M. le cardinal, at least not consciously."

"You must have committed some crime, however, since you are accused here of high treason."

"High treason?" cried Bonacieux, terrified. "High treason? And how can a poor mercer who detests the Huguenots and abhors the Spanish be accused of high treason? Consider, Monsieur, the thing is materially impossible."

"M. Bonacieux," said the commissary, looking at the accused as if his little eyes had the faculty of reading the very depths of hearts, "M. Bonacieux, do you have a wife?"

"Yes, Monsieur," replied the mercer, trembling all over, feeling that it was here that matters would become embroiled, "that is to say, I had one."

"How's that? You had one? What did you do with her, if you don't have her anymore?"

"She was abducted from me, Monsieur."

"She was abducted from you?" said the commissary. "Ah!"

Bonacieux felt at this "Ah!" that the matter was becoming more and more embroiled.

"She was abducted from you!" repeated the commissary. "And do you know the man who committed this ravishment?"

"I think I know him."

"Who is it?"

"Understand that I affirm nothing, Monsieur le commissaire, I merely suspect."

"Whom do you suspect? Come, answer frankly."

M. Bonacieux was in the greatest perplexity: should he deny everything or tell everything? If he denied everything, they might think he knew too much to admit it; if he told everything, he would give proof of his good will. So he decided to tell everything.

"I suspect," he said, "a tall, dark-haired man, of haughty bearing, who has all the marks of a great lord. He followed us several times, as it seems to me, when I waited for my wife outside the gate of the Louvre to bring her home."

The commissary seemed to feel a certain uneasiness.

"And his name?" he asked.

"Oh! as for his name, I know nothing, but if I ever meet him again, I will recognize him at once, I guarantee it, even out of a thousand persons."

The commissary's brow darkened more.

"You would recognize him out of a thousand, you say?" he continued.

"That is," Bonacieux picked up, seeing that he had made a misstep, "that is . . ."

"You replied that you would recognize him," said the commissary. "Very well, that's enough for today. Before we go further, someone must be informed that you know your wife's ravisher."

"But I didn't tell you I know him!" Bonacieux cried out in despair. "I told you, on the contrary . . ."

"Take the prisoner away," the commissary said to the two guards.

"And where must we bring him?" asked the clerk.

"To a cell."

"Which one?"

"Oh, my God, the first one you come to, provided it locks tight!" the commissary replied with an indifference that filled poor Bonacieux with horror.

"Alas! alas!" he said to himself, "misfortune hangs over my head! My wife must have committed some frightful crime. They think I'm her accomplice, and they will punish me along with her. She must have talked, she must have admitted that she told me everything—women are so weak! A cell, the first you come to! That's it! A night is soon past; and tomorrow, the wheel, the gallows! Oh, my God! my God! have mercy on me!"

Without paying the least attention to the lamentations of Master Bonacieux, lamentations to which they had anyhow become accustomed, the two guards took the prisoner by the arms and led him away, while the commissary hastily wrote a letter that his clerk waited for.

Bonacieux never closed an eye, not that his cell was so disagreeable, but because his worries were too great. He spent the whole night on his stool, shuddering at the least noise; and when the first rays of light slipped into his room, dawn seemed to him to have taken on funereal hues.

Suddenly he heard the bolts being drawn, and he gave a terrible start. He thought they had come for him in order to lead him to the scaffold. And so, when, instead of the executioner he was expecting, he saw appear purely and simply his commissary and his clerk from the day before, he was ready to throw himself on their necks.

"Your case has become extremely complicated since yesterday evening, my brave fellow," the commissary said to him, "and I advise you to tell the whole truth, for your repentance alone can avert the cardinal's wrath."

"But I'm quite ready to tell everything," cried Bonacieux, "at least everything I know. Question me, I beg you."

"Where is your wife, first of all?"

"But I've told you she was abducted from me."

"Yes, but since five o'clock yesterday afternoon, thanks to you, she has escaped."

"My wife has escaped?" cried Bonacieux. "Oh, the poor woman! Monsieur, if she has escaped, it's not my fault, I swear it."

"What were you doing, then, with M. d'Artagnan, your neighbor, with whom you had a long consultation during the day?"

"Ah, yes, Monsieur le commissaire, yes, that's true! And I admit I was wrong. I was with M. d'Artagnan."

"What was the goal of that visit?"

"To beg him to help me find my wife. I thought I had the right to reclaim her. I was wrong, it seems, and I ask you to pardon me for that."

"And what was M. d'Artagnan's reply?"

"M. d'Artagnan promised me his help, but I soon realized that he was betraying me."

"You're trying to bluff the law! M. d'Artagnan made a pact with you, and by virtue of that pact, he put to flight the policemen who had arrested your wife, and shielded her from all pursuit."

"M. d'Artagnan has abducted my wife? Ah! but what are you telling me?"

"Fortunately, M. d'Artagnan is in our hands, and you are going to confront him."

"Ah! my word, I could ask for nothing better," cried Bonacieux. "I won't be sorry to see a familiar face."

"Bring in M. d'Artagnan," the commissary said to the two guards.

The two guards brought in Athos.

"M. d'Artagnan," said the commissary, addressing Athos, "state what went on between you and Monsieur."

"But," cried Bonacieux, "this man you're showing me is not d'Artagnan!"

"What? This is not M. d'Artagnan?" cried the commissary.

"Not for all the world," replied Bonacieux.

"What is the gentleman's name?" asked the commissary.

"That I cannot tell you. I don't know him."

"What? You don't know him?"

"No."

"You have never seen him?"

"No, I have, but I don't know what he's called."

"Your name?" asked the commissary.

"Athos," replied the musketeer.

"But that's not the name of a man, it's the name of a mountain!" cried the poor interrogator, who was beginning to lose his head.

"It is my name," Athos said calmly.

"But you said your name was d'Artagnan."

"I?"

"Yes, you."

"That is to say, someone said to me: 'You are M. d'Artagnan?' I replied: 'You think so?' My guards shouted that they were sure of it. I did not want to vex them. Besides, I might have been mistaken."

"Monsieur, you insult the majesty of the law."

"Not at all," Athos said calmly.

"You are M. d'Artagnan."

"You see, you're telling me so again."

"But," M. Bonacieux cried in turn, "I tell you, Monsieur le commissaire, that there's not a moment's doubt. M. d'Artagnan is my lodger, and consequently, though he doesn't pay me the rent, and precisely because of that, I ought to know him. M. d'Artagnan is a young man of barely nineteen or twenty, and Monsieur is at least thirty. M. d'Artagnan is in M. des Essarts's guards, and Monsieur is in the company of M. de Tréville's musketeers: look at the uniform, Monsieur le commissaire, look at the uniform."

"That's true," murmured the commissary, "that's true, pardieu."

At that moment the door flew open, and a messenger, ushered in by one of the gatekeepers of the Bastille, handed the commissary a letter.

"Oh, the poor woman!" cried the commissary.

"How's that? What did you say? Who are you talking about? It's not my wife, I hope?"

"On the contrary, it is. You're in a fine mess now."

"Ah!" cried the exasperated mercer, "but be so kind as to tell me, Monsieur, how my case could be made worse by what my wife does while I'm in prison!"

"Because what she does is the result of a plan arranged between you, an infernal plan!"

"I swear to you, Monsieur le commissaire, that you are in the profoundest error, that I know nothing at all of what my wife is supposedly doing, that I am a perfect stranger to what she does, and that, if she has done something stupid, I renounce her, I deny her, I curse her."

"Ah, well," Athos said to the commissary, "if you have no further need of me here, send me somewhere else. Your M. Bonacieux is very tiresome."

"Take the prisoners back to their cells," said the commissary, indicating Athos and Bonacieux with the same gesture, "and see that they're guarded more strictly than ever."

"However," Athos said with his habitual calm, "if your business is with M. d'Artagnan, I don't see very well how I can replace him."

"Do as I said!" cried the commissary. "And the utmost secrecy! Understand?"

Athos followed his guards shrugging his shoulders, and M. Bonacieux pouring out lamentations that would have broken a tiger's heart.

The mercer was taken back to the same cell where he had spent the night, and was left there for the whole day. For the whole day Bonacieux wept like a real mercer, being no swords-man at all, as he told us himself.

In the evening, towards nine o'clock, just as he was mak-ing up his mind to go to bed, he heard footsteps in his corridor. These footsteps approached his cell, his door opened, guards appeared.

"Follow me," said an officer who came after the guards.

"Follow you?" cried Bonacieux. "Follow you at this hour? My God, where to?"

"Where we have orders to bring you."

"But that . . . that's not an answer."

"It is, however, the only one we can give you."

"Ah, my God, my God!" murmured the poor mercer, "this time I'm lost!"

And, mechanically and without resistance, he followed the guards who had come to fetch him.

He took the same corridor he had already taken, crossed a first courtyard, went through a second part of the building; fi-nally, at the door to the front courtyard, he found a carriage surrounded by four mounted guards. They made him get into this carriage, the officer sat down beside him, the door was locked, and the two found themselves in a rolling prison.

The carriage started off, slow as a funeral hearse. Through the locked grill, the prisoner made out houses and the pave-ment, that was all; but, true Parisian that he was, Bonacieux recognized each street by its hitching posts, signs, and street lamps. When they reached Saint-Paul, where the condemned prisoners of the Bastille were executed, he nearly fainted and crossed himself twice. He thought the carriage was going to stop there. The carriage went on, however.

Further on, he was seized by great terror again, as they passed beside the Saint-Jean cemetery, where state criminals were buried. One thing reassured him slightly, that before bury-ing them they generally cut off their heads, and his head was still on his shoulders. But when he saw the carriage go towards the place de Grève, when he made out the pointed roofs of the Hôtel de Ville, when the carriage turned under the arcade, he thought it was all over for him, wanted to confess to the officer, and, at his refusal, uttered cries so pitiable that the officer declared to him that if he went on deafening him like that he would gag him.

This threat reassured Bonacieux slightly: if he was to be executed on the Grève, it was not worth gagging him, because they had almost reached the place of execution. Indeed, the carriage crossed the fatal square without stopping. The only thing left to fear was the Croix-du-Trahoir. The carriage was going precisely that way.

This time there was no more doubt; it was at the Croix-du-Trahoir that they executed inferior criminals. Bonacieux had flattered himself in thinking he was worthy of Saint-Paul or the place de Grève: it was at the Croix-du-Trahoir that he was going to end his journey and his destiny! He could not yet see that ill-fated cross, but he somehow felt it coming towards him. When he was only twenty paces from it, he heard a hubbub, and the carriage stopped. This was more than poor Bonacieux could bear, crushed as he already was by the successive emotions he had suffered. He let out a feeble moan, which might have been taken for a dying man's last sigh, and fainted.

XIV

THE MAN FROM MEUNG

This gathering had been produced not by the expectation of a man to be hung, but by the contemplation of a hanged man.

The carriage, having stopped for a moment, started off again, passed through the crowd, continued on its way, went down the rue Saint-Honoré, turned into the rue des Bons-Enfants, and stopped in front of a low doorway.

The door opened, two guards received Bonacieux, supported by the officer, into their arms; he was pushed into an alley, made to climb a stairway, and deposited in an antechamber.

All these movements were performed for him in mechanical fashion.

He had walked as one walks in a dream; he had glimpsed things through a mist; his ears had perceived sounds without understanding them; he could have been executed at that moment without his making a gesture in his own defense or crying out to beg for mercy.

So he remained on the bench, his back leaning against the wall and his arms hanging down, just where his guards had deposited him.

However, as he looked around and saw no threatening objects, as nothing suggested that he was in any real danger, as the bench was comfortably upholstered, as the wall was covered in fine Cordovan leather, as great curtains of red damask hung before the window, held back by golden curtain loops, he gradually understood that his fright was exaggerated, and he began moving his head to the left, to the right, and up and down.

With this movement, which no one opposed, he plucked up a little courage and risked flexing one leg, then the other; finally, aiding himself with both hands, he got up from the bench and found himself on his feet.

At that moment, a benevolent-looking officer opened a portière, went on exchanging a few words with someone in the neighboring room, and, turning to the prisoner, said: "It's you who call yourself Bonacieux?"

"Yes, Monsieur l'officier," stammered the mercer, more dead than alive, "at your service."

"Come in," said the officer.

And he stood aside so that the mercer could pass. The latter obeyed without replying and went into the room, where he seemed to be expected.

It was a large office, the walls hung with offensive and defensive weapons, close and stuffy, and in which a fire already burned, though it was barely the end of the month of September. A square table, covered with books and papers, over which an immense map of the town of La Rochelle had been unrolled, occupied the middle of the room.

Standing before the fireplace was a man of medium height, of haughty and proud bearing, with piercing eyes, a broad forehead, a gaunt face elongated still more by an imperial surmounted by a pair of mustaches. Though the man was barely thirty-six or thirty-seven, his hair, mustache, and imperial were all going gray. This man had all the look of a man of war, minus the sword, and his buff boots still lightly covered with dust indicated that he had ridden on horseback during the day.

This man was Armand-Jean Duplessis, cardinal de Richelieu, not as he is represented to us, bent like an old man, suffering like a martyr, body broken, voice extinct, buried in a great armchair as in a premature grave, living only by the strength of his genius, and sustaining the war with Europe only by the eternal application of this thought; but such as he really was at that time, that is, an adroit and gallant cavalier, already weak of body, but sustained by that moral force which had made of him one of the most extraordinary men who ever existed; preparing finally, after having supported the duc de Nevers in his duchy at Mantua, after having taken Nîmes, Castres, and Uzés, to drive the English from the Île de Ré and lay siege to La Rochelle.

At first sight, then, nothing marked him as a cardinal, and it was impossible for those who did not know his face to guess before whom they found themselves.

The poor mercer remained standing at the door, while the eyes of the character we have just described fixed themselves on him and seemed to wish to penetrate to the bottom of the past.

"This is that Bonacieux?" he asked after a moment's silence.

"Yes, Monseigneur," replied the officer.

"Very well, give me those papers and leave us."

The officer took the designated papers from the table, handed them to him who had asked for them, bowed to the ground, and went out.

Bonacieux recognized these papers from his interrogation in the Bastille. From time to time, the man at the fireplace raised his eyes above the writings and plunged them like daggers to the bottom of the poor mercer's heart.

After ten minutes of reading and ten seconds of examination, the cardinal was decided.

"That head is no conspirator's," he murmured. "But never mind, let's still see."

"You are accused of high treason," the cardinal said slowly.

"I have already been apprised of that, Monseigneur," cried

Bonacieux, giving his questioner the title he had heard the officer give him, "but I swear to you that I know nothing about it."

The cardinal repressed a smile.

"You have conspired with your wife, with Mme de Chevreuse, and with Milord the duke of Buckingham."

"Indeed, Monseigneur," replied the mercer, "I've heard her mention all those names."

"And on what occasion?"

"She said that Cardinal Richelieu had lured the duke of Buckingham to Paris in order to ruin him and to ruin the queen along with him."

"She said that?" the cardinal shouted violently.

"Yes, Monseigneur. But I told her she was wrong to say such things, and that His Eminence was incapable . . ."

"Hold your tongue, imbecile," replied the cardinal.

"That's just what my wife said to me, Monseigneur."

"Do you know who abducted your wife?"

"No, Monseigneur."

"You have suspicions, however?"

"Yes, Monseigneur, but these suspicions seem to have displeased M. le commissaire, and I no longer have them."

"Your wife has escaped, did you know that?"

"No, Monseigneur, I learned it since I came to prison, and again through the medium of M. le commissaire—a very amiable man!"

The cardinal repressed a second smile.

"So you are unaware of what has become of your wife since her flight?"

"Absolutely, Monseigneur. But she must have returned to the Louvre."

"At one o'clock in the morning she had not yet returned."

"Ah, my God! But what's become of her then?"

"We'll find out, don't worry. Nothing is hidden from the cardinal; the cardinal knows everything."

"In that case, Monseigneur, do you think the cardinal will consent to tell me what has become of my wife?"

"Perhaps. But first you will have to confess all you know concerning your wife's relations with Mme de Chevreuse."

"But, Monseigneur, I know nothing, I've never seen her."

"When you went to fetch your wife at the Louvre, did she always go straight home with you?"

"Hardly ever. She had to deal with the cloth merchants I brought her to."

"And how many cloth merchants were there?"

"Two, Monseigneur."

"Where do they live?"

"One on the rue de Vaugirard, the other on the rue de La Harpe."

"Did you go into their shops with her?"

"Never, Monseigneur. I waited at the door."

"And what pretext did she give you for going in alone like that?"

"She never gave me any; she told me to wait, and I waited."

"You are an obliging husband, my dear M. Bonacieux," said the cardinal.

"He calls me his dear Monsieur!" the mercer said to himself. "Damn, things are going well!"

"Would you recognize those doors?"

"Yes."

"Do you know the numbers?"

"Yes"

"What are they?"

"25 rue de Vaugirard, and 75 rue de la Harpe."

"Very well," said the cardinal.

At these words he picked up a silver bell and rang. The officer came in.

"Go," he said in a low voice, "find Rochefort for me. Have him come at once, if he's back."

"The count is here," said the officer. "He asks urgently to speak with Your Eminence!"

"With Your Eminence?" murmured Bonacieux, who knew that this was the title usually given to M. le cardinal . . . "with Your Eminence?"

"Let him come in then, let him come in!" Richelieu said brusquely.

The officer rushed out of the room with that rapidity which all the cardinal's servants usually put into obeying him.

"With Your Eminence?" murmured Bonacieux, rolling his wild eyes.

Five seconds had not gone by since the officer's disappearance, when the door opened and a new character came in.

"It's he!" cried Bonacieux.

"He who?" asked the cardinal.

"The one who abducted my wife!"

The cardinal rang a second time. The officer reappeared.

"Put this man back into the hands of his two guards, and let him wait until I summon him before me."

"No, Monseigneur, no, it's not him!" cried Bonacieux. "No, I was wrong: it was somebody else who doesn't resemble him at all! Monsieur is an honest man."

"Take this imbecile away!" said the cardinal.

The officer took Bonacieux under the arm and brought him back to the antechamber, where he found his two guards.

The new character who has just been introduced followed Bonacieux impatiently with his eyes until he was gone, and once the door was closed again behind him, approached the cardinal briskly and said:

"They've seen each other."

"Who?" asked His Eminence.

"She and he."

"The queen and the duke?" cried Richelieu.

"Yes."

"Where?"

"At the Louvre."

"You're sure?"

"Perfectly sure."

"Who told you?"

"Mme de Lannoy, who is all for Your Eminence, as you know."

"Why didn't she say so sooner?"

"By chance, or by mistrust, the queen had Mme de Fargis sleep in her room, and kept her all day."

"Very well, we're beaten. Let us try to take our revenge."

"I will help you with all my soul, Monseigneur, rest assured."

"How did it happen?"

"At half-past midnight, the queen was with her women . . ."

"Where?"

"In her bedroom."

"Very well."

"When someone came to give her a handkerchief on the part of her seamstress . . ."

"And then?"

"The queen at once showed great emotion, and, despite the rouge with which she had painted her face, she turned pale."

"And then? And then?"

"She stood up, however, and said in an altered voice: 'Ladies, wait for me ten minutes, then I shall come back.' Then she opened the door to her alcove and went out."

"Why didn't Mme de Lannoy come to inform us that same instant?"

"Nothing was certain yet; besides, the queen had said, 'Ladies, wait for me,' and she did not dare disobey the queen."

"And how long was the queen out of the room?"

"Three-quarters of an hour."

"None of her women accompanied her?"

"Only Doña Estefania."

"And she came back afterwards?"

"Yes, but only to take a small rosewood box with her initial on it and go out at once."

"And when she came back later, did she bring the box?"

"No."

"Does Mme de Lannoy know what was in that box?"

"Yes: the diamond pendants His Majesty gave the queen."

"And she came back without the box?"

"Yes."

"So it is Mme de Lannoy's opinion that she gave them to Buckingham?"

"She's sure of it."

"How so?"

"During the day, Mme de Lannoy, in her quality as lady of the queen's wardrobe, had searched for that box, had seemed disturbed not to find it, and had ended by asking the queen about it."

"And the queen? . . ."

"The queen turned very red and replied that, having broken one of the pendants the day before, she had sent it to her jeweler to be mended."

"Someone should pass by and see if it's true or not."

"I did."

"Well, and the jeweler?"

"The jeweler has heard no mention of it."

"Good! Good! Rochefort, all is not lost, and perhaps . . . perhaps it's all for the better!"

"In fact, I do not doubt that the genius of Your Eminence . . ."

". . . will make up for the blunders of my agent, is that it?"

"That is just what I was about to say, if Your Eminence had allowed me to finish my phrase."

"Now, do you know where the duchess of Chevreuse and the duke of Buckingham are hiding?"

"No, Monseigneur, my people have been unable to tell me anything definite about that."

"But I know."

"You, Monseigneur?"

"Yes, or at least I have a suspicion. One of them has been staying at 25 rue de Vaugirard, and the other at 75 rue de la Harpe."

"Does Your Eminence wish me to have them both arrested?"

"It will be too late, they'll be gone."

"All the same, we can see."

"Take ten of my guards and search both houses."

"I'm on my way, Monseigneur."

And Rochefort rushed out of the room.

The cardinal, left alone, reflected for a moment and rang a third time.

The same officer reappeared.

"Bring in the prisoner," said the cardinal.

Master Bonacieux was ushered in again, and at a sign from the cardinal, the officer withdrew.

"You have deceived me," the cardinal said severely.

"I?" cried Bonacieux. "I, deceive Your Eminence?"

"When your wife went to the rue de Vaugirard and the rue de la Harpe, she was not going to see cloth merchants."

"Good God, and where was she going?"

"She was going to see the duchess of Chevreuse and the duke of Buckingham."

"Yes," said Bonacieux, recalling all his memories, "yes, that's it, Your Eminence is right. I said many times to my wife that it was surprising that cloth merchants should live in such houses, in houses that had no shop signs, and each time my wife burst out laughing. Ah! Monseigneur," Bonacieux went on, throwing himself at His Eminence's feet, "ah! you are indeed the cardinal, the great cardinal, the man of genius whom all the world reveres."

The cardinal, mediocre as was the triumph over such a vulgar being as Bonacieux, nonetheless enjoyed it for a moment; then, almost at once, as if a new thought had presented itself to his mind, a smile spread over his lips, and, holding out his hand to the mercer, he said:

"Get up, my friend, you're a brave man."

"The cardinal touched my hand! I have touched the great man's hand!" cried Bonacieux. "The great man has called me his friend!"

"Yes, my friend, yes!" said the cardinal, with that blandly benevolent tone he was able to take at times, but which fooled only those who did not know him. "And since you have been unjustly suspected, well, then you must have an indemnity. Here, take this pouch of a hundred pistoles, and forgive me."

"I should forgive you, Monseigneur?" said Bonacieux, hesitating to take the pouch, no doubt fearing that the supposed gift was only a joke. "But you're quite free to have me arrested, you're quite free to have me tortured, you're quite free to have me hung: you are the master, and I wouldn't have one little word to say about it. Forgive you, Monseigneur? Come now, don't even think of it!"

"Ah, my dear M. Bonacieux! You are being generous, I can see, and I thank you for it. So, then, take this pouch, and you won't go away too discontented?"

"I'll go away enchanted, Monseigneur."

"Good-bye, then, or rather, until we meet again, for I hope we shall meet again soon."

"Whenever Monseigneur wishes, and I am entirely at His Eminence's orders."

"It will be often, rest assured, for I find great charm in your conversation."

"Oh, Monseigneur!"

"Until then, M. Bonacieux, until then."

And the cardinal made him a sign of the hand, to which Bonacieux responded by bowing to the ground; then he backed his way out, and when he was in the antechamber, the cardinal heard him shouting his head off in his enthusiasm: "Viva Monseigneur! Viva His Eminence! Viva the great cardinal!" The cardinal listened, smiling, to this brilliant display of Master Bonacieux's enthusiastic feelings; then, when Bonacieux's cries were lost in the distance, he said:

"Good. There's a man who will henceforth get himself killed for me."

And the cardinal set about examining with the greatest attention the map of La Rochelle, which, as we have said, was spread over his desk, tracing with a pencil the line where the famous dike would pass, which eighteen months later would close the port of the besieged city.

While he was sunk most profoundly in his strategic meditations, the door opened again and Rochefort came in.

"Well?" the cardinal said brusquely, standing up with a promptness that proved the degree of importance he attached to the mission he had entrusted to the count.

"Well!" said the latter, "a young woman of twenty-six to twenty-eight and a man of thirty-five to forty were indeed lodged, one for four days and the other for five, in the houses Your Eminence indicated. But the woman left last night and the man this morning."

"It was them!" cried the cardinal, glancing at the clock.

"And now," he went on, "it's too late to run after them: the duchess is in Tours and the duke in Boulogne. They will have to be overtaken in London."

"What are Your Eminence's orders?"

"Not a word about what's happened; let the queen remain in perfect confidence; let her not know that we've learned her secret; let her believe that we're looking for some sort of conspiracy. Send me Séguier, the keeper of the seals."

"And what has Your Eminence done with that man?"

"Which man?" asked the cardinal.

"That Bonacieux."

"I've done all that could be done with him. I've made him his wife's spy."

The comte de Rochefort bowed, as one who recognizes the great superiority of his master, and withdrew.

Left alone, the cardinal sat down again, wrote a letter, which he sealed with his personal seal, then rang. The officer came in for the fourth time.

"Send for Vitray," he said, "and tell him to prepare for a journey."

A moment later, the man he had asked for was standing before him, all booted and spurred.

"Vitray," he said, "you are to leave posthaste for London. You will not stop for a moment on the way. You will give this letter to Milady. Here is an order for two hundred pistoles; go to my paymaster and have him pay you. There is as much to be had again if you're back here in six days and if you've properly carried out my commission."

The messenger, without a single word of response, bowed, took the letter and the order for two hundred pistoles, and left.

Here are the contents of the letter:

Milady,

Be present at the first ball where the duke of Buckingham will be present. He will have twelve diamond pendants on his doublet. Approach him and cut off two.

Inform me as soon as these pendants are in your possession.

XV

MEN OF THE ROBE AND MEN OF THE SWORD

The day after these events took place, Athos not having reappeared yet, M. de Tréville was informed of his disappearance by d'Artagnan and Porthos.

As for Aramis, he had asked for a five-day leave, and was said to be in Rouen on family business.

M. de Tréville was a father to his soldiers. The humblest and least known of them, once he put on the uniform of the company, was as certain of his help and support as his own brother would have been.

He thus went instantly to the criminal lieutenant. The officer who commanded the post at the Croix-Rouge was summoned, and from successive information it was learned that Athos was temporarily lodged in the Fort-l'Évêque.

Athos had passed through all the trials we have seen Bonacieux undergo.

We were present at the scene of the two captives' confrontation. Athos, who had said nothing up to then for fear that d'Artagnan, bothered in his turn, would not have time to do what he had to do, declared from that moment on that his name was Athos and not d'Artagnan.

He added that he knew neither M. nor Mme Bonacieux, that he had never spoken to the one or the other, that he had come at around ten o'clock in the evening to visit his friend, M. d'Artagnan, but that until that hour he had remained with M. de Tréville, with whom he had dined; twenty witnesses, he added, could attest to that fact, and he named several distinguished gentlemen, among them M. le duc de La Trémouille.

The second commissary was as stunned as the first by the simple and firm declaration of the musketeer, on whom he would have liked very much to take the revenge that men of the robe love to win from men of the sword; but the names of M. de Tréville and of M. de La Trémouille deserved consideration.

Athos was then sent to the cardinal, but unfortunately the cardinal was at the Louvre with the king.

This was precisely the moment when M. de Tréville, coming out from seeing the criminal lieutenant and the governor of the Fort-l'Évêque without having been able to find Athos, went to His Majesty.

We know what prejudices the king had against the queen, prejudices skillfully maintained by the cardinal, who, with regard to intrigues, was infinitely more wary of women than of men. One of the great causes of this particular prejudice was Anne d'Autriche's friendship with Mme de Chevreuse. These two women worried him more than the wars with Spain, the quarrels with England, and his financial difficulties. It was his view and his conviction that Mme de Chevreuse served the queen not only in her political intrigues, but, which tormented him much more, in her amorous intrigues.

At the first word of what the cardinal had said—that Mme de Chevreuse, exiled to Tours and thought to be in that town, had come to Paris, and had eluded the police for the five days she had stayed there—the king had flown into a furious temper. Capricious and unfaithful, the king wished to be called Louis the Just and Louis the Chaste. Posterity will have difficulty understanding this character, which history explains only by deeds and never by reasoning.

But when the cardinal added that not only had Mme de Chevreuse come to Paris, but also that the queen had renewed her friendship with her through the help of that mysterious sort of connection which was then known as a cabal; when he affirmed that, just as he, the cardinal, was about to unravel the most obscure threads of this intrigue, at the moment of catching the queen's emissary to the exiled lady red-handed, in flagrante delicto, provided with all necessary proofs, a musketeer had dared to violently disrupt the course of justice by falling, sword in hand, upon the honest men of law charged with the impartial examination of the affair in order to place it under the eyes of the king—Louis XIII could no longer contain himself. He made a step towards the queen's apartments with that pale and mute indignation which, when it burst out, brought this prince to the coldest cruelty.

And yet, in all this, the cardinal had still not said a word about the duke of Buckingham.

It was then that M. de Tréville came in, cold, polite, and impeccably dressed.

Alerted to what had just happened by the cardinal's presence and the king's altered looks, M. de Tréville felt as strong as Samson facing the Philistines.

Louis XIII already had his hand on the doorknob; at the sound of M. de Tréville's entrance, he turned.

"You've come in good time, Monsieur," said the king, who, when his passions had risen to a certain point, was incapable of dissembling. "I've been learning some fine things on your musketeers' account."

"And as for me," M. de Tréville said coldly, "I have some fine things to teach Your Majesty about his men of the robe."

"If you please?" the king said haughtily.

"I have the honor to inform Your Majesty," M. de Tréville went on in the same tone, "that a party of prosecutors, commissaries, and policemen, quite estimable men but, as it seems, quite set against the uniform, has allowed itself to arrest in a house, to lead through the open streets, and to throw into the Fort-l'Évêque, all on an order that they have refused to present to me, one of my musketeers, or rather of yours, Sire, a man of irreproachable conduct, of almost illustrious reputation, and favorably known to Your Majesty—M. Athos."

"Athos," the king said mechanically. "Yes, in fact, I know that name."

"If Your Majesty will recall," said M. de Tréville, "M. Athos is the musketeer who, in the regrettable duel known to you, had the misfortune of grievously wounding M. de Cahusac. By the way, Monseigneur," Tréville went on, turning to the cardinal, "M. de Cahusac is fully recovered, is he not?"

"Thank you!" said the cardinal, compressing his lips with anger.

"M. Athos had gone to visit one of his friends, who happened to be out," M. de Tréville went on, "a young Béarnais, a cadet in His Majesty's guards, M. des Essarts's company; but he had hardly settled himself in his friend's place and picked up a book while he waited, when a swarm of combined writ servers and soldiers came to lay siege to the house, broke down several doors . . ."

The cardinal made a sign to the king which meant: "This was on that business I mentioned to you."

"We know all that," replied the king, "for it was all done in our service."

"Then," said Tréville, "it was also in Your Majesty's service that they seized one of my innocent musketeers, placed him between two guards like a malefactor, and promenaded this gallant man through the midst of the insolent populace, though he has ten times spilt his blood in Your Majesty's service and is ready to shed more."

"Hah!" the king said, shaken, "so that's how things went?"

"M. de Tréville does not mention," the cardinal picked up with the greatest phlegm, "that an hour earlier this innocent musketeer, this gallant man, had turned his sword against four investigators I had delegated to prepare an affair of the highest importance."

"I defy Your Eminence to prove it," cried M. de Tréville, with all his Gascon frankness and all his military gruffness, "for an hour earlier M. Athos, who, I confide it to Your Majesty, is a man of the highest quality, did me the honor, after dining with me, of conversing in my hôtel drawing room with M. le duc de La Trémouille and M. le comte de Châlus, who happened to be there."

The king looked at the cardinal.

"Official reports are to be trusted," the cardinal replied aloud to His Majesty's mute interrogation, "and the ill-treated men have drawn up the following one, which I have the honor of presenting to Your Majesty."

"Is an official report from men of the robe worth the word of honor," Tréville replied proudly, "of a man of the sword?"

"Come, come, Tréville, be quiet," said the king.

"If His Eminence has some suspicion against one of my

musketeers," said Tréville, "the justice of M. le cardinal is known well enough for me to demand an investigation myself."

"The house where this police raid was carried out," the cardinal went on impassibly, "is, I believe, the lodging of a Béarnais who is the musketeer's friend."

"Your Eminence is referring to d'Artagnan?"

"I am referring to a young man who is your protégé, M. de Tréville."

"Yes, Your Eminence, that is exactly so."

"Do you not suspect this young man of having given bad advice . . ."

"To M. Athos, a man twice his age?" M. de Tréville interrupted. "No, Monseigneur. Besides, M. d'Artagnan spent the night with me."

"Ah, well!" said the cardinal, "did everybody spend the night with you?"

"Does His Eminence doubt my word?" asked Tréville, his brow flushed with anger.

"No, heaven forbid!" said the cardinal. "But, anyhow, at what hour was he with you?"

"Oh, that I can certainly tell Your Eminence, for I noticed as he came in that the clock read half-past nine, though I would have thought it was later."

"And at what hour did he leave your hôtel?"

"At half-past ten—an hour after the event."

"But, finally," replied the cardinal, who did not suspect Tréville's loyalty for a moment, and who felt that victory was slipping from his grasp, "but, finally, Athos was taken in that house on the rue des Fossoyeurs."

"Is it forbidden for a friend to visit a friend? for a musketeer of my company to fraternize with a guard from the company of M. des Essarts?"

"Yes, when the house where he fraternizes with that friend is suspect."

"The thing is that the house is suspect, Tréville," said the king. "Maybe you didn't know that?"

"Indeed, Sire, I was unaware of it. In any case, it may be suspect anywhere but in the part inhabited by M. d'Artagnan;

for I can assure you, Sire, that, if I can believe what he has said, there exists no more devoted servant of Your Majesty and no more profound admirer of M. le cardinal."

"Wasn't it this d'Artagnan who wounded Jussac one day in that unfortunate encounter which took place near the Carmes-Déchaussés?" the king asked, looking at the cardinal, who flushed with spite.

"And Bernajoux the next day. Yes, Sire, yes, that's right. Your Majesty has a good memory."

"Come, what shall we resolve on?" said the king.

"That concerns Your Majesty more than me," said the cardinal. "I say he is guilty."

"And I deny it," said Tréville. "But His Majesty has judges, and his judges will decide."

"That's right," said the king, "let's put the case before the judges: it's their business to judge, and they will judge."

"Only," Tréville picked up, "it's quite sad that in these unfortunate times of ours, the purest life, the most incontestable virtue, do not exempt a man from infamy and persecution. The army will also not be very content, I guarantee you, to be the butt of harsh treatment over police matters."

The word was imprudent, but M. de Tréville threw it out deliberately. He wanted an explosion, because powder makes fire, and fire makes light.

"Police matters!" cried the king, picking up M. de Tréville's words. "Police matters! And what do you know, Monsieur? Mix with your musketeers, and don't go cudgeling my brains. It seems, to hear you, that if one is so unfortunate as to arrest a musketeer, France is in danger. Eh! such ado over a musketeer! I'll have ten of them arrested, ventrebleu! a hundred, even; the whole company! And I won't have anyone breathe a word about it."

"From the moment Your Majesty finds them suspect," said Tréville, "the musketeers are guilty; and so, here you see me, Sire, prepared to surrender my sword. For, after accusing my soldiers, I do not doubt that M. le cardinal will end by accusing me myself. It will thus be better for me if I make myself a prisoner with M. Athos, who is arrested already, and M. d'Artagnan, who no doubt will be."

"Stubborn Gascon, will you have done?" said the king.

"Sire," replied Tréville, without lowering his voice in the least, "order them to give me back my musketeer, or else to try him."

"He will be tried," said the cardinal.

"Well, then, so much the better! For in that case I will ask His Majesty's permission to plead his cause."

The king feared a scandal.

"If His Eminence," he said, "has no personal motives . . ."

The cardinal saw where the king was going and headed him off:

"Pardon me," he said, "but the moment Your Majesty sees in me a prejudiced judge, I withdraw."

"Come," said the king, "will you swear to me by my father that M. Athos was with you during the event, and that he took no part in it?"

"By your glorious father and by yourself, who are what I love and venerate most in the world, I swear it!"

"Kindly consider, Sire," said the cardinal. "If we let the prisoner go like this, we will never be able to learn the truth."

"M. Athos will always be there," M. de Tréville picked up, "ready to answer when it pleases the men of the robe to question him. He will not desert, M. le cardinal; rest assured, I will answer for him myself."

"In fact, he won't desert," said the king, "he can always be found, as M. de Tréville says. Besides," he added, lowering his voice and casting a pleading glance at His Eminence, "let us give them a sense of security: it's politic."

This "politic" of Louis XIII made Richelieu smile.

"Give the order, Sire," he said, "you have the right of pardon."

"The right of pardon applies only to the guilty," said Tréville, who wanted to have the last word, "and my musketeer is innocent. It is thus not pardon that you will be granting, Sire, but justice."

"And he's in the Fort-l'Évêque?" said the king.

"Yes, Sire, and in secret, in a cell, like the lowest of criminals."

"Devil take it!" murmured the king. "What to do?"

"Sign the order to set him free, and all will be said," the cardinal picked up. "I think, like Your Majesty, that M. de Tréville's guarantee is more than sufficient."

Tréville bowed respectfully, with a joy that was not without an admixture of fear. He would have preferred stubborn resistance from the cardinal to this sudden leniency.

The king signed the order for release, and Tréville took it without delay.

As he was leaving, the cardinal gave him a friendly smile and said to the king:

"A good harmony reigns between leaders and soldiers in your musketeers, Sire; that is something quite profitable to the service and quite honorable for all."

"He'll keep playing me some bad turn or other," Tréville said to himself. "One never has the last word with such a man. But let's hurry, for the king may change his mind at any moment; and in the end it's harder to put a man back in the Bastille or the Fort-l'Évêque once he's out than to keep a prisoner there when you already have him."

M. de Tréville made a triumphal entry into the Fort-l'Évêque, where he freed the musketeer, whose peaceful indifference had never left him.

Then, the first time he saw d'Artagnan again, he said to him:

"You barely escaped. That pays you back for Jussac's wound. There's still Bernajoux's, but you shouldn't be too confident about that."

Moreover, M. de Tréville was right to be wary of the cardinal and to think that all was not over, for the captain of the musketeers had no sooner closed the door behind him than His Eminence said to the king:

"Now that there are just the two of us, we can talk seriously, if it please Your Majesty. Sire, M. de Buckingham was in Paris for five days and only left this morning."

XVI

In Which the Keeper of the Seals Séguier Searches More Than Once for the Bell in Order to Ring It the Way He Used To

It is impossible to have any idea of the impression that these few words made on Louis XIII. He alternately flushed and paled, and the cardinal saw at once that he had just won back at a single stroke all the terrain he had lost.

"M. de Buckingham in Paris!" he cried. "And what was he doing here?"

"Undoubtedly conspiring with our enemies the Huguenots and the Spanish."

"No, pardieu, no! Conspiring against my honor with Mme de Chevreuse, Mme de Longueville, and the Condés!"

"Oh, Sire, what an idea! The queen is too wise, and above all she loves Your Majesty too much."

"Woman is weak, M. le cardinal," said the king, "and as for loving me so much, I've formed my own opinion about that love."

"I maintain nonetheless," said the cardinal, "that the duke of Buckingham came to Paris for a wholly political scheme."

"And I am sure that he came for something else, M. le cardinal; but if the queen is guilty, let her tremble!"

"By the way," said the cardinal, "repugnant as it is for me to rest my mind on such a betrayal, Your Majesty reminds me of something: Mme de Lannoy, whom, on Your Majesty's orders, I have questioned several times, told me this morning that the night before last Her Majesty stayed up very late, that the next morning she wept a great deal, and that she spent the whole day writing."

"That's it!" said the king. "To him, no doubt. Cardinal, I must have the queen's papers."

"But how to take them, Sire? It seems to me that neither I nor Your Majesty can assume such a mission."

"How was it handled with the maréchale d'Ancre?" cried

the king in the highest degree of wrath. "Her wardrobes were searched, and finally she herself was searched."

"The maréchale d'Ancre was only the maréchale d'Ancre, a Florentine adventuress, Sire, nothing more; while Your Majesty's august spouse is Anne d'Autriche, queen of France—that is, one of the greatest princesses in the world."

"She's all the more guilty, M. le duc! The more she has forgotten the high position in which she has been placed, the lower she has descended. Besides, I decided long ago to put an end to all these little political and amorous intrigues. She also keeps a certain La Porte around her . . ."

"Whom I believe to be the linchpin in all this, I confess," said the cardinal.

"So you think, as I do, that she is deceiving me?" said the king.

"I think, and I repeat to Your Majesty, that the queen is conspiring against the power of her king, but I have never said against his honor."

"And I tell you against both at once; I tell you that the queen does not love me; I tell you that she loves another; I tell you that she loves that infamous duke of Buckingham! Why didn't you have him arrested while he was in Paris?"

"Arrest the duke? Arrest the prime minister of King Charles I!? Can you conceive of it, Sire? What a scandal! And if Your Majesty's suspicions, which I continue to doubt, turned out to have some substance, what a terrible scandal! What a hopeless scandal!"

"But since he's exposed himself as a vagabond and a pilferer, we ought . . ."

Louis XIII stopped himself, frightened by what he was about to say, while Richelieu, stretching his neck, waited in vain for the word that remained on the king's lips.

"We ought?"

"Nothing," said the king, "nothing. But you didn't lose sight of him all the while he was in Paris?"

"No, Sire."

"Where did he stay?"

"At 75 rue de la Harpe."

"Where's that?"

"Beside the Luxembourg."

"And you're sure that the queen and he did not see each other?"

"I think the queen is too attached to her duties, Sire."

"But they corresponded. It was to him that the queen was writing all day. M. le duc, I must have those letters!"

"However, Sire . . ."

"M. le duc, I want them, whatever the price."

"All the same, I will point out to Your Majesty . . ."

"Are you betraying me, too, then, M. le cardinal, opposing my will like this all the time? Are you also in concert with the Spaniard and the Englishman, with Mme de Chevreuse and the queen?"

"Sire," the cardinal answered with a sigh, "I thought I was safe from such suspicions."

"You have heard me, M. le cardinal. I want those letters."

"There is only one way."

"Which is?"

"It would be to entrust this mission to M. Séguier, the keeper of the seals. The thing falls completely within the duties of his office."

"Send someone to fetch him this very instant!"

"He should be in my rooms, Sire. I had asked him to pass by, and when I came to the Louvre, I left orders to have him wait, if he presented himself."

"Let someone go and fetch him this very instant!"

"Your Majesty's orders will be carried out. But . . ."

"But what?"

"But the queen may refuse to obey."

"My orders?"

"Yes, if she is unaware that these orders come from the king."

"Well, then, so that she won't doubt it, I'll go and inform her myself!"

"Your Majesty should not forget that I have done all I could to prevent a breach."

"Yes, Duke, I know you are very indulgent towards the

queen, too indulgent perhaps; and I warn you, we shall have to talk about that later."

"Whenever it please Your Majesty. But I will always be happy and proud to sacrifice myself to the good harmony that I wish to see reign between you and the queen of France."

"Very well, Cardinal, very well; but meanwhile send someone to fetch M. the keeper of the seals. I will go to the queen."

And Louis XIII, opening the connecting door, stepped into the corridor that led from his apartments to those of Anne d'Autriche.

The queen was in the midst of her women—Mme de Guitaut, Mme de Sablé, Mme de Montbazon, and Mme de Guéménée. In a corner was the Spanish lady-in-waiting, Doña Estefania, who had followed her from Madrid. Mme de Guéménée was reading, and everyone was listening attentively to the reader, with the exception of the queen, who, on the contrary, had called for this reading so that, while pretending to listen, she could follow the thread of her own thoughts.

These thoughts, all gilded as they were by a last glimmer of love, were no less sad for that. Anne d'Autriche, deprived of her husband's trust, pursued by the hatred of the cardinal, who could not forgive her for having spurned a more tender feeling, having before her eyes the example of the queen mother, whom that hatred had tormented all her life—though Marie de Medicis, if we are to believe the memoirs of the time, had begun by granting the cardinal the feeling that Anne d'Autriche always ended by refusing him—Anne d'Autriche had seen her most devoted servants, her most intimate confidants, her dearest favorites fall around her. Like those unfortunates who are endowed with a baneful gift, she brought misfortune to all she touched; her friendship was a fatal sign that called down persecution. Mme de Chevreuse and Mme de Vernet were in exile; finally, La Porte did not conceal from his mistress that he expected to be arrested any moment.

It was just when she was plunged in the deepest and darkest of these reflections that the door opened and the king came in.

The reader stopped that same instant, all the ladies stood up, and a profound silence fell.

As for the king, he made no demonstration of civility; he merely planted himself before the queen.

"Madame," he said in an altered voice, "you will receive a visit from M. le chancelier, who will communicate to you certain matters which I have entrusted to him."

The unfortunate queen, who was ceaselessly threatened with divorce, exile, and even court proceedings, paled behind her rouge, and could not help saying:

"But why this visit, Sire? What will M. le chancelier tell me that Your Majesty cannot tell me himself?"

The king turned on his heel without replying, and at almost that same instant the captain of the guards, M. de Guitaut, announced the visit of M. le chancelier.

When the chancelier appeared, the king had already left by another door.

The chancelier came in half smiling, half blushing. As we will probably come upon him again in the course of this story, it will do no harm if our readers make his acquaintance as this point.

The chancelier was a pleasant man. It was Des Roches le Masle, canon of Notre Dame, and formerly the cardinal's valet, who had proposed him to His Eminence as a completely devoted man. The cardinal trusted him and found he had done well.

Certain stories were told about him, among them this one:

After a stormy youth, he had withdrawn to a monastery to expiate, at least for a time, the follies of his adolescence.

But, on entering that holy place, the poor penitent had not managed to close the door quickly enough for the passions he was fleeing not to enter with him. He was relentlessly obsessed with them, and the superior, to whom he had confided this disgrace, wishing to defend him against them as far as he could, had recommended to him that he exorcise the tempting demon by running for the bell rope and ringing a full peal. At the denunciatory sound, the monks would be warned that temptation was besieging one of their brothers, and the whole community would start praying.

The advice seemed good to the future chancelier. He exorcised the evil spirit with a great reinforcement of prayers from the monks. But the devil does not let himself be dispossessed easily of a place where he has set up a garrison. As the exorcisms redoubled, he redoubled the temptations, so that the bell rang at full peal day and night, announcing the extreme desire for mortification experienced by the penitent.

The monks no longer had a moment's rest. During the day, they did nothing but go up and down the stairs that led to the chapel; at night, besides compline and matins, they were obliged to jump out of bed twenty times and prostrate themselves on the floor of their cells.

It is not known whether it was the devil who let go or the monks who grew weary, but after three months the penitent reappeared in the world with the reputation of the most terrible case of possession that had ever existed.

On leaving the monastery, he entered the magistracy, became a presiding judge in place of his uncle, embraced the cardinal's party, which showed no little sagacity; became chancelier, served His Eminence with zeal in his hatred of the queen mother and his vengeance on Anne d'Autriche; spurred on the judges in the Chalais affair, encouraged the efforts of M. de Laffemas, grand gibbeteer of France; and finally, invested with the cardinal's full confidence, a confidence he had so well earned, he had now received from him the singular commission for the carrying out of which he presented himself to the queen.

The queen was still standing when he came in, but she no sooner caught sight of him than she sat down in her chair again and made a sign to her women to sit down on their cushions and stools, and, in a tone of supreme hauteur, asked:

"What do you wish, Monsieur, and to what end do you present yourself here?"

"To carry out in the name of the king, Madame, and saving all the respect I have the honor of owing to Your Majesty, a thorough perquisition among your papers."

"How is that, Monsieur? A perquisition among my papers . . . Mine? What a shameful thing!"

"Pardon me, Madame, but in this circumstance I am only

an instrument made use of by the king. Did His Majesty not just leave here, and did he not ask you to prepare for this visit?"

"Search then, Monsieur; I am a criminal, it seems. Estefania, give him the keys to my tables and writing desks."

The chancelier made an inspection of this furniture for the sake of form, but he knew very well that the queen would not have locked the important letter she had spent the day writing in any piece of furniture.

Once the chancelier had opened and closed the drawers of the writing desk twenty times, he had, whatever hesitation he may have felt, he had, I say, to conclude the business, that is, to search the queen herself. The chancelier took three steps towards Anne d'Autriche, and in a very perplexed tone and with a highly embarrassed air, said:

"And now I am left with the principal perquisition."

"Which is that?" asked the queen, who did not understand or did not want to understand.

"His Majesty is certain that a letter was written by you during the day. He knows that it has not yet been sent to its addressee. This letter is to be found neither in your table nor in your writing desk, and yet this letter is somewhere."

"Will you dare lay hands on your queen?" said Anne d'Autriche, drawing herself up to her full height and fixing the chancelier with her eyes, whose expression had become almost threatening.

"I am a faithful subject of the king, Madame, and will do all that His Majesty orders."

"Well, then, it's true," said Anne d'Autriche, "and the spies of M. le cardinal have served him very well. I wrote a letter to-day, and that letter has not yet gone out. The letter is here."

And the queen brought her beautiful hand to her bodice.

"Give me the letter then, Madame," said the chancelier.

"I will give it only to the king, Monsieur," said Anne.

"If the king had wanted this letter handed to him, Madame, he would have asked you for it himself. But, I repeat to you, it is I who have been entrusted with demanding it from you, and if you do not give it up . . ."

"Well, then?"

"It is also I who have been entrusted to take it from you."

"What do you mean to say?"

"That my orders are far-reaching, Madame, and that I am authorized to search for the suspect paper even upon Your Majesty's person."

"What horror!" cried the queen.

"Then kindly behave more accommodatingly, Madame."

"This conduct is of an infamous violence, do you know that, Monsieur?"

"The king has ordered it, Madame, if you will excuse me."

"I will not endure it. No, no, I would rather die!" cried the queen, in whom the imperial blood of Spain and Austria rose up.

The chancelier made a deep bow. Then, with the very evident intention of not yielding an inch in the accomplishment of the commission entrusted to him, and as a hangman's valet might have done in the torture chamber, he approached Anne d'Autriche, in whose eyes at that same instant tears of rage welled up.

The queen was, as we have said, a woman of great beauty.

The mission could thus have been seen as a delicate one, but the king, by dint of his jealousy of Buckingham, had ceased to be jealous of anyone else.

No doubt Chancelier Séguier was looking around at that moment for the rope of the famous bell; but, not finding it, he resigned himself and reached his hand out towards the place where the queen had admitted the paper was to be found.

Anne d'Autriche took a step back, so pale one would have thought she was about to die; and, supporting herself with her left hand on a table that was behind her, to keep from falling, she drew a paper from her bosom with her right hand and held it out to the keeper of the seals.

"Here, Monsieur, this is that letter," cried the queen in a broken and shaking voice. "Take it, and rid me of your odious presence."

The chancelier, who for his part was trembling with an emotion easy to imagine, took the letter, bowed to the ground, and left.

The door had no sooner closed behind him than the queen fell half-fainting into the arms of her women.

The chancelier brought the letter to the king without reading a word of it. The king took it in a trembling hand, looked for the address, which was missing, turned very pale, opened it slowly, then, seeing from the first words that it was addressed to the king of Spain, read it very quickly.

It was a whole plan of attack against the cardinal. The queen called upon her brother and the emperor of Austria, offended as they were by the politics of Richelieu, who was eternally preoccupied with bringing down the house of Austria, to pretend to declare war on France and to impose the cardinal's dismissal as a condition of peace. But of love there was not a single word in the entire letter.

The king, quite joyful, inquired whether the cardinal was still in the Louvre. He was told that His Eminence was in the office awaiting His Majesty's orders.

The king went to him at once.

"You know, Duke," he said to him, "you were right and I was wrong. The whole intrigue is political, and there was never any question of love in that letter, which I have here. On the other hand, there is much question of you."

The cardinal took the letter and read it with the greatest attention; when he came to the end, he read it a second time.

"Well, Your Majesty," he said, "you see how far my enemies will go! You are threatened with two wars if you do not dismiss me. In your place, to tell the truth, Sire, I would yield to such strong entreaties, and for my part it would be a real blessing to retire from public affairs."

"What are you saying, Duke?"

"I am saying, Sire, that these excessive struggles and eternal labors are bad for my health. I am saying that, in all probability, I will be unable to bear the hardships of the siege of La Rochelle, and it would be better if you appointed either M. de Condé or M. de Bassompierre to it, or some other valiant man who is up to conducting a war, and not me, who am a man of the church and am ceaselessly being diverted from my vocation and made to apply myself to things for which I have no aptitude. You will be happier at home, Sire, and I have no doubt that you will be even more so abroad."

"Monsieur le duc," said the king, "I understand, rest assured. All those who are named in this letter will be punished as they deserve, and so will the queen herself."

"What are you saying, Sire? God forbid that for my sake the queen should experience the least vexation! She has always believed me her enemy, Sire, though Your Majesty can attest that I have always warmly taken her part, even against you. Oh! if she betrayed Your Majesty with regard to his honor, that would be another thing, and I would be the first to say: 'No pardon, Sire, no pardon for the guilty one!' Fortunately that is not at all the case, and Your Majesty has just received new proof of it."

"That's true, Monsieur le cardinal," said the king, "and you're right as always; but the queen nonetheless deserves my full wrath."

"It is you, Sire, who have incurred hers. And indeed, were she to pout seriously at Your Majesty, I would understand it. Your Majesty has treated her with a severity . . ."

"That is how I will always treat my enemies and yours, Duke, however highly placed they are and whatever risk I run in acting severely with them."

"The queen is my enemy, but not yours, Sire. On the contrary, she is a devoted spouse, submissive and irreproachable. Allow me, Sire, to intercede for her with Your Majesty."

"Let her humble herself, then, and come to me first!"

"On the contrary, Sire, set the example. Yours was the first wrong, since it was you who suspected the queen."

"I be the first to make it up?" said the king. "Never!"

"Sire, I beg you."

"Besides, how can I make it up first?"

"By doing something you know will please her."

"Such as?"

"Give a ball. You know how much the queen loves to dance. I guarantee you that her rancor will never withstand such thoughtfulness."

"Monsieur le cardinal, you know I have no love of worldly pleasures."

"The queen will only be the more grateful to you, since she knows your antipathy for this pleasure. Besides, it will be an occasion for her to put on those beautiful diamond pendants you gave her the other day for her birthday, and with which she has not yet had time to adorn herself."

"We'll see, Monsieur le cardinal, we'll see," said the king, who, in his joy at finding the queen guilty of a crime he was little concerned with and innocent of a fault he greatly feared, was quite ready to make peace with her. "We'll see, but, on my honor, you are too lenient."

"Sire," said the cardinal, "leave severity to ministers. Leniency is the royal virtue. Use it, and you will see that you won't regret it."

Upon which the cardinal, hearing the clock strike eleven, bowed deeply, asked the king's leave to retire, and begged him to make peace with the queen.

Anne d'Autriche, who, following the seizure of her letter, was expecting some reproach, was greatly astonished to see the king make attempts at reconciliation with her the next day. Her first impulse was to repel them. Her pride as a woman and her dignity as a queen had both been so cruelly injured that she could not make things up like that at the first stroke. But, conquered by the advice of her women, she finally seemed as though she was beginning to forget. The king profited from that first moment of reversal to tell her that he was intending to give a fête in the near future.

A fête was such a rare thing for poor Anne d'Autriche that, at his announcement, as the cardinal had thought, the last trace of her resentment disappeared, if not from her heart, at least from her face. She asked what day the fête would take place, but the king replied that he had to discuss that point with the cardinal.

Indeed, every day the king asked the cardinal when the fête would take place, and every day the cardinal, under some pretext or other, put off fixing the date.

Ten days passed that way.

On the eighth day after the scene we have just recounted, the cardinal received a letter, with a London stamp, which contained only these few lines:

> I have them; but I cannot leave London for lack of money. Send me five hundred pistoles, and four or five days after I receive them, I will be in Paris.

On the same day that the cardinal received this letter, the king asked him his usual question.

Richelieu counted on his fingers and said softly to himself: "She will come, she says, four or five days after she receives the money. It will take four or five days for the money to get there, four or five days for her to come back, which makes ten days. Now let us add something for contrary winds, bad luck, and feminine weaknesses, and say twelve days."

"Well, Monsieur le duc, have you made your calculation?"

"Yes, Sire. Today is the twentieth of September. The city aldermen are giving a fête on the third of October. That will work out perfectly, for it will not look as though you are making a step towards the queen."

Then the cardinal added: "By the way, Sire, don't forget to tell Her Majesty, on the eve of this fête, that you wish to see how her diamond pendants become her."

XVII

THE BONACIEUX HOUSEHOLD

This was the second time that the cardinal had returned to this point about the diamond pendants with the king. Louis XIII was struck by such insistence, and thought that this urging must conceal some mystery.

The king had been humiliated more than once by the cardinal, whose police, though they had not yet attained the perfection of modern police, were better informed than he himself about what was going on in his own household. So he hoped that he might draw some light from a conversation with Anne d'Autriche and then go back to His Eminence with some secret that the cardinal did or did not know, but which in either case would raise him infinitely in his minister's eyes.

So he went to find the queen, and, as was his habit, accosted her with new threats against those who surrounded her. Anne d'Autriche lowered her head and let the torrent flow without responding, hoping that it would finally come to a stop. But that was not what Louis XIII wanted; Louis XIII wanted a discussion that would yield some sort of light, convinced as he was that the cardinal had some ulterior motive and was contriving some terrible surprise for him, as His Eminence knew how to do. He reached that goal by his persistent accusations.

"Ah," cried Anne d'Autriche, "leave off these vague attacks, Sire. You are not telling me all that's in your heart. What have I done? Come, what crime have I committed? It is impossible that Your Majesty should make all this noise about a letter written to my brother."

The king, attacked in his turn with such directness, did not know how to respond. He thought it was the right moment to deliver the instructions he was supposed to give only on the eve of the fête.

"Madame," he said majestically, "there will soon be a ball at the Hôtel de Ville. To honor our worthy aldermen, I intend to have you appear in ceremonial dress, and above all adorned with the diamond pendants I gave you for your birthday. That is my reply."

The reply was terrible. Anne d'Autriche thought that Louis XIII knew everything, and that the cardinal had obtained from him this long dissimulation of seven or eight days, which moreover was in his character. She turned excessively pale, leaned on a console with her admirably beautiful hand, which then seemed made of wax, and, gazing at the king with terrified eyes, made not one syllable of reply.

"Do you hear, Madame," said the king, who enjoyed the full extent of this perplexity, but without suspecting its cause, "do you hear?"

"Yes, Sire, I hear," stammered the queen.

"You will appear at the ball?"

"Yes."

"With the pendants?"

"Yes."

The queen's pallor increased still more, if that was possible. The king noticed it and enjoyed it, with that cold cruelty which was one of the bad sides of his character.

"It's agreed, then," said the king, "and that is all I had to say to you."

"But what day will the ball take place?" asked Anne d'Autriche.

Louis XIII felt instinctively that he ought not to answer this question, the queen having asked it almost in a whisper.

"Why, very soon, Madame," he said, "but I can't remember the exact day. I'll ask the cardinal."

"So it was the cardinal who announced this fête to you?" cried the queen.

"Yes, Madame," replied the astonished king, "but why do you ask?"

"It was he who told you to invite me to appear with those pendants?"

"That is to say, Madame . . ."

"It was he, Sire, it was he!"

"Well, what matter if it was he or I? Is there any crime in the invitation?"

"No, Sire."

"You'll appear then?"

"Yes, Sire."

"Very well," said the king, withdrawing, "very well, I'll count on it."

The queen curtsied, less out of etiquette than because her knees were giving way under her.

The king went away delighted.

"I'm lost," murmured the queen, "I'm lost, because the cardinal knows everything, and it's he who is pushing the king, who knows nothing yet, but will soon know all. I'm lost! Oh, God, God, God!"

She knelt on a cushion and prayed, her head buried in her shaking arms.

Indeed, the situation was terrible. Buckingham had gone back to London, Mme de Chevreuse was in Tours. More closely watched than ever, the queen sensed dimly that one of her women had betrayed her, without being able to say which one. La Porte could not leave the Louvre. There was not a soul in the world she could trust.

Thus, faced with the ruin that threatened her and the abandonment she lived in, she burst into sobs.

"May I be of any use to Your Majesty?" a voice full of gentleness and pity said all at once.

The queen turned sharply, because there was no mistaking the expression of that voice: it was a friend who had spoken.

Indeed, in one of the doorways that opened onto the queen's apartments appeared the pretty Mme Bonacieux. She had been busy sorting gowns and linens in a side room when the king came in. She had not been able to leave, and had heard everything.

The queen let out a piercing cry on seeing herself caught, for in her agitation she did not at first recognize the young woman who had been given her by La Porte.

"Oh, don't be afraid of anything, Madame!" said the young woman, pressing her hands together and weeping at the queen's distress herself. "I am Your Majesty's, body and soul, and far as I am from her, inferior as my position is, I believe I have found a way to save Your Majesty from grief."

"You? Oh, heavens! You?" cried the queen. "But come, look me in the face. I'm betrayed on all sides; can I trust you?"

"Oh, Madame!" cried the young woman, falling to her knees, "upon my soul, I am ready to die for Your Majesty!"

This cry had come from the depths of the heart, and, as with the first, there was no mistaking it.

"Yes," Mme Bonacieux went on, "yes, there are traitors here. But, by the holy name of the Virgin, I swear to you that no one is more devoted to Your Majesty than I. You gave those pendants that the king keeps asking for to Buckingham, didn't you? Those pendants were in a little rosewood box that he held under his arm? Am I wrong? Isn't that so?"

"Oh, my God! my God!" murmured the queen, whose teeth were chattering with fear.

"Well, then," Mme Bonacieux went on, "we must get those pendants back!"

"Yes, we undoubtedly must," cried the queen, "but how to do it? how to manage it?"

"We must send someone to the duke."

"But who? . . . who? . . . Who can I trust?"

"Rely on me, Madame. Do me that honor, my queen, and I will find the messenger!"

"But I'll have to write!"

"Oh, yes! That is indispensable. Two words in Your Majesty's hand, and your personal seal."

"But those two words are my condemnation, divorce, exile!"

"Yes, if they fall into dishonorable hands! But I guarantee that those two words will be delivered to the right address."

"Oh, my God! So I must put my life, my honor, and my reputation in your hands?"

"Yes, yes, Madame, you must, and I will save them all!"

"But how? Tell me that, at least."

"My husband was set free two or three days ago. I haven't had time to see him yet. He's a worthy and honest man, who has neither hatred nor love for anyone. He'll do what I want. He'll go off on my orders, without knowing what he's carrying, and deliver Your Majesty's letter, without even knowing it is from Your Majesty, to the address you indicate."

The queen took the young woman by both hands on a passionate impulse, gazed at her as if to read to the bottom of her heart, and seeing only sincerity in her lovely eyes, embraced her tenderly.

"Do that," she cried, "and you will have saved my life, you will have saved my honor!"

"Oh, don't exaggerate the service I have the honor of rendering you! I have nothing to save of Your Majesty's, who is only the victim of perfidious plots."

"That's true, that's true, my child," said the queen, "you're right."

"Give me the letter then, Madame, time is short."

The queen rushed to a little table where she found ink, paper, and pens. She wrote two lines, sealed the letter with her seal, and handed it to Mme Bonacieux.

"And now," said the queen, "we're forgetting one necessary thing."

"What?"

"Money."

Mme Bonacieux blushed.

"Yes, that's true," she said, "and I'll confess to Your Majesty that my husband . . ."

"Your husband has none, that's what you want to say."

"No, he has, but he's terribly stingy, that's his failing. However, Your Majesty needn't worry, we'll find a way . . ."

"The thing is that I also have none," said the queen (those who have read the memoirs of Mme de Motteville will not be surprised by that response). "But wait."

Anne d'Autriche rushed behind her screen.

"Here," she said, "I'm assured that this is a very valuable ring. It came from my brother, the king of Spain. It is mine and I can dispose of it. Take this ring and exchange it for money, and let your husband set off."

"Within an hour you shall be obeyed."

"You see the address," added the queen, speaking so softly that what she said could barely be heard. "To Milord the duke of Buckingham, London."

"The letter will be delivered to him in person."

"Generous child!" cried Anne d'Autriche.

Mme Bonacieux kissed the queen's hands, hid the paper in her bodice, and disappeared with the lightness of a bird.

Ten minutes later, she was at home. As she had told the queen, she had not seen her husband since he was set free; she was thus unaware of the change that had been made in him with regard to the cardinal, a change wrought by His Eminence's flattery and money, corroborated afterwards by two or three visits from the comte de Rochefort, who had become Bonacieux's best friend and had made him believe without much difficulty that no blameworthy feelings had led to his wife's abduction, but that it was merely a political precaution.

She found M. Bonacieux alone. The poor man had with great difficulty restored order in the house, where he had found the furniture nearly all broken and the wardrobes nearly empty, the law not being one of the three things King Solomon mentioned as leaving no traces of their passage. As for the maid, she had fled at the time of her master's arrest. Terror had taken such possession of the poor girl that she never stopped walking between Paris and Burgundy, her native province.

The worthy mercer had sent notice to his wife of his happy return as soon as he came back to the house, and his wife in her response had congratulated him and told him that the first moment she could steal from her duties would be devoted entirely to paying him a visit.

That first moment had been delayed for five days, which, in any other circumstances, would have seemed rather too long to Master Bonacieux; but in the visit he had paid to the cardinal, and the visits Rochefort had made to him, he had found ample food for reflection, and, as we know, nothing makes the time pass so quickly as reflection.

The more so in that Bonacieux's reflections were all rose-colored. Rochefort called him his friend, his dear Bonacieux, and ceaselessly told him that the cardinal set the greatest store by him. The mercer already saw himself on the way to honor and fortune.

On her side, Mme Bonacieux had reflected, but, it must be said, on something quite other than ambition. Despite herself, her thoughts had for constant motive that handsome young man, so brave and seemingly so loving. Married at the age of eighteen to M. Bonacieux, living always in the midst of her husband's friends, who were hardly likely to inspire any sort of feeling in a young woman whose heart was loftier than her position, Mme Bonacieux had remained indifferent to vulgar seductions. But, at that time especially, the title of gentleman had great influence on the bourgeoisie, and d'Artagnan was a gentleman. Moreover, he wore the uniform of the guards, which, after the uniform of the musketeers, was the most esteemed among the ladies. He was, we repeat, handsome, young, adventurous; he spoke of love as a man who loves and longs to be loved; there was more there than was needed to turn a twenty-three-year-old head, and Mme Bonacieux had just reached that happy time of life.

The two spouses, as they had not seen each other for eight days, and during that week serious events had occurred on both sides, came together then with a certain uneasiness. Nonetheless, M. Bonacieux showed real joy and went to his wife with open arms.

Mme Bonacieux offered him her brow.

"Let's talk a little," she said.

"What's that?" said Bonacieux, surprised.

"Yes, to be sure, I have something of the highest importance to tell you."

"By the way, I also have several rather serious questions to ask you. Give me some explanation of your abduction, I beg you."

"That's hardly the point right now," said Mme Bonacieux.

"And what is the point, then? My imprisonment?"

"I learned of it the same day. But as you were incapable of any crime, as you were not an accomplice in any intrigue, as you knew nothing, finally, that could compromise either you or anyone else, I attached no more importance to that event than it deserved."

"That's easy enough for you to say, Madame!" Bonacieux picked up, offended by the slight interest he wife showed in him. "Do you know I was plunged for a day and a night into a cell of the Bastille?"

"A day and a night are soon past. Let's drop your imprisonment and come back to what has brought me here to you."

"How's that? What has brought you here to me? So it's not the wish to see again a husband from whom you have been separated for eight days?" asked the mercer, stung to the quick.

"That first, and then something else."

"Speak!"

"Something of the highest interest and on which our future fortunes may depend."

"Our fortunes have changed countenance greatly since I last saw you, Mme Bonacieux, and I wouldn't be surprised if in a few months they didn't become the envy of many folk."

"Yes, above all if you will follow the instructions I'm about to give you."

"Give me?"

"Yes, you. There is a good and holy action to be performed, Monsieur, and a lot of money to be made at the same time."

Mme Bonacieux knew that in mentioning money to her husband, she was taking him by his weak side.

But a man, though he be a mercer, who has once talked for ten minutes with Cardinal Richelieu, is no longer the same man.

"A lot of money to be made!" said Bonacieux, spreading his lips.

"Yes, a lot."

"How much, approximately?"

"Maybe a thousand pistoles."

"So what you're going to ask of me is something really serious?"

"Yes."

"What do I have to do?"

"You'll leave at once, I will give you a paper which you will not let go of under any pretext, and you will deliver it into the proper hands."

"And where will I leave for?"

"For London."

"I, for London? Come now, you're joking, I have no business in London."

"But others need you to go there."

"Who are these others? I warn you, I will no longer act blindly, and I want to know not only to what I'm exposing myself, but also for whom I'm exposing myself."

"An illustrious person is sending you, an illustrious person awaits you: the reward will exceed your desires, that is all I can promise you."

"More intrigues, always more intrigues! Thank you, but I

guard against them now, and M. le cardinal has enlightened me on the subject."

"The cardinal?" cried Mme Bonacieux. "You've seen the cardinal?"

"He sent for me," the mercer replied proudly.

"And you went there on his invitation, imprudent as you are!"

"I must say that I had no choice whether to go there or not, because I was between two guards. It is also true to say that, as I didn't know His Eminence then, I would have been quite delighted if I could have gotten out of that visit."

"So he mistreated you? He made threats against you?"

"He held out his hand to me and called me his friend—his friend! Do you hear, Madame? I am a friend of the great cardinal!"

"Of the great cardinal!"

"Would you perchance deny him the title, Madame?"

"I don't deny him anything, but I tell you that a minister's favor is ephemeral, and one has to be mad to attach oneself to a minister. There are powers above his, which do not rest on the caprice of a man or the outcome of an event. It is to those powers that one must rally."

"I am sorry, Madame, but I know no other power than that of the great man I have the honor of serving."

"You serve the cardinal?"

"Yes, Madame, and as his servant, I will not allow you to involve yourself in plots against the security of the State, or to assist the intrigues of a woman who is not French and who has a Spanish heart. Fortunately, the great cardinal is there; his vigilant eye keeps watch and penetrates to the bottom of the heart."

Bonacieux repeated word for word a phrase he had heard uttered by the comte de Rochefort. But the poor woman, who had counted on her husband, and who, in that hope, had answered for him to the queen, shuddered at it nonetheless, and at the danger she had almost thrown herself into, and at the powerlessness in which she found herself. However, knowing the weakness and above all the greediness of her husband, she did not despair of bringing him around to her purposes.

"So you are a cardinalist, Monsieur!" she cried. "You serve the party of those who ill-treat your wife and insult your queen!"

"Private interests are nothing in the face of the interests of all. I am for those who preserve the State," Bonacieux said emphatically.

This was another of the comte de Rochefort's phrases, which he had memorized and found occasion to drop.

"And do you know what this State you're talking about really is?" asked Mme Bonacieux, shrugging her shoulders. "Content yourself with being a bourgeois without any subtlety, and turn to the side that offers you the most advantages."

"Heh, heh!" said Bonacieux, patting a round-bellied pouch that gave out a silvery sound. "What do you say to that, Madame Preacher?"

"Where did that money come from?"

"Can't you guess?"

"From the cardinal?"

"From him and from my friend the comte de Rochefort."

"The comte de Rochefort! But he's the one who abducted me!"

"Maybe so, Madame."

"And you take money from that man?"

"Didn't you tell me that the abduction was entirely political?"

"Yes, but the purpose of that abduction was to make me betray my mistress, to extract statements from me by torture that might compromise the honor and perhaps even the life of my august mistress."

"Madame," Bonacieux picked up, "your august mistress is a perfidious Spaniard, and what the cardinal does is well done."

"Monsieur," said the young woman, "I knew you to be a coward, a miser, and an imbecile, but I did not know you to be dishonorable!"

"Madame," said Bonacieux, who had never seen his wife angry, and who retreated before such conjugal wrath, "Madame, what are you saying?"

"I am saying that you are a scoundrel!" Mme Bonacieux

went on, seeing that she was regaining some influence over her husband. "So you're involved in politics, are you! and cardinalist politics at that! So you've sold yourself body and soul to the devil for the sake of money!"

"No, to the cardinal."

"It's the same thing!" cried the young woman. "Whoever says Richelieu says Satan."

"Be quiet, Madame, be quiet, you might be heard!"

"Yes, you're right, and I'd be ashamed for you in your cowardice."

"But, see here, what are you asking of me?"

"I told you: that you leave this very instant, Monsieur, that you faithfully carry out the commission I deign to entrust to you, and on that condition I will forget everything, I will forgive, and more than that"—she held out her hand to him—"I will be your friend again."

Bonacieux was a poltroon and a miser, but he loved his wife. He was moved. A man of fifty does not hold a grudge for very long against a woman of twenty-three. Mme Bonacieux saw that he was wavering.

"Come, have you decided?" she said.

"But, my dear friend, think a little about what you're asking of me. London is far from Paris, very far, and maybe the commission you're entrusting to me is not without its dangers."

"What matter, if you avoid them!"

"Ah, no, Mme Bonacieux," said the mercer, "no, I decidedly refuse: intrigues scare me. I've seen the Bastille, I have. Brr! It's frightful, the Bastille! I get gooseflesh just thinking about it. They threatened to torture me. Do you know what torture is? Wooden wedges driven between your legs till the bones crack! No, I decidedly won't go. And, morbleu! why don't you go yourself? Because the truth is I think I've been mistaken about you up to now: I think you're a man, and among the maddest of them at that!"

"And you, you're a woman, a pathetic woman, stupid and besotted. Ah, you're afraid! Well, then, if you don't leave this very instant, I'll have you arrested by order of the queen, and I'll have them put you in that Bastille you're so afraid of."

Bonacieux lapsed into deep reflection. He maturely weighed these two angers in his head, the cardinal's and the queen's: the cardinal's came out enormously weightier.

"Have me arrested in the queen's name," he said, "and I will appeal to the cardinal."

This time Mme Bonacieux saw that she had gone too far, and she was appalled at having made such an advance. For a moment she contemplated in fear this stupid figure, with his invincible resoluteness, like that of fools when they are frightened.

"Well, then, so be it!" she said. "Perhaps you're right after all: men know far more about politics than women, and you above all, M. Bonacieux, who have talked with the cardinal. And yet it's a hard thing," she added, "that my husband, that a man whose affection I thought I could count on, treats me so disgracefully and won't satisfy my whim at all."

"It's that your whims may go too far," Bonacieux replied triumphantly, "and I distrust them."

"I'll give it up, then," the young woman said with a sigh. "Very well, let's not talk about it any more."

"If you'd at least tell me what I am to do in London," Bonacieux picked up, recalling a bit too late that Rochefort had strongly advised trying to worm the secrets out of his wife.

"There's no use your knowing," said the young woman, whom an instinctive mistrust now held back. "It was a matter of a trinket such as women like, a purchase on which there was a lot to be made."

But the more the young woman defended herself, the more Bonacieux thought, on the contrary, that the secret she refused to confide to him was important. He thus resolved to run that same instant to the comte de Rochefort and tell him that the queen was looking for a messenger to send to London.

"Excuse me if I leave you, my dear Mme Bonacieux," he said, "but, not knowing that you would come to see me, I had made an appointment with one of my friends. I'll be back in an instant, and if you will wait half a minute for me, as soon as I'm finished with that friend, I'll come to fetch you, and, as it's beginning to get late, I'll bring you back to the Louvre."

"Thank you, Monsieur," replied Mme Bonacieux. "You're not brave enough to be of any use to me, and I can very well return to the Louvre by myself."

"As you please, Mme Bonacieux," replied the ex-mercer. "Will I see you again soon?"

"No doubt. Next week, I hope, my service will leave me some free time, and I will profit from it to come and put our things in order, for they must be in a bit of a mess."

"Very well, I shall expect you. You're not vexed with me?"

"I? Not in the least."

"See you soon, then?"

"See you soon."

Bonacieux kissed his wife's hand and left quickly.

"Well, now," said Mme Bonacieux, once her husband had closed the street door and she was left alone, "all the imbecile needed was to be a cardinalist! And I, who had guaranteed the queen, I, who had promised my poor mistress . . . Ah, my God! My God! She'll take me for one of those scoundrels the palace is swarming with, who are put near her in order to spy on her! Ah, M. Bonacieux! I never loved you very much, but now it's far worse: I hate you! And, upon my word, you will pay me for it!"

Just as she said these words, a knock on the ceiling made her look up, and a voice that came to her through the floor-boards called to her:

"Dear Mme Bonacieux, open the little door to the alley for me, and I'll come down to you."

XVIII

THE LOVER AND THE HUSBAND

"Ah, Madame!" said d'Artagnan as he came through the door the young woman opened for him, "allow me to tell you, it's a sorry husband you've got there!"

"So you heard our conversation?" Mme Bonacieux asked sharply, looking worriedly at d'Artagnan.

"All of it."

"But, my God, how is it possible?"

"By a process known to me, and by means of which I also listened to the more lively conversation you had with the cardinal's beagles."

"And what did you understand of what we said?"

"A thousand things: first of all, that your husband, fortunately, is a ninny and a dolt; then, that you were in difficulties, for which I was quite glad, because it gives me an occasion to put myself at your service, and God knows I'm ready to go through fire for you; finally, that the queen needs a brave, intelligent, and devoted man to travel to London for her. I have at least two of the three qualities you need, and here I am."

Mme Bonacieux did not reply, but her heart leaped for joy, and a secret hope shone in her eyes.

"And what guarantee will you give me," she asked, "if I agree to entrust you with this mission?"

"My love for you. Speak, then, give your orders: what must I do?"

"My God! my God!" murmured the young woman. "Ought I to entrust you with such a secret, Monsieur? You're almost a boy!"

"Come, I see you need someone who can answer for me to you."

"I confess that would greatly reassure me."

"Do you know Athos?"

"No."

"Porthos?"

"No."

"Aramis?"

"No. Who are these gentlemen?"

"The king's musketeers. Do you know M. de Tréville, their captain?"

"Oh, yes! Him I know, not personally, but from having heard the queen speak of him more than once as a brave and loyal gentleman."

"You're not afraid that he'll betray you to the cardinal, are you?"

"Oh, no, certainly not!"

"Well, then, reveal your secret to him, and, important, precious, terrible as it may be, ask him if you can entrust it to me."

"But the secret doesn't belong to me, and I can't reveal it like that."

"You were going to entrust it to M. Bonacieux, weren't you?" d'Artagnan said spitefully.

"As one entrusts a letter to a hollow tree, a pigeon's wing, a dog's collar."

"And yet you see very well that I love you."

"So you say."

"I am a gallant man!"

"I believe it."

"I'm brave!"

"Oh, that I'm sure of!"

"Then put me to the test."

Mme Bonacieux gazed at the young man, held back by a last hesitation. But there was such ardor in his eyes, such persuasiveness in his voice, that she felt drawn to trust him. Besides, she found herself in one of those circumstances when one must risk all to win all. The queen would be ruined just as well by too great a discretion as by too great a confidence. Then, too, we must confess, the involuntary feeling she had for her young protector decided her to speak.

"Listen," she said to him, "I yield to your protestations and give way to your assurances. But I swear to you before God who hears us that if you betray me and my enemies pardon me, I will kill myself and accuse you of my death."

"And I swear to you before God, Madame," said d'Artagnan, "that if I am caught carrying out the orders you give me, I will die before doing or saying anything that will compromise anyone."

Then the young woman entrusted to him the terrible secret, part of which chance had already revealed to him across from the Samaritaine. This was their mutual declaration of love.

"I'll go," he said, "I'll go at once."

"What do you mean you'll go!" cried Mme Bonacieux. "What about your regiment, your captain?"

"By my soul, you've made me forget all that, dear Constance! Yes, you're right, I must ask for a leave."

"Another obstacle," Mme Bonacieux murmured woefully.

"Oh, don't worry," cried d'Artagnan after a moment's reflection, "I'll surmount this one!"

"How?"

"I'll go and find M. de Tréville this very evening, and charge him with asking this favor for me from his brother-in-law, M. des Essarts."

"Now, another thing."

"What?" asked d'Artagnan, seeing that Mme Bonacieux hesitated to go on.

"Perhaps you have no money?"

"Perhaps isn't the word," d'Artagnan said, smiling.

"In that case," Mme Bonacieux picked up, opening a wardrobe and taking from it the pouch that her husband had caressed so lovingly half an hour earlier, "take this pouch."

"The cardinal's?" cried d'Artagnan, bursting into laughter. As we remember, thanks to the removed floor tiles, he had not missed a single syllable of the conversation between the mercer and his wife.

"The cardinal's," replied Mme Bonacieux. "You see it comes in rather respectable guise."

"Pardieu!" cried d'Artagnan, "it will be twice as amusing to save the queen with His Eminence's money!"

"You are a kind and charming young man," said Mme Bonacieux. "Don't think that Her Majesty will be ungrateful."

"Oh, I'm already richly rewarded!" cried d'Artagnan. "I love you, and you allow me to tell you so; that's already more happiness than I dared hope for."

"Hush!" said Mme Bonacieux, shuddering.

"What?"

"Talking in the street."

"That's the voice . . ."

"Of my husband. Yes, I recognized it!"

D'Artagnan rushed to the door and slid the bolt.

"He won't come in before I've gone," he said, "and when I've gone, you can open it for him."

"But I must go, too. How can the disappearance of that money be justified if I'm here?"

"You're right, you'll have to leave."

"Leave how? He'll see us if we go out."

"Then you'll have to come up to my place."

"Ah!" cried Mme Bonacieux, "you say that in a tone that frightens me!"

Mme Bonacieux uttered these words with tears in her eyes. D'Artagnan saw those tears, and, troubled, moved, he threw himself on his knees.

"In my place," he said, "you'll be as safe as in a temple, I give you my word for it as a gentleman."

"Let's go," she said, "I trust you, my friend."

D'Artagnan carefully slid the bolt open again, and the two of them, light as shadows, slipped through the inner door into the alley, silently climbed the stairs, and went into d'Artagnan's room.

Once there, for greater security, the young man barricaded the door. They both went up to the window, and through a slat in the blind they saw M. Bonacieux talking with a man in a cloak.

At the sight of the man in the cloak, d'Artagnan leaped back and, half drawing his sword, rushed for the door.

It was the man from Meung.

"What are you doing?" cried Mme Bonacieux. "You'll ruin us!"

"But I've sworn to kill that man!" said d'Artagnan.

"Your life has been given up for the moment and no longer belongs to you. In the name of the queen, I forbid you to throw yourself into any danger that lies outside that of the journey."

"And don't you order anything in your own name?"

"And in my own name," said Mme Bonacieux with strong emotion, "and in my own name, I beg of you. But listen, I think they're talking about me."

D'Artagnan went up to the window and cocked his ear.

M. Bonacieux had opened his door and, seeing the place empty, had gone back to the man in the cloak, whom he had left alone for a moment.

"She's gone," he said. "She'll have returned to the Louvre."

"You're sure," asked the stranger, "that she didn't suspect your intentions in leaving?"

"No," replied M. Bonacieux with self-assurance, "she's too superficial a woman."

"Is the cadet of the guards at home?"

"I don't think so. As you see, his blinds are closed, and I don't see any light coming through the slats."

"Never mind, we must make sure."

"How?"

"By knocking on his door."

"I'll ask his valet."

"Go on."

Bonacieux went back to his place, passed through the same door that had just given passage to the two fugitives, went up to d'Artagnan's landing, and knocked.

No one answered. Porthos, in order to cut a grander figure, had borrowed Planchet for the night. As for d'Artagnan, he took care not to give a sign of life.

At the moment when Bonacieux's knuckle resounded on the door, the two young people felt their hearts leap.

"There's nobody home," said Bonacieux.

"Never mind, let's still go to your place; we'll be safer than in some doorway."

"Ah, my God!" murmured Mme Bonacieux, "we won't be able to hear anything!"

"On the contrary," said d'Artagnan, "we'll hear all the better."

D'Artagnan removed the three or four tiles that made his room another ear of Dionysius, spread a rug on the floor, knelt down, and made a sign to Mme Bonacieux to bend down to the opening as he had done.

"You're sure there's nobody there?" asked the stranger.

"I guarantee it," said Bonacieux.

"And you think your wife . . ."

"Has returned to the Louvre."

"Without speaking to anyone other than you?"

"I'm sure of it."

"It's an important point, you understand."

"So the news I've brought you is of some value?"

"Very great value, my dear Bonacieux, I won't conceal it from you."

"Then the cardinal will be pleased with me?"

"I have no doubt of it."

"The great cardinal!"

"You're sure that your wife didn't mention any proper names in her conversation with you?"

"I don't believe so."

"She didn't name Mme de Chevreuse, or M. de Buckingham, or Mme de Vernet?"

"No, she only told me that she wanted to send me to London to serve the interest of an illustrious person."

"The traitor!" murmured Mme Bonacieux.

"Hush!" said d'Artagnan, taking her hand, which she let him have without thinking of it.

"Never mind," the man in the cloak went on, "you're a ninny not to have pretended to accept the commission. You'd have the letter now; the threatened State would be saved, and you . . ."

"And I?"

"And you! Why, the cardinal would have granted you letters of nobility . . ."

"He told you so?"

"Yes, I know he wanted to give you that surprise."

"Don't worry," Bonacieux picked up, "my wife adores me, and there's still time."

"The ninny!" murmured Mme Bonacieux.

"Hush!" said d'Artagnan, squeezing her hand more strongly.

"How is there still time?" the man in the cloak picked up.

"I go back to the Louvre, I ask for Mme Bonacieux, I tell her I've thought it over, I take up the matter again, I obtain the letter, and I go running to the cardinal."

"Well, then, be quick! I'll come back soon to find out what comes of your efforts."

The unknown man left.

"The scoundrel!" said Mme Bonacieux, again addressing this epithet to her husband.

"Hush!" d'Artagnan repeated, squeezing her hand still more strongly.

Then a terrible howl interrupted the reflections of d'Artagnan and Mme Bonacieux. It was her husband, who had noticed the disappearance of his pouch and was crying thief.

"Oh, my God!" cried Mme Bonacieux, "he'll rouse the whole quarter."

Bonacieux shouted for a long time. But as such cries, given their frequency, attracted no one in the rue des Fossoyeurs, and, besides that, the mercer's house had been rather ill-famed for some time, Bonacieux, seeing that no one came, went out himself, still shouting, and his voice could be heard moving off in the direction of the rue du Bac.

"And now that he's gone, it's our turn to get away," said Mme Bonacieux. "Courage, but prudence above all, and remember your duty is to the queen."

"To her and to you!" cried d'Artagnan. "Don't worry, beautiful Constance, I'll come back worthy of her gratitude, but will I also come back worthy of your love?"

The young woman replied only with the bright flush that colored her cheeks. A few moments later, d'Artagnan left in his turn, also wrapped in a great cloak, the skirt of which was raised cavalierly by the scabbard of a long sword.

Mme Bonacieux's eyes followed him in that long, loving gaze with which a woman accompanies the man she feels she loves; but when he disappeared around the corner of the street, she fell to her knees, clasped her hands, and cried out:

"Oh, my God, protect the queen, protect me!"

XIX

THE CAMPAIGN PLAN

D'Artagnan went straight to M. de Tréville. He had realized that in a few minutes the cardinal would be informed by that damned unknown man, who seemed to be his agent, and he rightly thought that there was not a moment to lose.

The young man's heart was overflowing with joy. An occasion in which there was both glory to be achieved and money to be made had presented itself to him, and, as a first encouragement, had just brought him close to a woman he adored. Chance had thus done more for him, almost from the first stroke, than he would have dared ask of Providence.

M. de Tréville was in his reception room with his usual court of gentlemen. D'Artagnan, who was known as a familiar of the house, went straight to his office and had him notified that he was waiting for him on an important matter.

D'Artagnan had hardly been there five minutes when M. de Tréville came in. At first glance, and by the joy that was visible on his face, the worthy captain understood that something new was indeed afoot.

All the way there, d'Artagnan had asked himself if he should confide in M. de Tréville, or if he should only ask him to grant him carte blanche for a secret affair. But M. de Tréville had always been so perfect for him, he was so firmly devoted to the king and the queen, he so heartily hated the cardinal, that the young man decided to tell him everything.

"You asked for me, my young friend?" said M. de Tréville.

"Yes, Monsieur," said d'Artagnan, "and you will forgive me, I hope, for disturbing you, when you know what an important matter is involved."

"Tell me, then, I'm listening."

"It is a question of nothing less," said d'Artagnan, lowering his voice, "than the queen's honor and perhaps even her life."

"What's that you say?" asked M. de Tréville, looking around him to be sure they were alone, and returning his questioning gaze to d'Artagnan.

"I say, Monsieur, that chance has made me master of a secret . . ."

"Which I hope you will keep, young man, at the cost of your life."

"But which I must confide to you, Monsieur, for you alone can help me in the mission I have just received from Her Majesty."

"Is this secret yours?"

"No, Monsieur, it is the queen's."

"Are you authorized by Her Majesty to confide it to me?"

"No, Monsieur, on the contrary, I've been enjoined to the most profound secrecy."

"And why, then, are you about to betray it to me?"

"Because, as I told you, without you I can do nothing, and I'm afraid you will refuse me the grace I've come to ask of you if you don't know to what end I am asking it."

"Keep your secret, young man, and tell me what you want."

"I want you to obtain a two-week leave for me from M. des Essarts."

"Starting when?"

"This very night."

"You're leaving Paris?"

"I am going on a mission."

"Can you tell me where to?"

"To London.

"Is anyone interested in having you not reach your goal?"

"The cardinal, I believe, would give anything in the world to keep me from succeeding."

"And you're going alone?"

"I'm going alone."

"In that case, you won't get beyond Bondy. It is I who tell you so, Tréville's word of honor."

"Why not?"

"You'll be killed."

"I'll have died in the line of duty."

"But your mission will not be accomplished."

"That's true," said d'Artagnan.

"Believe me," Tréville went on, "in undertakings of this sort, it takes four for one to succeed."

"Ah, you're right, Monsieur!" said d'Artagnan. "But you're acquainted with Athos, Porthos, and Aramis, and you know whether I may have use of them."

"Without telling them the secret that I did not want to know?"

"We've sworn blind trust and unfailing devotion to each other once and for all. Besides, you can tell them that you have every confidence in me, and they'll be no more incredulous than you are."

"I can send each of them a two-week leave, that is all: to Athos, who is still suffering from his wound, to take the waters at Forges; to Porthos and Aramis, in order to follow their friend, whom they do not want to abandon in such a painful condition. The order for their leave will be proof that I authorize their journey."

"Thank you, Monsieur, you are good a hundred times over."

"Go and find them at once, then, and let it all be done tonight. Ah! and first of all, write me your request to M. des Essarts. You may have had a spy on your heels, and your visit, which in that case is already known to the cardinal, will be legitimized this way."

D'Artagnan wrote out his demand, and M. de Tréville, in receiving it into his hands, assured him that before two o'clock in the morning the four leaves would be at the travelers' respective domiciles.

"Be so good as to send mine to Athos," said d'Artagnan. "I'm afraid if I go home I may run into trouble."

"Rest assured. Good-bye and good journey! By the way!" said M. de Tréville, calling him back.

D'Artagnan retraced his steps.

"Do you have any money?"

D'Artagnan jingled the pouch he had in his pocket.

"Enough?"

"Three hundred pistoles."

"Very good; you could go to the end of the world on that. Off with you, then."

D'Artagnan bowed to M. de Tréville, who held out his hand to him. D'Artagnan shook it with a respect mixed with gratitude. Since his arrival in Paris, he had had nothing but praise for this excellent man, whom he had always found to be worthy, loyal, and magnanimous.

His first visit was to Aramis. He had not been back to his friend's place since the famous evening when he had followed Mme Bonacieux. More than that: he had scarcely seen the young musketeer, and each time he had met him, he had thought he noticed a profound sadness imprinted on his face.

This evening as well, Aramis sat looking sombre and dreamy. D'Artagnan asked him a few questions about this profound melancholy; Aramis excused himself with a commentary on the eighteenth chapter of St. Augustine, which he had to write in Latin for the following week, and which preoccupied him greatly.

The two friends had been talking for a few moments when a servant of M. de Tréville's came in carrying a sealed packet.

"What's that?" asked Aramis.

"The leave Monsieur requested," replied the lackey.

"I requested no leave."

"Be quiet and take it," said d'Artagnan. "And you, my friend, here's a half pistole for your trouble. Tell M. de Tréville that M. Aramis sincerely thanks him. Off you go."

The lackey bowed to the ground and left.

"What does this mean?" asked Aramis.

"Take what you'll need for a two-week journey and follow me."

"But I can't leave Paris at this moment, without knowing . . ."

Aramis stopped.

"What's become of her, is that it?" d'Artagnan continued.

"Who?" Aramis picked up.

"The woman who was here, the woman of the embroidered handkerchief."

"Who told you there was a woman here?" replied Aramis, turning pale as death.

"I saw her."

"And do you know who she is?"

"I think I can guess, at least."

"Listen," said Aramis, "since you know so much, do you know what's become of that woman?"

"I presume she's gone back to Tours."

"To Tours? Yes, that's it, you do know her. But why did she go back to Tours without saying anything to me?"

"Because she was afraid of being arrested."

"Why hasn't she written to me?"

"Because she's afraid of compromising you."

"D'Artagnan, you've restored me to life!" cried Aramis. "I thought I was scorned, betrayed. I was so happy to see her again! I couldn't believe she had risked her freedom for me, and yet what cause could have brought her back to Paris?"

"The same cause that's taking us to England today."

"And what cause is that?" asked Aramis.

"You'll find out one day, Aramis, but for the moment I'll imitate the discretion of the doctor's niece."

Aramis smiled, for he recalled the story he had told his friends on a certain evening.

"Well, then, since she has left Paris and you're sure of it, d'Artagnan, nothing else keeps me, and I'm ready to follow you. You say we're going to . . ."

"To Athos's place right now, and if you want to come, I even invite you to make haste, for we've already lost a lot of time. Inform Bazin, by the way."

"Is Bazin coming with us?" asked Aramis.

"Maybe. In any case, it will be good if he comes with us to Athos's right now."

Aramis summoned Bazin and ordered him to join them at Athos's place.

"Let's go, then," he said, taking his cloak, his sword, and his three pistols, and uselessly opening three or four drawers to see if he might not find a stray pistole. Then, once he was quite assured that the search was in vain, he followed d'Artagnan, asking himself how it could be that the young cadet of the guards knew as well as he who the woman to whom he had given hospitality was, and knew better than he what had become of her.

Only, on the way out, Aramis placed his hand on d'Artagnan's arm and looked at him fixedly.

"You haven't mentioned that woman to anyone?" he asked.

"No one in the world."

"Not even Athos and Porthos?"

"I didn't breathe the slightest word to them."

"Well done!"

And, at ease on this important point, Aramis continued on his way with d'Artagnan, and the two soon came to Athos's place.

They found him holding his leave in one hand and M. de Tréville's letter in the other.

"Can you explain to me the meaning of this leave and this letter that I've just received?" asked the astonished Athos.

My dear Athos,

Since your health absolutely demands it, I would like you to rest for two weeks. Go and take the waters at Forges or anywhere else you like, and get well quickly.

Yours affectionately,
Tréville

"Well, this leave and this letter mean that you must follow me, Athos."

"To the waters at Forges?"

"There or elsewhere."

"In the king's service?"

"The king's and the queen's: are we not in service to both Their Majesties?"

At that moment, Porthos came in.

"Pardieu," he said, "here's a strange thing: since when, in the musketeers, do they grant people leaves when they haven't asked for them?"

"Ever since they've had friends to ask for leaves for them," said d'Artagnan.

"Aha!" said Porthos, "it seems there's something new here?"

"Yes, we're leaving," said Aramis.

"For what country?" asked Porthos.

"By heaven, I know nothing about it," said Athos. "Ask d'Artagnan."

"For London, gentlemen," said d'Artagnan.

"For London!" cried Porthos. "And what are we going to do in London?"

"That I can't tell you, gentlemen; you will have to trust me."

"But it takes money to go to London," Porthos added, "and I don't have any."

"Neither do I," said Aramis.

"Neither do I," said Athos.

"But I do," d'Artagnan picked up, pulling his treasure from his pocket and placing it on the table. "There are three hundred pistoles in this pouch. Let's each take seventy-five; that's enough to go to London and back. Besides, don't worry, we won't all get to London."

"And why not?"

"Because in all probability some of us will be left by the roadside."

"So we're undertaking some sort of campaign?"

"And of the most dangerous kind, I warn you."

"Ah, well, since we risk getting ourselves killed," said Porthos, "I'd at least like to know why."

"You'll be no better off for that!" said Athos.

"However," said Aramis, "I'm of Porthos's opinion."

"Is the king in the habit of accounting to you? No, he just tells you: Gentlemen, there's fighting in Gascony or in Flanders. Go and fight. And you go. Why? You don't even bother about that."

"D'Artagnan is right," said Athos. "Here are our three leaves from M. de Tréville, and here are three hundred pistoles that come from I don't know where. Let's go where we're told to go and get ourselves killed. Is life worth asking so many questions? D'Artagnan, I'm ready to follow you."

"And so am I," said Porthos.

"And so am I," said Aramis. "Anyhow, I'm not sorry to leave Paris. I need some distraction."

"Well, rest assured, gentlemen, you'll have enough distraction," said d'Artagnan.

"And now, when do we leave?" asked Athos.

"At once," replied d'Artagnan, "there's not a minute to lose."

"Ho, there! Grimaud, Planchet, Mousqueton, Bazin!" cried the four young men, summoning their lackeys. "Grease our boots and bring the horses from the hôtel."

Indeed, each musketeer left his own horse and his lackey's at the general hôtel, as if in barracks.

Planchet, Grimaud, Mousqueton, and Bazin left in all haste.

"Now, let's draw up a campaign plan," said Porthos. "Where do we go first?"

"To Calais," said d'Artagnan. "That's the most direct line for getting to London."

"Well, then," said Porthos, "here's my advice."

"Speak."

"Four men traveling together will be suspect. D'Artagnan will give each of us his instructions: I'll go ahead on the road to Boulogne, to clear the way; Athos will leave two hours later by the road to Amiens; Aramis will follow us on the road to Noyon; and as for d'Artagnan, he can leave by whatever road he likes, in Planchet's clothes, while Planchet will follow us as d'Artagnan and in the uniform of the guards."

"Gentlemen," said Athos, "in my opinion it's not suitable for lackeys to have any part in such an affair. A gentlemen may betray a secret by chance, a lackey will almost invariably sell it."

"Porthos's plan seems impracticable to me," said d'Artagnan, "in that I myself don't know what instructions I can give you. I am the bearer of a letter, that's all. I do not have and cannot make three copies of this letter, since it is sealed. In my opinion, then, we must travel together. The letter is here in this pocket." And he showed them the pocket where the letter was. "If I am killed, one of you will take it, and you will continue on your way; if he is killed, it will be the next man's turn, and so on; provided one of us gets there, that's all that matters."

"Bravo, d'Artagnan! I'm of the same opinion," said Athos. "Besides, we must be consistent: I go to take the waters at Forges, you accompany me; instead of the waters at Forges, I go to take the waters at the sea; I'm a free man. They want to arrest us, I show M. de Tréville's letter, and you show your leaves; they attack us, we defend ourselves; they try us, we stubbornly insist that we have no other intention than to dip ourselves a certain number of times in the sea. They would have too easy a time with four isolated men, while four men together make a troop. We'll arm the four lackeys with pistols and muskets. If they send an army against us, we'll give battle, and the survivor, as d'Artagnan said, will carry the letter."

"Well spoken," cried Aramis. "You don't speak often, Athos, but when you do, it's like St. John Golden-mouth. I adopt Athos's plan. And you, Porthos?"

"I do, too," said Porthos, "if it suits d'Artagnan. D'Artagnan, as bearer of the letter, is naturally the leader of the undertaking; we'll do what he decides."

"Well, then," said d'Artagnan, "I decide that we adopt Athos's plan and that we leave in half an hour."

"Adopted!" the three musketeers picked up in chorus.

And each of them reached a hand out to the pouch, took seventy-five pistoles, and went to make his preparations for leaving at the agreed time.

XX

The Journey

At two o'clock in the morning, our four adventurers left Paris by the porte Saint-Denis. As long as it was night, they remained silent; despite themselves, they fell under the influence of the darkness and saw ambushes everywhere.

At the first rays of light, their tongues were loosened; with the sun, their gaiety returned. It was like the eve of a battle: their hearts throbbed, their eyes laughed; they felt that life, which they were perhaps about to leave, was, when all is said, a good thing.

The look of the caravan, moreover, was most imposing: the black horses of the musketeers, their martial appearance, that habit of the squadron which makes these noble soldier's companions march in step, would have given away the strictest incognito.

The valets followed, armed to the teeth.

Everything went well as far as Chantilly, where they arrived towards eight o'clock in the morning. It was time for breakfast. They dismounted in front of an inn recommended by a sign representing St. Martin giving half his cloak to a poor man. The lackeys were told not to unsaddle the horses and to be ready to leave again immediately.

They went into the common room and sat down at a table.

A gentleman who had just arrived by the road from Dammartin was sitting at the same table having breakfast. He started a conversation about rain and fair weather; the travelers replied. He drank their health; the travelers returned his civility.

But when Mousqueton came to announce that the horses were ready, and they got up from the table, the stranger proposed the cardinal's health to Porthos. Porthos replied that he could ask for nothing better, if the stranger in turn would drink to the king's health. The stranger cried that he knew no other king than His Eminence. Porthos called him a drunkard; the stranger drew his sword.

"That was a stupid thing to do," said Athos, "but never mind, there's no backing out now. Kill the man and catch up with us as quickly as you can."

And all three mounted their horses again and set off at a gallop, while Porthos was promising his adversary that he would perforate him with every hit known to fencing.

"That's one!" said Athos, after they had gone five hundred paces.

"But why did the man attack Porthos rather than anyone else?" asked Aramis.

"Because Porthos talks louder than the rest of us, and he took him for the leader," said d'Artagnan.

"I always said this young Gascon was a wellspring of wisdom," murmured Athos.

And the travelers continued on their way.

At Beauvais they stopped for two hours, as much to give their horses a breather as to wait for Porthos. After two hours, since Porthos had not come, nor any news of him, they set off again.

A league from Beauvais, at a place where the road narrowed between two banks, they met eight or ten men who, profiting from the fact that the roadway was unpaved in that place, made it look as though they were working at digging holes and opening out muddy ruts.

Aramis, fearing to dirty his boots in this artificial mire, apostrophized them severely. Athos wanted to restrain him, but it was too late. The workers set about jeering at the travelers, and their insolence made even the cool Athos lose his head and drive his horse at one of them.

Then the men all backed away to the ditch and there picked up hidden muskets; the result was that our seven travelers came under fire. Aramis got a bullet through the shoulder, and Mousqueton another that lodged itself in the fleshy parts beneath the lower back. However, Mousqueton was the only one who fell off his horse, not that he was seriously wounded, but, as he could not see the wound, he no doubt thought it was more dangerous than it was.

"It's an ambush," said d'Artagnan. "Don't waste your primer, keep going!"

Aramis, wounded as he was, clung to the mane of his horse, which carried him along with the others. Mousqueton's horse had rejoined them, and galloped in its place.

"That makes one spare horse for us," said Athos.

"I'd rather have a hat," said d'Artagnan. "Mine got blown off by a bullet. By heaven, it's lucky the letter I'm carrying wasn't in it!"

"Ah, but they're going to kill poor Porthos when he comes along!" said Aramis.

"If Porthos was still on his feet, he would have caught up with us by now," said Athos. "I'm of the opinion that that drunkard sobered up on the dueling ground."

And they galloped for another two hours, though the horses were so exhausted that it was to be feared they might soon refuse their service.

The travelers went cross-country, hoping to be less bothered that way, but at Crèvecoeur, Aramis declared that he could not go any farther. Indeed, it had taken all the courage he concealed under his elegant form and polished manners to get that far. He grew paler every moment, and they were obliged to support him on his horse. They set him down at the door of a tavern and left Bazin with him, who was, in any case, more cumbersome than useful in a skirmish, and set off again, hoping to spend the night in Amiens.

"Morbleu!" said Athos, when they were on the road again, reduced to two masters and Grimaud and Planchet. "Morbleu! I won't be their dupe again, and I guarantee you they won't make me open my mouth or draw my sword from here to Calais. I swear it . . ."

"Let's not swear," said d'Artagnan, "let's ride hard, if our horses will agree to it."

And the travelers dug their spurs into their horses' flanks, at which vigorous stimulation they recovered their strength. They reached Amiens at midnight and alighted at the sign of the Gilded Lily.

The innkeeper had the look of the most honest man on earth. He received the travelers with his candlestick in one hand and his cotton nightcap in the other; he wanted to lodge each of the travelers in a charming room, but unfortunately these charming rooms were at two ends of the inn. D'Artagnan and Athos refused. The host replied that there were no other rooms worthy of Their Excellencies; but the travelers declared that they would sleep in the common room, each on a mattress thrown on the floor. The host insisted; the travelers stood their ground; he had to do as they wished.

They had just made their beds and barricaded the door from inside when someone knocked at the courtyard shutter. They asked who was there, recognized the voices of their valets, and opened the shutter.

Indeed, it was Planchet and Grimaud.

"Grimaud can guard the horses by himself," said Planchet. "If the gentlemen wish, I will sleep across their doorsill; in that way, they'll be sure that no one will be able to get to them."

"And what will you sleep on?" asked d'Artagnan.

"Here's my bed," replied Planchet.

And he pointed to a bundle of straw.

"Come on, then," said d'Artagnan. "You're right: the host's face doesn't convince me; it's too ingratiating."

"I agree," said Athos.

Planchet climbed through the window and installed himself on the doorsill, while Grimaud went to lock himself in the stables, guaranteeing that at five o'clock in the morning, he and the four horses would be ready.

The night was rather quiet. Someone did try to open the door at two in the morning, but as Planchet awoke with a start and shouted: "Who goes there?" the person answered that he was mistaken and went away.

At four in the morning, they heard a great noise in the stables. Grimaud had wanted to wake up the stable boys, and the stable boys had given him a beating. When they opened the window, they saw the poor boy lying unconscious, his head split by the handle of a pitchfork.

Planchet went down to the courtyard, intending to saddle the horses, but the horses were foundered. Only Mousqueton's, which had traveled for five or six hours without its master the day before, might have continued the journey; but, by an inconceivable error, the veterinary surgeon who had been sent for, as it seemed, to bleed the host's horse, had bled Mousqueton's instead.

This was beginning to be disturbing: all these successive accidents were perhaps the result of chance, but they might also very well be the fruits of a plot. Athos and d'Artagnan came out, while Planchet went to see if there were three horses for sale in the neighborhood. At the gate stood two fully equipped horses, fresh and vigorous. They were just what he was after. He asked where the masters were; he was told that the masters had spent the night at the inn and were at that moment settling accounts with the host.

Athos went down to pay the bill, while d'Artagnan and Planchet waited at the street door. The innkeeper was in a low-ceilinged back room; Athos was asked to go there.

Athos went in unsuspectingly and took out two pistoles in order to pay. The host was alone and sitting at his desk, one of the drawers of which was half open. He took the money Athos handed him, turned it over and over in his hands, and all at once, crying out that the coin was false, declared that he would have them arrested, him and his companion, as counterfeiters.

"Knave!" said Athos, advancing towards him. "I'll cut your ears off!"

At that same instant, four men armed to the teeth came in by side doors and threw themselves upon Athos.

"It's a trap!" cried Athos at the top of his lungs. "Get away, d'Artagnan! quick! quick!" And he fired off two pistol shots.

D'Artagnan and Planchet did not need to hear it twice. They unhitched the two horses that were waiting by the gate, leaped onto them, sank their spurs into their flanks, and set off at a triple gallop.

"Do you know what became of Athos?" d'Artagnan asked Planchet on the run.

"Ah, Monsieur!" said Planchet, "I saw two of them fall at his two shots, and it seemed to me, through the glass door, that he was crossing blades with the others."

"Brave Athos!" murmured d'Artagnan. "And when you think that we have to abandon him! Besides, there may be as much waiting for us two steps from here. Keep on, Planchet, keep on! You're a brave man, too!"

"I told you, Monsieur," replied Planchet, "you can tell a Picard by the use of him; besides, I'm in my own country, and that excites me."

And the two of them, spurring for all they were worth, reached Saint-Omer at one stretch. In Saint-Omer, they gave their horses a breather with the bridles over their arms, for fear of a mishap, and ate a quick bite standing in the street, after which they set off again.

Within a hundred paces of the gates of Calais, d'Artagnan's horse collapsed under him, and there was no way to get it up again: blood flowed from its nose and eyes. There was still Planchet's, but it had stopped, and it was impossible to make it move again.

Fortunately, as we have said, they were a hundred paces from the town. They left their two mounts on the highway and ran to the port. Planchet pointed out to his master a gentleman who was just arriving with his valet and was no more than fifty paces ahead of them.

They quickly approached the gentleman, who seemed in a great bustle. His boots were covered with dust, and he inquired whether he might not cross to England that very moment.

"Nothing could be easier," replied the skipper of a ship that was ready to set sail. "But this morning orders came to let no one leave without the express permission of M. le cardinal."

"I have that permission," said the gentleman, taking a paper from his pocket. "Here it is."

"Have it certified by the governor of the port," said the skipper, "and give me your preference."

"Where can I find the governor?"

"At his country house."

"And where is that country house located?"

"A quarter of a league from town. Wait, you can see it from here, at the foot of that little rise, the one with a slate roof."

"Very good!" said the gentleman.

And, followed by his lackey, he set out for the governor's country house. D'Artagnan and Planchet followed the gentleman at a distance of about five hundred paces.

Once outside of town, d'Artagnan quickened his pace and caught up with the gentleman as he was entering a little wood.

"Monsieur," said d'Artagnan, "you seem to be in a great hurry?"

"One could not be in more of a hurry, Monsieur."

"I'm terribly sorry to hear it," said d'Artagnan, "for, as I am also in quite a hurry, I wanted to ask a favor of you."

"What favor?"

"To let me go first."

"Impossible," said the gentleman. "I've made sixty leagues in forty-four hours, and at noon tomorrow I must be in London."

"I did the same journey in forty hours, and at ten o'clock tomorrow morning I must be in London."

"Terribly sorry, Monsieur, but I arrived first, and I will not go second."

"Terribly sorry, Monsieur, but I arrived second, and I will go first."

"In the king's service!" said the gentleman.

"In my own service!" said d'Artagnan.

"You're picking a bad quarrel with me, it would seem."

"Parbleu! what would you like it to be?"

"What do you want?"

"Would you like to know?"

"Certainly."

"Well, then, I want the order you're carrying, seeing that I don't have one myself, and I need one."

"You're joking, I presume."

"I never joke."

"Let me pass!"

"You will not pass."

"My brave young man, I shall blow your head off. Ho, there, Lubin! My pistols!"

"Planchet," said d'Artagnan, "you take care of the valet, I'll take care of the master."

Planchet, emboldened by his first exploit, leaped upon Lubin, and, as he was strong and vigorous, knocked him flat on the ground and put his knee on his chest.

"Do your business, Monsieur," said Planchet. "I've already done mine."

Seeing that, the gentleman drew his sword and swooped upon d'Artagnan; but he had a strong opponent to contend with.

In three seconds, d'Artagnan had given him three strokes of the sword, saying at each stroke:

"One for Athos, one for Porthos, one for Aramis."

At the third stroke, the gentleman fell in a heap.

D'Artagnan thought he was dead, or at least unconscious, and went up to him to take the order; but just as he reached out to search him, the wounded man, who had not let go of his sword, thrust the point into his chest, saying:

"And one for you."

"And one for me! Saving the best for last!" d'Artagnan

cried, furious, and pinned him to the ground with a fourth stroke through the stomach.

This time the gentleman closed his eyes and passed out.

D'Artagnan rummaged in the pocket where he had seen him put the order of passage, and took it. It was in the name of the comte de Wardes.

Then, casting a last glance at the handsome young man, who was barely twenty-five years old, and whom he left lying there, insensible and perhaps dead, he heaved a sigh over the strange destiny that leads men to destroy each other for the interests of people who are strangers to them and who often do not even know that they exist.

But he was soon drawn out of these reflections by Lubin, who was howling and crying for help with all his might.

Planchet applied his hands to his throat and squeezed as hard as he could.

"Monsieur," he said, "as long as I hold him like this, he won't shout, I'm quite sure; but as soon as I let him go, he'll start shouting again. I make him out to be a Norman, and Normans are stubborn."

"Wait!" said d'Artagnan.

And taking his handkerchief, he gagged him.

"Now," said Planchet, "let's tie him to a tree."

The thing was done conscientiously. Then they dragged the comte de Wardes near his domestic, and as night was beginning to fall, and the bound man and the wounded man were both a few feet into the wood, it was evident that they would have to stay there until the morrow.

"And now," said d'Artagnan, "to the governor's!"

"But it seems you're wounded?" said Planchet.

"It's nothing. Let's deal with what's most urgent; then we can come back to my wound, which anyhow doesn't seem very dangerous to me."

And the two set off with great strides to the worthy functionary's country house.

M. le comte de Wardes was announced.

D'Artagnan was ushered in.

"You have an order signed by the cardinal?" asked the governor.

"Yes, Monsieur," replied d'Artagnan, "here it is."

"Hm! Yes, it is correct and well recommended," said the governor.

"That's simply explained," replied d'Artagnan. "I am among his most faithful followers."

"It seems His Eminence wants to keep someone from getting to England."

"Yes, a certain d'Artagnan, a gentleman from Béarn, who left Paris with three friends, intending to go to London."

"Do you know him personally?" asked the governor.

"Whom?"

"This d'Artagnan."

"Perfectly."

"Give me his description, then."

"Nothing could be easier."

And d'Artagnan gave him feature by feature the description of the comte de Wardes.

"Is anyone with him?" asked the governor.

"Yes, a valet named Lubin."

"We'll watch out for them, and if we lay hands on them, His Eminence can rest assured that they will be returned to Paris under a good escort."

"In so doing, Monsieur le gouverneur," said d'Artagnan, "you will have served the cardinal well."

"Will you see him on your return, Monsieur le comte?"

"Without a doubt."

"Tell him, please, that I am his humble servant."

"I shall not fail to do so."

And, delighted with this assurance, the governor certified the pass and gave it back to d'Artagnan.

D'Artagnan did not waste time in useless compliments; he bowed to the governor, thanked him, and left.

Once outside, he and Planchet hurried off and, making a long detour to avoid the wood, reentered town by a different gate.

The ship was still ready to depart. The skipper was waiting on the dock.

"Well?" he said, catching sight of d'Artagnan.

"Here is my certified pass," said the latter.

"And that other gentleman?"

"He won't be leaving today," said d'Artagnan, "but don't worry, I'll pay the passage for us both."

"In that case, let's go," said the skipper.

"Let's go!" d'Artagnan repeated.

And he and Planchet jumped into the skiff; five minutes later they were aboard.

It was time to take care of his wound. Fortunately, as d'Artagnan had thought, it was not very dangerous: the point of the sword had hit a rib and glanced off the bone; what's more, his shirt had become stuck to the wound at once, so that it had shed only a few drops of blood.

D'Artagnan was broken by fatigue. They laid out a mattress for him on the deck; he threw himself down on it and fell asleep.

At dawn the next day, he found himself still three or four leagues from the English coast. The breeze had been weak all night, and they had made little headway.

At ten, the ship dropped anchor in the port of Dover.

At half-past ten, d'Artagnan set foot on English soil, crying out: "Here I am at last!"

But that was not all: he had to get to London. In England, the post roads were rather well served. D'Artagnan and Planchet each took a nag, and a postilion raced ahead of them. In four hours they reached the gates of the capital.

D'Artagnan did not know London, d'Artagnan did not know a word of English, but he wrote the name of Buckingham on a piece of paper, and everyone showed him the way to the duke's mansion.

The duke was hunting at Windsor with the king.

D'Artagnan asked for the duke's confidential valet, who had accompanied him on all his travels and spoke perfect French. He told him that he had come from Paris on a matter of life and death, and that he had to speak with his master that very moment.

The confidence with which d'Artagnan spoke convinced Patrick—that was the name of this minister's minister. He had two horses saddled and took it upon himself to escort the young guard. As for Planchet, he had been taken down from his horse stiff as a pikestaff: the poor lad was at the end of his strength. D'Artagnan was like iron.

They arrived at the castle. There they found out that the king and Buckingham were hawking in the marshes some two or three leagues away.

In twenty minutes they reached the designated spot. Soon Patrick heard the voice of his master, who was calling his falcon.

"Whom should I announce to Milord the duke?" asked Patrick.

"The young man who picked a quarrel with him one night on the Pont Neuf, across from the Samaritaine."

"A singular introduction!"

"You'll see it's as good as any other."

Patrick set his horse at a gallop, came to the duke, and announced to him in the terms we have just mentioned that a messenger was waiting for him.

Buckingham recognized d'Artagnan instantly, and suspecting that news was being sent to him of something happening in France, took time enough only to ask where the man was who came bearing it; and having recognized the uniform of the guards from far off, he set his horse at a gallop and went straight to d'Artagnan. Patrick, out of discretion, kept himself apart.

"Nothing bad has happened to the queen?" cried Buckingham, pouring all his thought and all his love into the question.

"I believe not. However, I believe she is in some great peril from which Your Grace alone can save her."

"I?" cried Buckingham. "Why, I would be quite happy to be of some use to her! Speak! Speak!"

"Take this letter," said d'Artagnan.

"This letter? Who is this letter from?"

"From Her Majesty, I think."

"From Her Majesty?" said Buckingham, paling so much that d'Artagnan thought he was about to faint.

And he broke the seal.

"Why is it torn here?" he asked, showing d'Artagnan a place where it had been pierced through.

"Ah!" said d'Artagnan. "I hadn't noticed that. It was the sword of the comte de Wardes that made that neat hole as it went through my chest."

"You're wounded?" asked Buckingham as he broke the seal.

"Oh, it's nothing!" said d'Artagnan. "Just a scratch!"

"Good heavens, what's this I read!" cried the duke. "Patrick, stay here, or rather, join the king wherever he happens to be, and tell His Majesty that I humbly beg him to excuse me, but a matter of the highest importance calls me back to London. Come, Monsieur, come."

And they both set off at a gallop on the road to the capital.

XXI

THE COUNTESS DE WINTER

On the way there, the duke informed himself through d'Artagnan, not about all that had happened, but about what d'Artagnan knew. By comparing what he heard from the young man's lips with his own memories, he was able to form a fairly accurate idea of a situation the gravity of which, moreover, the queen's letter, short and inexplicit as it was, gave him the measure. But what surprised him most of all was that the cardinal, interested as he was in keeping the young man from setting foot in England, had not managed to stop him on the way. It was then, and on the showing of this surprise, that d'Artagnan told him of the precautions taken, and how, thanks to the devotion of his three friends, whom he had scattered all bleeding along the roadside, he had managed to get off with the sword stroke that had pierced the queen's letter, and which he had paid back to M. de Wardes in such terrible coin. While listening to this account, which was made in the greatest simplicity, the duke looked at the young man from time to time with an astonished air, as if he could not understand how so much prudence, courage, and devotion could combine with a face that indicated something less than twenty years of age.

The horses went like the wind, and in a few minutes they were at the gates of London. D'Artagnan had thought that, on reaching town, the duke would slow his horse's pace, but that was not so: he continued on his way at full tilt, little concerned with knocking over those who were in his way. Indeed, as they crossed the city, two or three accidents of that sort occurred, but Buckingham did not even turn his head to see what had become of those he had overturned. D'Artagnan followed him amidst shouts that strongly resembled curses.

On entering the courtyard of his house, Buckingham leaped from his horse and, without concerning himself about what would become of it, threw the bridle over its neck and rushed to the front steps. D'Artagnan did the same, with a little more concern, however, for those noble animals, whose worth he had been able to appreciate. But he had the consolation of seeing that three or four valets had already come running from the kitchens and stables, and at once took charge of their mounts.

The duke walked so quickly that d'Artagnan had difficulty following him. He passed through a series of reception rooms of an elegance that the greatest lords of France could not even conceive of, and came finally to a bedroom that was at once a miracle of taste and opulence. In the alcove of this room was a door set into the tapestry, which the duke opened with a little golden key that he wore around his neck on a chain of the same metal. Out of discretion, d'Artagnan had stayed behind; but the moment Buckingham crossed the threshold of this door, he turned and, seeing the young man's hesitation, said:

"Come, and if you have the good fortune to be admitted to Her Majesty's presence, tell her what you have seen."

Encouraged by this invitation, d'Artagnan followed the duke, who closed the door behind him.

The two then found themselves in a small chapel all hung

with Persian silk and gold brocade, brightly lit by a great number of candles. Above a sort of altar, and beneath a blue velvet canopy topped with white and red plumes, was a life-size portrait of Anne d'Autriche, of such perfect likeness that d'Artagnan cried out in surprise: one would have thought the queen was about to speak.

On the altar, and beneath the portrait, was the box containing the diamond pendants.

The duke went up to the altar, knelt as a priest might have done before Christ, then opened the box.

"Here," he said, drawing from the box a big bow of blue ribbon all sparkling with diamonds, "these are the precious pendants which I have sworn to be buried with. The queen gave them to me; the queen is taking them back again: her will, like God's, be done in all things."

Then he began kissing one after another the pendants he had to part with. All at once he let out a terrible cry.

"What is it?" d'Artagnan asked worriedly. "What is wrong with you, Milord?"

"All is lost," cried Buckingham, turning pale as a corpse. "Two of the pendants are missing; there are only ten here."

"Did Milord lose them, or does he think they were stolen from him?"

"They were stolen from me," the duke picked up, "and it is the cardinal's work. Here, you see, the ribbons that held them have been cut with scissors."

"If Milord has any suspicion of who committed the theft . . . Perhaps the person still has hold of them."

"Wait, wait!" cried the duke. "The only time I wore these pendants was at the king's ball eight days ago at Windsor. The countess de Winter, with whom I was on bad terms, approached me at that ball. This reconciliation was a jealous woman's vengeance. I haven't seen her since that day. This woman is an agent of the cardinal."

"He has them all over the world, then!" cried d'Artagnan.

"Oh, yes, yes!" said Buckingham, clenching his teeth with wrath. "Yes, he's a terrible opponent. But anyhow, when is this ball to take place?"

"Next Monday."

"Next Monday? Another five days; that's more time than we need. Patrick!" cried the duke, opening the door to the chapel. "Patrick!"

His confidential valet appeared.

"My jeweler and my secretary!"

The valet left with a promptness and a silence that bore witness to the habit he had acquired of obeying blindly and without reply.

But, though the jeweler had been summoned first, the secretary was the first to appear. He found Buckingham sitting at a table in his bedroom and writing out some orders with his own hand.

"Mr. Jackson," he said to him, "you will go at once to the lord chancellor and tell him that I entrust him with the carrying out of these orders. I want them to be issued at once."

"But, My Lord, if the lord chancellor asks me about the motives that have led Your Grace to so extraordinary a measure, what shall I reply?"

"That such is my good pleasure, and that I account to no one for my will."

"Would that be the answer he should transmit to His Majesty," the secretary picked up with a smile, "if perchance His Majesty were curious to know why no vessel may leave the ports of Great Britain?"

"You're right, sir," replied Buckingham. "In that case, he should say to the king that I have decided on war, and that this measure is my first act of hostility against France."

The secretary bowed and left.

"We can rest assured on that side," said Buckingham, turning back to d'Artagnan. "If the pendants have not left for France already, they will not arrive before you do."

"How is that?"

"I have just placed an embargo on all ships that are presently in His Majesty's ports, and without specific permission, not one of them will dare to raise anchor."

D'Artagnan gazed with stupefaction at this man who put the unlimited power vested in him by the king's confidence at the service of his love life. Buckingham saw, from the expression on the young man's face, what was going on in his thoughts, and he smiled.

"Yes," he said, "yes, Anne d'Autriche is my true queen. On a word from her, I would betray my country, I would betray my king, I would betray my God. She has asked me not to send the Protestants of La Rochelle the help I promised them, and I have not done so. I have broken my word, but what matter! I have obeyed her wish. Tell me, have I not been greatly rewarded for my obedience? For it is to that obedience that I owe her portrait."

D'Artagnan wondered at the fragile and unknown threads from which the fates of nations and the lives of men are sometimes hung.

He was in the depths of these reflections when the goldsmith came in. This was an Irishman, among the most skilled in his art, and who admitted himself that he earned a hundred thousand livres a year from the duke of Buckingham.

"Mr. O'Reilly," the duke of Buckingham said to him as he led him to the chapel, "look at these diamond pendants and tell me what they are worth apiece."

The goldsmith cast one glance at the elegant way they were mounted, added in the value of the diamonds, and replied without any hesitation:

"Fifteen hundred pistoles apiece, Milord."

"How many days would it take to make two pendants like these? You see that two are missing."

"Eight days, Milord."

"I will pay three thousand pistoles apiece for them; I need them by the day after tomorrow."

"Milord will have them."

"You are a precious man, Mr. O'Reilly, but that's not all: these pendants cannot be entrusted to anybody; they must be made in this palace."

"Impossible, Milord. I am the only one who can make them so that no difference will be seen between the new ones and the old ones."

"And so, my dear Mr. O'Reilly, you are my prisoner, and if

you should try to leave my palace right now, you would be unable to do so. Make your choice, then. Give me the names of the assistants you will need, and tell me what tools they should bring."

The goldsmith knew the duke, he knew that any remarks would be useless, and so he made his choice that same instant.

"Will I be permitted to inform my wife?" he asked.

"Oh, you will even be permitted to see her, my dear Mr. O'Reilly! Your captivity will be mild, rest assured. And as any inconvenience deserves compensation, here is an order for a thousand pistoles beyond the price of the pendants, to make you forget the trouble I'm causing you."

D'Artagnan could not get over his surprise at this minister who moved men and millions unstintingly.

As for the goldsmith, he wrote to his wife, sending her the order for a thousand pistoles, and telling her to send him in exchange his most skillful apprentice and an assortment of diamonds, of which he gave her the weight and water, along with a list of the tools he needed.

Buckingham led the goldsmith to the room intended for him, which in half an hour was transformed into a workshop. Then he placed a sentinel at each door with orders to let no one enter except his valet Patrick. It is unnecessary to add that the goldsmith O'Reilly and his apprentice were strictly forbidden to leave under whatever pretext.

With that taken care of, the duke went back to d'Artagnan.

"Now, my young friend," he said, "England is ours. What do you want, what would you like?"

"A bed," replied d'Artagnan. "For the moment, I must confess, that is what I need most."

Buckingham gave d'Artagnan a room adjoining his own. He wanted to keep the young man near at hand, not that he distrusted him, but to have someone to whom he could speak constantly of the queen.

An hour later the order was issued in London that no ship laden for France was to be allowed to leave port, not even the mail boat. In the eyes of all, this was a declaration of war between the two kingdoms.

Two days later, at eleven o'clock, the two diamond pendants were finished, so exactly copied, so perfectly the same, that Buckingham could not tell the new from the old, and those most experienced in such matters would have been as fooled as he was.

He immediately called d'Artagnan.

"Well," he said to him, "here are the diamond pendants you came for, and be my witness that I have done all that human power could do."

"Rest assured, Milord, I will say what I have seen. But is Your Grace giving me the pendants without the box?"

"The box would hamper you. Besides, the box is the more precious to me in that it is all I have left. You will say that I am keeping it."

"I will carry out your commission word for word, Milord."

"And now," Buckingham went on, gazing fixedly at the young man, "how shall I ever repay you?"

D'Artagnan blushed to the roots of his hair. He saw that the duke was seeking a way to make him accept something, and the idea that the blood of his companions and his own was going to be paid for in English gold was strangely repugnant to him.

"Let us understand each other, Milord," replied d'Artagnan, "and let us weigh the facts properly in advance, so that there is no mistake. I am in the service of the king and queen of France, and belong to the guards company of M. des Essarts, who is particularly attached to Their Majesties, as is his brother-in-law, M. de Tréville. I have thus done everything for the queen and nothing for Your Grace. What's more, I would perhaps have done none of it, if it were not a question of gratifying someone who is my own lady, as the queen is yours."

"Yes," the duke said, smiling, "and I even believe I know this other person. It is . . ."

"Milord, I have not named her," the young man interrupted sharply.

"That is so," said the duke. "Then it is to this person that I must be grateful for your devotion?"

"It is as you have said, Milord, for precisely at this time

when there is talk of war, I must confess that I see Your Grace only as an Englishman, and consequently as an enemy whom I would be still more delighted to meet on the battlefield than in the park at Windsor or the corridors of the Louvre; which, however, will not keep me from carrying out my mission point by point and from getting myself killed, if need be, to accomplish it—but, I repeat to Your Grace, without you personally having any more reason to thank me for what I have done for myself in this second interview than for what I already did for you in the first."

" 'Proud as a Scot,' we say," murmured Buckingham.

"And we say: 'Proud as a Gascon,' " replied d'Artagnan. "The Gascons are the Scots of France."

D'Artagnan bowed to the duke and prepared to leave.

"Well, so you're going off just like that? Where? And how?"

"True."

"Damn me! the French have their nerve!"

"I had forgotten that England is an island, and that you are the king of it."

"Go to the port, ask for a brig called the *Sund*, give this letter to the captain; he will land you in a small port where you will certainly not be expected and where one usually meets only fishing boats."

"That port is named?"

"Saint-Valery. But wait, wait! When you get there, you will go into a vile-looking inn with no name or sign, a real sailors' dive—you can't miss it, there's only one."

"And then?"

"You will ask for the host, and you will say 'Forward' to him."

"Which means?"

"*En avant*—that is the password. He will give you a saddled horse and show you the road you are to take. You will find four relays like this along the way. If you wish to give each of them your Paris address, the four horses will follow you; you already know two of them, and it seemed to me that you appreciated them as a fancier: they are the two we rode. You may take my word for it, the others are in no way inferior to them.

These four horses are equipped for campaigning. Proud as you may be, you will not refuse to accept one and to make your three companions accept the others. Besides, they will serve for making war on us. The end justifies the means, as you French say, I believe?"

"Yes, Milord, I accept," said d'Artagnan, "and if it please God, we will make good use of your presents."

"Now, your hand, young man. Perhaps we will meet soon on the battlefield, but in the meantime we part as good friends, I hope."

"Yes, Milord, but with the hope of soon becoming enemies."

"Don't worry, I promise you that."

"I count on your word, Milord."

D'Artagnan bowed to the duke and quickly made his way to the port.

Opposite the Tower of London, he found the designated boat, and handed his letter to the captain, who had it certified by the governor of the port and set sail at once.

Fifty boats were waiting to depart.

As they passed alongside one of them, d'Artagnan thought he recognized the lady from Meung, the one whom the unknown gentleman had called "Milady," and whom he, d'Artagnan, had found so beautiful. But thanks to the current of the river and the good wind that was blowing, his ship went so quickly that in a moment they were out of sight.

The next day, towards nine o'clock in the morning, they reached Saint-Valery.

D'Artagnan headed at once for the specified inn, which he recognized by the shouts coming from it: the war between England and France was being talked about as an imminent and unquestionable thing, and the joyful sailors were carousing.

D'Artagnan made his way through the crowd, went up to the host, and uttered the word "Forward." The host at once made a sign for him to follow, went out with him by a door that gave onto a courtyard, led him to the stable where a saddled horse was waiting for him, and asked him if he needed anything else.

"I need to know the road I'm to follow," said d'Artagnan.

"Go from here to Blangy, and from Blangy to Neufchâtel. At Neufchâtel, go into the inn of the Golden Harrow, give the innkeeper the password, and you will find a saddled horse ready, as you did here."

"Do I owe you anything?" asked d'Artagnan.

"It's all paid for," said the host, "and generously. Go on, then, and God be with you!"

"Amen!" replied the young man, setting off at a gallop.

Four hours later, he was in Neufchâtel.

He followed the instructions he had been given to the letter. At Neufchâtel, as at Saint-Valery, he found a mount already saddled and waiting for him. He went to transfer the pistols from the saddle he had just quitted to the one he was about to take: the holsters were already furnished with identical pistols.

"Your address in Paris?"

"Hôtel des Gardes, company of des Essarts."

"Very well," replied the man.

"What road must I take?" d'Artagnan asked in his turn.

"The road to Rouen; but leave the city on your right. You will stop at the little village of Ecouis. There is only one inn, the Shield of France. Don't judge it by its appearance; there will be a horse in its stables equal to this one."

"Same password?"

"Exactly."

"Good-bye, master."

"Good journey, sir! Is there anything you need?"

D'Artagnan shook his head and set off at full speed. At Ecouis the same scene repeated itself: he found a host just as obliging, a fresh and well-rested horse. He left his address as before, and set off at the same speed for Pontoise. At Pontoise he changed mounts a last time, and at nine o'clock he came galloping into M. de Tréville's courtyard.

He had made nearly sixty leagues in twelve hours.

M. de Tréville received him as if he had seen him that same morning; only, shaking his hand a bit more warmly than usual, he announced to him that M. des Essarts's company was on guard at the Louvre, and that he could report for duty.

XXII

The Ballet of the Merlaison

The next day, all the talk in Paris was about the ball that the city aldermen were giving for the king and queen, and at which Their Majesties would dance the famous ballet of the Merlaison, which was the king's favorite.

Indeed, for eight days everything at the Hôtel de Ville had been in preparation for this solemn evening. The city carpenter had set up scaffolding on which the invited ladies were to sit; the city grocer had furnished the halls with two hundred white wax torches, which was an unheard-of luxury for that time; finally, twenty violins had been called in, and the fee granted them had been fixed at double the ordinary rate, seeing that, according to this report, they were to play all night.

At ten o'clock in the morning, the sieur de La Coste, ensign of the king's guards, followed by two police officers and several archers of the corps, came to ask the city clerk, named Clément, for all the keys to the doors, rooms, and offices of the hôtel. The keys were handed over to him at once; each bore a tag to identify it, and from that moment on the sieur de La Coste was charged with guarding all the doors and all the drives.

At eleven o'clock, Duhallier, captain of the guards, came in his turn, bringing fifty archers with him, who immediately scattered through the Hôtel de Ville to the various doors assigned to them.

At three o'clock, two companies of guards arrived, one French, the other Swiss. The company of French guards was made up half of M. Duhallier's men and half of M. des Essarts's men.

At six o'clock in the evening, the guests began to arrive. As they went in, they were placed in the main hall on the prepared scaffolding.

At nine o'clock, Mme la Première Présidente arrived. As she was the most notable person after the queen, she was received by the city fathers and placed in a loge facing that which the queen was to occupy.

At ten o'clock, a light meal of preserves was set out for the king in the little hall on the side of the church of Saint Jean, facing the dresser containing the city silver, which was guarded by four archers.

At midnight, great cries and acclamations were heard: this was the king, who was making his way through the streets leading from the Louvre to the Hôtel de Ville, which were all lit by colored lanterns.

The aldermen, dressed in their woolen robes and preceded by six sergeants, each carrying a torch, went to meet the king, whom they came to on the steps, where the merchants' provost made him a speech of welcome, to which His Majesty responded by apologizing for being so late, placing the blame on M. le cardinal, who had kept him till eleven o'clock discussing affairs of state.

His Majesty, in ceremonial dress, was accompanied by His Royal Highness Monsieur, by the comte de Soissons, the Grand Prieur, the duc de Longueville, the duc d'Elbeuf, the comte d'Harcourt, the comte de La Roche-Guyon, M. de Liancourt, M. de Baradaqs, the comte de Cramail, and the chevalier de Souveray.

Everyone noticed that the king looked sad and preoccupied.

A dressing room had been prepared for the king and another for Monsieur. In each of these dressing rooms the costumes for various masques had been placed. The same had been done for the queen and for Mme la Présidente. The lords and ladies of Their Majesties' suite had to dress two by two in rooms prepared for that purpose.

Before going to his dressing room, the king gave instructions that he be informed the moment the cardinal appeared.

Half an hour after the king's entrance, new acclamations rang out: these announced the arrival of the queen. The aldermen did as they had done before, and, preceded by sergeants, went to meet their illustrious guest.

The queen came into the hall: it was noticed that, like the king, she looked sad and, above all, weary.

The moment she came in, the curtains of a small rostrum, which until then had remained closed, opened, and the pale head of the cardinal appeared. He was dressed as a Spanish cavalier. His eyes fastened themselves on the eyes of the queen, and a smile of terrible joy passed over his lips: the queen was not wearing her diamond pendants.

The queen stayed for some time to receive the compliments of the city fathers and answer the greetings of the ladies.

All at once the king appeared with the cardinal in one of the doors to the hall. The cardinal was speaking softly to him, and the king was very pale.

The king cut through the crowd and, without a mask, the ribbons of his doublet barely tied, approached the queen and said to her in an altered voice:

"Madame, if you please, why are you not wearing your diamond pendants, when you know it would have given me pleasure to see them?"

The queen looked around her and saw the cardinal standing behind the king, smiling a diabolical smile.

"Sire," the queen replied in an altered voice, "because in the midst of this great crowd I feared they might come to harm."

"But there you were wrong, Madame! If I made you a gift of them, it was so that you could adorn yourself with them. I tell you, you were wrong."

"Sire," said the queen, "I can send for them to the Louvre, where they are, and thus Your Majesty's desires will be fulfilled."

"Do so, Madame, do so, and that at once, for in an hour the ball will begin."

The queen bowed as a sign of submission and followed the ladies who were to lead her to her dressing room.

The king, for his part, went back to his own.

There was a moment of disorder and confusion in the hall.

Everyone had been able to notice that something had gone on between the king and the queen, but they had both spoken so softly that the people around them, who had moved back a few steps out of respect, had heard nothing. The violins were playing with all their might, but no one listened to them.

The king came out of his dressing room first: he was in the most elegant of hunting costumes, and Monsieur and the other lords were dressed like him. It was the costume that looked best on the king, and, dressed thus, he truly looked like the foremost gentleman of his kingdom.

The cardinal went up to the king and handed him a box. The king opened it and found there two diamond pendants.

"What does this mean?" he asked the cardinal.

"Nothing," replied the latter. "Only, if the queen has the pendants, which I doubt, count them, Sire, and if you find just ten, ask Her Majesty who could have stolen these two pendants from her."

The king looked questioningly at the cardinal, but he had no time to ask him anything. A cry of admiration came from all mouths. If the king looked like the foremost gentleman of his kingdom, the queen was quite certainly the most beautiful woman of France.

It is true that her huntress's outfit was wonderfully becoming to her. She had on a felt hat with blue feathers, a pearl gray velvet jacket fastened with diamond clasps, and a skirt of blue satin all embroidered in silver. On her left shoulder sparkled the pendants, held up by a bow of the same color as the feathers and the skirt.

The king trembled with joy and the cardinal with wrath. However, far away as they were from the queen, they could not count the pendants. The queen had them, but did she have ten or did she have twelve?

Just then the violins sounded the signal for the ballet. The king advanced towards Mme la Présidente, with whom he was to dance, and Monsieur with the queen. They took their places, and the ballet began.

The king danced facing the queen, and each time he passed close to her, he devoured the pendants with his gaze, but could not manage to count them. A cold sweat broke out on the cardinal's brow.

The ballet lasted an hour; it had sixteen figures.

The ballet ended amidst the applause of the entire hall, and each one conducted his lady to her place; but the king profited from his privilege of leaving his partner where she was, and went briskly to the queen.

"I thank you, Madame," he said to her, "for the deference

you have shown to my desires, but I believe you are missing two pendants, and I have brought them for you."

At those words, he held out to the queen the two pendants the cardinal had given him.

"What, Sire?" cried the young queen, feigning surprise. "You are giving me two more? But then I shall have fourteen!"

Indeed, the king counted, and the twelve pendants were there on Her Majesty's shoulder.

The king summoned the cardinal.

"Well, what is the meaning of this, M. le cardinal?" the king asked in a severe tone.

"It means, Sire," the cardinal replied, "that I wished to make Her Majesty accept these two pendants, and not daring to offer them to her myself, I adopted this method."

"And I am all the more grateful to Your Eminence," replied Anne d'Autriche, with a smile that showed she was not fooled by this ingenuous gallantry, "in that I am sure these two pendants cost you as dearly by themselves as the twelve others cost His Majesty."

Then, having bowed to the king and the cardinal, the queen made her way back to the room where she had dressed and where she was to undress.

The attention we were obliged to pay at the beginning of this chapter to the illustrious personages we have introduced in it has diverted us for a moment from the one to whom Anne d'Autriche owed the unprecedented triumph she had just won over the cardinal, and who, abashed, ignored, lost in the crowd massed at one of the doorways, watched from there this scene comprehensible only to four persons: the king, the queen, the cardinal, and himself.

The queen had just gone back to her room, and d'Artagnan was preparing to leave, when he felt a light touch on his shoulder. He turned and saw a young woman who made a sign for him to follow her. This young woman's face was covered by a black velvet half mask, but despite that precaution, which, moreover, had been taken rather for others than for him, he instantly recognized his usual guide, the light and witty Mme Bonacieux.

They had barely seen each other the evening before at

Germain's, where d'Artagnan had asked for her. The hurry the young woman had been in to bring the queen this excellent news of the fortunate return of her messenger had made it so that the two lovers barely exchanged a few words. D'Artagnan thus followed Mme Bonacieux, stirred by two feelings, love and curiosity. All along the way, and as the corridors became more and more deserted, d'Artagnan wanted to stop the young woman, hold her, look at her, if only for an instant; but, quick as a bird, she always slipped from his hands, and when he wanted to speak, her finger brought to her lips with a charmingly imperative little gesture reminded him that he was under the sway of a power that he had to obey blindly, and that forbade him even the slightest complaint. Finally, after a minute or two of twists and turns, Mme Bonacieux opened a door and ushered the young man into a completely dark dressing room. There she again made him a sign to keep mum, and opening a second door hidden behind a tapestry, the gaps of which suddenly let in a bright light, she disappeared.

D'Artagnan stood motionless for a moment, asking himself where he was, but soon a ray of light that penetrated from the other room, the warm and perfumed air that reached him, the conversation of two or three women in a language at once respectful and elegant, the word "majesty" repeated several times, clearly indicated to him that he was in a dressing room adjoining the queen's chamber.

The young man kept himself in the shadow and waited.

The queen appeared gay and happy, which seemed a great surprise to the persons around her, who were, on the contrary, accustomed to seeing her almost always anxious. The queen cast this joyful feeling back over the beauty of the fête, over the pleasure she had taken in the ballet, and as a queen is not to be contradicted, whether she smiles or weeps, they all outdid each other in praising the gallantry of the aldermen of the city of Paris.

Though d'Artagnan did not know the queen, he could tell her voice from the other voices, first by a slight foreign accent, then by that sense of domination naturally impressed upon all a sovereign's words. He heard her approach and move away from the open door, and two or three times he even saw the shadow of a body block the light.

Finally, all at once a hand and an arm of adorable form and whiteness passed through the tapestry. D'Artagnan understood that this was his reward. He threw himself on his knees, grasped that hand, and respectfully pressed his lips to it. Then the hand withdrew, leaving in his an object that he recognized as being a ring. The door closed again at once, and d'Artagnan found himself in the most complete darkness.

D'Artagnan put the ring on his finger and waited again. It was evident that all was not yet over. After the reward for his devotion came the reward for his love. Besides, the ballet had been danced, but the evening had barely begun: there was supper at three o'clock, and the Saint-Jean clock had already struck two hours and three-quarters some time ago.

Indeed, the sound of voices gradually diminished in the neighboring room; then people were heard going away; then the door to the dressing room where d'Artagnan was opened again, and Mme Bonacieux rushed in.

"You, at last!" cried d'Artagnan.

"Hush!" said the young woman, pressing her hand to the young man's lips. "Hush! And leave the same way you came."

"But where and when shall I see you again?" cried d'Artagnan.

"A note that you will find on returning home will tell you. Go, go!"

And at these words, she opened the door to the corridor and pushed d'Artagnan out of the dressing room.

D'Artagnan obeyed like a child, without resistance and without any objection, which showed that he really was in love.

XXIII

THE RENDEZVOUS

D'Artagnan returned home at a run, and though it was past three in the morning, and he had to go through some of the worst quarters of Paris, he met with no trouble. As we know, there is a special god for drunkards and lovers.

He found the door to his alley ajar, climbed his stairway, and knocked softly and in a way agreed upon between him and his lackey. Planchet, whom he had sent home from the Hôtel de Ville two hours earlier with instructions to wait up for him, came to open the door.

"Did someone bring a letter for me?" d'Artagnan asked abruptly.

"No one brought a letter, Monsieur," replied Planchet, "but there is one that came by itself."

"What do you mean, imbecile?"

"I mean that when I came home, though I had the key to your apartment in my pocket and that key had never left me, I found a letter on the green tablecloth in your bedroom."

"And where is that letter?"

"I left it where it was, Monsieur. It's not natural for letters to come into people's houses like that. If the window had still been open, or even half open, I wouldn't say so; but no, everything was hermetically shut. Watch out, Monsieur, for there's certainly some magic behind it."

Meanwhile, the young man rushed into the bedroom and opened the letter. It was from Mme Bonacieux, and read as follows:

There are warm thanks to be given you and transmitted to you. Be at Saint-Cloud this evening at around ten o'clock, across from the pavilion at the corner of M. d'Estrées's house.

C.B.

Reading this letter, d'Artagnan felt his heart dilate and contract in that sweet spasm which tortures and caresses the hearts of lovers.

It was the first such note he had ever received; it was the first rendezvous he had ever been granted. His heart, swollen with the drunkenness of joy, felt as though it was about to fail on the threshold of that earthly paradise known as love.

"Well, Monsieur?" said Planchet, who had seen his master blush and pale successively. "Well, didn't I guess right that it's some sort of wicked business?"

"You're mistaken, Planchet," replied d'Artagnan, "and as proof, here is an écu on which you can drink my health."

"I thank Monsieur for the écu he has given me, and promise to follow his instructions exactly; but it's still true that letters that get into locked houses like this . . ."

"Fall from heaven, my friend, fall from heaven."

"So Monsieur is content?" asked Planchet.

"My dear Planchet, I am the happiest of men!"

"And may I profit from Monsieur's happiness by going to bed?"

"Yes, go."

"May all the blessings of heaven fall upon Monsieur, but it's still true that that letter . . ."

And Planchet went off shaking his head with a doubtful air, which d'Artagnan's liberality had not managed to efface entirely.

Left alone, d'Artagnan read and reread his note, then kissed and rekissed twenty times those lines written by his beautiful mistress's hand. At last he went to bed, fell asleep, and dreamed golden dreams.

At seven in the morning, he woke up and called Planchet, who at the second call opened the door, his face still not properly cleansed of yesterday's worries.

"Planchet," d'Artagnan said to him, "I may be gone for the whole day, so you are free until seven o'clock in the evening; but at seven be ready with two horses."

"So," said Planchet, "it seems we're going to have our hide punctured in various places again."

"Take your musket and your pistols."

"Well, what did I tell you!" cried Planchet. "I was sure of it—that cursed letter!"

"Cheer up, imbecile, it's simply a little outing."

"Oh, yes! Like our pleasure trip the other day, where it rained bullets and sprouted snares."

"However, if you're afraid, M. Planchet," d'Artagnan picked up, "I'll go without you. I'd rather travel alone than have a trembling companion."

"Monsieur does me wrong," said Planchet, "though it seems to me he has seen me at work."

"Yes, but I thought you had used up all your courage at one go."

"Monsieur will see when the time comes that I still have more, only I beg Monsieur not to waste it, if he wants me to have it for long."

"Do you think you can spend a certain amount of it tonight?"

"I hope so."

"Well, then, I'll be counting on you!"

"I will be ready at the stated time; only I believe Monsieur has only one horse in the guards' stable."

"There may be only one at the moment, but this evening there will be four."

"It seems we remounted our way to Paris?"

"Exactly," said d'Artagnan.

And making Planchet a last admonitory gesture, he left.

M. Bonacieux was at his door. D'Artagnan's intention was to pass by without speaking to the worthy mercer, but the latter made so gentle and benign a bow that his tenant was forced not only to return it, but also to get into conversation with him.

Besides, how not show a little condescension to a husband whose wife has given you a rendezvous that same evening at Saint-Cloud, across from M. d'Estrées's pavilion! D'Artagnan approached with the most amiable air he could assume.

The conversation naturally turned to the poor man's incarceration. M. Bonacieux, who was not aware that d'Artagnan had overheard his conversation with the unknown man from Meung, told his young tenant about the persecutions of that monster of a M. de Laffemas, whom he never ceased to qualify throughout his account with the title of the cardinal's hangman, and went on at length about the Bastille, the bolts, the peepholes, the air vents, the bars, and the instruments of torture.

D'Artagnan listened to him with exemplary willingness; then, when he had finished, asked:

"And do you know who abducted Mme Bonacieux? For I have not forgotten that it is to that sorry circumstance that I owe the good fortune of having made your acquaintance."

"Ah!" said M. Bonacieux, "they took good care not to tell me that, and my wife for her part has sworn to me by all the gods in heaven that she doesn't know. But you yourself," M. Bonacieux went on in a tone of perfect joviality, "what became of you over the past few days? I haven't seen you, or your friends either, and I don't think it was on the cobblestones of Paris that you picked up all the dust that Planchet brushed from your boots yesterday."

"You're right, my dear M. Bonacieux, my friends and I went on a little journey."

"Far from here?"

"Oh, my God, no! Only forty leagues. We had to take M. Athos to the waters at Forges, where my friends stayed on."

"But you came back, didn't you?" M. Bonacieux picked up, giving his physiognomy its most mischievous air. "A handsome lad like you doesn't obtain long leaves from his mistress, and we were impatiently awaited in Paris, isn't that so?"

"By heaven," the young man said, laughing, "I confess it to you, all the more readily, my dear M. Bonacieux, in that I see one can hide nothing from you. Yes, I was awaited, and quite impatiently, I guarantee you."

A slight cloud passed over Bonacieux's brow, but so slight that d'Artagnan did not perceive it.

"And we're to be rewarded for our diligence?" the mercer went on, with a slight alteration in his voice, an alteration that d'Artagnan noticed no more than he had the momentary cloud that, an instant before, had darkened the worthy man's face.

"Ah, let's not play the saint!" d'Artagnan said, laughing.

"No, what I said to you," Bonacieux picked up, "was only so as to know if we'll be coming home late."

"Why this question, my dear landlord?" asked d'Artagnan. "Do you count on waiting up for me?"

"No, it's that since my arrest and the robbery committed upon me, I'm afraid each time I hear a door open, especially at night. What do you want, I'm no man of the sword, indeed not!"

"Well, don't be frightened if I come home at one, or two, or three in the morning; still less so if I don't come home at all."

This time Bonacieux turned so pale that d'Artagnan could not help noticing it and asked him what was wrong.

"Nothing," replied Bonacieux, "nothing. Since my misfortunes, I've become subject to weak spells that come over me all at once, and I just felt a shiver. Pay no attention to that, you who are only busy being happy."

"I must be very busy then, because that I am."

"Not yet, wait a little: you said this evening."

"Ah, well, this evening will come, thank God! And maybe you're waiting for it as impatiently as I am. Maybe this evening Mme Bonacieux will visit the conjugal dwelling."

"Mme Bonacieux is not free tonight," the husband replied gravely, "her service keeps her at the Louvre."

"Too bad for you, my dear landlord, too bad. When I'm happy, I want everyone in the world to be. But it seems that's not possible."

And the young man strode off, laughing loudly at the joke which he alone, as he thought, could understand.

"Have a good time!" replied Bonacieux in a sepulchral voice.

But d'Artagnan was already too far away to hear, and if he had heard, given the mood he was in, he would certainly not have noticed.

He headed for M. de Tréville's hôtel. His visit the evening before, it will be remembered, had been very brief and not very explicative.

He found M. de Tréville in the best of spirits. The king and queen had been charming to him at the ball. It is true that the cardinal had been thoroughly glum. He had retired at one o'clock in the morning, under the pretext of feeling indisposed. As for Their Majesties, they had not returned to the Louvre until six o'clock.

"Now," said M. de Tréville, lowering his voice and questioning all corners of the apartment with his eyes to see if they were quite alone, "now let's talk about you, my young friend, for it's obvious that your happy return has something to do with the joy of the king, the triumph of the queen, and the humiliation of His Eminence. You must watch out for yourself."

"What do I have to fear," replied d'Artagnan, "as long as I have the good fortune to enjoy Their Majesties' favor?"

"Everything, believe me. The cardinal is not a man to forget a trick, as long as he hasn't settled accounts with the trickster, and the trickster seems to me to be a certain Gascon of my acquaintance."

"Do you think the cardinal has gone as far as you and knows that it was I who was in London?"

"Devil take it! So you were in London? Is it from London that you brought back that handsome diamond sparkling on your finger? Take care, my dear d'Artagnan, an enemy's gift is not a good thing; isn't there some Latin verse about that? . . . Wait a moment . . ."

"Yes, no doubt," said d'Artagnan, who had never been able to stuff the barest rudiments into his head, and for ignorance had been his tutor's despair, "yes, no doubt, there must be one."

"There certainly is," said M. de Tréville, who had a smattering of letters, "and M. de Benserade recited it to me the other day . . . Hold on . . . Ah! I've got it:

timeo Danaos et dona ferentes.

"Which means: 'Beware the enemy who gives you presents.'"

"This diamond does not come from an enemy, Monsieur," d'Artagnan picked up, "it comes from the queen."

"From the queen! Oho!" said M. de Tréville. "Indeed, it is truly a royal jewel, worth a thousand pistoles if it's worth anything. Through whom did the queen give you this gift?"

"She gave it to me herself."

"Where was that?"

"In the dressing room adjoining the room where she changed costume."

"How?"

"By offering me her hand to kiss."

"You have kissed the queen's hand?" cried M. de Tréville, gazing at d'Artagnan.

"Her Majesty did me the honor of according me that grace!"

"And that in the presence of witnesses? Imprudent, three times imprudent!"

"No, Monsieur, rest assured, no one saw her," said d'Artagnan. And he told M. de Tréville how things had gone.

"Oh, women! women!" cried the old soldier. "I can tell them very well by their romantic imagination. Everything with a whiff of mystery charms them. So you saw an arm, that's all. You'll meet the queen and not recognize her; she'll meet you and not know who you are."

"No, but thanks to this diamond . . ." the young man picked up.

"Listen," said M. de Tréville, "do you want me to give you some advice, some good advice, some friendly advice?"

"I would be honored, Monsieur," said d'Artagnan.

"Well, then, go to the first goldsmith you come upon and sell that diamond for the price he offers. Jew though he be, you'll always get eight hundred pistoles for it. Pistoles have no name, young man, but that ring has a terrible one, and it may betray the man who wears it."

"Sell this ring? A ring that came from the queen? Never!" said d'Artagnan.

"Then turn the stone inwards, you poor fool, for everybody knows that a cadet from Gascony doesn't find such gems in his mother's jewelry box."

"So you think I have something to fear?" asked d'Artagnan.

"Let's say, young man, that somebody sleeping on a mine with a lighted fuse should consider himself safe compared to you."

"Devil take it!" said d'Artagnan, who was beginning to be worried by the certainty of M. de Tréville's tone. "Devil take it! What am I to do?"

"Keep on your guard at all times and before all else. The cardinal has a tenacious memory and a long arm; believe me, he'll play some trick on you."

"But what?"

"Eh, as if I know! Doesn't he have all the devil's wiles at his service? The least that can happen to you is that you get arrested."

"What? Would they dare to arrest a man in His Majesty's service?"

"Pardieu! they didn't bother much over Athos! In any case, young man, believe a man who has been thirty years at court: don't lull yourself into security or you're lost. Quite the contrary, and it's I who tell you this, see enemies everywhere. If someone picks a quarrel with you, avoid it, even if the one who picks it is a ten-year-old boy; if you're attacked by night or by day, beat a retreat, and without any shame; if you're crossing a bridge, test the planks, for fear one may give way under you; if you pass in front of a house under construction, look up, for fear a stone may fall on your head; if you come home late, have your lackey follow you, and let your lackey be armed—that is, if you're sure of your lackey. Distrust everyone, your friend, your brother, your mistress—above all your mistress."

D'Artagnan blushed.

"My mistress," he repeated mechanically. "And why her sooner than someone else?"

"Because mistresses are one of the cardinal's favorite means, and there is none more expeditious. A woman will sell you for ten pistoles—witness Delilah. You do know the Scriptures, hm?"

D'Artagnan thought of the rendezvous Mme Bonacieux had granted him for that same evening. But we must say, in praise of our hero, that the bad opinion M. de Tréville had of women in general did not awaken in him the least suspicion of his pretty landlady.

"By the way," asked M. de Tréville, "what's become of your three companions?"

"I was going to ask if you had any news of them."

"None, Monsieur."

"Well, I left them along my way: Porthos at Chantilly with a duel on his hands, Aramis at Crèvecoeur with a bullet in his shoulder, and Athos at Amiens with an accusation of counterfeiting on his head."

"So you see!" said M. de Tréville. "And you? How did you escape?"

"By a miracle, Monsieur, I must say, with a sword stroke in my chest, and by pinning M. le comte de Wardes to the Calais roadside like a butterfly to the wall."

"So you see again! De Wardes, one of the cardinal's men, Rochefort's cousin. Wait, my dear friend, I'm getting an idea."

"Say it, Monsieur."

"In your place, there's one thing I'd do."

"What?"

"While His Eminence was looking for me in Paris, I'd take the road to Picardy again, with no drums and trumpets, and go to find news of my three companions. Devil take it, they deserve a little attention on your part!"

"That's good advice, Monsieur. I'll leave tomorrow."

"Tomorrow? And why not tonight?"

"Tonight, Monsieur, I'm kept in Paris by an indispensable matter."

"Ah, young man! young man! Some little amour? Take care, I repeat to you: woman was the loss of us, each and every one, and she'll be the loss of us again, each and every one. Leave tonight, believe me."

"Impossible, Monsieur!"

"So you've given your word?"

"Yes, Monsieur."

"Then that's another thing. But promise me that if you're not killed tonight, you'll leave tomorrow."

"I promise."

"Do you need money?"

"I still have fifty pistoles. That's as much as I need, I think."

"But your companions?"

"They shouldn't have run out yet. When we left Paris we each had seventy-five pistoles in our pocket."

"Will I see you again before you leave?"

"No, I don't think so, Monsieur, unless something new turns up."

"Good journey, then!"

"Thank you, Monsieur."

And d'Artagnan took leave of M. de Tréville, touched more than ever by his paternal solicitude for his musketeers.

He went successively to the quarters of Athos, Porthos, and Aramis. None of them had come back. Their lackeys were also absent, and there was no news of the ones or the others.

He would have asked their mistresses about them, but he knew neither Porthos's nor Aramis's. As for Athos, he had none.

As he passed by the hôtel of the guards, he glanced into the stable: three of the four horses had already come. Planchet, quite dumbfounded, was in the process of currying them and had already finished two.

"Ah, Monsieur!" said Planchet, catching sight of d'Artagnan, "I'm so glad to see you!"

"And why is that, Planchet?" asked the young man.

"Do you trust our landlord, M. Bonacieux?"

"Me? Not in the least."

"Oh, how right you are, Monsieur!"

"But where does that question come from?"

"From the fact that, while you were talking with him, I was watching without listening to you. Monsieur, his face changed color two or three times."

"Bah!"

"Monsieur did not notice it, preoccupied as he was with the letter he had just received; but I, on the contrary, who had been put on my guard by the strange way that letter came into the house, I didn't miss a single movement of his physiognomy."

"And you found it?"

"Treacherous, Monsieur."

"Really!"

"What's more, as soon as Monsieur left him and disappeared around the corner, M. Bonacieux took his hat, locked his door, and went running down the street in the opposite direction."

"Indeed, you're right, Planchet, all that struck me as highly suspicious, and, rest assured, we will not pay the rent until the thing has been explained categorically."

"Monsieur is joking, but Monsieur will see."

"No help for it, Planchet, what's to come will come."

"So Monsieur will not give up his evening promenade?"

"Quite the contrary, Planchet, the more vexed I am with M. Bonacieux, the more intent I am on going to the rendezvous granted me by this letter which worries you so."

"Well, if that is Monsieur's determination . . ."

"Unshakable, my friend. So, then, at nine o'clock be ready here at the hôtel; I'll come to fetch you."

Seeing that there was no more hope of making his master give up his plan, Planchet heaved a deep sigh and set about currying the third horse.

As for d'Artagnan, as he was at bottom a very prudent lad, instead of going home, he went to dine with the Gascon priest who, at the time when the four friends were in distress, had given them a breakfast of chocolate.

XXIV

THE PAVILION

At nine o'clock d'Artagnan was at the hôtel of the guards. He found Planchet under arms. The fourth horse had arrived.

Planchet was armed with his musketoon and a pistol.

D'Artagnan had his sword and stuck two pistols in his belt; then they both mounted their horses and noiselessly rode off. It was after nightfall, and no one saw them leave. Planchet set out after his master and rode ten paces behind him.

D'Artagnan crossed the quais, went out through the porte de la Conférence, and continued along the road, much more beautiful then than now, that leads to Saint-Cloud.

As long as they were in the city, Planchet respectfully kept the distance he had imposed on himself; but once the road began to be more dark and deserted, he gradually drew closer, so that when they entered the bois de Boulogne, he found himself quite naturally riding side by side with his master. Indeed, we must not conceal the fact that the swaying of the tall trees and the glimmer of moonlight in the dark coppices caused him intense anxiety. D'Artagnan noticed that something extraordinary was going on in his lackey.

"Well, then, M. Planchet," he asked him, "how are we feeling?"

"Don't you find, Monsieur, that woods are like churches?"

"Why is that, Planchet?"

"Because you don't dare speak aloud in either of them."

"Why don't you dare speak aloud, Planchet? Because you're afraid?"

"Afraid of being heard, yes, Monsieur."

"Afraid of being heard? But our conversation is quite moral, my dear Planchet, and no one could find fault with it."

"Ah, Monsieur!" Planchet picked up, coming back to his mother idea, "that M. Bonacieux has something sly in his eyebrows and unpleasant in the play of his lips!"

"What the devil makes you think of Bonacieux?"

"Monsieur, a man thinks what he can and not what he wants."

"Because you're a poltroon, Planchet."

"Monsieur, don't confuse prudence with poltroonery; prudence is a virtue."

"And you are virtuous, aren't you, Planchet?"

"Monsieur, isn't that the barrel of a musket gleaming over there? Shall we duck our heads?"

"Truly," murmured d'Artagnan, who was beginning to remember M. de Tréville's advice, "truly, this creature will end by frightening me."

And he put his horse to a trot.

Planchet followed his master's movement, exactly as if he was his shadow, and found himself trotting beside him.

"Are we going to ride like this all night, Monsieur?" he asked.

"No, Planchet, because you happen to have arrived."

"How do you mean, I've arrived? And Monsieur?"

"I'm going a few steps further."

"And Monsieur is leaving me alone here?"

"Are you afraid, Planchet?"

"No, but I would only observe to Monsieur that the night will be very cold, that chills cause rheumatism, and that a lackey with rheumatism is a sorry servant, above all for so alert a master as Monsieur."

"Well, then, if you're cold, Planchet, you can go into one of the taverns you see there, and wait for me outside the door at six o'clock in the morning."

"Monsieur, I respectfully ate and drank the écu you gave me this morning, so that I don't have a wretched denier left in case I get cold."

"Here's a half pistole. Till tomorrow."

D'Artagnan got off his horse, threw the bridle over Planchet's arm, and walked off quickly, wrapping himself in his cloak.

"God, am I cold!" cried Planchet, once he had lost sight of his master, and hard-pressed as he was to warm up again, he hastened to knock at the door of a house decked out in all the attributes of a suburban tavern.

Meanwhile, d'Artagnan, who had plunged into a narrow crossroad, continued on his way and arrived in Saint-Cloud; but, instead of taking the main street, he circled behind the château, came to an extremely secluded sort of lane, and soon found himself facing the designated pavilion. The place was totally deserted. A high wall, at the corner of which this pavilion stood, dominated one side of the lane, and on the other a hedge protected a small garden against passersby. At the bottom of the garden stood a meagre hut.

He had come to the rendezvous, and since he had not been told to announce his presence by any signal, he waited.

There was no sound to be heard; one would have thought

one was a hundred leagues from the capital. D'Artagnan leaned back against the hedge after glancing behind him. Beyond the hedge, the garden, and the hut, a dark mist enveloped in its folds that immensity in which Paris slept, empty, gaping, an immensity in which a few specks of light shone, funereal stars in that hell.

But for d'Artagnan, all sights took on a happy form, all ideas wore a smile, all shadows were diaphanous. The hour of the rendezvous was about to strike.

Indeed, after a few moments, the belfry of Saint-Cloud slowly let fall ten strokes of its wide, booming maw.

There was something lugubrious in that bronze voice lamenting so in the middle of the night.

But each of the hours that made up the awaited hour vibrated harmoniously in the young man's heart.

His eyes were fixed on the little pavilion located at the corner of the street, all the windows of which were closed with shutters except for a single one on the second floor.

Through that window shone a gentle light which silvered the trembling foliage of two or three lindens that rose up, forming a group outside the park. Obviously, behind that little window, so graciously lit, the pretty Mme Bonacieux awaited him.

Lulled by that sweet notion, d'Artagnan, for his part, waited half an hour without any impatience, his eyes fixed on that charming little living room, of which he could make out a part of the ceiling with gilded moldings, attesting to the elegance of the rest of the apartment.

The belfry of Saint-Cloud rang half-past ten.

This time, without his understanding why, a shiver ran through d'Artagnan's veins. Perhaps the cold was beginning to affect him, and he mistook an entirely physical sensation for a moral one.

Then it occurred to him that he had misread and that the rendezvous was not until eleven.

He went up to the window, stood in a ray of light, took the letter from his pocket, and reread it. He had not been mistaken: the rendezvous was for ten o'clock.

He went back to his post, beginning to be troubled by the silence and the solitude.

It struck eleven.

D'Artagnan really began to fear that something had happened to Mme Bonacieux.

He clapped his hands three times, the usual signal of lovers, but no one answered him, not even an echo.

Then he thought with a certain vexation that the young woman might have fallen asleep while waiting for him.

He went up to the wall and tried to climb it, but the wall had been newly roughcast, and d'Artagnan uselessly broke his fingernails.

At that moment he noticed the trees, their leaves still silvered by the light, and as one of them hung over the road, he thought that from the midst of its branches he would be able to see into the pavilion.

The tree was an easy climb. Besides, d'Artagnan was barely twenty years old and still remembered his schoolboy skill. In an instant he was in the midst of the branches, and through the transparent windowpanes his eyes delved into the interior of the pavilion.

Strange thing, and it made d'Artagnan shiver from the soles of his feet to the roots of his hair: that gentle light, that calm lamp, lit up a scene of frightful disorder. One of the windowpanes was smashed, the door to the room had been broken down and hung in pieces from its hinges; a table that must have been covered with an elegant supper lay overturned on the floor; fragments of carafes and crushed fruit strewed the parquet; everything in the room bore witness to a violent and desperate struggle. D'Artagnan even thought he could make out in the midst of this strange pell-mell some shreds of clothing and a few bloodstains on the tablecloth and curtains.

He hurriedly climbed back down to the street, his heart pounding terribly. He wanted to see if he could find other traces of violence.

The mellow little light still shone through the calm of the night. D'Artagnan then saw—something he had not noticed at first, for nothing had prompted him to such an examination—

that the ground, trampled down here, dug up there, showed mingled traces of men's feet and horses' hooves. Moreover, the wheels of a carriage, which seemed to have come from Paris, had left deep ruts in the soft soil, which went no further than the pavilion and then returned to Paris.

Pursuing his search, d'Artagnan finally found a torn woman's glove near the wall. The glove, however, wherever it had not touched the muddy ground, was of an irreproachable freshness. It was one of those perfumed gloves such as lovers love to tear from a pretty hand.

As d'Artagnan pursued his investigations, an ever more abundant and icy sweat beaded his brow, his heart was gripped by a terrible anguish, his breath came in gasps; and yet he told himself, for reassurance, that this pavilion perhaps had nothing to do with Mme Bonacieux; that the young woman had given him a rendezvous in front of this pavilion, and not inside it; that she might have been kept in Paris by her service, or perhaps by her husband's jealousy.

But all these arguments were beaten down, destroyed, overturned by that sense of intimate grief which, on certain occasions, comes over our whole being and cries out to us, through every means we have of hearing, that a great misfortune is hovering over us.

Then d'Artagnan almost lost his senses. He ran down the main street, took the same path he had already taken, went as far as the ferry, and questioned the ferryman.

Towards seven o'clock in the evening, the ferryman had taken a woman across the river. She was wrapped in a black cloak and seemed to have the greatest interest in not being recognized. But, precisely because of the precautions she took, the ferryman had paid greater attention to her and had seen that the woman was young and pretty.

Then as now, there was a crowd of young and pretty women who went to Saint-Cloud and were interested in not being seen, and yet d'Artagnan never doubted for an instant that it was Mme Bonacieux whom the ferryman had noticed.

D'Artagnan profited from the lamp burning in the ferryman's hut to reread Mme Bonacieux's note once again and assure himself that he was not mistaken, that the rendezvous was indeed at Saint-Cloud and not somewhere else, in front of M. d'Estrées's pavilion and not in some other street.

Everything combined to prove to d'Artagnan that his forebodings had not deceived him and that a great misfortune had occurred.

He went back to the château at a run. It seemed to him that in his absence something new might have happened at the pavilion and that information awaited him there.

The lane was still deserted, and the same calm and sweet light streamed from the window.

D'Artagnan then thought of that mute and blind hovel which had undoubtedly seen and might perhaps speak.

The gate of the enclosure was locked, but he jumped over the hedge and, despite the barking of the chained-up dog, approached the hut.

To his first knocking there was no response.

A dead silence reigned in the hut, as in the pavilion. However, since this hut was his last resource, he persisted.

Soon he seemed to hear a slight noise inside, a timorous noise, which itself seemed to tremble lest it be heard.

Then d'Artagnan stopped knocking and pleaded, with an accent so full of care and of promises, of fright and cajolery, that his voice would have reassured the most fearful person. At last an old worm-eaten shutter opened, or rather half-opened, and closed again as soon as the light of a wretched lamp burning in a corner lit up d'Artagnan's baldric, sword hilt, and pistol butts. However, quick as the movement was, d'Artagnan had time to glimpse an old man's head.

"In the name of heaven," he said, "listen to me! I've been waiting for someone who hasn't come. I'm dying of worry. Has there been any trouble in the neighborhood? Speak!"

The window slowly opened, and the same face appeared again, only it was still paler than the first time.

D'Artagnan naively recounted his story, all but giving names. He said that he had had a rendezvous with a young woman in front of this pavilion, and that, seeing she did not come, he had climbed the linden and, by the light of the lamp, had seen the disorder of the room.

The old man listened attentively, nodding that it was all so. Then, when d'Artagnan finished, he shook his head with an air that foretold nothing good.

"What do you mean to say?" cried d'Artagnan. "In the name of heaven, explain yourself!"

"Oh, Monsieur," said the old man, "don't ask me anything! For if I tell you what I saw, it's sure that nothing good will happen to me."

"Then you did see something?" d'Artagnan picked up. "If so, in the name of heaven," he went on, tossing him a pistole, "tell me, tell me what you saw, and I give you my word as a gentleman that everything you say will remain locked in my heart."

The old man read such frankness and such grief in d'Artagnan's face that he made a sign for him to listen and told him in a low voice:

"It was just about nine o'clock. I had heard some noise in the street and wanted to find out what it might be, but as I approached my gate, I saw that someone was trying to get in. As I'm a poor man and have no fear of being robbed, I went to open it and saw three men a few steps away. In the shadow, there was a carriage with horses hitched to it and some riding horses. The riding horses evidently belonged to the three men, who were dressed as cavaliers.

"'Ah, my good gentlemen!' I cried, 'what do you want?'

"'You must have a ladder?' the one who seemed to be the leader of the escort asked me.

"'Yes, Monsieur, the same that I use to gather fruit.'

"'Give it to us and go back inside. Here's an écu for the trouble we're causing you. Only remember that if you say a word about what you're going to see and hear (because you'll look and listen no matter how we threaten you, I'm sure of that), you're a lost man.'

"At those words, he tossed me an écu, which I picked up, and took my ladder.

"In fact, after I closed the hedge gate behind them, I pretended to go back into the house, but I came out again at once by the back door and, slipping along in the shadows, got as far as that clump of elders, from the middle of which I could see everything without being seen.

"The three men had brought the carriage up without any noise. They pulled a little man out of it, fat, short, gray-haired, meanly dressed in dark clothes, who cautiously climbed the ladder, looked sneakily into the room, stealthily climbed down again, and murmured in a low voice:

"'It is she!'

"The one who had spoken to me went to the door of the pavilion at once, opened it with a key he had with him, closed it again, and disappeared. At the same time, the other two climbed the ladder. The little old man stayed by the doorway, the coachman held the carriage horses, and a lackey the saddle horses.

"Suddenly loud cries rang out in the pavilion; a woman rushed to the window and opened it in order to jump out. But as soon as she saw the two men, she threw herself back. The two men rushed into the room after her.

"Then I didn't see anything more, but I heard the noise of furniture being broken. The woman cried out and called for help. But her cries were soon stifled. The three men came back to the window carrying the woman in their arms; two went down the ladder and transferred her to the carriage. The little old man got in after her. The one who had stayed in the pavilion closed the window again, came out the door a moment later, and made sure the woman was indeed in the carriage. His two companions were already waiting on horseback. He jumped into the saddle in turn, the lackey took his place beside the coachman, the carriage drove off at a gallop, escorted by the three horsemen, and it was all over. From that moment on, I neither saw nor heard anything."

D'Artagnan, crushed by such terrible news, stood mute and motionless, while all the demons of wrath and jealousy howled in his heart.

"But, my good gentleman," continued the old man, on

whom this mute despair certainly made more effect than would have been produced by cries and tears, "come, don't grieve, they didn't kill her on you, that's the main thing."

"Do you have any idea," asked d'Artagnan, "who the leader of this infernal expedition was?"

"I don't know him."

"But if he spoke to you, it means you could see him."

"Ah, you're asking for his description?"

"Yes."

"A tall, dry man, dark-skinned, black mustaches, black eyes, the air of a gentleman."

"That's it," cried d'Artagnan, "him again! always him! He's my demon, it seems! And the other one?"

"Which?"

"The little one."

"Oh, that one's no gentleman, I guarantee! Besides, he wasn't wearing a sword, and the others treated him without any consideration."

"Some lackey," murmured d'Artagnan. "Ah, poor woman! poor woman! What have they done to her?"

"You've promised me secrecy," said the old man.

"And I renew my promise; don't worry, I'm a gentleman. A gentleman has only his word, and I've given you mine."

With distress in his soul, d'Artagnan went back down the road to the ferry. At times he could not believe that it was Mme Bonacieux, and he hoped to find her at the Louvre the next day; at times he feared she was having an intrigue with someone else, and that the jealous man had caught her and carried her off. He vacillated, he grieved, he despaired.

"Oh, if only I had my friends here," he cried, "I'd at least have some hope of finding her again! But who knows what's become of them!"

It was nearly midnight; the problem was to find Planchet. D'Artagnan successively opened the doors of every tavern in which he saw a glimmer of light; he did not find Planchet in any of them.

At the sixth he began to reflect that the search was somewhat rash. D'Artagnan had told his lackey to meet him only at six in the morning, and wherever he was, he was within his rights.

Besides, the idea occurred to the young man that by remaining in the neighborhood of the place where the abduction had occurred, he might obtain some elucidation of this mysterious affair. At the sixth tavern, as we have said, d'Artagnan thus stopped, ordered a bottle of first-class wine, leaned on his elbows in the darkest corner, and decided to wait like that till daybreak. But this time, too, his hopes were deceived, and though he listened with all his ears, he heard, amidst the oaths, gibes, and curses exchanged by the workers, lackeys, and wagoners who made up the honorable society he now shared, nothing that could put him on the trail of the poor abducted woman. He had no choice then, after downing his bottle out of idleness and so as not to arouse suspicion, but to try to find the most satisfactory position possible in his corner and sleep as well as he could. D'Artagnan was twenty, it will be recalled, and at that age sleep has inalienable rights, which it imperiously lays claim to, even over the most desperate hearts.

Towards six o'clock in the morning, d'Artagnan woke up with that malaise which usually comes with the break of day after a bad night. It did not take him long to straighten his clothes. He felt himself over to see whether anyone had profited from his sleep to rob him, and having found his diamond on his finger, his purse in his pocket, and his pistols in his belt, he stood up, paid for his bottle, and went out to see whether he might not have better luck in the search for his lackey in the morning than at night. Indeed, the first thing he saw through the damp and gray mist was honest Planchet, who, with the two horses in hand, was waiting for him at the door of a shady-looking little tavern that d'Artagnan had passed by without even suspecting its existence.

PORTHOS

Instead of going directly home, d'Artagnan alighted at M. de Tréville's door and quickly went up the stairs. This time he had decided to tell him all he had just been through. No doubt he would give him good advice in the whole affair. Then, too, as M. de Tréville saw the queen almost daily, he might perhaps draw some information from Her Majesty about the poor woman, who had undoubtedly been made to pay for her devotion to her mistress.

M. de Tréville listened to the young man's story with a gravity which proved that he saw something other than a love intrigue in this whole adventure; then, when d'Artagnan had finished, he said:

"Hm! all this smells of His Eminence a league away."

"But what to do?" asked d'Artagnan.

"Nothing, absolutely nothing, right now, except to leave Paris, as I told you, as soon as possible. I will see the queen, I will recount to her the details of this poor woman's disappearance, of which she is no doubt unaware. Those details will guide her on her side, and on your return perhaps I'll have some good news for you. Rely on me."

D'Artagnan knew that M. de Tréville, though a Gascon, was not in the habit of making promises, and that when by chance he promised something, he would do more than he promised. And so he bowed to him, full of gratitude for the past and for the future, and the worthy captain, who for his part took a keen interest in this young man who was so brave and so resolute, affectionately shook his hand and wished him a good journey.

Resolved to put M. de Tréville's advice into practice at once, d'Artagnan made his way to the rue des Fossoyeurs to supervise the packing of his bags. As he approached his house, he spotted M. Bonacieux in his morning suit, standing on his doorsill. Everything that the prudent Planchet had told him the day before about the sinister character of his landlord came back to d'Artagnan's mind then, and he looked at him more attentively than he had before. Indeed, over and above that yellowish and sickly pallor which indicated the infiltration of bile into the blood, and might, besides, be merely accidental, d'Artagnan noticed something slyly perfidious in the pattern of wrinkles on his face. A knave does not laugh in the same way as an honest man; a hypocrite does not weep the same tears as a man of good faith. All falsity is a mask, and however well made the mask is, one always manages, with a bit of attention, to distinguish it from a face.

So it seemed to d'Artagnan that M. Bonacieux was wearing a mask, and even that this mask was among the most disagreeable to be seen.

Consequently, overcome by his repugnance for the man, he was about to pass him by without speaking, when M. Bonacieux hailed him as he had the day before.

"Well, now, young man," he said to him, "it seems we're putting in some long nights! Seven o'clock in the morning, bedad! It strikes me that you're turning received custom on its head and coming home just when others go out."

"No one would make you the same reproach, Master Bonacieux," said the young man. "You are the model of orderly folk. It's true that when you've got a young and pretty wife, you needn't go chasing after happiness: it's happiness that comes looking for you, isn't that so, M. Bonacieux?"

Bonacieux turned pale as death and grinned painfully.

"Ha, ha!" said Bonacieux, "you're pleasant company! But where the devil were you running around last night, my young master? It seems the back roads weren't in very good condition."

D'Artagnan lowered his eyes to his completely mud-covered boots; but in that movement, his glance fell at the same time on the mercer's shoes and stockings. One would have said they had been soaked in the same quagmire; they were soiled with absolutely the same stains as his boots.

Then an idea suddenly flashed through d'Artagnan's mind. That little man, fat, short, gray-haired, that sort of lackey dressed in dark clothes, treated without consideration by the swordsmen who made up the escort, had been Bonacieux himself. The husband had presided over the abduction of his wife.

D'Artagnan felt a terrible desire to leap for the mercer's throat and strangle him; but, as we have said, he was an extremely prudent lad, and he contained himself. However, the change that had come over his face was so visible that Bonacieux was frightened and tried to back away; but he was standing just in front of the door, which was closed, and the obstacle he encountered forced him to stay where he was.

"Ah, but it's you who are joking, my good man!" said d'Artagnan. "It seems to me that if my boots could use a sponge down, your shoes and stockings also call for a brushing. Could you have been gadding about yourself, Master Bonacieux? Ah, devil take it! That would hardly be excusable in a man of your age and who, moreover, has a young and pretty wife like yours."

"Oh, my God, no!" said Bonacieux. "But yesterday I was in Saint-Mandé to obtain information about a maidservant, whom I cannot possibly do without, and as the roads were bad, I brought back all this mire, which I have not yet had time to make disappear."

The place Bonacieux designated as the end of his journey was a new proof in support of the suspicions d'Artagnan had conceived. Bonacieux had said Saint-Mandé, because Saint-Mandé is in absolutely the opposite direction from Saint-Cloud.

This probability was a first consolation for him. If Bonacieux knew where his wife was, then, by employing extreme means, one could always force the mercer to unclench his teeth and let out his secret. It was only a question of changing that probability into a certainty.

"Excuse me, my dear M. Bonacieux, if I impose on you unceremoniously, but nothing makes one so thirsty as lack of sleep, and I have a raging thirst. Allow me to take a glass of water in your house; you know that's something neighbors can't refuse."

And without waiting for his landlord's permission, d'Artagnan went briskly into the house and cast a quick glance at the bed. The bed was not unmade. Bonacieux had not slept in it. He had thus come back only an hour or two ago. He had gone with his wife wherever they had taken her, or at least to the first relay.

"Thank you, Master Bonacieux," said d'Artagnan, emptying his glass, "that's all I wanted from you. Now I'll go home, have Planchet brush my boots, and when he's done, I'll send him to you, if you like, to brush your shoes."

And he left the mercer quite dumbfounded with this singular good-bye, and asking himself if he had not run upon his own sword.

At the top of the stairs he found Planchet all alarmed.

"Ah, Monsieur!" cried Planchet the moment he caught sight of his master. "There's just been another one, and I thought you were never coming home!"

"What's the matter?" asked d'Artagnan.

"Oh, I'll give you a hundred, Monsieur, I'll give you a thousand guesses what visit I just received for you in your absence."

"When was that?"

"Half an hour ago, while you were at M. de Tréville's."

"And who was it that came? Come, speak."

"M. de Cavois."

"M. de Cavois?"

"Himself."

"He came to arrest me?"

"I suspect so, Monsieur, and that despite his fawning look."

"You say he had a fawning look?"

"That is, he was sweet as honey, Monsieur."

"Really?"

"He came, he said, on the part of His Eminence, who wishes you well, to beg you to go with him to the Palais-Royal."

"And you replied?"

"That the thing was impossible, given that you were away from home, as he could see."

"What did he say then?"

"That you should be sure to pass by his office sometime today. Then he added in a low voice: 'Tell your master that His Eminence is perfectly well disposed towards him, and that his fortune may depend on this interview.'"

"The trap is rather a clumsy one for the cardinal," the young man picked up with a smile.

"I saw it was a trap, too, and I replied that you would be heartbroken on your return."

" 'Where has he gone?' asked M. de Cavois.

" 'To Troyes in Champagne,' I replied.

" 'And when did he leave?'

" 'Last night.' "

"Planchet, my friend," d'Artagnan interrupted, "you are truly a precious man."

"You understand, Monsieur, I thought that if you wanted to see M. de Cavois, you would always be able to contradict me and say you never left. It would be I who had lied, in that case, and since I'm not a gentleman, I can always lie."

"Don't worry, Planchet, you'll keep your reputation as a truthful man: we're leaving in a quarter of an hour."

"That's the advice I was about to give Monsieur. And where are we going, if I'm not being too curious?"

"Pardieu! in the opposite direction from the one you said I went in. Besides, aren't you in as much of a hurry to have news of Grimaud, Mousqueton, and Bazin as I am to know what's become of Athos, Porthos, and Aramis?"

"Indeed so, Monsieur," said Planchet, "and I'll leave whenever you like. I think the provincial air will be better for us right now than the air of Paris. So then . . ."

"So then, pack our things, Planchet, and let's be going. I'll go on ahead with my hands in my pockets, so no one will suspect anything. Meet me at the hôtel of the guards. By the way, Planchet, I believe you're right as regards our landlord, and that he is decidedly a dreadful scoundrel."

"Ah, believe me, Monsieur, when I tell you something; I'm a physiognomist, so I am!"

D'Artagnan went downstairs first, as had been agreed. Then, so as to have nothing to reproach himself with, he went around to his friends' quarters one last time: there was no news of them; only one heavily perfumed letter in a small and elegant hand had come for Aramis. D'Artagnan took charge of it. Ten minutes later, Planchet rejoined him at the stables of the hôtel of the guards. So as not to lose time, d'Artagnan had already saddled his horse himself.

"Good," he said to Planchet, when the latter had joined the bags to their outfit, "now saddle the other three and let's go."

"Do you think we'll go more quickly with two horses each?" Planchet asked with his mocking air.

"No, mister bad joker," replied d'Artagnan, "but with our four horses we'll be able to bring back our three friends—that is, if we find them alive."

"Which will be great luck," replied Planchet, "but one mustn't finally despair of God's mercy."

"Amen," said d'Artagnan, mounting his horse.

And they both left the hôtel of the guards, going off in opposite directions, one to leave Paris by the porte de La Villette and the other by the porte de Montmartre, to meet again beyond Saint-Denis, a strategic maneuver which, having been carried out with equal punctuality, was crowned with the happiest results. D'Artagnan and Planchet entered Pierrefitte together.

Planchet, it must be said, was more courageous during the day than at night.

However, his natural prudence never abandoned him for a moment. He had forgotten none of the incidents of the first journey, and he took all those he met on the road for enemies. The result was that he constantly had his hat in his hand, which brought him some severe rebukes from d'Artagnan, who feared that, owing to this excessive politeness, he would be taken for a poor man's valet.

However, either because passersby were in fact touched by Planchet's urbanity, or because no one lay in wait along the young man's route, our two travelers reached Chantilly without any mishap, and dismounted at the Grand Saint Martin Hôtel, where they had stopped during their first journey.

The host, seeing a young man followed by a lackey and two saddle horses, stepped respectfully across the threshold. Now, as they had already gone eleven leagues, d'Artagnan thought it appropriate to stop, whether or not Porthos was in the hôtel. Then, too, it was perhaps not prudent to ask questions straight off about what had become of the musketeer. The result of these reflections was that d'Artagnan, without asking for news about anything at all, dismounted, entrusted the horses to his lackey, went into a small room meant for receiving those who wished to be alone, and asked his host for a bottle of his best wine and as fine a meal as he could prepare, a request that further corroborated the good opinion the innkeeper had formed of his traveler at first sight.

Thus d'Artagnan was served with miraculous celerity.

The regiment of the guards was recruited from among the foremost gentlemen of the realm, and d'Artagnan, followed by a lackey and traveling with four magnificent horses, could not fail to cause a sensation, despite the simplicity of his uniform. The host wanted to wait on him himself; seeing which, d'Artagnan had two glasses brought and entered upon the following conversation.

"By heaven, my good host," said d'Artagnan, filling the two glasses, "I asked you for your best wine, and if you've deceived me, you'll be punished where you sinned, seeing that, as I hate to drink alone, you are going to drink with me. Take this glass, then, and let us drink. Come now, what shall we drink to, so as not to wound any feelings? Let us drink to the prosperity of your establishment!"

"Your Lordship does me honor," said the host, "and I thank him quite sincerely for his good wishes."

"But don't be deceived," said d'Artagnan, "there is perhaps more egotism than you think in my toast: it is only in prosperous establishments that one is well received. In hôtels that go to seed, everything falls into disorder, and the traveler is the victim of his host's difficulties. Now, I, who travel a great deal, and above all on this road, would like to see all innkeepers make a fortune."

"Indeed," said the host, "it seems to me that this is not the first time I've had the honor of seeing Monsieur."

"Why, I've passed through Chantilly maybe ten times, and of those ten times, I've stopped with you at least three or four times. Wait, I was here some ten or twelve days ago. I was seeing off some friends, some musketeers, so much so that one of them got into a dispute with a stranger, an unknown man, a man who picked I don't know what sort of quarrel with him."

"Ah, yes, indeed," said the host, "and I recall him perfectly! Is Your Lordship not speaking of M. Porthos?"

"That is precisely the name of my traveling companion. My God, my dear host, tell me, has he suffered some misfortune?"

"Your Lordship must have noticed that he did not continue his journey."

"In fact, though he promised to rejoin us, we never saw him again."

"He did us the honor of remaining here."

"What? He did you the honor of remaining here?"

"Yes, Monsieur, in this hôtel. We're even rather worried."

"About what?"

"Certain expenses he has run up."

"Well, but if he has run up expenses, he'll pay them."

"Ah, Monsieur, you are truly pouring balm on my wounds! We have advanced extremely great sums, and this morning again the surgeon declared that if M. Porthos did not pay him, he would take it out of me, seeing that it was I who had sent for him."

"But is Porthos wounded then?"

"I am unable to tell you that, Monsieur."

"How do you mean, you're unable to tell me that? You should be better informed than anyone."

"Yes, but people in our condition do not say all we know, Monsieur, especially when we've been warned that our ears will answer for our tongue."

"Well, then, can I see Porthos?"

"Certainly, Monsieur. Take the stairs, go up to the second floor, and knock at number one. Only let him know that it's you."

"What? I should I let him know that it's me?"

"Yes, for misfortune might befall you."

"And what misfortune would you have befall me?"

"M. Porthos might take you for one of the household and, in a burst of anger, run you through with his sword or blow your brains out."

"What on earth have you done to him?"

"We have asked him for money."

"Ah, devil take it, now I understand! That's a request that

Porthos takes very badly when he's out of funds. But, as far as I know, he shouldn't be."

"That's what we thought as well, Monsieur. As the house is quite orderly, and we do our accounts every week, at the end of eight days we presented him with our bill, but it seems we happened upon the wrong moment, for, at the first word we uttered on the subject, he sent us to all possible devils. It's true that he had been playing cards the night before."

"So he had been playing cards the night before! And with whom?"

"Oh, my God, who knows? With a lord who was passing through and to whom he had proposed a game of lansquenet."

"That's it, the poor fellow must have lost everything."

"Including his horse, Monsieur, for when the stranger made ready to leave, we noticed that his lackey saddled M. Porthos's horse. We pointed it out to him then, but he told us we were mixing into what did not concern us and that the horse was his. We at once informed M. Porthos of what was happening, but he told us we were knaves to doubt the word of a gentleman, and that, since the latter had said the horse was his, it must have been so."

"That's him all right," murmured d'Artagnan.

"Then," continued the host, "I replied to him that, as we seemed destined not to understand each other in regard to payment, I hoped he would at least be so kind as to grant the favor of his custom to my colleague, the master of the Golden Eagle. But M. Porthos replied to me that, my hôtel being better, he wished to remain here.

"This reply was too flattering for me to insist on his departure. So I limited myself to asking that he give up his room, which is the finest in the hôtel, and content himself with a pretty little room on the fourth floor. But to this M. Porthos replied that, as he was expecting his mistress at any moment, and she was one of the grandest ladies of the court, I should understand that the room he did me the honor of inhabiting in my hôtel was still rather mediocre for such a person.

"However, while recognizing the truth of what he said, I

believed I had to insist. But without even bothering to enter into discussion with me, he took his pistol, placed it on the night table, and declared that at the first word anyone said to him about any movement at all, exterior or interior, he would blow the brains out of the one who would be so imprudent as to mix into something that concerned only him. And so, since that time, Monsieur, no one enters his room anymore except his domestic."

"So Mousqueton is here?"

"Yes, Monsieur, five days after his departure, he came back in an extremely bad humor. It seems he also had some inconvenience in his travels. Unfortunately, he's more nimble than his master, so that for his master's sake he turns everything upside down, seeing that, as he thinks he may be refused what he asks for, he takes everything he needs without asking."

"The fact is," replied d'Artagnan, "that I have always noticed a very superior devotion and intelligence in Mousqueton."

"That's possible, Monsieur. But if I should come in contact with such intelligence and devotion only four times a year, I'd be a ruined man."

"No, because Porthos will pay you."

"Hm!" said the innkeeper in a doubtful tone.

"He's the favorite of a very grand lady, who won't leave him in difficulties for a trifling sum like the one he owes you."

"If I dare say what I think about that . . ."

"What you think?"

"I'll say more: what I know."

"What you know?"

"And even what I'm sure of."

"And just what are you sure of?"

"I will say that I know this grand lady."

"You?"

"Yes, I."

"And how do you know her?"

"Oh, Monsieur, if I thought I could trust in your discretion . . ."

"Speak, and on my honor as a gentleman, you will not have to repent of your confidence."

"Well, then, Monsieur, as you well realize, many things get done out of anxiety."

"What did you do?"

"Oh, besides, it's nothing that's not within a creditor's rights."

"Well?"

"M. Porthos gave us a note for this duchess, and instructed us to put it in the post. His domestic hadn't come back yet. As he couldn't leave his room, he had no choice but to entrust us with his commissions."

"And so?"

"Instead of putting the letter in the post, which is never very certain, I profited from the occasion of one of my lads going to Paris, and ordered him to deliver the letter to the duchess herself. This was fulfilling the intentions of M. Porthos, who had so firmly charged us with this letter, was it not?"

"Nearly."

"Well, Monsieur, do you know what this grand lady is?"

"No. I've heard Porthos speak of her, that's all."

"Do you know what this supposed duchess is?"

"I repeat to you, I don't know her."

"She's an old procureuse of the Châtelet, Monsieur, by the name of Mme Coquenard, who is at least fifty and still gives herself airs of being jealous. It seemed quite a singular thing to me, a princess living on the rue aux Ours."

"How do you know all that?"

"Because she flew into a great rage on receiving the letter, saying that M. Porthos was fickle, and that he had been wounded in a duel over some woman."

"So he was wounded?"

"Ah, my God! What have I said?"

"You said that Porthos was wounded."

"Yes, but he strictly forbade me to say it!"

"Why so?"

"Why, Monsieur? Because he boasted that he was going to perforate that stranger you left him in dispute with, and, on the contrary, despite all his bluster, it was the stranger who laid him out on the tiles. Now, as M. Porthos is an extremely vainglorious man, except towards the duchess, whom he thought to interest by telling her the story of his adventure, he did not want to admit to anyone that he had been wounded in a duel."

"So it's a sword stroke that's keeping him in bed?"

"And a master stroke it was, I assure you. Your friend must have his soul well pinned to his body."

"You were there, then?"

"Monsieur, I followed them out of curiosity, so that I saw the combat without the combatants seeing me."

"And how did it go?"

"Oh, it wasn't a long affair, I warrant you. They put themselves on guard; the stranger made a feint, then a thrust, and all that so quickly that, by the time M. Porthos went to parry, he already had three inches of steel in his chest. He fell backwards. The stranger at once put his sword point to his throat, and M. Porthos, seeing himself at the mercy of his adversary, admitted that he was beaten. At which point the stranger asked him his name, and learning that he was M. Porthos and not M. d'Artagnan, offered him his arm, brought him back to the hôtel, mounted his horse, and disappeared."

"So it was M. d'Artagnan the stranger was after?"

"It seems so."

"And do you know what became of him?"

"No. I had never seen him till that moment, and we haven't seen him again since."

"Very well, I know what I wanted to know. Now, you say that Porthos's room is on the second floor, number one?"

"Yes, Monsieur, the inn's finest, a room I'd have had the chance to rent ten times already."

"Bah! Calm yourself," d'Artagnan said, laughing. "Porthos will pay you with the duchess Coquenard's money."

"Oh, Monsieur, procureuse or duchess, if she loosened her purse strings, this would be nothing; but she positively replied that she was weary of the demands and infidelities of M. Porthos, and that she wouldn't send him a denier."

"And have you delivered that reply to your guest?"

"We took great care not to: he would have seen how we carried out his commission."

"So he's still waiting for his money?"

"Oh, my God, yes! He wrote again yesterday, but this time it was his domestic who put the letter in the post."

"And you say the procureuse is old and ugly!"

"Fifty at least, Monsieur, and not at all pretty, so Pathaud says."

"In that case, don't worry, she'll let herself soften. Besides, Porthos can't owe you much."

"How do you mean, not much? Twenty pistoles already, not counting the doctor. Oh, he denies himself nothing, not him; one can see he's used to good living."

"Well, if his mistress abandons him, he'll find friends, I assure you. And so, my dear host, don't have any qualms, and go on giving him all the care his condition demands."

"Monsieur has promised me not to speak of the procureuse and not to say a word about the wound."

"It's agreed; you have my word."

"Oh, it's just that he'd kill me, you see!"

"Don't be afraid. He's not such a devil as he seems."

As he said these words, d'Artagnan went up the stairs, leaving his host a little more reassured regarding two things he seemed very attached to: his credit and his life.

At the top of the stairs, on the most conspicuous door of the corridor, a gigantic number 1 was drawn in black ink. D'Artagnan knocked once, and, at the invitation to move on that came to him from inside, he went in.

Porthos was lying in bed and playing a game of lansquenet with Mousqueton, to keep his hand in, while a spit loaded with partridges turned in front of the fire, and at either corner of the huge fireplace two pots simmered on chafing dishes, giving off a combined odor of stewed hare and stewed fish that delighted the nostrils. What's more, the top of a writing desk and the marble of a chest of drawers were covered with empty bottles.

At the sight of his friend, Porthos let out a great cry of joy, and Mousqueton, rising respectfully, yielded him his place and went to have a look at the two pots, of which he seemed to have personal oversight.

"Ah, pardieu, it's you!" Porthos said to d'Artagnan.

"Welcome, welcome, and excuse me if I don't come to greet you. But," he added, looking at d'Artagnan with a certain anxiety, "do you know what happened to me?"

"No."

"The host didn't tell you anything?"

"I asked after you and came straight up."

Porthos seemed to breathe more freely.

"And what did happen to you, my dear Porthos?" d'Artagnan went on.

"What happened to me was that, in lunging at my adversary, to whom I had already delivered three strokes, and whom I wanted to finish off with the fourth, my foot slipped on a stone, and I sprained my knee."

"Really?"

"Word of honor! Luckily for the rascal, for I'd wouldn't have left him otherwise than dead on the spot, I guarantee you."

"And what became of him?"

"Oh, I have no idea! He'd had enough and left without further ado. But you, my dear d'Artagnan, what's happened with you?"

"And so," d'Artagnan went on, "it's that sprain, my dear Porthos, that keeps you in bed?"

"Ah, my God, yes, that's all! Anyhow, in a few days I'll be on my feet."

"Why, then, didn't you have yourself transported to Paris? You must be excruciatingly bored here."

"That was my intention; but, my dear friend, there's something I must confess to you."

"What?"

"It's that, since I was excruciatingly bored, as you say, and I had the seventy-five pistoles that you gave me in my pocket, for the sake of distraction I invited a passing gentleman up and proposed that we have a game of cards. He accepted and, by heaven, my seventy-five pistoles went from my pocket to his, not to mention my horse, which he took into the bargain. But what about you, my dear d'Artagnan?"

"What do you want, my dear Porthos, you can't have all

the privileges. You know the saying: 'Lucky in love, unlucky at cards.' You're too lucky in love for the cards not to revenge themselves. But what are reverses of fortune to you? Don't you have your duchess, you lucky rascal, who can't fail to come to your aid?"

"Ah, well, you see, my dear d'Artagnan, I've had a streak of bad luck," Porthos replied with the most casual air in the world. "I wrote her to send me some fifty louis that I absolutely needed, seeing the position I was in."

"Well?"

"Well, she must be visiting her estates, because she didn't answer me."

"Really?"

"No, she didn't. So yesterday I sent her a second epistle more urgent than the first. But here you are, my most dear friend; let's talk about you. I admit, I was beginning to be a bit worried about you."

"But your host treats you well, it seems, my dear Porthos," said d'Artagnan, pointing to the full pots and the empty bottles.

"So so!" replied Porthos. "Three or four days ago the impertinent fellow showed me his bill, and I threw them out, him and his bill; so that I'm here as a sort of victor, a kind of conqueror. And, as you see, always fearing my position may be stormed, I'm armed to the teeth."

"However," d'Artagnan said, laughing, "it seems you make sorties from time to time."

And he pointed his finger at the bottles and pots.

"Not me, unfortunately!" said Porthos. "This wretched sprain keeps me in bed, but Mousqueton beats the bushes and brings back provisions. Mousqueton, my friend," Porthos went on, "you see reinforcements have come, we need an extra supply of victuals."

"Mousqueton," said d'Artagnan, "you must do me a service."

"What service, Monsieur?"

"You must give your recipe to Planchet. I might find myself besieged in my turn, and I wouldn't mind if he let me enjoy the same advantages you gratify your master with."

"Ah, my God, Monsieur," said Mousqueton with a modest air, "nothing could be simpler! It's a question of being adroit, that's all. I was brought up in the country, and my father, in his spare time, was a bit of a poacher."

"And what did he do the rest of the time?"

"Monsieur, he plied a trade which I have always found rather fortunate."

"What was it?"

"As it was the time of the wars of the Catholics and the Huguenots, and he saw the Catholics exterminating the Huguenots, and the Huguenots exterminating the Catholics, all in the name of religion, he made up a mixed belief for himself, which allowed him to be now a Catholic, now a Huguenot. He was in the habit of strolling, with his blunderbuss on his shoulder, behind the hedges that line the roads, and when he saw a lone Catholic coming, the Protestant religion would win over his mind at once. He would lower his blunderbuss in the traveler's direction; then, when he was ten paces away, he would begin a dialogue which almost always ended by the traveler relinquishing his purse in order to save his life. It goes without saying that, when he saw a Huguenot coming, he felt seized with such ardent Catholic zeal that he was unable to understand how, fifteen minutes ago, he could have doubted the superiority of our holy religion. For I, Monsieur, am a Catholic, my father, faithful to his principles, having made my elder brother a Huguenot."

"And how did this worthy man end up?" asked d'Artagnan.

"Oh, in the most unfortunate way, Monsieur! One day he found himself on a sunken lane between a Huguenot and a Catholic with whom he had already had dealings, and both of whom recognized him. They joined forces against him and hanged him from a tree. Then they came to boast of their fine escapade in the tavern of the nearest village, where my brother and I were drinking."

"And what did you do?" asked d'Artagnan.

"We let them talk," Mousqueton picked up. "Then, as they took opposite routes on leaving the tavern, my brother went to lie in ambush on the Catholic's way, and I on the Protestant's.

Two hours later it was all over, we had dealt with them both, while admiring our poor father's foresight in having taken the precaution of raising each of us in a different religion."

"Indeed, as you say, Mousqueton, your father seems to me to have been a most intelligent fellow. So you say that in his spare time the good man was a poacher?"

"Yes, Monsieur, and it was he who taught me to tie a snare and set a bottom line. The result was that when I saw our scoundrel of a host feeding us a heap of crude meat fit for yokels, and by no means suited to two stomachs as enfeebled as ours, I went back somewhat to my old trade. While strolling in the woods of M. le Prince, I set some snares in the runs; while lying on the banks of His Highness's ponds, I slipped some lines into the water. So that now, thank God, we're not lacking, as Monsieur can verify, in partridges and rabbits, carps and eels—all light and healthful foods, proper for sick men."

"But the wine," asked d'Artagnan, "who furnishes the wine? Is it your host?"

"Yes and no."

"How do you mean, yes and no?"

"He furnishes it, true, but he doesn't know he has that honor."

"Explain yourself, Mousqueton, your conversation is full of instructive things."

"It's like this, Monsieur. Chance brought it about that I met a Spaniard in my peregrinations who had seen many countries, the New World among others."

"What relation can the New World have with the bottles standing on this writing desk and that chest of drawers?"

"Patience, Monsieur, each thing in its turn."

"Fair enough, Mousqueton; I rely on you, and I'm listening."

"This Spaniard had a lackey in his service who had accompanied him on his voyage to Mexico. This lackey was my compatriot, so that we made friends all the more quickly, in that there were strong similarities of character between us. We both loved hunting more than anything, so that he told me how, in the plains of the pampas, the natives of the country hunt tigers and bulls with a simple slipknot, which they throw around the necks of these terrible animals. At first I refused to believe one could reach such a degree of skill as to throw the end of a rope accurately for twenty or thirty paces; but in the face of proof, the truth of the story had to be acknowledged. My friend placed a bottle thirty paces away, and he caught the neck in the slipknot every time. I took up the exercise, and as nature has granted me certain abilities, today I can throw a lasso as well as any man in the world. Well, do you understand? Our host has a very well-furnished cellar, but he never parts with the key. However, the cellar has a vent window. So I throw the lasso through this vent window; and as I now know where the good corner is, I draw from it. That, Monsieur, is how the New World turns out to have a relation with the bottles on that chest of drawers and this writing desk. Now, kindly taste our wine, and tell us, without reservation, what you think of it."

"Thank you, my friend, thank you, but unfortunately I've just had lunch."

"Well, then," said Porthos, "set the table, and while we two are having lunch, d'Artagnan can tell us what's become of him in the ten days since he left us."

"Gladly," said d'Artagnan.

While Porthos and Mousqueton lunched with the appetites of convalescents and that brotherly cordiality which draws men together in misfortune, d'Artagnan told how the wounded Aramis had been forced to stop at Crèvecoeur, how he had left Athos to fight it out in Amiens with four men who accused him of being a counterfeiter, and how he, d'Artagnan, had been forced to run the comte de Wardes through the belly in order to get to England.

But there d'Artagnan's confidences stopped. He only declared that, on his return from Great Britain, he had brought four magnificent horses, one for himself and one for each of his companions. Then he ended by declaring to Porthos that the one destined for him was already installed in the hôtel stable.

At that moment Planchet came in. He informed his master that the horses were sufficiently rested, and that it would be possible for them to spend the night in Clermont.

As d'Artagnan was all but reassured about Porthos and was longing for news of his two other friends, he held out his hand to the patient and informed him that he was setting out to continue his search. Moreover, as he counted on returning by the same route, if in seven or eight days Porthos was still at the Grand Saint Martin, he would pick him up on the way.

Porthos replied that, in all probability, his sprain would not allow him to leave in the meantime. Besides, he had to stay in Chantilly to await a reply from his duchess.

D'Artagnan wished him a prompt and good reply, and after commending Porthos to Mousqueton once again and settling his account with the host, he set out on his way with Planchet, already relieved of one of his spare horses.

XXVI

THE THESIS OF ARAMIS

D'Artagnan had said nothing to Porthos about his wound, or about his procureuse. Our Béarnais was a very wise lad, young as he was. He had therefore pretended to believe everything the vainglorious musketeer had told him, convinced that there is no friendship that cares about an overheard secret, above all when that secret has to do with pride; then one always has a certain moral superiority over those whose life one knows.

So d'Artagnan, in his plans for intrigues to come, and resolved as he was to make his three companions the instruments of his fortune, did not mind bringing together in his hand ahead of time the invisible threads by means of which he counted on leading them.

However, all along his way, a deep sadness gripped his heart: he thought of the young and pretty Mme Bonacieux, who was to have given him the reward for his devotion. But, we hasten to say, the young man's sadness came less from regret for his lost happiness than from the fear he felt lest some misfortune befall the poor woman. For him there was no doubt that she was the victim of the cardinal's vengeance, and, as we know, the cardinal's vengeance was terrible. What he did not know was how he himself had found grace in His Eminence's eyes, and that was no doubt what M. de Cavois would have revealed to him had he found him at home.

Nothing makes the time pass or shortens the way like a thought that absorbs in itself all the faculties of the one who is thinking. External existence is then like a sleep of which this thought is the dream. Under its influence, time has no more measure, space has no more distance. You leave one place and arrive at another, that is all. Of the interval in between, nothing more remains in your memory than a vague mist in which a thousand confused images of trees, mountains, and landscapes dissolve. It was in the grips of this hallucination that d'Artagnan covered, at whatever speed his horse wished to take, the six or eight leagues from Chantilly to Crèvecoeur, reaching that village without recalling anything he had met on the way.

Only there did memory return to him. He shook his head, spotted the tavern where he had left Aramis, and, setting his horse at a trot, drew up at the gate.

This time it was not a host but a hostess who received him. D'Artagnan was a physiognomist; he took in the fat, jolly figure of the mistress of the place at a single glance, and understood that he had no need to pretend with her, and that he had nothing to fear from such a joyful physiognomy.

"My good woman," d'Artagnan asked her, "can you tell me what has become of a friend of mine whom we were forced to leave here some twelve days ago?"

"A handsome young man of twenty-three or twenty-four, gentle, amiable, well-built?"

"Yes, and wounded in the shoulder."

"That's it!"

"Exactly."

"Well, Monsieur, he's still here."

"Ah, pardieu, my dear lady," said d'Artagnan, dismounting and throwing his horse's bridle over Planchet's arm, "you've restored me to life! Tell me where he is, that dear Aramis, so that I can embrace him, for I admit I can't wait to see him again!"

"Excuse me, Monsieur, but I doubt he can receive you at this moment."

"Why not? Is he with a woman?"

"Lord, what are you saying, poor lad! No, Monsieur, he is not with a woman."

"And who is he with, then?"

"With the curate of Montdidier and the superior of the Jesuits of Amiens."

"My God!" cried d'Artagnan, "has the poor lad taken a turn for the worse?"

"No, Monsieur, on the contrary, as a result of his illness he has been touched by grace and has decided to enter holy orders."

"Right," said d'Artagnan, "I'd forgotten he was only an interim musketeer."

"Does Monsieur still insist on seeing him?"

"More than ever."

"Well, then, Monsieur has only to take the stairway to the right in the courtyard, third floor, number five."

D'Artagnan dashed off in the direction indicated and found one of those outside stairways such as we still see today in the courtyards of old inns. But one did not reach the future abbé's quarters just like that. The access to Aramis's room was guarded no more nor less than the gardens of Armida. Bazin was stationed in the corridor and barred his way with all the more intrepidity in that, after many years of trial, he saw himself at last about to reach the result he had eternally striven for.

Indeed, poor Bazin's dream had always been to serve a man of the Church, and he awaited impatiently the moment ceaselessly glimpsed in the future when Aramis would finally throw his tabard to the nettles and take the cassock. The young man's daily renewed promise that the moment was not far off had been the only thing that had kept him in service to a musketeer, a service in which, he said, he could not fail to lose his soul.

Bazin was thus overjoyed. In all probability, this time his master would not retract. The combination of physical pain and moral pain had produced the long-desired effect: Aramis, suffering in both body and soul, had finally rested his eyes and thoughts on religion, and he had taken as a warning from heaven the double accident that had befallen him; that is, the sudden disappearance of his mistress and the wound in his shoulder.

We can well understand that, in his present frame of mind, nothing could have been more disagreeable to Bazin than the arrival of d'Artagnan, who might throw his master back into the whirlwind of worldly ideas that had so long carried him away. He thus resolved to defend the door bravely; and since, having been betrayed by the mistress of the inn, he could not say that Aramis was not there, he tried to prove to the new arrival that it would be the height of indiscretion to disturb his master in the pious conference he had entered upon that morning, which, according to Bazin, could not possibly end before evening.

But d'Artagnan took no account of Master Bazin's eloquent discourse, and as he did not care to enter into polemics with his friend's valet, he quite simply moved him aside with one hand and with the other turned the knob of door number five.

The door opened, and d'Artagnan went into the room.

Aramis, in a black robe, his head covered with a sort of round and flat cap that bore a fair resemblance to a calotte, was seated at an oblong table covered with scrolls of paper and enormous folio volumes. To his right sat the superior of the Jesuits and to his left the curate of Montdidier. The curtains were half drawn and admitted only a mysterious light, intended for blessed musings. All the worldly objects that might strike the eye when one enters a young man's room, above all if that young man is a musketeer, had disappeared as if by magic, and, no doubt for fear the sight of them might bring his master back to thoughts of this world, Bazin had spirited away the sword, the pistols, the plumed hat, the embroideries and laces of every sort and kind.

But in their place d'Artagnan thought he made out a scourge hanging in a dark corner from a nail in the wall.

At the noise d'Artagnan made on opening the door, Aramis raised his head and recognized his friend. But, to the young man's great astonishment, the sight of him did not seem to make a great impression on the musketeer, so detached was his spirit from earthly things.

"Good day, my dear d'Artagnan," said Aramis. "Believe me, I'm happy to see you."

"And I you," said d'Artagnan, "though I'm not quite sure yet that I'm speaking to Aramis."

"Himself, my friend, himself. But who could have made you doubt it?"

"I was afraid I'd mistaken the room, and I thought at first I was entering some churchman's quarters. Then another error came over me, seeing you in the company of these gentlemen: I thought you might be gravely ill."

The two men in black, who understood his intentions, shot d'Artagnan an almost threatening look; but d'Artagnan was not troubled by it.

"Perhaps I'm disturbing you, my dear Aramis," d'Artagnan went on, "for what I see leads me to believe that you are confessing to these gentlemen."

Aramis blushed imperceptibly.

"You, disturbing me? Oh, quite the contrary, dear friend, I swear to you! And as proof of what I say, allow me to rejoice at seeing you safe and sound."

"Ah, he's finally coming around," thought d'Artagnan, "and a lucky thing, too!"

"For Monsieur, who is my friend, has just escaped from grave danger," Aramis went on unctuously, indicating d'Artagnan to the two ecclesiastics.

"Praise God, Monsieur," they said, bowing in unison.

"I already have, my reverend sirs," the young man replied, returning their bow.

"You've come at a good moment, dear d'Artagnan," said Aramis, "and in taking part in the discussion, you will cast your own light on it. The superior of Amiens, the curate of Montdidier, and I are arguing over certain theological questions, the interest of which has long since captivated us. I would be charmed to have your opinion."

"The opinion of a man of the sword carries no weight,"

replied d'Artagnan, who was beginning to worry about the turn things were taking, "and you can content yourself, believe me, with the knowledge of these gentlemen."

The two men in black bowed again.

"On the contrary," Aramis picked up, "your opinion will be precious to us. Here's the question: the superior believes that my thesis must above all be dogmatic and didactic."

"Your thesis? So you're doing a thesis?"

"Of course," replied the Jesuit. "For the examination preceding ordination, a thesis is strictly required."

"Ordination?" cried d'Artagnan, who could not believe what the hostess and Bazin had both told him. "Ordination?"

And his stupefied eyes wandered over the three personages he had before him.

"Now," Aramis went on, taking the same graceful pose in his armchair as if he was in a salon, and complacently examining his hand, white and dimpled as a woman's, which he held up so that the blood would drain from it, "now, as you have heard, d'Artagnan, the superior would like my thesis to be dogmatic, while I, for my part, would like it to be idealist. That is why the superior is proposing this subject, which has never been treated before, and in which I acknowledge there is material for magnificent development: *Utraque manus in benedicendo clericis inferioribus necessaria est.*"

D'Artagnan, whose erudition we are familiar with, did not bat an eye at this citation, any more than he had at the one M. de Tréville had made to him concerning the presents d'Artagnan had received from M. de Buckingham.

"Which is to say," Aramis continued, to make it easier for him, "'Both hands are indispensable for priests of the lower orders when they give the blessing.'"

"An admirable subject!" cried the Jesuit.

"Admirable and dogmatic," repeated the curate, who, being about as strong in Latin as d'Artagnan, carefully kept an eye on the Jesuit, in order to lock steps with him and repeat his words like an echo.

As for d'Artagnan, he remained perfectly indifferent to the enthusiasm of the two men in black.

"Yes, admirable! *prorsus admirabile!*"* Aramis went on. "But it demands a thorough study of the Fathers and of the Scriptures. Now, I have confessed to these learned ecclesiastics, and that in all humility, that the watches of the corps of guards and the service of the king have made me neglect my studies somewhat. I would thus find myself more at ease, *facilius natans,*** with a subject of my own choice, which would be to these tough theological questions what ethics is to metaphysics in philosophy."

D'Artagnan was profoundly bored, as was the curate.

"What an exordium!" cried the Jesuit.

"Exordium," repeated the curate, in order to say something. "*Quemadmodum inter cœlorum immensitatem.*"†

Aramis gave d'Artagnan a sidelong glance and saw that his friend was yawning fit to dislocate his jaw.

"Let us speak French, father," he said to the Jesuit. "M. d'Artagnan will savor our words more fully."

"Yes, I'm tired out from the road," said d'Artagnan, "and all this Latin is beyond me."

"Very well," said the Jesuit, slightly vexed, while the curate, in a transport of relief, turned upon d'Artagnan a gaze filled with gratitude. "Now, then, see what advantage can be drawn from this gloss: Moses, the servant of God . . . He is no more than a servant, understand that well! Moses blessed with his hands. He had both arms held up for him while the Hebrews fought their enemies; thus he blessed with both hands. Besides, what says the Gospel: *imponite manus,* and not *manum*; lay on your hands, not your hand."

"Lay on your hands," the curate repeated with a gesture.

"To St. Peter, on the contrary, of whom the popes are successors," the Jesuit continued, "it was: *Porrige digitos*; hold up your fingers. Do you see now?"

"To be sure," Aramis replied in delight, "but it's a subtle thing."

---

* "Admirable indeed!"
** "Swimming more easily."
† "As amidst the immensity of the heavens."

"Your fingers!" the Jesuit repeated. "St. Peter blessed with his fingers. Thus the pope also blesses with his fingers. And with how many fingers does he bless? With three fingers, one for the Father, one for the Son, and one for the Holy Spirit."

They all crossed themselves. D'Artagnan thought he had better follow their example.

"The pope is the successor of St. Peter and represents the three divine powers. The rest, the *ordines inferiores* of the ecclesiastical hierarchy, bless in the name of the holy archangels and angels. The humblest clerics, such as our deacons and sacristans, bless with sprinklers, which simulate an indefinite number of blessing fingers. There you have a simple statement of the subject, *argumentum omni denudatum ornamento.** With it," the Jesuit went on, "I could produce two volumes the size of this one."

And in his enthusiasm he thumped the folio of St. Chrysostom, which made the table sag under its weight.

D'Artagnan shuddered.

"To be sure," said Aramis, "I do justice to the beauties of this thesis, but at the same time I find it overwhelming. I had chosen this text—tell me, my dear d'Artagnan, if it's not to your taste: *Non inutile est desiderium in oblatione,* or better still: A slight regret is not unbecoming in an offering to the Lord."

"Stop right there," cried the Jesuit, "for this thesis verges on heresy! There is almost the same proposition in the *Augustinus* of the heresiarch Jansenius, whose book will be burned sooner or later by the executioner's hands. Beware, my young friend! You are inclining towards false doctrines, my young friend, you will be lost!"

"You will be lost!" said the curate, shaking his head ruefully.

"You are touching upon that famous point about free will, which is a fatal stumbling block. You are coming abreast of the insinuations of the Pelagians and the semi-Pelagians."

"But, reverend father . . ." Aramis picked up, a bit stunned by the hail of arguments falling on his head.

* "The argument stripped of all ornament."

"How will you prove," the Jesuit went on without giving him time to speak, "that one must regret the world when one offers oneself to God? Listen to this dilemma: God is God, and the world is the devil. To regret the world is to regret the devil. There is my conclusion."

"It is mine as well," said the curate.

"But for pity's sake! . . ." said Aramis.

"*Desideras diabolum,* poor boy!" cried the Jesuit.

"He regrets the devil! Ah, my young friend," the curate continued, sighing, "do not regret the devil, I beseech you."

D'Artagnan was lapsing into idiocy. It seemed to him that he was in a madhouse, and that he was going to become as mad as those he was looking at. Only he was forced to keep silent, having no understanding of the language being spoken around him.

"But do listen to me," Aramis picked up, with a politeness behind which some slight impatience was beginning to show. "I am not saying I regret; no, I will never utter that phrase, which would not be orthodox . . ."

The Jesuit raised his arms to heaven, and the curate did the same.

"No, but agree at least that it is ungracious to offer the Lord only that which you are thoroughly disgusted with. Am I right, d'Artagnan?"

"I should say so, pardieu!" the latter cried.

The curate and the Jesuit jumped in their chairs.

"Here is my starting point. It is a syllogism: the world is not without its attractions; I am leaving the world; thus I am making a sacrifice. Now, the Scriptures say positively: Make a sacrifice unto the Lord."

"That is true," said the antagonists.

"Moreover," Aramis went on, pinching his ear to make it red, while he shook his hands to make them white, "moreover I've made a certain rondeau on the subject, which I transmitted to M. Voiture last year, and on which the great man has paid me a thousand compliments."

"A rondeau?" the Jesuit said disdainfully.

"A rondeau?" the curate repeated mechanically.

"Recite it, recite it," cried d'Artagnan, "it will be a bit of a change for us."

"Not so, for it is religious," replied Aramis, "it is versified theology."

"Devil take it!" said d'Artagnan.

"Here it is," said Aramis, with a modest little air that was not without a certain tinge of hypocrisy:

> You who lament the loss of past delight,
> And go on dragging out your hapless years,
> Offer up to God alone your tears,
> Then your sorrows all will find respite,
>   You who lament.

D'Artagnan and the curate seemed charmed. The Jesuit persisted in his opinion.

"Beware of profane taste in theological style. What indeed does St. Augustine say? *Severus sit clericorum sermo.*"*

"Yes, let the sermon be clear!" said the curate.

"Your thesis," the Jesuit hastened to interrupt, seeing that his acolyte had gone astray, "your thesis will please the ladies, that is all; it will have the success of one of Master Patru's pleadings."

"God grant it!" Aramis cried in transport.

"You see," cried the Jesuit, "the world still speaks in a loud voice within you, *altissima voce.*** You follow the world's ways, my young friend, and I tremble lest grace not suffice you."

"Cheer up, reverend father, I can answer for myself."

"Worldly presumption!"

"I know myself, father; my resolution is irrevocable."

"So you insist on pursuing this thesis?"

"I feel myself called upon to deal with it and not some other. I shall therefore continue, and tomorrow I hope you will be satisfied with the corrections I shall have made following your advice."

* "Austere be a cleric's conversation."
** "In the loudest voice."

"Work slowly," said the curate, "we leave you in excellent intentions."

"Yes, the ground is well sown," said the Jesuit, "and we need not fear that part of the seed has fallen upon stone, another part by the roadside, and that the fowls of the air have eaten the rest, *aves cœli comederunt illam.*"

"The plague choke you with your Latin!" said d'Artagnan, who felt at the end of his strength.

"Good-bye, my son," said the curate, "till tomorrow."

"Till tomorrow, my bold young man," said the Jesuit. "You promise to be one of the lights of the Church. Heaven grant that this light be not a devouring fire!"

D'Artagnan, who for an hour had been biting his nails with impatience, had gotten down to the quick.

The two men in black rose, bowed to Aramis and d'Artagnan, and moved towards the door. Bazin, who had remained standing and had listened to the whole controversy with pious jubilation, rushed to them, took the curate's breviary and the Jesuit's missal, and walked respectfully ahead of them to clear the way.

Aramis accompanied them to the foot of the stairs and immediately came back up to d'Artagnan, who was still somewhat dazed.

Left alone, the two friends first sat in embarrassed silence. However, one of them had to be the first to break it, and as d'Artagnan seemed resolved to leave that honor to his friend, Aramis said:

"You see, I've come back to my fundamental ideas."

"Yes, you've been touched by efficient grace, as one of those gentlemen said just now."

"Oh, these plans to retire were formed long ago, and you've already heard me speak of them, haven't you, my friend?"

"Of course, but I confess I thought you were joking."

"About such things? Oh, d'Artagnan!"

"Why, people joke about death, after all!"

"And wrong they are, d'Artagnan, for death is the doorway that leads to perdition or salvation."

"All right, but, please, let's not theologize, Aramis. You

must have had enough for the rest of the day, and as for me, I've all but forgotten the little Latin I ever knew; besides, I confess to you, I haven't eaten anything since ten o'clock this morning, and I'm as hungry as the very devil."

"We'll dine soon, my dear friend; only you'll remember that today is Friday, and on such a day I can neither see nor eat any meat. If you'll content yourself with my dinner, it's composed of cooked tetragons and fruit."

"What do you mean by tetragons?" d'Artagnan asked uneasily.

"I mean spinach," said Aramis. "But for you I'll add eggs, and that is a grave infraction of the rule, for eggs are meat, since they engender the chicken."

"It's hardly a succulent feast, but never mind; I'll put up with it in order to stay with you."

"I am grateful to you for the sacrifice," said Aramis, "and if it doesn't profit your body, you may be certain it will profit your soul."

"So, Aramis, you're decidedly entering religion. What will our friends say, what will M. de Tréville say? They'll treat you as a deserter, I warn you."

"I am not entering religion, I am re-entering it. It was the Church that I deserted for the world, for you know I did violence to myself in order to put on a musketeer's tabard."

"I know nothing about it."

"You're unaware of how I left the seminary?"

"Completely."

"Here is my story. Besides, the Scriptures say, 'Confess one to another,' and so I shall confess to you, d'Artagnan."

"And I give you absolution beforehand, so you can see I'm a good man."

"Do not joke about holy things, my friend."

"Speak, then, I'm listening."

"I had been in the seminary from the age of nine, I was going to be twenty in three days, I was going to be an abbé, and there was no more to be said. One evening I had gone, as was my habit, to a house I frequented with pleasure—one is young, one is weak, what do you want! An officer who looked with a jealous eye upon my reading the *Lives of the Saints* to the mistress of the house came in all at once and without being announced. As it happened, that evening I had translated an episode from Judith, and I had just communicated my verses to the lady, who paid me all sorts of compliments and, leaning over my shoulder, was rereading them with me. The pose, which was somewhat casual, I admit, offended this officer. He said nothing; but when I left, he came out after me and overtook me.

"'Monsieur l'abbé,'" he said, 'do you like canings?'

"'I cannot say, Monsieur,' I replied, 'no one has ever dared give me one.'

"'Well, then, listen to me, Monsieur l'abbé: if you go back to the house where I met you this evening, I will certainly dare!'

"I believe I was afraid, I became very pale, I felt my legs giving way, I sought for some reply but could find none and said nothing.

"The officer was waiting for that reply, and seeing it delayed, began to laugh, turned his back on me, and went into the house again. I returned to the seminary.

"I am a proper gentleman, and I am hot-blooded, as you may have noticed, my dear d'Artagnan. The insult was terrible, and, unknown though it was to the rest of the world, I felt it living and stirring in the bottom of my heart. I declared to my superiors that I did not feel myself sufficiently prepared for ordination, and, at my request, the ceremony was put off for a year.

"I went to find the best fencing master in Paris, made arrangements with him to take a lesson every day, and every day for a year I took that lesson. Then, on the anniversary of the day I was insulted, I hung my cassock on a nail, put on the full costume of a cavalier, and went to a ball given by a woman I was friends with, and where I knew that my man should be found. It was on the rue des Francs-Bourgeois, quite near to la Force.

"Indeed, my officer was there. I went up to him while he was singing a love song and looking tenderly at a woman, and interrupted him right in the middle of the second stanza.

"'Monsieur,' I said to him, 'is my going back to a certain

house on the rue Payenne as displeasing to you as ever, and will you still give me a caning if I take it into my head to disobey you?'

"The officer looked at me in astonishment, then said: 'What do you want of me, Monsieur? I do not know you.'

" 'I am,' I replied, 'the little abbé who reads the *Lives of the Saints* and translates Judith into verse.'

" 'Ah, yes, I remember!' the officer said jeeringly. 'What do you want of me?'

" 'I want you to take a moment to go for a little stroll with me.'

" 'Tomorrow morning, if you like, and it will be with the greatest pleasure.'

" 'No, not tomorrow morning, if you please, but right now.'

" 'If you absolutely insist . . .'

" 'Yes, I do insist.'

" 'Let us step out, then. Ladies,' said the officer, 'don't be upset. Only give me a moment to kill this gentleman, and I'll come back to finish the stanza for you.'

"We went out.

"I brought him to the rue Payenne, to the exact spot where a year ago, hour for hour, he had paid me the compliment I've reported to you. It was a superb moonlit night. We drew our swords, and at the first pass, I killed him dead."

"Devil take it!" said d'Artagnan.

"Now," Aramis went on, "as the ladies did not see their singer come back, and he was found in the rue Payenne with a great sword stroke through his body, they thought it was I who had done him up like that, and the thing caused a scandal. I was thus forced to renounce the cassock for a while. Athos, whose acquaintance I made at that time, and Porthos, who, beyond my fencing lessons, had taught me a few hearty thrusts, induced me to ask for a musketeer's tabard. The king had had a great liking for my father, who was killed at the siege of Arras, and the tabard was granted me. So you understand that today the moment has come for me to return to the bosom of the Church."

"And why today rather than yesterday or tomorrow? What's happened to you today that gives you such nasty ideas?"

"This wound, my dear d'Artagnan, was a warning to me from heaven."

"This wound? Bah, it's nearly healed, and I'm sure that's not what is making you suffer most right now."

"And what is?" asked Aramis, blushing.

"You have another in your heart, Aramis, a sharper and bloodier one, a wound made by a woman."

"Ah," he said, hiding his emotion under a feigned negligence, "don't speak of such things! Imagine me thinking of such things! Knowing the sorrows of love! *Vanitas vanitatem!** So my head has been turned, in your opinion, and by whom? By some young seamstress, by some chambermaid, whom I must have courted in garrison! Pah!"

"Forgive me, my dear Aramis, but I thought you aimed a little higher."

"Higher? And what am I to have so much ambition? A poor musketeer, quite beggarly and obscure, who hates servitude and finds himself completely out of place in the world!"

"Aramis, Aramis!" cried d'Artagnan, looking at his friend with a doubtful air.

"Dust, I return to dust. Life is filled with pain and humiliation," he went on, waxing gloomy. "The threads that bind it to happiness break one by one in man's hand, above all the golden threads. Oh, my dear d'Artagnan!" Aramis added, giving his voice a slight tinge of bitterness, "believe me, hide your wounds well when you have them. Silence is the last joy of the unfortunate. Beware of putting anyone on the trail of your sufferings. The curious suck up our tears as flies suck the blood of a wounded buck."

"Alas, my dear Aramis," said d'Artagnan, heaving a deep sigh in his turn, "it's my own story you're telling there!"

"How's that?"

* "Vanity of vanities!"

"Yes, a woman that I loved, that I adored, has just been taken from me by force. I don't know where she is, where they've taken her. She may be a prisoner, she may be dead."

"But at least you have the consolation of telling yourself that she has not left you voluntarily; that if you have no news of her, it's because all communication between you is forbidden, whereas . . ."

"Whereas . . ."

"Nothing," said Aramis, "nothing."

"So you're renouncing the world forever? The choice is made, the resolution taken?"

"Forever and ever. You are my friend today, tomorrow you will be no more than a shade for me; or, rather, you won't exist at all. As for the world, it is nothing but a grave."

"Devil take it! It's awfully sad what you're telling me."

"What do you want! My vocation draws me, it bears me away!"

D'Artagnan smiled and did not reply. Aramis went on:

"And yet, while I still hold to the earth, I would have liked to talk with you, about you, about our friends."

"And I," said d'Artagnan, "I would have liked to talk with you about yourself, but I see you so detached from everything. You say fie to love, your friends are shades, the world is a grave."

"Alas, you see it yourself!" Aramis said with a sigh.

"Then let us speak no more of it," said d'Artagnan, "and let us burn this letter, which doubtless informs you of some new infidelity of your seamstress or your chambermaid."

"What letter?" Aramis cried sharply.

"A letter that came for you in your absence and that was given to me for you."

"But who is the letter from?"

"Oh, from some tearful maid, some seamstress in despair— Mme de Chevreuse's chambermaid perhaps, who was obliged to return to Tours with her mistress, and who, to make herself elegant, must have stolen some scented paper and sealed her letter with a duchess's coronet."

"What are you saying?"

"Wait, I must have lost it!" the young man said slyly, pretending to search himself. "Fortunately, the world is a grave, men—and consequently women—are shades, and love is a sentiment you say fie to!"

"D'Artagnan, d'Artagnan!" cried Aramis, "you're killing me!"

"Ah, here it is after all!" said d'Artagnan.

And he pulled the letter from his pocket.

Aramis leaped over, seized the letter, read or rather devoured it. His face shone.

"It seems the maid has a pretty style," the messenger said nonchalantly.

"Thanks, d'Artagnan!" cried Aramis, almost in delirium. "She was forced to return to Tours. She's not unfaithful to me, she loves me still. Come here, my friend, come here till I embrace you. I'm choking with happiness!"

And the two friends started dancing around the venerable St. Chrysostom, boldly trampling on the pages of the thesis, which had slipped to the floor.

At that moment, Bazin came in with the spinach and the omelette.

"Away, wretch!" cried Aramis, throwing his calotte in his face. "Go back where you came from, take away these horrible vegetables and that frightful concoction! Order us a stuffed hare, a fat capon, a leg of lamb with garlic, and four bottles of old burgundy."

Bazin, who gazed at his master and was quite unable to understand this change, let the omelette slide sadly into the spinach, and the spinach onto the floor.

"This is the moment for consecrating our existence to the King of Kings," said d'Artagnan, "if you insist on doing him a courtesy: *Non inutile desiderium in oblatione.*"

"Go to the devil with your Latin! My dear d'Artagnan, let's have a drink, morbleu, a cool drink, a big drink, and tell me a little of what's going on out there."

XXVII

The Wife of Athos

"It remains now to have news of Athos," d'Artagnan said to the high-spirited Aramis, when he had brought him up to date on what had gone on in the capital since their departure, and an excellent dinner had made the one forget his thesis and the other his fatigue.

"So you think something bad may have happened to him?" asked Aramis. "Athos is so coolheaded, so brave, and handles his sword so well."

"Yes, of course, and no one acknowledges his courage and skill more readily than I do, but I like the shock of lances on my sword better than the shock of sticks. I'm afraid Athos may have been trounced by the flunkeys. Valets are the sort that strike hard and don't quit early. That, I admit to you, is why I'd like set off again as soon as possible."

"I'll try to go with you," said Aramis, "though I hardly feel up to mounting a horse. Yesterday I tried out the discipline you see hanging on the wall there, and the pain kept me from continuing that pious exercise."

"Then again, my dear friend, no one has ever heard of curing the blow of a blunderbuss with the blows of a whip. But you were sick, and sickness weakens the head, so I excuse you for it."

"And when are you leaving?"

"Tomorrow at daybreak. Rest as well as you can tonight, and tomorrow, if you can, we'll leave together."

"Till tomorrow, then," said Aramis, "because, though you're made of iron, you must need some rest."

The next day, when d'Artagnan came into Aramis's room, he found him at his window.

"What are you looking at?" asked d'Artagnan.

"By heaven, I'm admiring those three magnificent horses that the stable boys are holding by the bridle. It would be a princely pleasure to travel on such mounts."

"Well, my dear Aramis, you shall give yourself that pleasure, for one of those horses is yours."

"Ah, really? Which one?"

"Whichever of the three you want: I have no preference."

"And the rich caparison that's covering him is mine as well?"

"Of course."

"You're joking, d'Artagnan."

"I haven't joked since you began speaking French."

"Those gilded holsters, that velvet housing, that silver-studded saddle are mine?"

"All yours, as the horse that's pawing the ground is mine, and the one that's prancing is Athos's."

"Damn! They're three superb beasts!"

"I'm flattered that they're to your taste."

"So it was the king who made you this gift?"

"It certainly wasn't the cardinal. But don't worry about where they came from, just think that one of the three belongs to you."

"I'll take the one the red-haired valet is holding."

"Excellent!"

"By God," cried Aramis, "there goes what's left of my pain! I could mount him with thirty bullets in my body. Ah, upon my soul, what handsome stirrups! Ho, there, Bazin! Come here this very instant!"

Bazin appeared, mournful and languishing, in the doorway.

"Polish my sword, straighten my hat, brush my cloak, and load my pistols!" said Aramis.

"That last order is unnecessary," d'Artagnan interrupted. "There are loaded pistols in your holsters."

Bazin sighed.

"Come, Master Bazin, calm yourself," said d'Artagnan, "the kindom of heaven can be gained in all conditions."

"Monsieur was already such a good theologian," Bazin said almost tearfully. "He would have become a bishop and maybe even a cardinal."

"Ah, well, my poor Bazin, come now, reflect a little. What's the use of being a churchman, I ask you? You don't get out of going to war for that. You see very well that the cardinal is going to make his first campaign with a pot on his head and a pike in his fist. And what do you say of M. de Nogaret de La Valette? He, too, is a cardinal. Ask his lackey how many times he's shredded linen for his wounds."

"Alas!" sighed Bazin, "I know, Monsieur, everything is turned upside down in the world today."

During this time, the two young men and the poor lackey had gone downstairs.

"Hold my stirrup, Bazin," said Aramis.

And Aramis leaped into the saddle with his usual grace and lightness; but once the noble animal had wheeled and bucked a few times, his rider felt such unbearable pain that he grew pale and tottered. D'Artagnan, who, foreseeing this eventuality, had not taken his eyes off him, rushed to him, caught him in his arms, and brought him back to his room.

"Never mind, my dear Aramis," he said, "look after yourself, and I'll go alone in search of Athos."

"You're a man of bronze," Aramis said to him.

"No, I'm lucky, that's all. But how are you going to live while you wait for me? No more thesis, no more commentaries on fingers and blessings, eh?"

Aramis smiled.

"I shall compose verses," he said.

"Yes, verses with the scent of that note from Mme de Chevreuse's maid. Teach Bazin prosody; it will console him. As for the horse, ride him a little every day, and that will get you accustomed to maneuvers."

"Oh, don't worry about that!" said Aramis. "You'll find me ready to follow you."

They said good-bye, and ten minutes later, after entrusting his friend to the care of Bazin and the hostess, d'Artagnan trotted off in the direction of Amiens.

How would he find Athos? And would he even find him?

The position he had left him in was critical; he might well have succumbed. That notion, which clouded his face, drew some sighs from him, and made him quietly utter oaths of vengeance. Of all his friends, Athos was the oldest, and hence the furthest from him, seemingly, in his tastes and sympathies.

And yet he had a marked preference for this gentleman. The noble and distinguished air of Athos, those flashes of greatness that shot now and then from the darkness in which he voluntarily enclosed himself, that unalterable evenness of temper which made him the most easygoing companion on earth, that forced and biting gaiety, that bravery which might have been called blind had it not been the result of the rarest coolheadedness—all these qualities drew more than esteem, more than friendship from d'Artagnan, they drew his admiration.

Indeed, even held up to M. de Tréville, the elegant and noble courtier, Athos, on days when he was in his best humor, could sustain the comparison advantageously. He was of average height, but that height was so admirably borne and so well proportioned that more than once, in his contests with Porthos, whose physical strength was proverbial among the musketeers, he had forced the giant to yield. His head, with its piercing eyes, its straight nose, its chin formed like that of Brutus, had an indefinable character of grandeur and grace. His hands, which he took no care of, were the despair of Aramis, who cultivated his with a great deal of almond butter and scented oil. The sound of his voice was at once penetrating and melodious. Then, too, what was indefinable in Athos, who always made himself obscure and small, was that delicate knowledge of the world and of the ways of the most brilliant society, that well-born habit which showed through without his knowing it in the least of his actions.

If it was a question of dinner, Athos arranged it better than anyone in the world, placing each guest in the place and rank that his ancestors had made for him or that he had made for himself. If it was a question of heraldry, Athos knew all the noble families of the realm, their genealogy, their alliances, their coats of arms, and the origin of their coats of arms. Etiquette had no minutiae that were foreign to him, he knew the rights of the great landowners, he had a thorough knowledge of hunting and falconry, and one day, while discussing this great art, he had astonished King Louis XIII himself, though he was a past master of it.

Like all the great lords of that time, he rode and wielded arms to perfection. More than that: his education had been so little neglected, even with regard to scholastic studies, so rare at that time among gentlemen, that he smiled at the tags of Latin Aramis came out with, and that Porthos looked as if he understood. Two or three times, to the great astonishment of his friends, when Aramis had made some rudimentary mistake, he had put the verb into the right tense or the noun into the right case. Moreover, his probity was unassailable, in that age when men of war compromised so easily with their religion and their conscience, lovers with the rigorous delicacy of our day, and the poor with the seventh commandment of God. Athos was, then, a highly extraordinary man.

And yet one saw so distinguished a nature, so handsome a creature, so fine an essence, sink insensibly into material life, as old men sink into physical and moral imbecility. In his times of privation, and they were frequent, the whole luminous part of Athos would be extinguished, and his brilliant side would disappear as if into a dark night.

Then, with the demigod vanished, there remained barely a man. Head hung down, eye dull, speech heavy and labored, Athos would stare for long hours either at his bottle and glass, or at Grimaud, who, accustomed to obeying by signs, read even the smallest wish in his master's lifeless gaze and fulfilled it at once. If the four friends happened to meet during one of those moments, a single word, produced with violent effort, was all the share Athos would contribute to the conversation. In exchange, Athos alone drank like four men, and that without showing it other than by a deeper scowl and a more profound sadness.

D'Artagnan, whose inquisitive and penetrating mind we know, had so far been unable, interested as he was in satisfying his curiosity on the subject, to assign any cause to this dejection, or to keep track of its occurrences. Athos never received letters; Athos never took any step that was not known to all his friends.

It could not be said that this sadness came from wine, for, on the contrary, he drank only to combat the sadness, which this remedy, as we have said, made gloomier still. This excess of black bile could not be attributed to gambling, for, contrary to Porthos, who accompanied all the variations of luck with his songs or curses, Athos remained as impassive when he won as when he lost. In the circle of musketeers, he had been seen to win three thousand pistoles in one evening, lose them down to his gold-embroidered belt for gala days, and win it all back, plus a hundred louis more, without raising or lowering his handsome black eyebrow by half a line, without his hands losing their pearly hue, without his conversation, which was pleasant that evening, ceasing to be pleasant and calm.

Nor was it, as with our English neighbors, an atmospheric influence that clouded his face, for this sadness generally became more intense towards the fine days of the year: June and July were the terrible months for Athos.

The present caused him no grief; he shrugged his shoulders when anyone spoke to him of the future; his secret was therefore in the past, as had been vaguely mentioned to d'Artagnan.

The mysterious taint that spread over his whole being made still more interesting this man whose eyes and lips, even in the most complete drunkenness, had never revealed anything, however skillful the questions that were put to him.

"Ah, well," thought d'Artagnan, "poor Athos may be dead right now, and it will be my fault, for it was I who dragged him into this affair, of which he did not know the origin, of which he will not know the outcome, and from which he could not profit in any way."

"Not to mention, Monsieur," Planchet replied, "that we probably owe him our lives. Remember how he shouted: 'Get away, d'Artagnan, it's a trap!' And after he fired his two pistols, what a terrible racket he made with his sword! You'd have thought it was twenty men, or rather twenty raging devils!"

These words redoubled d'Artagnan's fervor, and he urged on his horse, which, having no need of urging, carried his rider along at a gallop.

Towards eleven in the morning they caught sight of Amiens; at half-past eleven, they were at the gate of the cursed inn.

D'Artagnan had often meditated that sort of sweet revenge on the perfidious host that is consoling, if only in anticipation.

He thus entered the hostelry with his hat pulled down over his eyes, his left hand on the hilt of his sword, and his riding crop whistling in his right hand.

"Do you recognize me?" he said to the host, who came forward to greet him.

"I do not have that honor, Monseigneur," replied the latter, his eyes still more dazzled by the splendid state in which d'Artagnan presented himself.

"Ah, so you don't know me?"

"No, Monseigneur."

"Well, then, two words will restore your memory. What have you done with that gentleman against whom you had the audacity to bring an accusation of counterfeiting two weeks ago?"

The host paled, for d'Artagnan had taken the most threatening attitude, and Planchet had modeled himself on his master.

"Ah, Monseigneur, don't speak of him to me!" cried the host in his most tearful voice. "Ah, Lord, how I've paid for that mistake! Ah, wretch that I am!"

"I ask you, what has become of that gentleman?"

"Deign to listen to me, Monseigneur, and be merciful. Come, sit down, I beg you!"

D'Artagnan, mute with wrath and anxiety, sat down, threatening as a judge. Planchet leaned back proudly in his chair.

"Here is the story, Monseigneur," the host went on, all atremble, "for now I recognize you. It was you who left when I had that unfortunate dispute with the gentleman you speak of."

"Yes, it was I. So you see very well that you can expect no clemency if you do not tell the whole truth."

"Kindly listen to me then, and you will know all of it."

"I'm listening."

"I had been warned by the authorities that a notorious counterfeiter would be coming to my inn with several of his companions, all of them disguised as guards or musketeers. Your horses, your lackeys, your looks, my lords, had all been described to me."

"And then, and then?" said d'Artagnan, who quickly realized where so exact a description had come from.

"Following the orders of the authorities, who sent me a reinforcement of six men, I took such measures as I believed necessary to secure the persons of the presumed counterfeiters."

"Go on!" said d'Artagnan, whose ears burned terribly at the word "counterfeiters."

"Forgive me, Monseigneur, for saying such things, but they are precisely my excuse. The authorities had frightened me, and you know that an innkeeper must get along with the authorities."

"But, once again, where is this gentleman? What has become of him? Is he dead or alive?"

"Patience, Monseigneur, I'm coming to that. What happened then you know, and your precipitous departure," the host added, with a subtlety that was by no means lost on d'Artagnan, "seemed to authorize the outcome. This gentleman friend of yours defended himself desperately. His valet, who, by an unforeseen misfortune, had picked a quarrel with some agents of the authorities, who were disguised as stable boys . . ."

"Ah, you wretch!" cried d'Artagnan. "You were all in it together, and I don't know what keeps me from exterminating you all!"

"Alas, no, Monseigneur, we were not in it together, as you shall soon see. Monsieur your friend (forgive me for not calling him by the honorable name he undoubtedly bears, but I do not know that name), Monsieur your friend, after having put two men out of combat with two pistol shots, beat a retreat while defending himself with his sword, with which he disabled another of my men and knocked me out with a blow of the flat side."

"You torturer, will you never finish?" said d'Artagnan. "Athos, what became of Athos?"

"While beating a retreat, as I have told Monseigneur, he found behind him the stairway to the cellar, and as the door was open, he took the key with him and barricaded it from inside. Since we knew where to find him, we left him there."

"Yes," said d'Artagnan, "you didn't insist on killing him outright, you only wanted to imprison him."

"Good God! imprison him, Monseigneur? Why, he imprisoned himself, I swear to you. First of all, he had made a nice job of it: one man had been killed on the spot, and two others had been seriously wounded. The dead man and the two wounded ones were carried off by their comrades, and I haven't heard another word about any of them. As for me, when I came to my senses, I went to find the governor, told him everything that had happened, and asked what I should do with the prisoner. But the governor seemed to have dropped from the sky. He told me he had no idea what I was talking about, that the orders I had received had not come from him, and that if I was so unfortunate as to tell anyone that he had something to do with this brawl, he would have me hanged. It seems I was mistaken, Monsieur, that I had arrested the wrong man, and that the one who should have been arrested had escaped."

"But Athos?" cried d'Artagnan, whose impatience was doubled by the authorities' abandoning of the thing. "What has become of Athos?"

"As I was in haste to repair the wrongs I had done the prisoner," the innkeeper went on, "I headed for the cellar in order to set him free. Ah, Monsieur, this was no longer a man, this was a devil! To the proposal of freedom, he replied that it was a trap set for him, and that he intended to lay down his conditions before coming out. I told him quite humbly, for I did not conceal from myself the bad position I had put myself in by laying hands on one of His Majesty's musketeers, I told him that I was ready to submit to his conditions."

" 'First of all,' he said, 'I want my valet returned to me fully armed.'

"We hastened to obey this order; for you understand, Monsieur, that we were disposed to do everything your friend wanted. M. Grimaud (this one had given his name, though he didn't speak much), M. Grimaud was therefore sent down to the cellar, wounded as he was. Then his master, having received him, barricaded the door again, and ordered us to go about our business."

"But where is he, finally?" cried d'Artagnan. "Where is Athos?"

"In the cellar, Monsieur."

"What, you wretch, you've kept him in the cellar all this time?"

"Merciful heavens, no, Monsieur! We, keep him in the cellar! You don't know what he's doing there in the cellar! Ah, if you could only make him come out, Monsieur, I'd be grateful to you all my life, I'd worship you like my patron saint!"

"So he's there, I can find him there?"

"Of course, Monsieur, he has stubbornly remained there. Every day we pass him bread through the vent window, and meat when he asks for it. But, alas, his greatest consumption is not of bread and meat. Once I tried to go down with two of my servants, but he flew into a terrible rage. I heard the sound of him cocking his pistols and of his domestic cocking his musketoon. Then, when we asked them what their intentions were, the master replied that he and his lackey had forty shots between them, and that they would shoot to the last sooner than allow a single one of us to set foot in the cellar. After that, Monsieur, I went to complain to the governor, who replied that I had gotten what I deserved, and that that would teach me to insult honorable noblemen who take lodgings with me."

"Meaning that all this time . . ." d'Artagnan picked up, unable to keep from laughing at the pitiable face of his host.

"Meaning that all this time, Monsieur," the latter went on, "we've been leading the saddest life you ever could see. For you should know, Monsieur, that all our provisions are in the cellar. There is our wine in bottles and our wine in casks, our beer, oil and spices, lard and sausages; and as we're forbidden to go down, we're forced to deny food and drink to travelers who come to us, so that our hostelry suffers losses every day. Another week with your friend in my cellar, and we're ruined."

"And justly so, you rascal. Tell me, couldn't you see perfectly well by the look of us that we were men of quality and not forgers?"

"Yes, Monsieur, yes, you're right," said the host. "But wait, wait, there he goes again!"

"Someone must have disturbed him," said d'Artagnan.

"But we have to disturb him," cried the host. "Two English gentlemen have just come to us."

"Well?"

"Well, the English like good wine, as you know, Monsieur. These two have called for the best. My wife must have begged M. Athos's permission to enter in order to satisfy these gentlemen, and he must have refused as usual. Ah, good heavens, what a racket!"

D'Artagnan did indeed hear a great noise coming from the direction of the cellar. He stood up and, preceded by the host, who was wringing his hands, and followed by Planchet, who kept his musketoon at the ready, approached the scene of the action.

The two gentlemen were exasperated. They had made a long journey and were dying of hunger and thirst.

"But this is tyranny," they cried in very good French, though with a foreign accent, "that this mad fellow will not let these good people have use of their wine. We'll break down the door, and if he's in too much of a rage, well, then we'll kill him."

"Hold on, gentlemen!" said d'Artagnan, drawing his pistols from his belt. "You won't kill anybody, if you please."

"Good, good," said the calm voice of Athos behind the door, "let those eaters of little children come in, and we shall see."

Brave as they seemed to be, the two English gentlemen looked at each other hesitantly. One would have thought the cellar was home to one of those scraggy ogres, gigantic heroes of popular legend, whose cave no one could force with impunity.

There was a moment of silence; but in the end the two Englishmen were ashamed to retreat, and the more cantankerous of the two went down the five or six steps of the stairway and gave the door a kick that would have cracked a wall.

"Planchet," said d'Artagnan, cocking his pistols, "I'll take care of the one up here, you take care of the one down there. So you want a fight, gentlemen? Well, then, we'll give you one!"

"My God," cried the muffled voice of Athos, "I believe I hear d'Artagnan!"

"That's right," said d'Artagnan, raising his voice in turn, "it's I myself, my friend."

"Ah, very good!" said Athos. "So we'll give these door-smashers a working over!"

The gentlemen had drawn their swords, but found themselves caught in a cross fire. They hesitated another instant; but, as the first time, pride won out, and a second kick split the door from top to bottom.

"Take cover, d'Artagnan, take cover," cried Athos, "take cover, I'm going to shoot!"

"Gentlemen," said d'Artagnan, whose wits never deserted him, "gentlemen, think it over! Be patient, Athos. You're getting into a nasty business, and you'll wind up riddled with holes. Here are my lackey and I, who will fire off three shots at you, and you'll get as many from the cellar. Then we still have our swords, which, I assure you, my friend and I handle passably well. Let me settle your affairs and my own. You'll have something to drink shortly, I give you my word on it."

"If there's anything left," growled the mocking voice of Athos.

The landlord felt cold sweat trickling down his spine.

"What do you mean, anything left!" he murmured.

"There will be, devil take it!" d'Artagnan picked up. "Don't worry, the two of them couldn't have drunk the whole cellar. Gentlemen, sheathe your swords."

"Well, then you put your pistols in your belt."

"Gladly."

And d'Artagnan set the example. Then, turning to Planchet, he made him a sign to uncock his musketoon.

The Englishmen, convinced, grumblingly sheathed their swords. They were told the story of Athos's imprisonment. And as they were decent gentlemen, they held that the landlord was in the wrong.

"Now, gentlemen," said d'Artagnan, "go back up to your room, and in ten minutes I guarantee you will be brought everything you could desire."

The Englishmen bowed and left.

"Now that I'm alone, my dear Athos," said d'Artagnan, "I beg you to open the door."

"This very instant," said Athos.

Then came a great noise of clattering logs and groaning beams: these were Athos's counterscarps and bastions, which the besieged man demolished himself.

A moment later, the door swung open, and in the doorway appeared the pale face of Athos, who looked over the surroundings with a rapid glance.

D'Artagnan threw himself on his neck and embraced him tenderly. Then he was about to drag him out of those damp quarters, when he noticed that Athos was swaying.

"Are you wounded?" he asked.

"Me? Not in the least. I'm dead drunk, that's all, and never has a man done better at it. Good God, mine host, I must have drunk at least a hundred and fifty bottles on my own!"

"Mercy!" cried the host. "If the valet drank only half what the master did, I'm ruined."

"Grimaud is a well-born lackey, who would never allow himself the same fare as I. He drank only from the kegs. Wait, I think he forgot to turn off the spigot. You hear? It's running."

D'Artagnan let out a burst of laughter that turned the host's shivering into a hot fever.

At the same time, Grimaud appeared in turn behind his master, the musketoon on his shoulder, his head wagging, like the drunken satyrs in Rubens's paintings. He was soaked front and back in a thick liquid that the host recognized as his best olive oil.

The cortege crossed the main dining room and went to install itself in the best room of the inn, which d'Artagnan occupied on his own authority.

Meanwhile, the host and his wife rushed with lamps to the cellar, which had so long been forbidden them and where a frightful spectacle awaited them.

Beyond the fortifications Athos had breached in order to come out, which were made up of logs, planks, and empty barrels piled up according to all the rules of strategic art, the bones of all the eaten hams could be seen here and there, swimming in pools of oil and wine, while a heap of broken bottles filled the whole left corner of the cellar, and a cask, the tap of which had been left open, was losing through that opening the last few drops of its blood. The image of devastation and death, as the ancient poet says, reigned there as over a field of battle.

Of fifty sausages hung from the joists, hardly ten remained.

Then the howls of the host and hostess pierced the cellar's vault. D'Artagnan himself was moved. Athos did not even turn his head.

But grief gave way to rage. The host armed himself with a spit and, in his despair, rushed into the room to which the two friends had retired.

"Wine!" said Athos, on catching sight of the host.

"Wine?" cried the stupefied host. "Wine? But you've drunk more than a hundred pistoles's worth on me! I'm a ruined man, lost, destroyed!"

"Bah!" said Athos, "we're constantly going thirsty!"

"If you'd been content with drinking, that would be one thing; but you've broken all the bottles."

"You shoved me into a heap that came crashing down. It's your fault."

"All my oil is lost!"

"Oil is a sovereign balm for wounds, and poor Grimaud simply had to bandage the ones you gave him."

"All my sausages gobbled up!"

"There's an enormous number of rats in that cellar."

"You're going to pay me for it all!" cried the exasperated host.

"You triple rascal!" said Athos, getting up. But he fell back again at once; he had just used up the last of his strength. D'Artagnan came to his aid by raising his riding crop.

The host backed away and dissolved in tears.

"That will teach you," said d'Artagnan, "to treat the guests God sends you in a more courteous fashion."

"God? . . . you mean the devil!"

"My dear friend," said d'Artagnan, "if you go on making

such noise, the four of us will shut ourselves up in your cellar, and we'll see if the damage is really as great as you say."

"Very well, gentlemen," said the host, "I'm wrong, I admit it. But every sin deserves mercy. You are noblemen, and I'm a poor innkeeper, you should take pity on me."

"Ah, if you talk like that," said Athos, "you'll break my heart, and the tears will pour from my eyes the way the wine poured from your barrels. We're not such devils as we seem. Come here and we'll talk."

The host approached uneasily.

"Come, I say, and don't be afraid," Athos went on. "At the moment when I was going to pay you, I had put my purse on the table."

"Yes, Monseigneur."

"That purse contained sixty pistoles. Where is it?"

"Deposited with the city clerk, Monseigneur: it was said to be counterfeit money."

"Well, then, have my purse returned to me, and keep the sixty pistoles."

"But Monseigneur knows very well that the clerk never lets go of what he has taken. If it was counterfeit money, there would still be hope; but unfortunately the coins were good."

"Settle with him, my good man, it no longer concerns me, the more so as I haven't got a single livre left."

"Wait," said d'Artagnan, "where is Athos's old horse?"

"In the stable."

"How much is he worth?"

"Fifty pistoles at the most."

"He's worth eighty. Take him, and there's an end to it."

"What? You're selling my horse?" said Athos. "You're selling my Bajazet? And what will I go campaigning on—Grimaud?"

"I've brought you another," said d'Artagnan.

"Another?"

"And a magnificent one!" cried the host.

"Well, then, if there's another that's handsomer and younger, take the old one, and let's drink!"

"Which wine?" asked the host, thoroughly satisfied.

"The one that's in the back, near the laths. There are still twenty-five bottles left, all the others got broken in my fall. Bring up six."

"Why, he's a tun of a man!" the host said to himself. "If he'd stay just two weeks and pay for what he drinks, I'd be back in business!"

"And don't forget," d'Artagnan went on, "to bring up four bottles of the same for the two English gentlemen."

"Now, d'Artagnan," said Athos, "while we wait for them to bring us the wine, tell me what's become of the others."

D'Artagnan told him how he had found Porthos in bed with a sprain, and Aramis at a table between two theologians. As he was finishing, the host came back with the requested bottles and a ham which, fortunately for him, had not gone to the cellar.

"Very good," said Athos, filling his glass and d'Artagnan's. "Here's to Porthos and Aramis. But you, my friend, what's the matter with you, and what has happened to you personally? I find you have an ominous look."

"Alas!" said d'Artagnan, "it's that I'm the unhappiest of us all!"

"You unhappy, d'Artagnan?" said Athos. "Come, how are you unhappy? Tell me."

"Later," said d'Artagnan.

"Later? And why later? Because you think I'm drunk, d'Artagnan? Remember this well: my ideas are never clearer than when I'm in my cups. Speak, then, I'm all ears."

D'Artagnan recounted his adventure with Mme Bonacieux.

Athos listened without batting an eye. When he finished, he said:

"That's all trifles, mere trifles!"

This was Athos's word.

"You always say 'trifles!' my dear Athos," said d'Artagnan. "It doesn't suit you, who have never been in love."

Athos's dead eye suddenly lit up; but this was only a flash; then it became as dull and vague as before.

"That's true," he said calmly, "I have never been in love."

"So you see very well, you heart of stone," said d'Artagnan, "that you're wrong to be hard on those of us who are tender-hearted."

"Tenderhearted is brokenhearted," said Athos.

"What are you saying?"

"I'm saying that love is a lottery in which the one who wins, wins death! You're very lucky to have lost, believe me, my dear d'Artagnan. And if I have one piece of advice to give you, it's to go on losing."

"She seemed to love me so much!"

"She seemed to."

"Oh, she did love me!"

"Child! There's no man who hasn't believed, like you, that his mistress loved him, and there's no man whose mistress hasn't deceived him."

"Except you, Athos, who have never had one."

"That's true," said Athos, after a moment's silence, "I've never had one. Let's drink!"

"Well, then, philosopher that you are," said d'Artagnan, "teach me, support me, I need to learn and to be consoled."

"Consoled for what?"

"For my unhappiness."

"Your unhappiness is laughable," said Athos, shrugging his shoulders. "I'd be curious to know what you'd say if I told you a love story."

"That happened to you?"

"Or to a friend of mine, what matter!"

"Tell me, Athos, tell me."

"Let's drink, it will be better."

"Drink and tell."

"In fact, that can be done," said Athos, emptying his glass and filling it again. "The two go perfectly together."

"I'm listening," said d'Artagnan.

Athos collected himself, and, as he collected himself, d'Artagnan saw him turn pale. He had reached that stage of drunkenness when vulgar drinkers fall down and sleep. He, however, dreamed aloud without sleeping. This drunken somnambulism had something frightening about it.

"You absolutely insist on it?" he asked.

"I beg you," said d'Artagnan.

"Let it be as you wish, then. A friend of mine—not I, but a friend of mine, you understand!" said Athos, interrupting himself with a sombre smile, "one of the counts of my province, that is, of Berry, as noble as a Dandolo or a Montmorency, fell in love at twenty-five with a girl of sixteen, as beautiful as love itself. An ardent mind showed through the naïveté of her age, the mind not of a woman but of a poet—she did not please, she intoxicated. She lived in a little village with her brother, who was a curate. The two were newly arrived in the area. Where they came from no one knew, but seeing her so beautiful and her brother so pious, no one thought of asking where they came from. Besides, they were said to be of good extraction. My friend, who was the lord of the place, might have seduced her or taken her by force if he liked: he was the master; who would have come to the aid of two strangers, two unknown people? Unfortunately, he was an honest man: he married her. The fool, the simpleton, the imbecile!"

"But why so, if he loved her?" asked d'Artagnan.

"Wait a moment," said Athos. "He brought her to his château and made her the first lady of his province. And, one must do her justice, she filled her rank perfectly."

"Well, then?"

"Well, then, one day when she was hunting with her husband," Athos went on in a low voice and speaking very quickly, "she fell from her horse and fainted. The count rushed to her aid, and, as she was suffocating in her clothes, he cut them open with his dagger and bared her shoulder. Guess what she had on her shoulder, d'Artagnan?" said Athos, with a loud burst of laughter.

"How should I know?" asked d'Artagnan.

"A fleur-de-lis," said Athos. "She was branded!"

And Athos emptied the glass he was holding at one draft.

"Horrible!" cried d'Artagnan. "What are you telling me?"

"The truth. My dear, the angel was a demon. The poor girl had been a thief."

"And what did the count do?"

"The count was a great lord, he had the right to render low

and high justice on his lands: he finished tearing off the count-ess's clothes, tied her hands behind her back, and hanged her from a tree."

"Good heavens, Athos, a murder!" cried d'Artagnan.

"Yes, a murder, no more nor less," said Athos, pale as death. "But I'm left without wine, it seems."

And Athos seized the last remaining bottle by the neck and emptied it at one draft, as he would have done an ordinary glass.

Then he let his head drop in both hands. D'Artagnan sat staring at him, stricken with horror.

"That cured me of beautiful, poetic, and loving women," said Athos, straightening up and not thinking of maintaining his fable about the count. "God grant you as much! Let's drink!"

"So she's dead?" stammered d'Artagnan.

"Parbleu!" said Athos. "But reach me your glass. Ham, you rascal," cried Athos, "we can't drink any more!"

"And her brother?" d'Artagnan added timidly.

"Her brother?" Athos picked up.

"Yes, the priest."

"Ah! I made inquiries about him in order to hang him, too, but he had anticipated me; he had quit his parish the evening before."

"Did anyone at least find out who the wretch was?"

"He was no doubt the beauty's first lover and accomplice, a worthy man, who may have pretended to be a priest in order to marry off his mistress and assure her future. He must have been drawn and quartered, or so I hope."

"Oh, my God, my God!" said d'Artagnan, stunned by this horrible adventure.

"Have some of this ham, d'Artagnan, it's exquisite," said Athos, cutting a slice, which he put on the young man's plate. "Too bad there weren't four like that in the cellar. I'd have drunk fifty bottles more!"

D'Artagnan could no longer bear this conversation; it would have driven him mad. He let his head drop in both hands and pretended to sleep.

"Young people don't know how to drink anymore," said Athos, looking at him with pity, "and yet he's one of the best! . . ."

XXVIII

THE RETURN

D'Artagnan was left stunned by Athos's terrible secret. However, many things still seemed obscure to him in this half revelation. First of all, it had been made by a man totally drunk to a man who was half so, and yet, despite the vagueness that rises to the brain from the vapors of two or three bottles of burgundy, d'Artagnan, on waking up the next morning, had Athos's every word as present to his mind as if they had been imprinted there just as they had fallen from his mouth. All this doubt only gave him a more intense desire to reach some certainty, and he went to his friend with the firm intention of renewing the evening's conversation; but he found Athos completely sober again—that is, the most subtle and impenetrable of men.

Moreover, after shaking hands with him, the musketeer anticipated his thoughts.

"I was rather drunk yesterday, my dear d'Artagnan," he said. "I felt it this morning in my tongue, which was still quite thick, and in my pulse, which was still quite agitated. I'll bet I came out with a thousand extravagances."

And in saying these words, he looked at his friend with a fixity that embarrassed him.

"Why, not at all," replied d'Artagnan. "If I remember rightly, you said nothing out of the ordinary."

"Ah, you astonish me! I thought I'd told you a most lamentable story."

And he looked at the young man as if he wanted to read to the very depths of his heart.

"By heaven," said d'Artagnan, "it seems I was drunker than you were, since I don't remember anything!"

Athos was not taken in by these words, and went on:

"You have not failed to notice, my dear friend, that each of us has his own sort of drunkenness, sad or gay. As for me, I have a sad drunkenness, and once I'm tipsy, my mania is to tell all sorts of lugubrious stories that my fool of a nurse stuffed into my brain. I have that failing—a capital failing, I agree—but apart from that, I'm an excellent drinker."

Athos said all this in such a natural way that d'Artagnan was shaken in his conviction.

"Oh, so that's it," the young man went on, trying to recover his grip on the truth, "so that's what I remember, though only as one remembers in a dream—we spoke about hanged men."

"Ah, there, you see," said Athos, turning pale and yet trying to laugh, "I was sure of it, hanged men are my personal nightmare."

"Yes, yes," d'Artagnan picked up, "now the memory is coming back to me: yes, it had to do . . . wait a minute . . . it had to do with a woman."

"You see," replied Athos, becoming almost livid, "it's my great story of the blond woman, and when I tell it, it means I'm dead drunk."

"Yes, that's it," said d'Artagnan, "the story of the blond woman, tall and beautiful, with blue eyes."

"Yes, and hanged."

"By her husband, who was a lord of your acquaintance," d'Artagnan went on, looking fixedly at Athos.

"Well, just see how you can compromise a man when you no longer know what you're saying," said Athos, shrugging his shoulders, as if he felt pity for himself. "Decidedly, I shall not get tipsy any more, d'Artagnan, it's too bad a habit."

D'Artagnan kept silent.

Then, abruptly changing the conversation, Athos said: "By the way, thank you for the horse you brought me."

"Is he to your taste?" asked d'Artagnan.

"Yes, but he was never a workhorse."

"You're mistaken. I did ten leagues with him in less than an hour and a half, and he looked as if he'd just made a turn around the place Saint-Sulpice."

"Ah, you're going to give me regrets."

"Regrets?"

"Yes, I got rid of him."

"How so?"

"Here's how it was: I woke up this morning at six o'clock. You were still sound asleep, and I didn't know what to do. I was still besotted with our debauch last night. I went down to the main dining room and caught sight of one of our Englishmen, who was bargaining with a horse dealer for a horse, his own having died yesterday of a stroke. I went over to him, and as I saw he was offering a hundred pistoles for a sorrel, I said to him:

" 'By God, my good sir, I also have a horse for sale.'

" 'And a very fine one at that,' he said, "I saw it yesterday, your friend's valet was holding it.'

" 'Do you find him worth a hundred pistoles?'

" 'Yes. And would you let me have him for that price?'

" 'No, but I'll play you for him.'

" 'Play me for him?'

" 'Yes.'

" 'At what?'

" 'At dice.'

"No sooner said than done, and I lost the horse. Ah, but to make up for it," Athos went on, "I won back the caparison!"

D'Artagnan made a rather glum face.

"Does that upset you?" asked Athos.

"Why, yes, I confess it does," replied d'Artagnan. "That horse was to make us recognizable one day in battle. It was a pledge, a souvenir. You did wrong, Athos."

"Eh, my dear friend, put yourself in my place!" the musketeer picked up. "I was dying of boredom. And then, on my honor, I don't like English horses. Look, if it's just a matter of being known by someone, well, then the saddle will do by itself—it's quite remarkable. As for the horse, we'll find some excuse for his disappearance. Devil take it, horses are mortal! Suppose mine got the glanders or the farcy."

D'Artagnan did not brighten up.

"It upsets me," Athos went on, "that you seem so attached to these animals, for I haven't reached the end of my story."

"What more have you done?"

"After losing my horse—nine to six, that was the throw—I had the idea of staking yours."

"Yes, but you confined yourself to the idea, I hope?"

"No, I put it into execution that very moment."

"Ah, don't tell me!" d'Artagnan cried anxiously.

"I staked him and lost."

"My horse?"

"Your horse; seven to eight; for want of a point . . . You know the proverb."

"Athos, you're out of your mind, I swear to you!"

"My dear, you should have told me that yesterday, when I was telling you my stupid stories, and not this morning. So I lost him with all possible equipment and harness."

"But that's awful!"

"Wait, you haven't heard everything yet. I'd make an excellent gambler, if I didn't get carried away; but I do get carried away, just as when I drink. So I got carried away . . ."

"But what could you stake? You had nothing left!"

"I did, I did, my friend. We still had that diamond sparkling on your finger. I had noticed it yesterday."

"This diamond!" cried d'Artagnan, quickly putting his hand to the ring.

"And as I'm a connoisseur, having had several of my own, I had estimated it at a thousand pistoles."

"I hope," d'Artagnan said seriously, half dead with fright, "that you made no mention of my diamond?"

"On the contrary, my dear friend. You understand, this diamond became our only resource. With it I could win back our harness and our horses, and, what's more, enough money for the road."

"Athos, you make me tremble!" cried d'Artagnan.

"So I mentioned your diamond to my partner, who had also noticed it. Devil take it anyhow, my dear, you wear a star from heaven on your finger, and you don't want anybody to pay attention to it! Impossible!"

"Finish, my dear, finish!" said d'Artagnan, "for, on my honor, your coolheadedness is killing me!"

"So we divided the diamond into ten parts of a hundred pistoles each."

"Ah, you're joking in order to test me!" said d'Artagnan, whom wrath was beginning to seize by the hair as Minerva seized Achilles in the *Iliad*.

"No, I'm not joking, mordieu! I'd like to have seen you in my place! It was two weeks since I'd laid eyes on a human face and was there besotting myself in converse with bottles."

"That's no reason to go staking my diamond," replied d'Artagnan, clenching his fist with a nervous spasm.

"Hear how it ended, then. Ten parts of a hundred pistoles each, in ten throws, with no revenge. In thirteen throws I lost everything. Thirteen throws! The number thirteen has always been fatal for me; it was on the thirteenth of July that . . ."

"Ventrebleu!" cried d'Artagnan, getting up from the table, the day's story making him forget that of the night before.

"Patience," said Athos, "I had a plan. The Englishman's an original, I'd seen him talking with Grimaud in the morning, and Grimaud informed me that he had made him proposals of entering into his service. I stake Grimaud with him, the silent Grimaud, divided into ten portions."

"A master stroke!" cried d'Artagnan, bursting into laughter in spite of himself.

"Grimaud himself, you understand! And with the ten parts of Grimaud, which aren't worth a ducaton in all, I win back the diamond. Tell me now if persistence isn't a virtue."

"By heaven, this is very funny!" cried the consoled d'Artagnan, holding his sides with laughter.

"You understand that, feeling myself in luck, I immediately began staking on the diamond."

"Ah, devil take it!" said d'Artagnan, turning gloomy again.

"I won back your harness, then your horse, then my harness, then my horse, then lost again. In short, I recovered your harness, then mine. That's where we're at. It was a superb throw, so I stopped there."

D'Artagnan gasped as if the entire hostelry had been lifted off his chest.

"So I still have my diamond?" he asked timidly.

"Intact, my dear friend! Plus the harnesses of your Bucephalus and mine."

"But what good are our harnesses without horses?"

"I have an idea for them."

"Athos, you make me tremble."

"Listen, you haven't gambled for a long time, have you, d'Artagnan?"

"And I have no desire to gamble."

"Don't swear to it. You haven't gambled for a long time, I said, so you should have a lucky hand."

"Well, what then?"

"Well, the Englishman and his companion are still here. I noticed that they felt very sorry about the harnesses. You seem to be keen on your horse. In your place, I'd stake your harness against your horse."

"But he won't want just one harness."

"Stake them both, pardieu! I'm no egotist like you."

"You'd do that?" asked d'Artagnan, hesitating. Athos's confidence was beginning to win him over without his knowing it.

"Word of honor, on a single throw."

"But since we've lost the horses, I had great hopes of keeping the harnesses."

"Stake your diamond, then."

"Oh, that's something else again! Never, never!"

"Devil take it," said Athos, "I'd gladly propose that you stake Planchet, but as it's already been done, the Englishman might not want any more of it."

"Decidedly, my dear Athos," said d'Artagnan, "I'd much rather risk nothing."

"Too bad," Athos said coldly, "the Englishman's stuffed with pistoles. Ah, my God, try one throw, one throw takes no time!"

"And what if I lose?"

"You'll win."

"But if I lose?"

"Well, then you'll give up the harnesses."

"It's worth a try," said d'Artagnan.

Athos went in search of the Englishman and found him in the stable, where he was studying the harnesses with a lustful eye. It was a good opportunity. He laid down his conditions: the two harnesses against the choice of a horse or a hundred pistoles. The Englishman made a quick calculation: the two harnesses were worth three hundred pistoles together. He went along.

D'Artagnan threw the dice all atremble and rolled a three; his paleness frightened Athos, who contented himself with saying:

"That was a sorry throw, friend. You'll have your horses all harnessed, Monsieur."

The triumphant Englishman did not even bother to shake the dice; he threw them on the table without looking, so sure he was of victory. D'Artagnan had turned away to hide his ill humor.

"Well, well, well," said Athos in his calm voice, "that's an extraordinary throw of the dice. I've seen it just four times in my life: two aces!"

The Englishman looked and was overcome with astonishment. D'Artagnan looked and was overcome with delight.

"Yes," Athos went on, "only four times: once at M. de Créquy's; another time at home in the country, in my château of . . . when I had a château; a third time at M. de Tréville's, where it surprised us all; and finally a fourth time in a tavern, where it fell to me, and I lost a hundred louis and a supper on it."

"So Monsieur is taking back his horse?" said the Englishman.

"To be sure," said d'Artagnan.

"So there's to be no revenge?"

"Our conditions stipulated no revenge, don't you remember?"

"That's true. The horse will be turned over to your valet, Monsieur."

"One moment," said Athos. "With your permission, Monsieur, I ask to have a word with my friend."

"Go on."

Athos drew d'Artagnan aside.

"Well," d'Artagnan said to him, "what more do you want of me, tempter? You want me to keep playing, is that it?"

"No, I want you to reflect."

"On what?"

"You're going to take back your horse, aren't you?"

"Certainly."

"You're wrong. I'd take the hundred pistoles. You know you staked the harnesses against your choice of the horse or a hundred pistoles."

"Yes."

"I'd take the hundred pistoles."

"Well, I'm taking the horse."

"And I repeat that you're wrong. What will we do with one horse for the two of us? I can't ride on the croup; we'll look like two sons of Aymon who have lost their brothers. You can't humiliate me by riding alongside me mounted on that magnificent steed. I wouldn't waver for an instant, I'd take the hundred pistoles, we need money to get back to Paris."

"I'm keen on that horse, Athos."

"And you're quite wrong, my friend. A horse will shy, a horse will stumble and break its knees, a horse will eat from a rack that a glandered horse has eaten from—and there goes your horse, or rather your hundred pistoles. The master has to feed his horse, whereas a hundred pistoles will feed their master."

"But how will we get back?"

"On our lackeys' horses, pardieu! It will always be clear from the look of our faces that we're people of quality."

"What a fine sight we'll be on those nags, while Aramis and Porthos go prancing along on their horses!"

"Aramis! Porthos!" cried Athos, and he started to laugh.

"What?" asked d'Artagnan, who did not understand his friend's hilarity.

"Never mind, never mind, let's go on," said Athos.

"So, your advice is? . . ."

"To take the hundred pistoles, d'Artagnan. With the hundred pistoles, we'll feast till the end of the month. We've suffered hardships, you see, and it will be good if we rest a bit."

"Me, rest? Ah, no, Athos, as soon as I'm in Paris, I'll set about searching for that poor woman!"

"Well, then, do you think your horse will be as much use to you in that as some good louis d'or? Take the hundred pistoles, my friend, take the hundred pistoles."

D'Artagnan needed only one reason to give in. This one seemed excellent to him. Besides, he was afraid that if he held out any longer, he would seem egotistical in Athos's eyes. So he acquiesced and took the hundred pistoles, which the Englishman counted out on the spot.

Then the only thought was of leaving. The peace treaty signed with the innkeeper cost six pistoles, over and above Athos's old horse. D'Artagnan and Athos took the horses of Planchet and Grimaud, and the two valets set out on foot, carrying the saddles on their heads.

Poorly mounted as the two friends were, they soon got ahead of their valets and arrived at Crèvecoeur. From afar they caught sight of Aramis leaning melancholically on his windowsill and, like "my sister Anne," watching the horizon dust up.

"Ho, hey, Aramis! What the devil are you doing there?" cried the two friends.

"Ah, it's you, d'Artagnan, it's you, Athos!" said the young man. "I was thinking how quickly the good things of this world pass, and my English horse, which is riding off and has just disappeared in a swirling cloud of dust, was a living image for me of the fragility of earthly things. Life itself can be summed up in three words: *Erat, est, fuit.*" *

"Which means at bottom?" asked d'Artagnan, who was beginning to suspect the truth.

"Which means that I've just made a fool's bargain: sixty louis for a horse which, by the way it moves, could make five leagues an hour at a trot."

* "It will be, it is, it was."

D'Artagnan and Athos burst out laughing.

"My dear d'Artagnan," said Aramis, "don't hold it too much against me, I beg you. Necessity knows no law; and besides, I'm the first to be punished, since that infamous horse dealer robbed me of at least fifty louis. Ah, the rest of you are good managers, you come on your lackeys' horses, and have your deluxe horses led by hand, slowly and in short stages."

Just then a wagon, which for several minutes had been looming up on the road from Amiens, came to a halt, and Grimaud and Planchet could be seen getting out with their saddles on their heads. The wagon was returning empty to Paris, and in exchange for their transportation, the two lackeys had promised to quench the wagoner's thirst on the way.

"What's this?" asked Aramis, seeing what was happening. "Nothing but saddles?"

"Now you understand?" asked Athos.

"My friends, it's just like me. I kept the harness, by instinct. Ho, there, Bazin! Bring my new harness here alongside these others."

"And what have you done with your curates?" asked d'Artagnan.

"My dear, I invited them to dinner the next day," said Aramis. "They have exquisite wine here, incidentally. I got them as tipsy as I could. Then the curate forbade me to quit the tabard, and the Jesuit begged me to get him into the musketeers."

"Without a thesis!" cried d'Artagnan. "Without a thesis! I demand the suppression of the thesis!"

"Since then," Aramis went on, "I've been living quite pleasantly. I began a poem in lines of one syllable. It's rather difficult, but the merit of all things lies in their difficulty. The subject matter is gallant. I'll read you the first canto; it's four hundred verses long and takes one minute."

"By heaven, my dear Aramis," said d'Artagnan, who detested verse almost as much as Latin, "add the merit of brevity to the merit of difficulty, and you'll be sure your poem has at least two merits."

"Then, too," Aramis went on, "it breathes of honest passions, you'll see. Ah, my friends, so we're returning to Paris? Bravo, I'm ready. We shall see the good Porthos again, so much the better. You don't believe I missed that great ninny? He's not one to have sold his horse, not even for a kingdom. I wish I could see him now, astride his beast and in his saddle. I'm sure he'd look like the Great Mogul."

They made a halt for an hour to give the horses a breather. Aramis settled his account, put Bazin in the wagon with his comrades, and they set out to find Porthos.

They found him on his feet, less pale than d'Artagnan had seen him on his first visit, and seated at a table where, though he was alone, a dinner for four had been laid. This dinner consisted of gallantly trussed meats, choice wines, and superb fruits.

"Ah, pardieu!" he said, getting up, "you've come at the perfect time, gentlemen, I'd just gotten to the soup! You shall dine with me."

"Oho!" said d'Artagnan. "Mousqueton never caught such bottles with his lasso, and here's a larded fricandeau, and a fillet of beef . . ."

"I'm recuperating," said Porthos, "I'm recuperating. Nothing weakens a man like these devilish sprains. Have you ever had a sprain, Athos?"

"Never. Only I remember that, during our scuffle in the rue Férou, I received a sword stroke which, after two weeks or so, produced exactly the same effect."

"But this dinner wasn't for you alone, my dear Porthos?" said Aramis.

"No," said Porthos. "I was expecting some local gentlemen, who just sent me word that they're not coming. You will replace them, and I'll lose nothing in the exchange. Ho, there, Mousqueton! Chairs! And double the bottles!"

"Do you know what we're eating here?" asked Athos, after ten minutes.

"Pardieu!" replied d'Artagnan, "I'm eating veal larded with cardoons and marrow."

"And I'm eating fillets of lamb," said Porthos.

"And I'm eating breast of chicken," said Aramis.

"You're all mistaken, gentlemen," replied Athos. "You are eating horse."

"Come, now!" said d'Artagnan.

"Horse!" cried Aramis with a disgusted grimace.

Porthos alone said nothing.

"Yes, horse. Isn't it true, Porthos, that we're eating horse? Maybe even with the caparisons!"

"No, gentlemen, I kept the harness," said Porthos.

"By heaven, we're all the same," said Aramis. "You'd think we passed the word around."

"What do you want," said Porthos, "that horse put my visitors to shame, and I didn't want to humiliate them!"

"Then, too, your duchess is still at the waters, isn't she?" d'Artagnan picked up.

"Still," replied Porthos. "Now, by heaven, the governor of the province, one of the gentlemen I was expecting today at dinner, seemed to me to have so strong a desire for the horse that I gave it to him."

"Gave?" cried d'Artagnan.

"Oh, my God, yes, gave! That's the word," said Porthos, "for he was certainly worth a hundred and fifty louis, and the tightwad would only pay me eighty."

"Without the saddle?" asked Aramis.

"Yes, without the saddle."

"You'll notice, gentlemen," said Athos, "that Porthos has once again made the best deal of us all."

Then there was a loud burst of laughter, which left poor Porthos quite stricken; but they soon explained the reason for this hilarity to him, and he noisily joined in it, as was his custom.

"So we're all in funds?" asked d'Artagnan.

"Not for my part," said Athos. "I found Aramis's Spanish wine so good that I had sixty bottles loaded into the lackeys' wagon, which has left me rather out of pocket."

"And I," said Aramis, "just imagine, I had given all but my last sou to the church of Montdidier and the Jesuits of Amiens. I had also made promises that I had to keep, masses ordered for myself and for you, gentlemen, which will be said, gentlemen, and from which I don't doubt we shall benefit wonderfully."

"And I," said Porthos, "do you think my sprain cost me nothing? Not to mention Mousqueton's wound, for which I was obliged to have the surgeon come twice a day, who made me pay double for his visits on the pretext that that imbecile Mousqueton had managed to get a bullet in a place not ordinarily shown to apothecaries. I've strongly advised him not to get wounded there any more."

"Well, well," said Athos, exchanging smiles with d'Artagnan and Aramis, "I see you've behaved grandly towards the poor lad: that's a good master for you."

"In short," Porthos went on, "with my expenses paid, I'll be left with a good thirty écus."

"And I've got a dozen pistoles," said Aramis.

"Well, well," said Athos, "it seems we're the Croesuses of society. How much have you got left of your hundred pistoles, d'Artagnan?"

"Of my hundred pistoles? First of all, I gave you fifty."

"You think so?"

"Pardieu!"

"Ah, that's true, I remember!"

"Then, I paid six to the host."

"What an animal that host is! Why did you give him six pistoles?"

"You told me to."

"It's true that I'm too good. In short, the balance?"

"Twenty-five pistoles," said d'Artagnan.

"And I," said Athos, pulling some small change from his pocket, "I . . ."

"You, nothing."

"By heaven, or so little it's not worth adding to the heap. Now, let's reckon up how much we have in all. Porthos?"

"Thirty écus."

"Aramis?"

"Ten pistoles."

"And you, d'Artagnan?"

"Twenty-five."

"Which makes in all?" asked Athos.

"Four hundred and sixty-five livres!" said d'Artagnan, who could calculate like Archimedes.

"When we get to Paris, we'll still have a good four hundred," said Porthos, "plus the harnesses."

"But our squadron horses?" said Aramis.

"Well, out of four lackeys' horses we can make two for masters, which we'll draw lots for. With the four hundred livres, we can make a half for one of the dismounted, then we can give the scourings of our pockets to d'Artagnan, who has a lucky hand, and who will go and stake them in the first gambling den he comes to, and there you are!"

"Let's dine," said Porthos, "it's getting cold."

The four friends, more at ease now about their future, did honor to the meal, the leftovers of which went to MM. Mousqueton, Bazin, Planchet, and Grimaud.

On reaching Paris, d'Artagnan found a letter from M. de Tréville informing him that, at his request, the king had just granted him the favor of joining the musketeers.

As that was d'Artagnan's only ambition in the world—except, of course, for the desire to find Mme Bonacieux again—he rushed all joyfully to his comrades, whom he had just left half an hour ago, and whom he found extremely sad and preoccupied. They had met in council at Athos's place, which always indicated a certain gravity in the circumstances.

M. de Tréville had just informed them that, it being His Majesty's firm intention to open the campaign on the first of May, they must prepare their outfits at once.

The four philosophers gazed dumbfounded at each other: M. de Tréville never joked in matters of discipline.

"And how much do you estimate these outfits will cost?" asked d'Artagnan.

"Oh, there's no two words about it," replied Aramis. "We've just made our calculations with a Spartan stinginess, and we'll need fifteen hundred livres each."

"Four times fifteen is sixty; that makes six thousand livres," said Athos.

"It seems to me," said d'Artagnan, "that with a thousand

livres each—true, I'm speaking not as a Spartan but as a procureur . . ."

The word "procureur" woke Porthos up.

"Wait, I've got an idea!" he said.

"That's already something: I haven't got even the shadow
of one," Athos said coldly, "but as for d'Artagnan, gentlemen,
the happiness of being one of us now has driven him mad—a
thousand livres! I declare that I need two thousand for myself
alone."

"Four times two is eight," Aramis then said, "so it's eight
thousand livres that we need for our outfits—of which outfits,
it's true, we already have the saddles."

"Plus," said Athos, waiting until d'Artagnan, who was going to thank M. de Tréville, had closed the door, "plus that fine
diamond sparkling on our friend's hand. Devil take it, d'Artagnan is too good a comrade to leave his brothers in a tight spot
when he's wearing a king's ransom on his middle finger!"

XXIX

The Chase After Outfits

The most preoccupied of the four friends was certainly
d'Artagnan, though d'Artagnan, in his quality as a guard, was
much easier to outfit than the gentlemen musketeers, who were
noblemen. But our cadet from Gascony, as we have been able
to see, was of a provident and almost miserly character, and
with that (try explaining contraries) almost vainglorious
enough to give points to Porthos. To this preoccupation of his
vanity, d'Artagnan joined at that moment a less egotistical
anxiety. The few inquiries he had been able to make about
Mme Bonacieux had brought him no news. M. de Tréville had
spoken of her to the queen; the queen did not know where the
mercer's young wife was and promised to have a search made
for her. But this promise was quite vague and hardly reassured
d'Artagnan.

Athos did not leave his room. He was determined not to
venture a single step to outfit himself.

"We still have fifteen days," he said to his friends. "Well, then, if I've found nothing at the end of those fifteen days, or rather if nothing has come to find me, since I'm too good a Catholic to blow my brains out with a pistol, I'll pick a nice quarrel with four of His Eminence's guards or eight Englishmen, and fight till one of them kills me, which, quantitatively speaking, cannot fail to happen. It will then be said that I died for the king, so that I'll have done my service without needing to outfit myself."

Porthos went on pacing, his hands behind his back, tossing his head and saying:

"I'll pursue my idea."

Aramis, worried and poorly curled, said nothing.

It can be seen from these disastrous details that desolation reigned in the community.

The lackeys, for their part, like the steeds of Hippolytus, shared the sorry plight of their masters. Mousqueton laid in a supply of crusts; Bazin, who had always been given to devotion, no longer left church; Planchet watched the flies flying; and Grimaud, whom the general distress could not induce to break the silence imposed by his master, heaved sighs that would have moved the hearts of stones.

The three friends—for, as we have said, Athos had sworn not to make a step to outfit himself—the three friends thus left early in the morning and came back late at night. They wandered through the streets, examining each paving stone to see if those who had passed there before them had not dropped some purse. One would have thought they were following trails, so attentive they were wherever they went. When they met, their desolate looks as much as said: "Have you found anything?"

However, as Porthos had been the first to find his idea, and as he had pursued it with persistence, he was the first to act. This worthy Porthos was a man of deeds. D'Artagnan caught sight of him one day heading for the church of Saint-Leu, and followed him instinctively. He went into the holy place after turning up his mustaches and stroking his imperial, which with him always signaled the boldest intentions. As d'Artagnan took some precautions to conceal himself, Porthos believed he had not been seen. D'Artagnan entered after him. Porthos went and leaned against the side of a pillar; d'Artagnan, still unseen, leaned on the other side.

A sermon was just being delivered, which meant that the church was filled with people. Porthos profited from this circumstance to ogle the ladies. Thanks to Mousqueton's good care, the exterior was far from betraying the distress of the interior; his hat was indeed a bit worn, his plume a bit faded, his embroideries a bit dull, his lace a bit frayed; but in the semidarkness all these trifles disappeared, and Porthos was still the handsome Porthos.

D'Artagnan noticed, on the bench closest to the pillar against which he and Porthos were leaning, a sort of ripe beauty, a bit yellow, a bit dry, but erect and haughty under her black lace mantilla. Porthos's eyes dropped furtively to this lady, then fluttered off through the nave of the church.

For her part, the lady, who blushed from time to time, cast a lightning quick glance at the fickle Porthos, and Porthos's eyes at once began fluttering away furiously. It was clear that this was a stratagem that stung the lady in the black mantilla to the quick, for she bit her lips till they bled, scratched the tip of her nose, and fidgeted desperately on her seat.

Seeing which, Porthos turned up his mustaches again, stroked his imperial a second time, and began making signs to a beautiful lady who was near the choir, and who was not only a beautiful lady, but also no doubt a grand lady, for behind her stood a little black boy who had brought her the cushion she was kneeling on, and a maid who was carrying an emblazoned bag that held the book from which she read her mass.

The lady in the black mantilla followed Porthos's glance through all its meanderings, and noticed that it had settled on the lady with the velvet cushion, the little black boy, and the maid.

Meanwhile, Porthos was playing a close game: one of winks of the eye, of fingers to the lips, of killing little smiles that really killed the scorned beauty.

And so, as a form of mea culpa, and beating her breast, she

sighed with such a vigorous "Hum!" that everyone, even the lady with the red cushion, turned to her. But Porthos held firm: though he had understood perfectly well, he played deaf.

The lady with the red cushion made a great effect, for she was extremely beautiful, on the lady with the black mantilla, who saw in her a rival truly to be feared; a great effect on Porthos, who found her prettier than the lady in the black mantilla; a great effect on d'Artagnan, who recognized her as the lady from Meung, Calais, and Dover, whom his persecutor, the man with the scar, had greeted with the name of Milady.

Without losing sight of the lady with the red cushion, d'Artagnan went on following Porthos's strategem, which amused him greatly. He guessed that the lady in the black mantilla was the procureuse of the rue aux Ours, the more easily as the church of Saint-Leu was not far from the said street.

He then guessed by induction that Porthos was seeking to take revenge for his defeat in Chantilly, when the procureuse had proved so recalcitrant in regard to her purse.

But in the midst of all that, d'Artagnan also noticed that not one face responded to Porthos's gallantries. It was all fantasy and illusion; but for a real love, for a veritable jealousy, is there any other reality than illusion and fantasy?

The sermon came to an end. The procureuse went towards the basin of holy water; Porthos got there ahead of her, and, instead of a finger, put his whole hand into it. The procureuse smiled, thinking that he had gone to that expense for her, but she was promptly and cruelly undeceived. When she was no more than three steps from him, he turned his head, fixing his eyes invariably on the lady with the red cushion, who had gotten up and was approaching, followed by her little black boy and her chambermaid.

When the lady with the red cushion was close to him, Porthos drew his hand all streaming from the basin; the devout beauty touched Porthos's immense hand with her slender hand, smiled as she made the sign of the cross, and left the church.

This was too much for the procureuse: she no longer doubted that this woman and Porthos were in gallant relations. If she had been a grand lady, she would have swooned; but as she was only a procureuse, she contented herself with saying to the musketeer with contained fury:

"Ah, M. Porthos, so you offer me no holy water?"

At the sound of that voice, Porthos gave a start, like a man waking up after a hundred-year nap.

"Ma . . . Madame!" he cried. "Is it really you? How is your husband, that dear M. Coquenard? Still as stingy as ever? Where were my eyes, then, that I didn't even notice you during the two hours the sermon lasted?"

"I was two steps away from you, Monsieur," replied the procureuse, "but you didn't notice me because you only had eyes for that beautiful lady to whom you just offered holy water."

Porthos feigned embarrassment.

"Ah!" he said, "you noticed . . ."

"One would have had to be blind not to see it."

"Yes," Porthos said casually, "she's a duchess friend of mine, with whom I have great difficulty meeting because of her husband's jealousy, and who had informed me that she would come to this paltry church in the depths of this godforsaken quarter just to see me."

"M. Porthos," said the procureuse, "would you kindly offer me your arm for five minutes? I should like to speak with you."

"How now, Madame?" said Porthos, winking to himself like a gambler laughing at the dupe he is about to trick.

At that moment, d'Artagnan passed by, following Milady. He threw Porthos a sidelong glance and caught that triumphant look.

"Aha!" he said to himself, reasoning according to the strangely easy morality of that gallant epoch, "there's one who may well be outfitted in time."

Porthos, yielding to the pressure of his procureuse's arm as a boat yields to the tiller, arrived at the cloister of Saint-Magloire, a little frequented passage closed at both ends by turnstiles. There was no one to be seen there during the day but beggars eating and children playing.

"Ah, M. Porthos!" cried the procureuse, when she was sure that no one who was a stranger to the usual population of the place could see or hear them. "Ah, M. Porthos, you are a great conqueror, it would seem!"

"I, Madame?" said Porthos, puffing out his chest. "And why so?"

"And all those signs just now, and the holy water? But she's a princess at the very least, this lady, with her little black boy and her chambermaid!"

"You are mistaken. My God, no," replied Porthos, "she's quite simply a duchess."

"And that footman waiting at the door, and that carriage with a coachman in grand livery waiting on his seat?"

Porthos had seen neither the footman nor the carriage, but Mme Coquenard, with her jealous woman's eye, had seen everything.

Porthos regretted that he had not made the woman with the red cushion a princess right from the start.

"Ah, you're the spoiled child of all the beauties, M. Porthos!" the procureuse went on with a sigh.

"But," replied Porthos, "you understand that, with a physique like that with which nature has endowed me, I can't help being a success with the ladies."

"My God, how quickly men forget!" cried the procureuse, raising her eyes to heaven.

"Less quickly than women, it seems to me," replied Porthos. "For in the end, Madame, I may say that I was your victim, when I lay bleeding, dying, and saw myself given up by the surgeons. I, the scion of an illustrious family, who had trusted in your friendship, nearly died of my wounds first and of hunger afterwards, in a wretched inn in Chantilly, and that without your deigning to reply to a single one of the ardent letters I wrote to you."

"But, M. Porthos . . ." murmured the procureuse, who felt that, judging by the conduct of the grand ladies of that time, she had been in the wrong.

"I, who had sacrificed the countess of Penaflor for you . . ."

"I know that very well . . ."

"The baroness of . . ."

"M. Porthos, do not crush me!"

"The duchess of . . ."

"M. Porthos, be generous!"

"You're right, Madame, I shall not finish the list."

"But it was my husband who would hear no talk of lending money."

"Mme Coquenard," said Porthos, "remember the first letter you wrote to me, which I have kept engraved in my memory."

The procureuse let out a groan.

"But it's also," she said, "that the sum you were asking to borrow was a bit too large."

"Mme Coquenard, I gave you the preference. I had only to write to the duchess of . . . I do not wish to speak her name, for it has never been my way to compromise a woman; but what I do know is that I had only to write to her and she would have sent me fifteen hundred."

The procureuse shed a tear.

"M. Porthos," she said, "I swear to you that you have punished me greatly, and that if in the future you find yourself in such a pass again, you will have only to turn to me."

"Fie upon it, Madame!" said Porthos, as if revolted. "Let us not speak of money, if you please, it is humiliating."

"So you don't love me anymore?" the procureuse said slowly and sadly.

Porthos kept a majestic silence.

"Is that how you answer me? Alas, I understand!"

"Consider your offense to me, Madame: it remains with me here," said Porthos, placing his hand on his heart and pressing hard on it.

"I'll make up for it. Come, my dear Porthos!"

"Besides, what was I asking of you, eh?" Porthos went on with a jovial shake of the shoulders. "A loan, nothing else. After all, I'm not an unreasonable man. I know you're not rich, Mme Coquenard, and your husband is obliged to leech onto poor clients in order to drag a few poor écus from them. Oh, if you were a countess, a marquise, or a duchess, that would be something else, and you would be unpardonable."

The procureuse was stung.

"Be it known to you, M. Porthos," she said, "that my strongbox, though it is only a procureuse's strongbox, is perhaps better lined than those of all your ruined fair ladies."

"Then you have doubly offended me," said Porthos, disengaging the procureuse's arm from his own, "for if you are rich, Mme Coquenard, then there is no more excuse for your refusal."

"When I say rich," the procureuse picked up, who saw that she had let herself get too carried away, "you mustn't take the word literally. I'm not exactly rich, but I am well off."

"Enough, Madame," said Porthos, "let us speak no more of that, I beg you. You have misunderstood me. All sympathy between us is extinguished."

"Ungrateful man!"

"Ah, I advise you to lodge a complaint!" said Porthos.

"Go off, then, with your beautiful duchess. I won't keep you any longer!"

"Ah, she's not such a withered hag yet, I believe!"

"Look here, M. Porthos, once more, and for the last time: do you still love me?"

"Alas, Madame!" said Porthos, in the most melancholy tone he could manage, "since we're about to embark on a campaign, a campaign in which my presentiments tell me that I shall be killed . . ."

"Oh, don't say such things!" cried the procureuse, bursting into sobs.

"Something tells me so," Porthos continued, melancholizing more and more.

"Say rather that you have a new love."

"Not so, I tell you frankly. No new object has touched me, and I even feel here, in the bottom of my heart, something that speaks for you. But in fifteen days, as you know or as you do not know, this fatal campaign will open; I shall be frightfully busy with my outfit. Then I must journey to see my family, in the depths of Brittany, in order to obtain the sum necessary for my departure."

Porthos detected a last struggle between love and greed.

"And," he went on, "as the duchess whom you have just seen in church has lands close to mine, we shall make the journey together. Journeys, as you know, seem much less long when you travel as two."

"So you have no friends in Paris, M. Porthos?" asked the procureuse.

"I thought I did," said Porthos, taking up his melancholy air, "but I have seen very well that I was mistaken."

"You have, M. Porthos, you have!" the procureuse picked up in a transport that surprised even herself. "Come to the house tomorrow. You are my aunt's son, and consequently my cousin; you come from Noyon in Picardy; you have several court cases in Paris and no procureur. Will you remember all that?"

"Perfectly, Madame."

"Come at dinnertime."

"Very well."

"And stand firm before my husband, who is a shrewd man for all his seventy-six years."

"Seventy-six years! damn! a fine age!" Porthos picked up.

"You mean a great age, M. Porthos. And so the poor dear man could leave me a widow from one minute to the next," the procureuse went on, casting a meaningful glance at Porthos. "Fortunately, according to our marriage contract, we've left everything to the last survivor."

"Everything?" asked Porthos.

"Everything."

"I see you are a woman of foresight, my dear Mme Coquenard," said Porthos, pressing the procureuse's hand tenderly.

"So we're reconciled, dear M. Porthos?" she said with a simper.

"For life," Porthos replied to the same tune.

"Good-bye, then, my traitor."

"Good-bye, my forgetful one."

"Till tomorrow, my angel!"

"Till tomorrow, flame of my life!"

XXX

MILADY

D'Artagnan had followed Milady without being seen by her. He saw her climb into her carriage, and heard her order her coachman to go to Saint-Germain.

It was useless to try to follow on foot a vehicle borne along at a trot by two vigorous horses. D'Artagnan went back to the rue Férou.

In the rue de Seine he ran into Planchet, who had stopped in front of a pastry shop and seemed to be in ecstasy before a brioche of the most appetizing shape.

He ordered him to go and saddle two horses in M. de Tréville's stables, one for d'Artagnan, the other for himself, Planchet, and to join him at Athos's—M. de Tréville having placed his stables once and for all at d'Artagnan's service.

Planchet headed off towards the rue du Vieux-Colombier and d'Artagnan towards the rue Férou. Athos was at home, sadly emptying one of the bottles of that famous Spanish wine he had brought back from his journey to Picardy. He made a sign to Grimaud to bring a glass for d'Artagnan, and Grimaud obeyed as usual.

D'Artagnan then told Athos all that had gone on in church between Porthos and the procureuse, and how their comrade was probably, at that moment, in the process of outfitting himself.

"As for me," Athos responded to this whole story, "I'm quite at ease; it won't be women who pay the cost of my harness."

"And yet a handsome, polished, grand lord like you, my dear Athos, should leave no princess or queen safe from your amorous darts."

"How young this d'Artagnan is!" said Athos, shrugging his shoulders.

And he made a sign to Grimaud to bring a second bottle.

At that moment, Planchet modestly stuck his head through the half-open door and announced to his master that the two horses were there.

"What horses?" asked Athos.

"Two that M. de Tréville is lending me for outings, and on which I am going to take a turn through Saint-Germain."

"And what are you going to do in Saint-Germain?" Athos asked further.

Then d'Artagnan told him about his encounter in church, and how he had found that woman who, along with the gentleman with the black cloak and the scar on his temple, had been his eternal preoccupation.

"That is to say, you're in love with her, as you were with Mme Bonacieux," said Athos, scornfully shrugging his shoulders, as if he felt pity for human weakness.

"Not at all!" cried d'Artagnan. "I'm merely curious to clarify the mystery that surrounds her. I don't know why, but I fancy that this woman, unknown as she is to me and as I am to her, has some effect on my life."

"In fact, you're right," said Athos. "I don't know any woman who is worth the trouble of looking for once she's lost. Mme Bonacieux is lost, too bad for her! Let her find herself!"

"No, Athos, no, you're mistaken," said d'Artagnan. "I love my poor Constance more than ever, and if I knew where she was, even if it were at the ends of the earth, I'd set out to take her from her enemies' hands. But I don't know; all my inquiries have been useless. What do you want, a man needs some distraction."

"Distract yourself with Milady, then, my dear d'Artagnan. I wish it with all my heart, if it will amuse you."

"Listen, Athos," said d'Artagnan, "instead of keeping yourself locked up here as if you were under arrest, get on a horse and come for an outing with me to Saint-Germain."

"My dear," replied Athos, "I ride my horses when I have them, otherwise I go on foot."

"Well, as for me," replied d'Artagnan, smiling at Athos's misanthropy, which in another man would certainly have offended him, "I'm less proud than you, I ride whatever I can find. And so, good-bye, my dear Athos."

"Good-bye," said the musketeer, making a sign to Grimaud to uncork the bottle he had just brought.

D'Artagnan and Planchet got into the saddle and took the road to Saint-Germain.

All along the way, what Athos had said to the young man about Mme Bonacieux kept coming to his mind. Though d'Artagnan was not of a very sentimental character, the mercer's pretty wife had made a real impression on his heart. As he said, he was willing to go to the ends of the earth in search of her. But the earth has many ends, being round, so that he did not know which way to turn.

In the meantime, he was going to try to find out who and what this Milady was. Milady had spoken to the man in the black cloak, therefore she knew him. Now, in d'Artagnan's mind, it was the man in the black cloak who had abducted Mme Bonacieux the second time, as he had abducted her the first time. D'Artagnan was only half lying, which means lying very little, when he said that in setting out in search of Milady, he was at the same time searching for Constance.

Lost in thought like this, and occasionally putting the spurs to his horse, d'Artagnan had covered the distance and come to Saint-Germain. He had just ridden past the pavilion in which which, ten years later, Louis XIV would be born. He was riding down a quite deserted street, looking right and left to see if he might pick up some trace of his beautiful Englishwoman, when on the ground floor of a pretty house, which, according to the custom of the time, had no window on the street, he caught sight of a familiar figure. This figure was pacing up and down a sort of terrace decorated with flowers. Planchet recognized him first.

"Eh, Monsieur," he said, turning to d'Artagnan, "can you place that mug that's gaping there?"

"No," said d'Artagnan, "and yet I'm sure it's not the first time I've seen it."

"I should say not, pardieu!" said Planchet. "It's that poor Lubin, the lackey of the comte de Wardes, the one you did up so well a month ago in Calais, on the road to the governor's summer house."

"Ah, yes, of course," said d'Artagnan, "now I recognize him! Do you think he recognizes you?"

"By heaven, Monsieur, he was so upset that I doubt he kept a very clear memory of me."

"Well, then, go and have a chat with the lad," said d'Artagnan, "and find out if his master is dead."

Planchet got off his horse, walked straight up to Lubin, who indeed did not recognize him, and the two lackeys started chatting with the best understanding in the world, while d'Artagnan pushed the two horses into a lane and, circling around the house, came back to attend the conference behind a hedge of hazels.

After a moment's observation behind the hedge, he heard the sound of horses and saw Milady's carriage pull up opposite him. There could be no mistake. Milady was in it. D'Artagnan flattened himself to his horse's neck, in order to see without being seen.

Milady leaned her charming blond head out the door and gave orders to her chambermaid.

The latter, a pretty girl of twenty or twenty-two, alert and lively, the perfect stage soubrette for a grand lady, jumped down from the footboard, which she had been sitting on following the custom of the time, and headed for the terrace where d'Artagnan had seen Lubin.

D'Artagnan followed the soubrette with his eyes and saw her going towards the terrace. But, by chance, an order from inside had called Lubin away, so that Planchet was left alone, looking all around to see by what path d'Artagnan had disappeared.

The chambermaid approached Planchet, whom she took for Lubin, and held out a little note to him.

"For your master," she said.

"For my master?" Planchet picked up, astonished.

"Yes, and it's very urgent. So take it quickly."

Thereupon she rushed for the carriage, which had swung around ahead of time to face the direction it had come from. She threw herself onto the footboard, and the carriage set off again.

Planchet turned the note over and over, then, accustomed to passive obedience, jumped from the terrace, went along the lane, and after twenty steps ran into d'Artagnan, who, having seen everything, was on his way to meet him.

"For you, Monsieur," said Planchet, presenting the note to the young man.

"For me?" asked d'Artagnan. "Are you sure of that?"

"Pardieu, yes, I'm sure of it! The soubrette said: 'For your master.' I have no other master than you, and so . . . A nice bit of a girl, by heaven, that soubrette!"

D'Artagnan opened the letter and read the following words:

> A person who is more interested in you than she can say would like to know on which day you will feel up to a stroll in the forest. Tomorrow, at the hotel of the Field of the Cloth of Gold, a lackey in black and red will await your reply.

"Oho!" d'Artagnan said to himself, "that's a bit hasty! It seems Milady and I are worried about the health of the same person. Well, Planchet, how is this good M. de Wardes doing? He's not dead, then?"

"No, Monsieur, he's doing as well as one can with four sword strokes in the body, for you, meaning no reproach, fetched the dear gentleman four good ones, and he's still quite weak, having lost nearly all his blood. As I had said to Monsieur, Lubin didn't recognize me, and he told me our adventure from beginning to end."

"Excellent, Planchet, you are the king of lackeys. Now back on your horse and let's catch up with the carriage."

It did not take long. After five minutes, they saw the carriage stopped by the side of the road. A richly dressed cavalier was standing at the door.

The conversation between Milady and the cavalier was so animated that d'Artagnan stopped on the other side of the carriage without anyone other than the pretty soubrette noticing his presence.

The conversation was conducted in English, a language d'Artagnan did not understand, but by the tone of it the young man guessed that the beautiful Englishwoman was extremely angry. She ended with a gesture that left him in no further doubt as to the nature of the conversation: it was the blow of a fan, delivered with such force that the little feminine accoutrement flew into a thousand pieces.

The cavalier let out a burst of laughter that seemed to exasperate Milady.

D'Artagnan thought it was the moment to intervene. He went up to the other door, respectfully removed his hat, and said:

"Madame, will you allow me to offer you my services? It seems to me that this cavalier has made you angry. Say the word, Madame, and I will take it upon myself to punish him for his lack of courtesy."

At his first words, Milady had turned, looking at the young man with astonishment, and when he finished, she said, in very good French:

"Monsieur, I would gladly put myself under your protection if the person quarreling with me were not my brother."

"Ah! Excuse me, then," said d'Artagnan, "you will understand that I was not aware of that, Madame."

"What is this featherbrain mixing into?" shouted the cavalier whom Milady had designated as her relation, bending down to the level of the coach door. "Why doesn't he go on his way?"

"Featherbrain yourself," said d'Artagnan, lowering himself in turn on the neck of his horse and replying through the door from his side. "I don't go on my way because it pleases me to stop here."

The cavalier addressed a few words in English to his sister.

"I speak French to you," said d'Artagnan. "Do me the favor, then, I beg you, of replying to me in the same language. You are Madame's brother, so be it, but fortunately you are not mine."

One might have thought that Milady, fearful as a woman ordinarily is, would intervene in this beginning of a provocation, so as to keep the quarrel from going too far; but, quite the contrary, she threw herself back in her carriage and shouted coldly to the coachman:

"To the hôtel!"

The pretty soubrette cast a worried glance at d'Artagnan, whose good looks seemed to have had an effect on her.

The carriage set off and left the two men face to face, with no material object separating them any longer.

The cavalier made a move as if to follow the carriage, but d'Artagnan, whose already boiling anger was increased still more when he recognized in him the Englishman who had won his horse at Amiens and had almost won his diamond ring from Athos, jumped for his bridle and stopped him.

"Eh, Monsieur," he said, "it seems you're even more featherbrained than I am, for it strikes me that you've forgotten there's already a little quarrel between us!"

"Aha!" said the Englishman, "it's you, my master. So you're forever playing one game or another?"

"Yes, and that reminds me that I have a revenge to take. We shall see, my dear sir, if you handle the rapier as adroitly as the dice cup."

"You can see very well that I have no sword," said the Englishman. "Do you mean to play the bravo against an unarmed man?"

"I certainly hope you have one at home," replied d'Artagnan. "In any case, I have two, and if you like, I'll play you for one."

"No need," said the Englishman, "I'm sufficiently furnished with these sorts of utensils."

"Well, then, my worthy gentleman," d'Artagnan picked up, "choose the longest one and come to show it to me this evening."

"Where, if you please?"

"Behind the Luxembourg. It's a charming quarter for outings of the sort I'm proposing to you."

"Very well, I'll be there."

"Your hour?"

"Six o'clock."

"By the way, you probably also have one or two friends?"

"Why, I have three who will be highly honored to play the same game as myself."

"Three? Perfect! How it all comes together!" said d'Artagnan. "That is precisely my count."

"Now, then, who are you?" asked the Englishman.

"I am M. d'Artagnan, a Gascon gentleman, serving in the guards, in the company of M. des Essarts. And you?"

"I am Lord de Winter, baron of Sheffield."

"Well, then, I am your humble servant, Monsieur le baron," said d'Artagnan, "though your names are quite hard to remember."

And spurring his horse, he set off at a gallop, and took the road back to Paris.

As he was in the habit of doing on such occasions, d'Artagnan dismounted right at Athos's place.

He found Athos lying on a large couch, where he was waiting, as he had said, for his outfit to come and find him.

He told Athos all that had just happened, minus the letter to M. de Wardes.

Athos was delighted when he learned he was going to fight an Englishman. We have mentioned that that was his dream.

They sent their lackeys at once to fetch Porthos and Aramis, and informed them of the situation.

Porthos drew his sword from its scabbard and started brandishing it at the wall, stepping back from time to time and flexing his knees like a dancer. Aramis, who was still at work on his poem, locked himself up in Athos's study and asked not to be bothered anymore until the moment for drawing swords.

Athos, by a sign to Grimaud, asked for a bottle.

As for d'Artagnan, he made up a little plan for himself, of which we shall see the execution later on, and which promised him a certain charming adventure, as could be seen by the smiles that passed over his face from time to time, lighting up its reverie.

XXXI

ENGLISHMEN AND FRENCHMEN

When the time came, they went with their lackeys behind the Luxembourg, to an enclosure abandoned to goats. Athos gave the goatherd a coin to keep out of the way. The lackeys were instructed to act as sentinels.

Soon a silent troop approached the same enclosure, came in, and joined the musketeers. Then, following the custom from across the Channel, introductions took place.

The Englishmen were all men of the highest quality. The bizarre names of their adversaries were thus a cause not only of surprise for them, but still more of concern.

"But, for all that," said Lord de Winter, when the three friends had been named, "we do not know who you are, and we shall not fight with such names. Why, these are the names of shepherds!"

"And thus false names, as you rightly suppose, Milord," said Athos.

"Which gives us all the more desire to know your real names," replied the Englishman.

"You gambled with us well enough without knowing them," said Athos, "so much so that you won our two horses from us."

"That's true, but we were only risking our pistoles; this time we are risking our blood: one gambles with anybody, one fights only with one's equals."

"Fair enough," said Athos. And he drew the Englishman he was to fight with aside and told him his name in a low voice.

Porthos and Aramis did the same.

"Does that suffice you," Athos asked his adversary, "and do you find me enough of a nobleman to do me the favor of crossing swords with me?"

"Yes, Monsieur," the Englishman said, bowing.

"Well, and now would you like me to tell you something?" Athos went on coldly.

"What?" asked the Englishman.

"You would have done better not to insist that I make myself known to you."

"Why is that?"

"Because I am thought dead, and I have reasons for wishing that no one know I am alive. I shall therefore be obliged to kill you, so that my secret will not be spread to the winds."

The Englishman stared at Athos, thinking he was joking; but Athos was not joking in the least.

"Gentlemen," he said, addressing both his companions and their adversaries, "are we ready?"

"Yes," the Englishmen and the Frenchmen replied with one voice.

"On guard, then," said Athos.

And at once eight swords flashed in the rays of the setting sun, and the combat began with a fury quite natural among men who were enemies twice over.

Athos fenced with as much calm and method as if he was in a fencing school.

Porthos, no doubt cured of his overconfidence by his adventure in Chantilly, played a game filled with subtlety and prudence.

Aramis, who had the third canto of his poem to finish, worked quickly, like a man in a great hurry.

Athos was the first to kill his adversary: he gave him only one stroke, but, as he had warned him, the stroke was fatal, it went through his heart.

Porthos was the second to bring his man down: he had pierced his thigh. Then, as the Englishman had yielded him his sword without offering any further resistance, Porthos took him in his arms and brought him to his carriage.

Aramis pressed his man so vigorously that, after falling back some fifty paces, he ended by taking flight for all he was worth and disappeared, to the hooting of the lackeys.

As for d'Artagnan, he had played a pure and simple defensive game. Then, when he had seen his adversary well wearied, he had sent his sword flying with a vigorous quarte thrust. The baron, seeing himself disarmed, retreated two or three steps; but as he did so, his foot slipped, and he fell backwards.

D'Artagnan was upon him in a single bound. Bringing the sword to his throat, he said to the Englishman:

"I could kill you, Monsieur, for you are certainly in my hands, but I grant you your life out of love for your sister."

D'Artagnan was overjoyed. He had just carried out the plan he had devised beforehand, and the elaboration of which had brought to his face those smiles we have mentioned.

The Englishman, delighted to be dealing with such a well-rounded gentleman, embraced him, patted the musketeers on the back a thousand times, and, as Porthos's adversary was already installed in the carriage, and Aramis's had bolted, they only had to think about the dead man.

As Porthos and Aramis undressed him in hopes that his wound was not fatal, a fat purse fell from his belt. D'Artagnan picked it up and held it out to Lord de Winter.

"What the devil to you want me to do with that?" said the Englishman.

"Give it to his family," said d'Artagnan.

"His family could not care less about such a trifle: they will inherit an income of fifteen thousand louis. Keep the purse for your lackeys."

D'Artagnan put the purse in his pocket.

"And now, my young friend, for you will permit me, I hope, to call you that," said Lord de Winter, "this very evening, if you wish, I will introduce you to my sister, Lady Clarick; for I would like her in turn to take you into her good graces, and, as she is not altogether out of favor at court, a word from her might not be entirely useless to you in the future."

D'Artagnan blushed with pleasure and bowed as a sign of assent.

Meanwhile, Athos came over to him.

"What are you going to do with that purse?" he said softly in his ear.

"Why, I was counting on giving it to you, my dear Athos."

"To me? Why so?"

"After all, you killed him: these are the spoils of war."

"I, an enemy's heir?" said Athos. "Whom do you take me for?"

"It's the custom in war," said d'Artagnan, "why shouldn't it be the custom in a duel?"

"Even on the battlefield," said Athos, "I have never done that."

Porthos shrugged his shoulders. Aramis, by a movement of his lips, approved of Athos.

"In that case," said d'Artagnan, "let's give the money to our lackeys, as Lord de Winter told us to do."

"Yes," said Athos, "let's give the purse, not to our lackeys, but to the Englishmen's."

Athos took the purse and tossed it to the coachman:

"For you and your comrades."

This grand manner in an utterly destitute man struck even Porthos himself, and this French generosity, recounted by Lord de Winter and his friend, had a great success everywhere, except with MM. Grimaud, Mousqueton, Planchet, and Bazin.

Lord de Winter, on leaving d'Artagnan, gave him his sister's address. She lived at number six on the place Royale, which was then a fashionable quarter. Moreover, he promised to come and fetch him in order to introduce him. D'Artagnan arranged a rendezvous for eight o'clock at Athos's.

This introduction to Milady took up much space in our Gascon's head. He recalled the strange way in which this woman had been involved in his destiny up to then. He was convinced that she was some sort of creature of the cardinal's, and yet he felt invincibly drawn to her, one of those feelings one cannot explain to oneself. His only fear was that Milady would recognize him as the man of Meung and Dover. In that case, she would know that he was a friend of M. de Tréville, and consequently belonged body and soul to the king, which would at once cost him some of his advantage, since, if he was known by Milady as she was known by him, he would be playing an even match with her. As for the budding intrigue between her and the comte de Wardes, our presumptuous Gascon was only mildly concerned with it, though the count was young, handsome, rich, and much in favor with the cardinal. It is not for nothing that one is twenty years old, and above all that one is born in Tarbes.

D'Artagnan began by going home to put on a flamboyant costume. Then he went back to Athos's, and, as was his habit, told him everything. Athos listened to his plans, shook his head, and, with a sort of bitterness, urged him to be prudent.

"What?" he said to him. "You've just lost one woman who you said was good, charming, perfect, and here you are running after another?"

D'Artagnan felt the truth of this reproach.

"I loved Mme Bonacieux with my heart, while I love Milady with my head," he said. "In having myself brought to her, I'm seeking above all to find out what role she plays at court."

"What role she plays, pardieu! It's not hard to guess, after all you've told me. She's some sort of emissary of the cardinal's: a woman who will draw you into a trap, where you'll very likely part with your head."

"Devil take it, my dear Athos, you have a black view of things, it seems to me."

"My dear, I distrust women—what do you want, I've paid for it!—and above all blond women. Didn't you say Milady is blond?"

"She has the most beautiful blond hair you could ever see."

"Ah, my poor d'Artagnan!" said Athos.

"Listen, I want to find out. Once I know what I want to know, I'll go away."

"Find out, then," Athos said phlegmatically.

Lord de Winter came at the appointed hour, but Athos, warned in time, had gone to the other room. He thus found d'Artagnan alone, and as it was nearly eight o'clock, he took the young man away.

An elegant carriage was waiting downstairs, and as it was harnessed to two excellent horses, in an instant they were at the place Royale.

Milady Clarick received d'Artagnan graciously. Her house was of a remarkable sumptuosity; and though most Englishmen, driven out by the war, were leaving France, or were on the point of leaving, Milady had just gone to new expenses in her home, which proved that the general measure that sent the English away did not concern her.

"You see before you," said Lord de Winter, introducing d'Artagnan to his sister, "a young gentleman who held my life in his hands, and who did not wish to make use of his advantage, though we were enemies twice over, since I had insulted him and I am also English. Thank him, then, Madame, if you have any friendship for me."

Milady frowned slightly. A barely visible cloud passed over

her brow, and so strange a smile came to her lips that the young man, who noticed this triple nuance, almost shuddered at it.

The brother noticed nothing. He had turned around to play with Milady's favorite monkey, who had pulled him by the doublet.

"You are welcome, Monsieur," said Milady, in a voice the singular softness of which contrasted with the symptoms of ill humor that d'Artagnan has just observed. "Today you have acquired eternal rights to my gratitude."

The Englishman then turned back again and recounted their combat without omitting a single detail. Milady listened with the greatest attention; yet one could easily see, despite the effort she made to hide her impressions, that this story was not at all pleasing to her. The blood rose to her face, and her little foot tapped impatiently under her dress.

Lord de Winter perceived nothing. When he had finished, he went over to a table where a bottle of Spanish wine and some glasses had been served on a tray. He filled two glasses and made a sign inviting d'Artagnan to drink.

D'Artagnan knew it was highly offensive to an Englishman to refuse to exchange toasts with him. He therefore went over to the table and took the second glass. However, he had not lost sight of Milady, and in the mirror caught the change that had just come over her face. Now that she thought she was no longer being looked at, a feeling resembling ferocity animated her physiognomy. She bit her handkerchief with her beautiful teeth.

That pretty little soubrette, whom d'Artagnan had already noticed, came in then. She spoke a few words in English to Lord de Winter, who at once asked d'Artagnan's permission to leave, excusing himself by the urgency of the matter that called him away, and entrusting his sister with obtaining his pardon.

D'Artagnan shook hands with Lord de Winter and went back to Milady. With a surprising mobility, the woman's face had resumed its gracious expression, only some little red spots scattered over her handkerchief indicated that she had bitten her lips till they bled.

Those lips were magnificent, the color of coral.

The conversation took a lively turn. Milady seemed to be completely recovered. She told him that Lord de Winter was only her brother-in-law, not her brother: she had married a younger son of the family, who had left her a widow with a child. That child was Lord de Winter's sole heir, if Lord de Winter never married. All this made visible to d'Artagnan a veil that enveloped something, but he could as yet make out nothing behind that veil.

Moreover, after half an hour of conversation, d'Artagnan was convinced that Milady was his compatriot: she spoke French with a purity and elegance that left no doubt in that regard.

D'Artagnan produced a flood of gallant remarks and protests of devotion. To all the platitudes that escaped our Gascon, Milady smiled benevolently. It came time to retire. D'Artagnan said good-bye to Milady and left the salon the happiest of men.

On the stairs he ran into the pretty soubrette, who brushed softly against him in passing, and, blushing to the roots of her hair, begged his pardon for having touched him, in a voice so sweet that the pardon was granted at once.

D'Artagnan went back the next day and was given an even better reception than the evening before. Lord de Winter was not there, and it was Milady who this time did him all the honors of the evening. She seemed to take a great interest in him, asked him where he was from, who his friends were, and if he had not sometimes thought of attaching himself to the service of M. le cardinal.

D'Artagnan, who, as we know, was extremely prudent for a lad of twenty, then remembered his suspicions of Milady. He praised His Eminence highly to her, told her that he would unfailingly have entered the cardinal's guards instead of the king's guards, if he had known M. de Cavois, for example, instead of M. de Tréville.

Milady changed the subject without any affectation, and asked d'Artagnan in the most casual way in the world if he had ever been to England.

D'Artagnan replied that he had been sent there by M. de Tréville to arrange for a remount of horses, and that he had even brought back four as a sample.

In the course of the conversation, Milady pressed her lips two or three times: she was dealing with a Gascon who played a close game.

D'Artagnan left at the same hour as the evening before. In the corridor he again ran into the pretty Kitty—that was the soubrette's name. She looked at him with an expression of mysterious benevolence that was quite unmistakable. But d'Artagnan was so preoccupied with the mistress that he noticed absolutely nothing but what came from her.

D'Artagnan went back to Milady's the next day and the day after that, and each time Milady gave him a more gracious welcome.

Each time, too, either in the antechamber, in the corridor, or on the stairs, he ran into the pretty soubrette.

But, as we have said, d'Artagnan paid no attention to poor Kitty's persistence.

XXXII

A Procureur's Dinner

Meanwhile, the duel in which Porthos had played so brilliant a role had not made him forget the dinner to which the procureur's wife had invited him. The next day, towards one o'clock, he had Mousqueton give him a last brushing off and made his way to the rue aux Ours, with the stride of a man who is in double good fortune.

His heart was throbbing, but not, like d'Artagnan's, with young and impatient love. No, a more material interest whipped up his blood; he was finally going to cross that mysterious threshold and climb that unknown stairway which the old écus of Master Coquenard had gone up one by one.

He was going to see in reality a certain chest that he had seen the image of twenty times in his dreams; a chest long and deep in form, padlocked, bolted, fixed to the floor; a chest he had heard spoken of so often, and which the hands of the procureuse—slightly dry, true, but not without elegance— were going to open to his admiring gaze.

And then he, a man wandering over the earth, a man without fortune, a man without family, a soldier accustomed to inns, taverns, posadas, a gourmet forced most of the time to content himself with chance mouthfuls, was going to sample family meals, savor a comfortable interior, and give himself up to those little attentions that are the more pleasant the tougher one is, as old soldiers say.

To come in the quality of a cousin and sit every day at a good table, smooth the old procureur's yellow and wrinkled brow, fleece the young clerks a bit by teaching them the finer points of basset, passe-dix, and lansquenet, and winning their month's savings from them by way of an honorarium for the lesson he would give them in an hour—all this smiled enormously upon Porthos.

The musketeer recalled now and then the bad reports on procureurs that were already current at that time and have long outlived it: stinginess, cheese paring, fasting—but since, after all, except for a few fits of economy, which Porthos had always found untimely, he had seen the procureuse be rather liberal (for a procureuse, that is), he hoped to find a household set up on a satisfactory footing.

At the door, however, the musketeer had a few doubts. The access was hardly meant to be enticing: a dark and stinking alley; a stairway poorly lit by a barred window, through which the gray light of the neighboring courtyard filtered; on the second floor, a low door studded with huge nails like the main door of the Grand Châtelet.

Porthos rapped with his knuckle. A tall clerk, pale and buried under a forest of virgin hair, came to open the door, and bowed with the air of a man forced to respect simultaneously in another the great size, indicative of strength, the military uniform, indicative of condition, and the bright red face, indicative of a habit of living well.

Another smaller clerk behind the first, another bigger clerk behind the second, a twelve-year-old errand boy behind the third.

Three and a half clerks in all, which, at that time, spoke for a well-patronized office.

Though the musketeer was only due to arrive at one o'clock, the procureuse had been on the lookout since noon, and was reckoning on the heart, and perhaps also the stomach, of her adorer to bring him there ahead of time.

Mme Coquenard thus came to the door of her private apartment almost at the same time that her guest came to the door from the stairs, and the worthy lady's appearance got him out of a great quandary. The clerks were all eyeing him curiously, and he, not knowing very well what to say to this ascending and descending scale, found himself tongue-tied.

"It's my cousin!" cried the procureuse. "Come in, come in, M. Porthos."

Porthos's name had its effect on the clerks, who started to laugh; but Porthos turned around, and all the faces resumed their gravity.

They reached the procureur's study after passing through the antechamber where the clerks were, and the office where they ought to have been: the latter was a sort of dark hall furnished with waste paper. On leaving the office, they passed the kitchen on the right and entered the reception room.

All these rooms leading one to the other hardly inspired any good ideas in Porthos. Talk could be heard from far off through all those open doors; then, in passing, he had cast a rapid and investigative glance into the kitchen, and confessed to himself, to the shame of the procureuse and his own great regret, that he had not seen that fire, that animation, that bustle which usually reign in such a sanctuary of gluttony before the start of a good meal.

The procureur had no doubt been informed of this visit, for he showed no surprise on seeing Porthos, who went up to him with a rather jaunty air and bowed courteously.

"We are cousins, it seems, M. Porthos?" said the procureur, raising himself in his rattan wheelchair with the help of his arms.

The old man, enveloped in a great black doublet in which his slender body swam, was green and dry. His little gray eyes glittered like carbuncles and seemed, along with his grimacing mouth, to be the only part of his face that had any life left in it. Unfortunately, the legs had begun to refuse their service to the rest of this bony mechanism; in the five or six months since this weakening had made itself felt, the worthy procureur had very nearly become the slave of his wife.

The cousin was accepted with resignation, that was all. A spry Master Coquenard would have declined any relation with M. Porthos.

"Yes, Monsieur, we are cousins," said the unfazed Porthos, who, besides, had never counted on being received enthusiastically by the husband.

"Through the female side, I believe?" the procureur said maliciously.

Porthos felt none of this mockery and took it for a naïveté at which he laughed into his thick mustache. Mme Coquenard, who knew that a naive procureur was an extremely rare variety of the species, smiled slightly and blushed deeply.

Since Porthos's arrival, Master Coquenard had been casting his eyes uneasily on a large cupboard placed opposite his oak desk. Porthos understood that this cupboard, though it did not correspond at all to the form of the one he had seen in his dreams, must be the blessed chest, and he applauded the fact that the reality was six feet taller than the dream.

Master Coquenard did not push his genealogical investigations any further, but, shifting his uneasy gaze from the cupboard to Porthos, contented himself with saying:

"Before leaving for the country, Monsieur our cousin will surely do us the favor of dining with us once, will he not, Mme Coquenard?"

This time Porthos received the blow right in the stomach, and felt it. It seemed that, for her part, Mme Coquenard was also not insensible of it, for she added:

"My cousin will not come again if we treat him badly; but, on the contrary, he has too little time to spend in Paris, and therefore to see us, for us not to insist that he give us almost every moment he can spare before his departure."

"Oh, my legs, my poor legs, where have you gone?" murmured Coquenard. And he attempted to smile.

This help, which had come to Porthos just as he was attacked in his gastronomic hopes, filled the musketeer with exceeding gratitude towards his procureuse.

Soon dinnertime came. They went to the dining room, a big dark room located opposite the kitchen.

The clerks, who, it seemed, had sensed unaccustomed fragrances in the house, were of military precision, and held their stools in their hands, ready as they were to sit down. One could see them moving their jaws ahead of time with frightful aptitude.

"Tudieu!" thought Porthos, casting a glance at the three starvelings, for the errand boy, as one might well think, was not admitted to the honors of the magisterial table, "tudieu! if I were my cousin, I wouldn't keep such gourmandizers. You'd think they were castaways who haven't eaten for six weeks."

Master Coquenard came in, pushed in his wheelchair by Mme Coquenard, whom Porthos, in his turn, went to help in rolling her husband up to the table.

He had no sooner come in than he began twitching his nose and jaws after the example of his clerks.

"Oho!" he said, "here's an enticing soup!"

"What the devil do they find so extraordinary in this soup?" Porthos said to himself, looking at a pale broth, abundant but perfectly blind, on which a few sparse crusts floated like the islands of an archipelago.

Mme Coquenard smiled, and, at a sign from her, everyone sat down eagerly.

Master Coquenard was served first, then Porthos; then Mme Coquenard filled her plate and distributed the crusts, without broth, to the impatient clerks.

At that moment the dining room door creaked open by itself, and through the gap Porthos made out the little clerk, who, unable to take part in the feast, was eating his bread in the combined odors of the kitchen and the dining room.

After the soup, the servant girl brought a boiled chicken, a magnificence that made the guests' eyes widen so much they looked as though they might pop.

"One can see you love your family, Mme Coquenard," said the procureur with an almost tragic smile. "This is quite a courtesy you've done your cousin."

The poor chicken was scrawny and clothed in that sort of thick, bristly hide that the bones can never pierce, for all their efforts. It must have taken a long time to find her on her perch, where she had withdrawn to die of old age.

"Devil take it," thought Porthos, "there's a sorry sight for you! I repect old age, but I'm not partial to having it boiled or roasted."

And he looked around to see if his opinion was shared. But, quite to the contrary, he saw only burning eyes, devouring in advance this sublime chicken that was the object of his contempt.

Mme Coquenard drew the platter towards her, skillfully detached the two big black feet, which she put on her husband's plate, severed the neck, which, together with the head, she set aside for herself, removed a wing for Porthos, and gave the animal back to the girl who had just brought it, so that it returned to the kitchen almost intact, and disappeared before the musketeer had time to examine the variations that disappointment brought to the faces around him, according to the characters and temperaments of those who felt it.

Instead of the chicken, a dish of broad beans made its entrance, an enormous dish, in which a few mutton bones, which one might at first have believed were accompanied by meat, made a semblance of appearing.

But the clerks were not fooled by this deception, and the look on their faces turned from mournful to resigned.

Mme Coquenard distributed this food to the young men with the moderation of a good housewife.

It came time for wine. From an extremely narrow stoneware bottle, Master Coquenard poured a third of a glass for each of the young men, and about as much again for himself, and the bottle passed at once to the side of Porthos and Mme Coquenard.

The young men filled this third of wine with water; then, when they had drunk half the glass, filled it again, and kept doing the same, thus coming, by the end of the meal, to swallowing a drink that had gone from the color of ruby to that of pink topaz.

Porthos timidly ate his chicken wing, and shivered when he felt the procureuse's knee, which had just found his under the table. He also drank half a glass of this much spared wine, which he recognized as the horrible vintage of Montreuil, the terror of experienced palates.

Master Coquenard watched him swallow this wine straight, and sighed.

"Would you care for some broad beans, cousin Porthos?" said Mme Coquenard, in a tone that said, "Believe me, you shouldn't eat them."

"The devil if I'll taste them!" Porthos murmured softly . . . Then aloud: "Thank you, cousin, I'm no longer hungry."

Silence ensued. Porthos did not know where to look. The procureur repeated several times:

"Ah, Mme Coquenard, I give you my compliments, your dinner was a veritable feast! God, how I've eaten!"

Master Coquenard had eaten his soup, the chicken's black feet, and the one mutton bone on which there was a little meat.

Porthos thought they were hoaxing him, and began to frown and twist his mustache, but Mme Coquenard's knee came quite gently to counsel patience.

The silence and the interruption of the service, which remained incomprehensible for Porthos, had, on the contrary, a terrible significance for the clerks: at a glance from the procureur, accompanied by a smile from Mme Coquenard, they slowly got up from the table, folded their napkins still more slowly, then bowed and left.

"Go, young men, go and digest while you work," the procureur said gravely.

Once the clerks were gone, Mme Coquenard got up and took from the buffet a piece of cheese, some quince preserves, and a cake she had made herself from almonds and honey.

Master Coquenard frowned, because he saw too much

food; Porthos pressed his lips, because he saw there was nothing to eat.

He looked to see if the dish of broad beans was still there: the dish of broad beans had disappeared.

"A decided feast," cried Master Coquenard, fidgeting in his chair, "a veritable feast, *epulæ epularum*!* Lucullus dining with Lucullus!"

Porthos eyed the bottle, which was close to him, and hoped that with wine, bread, and cheese he would have enough to eat. But the wine was gone, the bottle was empty. M. and Mme Coquenard seemed not to notice it.

"Very well," Porthos said to himself, "I'm forewarned."

He passed his tongue over a small spoonful of preserves and sank his teeth into Mme Coquenard's sticky pastry.

"Now," he said to himself, "the sacrifice is consummated. Ah, if it weren't for the hope of looking with Mme Coquenard into her husband's cupboard!"

Master Coquenard, after the delights of such a meal, which he called an excess, felt the need for a siesta. Porthos hoped it would take place on the spot and in that same locale; but the cursed procureur would hear none of it: he had to be taken to his room, and he shouted so long as he was not facing his cupboard, on the edge of which, for still greater precaution, he placed his feet.

The procureuse took Porthos to a neighboring room, and they began laying the foundations for a reconciliation.

"You could come to dine three times a week," said Mme Coquenard.

"Thanks," said Porthos, "but I don't like to overdo things. Besides, I have to think about my outfit."

"That's true," said the procureuse, sighing, ". . . it's that wretched outfit."

"Alas, yes," said Porthos, "that it is!"

"But what does an outfit consist of in your corps, M. Porthos?"

* "A banquet of banquets."

"Oh, lots of things," said Porthos. "The musketeers, as you know, are elite soldiers, and they need lots of things that would be useless for the guards or the Switzers."

"But, still, tell me in detail."

"But that may come to . . ." said Porthos, who preferred discussing the total than the particulars.

The procureuse waited tremblingly.

"To how much?" she asked. "I hope it won't be more than . . ."

She stopped; words failed her.

"Oh, no!" said Porthos, "it won't go over two thousand five hundred livres. I even think that, with some economies, I could get away with two thousand."

"Good God, two thousand livres!" she cried. "But that's a fortune!"

Porthos made a most significant grimace. Mme Coquenard understood it.

"I asked for details," she said, "because, having many relations and clients in trade, I was almost sure I could get the things at a hundred percent less than you would pay for them yourself."

"Aha!" said Porthos, "if that's what you meant to say!"

"Yes, dear M. Porthos! So, then, don't you need a horse first of all?"

"Yes, a horse."

"Well, I've got just the thing for you."

"Ah!" said Porthos, beaming, "then that takes care of my horse. Then I need all the harness, which is made up of things that only a musketeer can buy, and, besides, won't amount to more than three hundred livres."

"Three hundred livres. Well, let's make it three hundred livres then," the procureuse said with a sigh.

Porthos smiled. It will be remembered that he had the saddle that came to him from Buckingham, so this was three hundred livres that he slyly counted on putting in his pocket.

"Then," he went on, "there's my lackey's horse and my valise. As for weapons, you needn't worry about that, I've got them."

"A horse for your servant?" picked up the hesitant procureuse. "But that's rather grand of you, my friend."

"Eh, Madame!" Porthos said proudly, "am I some sort of
yokel, by any chance?"

"No, I only meant to say that a handsome mule sometimes
looks as good as a horse, and it seems to me that in procuring
you a handsome mule for Mousqueton . . ."

"Let it be a handsome mule," said Porthos. "You're right.
I've seen Spanish grandees whose entire suite was on mule-
back. But then, you understand, Mme Coquenard, a mule with
plumes and bells?"

"Don't worry," said the procureuse.

"There remains the valise," Porthos continued.

"Oh, that needn't trouble you at all," cried Mme
Coquenard. "My husband has five or six valises. You can
choose the best of them. There's one he especially preferred for
his travels, and it's so big you could put a whole world in it."

"It's empty, then, this valise of yours?" Porthos asked
naively.

"Certainly it's empty," the procureuse replied naively.

"Ah, but what I need is a well-furnished valise, my dear."

Mme Coquenard heaved some fresh sighs. Molière had not
yet written his play *The Miser*. Mme Coquenard was thus a
step ahead of Harpagon.

Then the remainder of the outfit was successively haggled
over in the same way, and the result of the scene was that the
procureuse would ask her husband for a loan of eight hundred
livres in cash, and would furnish the horse and the mule that
would have the honor of carrying Porthos and Mousqueton to
glory.

With these conditions agreed upon, along with the stipulated interest and the period of repayment, Porthos took leave
of Mme Coquenard. The lady tried to keep him there by making soft eyes at him, but Porthos used the duties of the service
as a pretext, and the procureuse had to yield to the king.

The musketeer returned home with a very ill-humored
hunger.

XXXIII

Soubrette and Mistress

Meanwhile, as we have said, despite the cries of his conscience and the wise advice of Athos, d'Artagnan fell more in love with Milady by the hour. And so he went every day without fail to pay her court, to which the adventurous Gascon was convinced she could not fail to respond sooner or later.

One day as he arrived, nose to the winds, light as a man expecting a shower of gold, he met the soubrette under the gateway. But this time the pretty Kitty was not content with smiling at him in passing. She gently took his hand.

"Right," thought d'Artagnan, "she's been entrusted with some message for me from her mistress; she's going to set up some rendezvous for me that she didn't dare mention aloud."

And he looked at the lovely girl with the most triumphant air he could muster.

"I'd like to say a couple of words to you, Monsieur le chevalier," the soubrette stammered.

"Speak, my girl, speak," said d'Artagnan, "I'm listening."

"It's impossible here. What I have to say to you is too long and above all too secret."

"Well, then, what are we to do?"

"If Monsieur le chevalier would kindly follow me," Kitty said timidly.

"Wherever you like, my lovely girl."

"Come, then."

And Kitty, who had never let go of d'Artagnan's hand, led him to a dark and winding stairway and, after going up fifteen steps, opened a door.

"Go in, Monsieur le chevalier," she said. "Here we will be alone and we can talk."

"And what room is this, my lovely girl?" asked d'Artagnan.

"It is my bedroom, Monsieur le chevalier. It communicates with my mistress's bedroom by that door. But don't worry, she won't be able to hear what we say; she never goes to bed before midnight."

D'Artagnan glanced around him. The little room was charming in its taste and cleanliness; but, despite himself, his eyes fastened on the door that Kitty had said led to Milady's bedroom.

Kitty guessed what was going on in the young man's soul and heaved a sigh.

"So you really love my mistress, Monsieur le chevalier?" she said.

"Oh, more than I can say! I'm mad about her!"

Kitty heaved a second sigh.

"Alas, Monsieur," she said, "that is a real pity!"

"What the devil do you find so sad about it?" asked d'Artagnan.

"It's just that my mistress doesn't love you at all, Monsieur," replied Kitty.

"Hm!" said d'Artagnan. "Did she order you to tell me that?"

"Oh, no, Monsieur! It was I who, out of concern for you, took the decision to inform you of it."

"Thanks, my good Kitty, but for the intention alone, because the secret itself, you'll agree, is hardly pleasant."

"You mean to say that you don't believe what I've told you, isn't that so?"

"It's always hard to believe such things, my lovely girl, if only out of vanity."

"So you don't believe me?"

"I confess that, until you deign to give me some proof of what you assert . . ."

"What do you say to this?"

And Kitty drew a small note from her bosom.

"For me?" asked d'Artagnan, quickly snatching the letter.

"No, for another man."

"Another man?"

"Yes."

"His name! His name!" cried d'Artagnan.

"Look at the address."

"M. le comte de Wardes."

The memory of the scene in Saint-Germain came at once to

the presumptuous Gascon's mind. With a movement quick as thought, he tore open the envelope, despite the cry that Kitty uttered on seeing what he was about to do, or rather, what he was doing.

"Oh, my God! Monsieur le chevalier," she said, "what are you doing?"

"I? Nothing!" said d'Artagnan, and he read:

> You have not replied to my first note. Are you then so unwell, or might you have forgotten what eyes you made at me during Mme de Guise's ball? Here is your chance, count! Do not let it slip away.

D'Artagnan paled. It was his vanity that was wounded, but he thought it was his love.

"Poor dear M. d'Artagnan!" said Kitty, in a voice filled with compassion, and pressing the young man's hand again.

"You feel sorry for me, kind child?" said d'Artagnan.

"Oh, yes, with all my heart! For I know what love is myself!"

"You know what love is?" said d'Artagnan, looking at her for the first time with a certain attention.

"Alas, yes!"

"Well, then, instead of feeling sorry for me, you'd do better to help me take revenge on your mistress."

"And what sort of revenge would you like to take?"

"I'd like to conquer her, to supplant my rival."

"I'll never help you in that, Monsieur le chevalier," Kitty said sharply.

"And why not?" asked d'Artagnan.

"For two reasons."

"Which are?"

"First, that my mistress will never love you."

"How do you know?"

"You have offended her heart."

"I? How could I have offended her—I, who, ever since I've known her, have lived at her feet like a slave! Speak, I beg you!"

"I will never confess that except to the man . . . who can read to the bottom of my soul!"

D'Artagnan looked at Kitty for the second time. The young girl was of a freshness and beauty that many a duchess would have purchased with her coronet.

"Kitty," he said, "I'll read to the bottom of your soul whenever you like; don't insist on that, my dear child."

And he gave her a kiss that made the poor girl turn red as a cherry.

"Oh, no!" cried Kitty, "you don't love me! It's my mistress you love, you just told me so."

"And does that keep you from telling me the second reason?"

"The second reason, Monsieur le chevalier," Kitty picked up, emboldened first of all by the kiss and then by the look in the young man's eyes, "is that in love it's every man for himself."

Only then did d'Artagnan remember the languishing glances Kitty gave him, the meetings in the antechamber, on the stairs, in the corridor, those brushings of the hand each time she met him, and those stifled sighs. But, absorbed by the desire to please the grand lady, he had scorned the soubrette: he who hunts the eagle bothers not with the sparrow.

But this time our Gascon saw at a glance the whole advantage to be derived from this love, which Kitty had just confessed in such a naive and barefaced way: interception of letters addressed to the comte de Wardes; intelligence on site; entry at any hour to Kitty's room, adjacent to that of her mistress. The deceiver, as we see, was already sacrificing the poor girl in his mind to get Milady willy-nilly.

"Well, now, my dear Kitty," he said to the young girl, "would you like me to give you proof of that love you doubt?"

"Of what love?" asked the young girl.

"The love I'm quite ready to feel for you."

"And what is that proof?"

"Would you like me to spend with you tonight the time I usually spend with your mistress?"

"Oh, yes!" said Kitty, clapping her hands. "Very gladly!"

"Well, then, my dear girl," said d'Artagnan, establishing himself in an armchair, "come here till I tell you that you're the prettiest soubrette I've ever seen!"

And he told it to her so much and so well that the poor girl, who asked nothing better than to believe him, did believe him . . . However, to d'Artagnan's great astonishment, the pretty Kitty defended herself with a certain determination.

Time passes quickly when it comes to attack and defense.

It struck midnight, and at almost the same time the little bell rang in Milady's bedroom.

"Good God!" cried Kitty, "that's my mistress summoning me! Go, go quickly!"

D'Artagnan stood up, took his hat as though he intended to obey; then, quickly opening the door to a large wardrobe, instead of the door to the stairs, he ducked in amidst Milady's dresses and robes.

"What on earth are you doing?" cried Kitty.

D'Artagnan, who had taken the key beforehand, locked himself up in the wardrobe without answering.

"Well!" cried Milady in a harsh voice, "are you asleep that you don't come when I ring?"

And d'Artagnan heard the communicating door open violently.

"Here I am, Milady, here I am," cried Kitty, rushing to meet her mistress.

They both went into the bedroom, and as the communicating door remained open, d'Artagnan could hear Milady scolding her maid for a while longer; then she finally calmed down, and, while Kitty tended to her mistress, the conversation turned to him.

"Well," said Milady, "I didn't see our Gascon this evening."

"What, Madame," said Kitty, "you mean he didn't come? Will he turn fickle before he's made happy?"

"Oh, no, he must have been hindered by M. de Tréville or M. des Essarts. I know myself, Kitty, and that one is hooked."

"What will Madame do with him?"

"What will I do with him! . . . Don't worry, Kitty, there's something between that man and me that he doesn't know . . .

he nearly made me lose my credit with His Eminence . . . Oh, I will have my revenge!"

"I thought Madame was in love with him."

"In love with him? I detest him! A ninny, who has Lord de Winter's life in his hands and doesn't kill him, and who costs me three hundred thousand livres in income!"

"That's true," said Kitty, "your son was his uncle's sole heir, and until his coming of age, you would have had the enjoyment of his fortune."

D'Artagnan shuddered to the marrow of his bones, listening to this suave creature reproach him, in that strident voice she had so much trouble concealing in conversation, for not having killed a man he had seen her heap with friendship.

"And so," Milady went on, "I would already have taken revenge on him, if the cardinal, I don't know why, hadn't urged me to spare him."

"Oh, yes, but Madame didn't spare that little woman he was in love with."

"Oh, the mercer's wife from the rue des Fossoyeurs—hasn't he already forgotten she existed? A fine vengeance, by heaven!"

Cold sweat trickled down d'Artagnan's brow: she was a monster, this woman.

He went back to listening, but unfortunately the night's preparations were finished.

"Very well," said Milady, "go to your room, and tomorrow try finally to get a response to that letter I gave you."

"For M. de Wardes?" asked Kitty.

"Of course, for M. de Wardes."

"There's one," said Kitty, "who strikes me as being quite the contrary of that poor M. d'Artagnan."

"Leave me, Mademoiselle," said Milady, "I dislike personal remarks."

D'Artagnan heard the door close again, then the sound of two bolts that Milady slid shut in order to lock herself in. On her own side, but as softly as she could, Kitty turned the key in the lock. D'Artagnan then pushed open the door of the wardrobe.

"Oh, my God!" Kitty said softly. "What's the matter with you? How pale you are!"

"The abominable creature!" murmured d'Artagnan.

"Silence! silence! leave now!" said Kitty. "There's only one partition between my room and Milady's; in the one you hear everything that's said in the other."

"That's just why I won't leave," said d'Artagnan.

"What?" said Kitty, blushing.

"Or at least I'll leave . . . later."

And he drew Kitty to him. There was no way to resist; resistance makes so much noise! And so Kitty yielded.

This was an impulse of vengeance on Milady. D'Artagnan found it was right to say that vengeance is the pleasure of the gods. And so, with a little heart, he would have been content with this new conquest; but d'Artagnan only had his ambition and his pride.

However, it must be said in praise of him, the first use he made of his influence over Kitty was to try to find out from her what had become of Mme Bonacieux, but the poor girl swore to d'Artagnan on the crucifix that she had no idea, that her mistress never let her into more than half of her secrets; only she believed she could guarantee that she was not dead.

As for what it was that had nearly made Milady lose her credit with the cardinal, Kitty knew no more about that; but this time d'Artagnan was ahead of her: as he had seen Milady on a detained ship the moment he himself was leaving England, he suspected that this time it was a question of the diamond pendants.

But what was clearest of all here was that the real hatred, the deep hatred, the inveterate hatred Milady felt for him came from the fact that he had not killed her brother-in-law.

D'Artagnan returned to Milady's the next day. She was in a very bad humor. D'Artagnan suspected it was the lack of a response from M. de Wardes that vexed her so. Kitty came in, but Milady received her very harshly. A glance she cast at d'Artagnan was meant to say: you see what I suffer on your account.

However, towards the end of the evening, the beautiful lioness softened; she listened smiling to d'Artagnan's sweet talk; she even gave him her hand to kiss.

D'Artagnan left no longer knowing what to think. But as he was a lad who could not be made to lose his head easily, while paying court to Milady he had contrived a little plan in his mind.

He found Kitty at the door, and, as the evening before, went up to her room in order to get news. Kitty had been severely scolded; she had been accused of negligence. Milady simply could not understand M. de Wardes's silence, and had ordered her to come to her room at nine o'clock in the morning to take a third letter.

D'Artagnan made Kitty promise to bring him that letter the next morning. The poor girl promised to do everything her lover wanted: she was mad.

Things went as the evening before: d'Artagnan locked himself in his wardrobe, Milady called, did her nightly preparations, sent Kitty away, and locked her door again. As the evening before, d'Artagnan did not return home until five o'clock in the morning.

At eleven o'clock, he saw Kitty arrive. She was holding a new note from Milady. This time the poor girl did not even try to keep it from d'Artagnan; she let him do as he liked; she belonged body and soul to her handsome soldier.

D'Artagnan opened the note and read the following:

This is the third time I am writing to you to tell you that I love you. Take care that I do not write you a fourth time to tell you that I detest you.

If you repent of the way you have behaved with me, the young girl who hands you this letter will tell you how a gallant man may obtain his pardon.

D'Artagnan flushed and paled several times while reading this note.

"Oh, you love her still!" said Kitty, who had not taken her eyes off the young man for a moment.

"No, Kitty, you're mistaken, I no longer love her; but I want to avenge myself for her contempt."

"Yes, I know your vengeance—you told it to me."

"What is it to you, Kitty? You know very well that I love only you."

"How can I know that?"

"By my contempt for her."

Kitty sighed.

D'Artagnan took a pen and wrote:

Madame,

Up to now I have doubted that your first two notes were indeed addressed to me, so unworthy did I deem myself of such an honor. Moreover, I was so unwell that I would in any case have hesitated to reply to them.

But today I must indeed believe in the excess of your kindness, since not only your letter, but your maid as well, assure me that I have the happiness of being loved by you.

She has no need to tell me how a gallant man may obtain his pardon. I shall come to ask you for mine this evening at eleven o'clock. To tarry a day longer would now be, in my eyes, to offend you anew.

He whom you have made the happiest of men,

Comte de Wardes

This note was first of all a forgery; it was also an indelicacy; from the point of view of our present-day morals, it was even something of a disgrace; but people of that time were less dainty than they are now. Besides, d'Artagnan knew by her own admission that Milady was guilty of treachery in more important matters, and he had only the slenderest respect for her. And yet, despite such small respect, he felt a mad passion burning in him for this woman. A passion drunk with contempt, but a passion or thirst all the same.

D'Artagnan's intention was quite simple: through Kitty's bedroom he would reach her mistress's; he would profit from the first moment of surprise, of shame, of terror, to conquer her; he might also fail, but something surely had to be left to chance. In eight days the campaign would begin, and he would have to leave. D'Artagnan had no time to spin out a perfect love.

"Here," said the young man, handing the sealed note to Kitty, "give this letter to Milady. It's the reply from M. de Wardes."

Poor Kitty turned pale as death; she guessed what was in the letter.

"Listen, my dear girl," d'Artagnan said to her, "you understand that all this has to end in one way or another. Milady may find out that you gave the first note to my valet instead of the count's valet, that it was I who opened the others that should have been opened by M. de Wardes. Then Milady will throw you out, and you know her, she's not a woman to limit her vengeance to that."

"Alas!" said Kitty, "for whom have I exposed myself to all this?"

"For me, I know very well, my lovely," said the young man, "and I'm very grateful to you for it, I swear to you."

"But what on earth is in your note?"

"Milady will tell you."

"Ah! you don't love me!" cried Kitty. "And I am so unhappy!"

To this reproach there is a response by which women are always fooled. D'Artagnan responded in such a way that Kitty remained in the greatest delusion.

She wept a great deal, however, before deciding to give Milady the letter; but she finally did decide. That was all d'Artagnan wanted.

Besides, he promised her that he would leave her mistress early, and that on leaving her mistress, he would come up to her room.

This promise thoroughly consoled poor Kitty.

XXXIV

WHICH TREATS OF THE OUTFITTING OF ARAMIS AND PORTHOS

Since the four friends began the chase after their outfits, there had been no fixed meeting between them. They dined apart from one another, wherever they happened to be, or rather wherever they could. Duty, for its part, also took up a portion of this precious time, which was so quickly running out. They had agreed to meet just once a week, towards one o'clock, at Athos's lodgings, seeing that the latter, according to the oath he had taken, no longer crossed his doorsill.

The day when Kitty came to d'Artagnan's was the day of the meeting.

Kitty had barely left when d'Artagnan set out for the rue Férou.

He found Athos and Aramis philosophizing. Aramis had half a mind to return to the cassock. Athos, as was his habit, neither dissuaded nor encouraged him. Athos was for allowing each one his free will. He never gave advice unless he was was asked. And even then one had to ask him twice.

"In general, people ask for advice," he used to say, "only so as not to follow it; or, if they do follow it, it's only so as to have someone to blame for having given it."

Porthos arrived a moment after d'Artagnan. The four friends thus found themselves together.

Their four faces expressed four different feelings: Porthos's tranquillity, d'Artagnan's hope, Aramis's worry, Athos's unconcern.

After a moment of conversation, in which Porthos let it be glimpsed that a highly placed person had kindly agreed to get him out of his difficulty, Mousqueton came in.

He came to beg Porthos to return to his lodgings, where, he said with a most pitiable air, his presence was urgently needed.

"Is it my outfit?" asked Porthos.

"Yes and no," replied Mousqueton.

"But what, finally, do you mean to say?"

"Come, Monsieur."

Porthos got up, bowed to his friends, and went out after Mousqueton.

A moment later, Bazin appeared in the doorway.

"What do you want of me, my friend?" asked Aramis, with that gentleness of expression which was noticeable in him each time his thoughts led him back to the Church.

"A man is awaiting Monsieur at home," replied Bazin.

"A man? What man?"

"A beggar."

"Give him alms, Bazin, and tell him to pray for a poor sinner."

"This beggar wants by all means to speak to you, and claims that you will be very glad to see him."

"Didn't he have anything particular to tell me?"

"He did. 'If M. Aramis hesitates to come to see me,' he said, 'announce to him that I have just come from Tours.'"

"From Tours?" cried Aramis. "Gentlemen, a thousand pardons, but this man has no doubt brought me news I've been waiting for."

And, getting up at once, he quickly left.

Athos and d'Artagnan remained.

"I think those good fellows have found what they were after. What do you think, d'Artagnan?" said Athos.

"I know that Porthos was well on his way," said d'Artagnan, "and, as for Aramis, to tell the truth, I was never seriously worried about him. But you, my dear Athos, you who so generously gave away the Englishman's pistoles, which were your legitimate property, what are you going to do?"

"I'm very glad to have killed that rascal, my boy, seeing that it's blessed bread to kill an Englishman, but if I had pocketed his pistoles, they would weigh on me like remorse."

"Come now, my dear Athos! You really have the most inconceivable ideas!"

"Let's drop it! What's this I hear from M. de Tréville, who honored me with a visit yesterday, about you haunting those suspicious Englishmen who are protected by the cardinal?"

"That is, I've been visiting a certain Englishwoman, the one I've told you about."

"Ah, yes, the blond woman about whom I gave you advice which you have naturally been careful not to follow."

"I gave you my reasons."

"Yes. You see your outfit in it, I believe, from what you told me."

"Not at all! I've learned for certain that this woman had something to do with the abduction of Mme Bonacieux."

"Yes, and I can understand that. To find one woman, you pay court to another: that's the longest way, but the most amusing."

D'Artagnan was on the point of telling Athos everything, but one thing stopped him: Athos was a strict gentleman on the point of honor, and there were, in this whole little plan our lover had made up regarding Milady, certain things which—he was sure of it beforehand—would not win the puritan's assent. He thus preferred to keep silent, and as Athos was the least curious man on earth, d'Artagnan's confidences stopped there.

We shall therefore leave the two friends, who had nothing very important to say to each other, and follow Aramis.

At the news that the man who wished to speak to him had just come from Tours, we have seen with what rapidity the young man went after, or rather ahead of, Bazin. He made it from the rue Férou to the rue de Vaugirard in a single bound.

On going into his place, he indeed found a small man with intelligent eyes, but clothed in rags.

"It's you who are asking for me?" said the musketeer.

"That is, I am asking for M. Aramis: is it you who call yourself that?"

"Himself. Do you have something to give me?"

"Yes, if you will show me a certain embroidered handkerchief."

"Here it is," said Aramis, taking a key from his bosom and opening a small ebony chest inlaid with mother-of-pearl, "here it is, take it."

"Very well," said the beggar, "send your lackey away."

Indeed, Bazin, curious to know what the beggar wanted with his master, had matched his pace and arrived at almost the same time. But this celerity was of little use to him. At the beggar's invitation, his master made a sign for him to withdraw, and he was forced to obey.

With Bazin gone, the beggar cast a rapid glance around to make sure that no one could either see or hear him, and, opening his ragged coat, poorly secured by a leather belt, set about unstitching the top of his doublet, from which he drew a letter.

Aramis let out a cry of joy on seeing the seal, kissed the handwriting, and with an almost religious respect, opened the epistle, which contained the following:

> My friend, fate wills that we be separated for some time still; but the lovely days of youth are not lost forever. Do your duty in the camp; I shall do mine elsewhere. Take what the bearer will give you; make the campaign as a fine and true gentleman, and think of me, who tenderly kiss your dark eyes.
>
> Adieu, or rather, au revoir!

The beggar went on unstitching. One by one, he drew a hundred and fifty Spanish double pistoles from his dirty clothes and lined them up on the table. Then he opened the door, bowed, and left before the stupefied young man dared say a word to him.

Aramis then reread the letter, and noticed that it had a *post-scriptum*.

> P.S. You may welcome the bearer, who is a count and a Spanish grandee.

"Golden dreams!" cried Aramis. "Oh, beautiful life! Yes, we're still young! Yes, we shall still have happy days! Oh, to you, my love, my blood, my life! All, all, all, my beautiful mistress!"

And he kissed the letter passionately, without even looking at the gold that glittered on the table.

Bazin scratched at the door. Aramis had no more reason to keep him away; he let him come in.

Bazin was left stunned by the sight of the gold, and forgot that he had come to announce d'Artagnan, who, curious to know what this beggar was all about, went to Aramis on leaving Athos.

Now, as d'Artagnan did not stand on ceremony with Aramis, seeing that Bazin forgot to announce him, he announced himself.

"Ah, devil take it, my dear Aramis," said d'Artagnan, "if that's the sort of prunes they send us from Tours, give my compliments to the gardener who picked them!"

"You're mistaken, my dear," said the ever discreet Aramis, "it's my bookseller, who has just sent me the fee for that poem in one-syllable lines that I began down there."

"Ah, really!" said d'Artagnan. "Well, your bookseller is generous, my dear Aramis, that's all I can say."

"What, Monsieur!" cried Bazin. "A poem selling for so much? It's incredible! Oh, Monsieur, just keep on going, you may become the equal of M. de Voiture and M. de Benserade! I like that, I do. A poet—that's almost an abbé. Ah, M. Aramis, be a poet, then, I beg you!"

"Bazin, my friend," said Aramis, "I believe you're mixing into the conversation."

Bazin understood that he was in the wrong. He hung his head and left.

"Ah," said d'Artagnan with a smile, "you sell your productions for their weight in gold. You're a lucky man, my friend. But take care, you're going to lose that letter that's sticking out of your tabard, and which is undoubtedly from your bookseller."

Aramis blushed to the roots of his hair, pushed the letter back in, and buttoned up his doublet.

"My dear d'Artagnan," he said, "if you're willing, we'll go to find our friends. And since I'm rich, today we'll start dining together again, while we wait for you all to become rich in turn."

"By heaven," said d'Artagnan, "with great pleasure! We haven't had a proper dinner for a long time. And since, for my own part, I have a somewhat risky expedition to make this evening, I won't be sorry, I'll confess, to work myself up a bit with a few bottles of old burgundy."

"Let it be old burgundy; I don't detest it either," said Aramis, from whom the sight of the gold had removed, as if by sleight of hand, all thoughts of retirement.

And having put three or four double pistoles in his pocket to answer to the needs of the moment, he locked up the rest in the ebony chest inlaid with mother-of-pearl, where he had already put the famous handkerchief that had served him as a talisman.

The two friends went first to see Athos, who, faithful to the oath he had taken not to go out, undertook to have dinner brought to his place. As he had a perfect understanding of gastronomic details, d'Artagnan and Aramis had no difficulty in leaving this important task to him.

They were on their way to see Porthos when, at the corner of the rue du Bac, they ran into Mousqueton, who, with a pitiable look, was driving a mule and a horse before him.

D'Artagnan let out a cry of surprise, which was not without an admixture of joy.

"Ah, my yellow horse!" he cried. "Aramis, look at this horse!"

"What a frightful old cob!" said Aramis.

"Well, my dear," d'Artagnan picked up, "that's the horse I came to Paris on!"

"What? Monsieur knows this horse?" said Mousqueton.

"The color's original," said Aramis. "It's the only one I've ever seen with a hide like that."

"I can well believe it," d'Artagnan picked up. "I sold him for three écus, and it must have been for the hide, because the carcass certainly wasn't worth eighteen livres. But how did you wind up with this horse, Mousqueton?"

"Ah!" said the valet, "don't speak of it, Monsieur. It's a frightful trick of our duchess's husband!"

"How's that, Mousqueton?"

"Yes, we're looked upon with a very kindly eye by a lady of quality, the duchess of . . . But, forgive me, my master has urged me to be discreet. She had forced us to accept a little souvenir, a magnificent Spanish jennet and an Andalusian mule that was a wonder to behold. The husband found out about it, confiscated the two magnificent beasts as they were being sent to us, and substituted these horrible animals for them!"

"Which you are bringing back to him?" asked d'Artagnan.

"Exactly!" replied Mousqueton. "You understand that we can hardly accept such mounts in exchange for the ones that were promised us."

"No, pardieu, though I'd love to have seen Porthos on my Buttercup; it would have given me an idea of how I looked myself when I arrived in Paris. But don't let us detain you, Mousqueton. Go, go, and carry out your master's commission. Is he at home?"

"Yes, Monsieur," said Mousqueton, "but very grumpy, I can tell you!"

And he continued on his way towards the quai des Grands-Augustins, while the two friends went to ring at the unfortunate Porthos's door. The latter had seen them crossing the courtyard and took care not to open. So they rang in vain.

Meanwhile, Mousqueton continued on his route, and, crossing the Pont-Neuf, constantly driving the two nags before him, came to the rue aux Ours. On arriving there, following his master's orders, he tied the horse and the mule to the procureur's door knocker. Then, without worrying about their future fate, he went to find Porthos and announced to him that his commission had been carried out.

After a while, the two wretched beasts, who had not eaten since morning, made so much noise by raising the knocker and letting it fall that the procureur ordered his errand boy to go and find out from the neighbors whom the horse and mule belonged to.

Mme Coquenard recognized her present, and at first could not understand this restitution; but soon a visit from Porthos enlightened her. The wrath that shone in the musketeer's eyes, despite the restraint he imposed on himself, frightened his sensitive lady love. Indeed, Mousqueton had not concealed from his master that he had run into d'Artagnan and Aramis, and that d'Artagnan had recognized the yellow horse as the Béarnais nag on which he had come to Paris, and which he had sold for three écus.

Porthos left after arranging a rendezvous with the procureuse in the cloister of Saint-Magloire. The procureur, seeing that Porthos was leaving, invited him to dinner, an invitation that the musketeer declined with a majestic air.

Mme Coquenard went all atremble to the cloister of Saint-Magloire, for she had guessed what reproaches awaited her there; but she was fascinated by Porthos's grand manner.

All the imprecations and reproaches that a man wounded in his vanity could pour down on a woman's head, Porthos poured down on the bent head of the procureuse.

"Alas!" she said, "I did my best. One of our clients is a horse merchant. He owed the office money and proved recalcitrant. I took the mule and the horse for what he owed us—he had promised me two royal mounts."

"Well, Madame," said Porthos, "if he owed you more than five écus, your horse dealer is a thief."

"It's not forbidden to look for a bargain, M. Porthos," said the procureuse, looking for an excuse.

"No, Madame, but those who look for bargains must allow others to look for more generous friends."

And, turning on his heel, Porthos took a step away.

"M. Porthos! M. Porthos!" cried the procureuse. "I was wrong, I admit it, I shouldn't have bargained when it was a question of outfitting a cavalier like you!"

Porthos, without replying, took a second step away.

The procureuse thought she saw him in a dazzling cloud, all surrounded by duchesses and marquises, who were throwing sacks of gold at his feet.

"Stop, in heaven's name, M. Porthos!" she cried. "Stop and let's talk."

"Talking with you brings me misfortune," said Porthos.

"But, tell me, what are you asking for?"

"Nothing, for it comes down to the same thing as asking you for something."

The procureuse hung on Porthos's arm, and, carried away by her sorrow, cried to him:

"M. Porthos, I am ignorant of all that. Do I know what a horse is? Do I know what harness is?"

"You should have left it to me, who do know, Madame. But you wanted to be economical and, consequently, to lend at usury."

"It was a wrong thing, M. Porthos, and I'll make up for it, on my word of honor."

"How so?" asked the musketeer.

"Listen. Tonight M. Coquenard is going to see M. le duc de Chaulnes, who has summoned him. It's for a consultation that will last at least two hours. Come, we'll be alone, and we'll settle our accounts."

"Capital! Now you're talking, my dear!"

"You'll forgive me?"

"We'll see," Porthos said majestically.

And the two separated, saying: till this evening.

"Devil take it!" thought Porthos, walking away. "It seems I'm finally getting close to Master Coquenard's cupboard."

XXXV

AT NIGHT ALL CATS ARE GRAY

That evening, awaited so impatiently by Porthos and by d'Artagnan, finally came.

D'Artagnan, as usual, appeared at Milady's towards nine o'clock. He found her in a charming humor; never had she received him so well. Our Gascon saw at first glance that his note had been delivered and had had its effect.

Kitty came in bringing sherbets. Her mistress gave her a charming look, smiled her most gracious smile at her, but, alas! the poor girl was so sad that she did not even notice Milady's benevolence.

D'Artagnan looked from one woman to the other, and was forced to admit that nature had made a mistake in forming them: to the grand lady she had given a vile and venal soul; to the soubrette she had given the heart of a duchess.

At ten o'clock Milady began to look restless. D'Artagnan

understood what this meant. She glanced at the clock, got up, sat down again, smiled at d'Artagnan with a look that meant to say: you are very nice, of course, but you would be so charming if you left!

D'Artagnan got up and took his hat; Milady gave him her hand to kiss. The young man felt her press his hand and understood that it was with a feeling not of coquetry but of gratitude for his departure.

"She's devilishly in love with him," he murmured. Then he left.

This time Kitty was not waiting for him anywhere, either in the antechamber, or in the corridor, or under the gateway. D'Artagnan had to find the stairway and the little bedroom on his own.

Kitty was sitting with her face buried in her hands, weeping. She heard d'Artagnan come in, but she did not raise her head. The young man went to her and took her hands, and then she burst into sobs.

As d'Artagnan had guessed, Milady, on receiving the letter, had, in the delirium of her joy, told her maid everything. Then, in reward for the way she had carried out her commission this time, she had given her a purse. Kitty, on returning to her room, had thrown the purse into a corner, where it lay wide open, spewing out three or four gold pieces on the rug.

At the sound of d'Artagnan's voice, the poor girl raised her head. D'Artagnan himself was startled at the distortion of her face. She pressed her hands together with a look of supplication, but without daring to say a word.

Little sensitive as d'Artagnan's heart was, he felt touched by this mute suffering; but he was too keen on his plans, and above all on this one, to change anything in the program he had laid out in advance. He thus left Kitty no hope of making him relent, only he presented his act to her as a simple matter of vengeance.

This vengeance, moreover, became the more easy in that Milady, no doubt to conceal her blushes from her lover, had told Kitty to put out all the lights in the apartment, and even in her own bedroom. Before daybreak, M. de Wardes was to leave, still in darkness.

A moment later, Milady could be heard going to her bedroom. D'Artagnan leaped for his wardrobe at once. He had barely ducked into it when the little bell rang.

Kitty went to her mistress's room and did not leave the door open; but the partition was so thin that almost everything said between the two women could be heard.

Milady seemed drunk with joy. She made Kitty repeat the smallest details of the supposed interview between the soubrette and de Wardes, how he had received her letter, how he had responded, what had been the expression of his face, whether he had seemed truly amorous. And to all these questions, poor Kitty, forced to keep a good countenance, responded in a choking voice, of which her mistress did not even notice the sorrowful tone—so egotistical is happiness.

Finally, as the hour of her meeting with the count approached, Milady indeed had all the lights put out, and ordered Kitty to go back to her room and let de Wardes in as soon as he appeared.

Kitty did not have to wait long. The moment d'Artagnan saw through the keyhole of his wardrobe that the whole apartment was in darkness, he leaped from his hiding place, just as Kitty was closing the communicating door.

"What was that noise?" asked Milady.

"It is I," said d'Artagnan in a low voice, "I, the comte de Wardes."

"Oh, my God, my God!" murmured Kitty. "He couldn't even wait for the hour he had fixed himself!"

"Well!" said Milady, in a trembling voice, "why doesn't he come in? Count, Count," she added, "you know very well I'm expecting you!"

At this summons, d'Artagnan gently moved Kitty aside and sprang into Milady's bedroom.

If rage and pain can torture any soul, it is that of the lover who, under a name not his own, receives protestations of love addressed to his fortunate rival.

D'Artagnan was in a painful situation that he had not foreseen, jealousy gnawed at his heart, and he suffered almost as much as poor Kitty, who at that same moment was weeping in the neighboring room.

"Yes, Count," said Milady in her gentlest voice, pressing his hand tenderly in hers, "yes, I am happy in the love which your glances and your words have expressed to me each time we've met. I love you, too. Oh, tomorrow, tomorrow I want some pledge from you which will prove that you think of me, and as you might forget me, take this."

And she slipped a ring from her finger onto d'Artagnan's.

D'Artagnan remembered having seen this ring on Milady's hand: it was a magnificent sapphire surrounded by brilliants.

D'Artagnan's first impulse was to give it back, but Milady added:

"No, no, keep this ring out of love for me. Besides, in accepting it," she added with feeling, "you will be doing me a greater service than you could ever imagine."

"This woman is full of mysteries," d'Artagnan murmured to himself.

At that moment he felt ready to reveal all. He opened his mouth to tell Milady who he was and with what vengeful purpose he had come, but she added:

"Poor angel, that monster of a Gascon nearly killed you!"

He was that monster.

"Oh!" Milady went on, "do you still suffer from your wounds?"

"Yes, very much," said d'Artagnan, who did not quite know how to reply.

"Don't worry," murmured Milady, "I will avenge you myself, and cruelly!"

"Damn!" d'Artagnan said to himself. "It's not yet the moment for confessions."

It took d'Artagnan some time to get over this little dialogue. But all the ideas of vengeance he had brought with him had vanished completely. This woman exercised an incredible power over him. He both hated her and adored her. He had never thought that two so contrary feelings could inhabit the same heart and, in coming together, form a strange and some-how diabolical love.

However, it had just struck one; they had to separate. D'Artagnan, at the moment of leaving Milady, felt only a sharp regret to be going away, and, in the passionate farewell they addressed to each other, a new meeting was agreed upon for the next week. Poor Kitty hoped to be able to say a few words to d'Artagnan as he passed through her room, but Milady saw him off herself in the dark and left him only on the stairs.

The following morning, d'Artagnan ran to Athos's. He was caught up in so singular an adventure that he wanted to ask his advice. He told him everything. Athos frowned several times.

"Your Milady," he said to him, "seems to me to be an infamous creature, but nonetheless you were wrong to deceive her. In one way or another, you've got a terrible enemy on your hands."

And as he spoke with him, Athos kept looking at the sapphire surrounded with diamonds that d'Artagnan was wearing on his finger in place of the queen's ring, which had been carefully put away in a jewelry box.

"You're looking at this ring?" asked the Gascon, proud to show off so rich a present before the eyes of his friends.

"Yes," said Athos, "it reminds me of a family jewel."

"It's beautiful, isn't it?" said d'Artagnan.

"Magnificent!" replied Athos. "I didn't think there could be two sapphires of so fine a water. Did you pawn your diamond for it?"

"No," said d'Artagnan, "it's a gift from my beautiful Englishwoman, or rather my beautiful Frenchwoman: for, though I've never asked her, I'm convinced she was born in France."

"That ring came to you from Milady?" cried Athos, with a voice in which it was easy to detect strong emotion.

"Herself. She gave it to me last night."

"Show me the ring," said Athos.

"Here it is," replied d'Artagnan, taking it from his finger. Athos examined it and turned very pale. Then he tried it on the ring finger of his left hand. It went on the finger as if it had been made for it. A cloud of anger and vengeance passed over the usually calm brow of the gentleman.

"It can't possibly be the same," he said. "How could that ring wind up in the hands of Milady Clarick? And yet it's hardly likely that two jewels could be so much alike."

"You know this ring?" asked d'Artagnan.

"I thought I recognized it," said Athos, "but no doubt I'm mistaken."

And he handed it back to d'Artagnan, yet without ceasing to look at it.

"Listen, d'Artagnan," he said after a moment, "either take that ring off, or turn the stone inside; it reminds me of such cruel memories that I won't have wits enough to talk with you. Didn't you come to ask my advice, didn't you say to me that you had trouble deciding what you should do? . . . But wait . . . hand me that sapphire: the one I mentioned to you should have a scrape on one of its facets as the result of an accident."

D'Artagnan took the ring off again and handed it to Athos. Athos shuddered.

"Here," he said, "you see, isn't it strange?"

And he showed d'Artagnan the scratch that he had remembered should be there.

"But who did you have this sapphire from, Athos?"

"My mother, who had it from her mother. As I told you, it's an old jewel . . . which should never have left the family."

"And you . . . sold it?" d'Artagnan asked hesitantly.

"No," Athos picked up with a singular smile, "I gave it away during a night of love, as it was given to you."

D'Artagnan waxed pensive in his turn. He seemed to see abysses of a dark and unknown depth in Milady's soul.

He put the ring not on his finger but in his pocket.

"Listen," Athos said to him, taking his hand, "you know that I love you, d'Artagnan. If I had a son, I couldn't love him more than you. Well, then, believe what I say: give up that woman. I don't know her, but a sort of intuition tells me that she's a lost creature, and that there is something fatal in her."

"And you're right," said d'Artagnan. "So I'll break with her. I confess to you that the woman really frightens me."

"Will you have the courage?" asked Athos.

"I will," replied d'Artagnan, "and even at once."

"Well, true enough, my lad, you're right," said the gentleman, pressing the Gascon's hand with an almost paternal affection. "God grant that this woman, who has barely entered your life, leaves no baneful trace on it!"

And Athos bowed his head to d'Artagnan, as a man who means to make it understood that he is not sorry to be left alone with his thoughts.

On returning home, d'Artagnan found Kitty waiting for him. A month of fever could not have changed the poor girl more than had that one night of insomnia and grief.

She had been sent by her mistress to the false de Wardes. Her mistress was mad with love, drunk with joy; she wanted to know when the count would grant her a second meeting.

And poor Kitty, pale and trembling, awaited d'Artagnan's reply.

Athos had great influence over the young man. His friend's advice, together with the cries of his own heart, had determined him, now that his pride had been saved and his vengeance satisfied, not to see Milady again. For his whole reply, then, he took a pen and wrote the following letter:

Do not count on me, Madame, for the next rendezvous: since my convalescence, I have so much business of the same sort that I have had to put it in a certain order. When your turn comes, I shall have the honor of informing you of it.

I kiss your hands.

Comte de Wardes

Not a word of the sapphire. Did the Gascon want to keep it as a weapon against Milady? Or else, to be frank, was he not keeping this sapphire as a last resource for outfitting himself?

It would be wrong, however, to judge the actions of one

age from the point of view of another. What would be regarded today as shameful for a gallant man was at that time
quite a simple and natural thing, and the cadets of the best
families generally had themselves kept by their mistresses.

D'Artagnan handed the unsealed letter to Kitty, who first
read it without understanding, and nearly became mad with
joy on reading it a second time.

Kitty could not believe in this happiness. D'Artagnan was
forced to repeat aloud the assurances that the letter gave her in
writing. And whatever the danger the poor girl was running,
given the fiery nature of Milady, in delivering this note to her
mistress, she nevertheless went back to the place Royale as fast
as her legs would carry her.

The heart of the best woman is pitiless towards the sufferings of a rival.

Milady opened the letter with an eagerness equal to that
with which Kitty had brought it. But at the first word, she became livid; then she crumpled the paper; then she turned to
Kitty with lightning in her eyes.

"What is this letter?" she said.

"Why, it's the reply to Madame's," Kitty replied, trembling
all over.

"Impossible!" cried Milady. "It's impossible that a gentleman should write such a letter to a woman!"

Then, shuddering all at once:

"My God!" she said, "could he know?..." And she
stopped.

She ground her teeth, her face was the color of ash. She
tried to take a step towards the window to get some air, but
she could only hold out her arms; her legs gave way, and she
collapsed onto a chair.

Kitty thought she was unwell and rushed to open her
bodice. But Milady sat up quickly.

"What do you want?" she said. "Why are you putting
your hands on me?"

"I thought Madame was unwell, and I wanted to help
her," replied the maid, frightened at the terrible expression
that had come over her mistress's face.

"Unwell? I? I? Do you take me for a weak female? When I am insulted, I do not become unwell, I become vengeful! Do you hear?"

And she made a sign with her hand for Kitty to leave.

XXXVI

THE DREAM OF VENGEANCE

That evening Milady gave orders to admit M. d'Artagnan as soon as he came, as was her custom. But he did not come.

The next day Kitty went to see the young man again and told him all that had happened the evening before. D'Artagnan smiled; this jealous anger of Milady was his vengeance.

That evening Milady was still more impatient than the day before. She repeated her orders concerning the Gascon; but, as the day before, she waited in vain.

The next day Kitty appeared at d'Artagnan's, no longer joyful and alert as on the two previous days, but desperately sad.

D'Artagnan asked the poor girl what was wrong, but her only reply was to take a letter from her pocket and hand it to him.

This letter was in Milady's hand, only this time it was actually addressed to d'Artagnan and not to M. de Wardes.

He opened it and read the following:

Dear M. d'Artagnan,

It is wrong to neglect one's friends like this, above all when one is about to leave them for so long. My brother-in-law and I waited in vain yesterday and the day before. Will it be the same this evening?

Your very grateful,

Lady Clarick

"It's quite simple," said d'Artargnan, "and I've been expecting this letter. My credit goes up as the comte de Wardes's goes down."

"You mean you'll go?" asked Kitty.

"Listen, my dear child," said the Gascon, who was seeking to excuse himself in his own eyes for breaking his promise to Athos, "you understand that it would be impolitic not to accept such an outright invitation. Milady, seeing that I do not come back, will be unable to understand the breaking off of my visits. She may suspect something, and who can say how far the vengeance of a woman of such temper will go?"

"Oh, my God!" said Kitty. "You know how to present things so that you're always right. But you'll court her again; and if you manage to please her this time, under your own name and your own face, it will be much worse than the first time!"

Instinct made the poor girl guess part of what was going to happen.

D'Artagnan reassured her as best he could and promised her that he would remain insensible to Milady's seductions.

He sent word to her that he could not be more grateful for her kindness and that he would obey her orders; but he did not dare write to her for fear of being unable to disguise his handwriting sufficiently for eyes as experienced as Milady's.

At the stroke of nine, d'Artagnan was at the place Royale. It was obvious that the domestics who were waiting in the antechamber had been forewarned, for as soon as d'Artagnan appeared, even before he asked if it was possible to see Milady, one of them ran to announce him.

"Show him in," said Milady, in a voice so curt but so piercing that d'Artagnan heard it in the antechamber.

He was admitted.

"I am at home to no one," said Milady, "understand? No one."

The lackey went out.

D'Artagnan cast a curious glance at Milady: she was pale and her eyes were tired, either from tears or from insomnia. The number of lights had been intentionally diminished, and yet the young woman could not manage to conceal the traces of the fever that had devoured her for two days.

D'Artagnan went up to her with his usual gallantry. She

made a supreme effort to receive him, but never had a more distorted physiognomy belied a more amiable smile.

To d'Artagnan's questions about her health, she replied: "Bad, very bad."

"But in that case," said d'Artagnan, "I am being indiscreet, you no doubt have need of rest, and I shall withdraw."

"Not at all," said Milady. "On the contrary, stay, M. d'Artagnan, your amiable company will distract me."

"Oho!" thought d'Artagnan. "She's never been so charming. We must beware!"

Milady assumed the most affectionate air she could manage, and put all possible brilliance into her conversation. At the same time, that fever which had left her for an instant came back to restore the brightness to her eyes, the color to her cheeks, the crimson to her lips. D'Artagnan found again that Circe who had already wrapped him in her enchantments. His love, which he thought extinguished and which was only napping, awakened in his heart. Milady smiled, and d'Artagnan felt he would damn himself for that smile.

There was a moment when he felt something like remorse for what he had done to her.

Milady gradually became more communicative. She asked d'Artagnan if he had a mistress.

"Alas!" said d'Artagnan, with the most sentimental air he could assume, "could you be so cruel as to ask me such a question? I, who, ever since I first saw you, have breathed and sighed only through you and for you?"

Milady smiled a strange smile.

"So you love me?" she asked.

"Do I need to tell you so? Haven't you noticed it?"

"Yes, I have. But you know, the prouder the heart, the harder it is to win."

"Oh, I'm not afraid of difficulties!" said d'Artagnan. "It is only impossibilities that frighten me."

"Nothing is impossible," said Milady, "for true love."

"Nothing, Madame?"

"Nothing," replied Milady.

"Devil take it," d'Artagnan said to himself, "that's a different tune! Is she falling in love with me, by chance, the capricious lady, and would she be disposed to give me some other sapphire for myself, like the one she gave me when she took me for de Wardes?"

D'Artagnan quickly brought his chair closer to Milady's.

"Well, now," she said, "what would you do to prove this love you speak of?"

"Anything that was asked of me. Give the order, and I'm ready."

"For anything?"

"For anything!" cried d'Artagnan, who knew ahead of time that he was not risking much in committing himself like this.

"Well, then, let's talk a little," Milady said in her turn, bringing her chair closer to d'Artagnan's.

"I'm listening, Madame," the latter said.

Milady remained anxious and as if undecided for a moment; then she seemed to make a decision.

"I have an enemy," she said.

"You, Madame?" cried d'Artagnan, acting surprised. "My God, is it possible, good and beautiful as you are?"

"A mortal enemy."

"Really?"

"An enemy who has insulted me so cruelly that there is war to the death between him and me. Can I count on you as an ally?"

D'Artagnan understood then and there where the vindictive creature was heading.

"You can, Madame," he said emphatically. "My arm and my life are yours, as is my love."

"In that case," said Milady, "since you are as generous as you are loving . . ."

She paused.

"Well?" asked d'Artagnan.

"Well," picked up Milady, after a moment's silence, "from now on stop speaking of impossibility."

"Do not overwhelm me with happiness," cried d'Artagnan, throwing himself on his knees and covering with kisses the hands that were surrendered to him.

"Avenge me on that infamous de Wardes," Milady murmured between her teeth, "and I'll know very well how to get rid of you afterwards, you double fool, you walking sword blade!"

"Fall willingly into my arms after having jeered at me so impudently, you dangerous and hypocritical woman," d'Artagnan thought for his part, "and afterwards I and the man you want to kill by my hand will both laugh at you."

D'Artagnan raised his head.

"I am ready," he said.

"You've understood me, then, my dear M. d'Artagnan?" said Milady.

"I could guess from one look of yours."

"And so you will put your arm to use for me, that arm which has already won so much renown?"

"This very instant."

"But," said Milady, "how shall I reward such service? I know what lovers are like; they are people who never do anything for nothing."

"You know the only response I desire," said d'Artagnan, "the only one worthy of you and of me!"

And he drew her gently towards him.

She hardly resisted.

"Calculator!" she said, smiling.

"Ah!" cried d'Artagnan, truly carried away by the passion that this woman had the gift of kindling in his heart, "ah! it's that my happiness seems so improbable to me, and since I'm always afraid to see it fly off like a dream, I'm in haste to make it a reality."

"Well, then, try to deserve this supposed happiness."

"I am at your orders," said d'Artagnan.

"Is that so?" asked Milady, with a final doubt.

"Name for me the infamous one who could make your lovely eyes weep."

"Who told you I wept?" she asked.

"It seemed to me . . ."

"Women like me never weep," said Milady.

"So much the better! Come, tell me his name."

"Realize that his name is the whole of my secret."

"I still must know what it is."

"Yes, you must. See how I trust you!"

"You fill me with joy. What is his name?"

"You know it."

"Really?"

"Yes."

"It's not one of my friends?" d'Artagnan picked up, feigning hesitation to make her believe in his ignorance.

"So you'd hesitate if it was one of your friends?" cried Milady. And a threatening gleam flashed in her eye.

"No, not even if it was my brother!" cried d'Artagnan, as if carried away by enthusiasm.

Our Gascon advanced without risk, because he knew where he was going.

"I love your devotion," said Milady.

"Alas! is that all you love in me?" asked d'Artagnan.

"I love you, too, you yourself," she said, taking his hand.

And the ardent pressure made d'Artagnan shudder, as if by that touch the fever that burned in Milady passed over to him.

"You? You love me?" he cried. "Oh, if it were so, it would make me lose my reason!"

And he threw his arms around her. Her lips did not try to avoid his kiss, though she did not return it.

Her lips were cold. It seemed to d'Artagnan that he had just kissed a statue.

But he was nonetheless drunk with joy, electrified with love. He almost believed in Milady's tenderness; he almost believed in de Wardes's crime. If de Wardes had been in his hands at that moment, he would have killed him.

Milady seized the occasion.

"His name is . . ." she said in her turn.

"De Wardes, I know it!" cried d'Artagnan.

"And how do you know it?" asked Milady, seizing him by both hands and trying to read the depths of his soul through his eyes.

D'Artagnan realized that he had gotten carried away and had made a blunder.

"Tell me, tell me, tell me!" Milady repeated. "How do you know it?"

"How do I know it?" said d'Artagnan.

"Yes."

"I know it because yesterday, in a salon where I happened to be, de Wardes displayed a ring which he said he had from you."

"The scoundrel!" cried Milady.

The epithet, as we can well understand, echoed to the bottom of d'Artagnan's heart.

"Well?" she went on.

"Well, I will avenge you on that scoundrel," d'Artagnan picked up, giving himself the airs of Don Japhet of Armenia.

"Thank you, my brave friend!" cried Milady. "And when will I be avenged?"

"Tomorrow, at once, whenever you like."

Milady was about to cry "At once," but she reflected that such haste would not be very becoming for d'Artagnan.

Besides, she had a thousand precautions to take, a thousand counsels to give her defender, so that he would avoid explanations with the count in front of witnesses. All of this was settled by a word from d'Artagnan.

"Tomorrow," he said, "you will be avenged, or I will be dead."

"No!" she said. "You will avenge me, and you will not die. He's a coward."

"With women, perhaps, but not with men. I know something about it."

"But it seems to me that in your fight with him, you had no reason to complain to fortune."

"Fortune is a courtesan: favorable yesterday, she may betray me tomorrow."

"Which means you're hesitant now."

"No, I'm not hesitant, God forbid! But would it be fair to let me go to a possible death without having given me at least a little more than mere hope?"

Milady replied with a glance that meant: "Is that all? Speak up, then." And accompanying the glance with explanatory words, she said tenderly:

"You're quite right."

"Oh, you're an angel!" said the young man.

"So it's all agreed?" she said.

"Except what I'm asking of you, my dear soul!"

"But since I've told you that you can trust in my affection?"

"I have no tomorrow to wait for."

"Quiet! I hear my brother. There's no use in him finding you here."

She rang; Kitty appeared.

"Leave by this door," she said, pushing open a little hidden door, "and come back at eleven. We'll finish our discussion. Kitty will show you to my room."

The poor child thought she would fall over when she heard these words.

"Well, what are you doing, Mademoiselle, standing there motionless as a statue? Come, show the chevalier out. And this evening, at eleven, you heard me!"

"Eleven o'clock seems to be her time for appointments," thought d'Artagnan. "It's an acquired habit."

Milady held out a hand, which he kissed tenderly.

"Now, then," he said, going out, and scarcely responding to Kitty's reproaches, "now then, let's have no foolishness. This woman is decidedly a great villain: let's be careful!"

XXXVII

Milady's Secret

D'Artagnan had left the hôtel instead of going up at once to Kitty's, despite the solicitations the young girl had made to him, and that for two reasons: first, because in that way he avoided reproaches, recriminations, entreaties; second, because he was not sorry for the chance to examine his own thoughts a little, and, if possible, that woman's as well.

What was clearest in it all was that d'Artagnan loved Milady madly and that she did not love him in the least. D'Artagnan instantly understood that the best thing to do would be to go home and write Milady a long letter confessing that up to now he and de Wardes were one and the same, and that consequently he could not take it upon himself, under pain of suicide, to kill de Wardes. But he was also spurred on by a fierce desire for vengeance. He wanted to possess this woman once more under his own name, and as this vengeance seemed to him to have a certain sweetness, he was unwilling to renounce it.

He made the tour of the place Royale five or six times, turning every ten steps to look at the light in Milady's apartment, which could be seen through the blinds. It was obvious that this time the young woman was in less of a hurry to go to her room than she had been the first time.

At last the light went out.

Along with that glimmer, the last irresolution was extinguished in d'Artagnan's heart. He recalled the details of the previous night, and, his heart leaping, his head on fire, went back to the hôtel and hurried to Kitty's room.

The young girl, pale as death, trembling all over, wanted to stop her lover; but Milady, her ears pricked up, had heard the noise d'Artagnan made. She opened the door.

"Come," she said.

All this was so incredibly impudent, so monstrously brazen, that d'Artagnan could scarcely believe what he saw and heard. He thought he was being dragged into one of those fantastic intrigues such as are fulfilled in dreams.

He rushed to Milady nonetheless, yielding to that attraction which a magnet exerts upon iron.

The door closed behind them.

Kitty threw herself against it from her side.

Jealousy, fury, offended pride, all the passions, finally, that struggle over the heart of a woman in love, urged her to give him away. But she would be lost if she admitted having lent a hand in such a machination; and, above all, d'Artagnan would be lost to her. This last loving thought advised her to make this last sacrifice.

D'Artagnan, for his part, had reached the fulfillment of all his wishes: it was no longer a rival that was loved in him, it was he himself who seemed to be loved. A secret voice told him at the very bottom of his heart that he was only an instrument of vengeance that one caressed while waiting for it to kill, but pride, but vanity, but madness silenced that voice, stifled that murmur. Then our Gascon, with the dose of confidence we know in him, compared himself with de Wardes and asked why, when all was said, he, too, should not be loved for himself alone.

He thus abandoned himself entirely to the sensations of the moment. For him, Milady was no longer that woman of fatal intentions who had frightened him momentarily, she was an ardent and passionate mistress abandoning herself entirely to a love that she herself seemed to feel. Some two hours went by like this.

However, the transports of the two lovers subsided. Milady, who did not have the same motives for forgetting as d'Artagnan, came back to reality first and asked the young man if the measures that were to lead to a meeting between him and de Wardes the next day had been well fixed in his mind beforehand.

But d'Artagnan, whose ideas had taken quite a different course, forgot himself like a fool and answered gallantly that it was rather late to be concerned with duels at sword point.

This coolness towards the only interests that concerned her frightened Milady, whose questions became more insistent.

Then d'Artagnan, who had never seriously thought about this impossible duel, tried to change the subject, but he was no longer up to it.

Milady confined him to the limits she had traced out beforehand with her irresistible mind and her iron will.

D'Artagnan thought himself witty in advising Milady to pardon de Wardes and give up the furious plans she had made.

But at his first words, the young woman shuddered and moved away.

"Might you be afraid, dear d'Artagnan?" she said in a shrill and jeering voice that rang out strangely in the darkness.

"Don't think of it, dear soul!" replied d'Artagnan. "But, finally, what if this poor comte de Wardes was less guilty than you think?"

"In any case," Milady said gravely, "he deceived me, and from the moment he deceived me, he deserved to die."

"He will die, then, since you condemn him!" said d'Artagnan, in so firm a tone that it seemed to Milady the expression of an unflagging devotion.

She drew close to him at once.

We cannot say how long the night lasted for Milady; but d'Artagnan thought he had been with her for barely two hours when daylight appeared through the slats of the blinds and soon invaded the room with its pallid gleam.

Then Milady, seeing that d'Artagnan was going to leave her, reminded him of the promise he had made to avenge her on de Wardes.

"I am quite ready to," said d'Artagnan, "but first I would like to be sure of one thing."

"What is it?" asked Milady.

"That you love me."

"I've given you proof of that, it seems to me."

"Yes, and so I am yours body and soul."

"Thank you, my brave lover! But just as I have proved my love for you, you will prove yours in turn, will you not?"

"Certainly. But if you love me as you say," d'Artagnan picked up, "aren't you a little afraid for me?"

"What have I to fear?"

"Why, that I might be seriously wounded, even killed."

"Impossible," said Milady, "you're so valiant a man and so keen a sword."

"So you wouldn't prefer," d'Artagnan continued, "a means that would avenge you just as well, while making combat unnecessary?"

Milady gazed silently at her lover: the pale gleam of the first rays of light gave her bright eyes a strangely baleful expression.

"Really," she said, "I believe you're actually hesitating now."

"No, I'm not hesitating. But I really feel sorry for this poor comte de Wardes, since you no longer love him, and it seems to me that a man must be so cruelly punished by the loss of your love alone that he needs no further punishment."

"Who told you I loved him?" asked Milady.

"At least I can now believe without too much self-conceit that you love another," the young man said in a caressing tone, "and, I repeat to you, I'm concerned for the count."

"You?" asked Milady.

"Yes, I."

"And why you?"

"Because I alone know . . ."

"What?"

"That he is far from being, or rather from having been, as guilty towards you as he seems."

"Indeed!" said Milady in an uneasy tone. "Explain yourself, for I really don't know what you mean to say."

And she looked at d'Artagnan, who held her in his embrace, with eyes that seemed gradually to take fire.

"Yes, I am a gallant man!" said d'Artagnan, resolved to have done. "And since your love is mine, since I am sure of possessing it, for I do possess it, do I not? . . ."

"Entirely. Go on."

"Well, I feel quite transported, but a confession weighs me down."

"A confession?"

"If I doubted your love, I wouldn't make it; but you do love me, my beautiful mistress, you do love me, don't you?"

"Of course."

"Then if, by excess of love, I have made myself guilty before you, you will forgive me?"

"Perhaps."

D'Artagnan tried, with the sweetest smile he could manage, to bring his lips close to Milady's lips, but she pushed him away.

"This confession," she said, turning pale, "what is this confession?"

"You gave de Wardes a rendezvous last Thursday, in this same bedroom, did you not?"

"I? No, that's not so!" said Milady, in so firm a tone of voice and with so impassive a face that if d'Artagnan had not been perfectly certain, he would have doubted.

"Don't lie, my beautiful angel," d'Artagnan said, smiling, "there's no use."

"What's that? Speak! You're killing me!"

"Oh, don't worry, you're not guilty before me, and I've already forgiven you!"

"Go on! Go on!"

"De Wardes has nothing to boast of."

"Why? You yourself told me that that ring . . ."

"That ring, my love, is in my possession. Thursday's comte de Wardes and today's d'Artagnan are the same person."

The imprudent young man was expecting surprise mixed with modesty, a little storm that would resolve itself in tears; but he was strangely mistaken, and his error was not long in appearing.

Pale and terrible, Milady drew herself up and, pushing d'Artagnan away with a violent blow to the chest, sprang out of bed.

It was nearly day.

D'Artagnan held her back by her negligee of fine Indies cotton in order to beg her forgiveness, but she made a strong and resolute movement to escape. Then the batiste tore, baring her shoulders, and on one of those beautifully rounded white shoulders d'Artagnan, with an inexpressible shock, recognized the fleur-de-lis, that indelible mark imprinted by the executioner's infamatory hand.

"Good God!" cried d'Artagnan, letting go of the negligee.

And he remained mute, immobile, frozen on the bed.

But Milady sensed her denunciation in d'Artagnan's very horror. No doubt he had seen all. The young man now knew her secret, a terrible secret, which no one in the world knew except him.

She turned, no longer like a furious woman, but like a wounded panther.

"Ah, you scoundrel!" she said. "You have basely betrayed me, and what's more you know my secret! You shall die!"

And she ran to an inlaid box sitting on her dressing table, opened it with a feverish and trembling hand, took from it a small dagger with a gold hilt and a sharp, slender blade, and with one bound flung herself at the half-naked d'Artagnan.

Though the young man was brave, as we know, he was frightened of that distorted face, those horribly dilated pupils, and those bleeding lips. He shrank back against the head-board, as he would have done at the approach of a snake slithering towards him. His sweating hand happened upon his sword, and he drew it from the scabbard.

But, not worried by the sword, Milady tried to climb back onto the bed in order to strike him, and did not stop until she felt the sharp point at her throat.

Then she tried to seize the sword with both hands; but d'Artagnan kept moving it out of her grasp, and, pointing it now at her eyes, now at her breast, he managed to slip to the foot of the bed, seeking the door to Kitty's room in order to make his retreat.

Milady, meanwhile, kept hurling herself at him with horrible paroxysms, roaring in a frightful way.

All this resembled a duel, however, and so d'Artagnan gradually recovered himself.

"Very well, lovely lady, very well," he said, "but for God's sake calm yourself, or I'll draw you a second fleur-de-lis on the other shoulder!"

"Vile wretch!" screamed Milady.

But d'Artagnan, still seeking the door, kept on the defensive.

At the noise they were making—she overturning furniture to get at him, he hiding behind furniture to escape her—Kitty opened the door. D'Artagnan, who had constantly maneuvered so as to get close to that door, was only three steps away from it. With a single bound he leaped from Milady's room to her maid's, and, quick as lightning, closed the door, leaning all his weight against it, while Kitty slid the bolts.

Then, with far more than a woman's strength, Milady tried to break down the barrier that confined her to her room. Once she felt that it was impossible, she stabbed the door repeatedly with her dagger, sometimes piercing the entire thickness of the wood.

Each stab was accompanied by a terrible curse.

"Quick, Kitty, quick," d'Artagnan said in a low voice, once the bolts were in place, "get me out of the hôtel! If we give her time to catch her breath, she'll have me killed by the lackeys."

"But you can't go out like that," said Kitty, "you're quite naked."

"That's true," said d'Artagnan, who only then noticed the costume he happened to be wearing, "that's true. Dress me however you can, but let's hurry. You understand, it's a matter of life and death!"

Kitty understood only too well. With one flick of the wrist, she rigged him out in a flowery dress, a big head scarf, and a short cape, and she gave him a pair of slippers into which he slipped his bare feet. Then she led him down the stairs. They were just in time. Milady had already rung and awakened the whole hôtel. The gatekeeper drew the latch at the sound of Kitty's voice just as Milady, half naked herself, shouted from the window:

"Don't open!"

XXXVIII

HOW, WITHOUT STIRRING, ATHOS FOUND HIS OUTFIT

The young man ran off, while she went on threatening him with an impotent gesture. Just as she lost sight of him, Milady fell into a faint in her room.

D'Artagnan was so distraught that, without worrying about what would become of Kitty, he crossed half of Paris at a run and stopped only when he was at Athos's door. The disorder of his mind, the terror that spurred him on, the shouts of some patrols that set off in pursuit of him, and the hoots of some passersby who, despite the late hour, were going about their business, only quickened his pace.

He crossed the courtyard, climbed the two stories to Athos, and pounded on the door fit to break it down.

Grimaud came to open, his eyes puffy with sleep. D'Artagnan rushed into the antechamber with such force that he almost knocked him over on the way.

Despite the poor lad's habitual mutism, this time he found his tongue.

"Hey, hey, there!" he cried. "What do you want, you slut! What are you after, you strumpet!"

D'Artagnan lifted his head scarf and freed his hands from under the cape. At the sight of his mustaches and his bared sword, the poor devil realized he was dealing with a man.

He thought then that it was some assassin.

"Help! Help! Save me!" he cried.

"Shut up, wretch!" said the young man. "I'm d'Artagnan, don't you recognize me? Where is your master?"

"You, M. d'Artagnan?" cried the terrified Grimaud. "Impossible!"

"Grimaud," said Athos, coming from his room in a dressing gown, "I believe you have allowed yourself to speak."

"Ah! Monsieur! it's just that . . ."

"Silence."

Grimaud contented himself with pointing out d'Artagnan to his master.

Athos recognized his comrade, and, phlegmatic as he was, let out a burst of laughter that was well motivated by the masquerade before his eyes: scarf askew, skirts falling over the shoes, sleeves pulled up, and mustaches bristling with emotion.

"Don't laugh, my friend," cried d'Artagnan, "in heaven's name, don't laugh, for, upon my soul, I'll tell you, there's nothing to laugh at."

And he uttered these words with such a solemn air and such genuine fright that Athos immediately took him by the hands, crying:

"Are you wounded, my friend? You're very pale."

"No, but a terrible thing has just happened to me. Are you alone, Athos?"

"Pardieu! who do you suppose could be with me at this hour?"

"Good, good."

And d'Artagnan hurried into Athos's room.

"Well, speak!" said the latter, closing the door and sliding the bolts so that they would not be disturbed. "Is the king dead? Have you killed the cardinal? You're all upset. Come, come, tell me, for I'm truly dying of worry."

"Athos," said d'Artagnan, taking off his woman's clothing and appearing in his undershirt, "prepare yourself to hear a shocking, incredible story."

"First take this dressing gown," the musketeer said to his friend.

D'Artagnan put on the dressing gown, mistaking one sleeve for another, so agitated he still was.

"Well, then?" said Athos.

"Well, then," replied d'Artagnan, bending to Athos's ear and lowering his voice, "Milady has the mark of the fleur-de-lis on her shoulder."

"Ah!" cried the musketeer, as if he had received a bullet in the heart.

"Listen," said d'Artagnan, "are you sure the *other one* is really dead?"

"The *other one*?" said Athos, in so faint a voice that d'Artagnan could barely hear him.

"Yes, the one you told me about that day in Amiens."

Athos heaved a sigh and let his head sink in his hands.

"This one," d'Artagnan went on, "is a woman of twenty-six or twenty-eight."

"Blond," said Athos, "isn't she?"

"Yes."

"Light blue eyes, of a strange brightness, with dark eyebrows and lashes?"

"Yes."

"Tall, well built? She's missing a tooth next to the left eye tooth."

"Yes."

"The fleur-de-lis is small, of a reddish color, and as if washed out by the layers of paste applied to it."

"Yes."

"But you say she's English!"

"She's called Milady, but she may be French. Anyhow, Lord de Winter is only her brother-in-law."

"I want to see her, d'Artagnan."

"Beware, Athos, beware! You wanted to kill her. She's a woman who will do the same to you, and she won't miss."

"She won't dare say a word, for she'd be denouncing herself."

"She's capable of anything! Have you ever seen her furious?"

"No," said Athos.

"A tigress, a panther! Ah, my dear Athos! I'm afraid I've brought down a terrible vengence on us both!"

D'Artagnan then told everything: the mad anger of Milady and her threats of death.

"You're right, and, upon my soul, my life wouldn't be worth a hair," said Athos. "Fortunately, we're leaving Paris the day after tomorrow. We'll be going, in all probability, to La Rochelle, and once we've left . . ."

"She'll follow you to the ends of the earth, Athos, if she recognizes you. So let her hatred vent itself on me alone."

"Ah, my dear, what do I care if she kills me!" said Athos. "Do you think by any chance that I set much store on life?"

"There's some horrible mystery behind all this. Athos, this woman is the cardinal's spy, I'm sure of it!"

"In that case, watch out for yourself. If the cardinal doesn't hold you in the highest admiration on account of that London business, he certainly hates you; but since, when all is said, he cannot reproach you openly for anything, and hatred must be satisfied, above all when it's a cardinal's hatred, watch out for yourself! If you go out, don't go out alone; if you eat, take your precautions; distrust everything, finally, even your own shadow."

"Fortunately," said d'Artagnan, "it's only a question of getting through the evening of the day after tomorrow without mishap, for once we're in the army, I hope we'll have nothing to fear except our fellow men."

"In the meantime," said Athos, "I'm giving up my planned reclusion and will go everywhere with you. You've got to go back to the rue des Fossoyeurs. I'll accompany you."

"Close as it is," said d'Artagnan, "I can't go back there like this."

"Right enough," said Athos. And he rang.

Grimaud came in.

Athos made him a sign to go to d'Artagnan's place and bring back some clothes.

Grimaud replied by a sign indicating that he understood perfectly, and left.

"Well, now, none of this gets us any closer to being outfitted, my dear friend," said Athos. "For, if I'm not mistaken, you left all your gear with Milady, who doubtless has no intention of returning it. Luckily, you have the sapphire."

"The sapphire is yours, my dear Athos! Didn't you tell me it was a family ring?"

"Yes, my father bought it for two thousand écus, as he told me once. It was one of the wedding gifts he gave to my mother, and it is magnificent. My mother gave it to me, and I, fool that I was, rather than keeping the ring as a sacred relic, gave it away in turn to that wretched woman."

"Then take back the ring, my dear. I understand that you must be attached to it."

"Take back that ring after it has passed through such infamous hands? Never! The ring is befouled, d'Artagnan."

"Sell it, then."

"Sell a jewel that comes from my mother? I confess to you, I would regard that as a profanation."

"Pawn it, in that case. They'll lend you well over a thousand écus on it. With that sum you'll be on top of your affairs, and with the first money that comes in, you can redeem it, and you'll get it back cleansed of its old stains, because it will have passed through the hands of usurers."

Athos smiled.

"My dear d'Artagnan, you are a charming companion," he said. "With your eternal gaiety, you lift the spirits of the afflicted. Well, then, yes, let's pawn the ring, but on one condition!"

"What is it?"

"That there will be five hundred écus for you and five hundred for me."

"Are you dreaming, Athos? I don't need a quarter of that amount, being in the guards, and I'll get it by selling my saddle. What do I need? A horse for Planchet, that's all. And you're forgetting that I also have a ring."

"To which you're more attached, as it seems to me, than I am to mine. At least I believe I've noticed that."

"Yes, for in extreme circumstances, it could get us not only out of some great difficulty, but also out of some great danger. It's not only a precious diamond, but also a charmed talisman."

"I don't understand you, but I believe what you say. Getting back to my ring, then, or rather to yours: you will take half of the amount we get for it, or I'll throw it into the Seine, and I doubt whether, as with Polycrates, any fish will be so obliging as to return it to us."

"Well, then, I accept!" said d'Artagnan.

At that moment Grimaud came in, accompanied by Planchet. The latter, worried about his master and curious to know what had happened to him, had profited from the occasion and brought the clothes himself.

D'Artagnan got dressed; Athos did the same. Then, when they were both ready to go out, Athos made Grimaud the sign of a man taking aim. The latter took down his musketoon and prepared to accompany his master.

Athos and d'Artagnan, followed by their valets, reached the rue des Fossoyeurs without incident. Bonacieux was in the doorway. He gave d'Artagnan a mocking look.

"Ah, my dear tenant!" he said. "Hurry up, you have a beautiful young girl waiting for you, and you know women don't like to be kept waiting!"

"It's Kitty!" cried d'Artagnan.

And he raced down the alley.

In fact, he found the poor child on the landing outside his room, pressed up against the door, and trembling all over. As soon as she saw him, she said:

"You promised me your protection, you promised to save me from her anger, remember it's you who have been my ruin!"

"Yes, of course," said d'Artagnan, "don't worry, Kitty. But what happened after I left?"

"How do I know?" said Kitty. "The lackeys came running at her cries. She was wild with anger. She vomited up every curse there is against you. Then I thought she'd remember that you got to her room through mine, and she'd think I was your accomplice. I took the little money I had, and my most precious rags, and ran away."

"Poor child! But what am I to do with you? I'm leaving the day after tomorrow."

"Anything you like, Monsieur le chevalier, get me out of Paris, get me out of France!"

"But I can't take you with me to the siege of La Rochelle," said d'Artagnan.

"No, but you can find me a place in the provinces, with some lady of your acquaintance—where you come from, for instance."

"Ah, my dear friend, where I come from the ladies don't have chambermaids. But wait, I know what to do. Planchet, go and find Aramis for me. He must come at once. We have something very important to tell him."

"I understand," said Athos. "But why not Porthos? It seems to me that his marquise . . ."

"Porthos's marquise has herself dressed by her husband's clerks," said d'Artagnan, laughing. "Besides, Kitty wouldn't want to live on the rue aux Ours, would you, Kitty?"

"I'll live wherever you like," said Kitty, "provided I'm well hidden and nobody knows where I am."

"Now that we're going to part, Kitty, and you are therefore no longer jealous over me . . ."

"Monsieur le chevalier," said Kitty, "far or near, I will always love you."

"Where the devil will constancy find its nesting place?" murmured Athos.

"I, too," said d'Artagnan, "I, too, will always love you, rest assured. But come, answer me. I attach great importance to the question I'm asking you now: did you ever hear mention of a young lady who was abducted one night?"

"Wait a moment . . . Oh, my God! Monsieur le chevalier, are you still in love with that woman?"

"No, one of my friends is in love with her. In fact, it's Athos here."

"I?" cried Athos, with an accent like that of a man who sees that he is about to tread on a snake.

"Of course, you!" said d'Artagnan, squeezing Athos's hand. "You know very well what interest we all take in that poor little Mme Bonacieux. Besides, Kitty won't say anything, will you, Kitty? You understand, my child," d'Artagnan went on, "she's the wife of that ugly ape you saw on the doorstep when you came here."

"Oh, my God," cried Kitty, "you remind me of how frightened I was! If only he didn't recognize me!"

"What do you mean, recognize? So you've seen that man before?"

"He came to Milady's twice."

"Of course! When was that?"

"Why, some fifteen or eighteen days ago."

"Exactly."

"And last evening he came back."

"Last evening."

"Yes, a moment before you came yourself."

"My dear Athos, we're enveloped in a web of spies! And do you think he recognized you, Kitty?"

"I pulled down my scarf when I saw him, but maybe it was too late."

"Go down, Athos, and see if he's still at the door. He distrusts you less than he does me."

Athos went down and came back up at once.

"He's gone," he said, "and the house is locked."

"He went to make his report and say that right now all the pigeons are in the dovecote."

"Well, then, let's fly away," said Athos, "and leave Planchet here to bring us news."

"Wait a minute! What about Aramis? We've just sent for him."

"That's right," said Athos, "let's wait for Aramis."

At that moment, Aramis came in.

They explained the affair to him and told him how urgent

it was for him to find a place for Kitty among all his high-born acquaintances.

Aramis reflected for a moment and said, blushing:

"This will really be doing you a service, d'Artagnan?"

"I'll be grateful to you all my life."

"Well, then, Mme de Bois-Tracy has asked me for a reliable chambermaid, for one of her friends who lives in the provinces, I believe. If you, my dear d'Artagnan, can answer to me for Mademoiselle . . ."

"Oh, Monsieur!" cried Kitty, "I'll be completely devoted to the person who gives me the means of leaving Paris, you can be sure of that."

"In that case," said Aramis, "it's all for the best."

He sat down at a table, wrote a little note, which he sealed with a ring, and handed it to Kitty.

"Now, my child," said d'Artagnan, "you know that this place is no better for us than it is for you. And so, let us part. We shall meet again in better days."

"And whenever we meet again, and wherever it may be," said Kitty, "you will find I still love you as I do today."

"A gambler's oath," said Athos, while d'Artagnan went to see Kitty down the stairs.

A moment later, the three young men separated, arranging a rendezvous for four o'clock at Athos's and leaving Planchet to guard the house.

Aramis went home, and Athos and d'Artagnan concerned themselves with pawning the sapphire.

As our Gascon had foreseen, they easily got three hundred pistoles for the ring. Moreover, the Jew declared that if they wanted to sell it to him, as it would make him a magnificent set with a pair of earrings, he would give as much as five hundred pistoles for it.

Athos and d'Artagnan, with the diligence of two soldiers and the knowledge of two connoisseurs, spent barely three hours buying a whole musketeer's outfit. Besides, Athos was of good character and a great lord to his fingertips. Each time something suited him, he paid the price that was asked without even trying to knock it down. D'Artagnan was going to make some observations about that, but Athos placed his hand on his shoulder, smiling, and d'Artagnan understood that it was fine for a little Gascon gentleman like him to haggle, but not for a man who had the airs of a prince.

The musketeer found himself a superb Andalusian horse, black as jade, with flaming nostrils, fine and elegant legs, which was going on six years old. He examined it and found it flawless. He was asked a thousand livres.

Perhaps he could have had it for less; but while d'Artagnan was debating the price with the horse dealer, Athos counted out the hundred pistoles on the table.

Grimaud got a Picard horse, thickset and strong, that cost three hundred livres.

But once the saddle for the latter horse and arms for Grimaud were bought, not a sou was left of Athos's hundred and fifty pistoles. D'Artagnan offered to let his friend take a bite out of his own share, which he could pay back later.

But Athos's only response was a shrug of the shoulders.

"How much did the Jew offer to buy the sapphire outright?" he asked.

"Five hundred pistoles."

"In other words, two hundred pistoles more—a hundred for you, a hundred for me. Why, that's a veritable fortune, my friend. Go back to the Jew."

"You mean you want to . . ."

"That ring will decidedly bring back too many sad memories to me. And then, we'll never have the three hundred pistoles to give him, so we're just losing two hundred pistoles on the deal. Go and tell him the ring is his, d'Artagnan, and come back with the two hundred pistoles."

"Think it over, Athos."

"Ready money is precious these days, and we must know how to make sacrifices. Go, d'Artagnan, go. Grimaud will accompany you with his musketoon."

Half an hour later, d'Artagnan came back with the two thousand livres and without any incidents on the way.

Thus Athos found resources in his household that he was not expecting at all.

XXXIX

A Vision

At four o'clock, the four friends met at Athos's. Their concerns about outfitting themselves had vanished entirely, and each face kept the expression only of its own secret concerns, for behind every present happiness a future fear lies hidden.

All at once Planchet came in, bringing two letters addressed to d'Artagnan.

One was a little note nicely folded lengthwise, with a pretty seal of green wax bearing the impression of a dove carrying an olive branch.

The other was a big square epistle resplendent with the terrible coat of arms of His Eminence the cardinal-duke.

At the sight of the little letter, d'Artagnan's heart leaped, for he thought he recognized the handwriting; and though he had seen that handwriting only once, the memory of it had remained in the depths of his heart.

He thus took the little epistle and quickly unsealed it. It told him:

> Go for a ride next Wednesday, between six and seven in the evening, on the road to Chaillot, and look carefully into the passing carriages, but if you value your life and that of people who love you, do not say a word, do not make a gesture that could lead anyone to think you have recognized her who is exposing herself to so much in order to catch a momentary glimpse of you.

No signature.

"It's a trap," said Athos. "Don't go, d'Artagnan."

"And yet," said d'Artagnan, "I seem to recognize the handwriting."

"It may be a counterfeit," replied Athos. "Between six and seven, at this time of year, the road to Chaillot is completely deserted: you might as well go for a walk in the forest of Bondy."

"But what if we should all go!" said d'Artagnan. "Devil

take it, they'll never devour all four of us, plus four lackeys, plus the horses, plus the weapons."

"Then, too, it will be an occasion for showing off our outfits," said Porthos.

"But if it's a woman writing," said Aramis, "and that woman wishes not to be seen, think how you'll compromise her, d'Artagnan—which is a bad thing on a gentleman's part."

"We'll drop back," said Porthos, "and he can go ahead by himself."

"Yes, but a pistol is quickly fired from a galloping carriage."

"Bah!" said d'Artagnan, "they'll miss me. Then we'll catch up with the carriage and exterminate whomever we find in it. That will always be so many fewer enemies."

"He's right," said Porthos. "Battle! Besides, we've got to try out our weapons."

"Yes, let's give ourselves that pleasure," said Aramis, with his gentle and nonchalant air.

"As you wish," said Athos.

"Gentlemen," said d'Artagnan, "it's half-past four, and we barely have time to be on the road to Chaillot by six."

"Then, too, if we leave too late, nobody will see us," said Porthos, "and that will be a pity. Let's get ready, gentlemen."

"But the second letter," said Athos, "you're forgetting about that. It seems to me, however, that the seal suggests it's well worth opening. As for me, I declare to you, my dear d'Artagnan, that I'm more worried about it than about that little bauble you've just slipped so daintily into your bosom."

D'Artagnan blushed.

"Well, gentlemen," said the young man, "let's see what His Eminence wants with me."

And d'Artagnan unsealed the letter and read:

M. d'Artagnan, king's guard, company of des Essarts, is expected at the Palais Cardinal this evening at eight o'clock.

La Houdinière,
Captain of the Guards

"Devil take it!" said Athos, "that's a much more worrisome rendezvous than the other!"

"I'll go to the second on coming from the first," said d'Artagnan. "The one is for seven o'clock, the other for eight; there will be time for all of it."

"Hm! I wouldn't go," said Aramis. "A gallant chevalier cannot miss a rendezvous accorded by a lady; but a prudent gentleman can be excused for not reporting to His Eminence, above all when he has some reason to believe that he is not going to receive any compliments there."

"I'm of Aramis's opinion," said Porthos.

"Gentlemen," replied d'Artagnan, "I already received a similar invitation from His Eminence through M. de Cavois, I ignored it, and the next day I suffered a great misfortune! Constance disappeared. Come what may, I'll go."

"If you're set on it," said Athos, "do it."

"But the Bastille?" said Aramis.

"Bah! you'll get me out," replied d'Artagnan.

"Of course," Aramis and Porthos picked up with admirable aplomb and as if it was the simplest of things, "of course we'll get you out; but, in the meantime, as we have to leave the day after tomorrow, you'd do better not to risk the Bastille."

"Let's do better," said Athos, "let's not leave him all evening, let's each wait at a door of the palace with three musketeers behind us. If we see some carriage come out with its curtains drawn and looking half suspicious, we'll fall upon it. It's a long time since we've had a bone to pick with the guards of M. le cardinal, and M. de Tréville must think we've died."

"Decidedly, Athos," said Aramis, "you were made to be a general. What do you say of the plan, gentlemen?"

"Admirable!" the young men repeated in chorus.

"Well, then," said Porthos, "I'll run to the hôtel; I'll warn our comrades to be ready by eight o'clock; the rendezvous will be on the place du Palais Cardinal. Meanwhile, have the lackeys saddle the horses."

"I have no horse," said d'Artagnan. "I'll go and take one from M. de Tréville."

"That's unnecessary," said Aramis, "you can take one of mine."

"How many do you have, then?" asked d'Artagnan.

"Three," replied Aramis, smiling.

"My dear fellow," said Athos, "you are certainly the most well-mounted poet in France and Navarre!"

"Listen, my dear Aramis, you don't know what to do with three horses, do you? I don't understand why you even bought three horses."

"In fact, I only bought two," said Aramis.

"So the third fell on you from the sky?"

"No, the third was brought to me just this morning by a servant without livery, who didn't want to tell me whom he belonged to, and who informed me that he had received orders from his master . . ."

"Or his mistress," interrupted d'Artagnan.

"That's of no importance," said Aramis, blushing. "And who informed me, I say, that he had received orders from his mistress to put this horse in my stable without telling me where it came from."

"Such things only happen to poets," Athos said gravely.

"Well, in that case, we'll do better," said d'Artagnan. "Which of the two horses will you ride—the one you bought, or the one that was given to you?"

"The one that was given to me, without question. You understand, d'Artagnan, I cannot insult . . ."

"The unknown donor," d'Artagnan picked up.

"Or mysterious donatrice," said Athos.

"So the one you bought has become useless to you?"

"Nearly."

"And you chose it yourself?"

"And with the greatest care. The safety of the rider, as you know, almost always depends on his horse."

"Well, then, let me have it for the price you paid!"

"I was going to offer it to you, my dear d'Artagnan, giving you all the time you need to pay me back for this trifle."

"And how much did it cost you?"

"Eight hundred livres."

"Here are forty double pistoles, my dear friend," said d'Artagnan, taking the sum from his pocket. "I know it's the money you were paid for your poems."

"So you're in funds?" asked Aramis.

"Rich, extremely rich, my dear!"

And d'Artagnan clinked the rest of the pistoles in his pocket.

"Send your saddle to the hôtel of the musketeers, and your horse will be brought here along with ours."

"Very good. But it will soon be five o'clock, we must hurry."

A quarter of an hour later, Porthos appeared at one end of the rue Férou on a magnificent jennet. Mousqueton followed him on an Auvergne horse, small but sturdy. Porthos shone with joy and pride.

At the same time, Aramis appeared at the other end of the street, mounted on a superb English steed. Bazin followed him on a roan, leading a vigorous Mecklenburg stallion by the reins: this was d'Artagnan's mount.

The two musketeers met at the door; Athos and d'Artagnan watched them from the window.

"Devil take it!" said Aramis, "that's a superb horse you've got there, my dear Porthos."

"Yes," replied Porthos, "it's the one they should have sent me in the first place: a bad joke on the husband's part exchanged him for the other; but the husband has since been punished, and I have obtained full satisfaction."

Planchet and Grimaud then appeared in their turn, taking their masters' mounts in hand. D'Artagnan and Athos went downstairs, got into the saddle beside their companions, and the four set off: Athos on the horse he owed to his wife, Aramis on the horse he owed to his mistress, Porthos on the horse he owed to his procureuse, and d'Artagnan on the horse he owed to his good luck—the best mistress of them all.

The valets followed after.

As Porthos had thought, the cavalcade made a good effect; and if Mme Coquenard had found herself in Porthos's path and could have seen what a grand air he had on his handsome

Spanish jennet, she would not have regretted the bleeding she had inflicted on her husband's strongbox.

Near the Louvre the four friends met M. de Tréville, who was coming back from Saint-Germain. He stopped them to compliment them on their turnout, which in an instant drew around them a gaping crowd of several hundred people.

D'Artagnan profited from the occasion to speak with M. de Tréville about the letter with the big red seal and the ducal arms. Naturally, he did not breathe a word about the other letter.

M. de Tréville approved of the decision he had taken, and assured him that, if he did not show up the next day, he would manage to find him, wherever he might be.

At that moment, the clock of the Samaritaine struck six. The four friends excused themselves on account of their rendezvous and took leave of M. de Tréville.

A short gallop brought them to the road to Chaillot. Night was beginning to fall. Carriages passed back and forth. D'Artagnan, guarded by his friends from several paces away, plunged his eyes into the depths of each carriage and saw no face he knew.

At last, after a quarter of an hour's wait and as twilight settled in, a carriage appeared, coming at a great gallop along the road from Sèvres. A presentiment told d'Artagnan that this carriage held the person who had given him the rendezvous. The young man was quite astonished himself to feel his heart beating so violently. Almost at once a woman's head emerged from the coach door, two fingers to her lips, as if enjoining silence or blowing a kiss. D'Artagnan uttered a faint cry of joy: the woman, or rather the apparition, for the carriage passed with the speed of a vision, was Mme Bonacieux.

With an involuntary movement, and despite the warning he had been given, d'Artagnan set his horse at a gallop and in a few bounds caught up with the carriage; but the window of the coach door was hermetically sealed: the vision had disappeared.

D'Artagnan then remembered the injunction: "If you value your life and that of those who love you, remain motionless and as if you had not seen anything."

He stopped, trembling not for himself but for the poor woman, who had evidently exposed herself to great danger in giving him this rendezvous.

The carriage continued on its way, still going at breakneck speed, plunged into Paris, and disappeared.

D'Artagnan remained dumbfounded on the same spot, not knowing what to think. If it was Mme Bonacieux, and if she was returning to Paris, why this fleeting rendezvous, why this simple exchange of glances, why this lost kiss? If, on the other hand, it was not she, which was still quite possible, for the little remaining light made error easy, if it was not she, would this not be the beginning of a move against him, using as bait this woman whom he was known to love?

The three companions approached him. All three had distinctly seen a woman's head appear in the coach door, but none of them except Athos knew Mme Bonacieux. Athos's opinion, however, was that it was certainly she; but, being less preoccupied than d'Artagnan by that pretty face, he thought he had seen a second head, a man's head, in the carriage.

"If so," said d'Artagnan, "they're no doubt transporting her from one prison to another. But what do they mean to do to the poor creature, and how will I ever join her again?"

"Friend," Athos said gravely, "remember that the dead are the only ones we're in no danger of meeting again on earth. You and I both know something about that, don't we? Now, if your mistress isn't dead, if it was her we just saw, you'll find her again one day or another. And, by God," he added with a typically misanthropic note, "maybe sooner than you'd like."

It struck half-past seven. The carriage had been some twenty minutes late for the rendezvous. D'Artagnan's friends reminded him that he had a visit to pay, observing at the same time that it was still possible to cancel it.

But d'Artagnan was both stubborn and curious. He had taken it into his head that he would go to the Palais Cardinal and would find out what His Eminence wanted to say to him. Nothing could make him change his decision.

They came to the rue Saint-Honoré, and on the place du Palais Cardinal they found the dozen musketeers they had summoned pacing up and down while waiting for their comrades. Only then were they informed of what it was all about.

D'Artagnan was well known to the honorable corps of the king's musketeers, in which it was understood that he would one day take his place. He was thus looked upon beforehand as a comrade. The result of all this was that each of them wholeheartedly accepted the mission for which he had been summoned. Besides, it was a question, in all probability, of doing the cardinal and his men a bad turn, and for such expeditions these worthy gentlemen were always ready.

Athos divided them into three groups, took command of one, gave the second to Aramis, and the third to Porthos. Then each group went to lie in ambush facing one of the exits.

D'Artagnan, for his part, bravely entered by the main gate.

Though he felt himself vigorously supported, it was not without uneasiness that the young man climbed the grand stairway step by step. His conduct with Milady bore a slight resemblance to treachery, and he suspected that there were political relations between this woman and the cardinal. Moreover, de Wardes, whom he had done up so badly, was among His Eminence's faithful, and d'Artagnan knew that if His Eminence was terrible to his enemies, he was strongly attached to his friends.

"If de Wardes has told the cardinal about our whole affair, which is not unlikely, and if he has recognized me, which is probable, I must look upon myself as little short of a condemned man," d'Artagnan said to himself, shaking his head. "But why has he waited till today? It's quite simple. Milady must have complained against me, with that hypocritical grief that makes her so interesting, and this last crime must have made the cup run over.

"Luckily," he added, "my good friends are down there, and they won't let me be taken away without defending me. However, M. de Tréville's company of musketeers can't make war alone against the cardinal, who disposes of forces from all over France, and before whom the queen is without power and the king without will. D'Artagnan, my friend, you're brave, you have excellent qualities, but women will be the ruin of you!"

He reached that sad conclusion just as he was entering the antechamber. He handed his letter to the usher on duty, who let him into the waiting room and disappeared into the interior of the palace.

In the waiting room there were five or six of M. le cardinal's guards, who, recognizing d'Artagnan and knowing that it was he who had wounded Jussac, looked at him with odd smiles.

These smiles seemed to d'Artagnan to augur ill; only, as our Gascon was not easily intimidated, or rather, thanks to the great pride natural to people from his province, he did not let what was happening in his soul be easily seen, when what was happening was something like fear, he planted himself proudly before the guards and waited, hand on hip, in an attitude not lacking in majesty.

The usher came back and made a sign for d'Artagnan to follow him. It seemed to the young man that the guards whispered among themselves as they watched him walk away.

He followed a corridor, passed through a large salon, went into a library, and found himself facing a man sitting at a desk and writing.

The usher showed him in and withdrew without saying a word. D'Artagnan thought at first that he was dealing with some judge who was examining his case, but he noticed that the man at the desk was writing, or rather correcting, lines of unequal length, scanning the words on his fingers. He saw that he was facing a poet. After a moment, the poet closed his manuscript, on the cover of which was written: *Mirame, a Tragedy in Five Acts,* and raised his head.

D'Artagnan recognized the cardinal.

XL

THE CARDINAL

The cardinal rested his elbow on his manuscript, cheek in hand, and looked at the young man for a moment. No one had a more deeply searching eye than Cardinal Richelieu, and d'Artagnan felt that gaze running through his veins like a fever.

However, he stood up to it well, holding his hat in his hand, and awaiting His Eminence's good pleasure, without too much pride, but also without too much humility.

"Monsieur," the cardinal said to him, "you are a certain d'Artagnan from Béarn?"

"Yes, Monseigneur," replied the young man.

"There are several branches of the d'Artagnans in Tarbes and its environs," said the cardinal. "To which do you belong?"

"I am the son of the man who fought in the wars of religion on the side of the great King Henri, father of His Gracious Majesty."

"Just so. It is you who, some seven or eight months ago, set out from your province to seek your fortune in the capital?"

"Yes, Monseigneur."

"You came via Meung, where something happened to you, I do not quite know what, but something."

"Monseigneur," said d'Artagnan, "here is what happened to me . . ."

"Never mind, never mind," the cardinal picked up, with a smile which indicated that he knew the story as well as the one who wanted to tell it to him. "You were recommended to M. de Tréville, were you not?"

"Yes, Monseigneur. But, as a matter of fact, in that unfortunate business in Meung . . ."

"The letter got lost," His Eminence interrupted. "Yes, I know that. But M. de Tréville is a skillful physiognomist, who can judge men at first sight, and he placed you in the company of his brother-in-law, M. des Essarts, while letting you hope that one day or another you would enter the musketeers."

"Monseigneur is perfectly informed," said d'Artagnan.

"Since that time many things have happened to you: you strolled behind the Chartreux one day when it would have been better for you to be elsewhere; then, you made a trip with your friends to the waters at Forges; they stopped on the way, but you continued your journey. It is quite simple: you had business in England."

"Monseigneur," said d'Artagnan, quite dumbstruck, "I was going . . ."

"To hunt in Windsor, or wherever, that is nobody's concern. I know it, because it is my job to know everything. On your return, you were received by an august person, and I am pleased to see that you have kept the souvenir she gave you."

D'Artagnan put his hand to the diamond he had received from the queen and quickly turned the stone inwards; but it was too late.

"The next day, you received a visit from Cavois," the cardinal went on. "He came to ask you to come to the palace; you did not pay him that visit, and you were wrong."

"Monsiegneur, I feared I had incurred Your Eminence's disfavor."

"And why is that, Monsieur? For having followed the orders of your superiors with more intelligence and courage than another would have done, to incur my disfavor when you deserved only praise? It is those who do not obey that I punish, not those who, like you, obey . . . too well . . . And for proof, recall the date of the day I sent word for you to come and see me, and search your memory for what happened that same evening."

It was that same evening that the abduction of Mme Bonacieux took place. D'Artagnan shuddered. And he remembered that half an hour ago the poor woman had passed by him, no doubt carried off again by the same power that had made her disappear.

"Finally," the cardinal continued, "as I had not heard mention of you for some time, I wanted to know what you were doing. Besides, you certainly owe me some thanks: you have noticed yourself how you have been spared in all these circumstances."

D'Artagnan bowed respectfully.

"That," the cardinal continued, "came not only from a natural sense of fairness, but also from a plan I had drawn up for myself in your regard."

D'Artagnan was more and more astonished.

"I was going to present that plan to you on the day you received my first invitation, but you did not come. Fortunately, nothing has been lost by the delay, and today you shall hear it.

Sit down here, in front of me, M. d'Artagnan: you are gentleman enough not to listen standing."

And the cardinal pointed out a chair to the young man,
who was so astonished by what was happening that he waited
for a second sign from his interlocutor before obeying.

"You are brave, M. d'Artagnan," His Eminence went on.
"You are prudent, which is better still. I like men of both head
and heart. Don't be afraid," he said, smiling, "by men of heart,
I mean men of courage. But, young as you are, and only just
entering the world, you have powerful enemies. If you are not
careful, they will destroy you."

"Alas, Monseigneur," replied the young man, "they can do
so very easily, no doubt, for they are strong and well supported, while I am quite alone!"

"Yes, that's true. But, alone as you are, you have already
done much, and you will do more, I have no doubt. However,
I believe you need to be guided in the adventurous career you
have undertaken; for, if I am not mistaken, you have come to
Paris with the ambitious idea of making a fortune."

"I am at the age of wild hopes, Monseigneur," said d'Artagnan.

"Only fools have wild hopes, Monsieur, and you are an intelligent man. Listen, what would you say to becoming an ensign in my guards, and to commanding a company after the
campaign?"

"Ah, Monseigneur!"

"You accept, do you not?"

"Monseigneur," d'Artagnan repeated with an embarrassed
look.

"What, you refuse?" the cardinal cried in astonishment.

"I am in His Majesty's guards, Monseigneur, and I have no
reason to be discontented."

"But it seems to me," said His Eminence, "that my own
guards are also His Majesty's guards, and that, provided one
serves in a French corps, one serves the king."

"Monseigneur, Your Eminence has misunderstood my
words."

"You want a pretext, is that it? I understand. Well, then,

you have that pretext. Advancement, the opening of the campaign, the chance I am offering you, so much for the world; for yourself, a need of sure protection. For it is well that you know, M. d'Artagnan, I have received serious complaints against you. You do not devote your days and nights exclusively to the king's service."

D'Artagnan blushed.

"Moreover," the cardinal continued, placing his hand on a sheaf of papers, "I have here a whole file concerning you; but, before reading it, I wanted to speak with you. I know you to be a man of determination, and your services, properly guided, instead of leading you to harm, could reward you greatly. Come, reflect and decide."

"Your goodness overwhelms me, Monseigneur," replied d'Artagnan, "and I acknowledge a greatness of soul in Your Eminence that makes me small as a worm; but, finally, since Your Eminence permits me to speak frankly . . ."

D'Artagnan paused.

"Yes, speak."

"Well, then, I will say to Your Eminence that all my friends are in the musketeers or the king's guards, and that my enemies, by some inconceivable fatality, are Your Eminence's men. I will thus be ill-received here and ill-regarded there, if I accept what Monseigneur is offering me."

"Might you already have the proud idea that I am not offering you as much as you are worth, Monsieur?" said the cardinal with a scornful smile.

"Monseigneur, Your Eminence is a hundred times too kind to me, and I think, on the contrary, that I have by no means done enough yet to be worthy of his kindness. I shall serve under Your Eminence's eyes, and if I have the good fortune to conduct myself at this siege in such fashion that I deserve to attract your attention, well, then afterwards I shall at least have some brilliant action behind me to justify the protection with which you would so kindly honor me. Everything in its time, Monseigneur. Perhaps later I shall have the right to give myself; at the moment it would look as if I were selling myself."

"In other words, you refuse to serve me, Monsieur," said

the cardinal, with a spiteful tone in which, however, a certain esteem could be detected. "Remain free, then, and keep your hatreds and your sympathies."

"Monseigneur . . ."

"Very well, very well," said the cardinal, "I do not hold it against you. But you understand, it is enough to defend one's friends and reward them; one owes nothing to one's enemies. And yet I will give you one piece of advice: watch out for yourself, M. d'Artagnan, for the moment I withdraw my hand from you, your life will not be worth a straw."

"I will do my best, Monseigneur," the Gascon replied with noble self-assurance.

"Reflect later, if at a certain moment misfortune befalls you," Richelieu said meaningfully, "that it was I who sought you out, and that I have done what I could to keep that misfortune from befalling you."

"Whatever may befall," said d'Artagnan, placing his hand on his heart and bowing, "I shall be eternally grateful to Your Eminence for what he has done for me at this moment."

"Very well, then, as you have said, M. d'Artagnan, we shall see each other after the campaign. I shall be keeping an eye on you, for I shall be there," the cardinal went on, pointing out to d'Artagnan the magnificent suit of armor he was to wear, "and on our return, we shall make our reckoning!"

"Ah, Monseigneur!" cried d'Artagnan, "spare me the weight of your disfavor; remain neutral, Monseigneur, if you find that I act as a gallant man."

"Young man," said Richelieu, "if I can say to you again what I have said to you today, I promise you that I will say it."

This last word from Richelieu expressed a terrible doubt. It dismayed d'Artagnan more than a threat, for it was a warning. So the cardinal was seeking to save him from some misfortune that threatened him. He opened his mouth to reply, but the cardinal dismissed him with a haughty gesture.

D'Artagnan left; but at the door his heart nearly failed him, and he was about to turn back. However, the grave and stern face of Athos appeared to him: if he made the pact with the cardinal that the latter was proposing to him, Athos would never give him his hand, Athos would disavow him.

It was this fear that held him back, so strong is the influence of a truly great character on all around him.

D'Artagnan went down the same stairway he had gone up, and found Athos and the four musketeers at the door, waiting for his return and beginning to worry. A word from d'Artagnan reassured them, and Planchet ran to inform the other posts that there was no need to mount guard any longer, seeing that his master had emerged safe and sound from the Palais Cardinal.

Back at Athos's, Aramis and Porthos asked about the causes of this strange rendezvous; but d'Artagnan contented himself with telling them that M. de Richelieu had invited him in order to propose that he join his guards with the rank of ensign, and that he had refused.

"And right you were," cried Porthos and Aramis with one voice.

Athos fell into deep thought and made no reply. But when he was alone with d'Artagnan, he said:

"You've done what you should have done, but perhaps you were wrong."

D'Artagnan heaved a sigh, for this voice answered to a secret voice in his soul, which told him that great misfortunes were in store for him.

The next day was spent in preparations for departure. D'Artagnan went to say good-bye to M. de Tréville. At that time it was still thought that the separation of the guards and musketeers would be momentary; the king was holding his parliament that same day and was to set out on the next. M. de Tréville thus contented himself with asking d'Artagnan if he had need of him, but d'Artagnan proudly replied that he had all he required.

Night brought together all the comrades of the company of M. des Essarts's guards and the company of M. de Tréville's musketeers, who had become friends. They were separating, to see each other again when it pleased God and if it pleased God.

The night was thus a most rollicking one, as one might think, for in such cases extreme anxiety can only be combated by extreme insouciance.

The next day, at the first sound of the trumpets, the friends parted: the musketeers rushed to the hôtel of M. de Tréville, the guards to that of M. des Essarts. Each captain at once led his company to the Louvre, where the king held his review.

The king was sad and seemed unwell, which took from him some of his noble bearing. Indeed, the evening before, he had come down with a fever in the midst of the parliament and while he was holding his bed of justice. He was nonetheless determined to leave that same evening; and, despite the observations that had been made to him, he had wished to hold his review, hoping to defeat the illness that was beginning to come over him by striking a vigorous first blow.

After the review, the guards set out on the march alone; the musketeers were to leave only with the king, which allowed Porthos, in his superb outfit, to go around to the rue aux Ours.

The procureuse saw him pass by in his new uniform and on his handsome horse. She loved Porthos too much to let him go like that; she made a sign for him to dismount and come to her. Porthos was magnificent: his spurs jingled, his breastplate shone, his sword clanked proudly against his thigh. This time the clerks felt no desire to laugh, so much did Porthos have the look of a clipper of ears.

The musketeer was brought to see M. Coquenard, whose little gray eye gleamed with anger on seeing his cousin all flaming new. Yet he had one inner consolation: everyone was saying it would be a hard campaign. He hoped very quietly, at the bottom of his heart, that Porthos would be killed.

Porthos presented his compliments to Master Coquenard and bade him farewell. Master Coquenard wished him every sort of prosperity. As for Mme Coquenard, she could not hold back her tears. But no bad conclusions were drawn from her grief. She was known to be very attached to her relatives, over whom she had always had such bitter disputes with her husband.

But the real farewells took place in Mme Coquenard's bedroom: they were heartrending.

As long as the procureuse could follow her lover with her eyes, she waved her handkerchief, leaning so far out her window that it looked as if she wanted to throw herself from it. Porthos took all these marks of affection like a man who was used to such demonstrations. But as he turned the corner of the street, he took off his hat and waved it in a sign of farewell.

For his part, Aramis wrote a long letter. To whom? No one knew. In the neighboring room, Kitty, who was to leave that same evening for Tours, waited for this mysterious letter.

Athos drank the last bottle of his Spanish wine in little sips.

In the meantime, d'Artagnan was marching with his company.

On reaching the faubourg Saint-Antoine, he turned and looked gaily at the Bastille; but, as he was only looking at the Bastille, he did not see Milady, mounted on a dun-colored horse, who pointed him out to two evil-looking men, who approached the ranks at once in order to identify him. To their questioning look, Milady replied by a sign that he was the man. Then, certain that there could no longer be any mistake in the carrying out of her orders, she spurred her horse and disappeared.

The two men then followed the company and, on leaving the faubourg Saint-Antoine, mounted two horses that an unliveried servant was holding by the reins in readiness for them.

XLI

THE SIEGE OF LA ROCHELLE

The siege of La Rochelle was one of the great political events of the reign of Louis XIII, and one of the great military undertakings of the cardinal. It is thus worthwhile, and even necessary, for us to say a few words about it. Besides, many details of this siege are bound up in too important a way with the story we have undertaken to tell for us to pass over them in silence.

The cardinal's political objectives, when he undertook this siege, were extensive. Let us present them first, and then go on to some particular objectives, which were perhaps of no less influence on His Eminence than the former.

Of the important towns given to the Huguenots by Henri IV as safe havens, the only one left was La Rochelle. It was thus a question of destroying this last bulwark of Calvinism, a dangerous leavening, into which ferments of civil rebellion and foreign war were constantly being mixed.

Spanish, English, and Italian malcontents, adventurers from all nations, soldiers of fortune of every sect, ran at the first call to put themselves under the banners of the Protestants, and made up a sort of vast association that branched out at leisure over every part of Europe.

La Rochelle, which had acquired a new importance from the ruin of the other Calvinist towns, was thus a hotbed of dissension and ambition. What was more, its port was the last port open to the English in the realm of France. In closing it to England, our eternal enemy, the cardinal completed the work of Joan of Arc and the duc de Guise.

And so Bassompierre, who was at once Protestant and Catholic, Protestant by conviction and Catholic as commander of the Order of the Holy Spirit; Bassompierre, who was German by birth and French at heart; Bassompierre, finally, who commanded his own army at the siege of La Rochelle, said, in charging at the head of several other Protestant noblemen like himself:

"You'll see, gentlemen, that we shall be fools enough to take La Rochelle!"

And Bassompierre was right: the cannonade of the Île de Ré foreshadowed the dragonnades of the Cévennes; the taking of La Rochelle was the preface to the revocation of the Edict of Nantes.

But, as we have said, alongside these objectives of the leveling and simplifying minister, which belong to history, the chronicler is forced to acknowledge the petty aims of the lover and jealous rival.

Richelieu, as everyone knows, had been in love with the queen. Whether that love had a simple political goal for him, or was quite naturally one of those deep passions that Anne d'Autriche inspired in those around her, we are unable to say; but in any case we have seen, from previous developments in this story, that Buckingham had won out over him, and that, on two or three occasions, particularly that of the pendants, thanks to the devotion of the three musketeers and the courage of d'Artagnan, he had been cruelly outwitted.

It was thus a question, for Richelieu, not only of ridding France of an enemy, but of revenging himself on a rival; moreover, the vengeance had to be great and terrible, and worthy in every way of a man who held the forces of an entire realm like a sword in his hand.

Richelieu knew that, in fighting England, he was fighting Buckingham; that in triumphing over England, he was triumphing over Buckingham; finally, that in humiliating England, he was humiliating Buckingham in the queen's eyes.

Buckingham, for his part, while putting forward the honor of England, was moved by interests absolutely identical to the cardinal's. Buckingham was also pursuing private vengeance. Under no pretext could Buckingham have returned to France as an ambassador; he would return, then, as a conqueror.

The result was that the real stake in this game, which the two most powerful kingdoms were playing for the good pleasure of two enamored men, was a mere glance from Anne d'Autriche.

The advantage had first gone to the duke of Buckingham. Arriving unexpectedly in sight of the Île de Ré with ninety vessels and some twenty thousand men, he had surprised the comte de Toiras, who commanded the island for the king. After a bloody battle, his landing had been effected.

Let us relate in passing that the baron de Chantal perished in this battle, leaving as an orphan a little girl eighteen months old.

This little girl was later Mme de Sévigné.

The comte de Toiras withdrew to the Saint-Martin citadel with the garrison and threw a hundred men into a small fort known as the fort of La Prée.

This outcome had hastened the cardinal's resolve, and while waiting until the king and he could come to take command of the siege of La Rochelle, which was decided on, he had sent Monsieur to direct the first operations, and had rushed all the troops he could dispose of to the theater of war.

Our friend d'Artagnan was part of this detachment sent as a vanguard.

The king, as we have said, was to follow as soon as he had held his bed of justice; but on getting up from this bed of justice on the twenty-eighth of June, he felt that he had caught a fever. He insisted on setting out nontheless, but, his condition having worsened, he was forced to stop at Villeroi.

Now, where the king stopped, the musketeers also stopped. The result was that d'Artagnan, who was purely and simply a guard, found himself separated, at least momentarily, from his good friends Athos, Porthos, and Aramis. This separation, which was only a vexation for him, would certainly have become a serious concern if he could have guessed what unknown dangers surrounded him.

He nonetheless reached the camp set up before La Rochelle without incident, towards the tenth of September of the year 1627.

Everything was in the same state: the duke of Buckingham and his Englishmen, masters of the Île de Ré, continued to besiege the citadel of Saint-Martin and the fort of La Prée, but without success, and the hostilities with La Rochelle had begun two or three days earlier over a fort that the duc d'Angoulême had just built near the town.

The guards, under the command of M. des Essarts, took quarters with the Minimes.

But, as we know, d'Artagnan, preoccupied with the ambition of going over to the musketeers, had made few friends among his comrades. He thus found himself isolated and given over to his own reflections.

These reflections were hardly cheerful. For the year since his arrival in Paris, he had been embroiled in public affairs; his private affairs had not gone very far in terms of love and fortune.

In terms of love, the only woman he had loved was Mme Bonacieux, and Mme Bonacieux had disappeared without his being able to discover yet what had become of her.

In terms of fortune, he, puny as he was, had made an enemy of the cardinal, that is, of a man before whom the greatest men of the realm trembled, starting with the king.

This man could crush him, and yet he had not done so. For a mind as perspicacious as d'Artagnan's, this indulgence was the light by which he saw into a better future.

Then, he had made yet another enemy, less to be feared, he thought, but who he felt instinctively was not to be scorned. That enemy was Milady.

In exchange for all that, he had acquired the protection and benevolence of the queen, but the benevolence of the queen, at the current time, was one more cause of persecution; and her protection, as we know, protected very poorly—witness Chalais and Mme Bonacieux.

Thus the clearest gain he had made in all this was the five- or six-thousand-livre diamond he wore on his finger; and even that diamond, supposing that d'Artagnan, in his ambitious plans, wanted to keep it in order to use it one day as a sign of recognition with the queen, meanwhile, since he could not dispose of it, had no more value than the pebbles he was trampling underfoot.

We say trampling underfoot, for d'Artagnan was making these reflections while walking alone down a pretty little path that led to the camp in the village of Angoutin. But these reflections had led him further than he thought, and the day was beginning to decline when, in the last ray of the setting sun, behind a hedge, he seemed to see the gleam of a musket barrel.

D'Artagnan had a sharp eye and a quick mind. He understood that the musket had not come there by itself, and that the one carrying it had not hidden behind a hedge with friendly intentions. He decided to clear off, but then, on the other side of the road, behind a rock, he noticed the tip of another musket.

It was evidently an ambush.

The young man cast a glance at the first musket and saw with a certain uneasiness that it was taking aim at him, but as soon as he saw the mouth of the barrel stop moving, he threw himself to the ground. At the same time, the shot rang out, and he heard the whistle of a bullet passing over his head.

There was no time to lose. D'Artagnan leaped up, and at that same moment the bullet of the other musket sent the pebbles flying at the very place on the path where he had been lying face down.

D'Artagnan was not one of those uselessly brave men who court a ridiculous death so that it will be said of them that they did not yield an inch; besides, it was not a question of courage here: d'Artagnan had fallen into a trap.

"If there's a third shot," he said to himself, "I'm done for!"

And taking to his heels at once, he ran off in the direction of the camp, with the swiftness of the folk of his province, so renowned for their agility. But fast as he ran, the first one who had fired, having had time to reload his gun, fired a second shot at him, so well aimed this time that it went through his hat and sent it flying ten feet in front of him.

However, as d'Artagnan had no other hat, he picked it up as he ran, reached his quarters quite out of breath and pale, sat down without saying anything to anyone, and began to reflect.

This event could have three causes:

The first and most natural would be an ambush by the Rochelois, who would not have been sorry to kill one of His Majesty's guards, first because that was one less enemy, and then because that enemy might have a well-stuffed purse in his pocket.

D'Artagnan picked up his hat, examined the bullet hole, and shook his head. The bullet was not a musket ball; it was a ball from an arquebus. The accuracy of the shot had already made him think it had been fired by a personal weapon: this was not, then, a military ambush, since the ball was of the wrong caliber.

It could be a nice souvenir from M. le cardinal. It will be recalled that, at the very moment when, thanks to that blessed ray of sunlight, he caught sight of the gun barrel, he was marveling at His Eminence's forebearance regarding him.

But d'Artagnan shook his head. With men towards whom

he had only to reach out his hand, His Eminence rarely had recourse to such methods.

It could be the vengeance of Milady.

That was more probable.

He tried in vain to recall either the features or the dress of the assassins, but he had gotten away from them so quickly that he had not had time to notice anything.

"Ah, my poor friends!" murmured d'Artagnan. "Where are you? How I miss you!"

D'Artagnan spent a very bad night. Three or four times he woke up with a start, imagining that a man was approaching his bed to put a dagger in him. Yet day came without the darkness having brought any mishap.

But d'Artagnan was well aware that what was put off was not forgotten.

D'Artagnan remained in his quarters all day. He gave himself the excuse that the weather was bad.

The day after that, the drums beat assembly. The duc d'Orléans was visiting the posts. The guards rushed to arms, and d'Artagnan fell in among his comrades.

Monsieur passed along the front line. Then all the superior officers approached him to pay their respects, M. des Essarts, the captain of the guards, like the others.

After a moment it seemed to d'Artagnan that M. des Essarts was making a sign for him to approach. He waited for a second gesture from his superior, fearing he was mistaken, but, the gesture being repeated, he left the ranks and went to receive his orders.

"Monsieur is going to ask for men willing to take on a dangerous mission, but one that will bring honor to those who carry it out, and I made a sign to you so that you would keep yourself ready."

"Thank you, Captain!" replied d'Artagnan, who asked for nothing better than to distinguish himself in the eyes of the lieutenant general.

In fact, the Rochelois had made a sortie during the night and had retaken a bastion that the royalist army had captured two days before. It was a question of sending out a forlorn hope to see how the army was guarding this bastion.

Indeed, after a few moments, Monsieur raised his voice and said:

"For this mission I need three or four volunteers led by a dependable man."

"As for the dependable man, I have him here, Monseigneur," said M. des Essarts, pointing to d'Artagnan. "And as for the four or five volunteers, Monseigneur has only to make known his intentions, and he will not lack for men."

"Four men willing to go and get themselves killed with me!" said d'Artagnan, raising his sword.

Two of his comrades from the guards leaped forward at once, and two soldiers joined them, making up the number called for. D'Artagnan then rejected all others, not wishing to do an injustice to those who had the priority.

It was not known whether, after taking the bastion, the Rochelois had evacuated it or had left a garrison there. The place therefore had to be examined rather closely in order to find out.

D'Artagnan set out with his four companions and followed the trench. The two guards marched beside him, and the soldiers came behind.

Thus, under cover of the revetments, they came to within a hundred paces of the bastion! There d'Artagnan, turning around, saw that the two soldiers had disappeared.

He thought they had lagged behind out of fear and continued his advance.

At the turning of the counterscarp, they found themselves some sixty paces from the bastion.

There was no one to be seen, and the bastion seemed abandoned.

The three forlorn lads were debating whether they should go further on when, all at once, a belt of smoke surrounded the stone giant, and a dozen bullets went whistling past d'Artagnan and his two companions.

They knew what they wanted to know: the bastion was guarded. A longer stay in that dangerous place would thus have been a useless imprudence. D'Artagnan and the two guards did an about-face and beat a retreat that looked more like a rout.

On reaching the corner of the trench that would serve them as a rampart, one of the guards fell with a bullet through his chest. The other, who was safe and sound, continued his run to the camp.

D'Artagnan did not want to abandon his companion like that, and bent over him to pick him up and help him get back to their lines; but at that moment two gunshots rang out: one bullet shattered the head of the already wounded guard, and the other flattened itself against a rock after having passed within two inches of d'Artagnan.

The young man turned around quickly, for this attack could not be coming from the bastion, which was masked by the corner of the trench. The notion of the two soldiers who had abandoned them came back to his mind, and he recalled his assassins of two days ago. He decided this time to find out what it was all about, and fell on the body of his comrade as if he was dead. He immediately saw two heads rise above an abandoned earthwork thirty paces away: they were the heads of our two soldiers. D'Artagnan had not been mistaken. These two men had followed him only in order to assassinate him, hoping that the young man's death would be laid to the enemy's account.

But since he might merely be wounded and might denounce their crime, they came to finish him off. Fortunately, deceived by d'Artagnan's ruse, they neglected to reload their guns.

When they were ten paces from him, d'Artagnan, who in falling had been very careful not to let go of his sword, rose up all at once and in one bound was on top of them.

The assassins understood that if they ran towards the camp without having killed their man, they would be accused by him. Their first idea was therefore to go over to the enemy. One of them seized his gun by the barrel and wielded it as a club: he aimed a terrible blow at d'Artagnan, who avoided it by throwing himself to the side; but by this movement he opened the way for the bandit, who rushed at once towards the bastion. As the Rochelois who were guarding it had no idea of the intentions of this man running towards them, they opened fire on him, and he fell, struck by a bullet that broke his shoulder.

During this time, d'Artagnan had thrown himself upon the second soldier, attacking him with his sword. The fight did not last long; the wretch had nothing to defend himself with but his discharged arquebus. The guard's sword slid along the barrel of the now useless weapon and pierced the assassin's thigh. He fell. D'Artagnan immediately brought the point of his blade to his throat.

"Oh, don't kill me!" cried the bandit. "Mercy, mercy, officer, and I'll tell you everything!"

"Is your secret at least worth the trouble of my letting you live?" asked the young man, restraining his arm.

"Yes, if you judge that existence is worthwhile when one is twenty-two, as you are, and can attain all, being handsome and brave as you are."

"Scoundrel!" said d'Artagnan. "Come on, talk quickly, who ordered you to kill me?"

"A woman I don't know, but who is called Milady."

"But if you don't know this woman, how do you know her name?"

"My comrade knew her and called her that. It was him she dealt with, not me. He even has a letter from this person in his pocket, which should have great importance for you, from what I've heard him say."

"But how did you end up as the second half of this trap?"

"He proposed to me that we pull it off together, and I accepted."

"And how much did she give you for this pretty expedition?"

"A hundred louis."

"Well, how nice," the young man said, laughing, "she finds me worth something at least—a hundred louis! That's a lot for two scoundrels like you, so I can understand that you accepted, and I will grant you mercy, but on one condition!"

"What is it?" asked the uneasy soldier, seeing that all was not over.

"That you go and find me the letter your comrade has in his pocket."

"But," cried the bandit, "that's just another way of killing me! How do you want me to go and find that letter under fire from the bastion?"

"All the same, you'll have to make up your mind to go and find it, or I swear to you that you will die by my hand."

"Mercy, Monsieur, have pity! In the name of that young lady you love, whom you perhaps think is dead, but who isn't!" cried the bandit, throwing himself on his knees and leaning on his hand, for he was beginning to lose his strength along with his blood.

"And how do you know that there is a woman I love, and that I thought the woman was dead?" asked d'Artagnan.

"From the letter my comrade has in his pocket."

"You see very well, then, that I must have that letter," said d'Artagnan. "And so, no more delay, no more hesitation, or else, repugnant as it is to me to dip my sword a second time in the blood of a scoundrel like you, I swear on my faith as an honest man . . ."

And at these words d'Artagnan made such a threatening gesture that the wounded man stood up.

"Stop! Stop!" he cried, taking courage out of terror. "I'll go . . . I'll go! . . ."

D'Artagnan took the soldier's arquebus, made him walk ahead of him, and pushed him towards his companion, prodding him in the back with the point of his sword.

It was a frightful thing to see the wretch, leaving a long trail of blood behind him as he went, pale in the face of death, trying to drag himself without being seen to the body of his accomplice, which lay twenty paces away!

Terror was so painted on his face, covered in cold sweat, that d'Artagnan took pity on him, and, looking at him with contempt, said:

"Well, then, I'll show you the difference between a man of courage and a coward like you! Stay here, and I'll go."

And with an agile step, his eye on the lookout, observing

the movements of the enemy, availing himself of all the accidents of the terrain, d'Artagnan reached the second soldier.

There were two ways of achieving his goal: to search him on the spot, or to carry him off, using his body as a shield, and search him in the trench.

D'Artagnan preferred the second method, and took the assassin on his back at the very moment when the enemy opened fire.

A slight shock, the dull noise of three bullets piercing flesh, a last cry, a shudder of agony, proved to d'Artagnan that the man who had wanted to assassinate him had just saved his life.

He began his inventory at once: a leather wallet, a purse evidently containing part of the sum the bandit had received, a dice cup, and dice made up the dead man's inheritance.

He left the cup and the dice where they fell, threw the purse to the wounded man, and avidly opened the wallet.

Amidst various papers of no importance, he found the following letter. It was the one he had gone to find at the risk of his life:

> Since you have lost track of that woman, and she is now safely in a convent which you should never have let her reach, try at least not to miss the man; otherwise, you know that I have a long arm, and that you will pay dearly for the hundred louis you got from me.

No signature. Nevertheless, it was evident that the letter was from Milady. He therefore kept it as convicting evidence, and, in safety behind the corner of the trench, began questioning the wounded man. The latter confessed that he had been directed, together with his comrade, the same one who had just been killed, to abduct a young woman who was to leave Paris by the porte de La Villette, but that, having stopped for a drink in a tavern, they had missed the carriage by ten minutes.

"But what would you have done with this woman?" d'Artagnan asked in anguish.

"We were to put her in a house on the place Royale," said the wounded man.

"Yes, yes," murmured d'Artagnan, "that's it—in Milady's own house!"

Then the young man understood with a shudder what a terrible thirst for vengeance drove this woman to destroy him, as well as those who loved him, and how much she knew about the affairs of court, since she had found out everything. No doubt she owed this information to the cardinal.

But, in the midst of all this, he understood, with a very real sense of joy, that the queen had ended by discovering the prison where poor Mme Bonacieux was paying for her devotion, and that she had taken her from that prison. And so the letter he had received from the young woman, and her passing by like an apparition on the road to Chaillot, were explained to him.

Hence, as Athos had predicted, it was possible to find Mme Bonacieux again, and a convent was not impregnable.

This idea finished restoring clemency to his heart. He turned to the wounded man, who was anxiously following all the changing expressions of his face, and holding out his arm to him, said:

"Come, I don't want to abandon you like this. Lean on me and let's go back to camp."

"Yes," said the wounded man, who could hardly believe in so much magnanimity, "but isn't it just to have me hanged?"

"You have my word," said d'Artagnan, "and I am granting you your life for the second time."

The wounded man dropped to his knees and once again kissed the feet of his savior. But d'Artagnan, who no longer had any motive for remaining so close to the enemy, cut short the expressions of his gratitude.

The guard who had gone back at the first blast from the Rochelois had announced the death of his four companions. There was thus great astonishment and great joy in the regiment when they saw the young man reappear safe and sound.

D'Artagnan explained his companion's wound by a sortie of his own improvisation. He told of the death of the other soldier and the dangers they had run. This account was the occasion of a veritable triumph for him. The whole army spoke of the expedition for a day, and Monsieur sent him his compliments on it.

Moreover, as every fair deed brings its own reward, d'Artagnan's fair deed had the result of restoring to him the tranquillity he had lost. Indeed, d'Artagnan believed he could be tranquil, since, of his two enemies, one was killed and the other was devoted to his interests.

This tranquillity proved one thing: that d'Artagnan did not yet know Milady.

XLII

THE WINE OF ANJOU

After almost despairing news of the king, the rumor of his convalescence began to spread through the camp; and as he was in great haste to come to the siege in person, it was said that, as soon as he could get back on a horse, he would set out on his way again.

During this time, Monsieur, who knew that one day or another he was going to be replaced in his command, either by the duc d'Angoulême, or by Bassompierre or Schomberg, who were disputing for the command, did very little, wasted his days in tentative efforts, and did not dare risk any major undertaking to drive the English from the Île de Ré, where they were still besieging the citadel of Saint-Martin and the fort of La Prée, while the French, for their part, were besieging La Rochelle.

D'Artagnan, as we have said, had become more tranquil, as always happens after passing through danger, when the danger seems to have vanished. He had only one worry left, which was that he had had no news of his friends.

But, one morning at the beginning of the month of November, everything was explained to him by this letter, dated from Villeroi:

Monsieur d'Artagnan,

MM. Athos, Porthos, and Aramis, after having a good time at my place and becoming quite lively, made so great a racket that the provost of the castle, a very rigid man, has confined them to barracks for several days. But I am carrying out the orders they gave me to send you a dozen bottles of my Anjou wine, which they made much of. They wish you to drink their health with their favorite wine.

I have done so, and remain, Monsieur, with great respect,

Your most humble and obedient servant,

Godeau,
Hosteler to the gentlemen musketeers

"Excellent!" cried d'Artagnan. "They think of me in their pleasures as I think of them in my troubles. I'll certainly drink their health, and wholeheartedly, but I won't drink alone."

And d'Artagnan ran to two of the guards with whom he had become more friendly than with the others to invite them to drink the delicious little Anjou wine that had just arrived from Villeroi. One of the two guards already had an invitation for that evening, and the other for the next. The gathering was thus set for the day after that.

On returning, d'Artagnan sent the twelve bottles of wine to the guards' pothouse, ordering that they be carefully kept. Then, on the day of the solemnity, as the dinner hour had been set for noon, d'Artagnan sent Planchet at nine o'clock to prepare everything.

Planchet, quite proud to be raised to the dignity of maître d'hôtel, intended to prepare everything like an intelligent man. To that end, he took on the valet of one of his master's guests, named Fourreau, and that false soldier who had wanted to kill d'Artagnan, and who, belonging to no corps, had entered into his service, or rather Planchet's, since d'Artagnan had spared his life.

When the hour of the feast came, the two guests arrived, took their places, and the dishes lined themselves up on the table. Planchet served with a napkin over his arm, Fourreau uncorked the bottles, and Brisemont (that was the convalescent's name) decanted the wine into carafes, for it seemed to have thrown a sediment owing to the bumps in the road. The first bottle of this wine was a bit clouded at the bottom. Brisemont poured the lees into a glass, and d'Artagnan allowed him to drink it; for the poor fellow still did not have much strength.

The guests, after finishing the soup, were about to bring the first glass to their lips, when all at once the cannon thundered from Fort Louis and the Port-Neuf. The guards, thinking it was some unexpected attack either from the besieged forces or from the English, jumped for their swords at once. D'Artagnan, no less nimble, did the same, and all three left at a run to report to their posts.

But they were hardly out of the pothouse when they found themselves staring at the cause of the great commotion. Cries of "Long live the king!" and "Long live the cardinal!" rang out on all sides, and drums were beating in all directions.

Indeed, the king, impatient as we have said, had just doubled two days' marches and arrived at that very moment with all his household and a reinforcement of ten thousand troops. His musketeers preceded and followed him. D'Artagnan, lined up with his company, saluted his friends with an expressive gesture. They responded with their eyes, as did M. de Tréville, who had recognized him first thing.

Once the reception ceremony was over, the four friends were soon in each other's arms.

"Pardieu!" cried d'Artagnan, "you couldn't possibly have arrived more opportunely; the food won't even have had time to get cold! Isn't that so, gentlemen?" the young man added, turning to the two guards, whom he introduced to his friends.

"Aha! it seems we're banqueting!" said Porthos.

"I hope," said Aramis, "that there are no women at your dinner!"

"Is there any drinkable wine in your shanty?" asked Athos.

"Pardieu! There's yours, my dear friend!" replied d'Artagnan.

"Our wine?" said Athos, astonished.

"Yes, the wine you sent me."

"We sent you wine?"

"But you know very well, that little wine from the slopes of Anjou."

"Yes, I know very well which wine you mean."

"Your favorite wine."

"To be sure, when I don't have champagne or chambertin."

"Well, for lack of champagne and chambertin, you can content yourself with this."

"So we sent you Anjou wine, gourmets that we are?" said Porthos.

"No, I was sent the wine in your name."

"In our name?" said the three musketeers.

"Was it you who had the wine sent, Aramis?" asked Athos.

"No, and you, Porthos?"

"No, and you, Athos?"

"No."

"If it wasn't you," said d'Artagnan, "it was your hosteler."

"Our hosteler?"

"Why, yes! Your hosteler, Godeau, hosteler to the musketeers."

"By heaven, let it come from wherever it likes, it's no matter," said Porthos. "Let's try it, and if it's good, we'll drink it."

"No," said Athos, "we won't drink wine from an unknown source."

"You're right, Athos," said d'Artagnan. "None of you directed the hosteler Godeau to send me wine?"

"No! And yet he sent it to you in our name?"

"Here's the letter!" said d'Artagnan.

And he handed the note to his comrades.

"That's not his writing!" cried Athos. "I know his hand. It was I who settled accounts for the community before we left."

"A false letter," said Porthos. "We were never confined to barracks."

"D'Artagnan," asked Aramis in a reproachful tone, "how could you believe we made a racket? . . ."

D'Artagnan turned pale, and a convulsive trembling shook all his limbs.

"You frighten me," said Athos. "What's happened?"

"Run quickly, quickly, my friends!" cried d'Artagnan. "A horrible suspicion has just occurred to me! Can this be another attempt at vengeance from that woman?"

This time it was Athos who turned pale.

D'Artagnan rushed to the pothouse, the three musketeers and the two guards behind him.

The first thing that struck d'Artagnan's eyes on going into the dining room was Brisemont lying on the floor and rolling about in atrocious convulsions.

Planchet and Fourreau, pale as death, were trying to help him, but it was obvious that all help was useless: the dying man's features were twisted in agony.

"Ah!" he cried out on seeing d'Artagnan, "ah! it's abominable! You seemed to grant me mercy, and now you've poisoned me!"

"I?" cried d'Artagnan. "I, you poor wretch? What are you saying?"

"I say it was you who gave me that wine, I say it was you who told me to drink it, I say you wanted to revenge yourself on me, I say it's abominable!"

"Don't think it, Brisemont," said d'Artagnan, "don't think it. I swear to you, I protest to you . . ."

"Oh! but God is there! God will punish you! My God, some day let him suffer what I'm suffering!"

"On the Gospel," cried d'Artagnan, rushing to the dying man, "I swear to you, I didn't know the wine was poisoned, and I was going to drink it just like you."

"I don't believe you," said the soldier.

And in redoubled torment, he expired.

"Abominable! Abominable!" murmured Athos, while Porthos broke the bottles and Aramis gave somewhat belated orders to send for a confessor.

"Oh, my friends," said d'Artagnan, "you've just saved my life again, and not only mine, but these gentlemen's as well! Gentlemen," he went on, addressing the guards, "I ask you to keep silent about this whole adventure. Great personages may have had a hand in what you've seen, and the evil of it all will fall back on us."

"Ah, Monsieur!" stammered Planchet, more dead than alive, "ah, Monsieur! I've had a narrow escape!"

"What, you rascal," cried d'Artagnan. "So you were going to drink my wine?"

"To the king's health, Monsieur, I would have drunk one little glass, if Fourreau hadn't told me that someone was calling me."

"Alas!" said Fourreau, whose teeth were chattering with terror. "I wanted him out of the way so that I could drink by myself!"

"Gentlemen," said d'Artagnan, addressing the guards, "you understand that such a feast could not help but be rather sad after what has just happened. Please accept all my excuses and put off the party till another day."

The two guards courteously accepted d'Artagnan's excuses, and, understanding that the four friends wished to remain alone, they withdrew.

Once the young guard and the three musketeers were without witnesses, they looked at each other with an air which meant to say that each of them understood the gravity of the situation.

"First of all," said Athos, "let's leave this room. A dead man is bad company, especially one who has died a violent death."

"Planchet," said d'Artagnan, "I entrust the poor devil's body to you. Let him be buried in hallowed ground. He committed a crime, it's true, but he repented of it."

And the four friends went out, leaving to Planchet and Fourreau the task of rendering mortuary honors to Brisemont.

The host gave them another room, in which he served them boiled eggs and water, which Athos went to draw from the well himself. In a few words, Porthos and Aramis were let in on the situation.

"Well, then," d'Artagnan said to Athos, "you see, my dear friend, that it's war to the death."

Athos shook his head.

"Yes, yes," he said, "I see it very well; but do you think she's the same one?"

"I'm sure of it."

"I confess to you that I still have doubts."

"But what about the fleur-de-lis on her shoulder?"

"She's an Englishwoman who must have committed some misdeed in France, and she must have been branded in consequence of her crime."

"Athos, she's your wife, I tell you," d'Artagnan repeated. "Don't you remember how close the two descriptions are?"

"Yet I'd have thought the other one was dead—I hanged her well enough."

This time it was d'Artagnan who shook his head.

"But what to do, finally?" said the young man.

"The fact is that we can't remain like this, with a sword eternally hanging over our heads," said Athos. "We must get out of this situation."

"But how?"

"Listen, try to find her again and have it out with her. Tell her: peace or war! My word as a gentleman that I will never say anything about you and never do anything against you; on your side, a solemn oath to remain neutral regarding me. If not, I'll go to the chancelier, I'll go to the king, I'll go to the executioner, I'll rouse the court against you, I'll denounce you as a branded woman, I'll have you tried, and if they acquit you, well, then, on my word as a gentleman, I'll kill you at some corner post as I'd kill a mad dog."

"I rather like that way," said d'Artagnan, "but how can I find her?"

"Time, my dear, time will afford the opportunity, time is man's martingale: the more binding it is, the more you gain when you know how to wait."

"Yes, but to wait surrounded by assassins and poisoners . . ."

"Bah!" said Athos. "God has preserved us up to now, God will go on preserving us."

"Us, yes. But anyhow we're men, and, all things considered, it's our job to risk our lives; while she! . . ." he added in a low voice.

"She who?" asked Athos.

"Constance."

"Mme Bonacieux? Ah, that's right," said Athos. "My poor friend, I'd forgotten you were in love!"

"Well," said Aramis, "but haven't you seen from that same letter you found on the wretched dead man that she's in a convent? It's very good to be in a convent, and once the siege of La Rochelle is over, I promise you that for my part . . ."

"Right!" said Athos. "Right! Yes, my dear Aramis, we know you have religious leanings."

"I am only an interim musketeer," Aramis said humbly.

"It appears he hasn't had news from his mistress for a long time," Athos said softly, "but pay no attention, we know all that."

"Well," said Porthos, "it seems to me there would be a very simple way."

"What is it?" asked d'Artagnan.

"You say she's in a convent?" Porthos went on.

"Yes."

"Well, once the siege is over, we'll abduct her from the convent."

"But we still have to know which convent it is."

"That's true," said Porthos.

"But I'm thinking," said Athos, "didn't you claim, my dear d'Artagnan, that it was the queen who chose this convent for her?"

"Yes, or so I think."

"Well, then Porthos will help us with that."

"How so, if you please?"

"Why, through your marquise, your duchess, your princess: she must have a long arm."

"Shh!" said Porthos, putting a finger to his lips. "I think she's a cardinalist, and she mustn't learn anything about it."

"In that case," said Aramis, "I'll take charge of finding out the news."

"You, Aramis?" cried the three friends. "And how is that?"

"Through the queen's chaplain, with whom I have close ties . . ." said Aramis, blushing.

And on this assurance, the four friends, who had finished their modest meal, separated with a promise to see each other that same evening. D'Artagnan returned to the Minimes, and the three musketeers went back to the king's sector, where they had to have their quarters prepared.

XLIII

THE INN OF THE RED DOVECOTE

Having barely reached camp, the king, who was in great haste to confront the enemy, and who, with a better right than the cardinal, shared his hatred of Buckingham, wanted to make all the arrangements, first for driving the English from the Île de Ré, and then for pressing the siege of La Rochelle. But, in spite of himself, he was held up by the dissensions that broke out between MM. de Bassompierre and Schomberg and the duc d'Angoulême.

MM. Bassompierre and Schomberg were maréchals de France, and claimed their right to command the army under the king's orders; but, fearing that Bassompierre, a Huguenot at heart, would not press hard enough against the English and the Rochelois, his brothers in religion, the cardinal, on the contrary, backed the duc d'Angoulême, whom the king, at his instigation, had named lieutenant general. The result was that, to avoid seeing MM. Bassompierre and Schomberg desert the army, they were obliged to make each of them a separate commander. Bassompierre set up his quarters to the north of the town, from La Leu to Dompierre; the duc d'Angoulême from Dompierre to Périgny; and M. de Schomberg to the south, from Périgny to Angoutin.

Monsieur had his quarters at Dompierre.

The king had his quarters now at Etré, now at La Jarrie.

Finally, the cardinal had his quarters on the dunes, at the pont de La Pierre, in a simple house without any entrenchment.

In this way, Monsieur kept an eye on Bassompierre, the king on the duc d'Angoulême, and the cardinal on M. de Schomberg.

Once this organization was established, they set about driving the English from the Île de Ré.

The circumstances were favorable. The English, who above all had need of good provisions in order to be good soldiers, had been eating only salted meat and bad biscuits, and had many sick men in their camp. Moreover, the sea, very rough at that time of year on the whole Atlantic coast, brought some little boat to harm every day, and the beach, from the point of l'Aiguillon to the trenches, was literally covered, at each low tide, with the wreckage of pinnaces, luggers, and feluccas. As a result, even if the king's men kept to their camp, it was obvious that one day or another Buckingham, who only stayed on the Île de Ré out of stubbornness, would be obliged to raise the siege.

But, as M. de Toiras announced that everything was being prepared in the enemy camp for a fresh assault, the king decided that it must be brought to an end and gave the necessary orders for a decisive engagement.

As it is not our intention to give a day-by-day account of the siege, but, on the contrary, to report only the events that have to do with the story we are telling, we shall content ourselves with saying in two words that the undertaking succeeded, to the great astonishment of the king and the great glory of M. le cardinal. The English, driven back foot by foot, beaten at every encounter, crushed in the passage of the Île de Loix, were obliged to re-embark, leaving two thousand men on the battlefield, among them five colonels, three lieutenant colonels, two hundred and fifty captains, and twenty gentlemen of quality, four cannon, and sixty banners that were taken to Paris by Claude de Saint-Simon and hung with great pomp from the vaults of Notre-Dame.

Te Deums were sung in camp, and from there spread throughout France.

The cardinal was thus left free to pursue the siege without having anything to fear from the English—at least for the moment.

But, as we have just said, the respite was only momentary.

An envoy from the duke of Buckingham by the name of Montaigu had been captured, and they had acquired proof of a league between the Empire, Spain, England, and Lorraine.

This league was directed against France.

Moreover, in Buckingham's quarters, which he had been forced to abandon more precipitately than he had thought, they found papers confirming this league, and which, as M. le cardinal insists in his *Memoirs*, strongly compromised Mme de Chevreuse, and consequently the queen.

It was on the cardinal that all the responsibility weighed, for one is not an absolute minister without being responsible; and so all the resources of his vast genius were strained night and day, and taken up with listening to the least rumor that arose in one of the great kingdoms of Europe.

The cardinal was aware of Buckingham's activity and above all of his hatred. If the league that threatened France triumphed, all his influence would be lost: Spanish policy and Austrian policy would have their representatives in the cabinet at the Louvre, where they now had only partisans; he, Richelieu, the French minister, the national minister par excellence, would be ruined. The king, who, while obeying him like a child, hated him as a child hates its schoolmaster, would abandon him to the combined vengeance of Monsieur and the queen. He would thus be lost, and perhaps France along with him. He had to guard against all that.

And so one saw his couriers, who became more numerous every moment, succeeding each other day and night in that little house at the pont de La Pierre where the cardinal had taken up his residence.

There were monks so ill suited to the habit that it was easy to tell they belonged above all to the church militant; women slightly hindered by their pages' costumes, and whose baggy trousers could not entirely conceal their rounded forms; finally, peasants with blackened hands but slender legs, who smelled of quality for leagues around.

Then there were less agreeable visits, for the rumor spread two or three times that the cardinal had nearly been assassinated.

It is true that His Eminence's enemies said he himself had set these bungling assassins afield, so that, if the case presented itself, he would have the right to reprisals. But neither ministers nor their enemies are to be believed.

Moreover, this did not stop the cardinal, whose personal bravery had never been contested even by his most dogged detractors, from making many night journeys, now to communicate important orders to the duc d'Angoulême, now to go and discuss things with the king, now to confer with some messenger whom he did not want to let into his quarters.

For their part, the musketeers, who did not have much to do at the siege, were not strictly controlled and led a merry life. This was all the easier for them—for our three companions especially—in that, being friends of M. de Tréville, they easily obtained special permissions from him to stay out late and to remain after the closing of the camp.

One evening, when d'Artagnan, who was in the trenches, was unable to accompany them, Athos, Porthos, and Aramis, mounted on their chargers, wrapped in their war cloaks, one hand on their pistol butts, were coming back from a tavern that Athos had discovered two days earlier on the road to La Jarrie, and which was called the Red Dovecote. They were going along the road that led to camp, keeping themselves on guard, as we have said, for fear of an ambush, when, about a quarter of a league from the village of Boisnar, they thought they heard the sound of hoofbeats coming towards them. The three stopped at once, drew close together, and waited, keeping to the middle of the way. After a moment, and just as the moon came out from behind a cloud, they saw two horsemen appear around a turning of the road, who, on catching sight of them, also stopped, seeming to deliberate on whether they should continue on their way or turn back. This hesitation aroused some suspicions in the three friends, and Athos, advancing a few paces, called out in a firm voice:

"Who goes there?"

"Who goes there yourself?" answered one of the two horsemen.

"That's no answer!" said Athos. "Who goes there? Answer, or we'll charge!"

"Take care what you are about to do, gentlemen!" then said a vibrant voice that seemed accustomed to command.

"It's some superior officer making his night rounds," said Athos. "What do you wish to do, gentlemen?"

"Who are you?" said the same voice with the same tone of command. "Answer in your turn, or your disobedience may get you into trouble."

"King's musketeers," said Athos, more and more convinced that he who was questioning them had the right to do so.

"What company?"

"M. de Tréville's."

"I order you to advance and account to me for what you are doing here at this hour."

The three companions advanced, their ears back somewhat, for all three were now convinced that they were dealing with someone more powerful than themselves. Moreover, they left it to Athos to be their spokesman.

One of the two horsemen, the one who had spoken second, was ten paces in front of his companion. Athos made a sign for Porthos and Aramis to stay behind in their turn and advanced alone.

"Excuse us, officer," said Athos, "but we did not know whom we were dealing with, and you could see that we were on our guard."

"Your name?" asked the officer, who covered part of his face with his cloak.

"But you yourself, Monsieur," said Athos, who was beginning to rebel against this inquisition, "kindly give me some proof that you have the right to question me."

"Your name?" the horseman asked a second time, letting his cloak fall so as to uncover his face.

"M. le cardinal!" cried the stupefied musketeer.

"Your name?" His Eminence asked for the third time.

"Athos," said the musketeer.

The cardinal made a sign to his equerry, who approached.

"These three musketeers will follow us," he said in a low voice. "I do not want it known that I have left camp, and, by having them follow us, we will be sure that they will not tell anyone."

"We are gentlemen, Monseigneur," said Athos. "Ask us

for our word and do not trouble yourself further. Thank God, we know how to keep a secret."

The cardinal fixed his piercing eyes on this bold interlocutor.

"You have a sharp ear, M. Athos," said the cardinal, "but now listen to this: it is not out of mistrust that I ask you to follow me; it is for my own safety. No doubt your companions are MM. Porthos and Aramis?"

"Yes, Your Eminence," said Athos, while the two musketeers who had remained behind approached, hat in hand.

"I know you, gentlemen," said the cardinal, "I know you: I know that you are not exactly my friends, and I am sorry for that, but I know that you are brave and loyal gentlemen, and that you can be trusted. M. Athos, do me the honor, then, of accompanying me, you and your two friends, and then I shall have an escort that His Majesty would envy, if we should meet him."

The three musketeers bowed all the way to their horses' necks.

"Well, on my honor," said Athos, "Your Eminence is right to bring us with him! We have met some frightful faces on the road, and we have even had a quarrel with four of those faces at the Red Dovecote."

"A quarrel? Over what, gentlemen?" asked the cardinal. "I dislike quarrelers, you know!"

"That is precisely why I have the honor of informing Your Eminence of what has just happened; for you might learn of it from others than us, and, on false report, believe that we are at fault."

"And what was the outcome of this quarrel?" asked the cardinal, frowning.

"Why, my friend Aramis, here, received a slight wound in the arm, which will not hinder him, as Your Eminence may see, from mounting the assault tomorrow, if Your Eminence orders the escalade."

"But you are not men to let yourselves be wounded like that," said the cardinal. "Come, be frank, gentlemen; you certainly gave a few in return. Confess yourselves: you know I have the right to give absolution."

"As for me, Monseigneur," said Athos, "I didn't even draw

my sword. I took the one I was dealing with by the waist and threw him out the window. It seems that in the fall," Athos continued somewhat hesitantly, "he broke his thigh."

"Aha!" said the cardinal. "And you, M. Porthos?"

"As for me, Monseigneur, knowing that dueling is forbidden, I picked up a bench and gave one of those brigands a blow with it, which I think broke his shoulder."

"Very well," said the cardinal. "And you, M. Aramis?"

"As for me, Monseigneur, since I am of a very gentle nature, and besides, as Monseigneur may not know, am on the point of entering holy orders, I was trying to get my comrades away, when one of those scoundrels treacherously stabbed me in the left arm. Then I lost patience. I drew my sword in turn, and as he came back to the charge, I believe I felt that, in throwing himself upon me, he ran himself through. All I know for certain is that he fell, and it seemed to me that he was carried out with his two companions."

"Devil take it, gentlemen," said the cardinal, "three men put out of action in a tavern brawl! You don't go about things lightly. And what was the quarrel about?"

"The scoundrels were drunk," said Athos, "and knowing that a woman had arrived at the tavern that evening, they wanted to force her door."

"To force her door?" said the cardinal. "To do what?"

"To do her violence, no doubt," said Athos. "I had the honor of telling Your Eminence that the scoundrels were drunk."

"And was this woman young and pretty?" asked the cardinal with a certain uneasiness.

"We did not see her, Monseigneur," said Athos.

"You did not see her—ah, very good!" the cardinal picked up sharply. "You did well to defend a woman's honor, and, as I am going to the inn of the Red Dovecote myself, I shall find out if you have told me the truth."

"Monseigneur," Athos said proudly, "we are gentlemen, and would not tell a lie to save our own heads."

"Nor do I doubt what you tell me, M. Athos, not for a single instant do I doubt it. But," he added, to change the subject, "was this lady alone, then?"

"This lady was closeted with a cavalier," said Athos. "But as this cavalier did not show himself, in spite of the noise, it is to be presumed that he is a coward."

"'Judge not rashly,' says the Gospel," the cardinal replied.

Athos inclined his head.

"Very well, gentlemen," His Eminence continued, "now I know what I wanted to know. Follow me."

The three musketeers fell in behind the cardinal, who wrapped his face once more in his cloak and set his horse at a walk, keeping eight or ten paces ahead of his four companions.

They soon reached the silent and solitary inn. No doubt the host knew what illustrious visitor he was expecting, and had consequently sent away all intruders.

Ten paces from the door, the cardinal made a sign for his equerry and the three musketeers to stop. A saddled horse was tied to the outside shutter. The cardinal knocked three times and in a certain way.

A man wrapped in a cloak came out at once and exchanged a few quick words with the cardinal, after which he got back on his horse and rode off in the direction of Surgères, which was also the direction to Paris.

"Come here, gentlemen," said the cardinal, addressing the three musketeers. "You have told me the truth, and if our meeting tonight is not advantageous to you, it will not be my fault. Meanwhile, follow me."

The cardinal dismounted; the three musketeers did the same. The cardinal threw the bridle of his horse into his equerry's hands; the three musketeers tied the bridles of theirs to the shutters.

The host stood in the doorway. For him, the cardinal was no more than an officer coming to visit a lady.

"Do you have some room on the ground floor where these gentlemen can wait for me by a good fire?" asked the cardinal.

The host opened the door to a large room, in which a wretched stove had just been replaced by a large and excellent fireplace.

"I have this one," he replied.

"Very good," said the cardinal. "Go in here, gentlemen, and kindly wait for me. I won't be more than half an hour."

And while the three musketeers went into the ground-floor room, the cardinal, without asking for further information, went upstairs like a man who had no need to be shown the way.

XLIV

OF THE USEFULNESS OF STOVEPIPES

It was evident that, without suspecting it, and moved only by their chivalrous and adventurous character, our three friends had just rendered a service to someone whom the cardinal honored with his special protection.

Now, who was this someone? That was the question the three musketeers asked themselves first of all. Then, seeing that none of the responses their own intelligence could offer them were satisfactory, Porthos called the host and asked for dice.

Porthos and Aramis sat at a table and began to play. Athos paced the room and reflected.

While pacing and reflecting, Athos went back and forth before the broken-off stovepipe, the other end of which went to the room above, and each time he went back and forth, he heard a murmur of speech, which ended by catching his attention. Athos stepped closer and made out several words which doubtless seemed to him worthy of so great an interest that he made a sign to his companions to be quiet, while he himself remained bent down with his ear cocked at the level of the lower opening.

"Listen, Milady," said the cardinal, "it's an important matter. Sit down here and let's talk."

"Milady!" murmured Athos.

"I am listening to Your Eminence with the greatest attention," replied a woman's voice that made the musketeer shiver.

"A small boat with an English crew, whose captain is my man, is waiting for you in the mouth of the Charente, at the Fort de La Pointe. It will set sail tomorrow morning."

"Then I must go there tonight?"

"This very moment—that is, once you've received my instructions. Two men, whom you will find at the door as you leave, will serve as your escort. You will allow me to leave first, then half an hour later you will leave yourself."

"Yes, Monseigneur. Now let's get back to the mission you wish to entrust me with. And, as I am anxious to go on deserving Your Eminence's confidence, kindly present it to me in clear and precise terms, so that I make no mistake."

There was a moment of deep silence between the two interlocutors. It was evident that the cardinal was weighing in advance the terms in which he was going to speak, and that Milady was gathering all her intellectual faculties to understand the things she was going to hear and engrave them in her memory once they were spoken.

Athos profited from this moment to tell his comrades to lock the door from inside and made them a sign to come and listen with him.

The two musketeers, who liked their comfort, brought chairs for themselves and a chair for Athos. All three then sat down, their heads together and their ears pricked up.

"You are going to leave for London," the cardinal went on. "Once in London, you will go to find Buckingham."

"I would observe to His Eminence," said Milady, "that since the affair of the diamond pendants, for which the duke has always suspected me, His Grace distrusts me."

"But this time," said the cardinal, "it is no longer a question of gaining his confidence, but of presenting yourself to him frankly and loyally as a negotiator."

"Frankly and loyally," repeated Milady, with an inexpressible accent of duplicity.

"Yes, frankly and loyally," the cardinal picked up in the same tone. "This whole negotiation must be done in the open."

"I will follow His Eminence's instructions to the letter, and am only waiting for him to give them to me."

"You will go to find Buckingham on my behalf, and you will tell him that I know all the preparations he has made, but that I am hardly troubled by them, seeing that at the first move he ventures, I will ruin the queen."

"Will he believe that Your Eminence is in a position to carry out such a threat?"

"Yes, for I have proofs."

"I must be able to present those proofs for his evaluation."

"Of course. You will tell him that I am going to publish the report of Bois-Robert and the marquis de Beautru on the interview the duke had with the queen in the home of Mme le connétable, on the evening when Mme le connétable gave a masked fête. You will tell him, so that he has no doubts at all, that he came in the costume of the Grand Mogul, which was to be worn by the chevalier de Guise, and which he bought from the latter for the sum of three thousand pistoles."

"Very well, Monseigneur."

"All the details of his entry into the Louvre and his leaving during the night, when he was introduced at the palace in the costume of an Italian fortune-teller, are known to me. You will tell him, so that he does not still doubt the authenticity of my information, that under his cloak he had on a long white robe sprinkled with black teardrops and skulls and crossbones: for, in case of surprise, he was to pass himself off as the ghost of the White Lady, who, as everyone knows, returns to the Louvre each time some great event is about to take place."

"Is that all, Monseigneur?"

"Tell him that I also know all the details of the adventure in Amiens, and that I shall make a little novel of it, wittily written, with a plan of the garden, and portraits of the principal actors in that nocturnal scene."

"I shall tell him that."

"Tell him also that I have Montaigu, that Montaigu is in the Bastille, that no letter was found on him, true, but that torture may make him tell what he knows, and even . . . what he does not know."

"Excellent."

"Add, finally, that His Grace, in the precipitation with which he set about quitting the Île de Ré, forgot in his quarters a certain letter from Mme de Chevreuse, which is singularly compromising to the queen, in so far as it proves not only that Her Majesty can love the enemies of the king, but also that she is conspiring with the enemies of France. You have remembered everything I've told you, have you not?"

"Your Eminence will be the judge: the ball at Mme le connétable's, the night at the Louvre, the evening in Amiens, the arrest of Montaigu, the letter of Mme de Chevreuse."

"That's it," said the cardinal, "that's it: you have a very felicitous memory, Milady."

"But," said she to whom the cardinal had just addressed this flattering compliment, "if, in spite of all these reasons, the duke does not give up and continues to threaten France?"

"The duke is madly in love, or rather, foolishly in love," Richelieu picked up with profound bitterness. "Like the ancient paladins, he undertook this war only to win a glance from his fair one. If he knows that this war may cost the honor and even the liberty of the lady of his thoughts, as they say, I guarantee you that he will think twice about it."

"And yet," said Milady, with a persistence which proved that she wanted to see clearly to the end of the mission she was being entrusted with, "and yet, what if he persists?"

"If he persists . . ." said the cardinal. "But it's not probable."

"But it's possible," said Milady.

"If he persists . . ." His Eminence paused and then went on: "If he persists, well, then I shall hope for one of those events that change the face of states."

"If His Eminence will cite me some examples of these events in history," said Milady, "perhaps I will be able share his confidence in the future."

"Well, take, for example," said Richelieu, "when, in 1610, for a cause rather like the one that moves the duke, King Henri IV, of glorious memory, set about invading Flanders and Italy at the same time, in order to strike at Austria from both sides. Well, didn't an event come along that saved Austria? Why should the king of France not have the same luck as the emperor?"

"Your Eminence is referring to the stab of a knife on the rue de la Ferronerie?"

"Exactly," said the cardinal.

"Is Your Eminence not afraid that the torture and death of

Ravaillac may frighten off those who would think even for an instant of imitating him?"

"In all times and in all countries, especially if those countries are divided by religion, there will always be fanatics who ask for nothing better than to be made martyrs. But wait, it just occurs to me right now that the Puritans are furious with the duke of Buckingham, and their preachers are calling him the Antichrist."

"Well?" asked Milady.

"Well," the cardinal went on with an air of indifference, "it will only be a question, for the moment, for example, of finding a woman, beautiful, young, and clever, who has some reason to revenge herself on the duke. Such a woman can be found: the duke is a ladies' man, and if he has sown much love by his promises of eternal constancy, he must also have sown much hatred by his eternal infidelity."

"No doubt such a woman can be found," Milady said coldly.

"Well, such a woman, who would put the knife of Jacques Clément or Ravaillac into the hands of some fanatic, would save France."

"Yes, but she would be an accomplice in the assassination."

"Have they ever discovered the accomplices of Jacques Clément or Ravaillac?"

"No, for they were perhaps too highly placed for anyone to dare to go looking for them where they were. They will not burn down the Palais de Justice for everybody, Monseigneur."

"So you believe that the fire in the Palais de Justice was caused by something other than chance?" asked Richelieu, in the tone in which he would have asked a question of no importance.

"I, Monseigneur?" replied Milady. "I believe nothing; I am citing a fact, that's all. Only I say that if I were called Mlle de Monpensier or Queen Marie de Medicis, I would take fewer precautions than I take being called simply Lady Clarick."

"That is fair enough," said Richelieu. "And what would you like, then?"

"I would like an order that would ratify in advance all that I believe must be done for the greater good of France."

"But first we would have to find the woman I mentioned, who will revenge herself on the duke."

"She has been found," said Milady.

"Then we must find the wretched fanatic who will serve as an instrument of God's justice."

"He will be found."

"Well," said the duke, "then will be the time to demand the order you have just asked for."

"Your Eminence is right," said Milady, "and it is I who was wrong to see in the mission with which you have honored me anything other than what it really is, that is, to announce to His Grace, on behalf of His Eminence, that you know the different disguises by means of which he managed to approach the queen during the fête given by Mme le connétable; that you have proofs of the interview in the Louvre granted by the queen to a certain Italian astrologer, who was none other than the duke of Buckingham; that you have commissioned a most witty little novel on the adventure in Amiens, with a plan of the garden where this adventure took place, and portraits of the actors who figured in it; that Montaigu is in the Bastille, and that torture may make him say things he remembers, and even things he may have forgotten; finally, that you are in possession of a certain letter from Mme de Chevreuse, found in His Grace's quarters, which singularly compromises not only her who wrote it, but also her in whose name it was written. Then, if he persists despite all that, since my mission is limited to what I have just told you, all I will be able to do is pray that God perform a miracle to save France. That is so, is it not, Monseigneur, and there is nothing more for me to do?"

"That is quite so," the cardinal replied drily.

"And now," said Milady, without seeming to notice the change in the duke's tone with her, "now that I have received Your Eminence's instructions concerning his enemies, will Monseigneur allow me to say two words about my own?"

"So you have enemies?" asked Richelieu.

"Yes, Monseigneur, enemies against whom you owe me all your support, for I made them in Your Eminence's service."

"And who are they?" asked the duke.

"First of all, a little intriguer by the name of Bonacieux."

"She is in the prison of Mantes."

"That is to say, she was," picked up Milady, "but the queen intercepted an order from the king, by means of which she had her transferred to a convent."

"A convent?" asked the duke.

"Yes, a convent."

"And which one?"

"I don't know, the secret has been well kept."

"I will find out!"

"And Your Eminence will tell me which convent this woman is in?"

"I see no objection to that," said the cardinal.

"Good. Now, I have another enemy whom I find much more to be feared than this little Mme Bonacieux."

"Who is it?"

"Her lover."

"What is his name?"

"Oh, Your Eminence knows him well!" cried Milady, carried away by wrath. "He is the evil genius of us both. It was he who, in an encounter with Your Eminence's guards, decided the victory in favor of the musketeers; it was he who gave three sword strokes to de Wardes, your emissary, and who thwarted the affair of the diamond pendants; it was he, finally, who, knowing it was I who had Mme Bonacieux abducted from him, swore my death."

"Aha!" said the cardinal. "I know who you mean."

"I mean that scoundrel d'Artagnan."

"He's a bold fellow," said the cardinal.

"And it is just because he's a bold fellow that he's the more to be feared."

"We must have some proof of his dealings with Buckingham," said the cardinal.

"Some proof!" cried Milady. "I can give you ten!"

"Well, then, it's the simplest thing in the world! Furnish me with this proof, and I will send him to the Bastille."

"Very well, Monseigneur, but what then?"

"When one is in the Bastille, there is no what then," said the cardinal in a hollow voice. "Ah, pardieu!" he went on, "if it was as easy for me to get rid of my enemy as it is for me to get rid of yours, and if it was against such men that you were asking me for impunity! . . ."

"Monseigneur," picked up Milady, "tit for tat, life for life, man for man: give me this one, I'll give you the other."

"I don't know what you mean to say," replied the cardinal, "and I don't even want to know; but I have a wish to be nice to you, and I see no objection to giving you what you ask with regard to so mean a creature—all the more so since, as you tell me, this little d'Artagnan is a libertine, a duelist, and a traitor."

"A despicable man, Monseigeur, a despicable man!"

"Then give me some paper, a pen and ink," said the cardinal.

"Here, Monseigneur."

There was a moment of silence, which suggested that the cardinal was busy searching for the terms in which the note ought to be written, or was even writing it. Athos, who had not missed a word of the conversation, took his two companions by the hand and led them to the other end of the room.

"Well," said Porthos, "what do you want? Why don't you let us listen to the end of the conversation?"

"Shh!" said Athos, speaking in a low voice. "We've heard all we needed to hear. Besides, I'm not keeping you from listening to the rest, but I must leave."

"You must leave?" said Porthos. "But if the cardinal asks for you, what will we say?"

"You won't wait for him to ask for me; you will tell him beforehand that I went to clear the way, because certain words of our host led me to think the road wasn't safe. I'll say a couple of words to the cardinal's equerry. The rest is my concern, don't bother about it."

"Be careful, Athos!" said Aramis.

"Don't worry," replied Athos, "you know I'm coolheaded."

Porthos and Aramis went back to their places by the stovepipe.

As for Athos, he left without any secrecy, went to take his horse, which was tied with those of his two friends to the latches of the shutters, convinced the equerry in four words of the need of an advance guard for the return, made a showy inspection of the priming of his pistols, took his sword in his teeth, and desperately set off down the road to camp.

XLV

A Conjugal Scene

As Athos had foreseen, the cardinal came down without delay. He opened the door to the room that the three musketeers had been ushered into, and found Porthos playing a hot game of dice with Aramis. With a rapid glance he searched all the corners of the room and saw that one of his men was missing.

"What's become of Athos?" he asked.

"Monseigneur," replied Porthos, "he went to clear the way after some remarks from our host that made him think the road was not safe."

"And you, what have you been doing, M. Porthos?"

"I've won six pistoles from Aramis."

"And now you can return with me?"

"We are at Your Eminence's orders."

"To horse, then, gentlemen, for it's getting late."

The equerry was at the door, holding the cardinal's horse by the bridle. A little further off a group of two men and three horses appeared in the darkness. These two men were those who were to conduct Milady to the Fort de La Pointe and see her aboard ship.

The equerry confirmed to the cardinal what the two musketeers had already told him concerning Athos. The cardinal made an approving gesture and set out on his way again, surrounding himself on his return with the same precautions he had taken at his departure.

Let us leave him on the road to camp, protected by the equerry and the two musketeers, and go back to Athos.

He had continued at the same speed for a hundred paces; but, once out of sight, he had swung his horse to the right, made a detour, and come back to a copse twenty paces from the inn, to watch the little troop pass by. Having recognized the wide-brimmed hats of his companions and the gilded fringe of M. le cardinal's cloak, he waited until the horsemen had turned the corner of the road, and, having lost sight of them, went galloping back to the inn, where the door was opened to him without difficulty.

The host recognized him.

"My officer forgot to give the lady upstairs some important instructions," said Athos. "He sent me to make good his forgetfulness."

"Go on up," said the host. "She's still in her room."

Athos profited from the permission, went upstairs with the lightest step he could manage, came to the landing, and, through the half-open door, saw Milady tying her bonnet.

He went into the room and shut the door behind him.

At the sound of the sliding bolt, Milady turned around.

Athos was standing in front of the door, wrapped in his cloak, his hat pulled down over his eyes.

Seeing this figure as mute and immobile as a statue, Milady was afraid.

"Who are you, and what do you want of me?" she cried.

"So it's really she!" murmured Athos.

And, letting his cloak fall and taking off his hat, he went towards Milady.

"Do you recognize me, Madame?" he asked.

Milady took one step forward, then recoiled as if she had seen a snake.

"Come," said Athos, "that's good, I see you do recognize me."

"The comte de La Fère!" murmured Milady, turning pale and backing away until the wall prevented her from going further.

"Yes, Milady," replied Athos, "the comte de La Fère in

person, come back from the other world on purpose to have the pleasure of seeing you. Let's sit down, then, and talk, as Monseigneur le cardinal says."

Milady, overcome by an inexpressible terror, sat down without saying a word.

"So you are a demon sent to earth?" said Athos. "Your power is great, I know; but you also know that, with God's help, men have often defeated the most terrible demons. You have already crossed my path; I believed I had crushed you, Madame; but, either I'm mistaken, or hell has resuscitated you."

At these words, which reminded her of frightful memories, Milady bowed her head with a low moan.

"Yes, hell has resuscitated you," Athos went on, "hell has made you rich, hell has given you another name, hell has almost fashioned another face for you; but it has not wiped out the stains on your soul, nor the brand on your body."

Milady stood up as if moved by a spring, and her eyes flashed lightning. Athos remained seated.

"You believed me dead, didn't you, as I believed you dead? And this name of Athos hid the comte de La Fère, as the name of Milady Clarick hid Anne de Breuil! Wasn't that what you called yourself when your honorable brother married us? Our position is truly strange," Athos continued, laughing. "We have both lived up to now only because each of us thought the other dead, and a memory is less disturbing than a live creature, though a memory can sometimes be a devouring thing!"

"But, finally," said Milady in a hollow voice, "who has brought you to me, and what do you want of me?"

"I want to tell you that, while remaining invisible to your eyes, I myself have not lost sight of you."

"You know what I have done?"

"I can recount your actions for you day by day, from your entry into the cardinal's service to this very evening."

A smile of incredulity passed over Milady's pale lips.

"Listen: it was you who cut the two diamond pendants from the duke of Buckingham's shoulder; it was you who had Mme Bonacieux abducted; it was you who, enamoured of de

Wardes, and thinking you were spending the night with him, opened your door to M. d'Artagnan; it was you who, believing de Wardes had deceived you, wanted to have him killed by his rival; it was you who, when that rival discovered your infamous secret, wanted to kill him in turn by means of two assassins whom you sent in pursuit of him; it was you who, seeing that the bullets had missed their target, sent poisoned wine with a false letter, to make your victim believe that the wine came from his friends; it was you, finally, who, here in this room, sitting in this chair that I am now sitting in, just undertook with the cardinal de Richelieu to have the duke of Buckingham assassinated, in exchange for the promise he made you to let you assassinate d'Artagnan."

Milady was livid.

"Are you Satan himself?" she said.

"Perhaps," said Athos. "But, in any case, listen very well to this: assassinate the duke of Buckingham, or have him assassinated, it matters little to me! I don't know him, and besides, he's an Englishman. But do not touch with the tip of your finger a single hair on the head of d'Artagnan, who is a faithful friend whom I love and defend, or, I swear to you on my father's bones, that attempted crime will be your last."

"M. d'Artagnan has cruelly offended me," Milady said in a hollow voice. "M. d'Artagnan will die."

"Really, is it possible for someone to offend you, Madame?" Athos said, laughing. "He offended you, and he will die?"

"He will die," repeated Milady. "She first, then he."

Athos felt his head spinning: the sight of this creature, who had nothing of the woman about her, brought back terrible memories to him. He thought of how one day, in a less dangerous situation than the one he now found himself in, he had meant to sacrifice her to his honor. His desire for murder flared up in him again and invaded him like a burning fever: he stood up in his turn, brought his hand to his belt, drew a pistol, and cocked it.

Milady, pale as a corpse, wanted to cry out, but her frozen tongue could produce no more than a hoarse sound that had nothing of human speech about it and seemed like the rasping of a wild beast. Pressed against the dark tapestry, she appeared, with her dishevelled hair, like a ghastly image of terror.

Athos slowly raised his pistol, stretched out his arm until the weapon almost touched Milady's forehead, then, in a voice all the more terrible in that it had the supreme calm of inflexible resolution, said:

"Madame, you are going to give me the paper that the cardinal signed for you this very instant, or, by my soul, I will blow your brains out."

With another man, Milady might have harbored some doubt, but she knew Athos. Yet she remained motionless.

"You have one second to make up your mind," he said.

Milady saw by the contraction of his face that the shot was about to be fired. She quickly brought her hand to her breast, took out a paper, and handed it to Athos.

"Take it," she said, "and be cursed!"

Athos took the paper, put the pistol back in his belt, went to a lamp to make sure it was the right one, unfolded it, and read:

It is by my orders and for the good of the State that the bearer of this present has done what he has done.

3 December 1627

Richelieu

"And now," said Athos, picking up his cloak and putting his hat back on his head, "now that I have drawn your teeth, viper, bite if you can."

And he left the room without looking back.

At the door, he found the two men and the horse they were holding by the bridle.

"Gentlemen," he said, "Monseigneur's orders, as you know, are to conduct this woman, with no loss of time, to the Fort de La Pointe, and not to leave her until she is on shipboard."

As these words indeed accorded with the orders they had received, they bowed their heads in a sign of assent.

As for Athos, he swung lightly into the saddle and set off

at a gallop. Only instead of following the road, he went cross country, spurring his horse vigorously, and pausing now and then to listen.

In one of these pauses, he heard the hoofbeats of several horses on the road. He had no doubt that it was the cardinal and his escort. He at once raced ahead another stretch, rubbed his horse down with heather and leaves, and placed himself in the middle of the road about two hundred paces from the camp.

"Who goes there?" he cried from far off, when he caught sight of the horsemen.

"It's our brave musketeer, I believe," said the cardinal.

"Yes, Monseigneur," replied Athos, "the man himself."

"M. Athos," said Richelieu, "accept all my thanks for the good protection you have afforded us. Gentlemen, we have arrived. Take the gate to the left; the password is *Roi et Ré.*"

As he said these words, the cardinal bowed his head to the three friends and went to the right, followed by his equerry; for, on that night, he slept in camp himself.

"Well!" Porthos and Aramis said together, once the cardinal was out of earshot. "Well, he signed the paper she asked for."

"I know," Athos said calmly. "I have it here."

And the three friends did not exchange a single word more until they reached their sector, except for giving the password to the sentries.

Only they sent Mousqueton to tell Planchet that his master was invited, the moment he was relieved from the trenches, to come to the quarters of the musketeers.

On the other hand, as Athos had foreseen, Milady, finding the men waiting for her at the door, made no difficulty in following them. She had wanted for a moment to be taken to the cardinal again and to tell him all, but a revelation on her part would bring a revelation on Athos's part: she might well say that Athos had hanged her, but Athos would say that she was branded. She thought it was more worthwhile to keep silent, leave discreetly, carry out with her usual skill the difficult mission she had been entrusted with, and then, with everything done to the cardinal's satisfaction, to come and claim her revenge.

As a consequence, after traveling all night, at seven o'clock in the morning she was at the Fort de La Pointe, at eight o'clock she was aboard ship, and at nine o'clock the vessel, which, with letters of marque from the cardinal, was supposedly bound for Bayonne, raised anchor and set sail for England.

XLVI

THE SAINT-GERVAIS BASTION

On coming to his three friends' quarters, d'Artagnan found them all gathered in the same room: Athos was reflecting, Porthos was curling his mustache, Aramis was saying his prayers from a charming little book of hours bound in blue velvet.

"Pardieu, gentlemen," he said, "I hope that what you have to tell me is worth the trouble! Otherwise I warn you that I won't forgive you for making me come, instead of letting me rest after a night spent in capturing and demolishing a bastion. Ah, if only you had been there, gentlemen! We had a hot time of it!"

"We were elsewhere, where it wasn't exactly cold!" replied Porthos, giving his own particular twist to his mustache.

"Shh!" said Athos.

"Oho!" said d'Artagnan, understanding the musketeer's slight frown, "it seems there's something new here."

"Aramis," said Athos, "you had lunch the day before yesterday at the inn of the Parpaillot, I believe?"

"Yes."

"How is it there?"

"Well, it was a very bad meal in my opinion; the day before yesterday was a fast day, and they had nothing but meat."

"How's that?" said Athos. "A seaport without fish?"

"They say," Aramis picked up, returning to his pious reading, "that the dike M. le cardinal has built drives them out to sea."

"But that's not what I was asking you, Aramis," said Athos. "I was asking if you were quite free, if no one disturbed you?"

"It seems to me that we didn't have too many pests. Yes, in fact, for what you're getting at, Athos, we'd do rather well at the Parpaillot."

"To the Parpaillot, then," said Athos, "for here the walls are like sheets of writing paper."

D'Artagnan, who was used to his friend's way of doing things, and who recognized at a word, at a gesture, at a sign from him, that the circumstances were serious, took Athos's arm and went out with him without saying a word. Porthos followed them, chatting with Aramis.

On the way they ran into Grimaud. Athos made a sign for him to follow them; Grimaud, as was his habit, obeyed in silence. The poor boy had ended up by almost forgetting how to speak.

They came to the Parpaillot pothouse. It was seven o'clock in the morning; dawn was breaking. The three friends ordered breakfast and went into a room where, according to the host, they would not be disturbed.

Unfortunately, it was a poorly chosen hour for a conciliabule. Reveille had just sounded, everyone was shaking off the night's sleep, and, to drive away the damp morning air, came to the tavern for a drop to drink: dragoons, Switzers, guards, musketeers, light horse succeeded each other with a speed that must have been very profitable for the host, but which fulfilled the aims of our four friends rather poorly. And so they responded quite gloomily to the greetings, toasts, and jests of their companions.

"Enough!" said Athos. "We're going to have a nice little quarrel, and we don't need that right now. D'Artagnan, tell us about your night; we'll tell you about ours afterwards."

"Indeed," said a light horseman, who sidled up to them holding a glass of brandy, which he slowly sipped, "indeed, you were in the trenches last night, gentlemen of the guard, and it seems to me you had a bone to pick with the Rochelois?"

D'Artagnan looked at Athos to see if he should reply to this intruder who had mixed into the conversation.

"Well," said Athos, "don't you hear M. de Busigny, who has

done you the honor of addressing you? Tell what happened last night, since these gentlemen wish to know."

"Habend you tekken a pastion?" asked a Switzer, who was drinking rum from a beer glass.

"Yes, Monsieur," replied d'Artagnan, bowing, "we had that honor. As you may have heard, we even introduced a keg of powder under one corner, which, on exploding, made a very pretty breach; not to mention that, since the bastion wasn't built yesterday, the rest of the structure was quite badly shaken."

"And what bastion was it?" asked a dragoon, who had a goose spitted on his sabre that he had brought to be cooked.

"The Saint-Gervais bastion," replied d'Artagnan, "from the cover of which the Rochelois were harassing our workmen."

"And was it a hot business?"

"Why, yes. We lost five men in it, and the Rochelois eight or ten."

"Balzampleu!" cried the Switzer, who, though the German language possesses an admirable collection of oaths, had acquired the habit of cursing in French.

"But it's likely," said the light horseman, "that they'll send pioneers this morning to put the bastion back into shape."

"Yes, it's likely," said d'Artagnan.

"Gentlemen," said Athos, "a bet!"

"Ach, ja, a pet!" said the Switzer.

"What is it?" asked the light horseman.

"Wait," said the dragoon, placing his sabre like a spit on the two massive andirons that held up the fire in the hearth, "count me in. You woeful hosteler! A dripping pan at once! I don't want to lose a drop of grease from this estimable fowl!"

"Und he's right," said the Switzer, "goose grease makes fery gut gondiments."

"There!" said the dragoon. "Now, what about the bet? We're listening, M. Athos!"

"Yes, the bet!" said the light horseman.

"Well, then, M. de Busigny, I bet you," said Athos, "that I and my three companions, MM. Porthos, Aramis, and d'Artagnan, will go to have lunch in the Saint-Gervais bastion, and that we'll hold it for an hour by the clock, whatever the enemy does to dislodge us."

Porthos and Aramis looked at each other. They were beginning to understand.

"But," said d'Artagnan, leaning over to Athos's ear, "you're going to get us killed quite mercilessly."

"We're still more killed if we don't go," replied Athos.

"Ah, by heaven, gentlemen," said Porthos, throwing himself back in his chair and twirling his mustache, "there's a splendid bet, I should hope!"

"I accept!" said M. de Busigny. "Now it's a matter of setting the stakes."

"There are four of you, gentlemen," said Athos, "and four of us: dinner for eight, all you can eat—does that suit you?"

"Wonderfully," replied M. de Busigny.

"Perfectly," said the dragoon.

"Dat zoots me," said the Switzer.

The fourth listener, who had played a mute role throughout this conversation, nodded his head as a sign that he agreed to the proposition.

"The gentlemen's lunch is ready," said the host.

"Well, bring it then!" said Athos.

The host obeyed. Athos called Grimaud, showed him a big basket lying in a corner, and made a gesture of wrapping the food that had been brought in napkins.

Grimaud understood instantly that it was a question of a picnic, took the basket, packed up the food, added some bottles, and slung the basket over his arm.

"But where are you going to eat my lunch?" asked the host.

"What does it matter to you," said Athos, "provided we pay you for it?"

And he majestically tossed two pistoles on the table.

"Do you want the change, officer?" asked the host.

"No, just add two bottles of champagne, and the difference will go for the napkins."

The host did not make as good a deal as he had thought at first, but he compensated himself for it by slipping the four guests two bottles of Anjou wine instead of two bottles of champagne.

"M. de Busigny," said Athos, "would you kindly set your watch by mine, or allow me to set mine by yours?"

"Excellent, Monsieur!" said the light horseman, pulling from his watch pocket an extremely handsome watch set round with diamonds. "Seven-thirty," he said.

"Seven-thirty-five," said Athos. "We shall know that I am five minutes ahead of you, Monsieur."

And, bowing to the dumbfounded bystanders, the four young men took the road to the Saint-Gervais bastion, followed by Grimaud, who was carrying the basket, not knowing where he was going, but, in the passive obedience he had grown used to with Athos, not even dreaming of asking.

As long as they were within the camp enclosure, the four friends did not exchange a word. Besides, they were being followed by the curious, who, learning of the bet that had been made, wanted to know how they would make out.

But once they had crossed the line of circumvallation and found themselves in the open country, d'Artagnan, who had no idea what it was all about, thought it was time he asked for an explanation.

"And now, my dear Athos," he said, "do me the kindness of letting me know where we're going."

"You can see very well," said Athos, "we're going to the bastion."

"But what are we going to do there?"

"You know very well, we're going to have lunch."

"But why didn't we have lunch at the Parpaillot?"

"Because we have very important things to tell you, and it was impossible to talk for five minutes in that inn, with all those importunate fellows coming, going, bowing, embracing. Here, at least," Athos went on, pointing to the bastion, "they won't come to disturb us."

"It seems to me," said d'Artagnan, with that prudence which combined so well and so naturally in him with an exceeding bravery, "it seems to me that we could have found some out-of-the-way place in the dunes, by the seashore."

"Where the four of us would have been seen conferring together, so that in a quarter of an hour the cardinal would have been warned by his spies that we were holding a council."

"Yes," said Aramis, "Athos is right: *Animadvertuntur in desertis.*"*

"A desert wouldn't have been bad," said Porthos, "but it was a question of finding one."

"There is no desert where a bird can't fly over your head, or a fish leap out of the water, or a rabbit spring from its form, and I believe that bird, fish, and rabbit are all spies for the cardinal. So it's better if we continue our undertaking, from which, anyhow, we can no longer retreat without shame. We've made a bet, a bet that could not be foreseen, and of which I defy anyone to guess the veritable cause: to win it, we are going to hold out for one hour in the bastion. Where we will or will not be attacked. If we're not, we'll have plenty of time to talk, and nobody will hear us, for I guarantee that the walls of this bastion do not have ears. If we are, we'll talk over our affairs anyway, and moreover, in defending ourselves, we will cover ourselves with glory. You can see very well that it's all profit."

"Yes," said d'Artagnan, "but we'll undoubtedly catch a bullet."

"Ah, my dear," said Athos, "you know very well that the bullets most to be feared are not those of the enemy."

"But it seems to me that, for such an expedition, we should at least have brought our muskets."

"You're a ninny, Porthos, my friend. Why load ourselves down with useless baggage?"

"In the face of the enemy, a good, high-caliber musket, a dozen cartridges, and a powder flask don't strike me as useless."

"Oh, well," said Athos, "didn't you hear what d'Artagnan said?"

"What did d'Artagnan say?" asked Porthos.

"D'Artagnan said that, in the attack last night, there were eight or ten French killed and as many Rochelois."

* "They were noticed in desert places."

"So?"

"They had no time to strip them, did they? Seeing that they had other more pressing things to do at the moment."

"Well?"

"Well, we shall find their muskets, their powder flasks, and their cartridges, and instead of four musketoons and a dozen bullets, we'll have fifteen guns and a hundred rounds of ammunition."

"Oh, Athos," said Aramis, "you are truly a great man!"

Porthos inclined his head in a sign of concurrence.

D'Artagnan alone seemed unconvinced.

Grimaud clearly shared the young man's doubts; for, seeing that they kept on walking towards the bastion, something he had doubted up to then, he pulled his master by the coattail.

"Where are we going?" he asked with a gesture.

Athos pointed to the bastion.

"But," said the silent Grimaud, still in the same dialect, "we'll be skinned alive."

Athos raised his eyes and finger to heaven.

Grimaud set his basket on the ground and sat down beside it, shaking his head.

Athos took a pistol from his belt, checked that it was well primed, cocked it, and brought the barrel to Grimaud's ear.

Grimaud found himself standing up again as if on a spring.

Athos then made a sign to him to pick up the basket and walk ahead of them.

Grimaud obeyed.

All the poor lad gained from this momentary pantomime was that he passed from the rear guard to the advance guard.

On reaching the bastion, the four friends turned around.

More than three hundred soldiers of every stripe were gathered at the gate of the camp, and in a separate group they could make out M. de Busigny, the dragoon, the Switzer, and the fourth bettor.

Athos took off his hat, put it on the tip of his sword, and waved it in the air.

The spectators all returned his salute, accompanying this courtesy with a great hurrah that carried all the way to their ears.

After which, the four of them disappeared into the bastion, where they had been preceded by Grimaud.

XLVII

THE COUNCIL OF THE MUSKETEERS

As Athos had foreseen, the bastion was occupied only by a dozen dead men, both French and Rochelois.

"Gentlemen," said Athos, who had taken command of the expedition, "while Grimaud is setting the table, let's begin by gathering up the guns and cartridges. Besides, we can talk while we're performing this task. These gentlemen," he added, pointing to the dead men, "are not listening to us."

"But we could always throw them into the ditch," said Porthos, "after assuring ourselves that they have nothing in their pockets."

"Yes," said Aramis, "Grimaud will take care of that."

"Ah, well," said d'Artagnan, "then let Grimaud search them and throw them over the walls."

"That we mustn't do," said Athos. "They may be of use to us."

"These dead men may be of use to us?" said Porthos. "Ah, no, you're losing your wits, my friend."

"'Judge not rashly,' say the Gospels and M. le cardinal," replied Athos. "How many guns, gentlemen?"

"Twelve," replied Aramis.

"How many rounds of ammunition?"

"A hundred."

"That's all we need. Let's load the weapons."

The four musketeers set to work. Just as they finished loading the last gun, Grimaud made a sign that lunch was served.

Athos replied, still by a gesture, that it was a good thing, and pointed out to Grimaud a sort of pepperbox where the latter understood he should stand watch. Only, to sweeten the boredom of sentry duty, Athos allowed him to take a loaf of bread, two cutlets, and a bottle of wine.

"And now, to lunch," said Athos.

The four friends sat cross-legged on the ground, like Turks or tailors.

"Ah!" said d'Artagnan, "now that you have no more fear of being overheard, I hope you will let us in on your secret, Athos."

"I hope to furnish you with both pleasure and glory, gentlemen," said Athos. "I've taken you on a charming stroll; here we have a most succulent lunch. And there are five hundred people back there, as you can see through the loopholes, who take us either for fools or for heroes, two classes of imbeciles that are rather similar."

"But the secret?" asked d'Artagnan.

"The secret," said Athos, "is that I saw Milady last evening."

D'Artagnan was bringing his glass to his lips, but at the name of Milady, his hand shook so much that he set it down, so as not so spill the contents.

"You saw your wi . . ."

"Quiet!" interrupted Athos. "You forget, my dear, that these gentlemen are not initiated, as you are, into the secret of my family affairs. I saw Milady."

"And where was that?" asked d'Artagnan.

"Some two leagues from here, at the inn of the Red Dovecote."

"In that case I'm done for," said d'Artagnan.

"No, not quite yet," Athos picked up, "for by now she must have left the shores of France."

D'Artagnan drew a deep breath.

"But," asked Porthos, "who is this Milady after all?"

"A charming woman," said Athos, sipping a glass of fizzy wine. "That knave of a hosteler!" he cried. "He gave us Anjou wine instead of champagne, and thinks we'll let ourselves be fooled! Yes," he went on, "a charming woman, who had the kindest intentions towards our friend d'Artagnan, who did her I don't know what foul turn, for which she has attempted to revenge herself, a month ago by having him shot, a week ago by trying to poison him, and yesterday by asking the cardinal for his head."

"What? By asking the cardinal for my head?" cried d'Artagnan, pale with terror.

"That," said Porthos, "is the Gospel truth. I heard it with my own two ears."

"So did I," said Aramis.

"In that case," said d'Artagnan, letting his arm drop in discouragement, "it's useless to struggle any longer. I may as well blow my brains out and be done with it!"

"That's the last stupid thing you should do," said Athos, "seeing that it's the only one without remedy."

"But I'll never escape," said d'Artagnan, "with enemies like that. First of all, my unknown man from Meung; then de Wardes, to whom I gave three strokes of the sword; then Milady, whose secret I've found out; and, finally, the cardinal, whose vengeance I thwarted."

"Well," said Athos, "that only makes four, and we are four, one on one. Pardieu! if we believe the signals Grimaud is making to us, we're going to have a lot more people to deal with. What is it, Grimaud? Considering the seriousness of the circumstances, I allow you to speak, my friend, but please be laconic. What do you see?"

"A troop."

"How many men?"

"Twenty."

"What sort?"

"Sixteen pioneers, four soldiers."

"How far away?"

"Five hundred paces."

"Good, we still have time to finish this chicken and drink a glass of wine to your health, d'Artagnan!"

"To your health!" repeated Porthos and Aramis.

"Oh, very well, to my health! Though I don't think your wishes will be much use to me."

"Bah!" said Athos. "God is great, as the votaries of Mohammed say, and the future is in His hands."

Then, draining his glass, which he set down next to him, Athos stood up nonchalantly, took the first gun he came upon, and went to a loophole.

Porthos, Aramis, and d'Artagnan did the same. As for Grimaud, he was ordered to place himself behind the four friends in order to reload the weapons.

After a moment, they saw the troop appear. It was following a sort of connecting trench, which communicated between the bastion and the town.

"Pardieu!" said Athos, "it's hardly worth bothering ourselves over twenty rascals armed with picks, hoes, and shovels! Grimaud need only have made a sign for them to go away, and I'm sure they would have left us in peace."

"I doubt it," observed d'Artagnan, "for they're advancing quite determinedly from this side. Besides, there are four soldiers with the workers and a corporal, all armed with muskets."

"That's because they haven't seen us," said Athos.

"By heaven," said Aramis, "I confess I'm loath to fire on those poor devils of civilians!"

"It's a bad priest," replied Porthos, "who takes pity on heretics!"

"In fact, Aramis is right," said Athos. "I'm going to warn them."

"What the devil are you doing?" cried d'Artagnan. "You'll get yourself shot, my dear."

But Athos took no account of that advice and climbed up to the breach, his gun in one hand and his hat in the other.

"Gentlemen," he called out, courteously saluting the soldiers and workers, who, astonished at his appearance, stopped some fifty paces from the bastion, "gentlemen, some friends of mine and I are just having lunch in this bastion. Now, you know there is nothing more unpleasant than to be disturbed at lunch. We therefore ask you, if you absolutely must muck about here, to wait until we've finished our meal, or to come back later, unless you have a salutary desire to quit the rebellious side and come to drink the health of the king of France with us."

"Watch out, Athos!" cried d'Artagnan. "Don't you see they're taking aim at you?"

"True, true," said Athos, "but these civilians are very bad shots, and they don't care about hitting me."

Indeed, that very instant, four shots were fired, and bullets flattened themselves around Athos, but not one hit him.

Four shots replied to them at almost the same moment, but they were better aimed than those of the attackers: three soldiers were killed outright, and one of the workers was wounded.

"Grimaud, another musket!" said Athos, still in the breach.

Grimaud obeyed at once. For their part, the three friends had already loaded their weapons. A second volley followed the first: the corporal and two pioneers fell dead; the rest of the troop took flight.

"Come, gentlemen, a sortie!" said Athos.

And the four friends, rushing out of the fort, made their way to the battlefield, gathered up the four muskets of the soldiers and the corporal's half pike, and, convinced that the fugitives would not stop before they reached town, made their way back to the bastion, bringing with them the trophies of their victory.

"Reload the guns, Grimaud," said Athos, "and we, gentlemen, will return to our lunch and our conversation. Where were we?"

"I remember," said d'Artagnan, who was greatly concerned with the itinerary Milady was to follow.

"She's going to England," replied Athos.

"What for?"

"To assassinate Buckingham, or have him assassinated."

D'Artagnan uttered an exclamation of surprise and indignation.

"But that is infamous!" he cried.

"Oh, as for that," said Athos, "I beg you to believe that it worries me very little. Now that you've finished, Grimaud," Athos went on, "take our corporal's half pike, tie a napkin to it, and plant it at the top of our bastion, so that the rebellious Rochelois see that they're dealing with brave and loyal soldiers of the king."

Grimaud obeyed without reply. A moment later the white flag was floating above the heads of the four friends. Thunderous applause broke out at its appearance; half the camp was at the gates.

"How's that?" d'Artagnan picked up. "It worries you very little that she will kill Buckingham or have him killed? But the duke is our friend!"

"The duke is English, the duke is fighting against us; let her do as she likes with the duke, I care as much as for an empty bottle."

And Athos tossed the bottle he was holding some fifteen feet away, having just drained it to the last drop into his glass.

"Wait a minute," said d'Artagnan, "I'm not abandoning Buckingham like this. He gave us very fine horses."

"And above all very fine saddles," added Porthos, who at that very moment was wearing the gold braid of his on the shoulder of his cloak.

"Then, too," observed Aramis, "God wishes the conversion and not the death of the sinner."

"Amen," said Athos, "and we will come back to that later, if such is your pleasure; but what concerned me most for the moment—and I'm sure you will understand me, d'Artagnan—was getting hold of a sort of blank permit the woman had extorted from the cardinal and by means of which she could get rid of you, and maybe of us, with impunity."

"This creature is a real demon!" exclaimed Porthos, holding out his plate to Aramis, who was cutting up a chicken.

"And this blank permit," said d'Artagnan, "this blank permit remained in her hands?"

"No, it came into mine—I won't say without difficulty, though, for I would be lying."

"My dear Athos," said d'Artagnan, "I can no longer count how many times I've owed you my life."

"So you left us in order to go to her?" asked Aramis.

"Exactly."

"And you have this letter from the cardinal?" asked d'Artagnan.

"Here it is," said Athos.

And he took the precious paper from the pocket of his tabard.

D'Artagan unfolded it, not even trying to conceal the trembling of his hand, and read:

> It is by my orders and for the good of the State that the bearer of this present has done what he has done.
>
> 5 December 1627
>
>   Richelieu

"Indeed," said Aramis, "that is an absolution according to all the rules."

"This paper must be torn up!" cried d'Artagnan, who seemed to read his death sentence in it.

"Quite the contrary," said Athos, "it must be carefully kept. I wouldn't give this paper away if they covered it with gold pieces."

"And what is she going to do now?" asked the young man.

"Why," Athos said casually, "she will probably write to the cardinal that a damned musketeer by the name of Athos got her safe conduct away from her. She will advise him in the same letter to get rid of him and of his two friends, Porthos and Aramis, along with him. The cardinal will recall that those are the same men he met on the road. Then, one fine morning, he'll have d'Artagnan arrested, and, so that he won't be bored all alone, he'll send us to keep him company in the Bastille."

"Really now!" said Porthos. "It seems to me you're making some sorry jokes there, my dear."

"I'm not joking," replied Athos.

"Do you know," said Porthos, "that to wring that damned Milady's neck would be less of a sin than to wring the necks of these poor devils of Huguenots, who have never committed any other crime than singing psalms in French that we sing in Latin?"

"What says the abbé?" Athos asked calmly.

"I say that I'm of Porthos's opinion," replied Aramis.

"And so am I!" said d'Artagnan.

"Luckily, she's far away," observed Porthos, "for I confess she'd trouble me greatly here."

"She troubles me as much in England as in France," said Athos.

"She troubles me wherever she is," d'Artagnan continued.

"But since you had her," said Porthos, "why didn't we drown her, strangle her, hang her? It's only the dead who don't come back."

"Do you think so, Porthos?" replied the musketeer, with a gloomy smile that d'Artagnan alone understood.

"I've got an idea," said d'Artagnan.

"Let's have it," said the musketeers.

"To arms!" cried Grimaud.

The young men got up quickly and ran for their guns.

This time a small troop of some twenty or twenty-five men was coming; but these were no longer workers, they were garrison soldiers.

"How about returning to camp?" said Porthos. "It strikes me as an unequal match."

"Impossible for three reasons," replied Athos. "First, we haven't finished lunch; second, we still have important things to say; third, there are another ten minutes before the hour is up."

"Listen," said Aramis, "we still have to draw up a plan of battle."

"It's quite simple," replied Athos. "As soon as the enemy is within musket range, we open fire. If he keeps on coming, we fire again. If what's left of the troop still wants to mount an assault, we let the besiegers get as far as the ditch, and then we push over that section of wall, which is holding up only by a miracle of equilibrium, onto their heads."

"Bravo!" cried Porthos. "Decidedly, Athos, you are a born general, and the cardinal, who thinks he's a great man of war, is nothing in comparison."

"Gentlemen," said Athos, "no duplication of effort, please. Each of you aim at his own man."

"I've got mine," said d'Artagnan.

"And I mine," said Porthos.

"Idem," said Aramis.

"Fire!" said Athos.

The four shots made a single bang, and four men fell.

The drum began beating at once, and the little troop rushed to the charge.

Then the shots succeeded each other without regularity, but always with the same accuracy. However, as if they knew the numerical weakness of the friends, the Rochelois kept advancing at a run.

With three more shots, two men fell; yet the advance of those who remained standing was not slowed.

On reaching the bastion, the enemy still numbered twelve or fifteen. A last volley greeted them but did not stop them: they leaped into the ditch and prepared to scale the breach.

"Come, my friends," said Athos, "let's finish them off with one blow. To the wall! To the wall!"

And the four friends, backed up by Grimaud, set about pushing with their gun barrels at an enormous section of wall, which leaned over as if the wind was pushing it, and, breaking loose from its base, fell with a horrible noise into the ditch. Then a great cry was heard, a cloud of dust rose into the sky, and all was over.

"Have we crushed every last one of them?" asked Athos.

"By heaven, it looks that way to me," said d'Artagnan.

"No," said Porthos, "there go two or three of them limping for safety."

Indeed, three or four of the wretches, covered with mire and blood, fled down the sunken road to town. They were all that remained of the little troop.

Athos looked at his watch.

"Gentlemen," he said, "we've been here an hour, and now the bet is won. But we must be good sports. Besides, d'Artagnan hasn't told us his idea yet."

And the musketeer, with his usual coolheadedness, went to sit down before the remains of the lunch.

"My idea?" asked d'Artagnan.

"Yes, you were saying that you had an idea," replied Athos.

"Ah, I've got it!" d'Artagnan picked up. "I go over to England a second time, find M. de Buckingham, and warn him of the plot on his life that's being hatched."

"That you will not do, d'Artagnan," Athos said coldly.

"And why not? Haven't I already done it once?"

"Yes, but at that time we were not at war; at that time, M. de Buckingham was an ally and not an enemy. What you want to do would qualify as treason."

D'Artagnan understood the force of this argument and fell silent.

"But," said Porthos, "it seems to me that I also have an idea."

"Silence for M. Porthos's idea!" said Aramis.

"I ask M. de Tréville for a leave of absence, under some pretext that you will come up with—pretexts are not my strong point. Milady doesn't know me. I approach her without alarming her, and when I have my beauty, I strangle her."

"Well, now," said Athos, "I'm pretty close to adopting Porthos's idea!"

"Fie on it!" said Aramis. "Killing a woman! No, wait, I've got a real idea."

"Let's have your idea, Aramis!" demanded Athos, who showed great deference towards the young musketeer.

"We must warn the queen."

"Ah, yes, by heaven!" Porthos and d'Artagnan cried together. "I think we've hit upon the way!"

"Warn the queen?" asked Athos. "And how will we do that? Do we have any connections at court? Can we send somebody to Paris without the camp knowing it? It's a hundred and forty leagues from here to Paris. Our letter won't have reached Angers before we're all locked up."

"As for having a letter delivered safely to Her Majesty," proposed Aramis, blushing, "I can take care of that. I know a clever person in Tours . . ."

Aramis stopped on seeing Athos smile.

"Well, so you wouldn't adopt this method, Athos?" asked d'Artagnan.

"I don't reject it entirely," said Athos, "but I'd merely like to point out to Aramis that he can't leave camp; that anyone other than one of us is unsafe; that, two hours after the messenger leaves, every trusty, every alguazil, every black cap of the cardinal's will know your letter by heart, and they'll arrest you and your clever person."

"Not to mention," objected Porthos, "that the queen will save M. de Buckingham, but she's not going to save the rest of us."

"Gentlemen," said d'Artagnan, "Porthos's objection is sensible."

"Aha! What's going on in town now?" asked Athos.

"They're beating the call to arms."

The four friends listened, and the sound of the drum did in fact reach them.

"You'll see, they're going to send a whole regiment against us," said Athos.

"You don't count on holding out against a whole regiment, do you?" asked Porthos.

"Why not?" said the musketeer. "I feel up to it, and I'd hold out against a whole army, if only we'd had the foresight to bring a dozen bottles more."

"I think the drum is coming closer," said d'Artagnan.

"Let it come," said Athos. "It's a quarter of an hour distance from here to town, and therefore from town to here. That's more than enough time for us to draw up our plan. If we leave here, we'll never find so convenient a place. Wait, gentlemen, the right idea has just come to me."

"Say it, then."

"Let me give Grimaud a few indispensable orders."

Athos made a sign for his valet to approach.

"Grimaud," said Athos, pointing to the dead men lying about in the bastion, "you're going to take these gentlemen, you're going to stand them up against the wall, and you're going to put their hats on their heads and their guns in their hands."

"Oh, you great man," cried d'Artagnan, "I understand you!"

"You understand?" asked Porthos.

"And you, Grimaud, do you understand?" asked Aramis.

Grimaud made a sign that he did.

"That's all that matters," said Athos. "Let's get back to my idea."

"I would like to understand, though," observed Porthos.

"There's no need."

"Yes, yes, Athos's idea," d'Artagnan and Aramis said at the same time.

"This Milady, this woman, this creature, this demon has a brother-in-law, I believe, from what you tell me, d'Artagnan."

"Yes, I even know him quite well, and I also think he doesn't have much sympathy for his sister-in-law."

"There's no harm in that," replied Athos, "and if he detested her that would be all the better."

"In that case we're fully gratified."

"However," said Porthos, "I'd really like to understand what Grimaud is doing."

"Quiet, Porthos!" said Aramis.

"What is this brother-in-law's name?"

"Lord de Winter."

"Where is he now?"

"He went back to London at the first rumor of war."

"Well, there's just the man we need!" said Athos. "It's he whom we ought to warn. We'll let him know that his sister-in-law is on the point of assassinating someone, and we'll beg him not to lose sight of her. I hope there's some establishment in London like the Madelonnettes or the Reformed Girls. He can put his sister-in-law there, and we'll rest easy."

"Yes," said d'Artagnan, "until she gets out."

"Ah, by heaven," Athos picked up, "you're asking too much, d'Artagnan! I've given you all I had, and I warn you my sack has a bottom."

"I think this is the best idea," said Aramis. "We'll warn both the queen and Lord de Winter."

"Yes, but whom will we have carry the letters to Tours and to London?"

"I can vouch for Bazin," said Aramis.

"And I for Planchet," said d'Artagnan.

"Indeed," said Porthos, "if we can't leave camp, our lackeys can."

"Certainly," said Aramis. "We'll write the letters today, give them money, and they'll go."

"We'll give them money?" Athos picked up. "You have money, then?"

The four friends looked at each other, and a cloud passed over their faces, which had brightened for a moment.

"To arms!" cried d'Artagnan. "I see black spots and red spots moving about over there. What were you saying about a regiment, Athos? It's a veritable army!"

"By heaven, yes," said Athos, "there they are. See the sly fellows coming without drums and trumpets! Aha! you're done, Grimaud?"

Grimaud made a sign that he was, and pointed out a dozen dead men whom he had placed in the most picturesque attitudes: some at port arms, others taking aim, others with swords in their hands.

"Bravo!" said Athos. "That does honor to your imagination!"

"All the same," said Porthos, "I'd still like to understand."

"Let's decamp first," interrupted d'Artagnan, "you'll understand later."

"One moment, gentlemen, one moment! Let's give Grimaud time to clear away the dishes."

"Ah!" said Aramis, "look, the black spots and red spots are growing visibly bigger, and I'm of d'Artagnan's opinion. I think we have no time to waste in getting back to camp."

"By heaven," said Athos, "I have nothing against retreating: we bet on an hour, and we've stayed an hour and a half. There's nothing to talk about. Let's go, gentlemen, let's go!"

Grimaud had already taken the lead with the basket and the dessert.

The four friends followed him out and went a dozen paces.

"Eh!" cried Athos, "what the devil are we doing, gentlemen?"

"Did you forget something?" asked Aramis.

"What about the flag, morbleu! A flag can't be allowed to fall into the enemy's hands, even if the flag is only a napkin."

And Athos rushed back into the bastion, climbed up to the platform, and removed the flag. Only, as the Rochelois had come within musket range, they fired off a terrible volley at this man who, as if for his own pleasure, had exposed himself to their shots.

But one would have thought that Athos was wearing some sort of charm, for the bullets went whistling all around him, but not one hit him.

Athos waved his standard, turning his back to the men from the town and saluting those from the camp. Great shouts rang out from both sides, on one side shouts of anger, on the other shouts of enthusiasm.

A second volley followed the first, and three bullets, piercing it, turned the napkin into a real flag. A clamor came from the whole camp, who cried out:

"Climb down, climb down!"

Athos climbed down. His comrades, who were waiting anxiously, were overjoyed to see him appear.

"Come on, Athos, come on," said d'Artagnan, "step on it, step on it! Now that we've found everything except money, it would be stupid to get killed."

But Athos walked on majestically, whatever remarks his companions made to him, and they, finding all remarks useless, fell into step with him.

Grimaud and his basket had taken a good lead and were both out of range.

After a moment, they heard the noise of a wild fusillade.

"What's that?" asked Porthos. "What are they shooting at? I don't hear bullets whistling, and I don't see anybody."

"They're shooting at our dead men," replied Athos.

"But our dead men don't shoot back."

"Exactly. So they'll think it's an ambush, they'll talk things over, they'll send a white flag, and by the time they've discovered the joke, we'll be out of range of their bullets. That's why there's no point getting a stitch in your side from hurrying."

"Oh, I understand!" cried the marveling Porthos.

"That's quite fortunate!" said Athos, shrugging his shoulders.

On their side, the French, seeing the four friends coming back at a walk, burst into shouts of enthusiasm.

Finally, a new musket volley was heard, and this time the

bullets flattened themselves on the pebbles around the four friends and whistled lugubriously in their ears. The Rochelois had just finally taken the bastion.

"They're clumsy fellows," said Athos. "How many did we kill? Twelve?"

"Or fifteen."

"How many did we crush?"

"Eight or ten."

"And in exchange for all that, not a single scratch? Ah, no! What's that on your hand, d'Artagnan? Blood, it seems to me?"

"It's nothing," said d'Artagnan.

"A stray bullet?"

"Not even."

"What is it then?"

As we have said, Athos loved d'Artagnan like his own son, and this gloomy and inflexible character sometimes had a father's worries about the young man.

"A scratch," replied d'Artagnan. "My fingers got caught between two stones, one in the wall and one on my finger, and the skin was cut."

"That's what comes of having diamonds, my dear master," Athos said disdainfully.

"Ah, wait," cried Porthos, "there is indeed a diamond, and since there is a diamond, why the devil are we complaining about having no money?"

"Yes, why, in fact!" said Aramis.

"Well done, Porthos! There's an idea for once."

"Of course," said Porthos, puffing himself up at Athos's compliment, "since there's a diamond, let's sell it."

"But," said d'Artagnan, "it's the queen's diamond."

"All the more reason," Athos picked up. "The queen saving M. de Buckingham, her love—nothing could be more just; the queen saving us, her friends—nothing could be more moral. Let's sell the diamond. What thinks M. l'abbé? I'm not asking Porthos's opinion, he's already given it."

"I think," said Aramis, blushing, "that as his ring does not come from a mistress, and consequently is not a token of love, d'Artagnan can sell it."

"My dear, you speak like theology personified. And so your opinion is . . . ?"

"To sell the diamond," replied Aramis.

"Well, then," d'Artagnan said gaily, "let's sell it and say no more about it."

The fusillade continued, but the friends were out of range, and the Rochelois only shot at them for the sake of their conscience.

"By heaven," said Athos, "that idea came to Porthos just in time! Here we are in camp. And so, gentlemen, not a word more of this affair. We're being observed, they're coming to meet us, and we're going to be carried in triumph."

Indeed, as we have said, the whole camp was stirred up. More than two thousand people had watched, like a performance, the four friends' successful fanfaronnade, a fanfaronnade of which they were far from suspecting the real motive. All that was heard was the cry: "Long live the guards! Long live the musketeers!" M. du Busigny came first to shake Athos's hand and acknowledge that the bet was lost. The dragoon and the Switzer followed him, and all their comrades followed the dragoon and the Switzer. There was no end of congratulations, handshakes, embraces, and inextinguishable laughter at the expense of the Rochelois—so great a tumult, finally, that M. le cardinal thought it was a riot and sent La Houdinière, the captain of his guards, to find out what was happening.

The thing was recounted to the messenger with all the efflorescence of enthusiasm.

"Well?" asked the cardinal, on seeing La Houdinière.

"Well, Monseigneur," said the latter, "three musketeers and a guard made a bet with M. de Busigny that they could go to have lunch in the Saint-Gervais bastion, and, while lunching, they held the place for two hours against the enemy and killed I don't know how many Rochelois."

"Did you find out the names of these three musketeers?"

"Yes, Monseigneur."

"What are they?"

"They are MM. Athos, Porthos, and Aramis."

"Ever the same brave three!" murmured the cardinal. "And the guard?"

"M. d'Artagnan."

"Ever the same young rascal! Decidedly, these four men must be mine."

That same evening, the cardinal spoke with M. de Tréville of the morning's exploit, which was the only subject of conversation throughout the camp. M. de Tréville, who had the story of the adventure from the very mouths of those who had been its heroes, told it in full detail to His Eminence, without forgetting the episode of the napkin.

"Very well, M. de Tréville," said the cardinal, "keep that napkin for me, I beg you. I will have three gold fleurs-de-lis embroidered on it, and will give it to your company as a standard."

"Monseigneur," said M. de Tréville, "that would be an injustice to the guards: M. d'Artagnan does not belong to me, but to M. des Essarts."

"Well, then, take him," said the cardinal. "It's not fair that these four brave soldiers, since they love each other so much, do not serve in the same company."

That very evening, M. de Tréville announced this good news to the three musketeers and d'Artagnan, inviting the four of them to lunch the next day.

D'Artagnan could not contain himself for joy. As we know, the dream of his whole life was to be a musketeer.

The three friends were very joyful.

"By heaven!" said d'Artagnan to Athos, "you had a triumphant idea there, and, as you said, we've gained glory by it, and we were also able to have a conversation of the highest importance."

"Which we can take up again now, without anyone suspecting us; for, with God's help, from now on we'll be taken for cardinalists."

That same evening, d'Artagnan went to pay his respects to M. des Essarts, and to acquaint him with the advancement he had obtained.

M. des Essarts, who liked d'Artagnan very much, then offered to be of service to him, this change of corps bringing with it expenses for outfitting.

D'Artagnan declined; but, finding it a good occasion, gave him his diamond and asked him to have it appraised, as he wished to turn it into money.

The next day, at eight o'clock in the morning, M. des Essarts's valet came to see d'Artagnan, and handed him a pouch containing seven thousand livres in gold.

That was the price of the queen's diamond.

XLVIII

A FAMILY MATTER

Athos had found the term: "a family matter." A family matter was not subject to the cardinal's investigation; a family matter was nobody's concern; one could be occupied with a family matter in front of all the world.

And so, Athos had found the term: a family matter.

Aramis had found the idea: the valets.

Porthos had found the means: the diamond.

D'Artagnan alone had found nothing, he who was usually the most inventive of the four. But it must also be said that the mere name of Milady paralyzed him.

Ah, no, we are mistaken! He had found a buyer for the diamond.

The lunch with M. de Tréville was of a charming gaiety. D'Artagnan already had his uniform. As he was about the same size as Aramis, and as Aramis, generously paid, as will be remembered, by the bookseller who had bought his poem, had had doubles made of everything, he had handed over a complete outfit to his friend.

D'Artagnan would have had all his wishes fulfilled, if he had not seen Milady looming up like a dark cloud on the horizon.

After lunch, they agreed to meet that evening in Athos's quarters and there settle the matter.

D'Artagnan spent the day displaying his musketeer's garb in all the streets of the camp.

That evening, at the appointed hour, the four friends came together. There were only three things left to decide:

what to write to Milady's brother;

what to write to the clever person in Tours;

and which of the lackeys would carry the letters.

Each of them offered his own. Athos spoke of the discretion of Grimaud, who only spoke when his master unstitched his lips; Porthos boasted of the strength of Mousqueton, who was big enough to thrash four men of ordinary constitution; Aramis, confident of Bazin's cleverness, made a pompous speech in praise of his candidate; finally, d'Artagnan had complete faith in Planchet's bravery, and recalled the way he had behaved himself in the thorny business at Boulogne.

These four virtues disputed the prize for a long time, and gave rise to magnificent speeches, which we will not record here for fear of being tedious.

"Unfortunately," said Athos, "the one we send should combine all four of these qualities in himself."

"But where can such a lackey be found?"

"Nowhere!" said Athos. "I know it very well: so take Grimaud."

"Take Mousqueton."

"Take Bazin."

"Take Planchet. Planchet is brave and clever: that's already two of the four qualities."

"Gentlemen," said Aramis, "the main thing is not to know which of our four lackeys is the most discreet, the most strong, the most clever, or the most brave; the main thing is to know which of them loves money the most."

"What Aramis says makes great sense," Athos picked up. "One must speculate on people's defects, not on their virtues. Monsieur l'abbé, you are a great moralist!"

"To be sure," replied Aramis, "for we need to be well served not only so as to succeed, but also so as not to fail; for, in case of failure, it will be the head, not of the lackeys . . ."

"Not so loud, Aramis!" said Athos.

"Right, not of the lackeys," Aramis went on, "but of the master, and even the masters! Are our valets devoted to us enough to risk their lives for us? No."

"By heaven," said d'Artagnan, "I'd almost vouch for Planchet."

"Well, then, my dear friend, add to his natural devotion a good sum of money, which will give him some independence, and instead of vouching for him once, you can vouch for him twice."

"Ah, good God, you'll be deceived all the same!" said Athos, who was an optimist when it came to things, but a pessimist when it came to men. "They'll promise everything to get the money, and along the way fear will keep them from acting. Once caught, they'll be squeezed; squeezed, they'll confess. Devil take it, we're not children! To go to England," Athos lowered his voice, "one must cross through France, which is strewn with the cardinal's spies and creatures. One must have a pass to take ship. One must know enough English to ask the way to London. It all looks rather difficult to me."

"Not at all," said d'Artagnan, who was very keen on having the thing accomplished. "On the contrary, to me it looks easy. It goes without saying, parbleu, that if we write enormities to Lord de Winter about the horrors of the cardinal ..."

"Not so loud!" said Athos.

"About intrigues and state secrets," d'Artagnan went on, complying with the recommendation, "it goes without saying that we'll all be broken on the wheel. But, for God's sake, don't forget, as you yourself have said, Athos, that we are writing to him about a family matter; that we are writing to him with the sole purpose of having him make it so that Milady, once she reaches London, is unable do us harm. So I'll write him a letter more or less in these terms ..."

"Let's hear," said Aramis, putting on a critical face beforehand.

"'Dear Sir and Good Friend ...'"

"Oh, yes! 'Good friend,' to an Englishman," interrupted Athos. "A fine beginning! Bravo, d'Artagnan! For that word alone you'll be drawn and quartered, if not broken on the wheel."

"Well, all right, I'll just say, 'Dear Sir.'"

"You could even say 'Milord,'" continued Athos, who was a stickler for proprieties.

"'Milord, do you remember that little enclosure with the goats behind the Luxembourg?'"

"Fine! Now it's the Luxembourg! They'll think it's an allusion to the queen mother! Isn't that clever," said Athos.

"Well, then we'll simply put: 'Milord, do you remember a certain little enclosure where your life was spared?'"

"My dear d'Artagnan," said Athos, "you'll never be more than a very bad author! 'Where your life was spared!' Fie on it, that's improper! One does not remind a gallant man of such services. A good turn remembered is an insult rendered."

"Ah, my dear," said d'Artagnan, "you are unbearable! If I have to write under your censorship, by heaven, I give up!"

"And right you are. Handle the musket and the sword, my dear, you do gallantly at both excercises, but pass the pen to M. l'abbé, that is his concern."

"Ah, yes, indeed," said Porthos, "pass the pen to Aramis, who writes theses in Latin, so he does."

"Very well," said d'Artagnan, "write the note for us, Aramis. But, by our Holy Father the Pope, keep it concise, for I'm going to pluck you in my turn, I warn you."

"I ask for nothing better," said Aramis, with that naive confidence that every poet has in himself. "But first fill me in on it: I've certainly heard here and there that his sister-in-law is a minx; I even had proof of it when I listened to her conversation with the cardinal."

"Not so loud, sacrebleu!" said Athos.

"But," Aramis continued, "the details escape me."

"And me, too," said Porthos.

D'Artagnan and Athos looked at each other for a time in silence. Finally Athos, after collecting himself, and turning still paler than he usually was, made a sign of acquiescence. D'Artagnan understood that he could speak.

"Well, here's what there is to say," d'Artagnan began. "'Milord, your sister-in-law is a villain, who wanted to have you killed in order to take your inheritance. But she could not marry your brother, having already married in France, and having been . . .'"

D'Artagnan paused, as if searching for the right word, and looked at Athos.

"Driven out by her husband," said Athos.

"Because she had been branded," d'Artagnan continued.

"Bah!" cried Porthos. "Impossible! She wanted to have her brother-in-law killed?"

"Yes."

"She was married?" asked Aramis.

"Yes."

"And her husband saw that she had the fleur-de-lis on her shoulder?" cried Porthos.

"Yes."

Athos had uttered each of these three "yesses" with a gloomier intonation.

"And who saw this fleur-de-lis?" asked Aramis.

"D'Artagnan and I, or rather, to observe chronological order, I and d'Artagnan," replied Athos.

"And this frightful creature's husband is still alive?" asked Aramis.

"Still alive."

"You're sure of it?"

"Quite sure."

There was a moment of chilled silence, during which each of them felt himself affected according to his own nature.

"This time," Athos picked up, breaking the silence first, "d'Artagnan has given us an excellent program, and that is what we must write first."

"Devil take it, you're right, Athos!" said Aramis. "And writing it is a thorny problem. M. le chancelier himself would be hard put to write an epistle to that effect, and yet M. le chancelier draws up very nice police reports. Never mind! Keep quiet, I'm writing."

Aramis indeed took up the pen, reflected for a few moments, and set about writing eight or ten lines in a charming little feminine hand. Then, in a soft and slow voice, as if each word had been scrupulously weighed, he read the following:

Milord,

The person who writes you these lines had the honor of crossing swords with you in a small enclosure on the rue d'Enfer. As you have been quite willing, several times since then, to call yourself this person's friend, he owes it to you to repay that friendship with a piece of good advice. Two times you have nearly fallen victim to a close relative, whom you believe to be your heir, because you are unaware that before contracting a marriage in England, she had already married in France. The third time, which is this one, you may succumb. Your relative has left La Rochelle for England during the night. Watch out for her arrival, for she has great and terrible designs. If you absolutely insist on knowing what she is capable of, you may read her past on her left shoulder.

"Well, that's just perfect!" said Athos. "You have the pen of a secretary of state, my dear Aramis. Lord de Winter will certainly be on his guard now, if the warning manages to reach him; and if it should fall into the hands of His Eminence himself, we will not be compromised. But as the valet who is to take it could make us believe he went to London when he stopped at Châtellerault, we'll give him only half the sum, promising him the other half in return for the reply. Have you got the diamond?" asked Athos.

"I've got better than that, I've got the money."

And d'Artagnan tossed the pouch on the table. At the sound of the gold, Aramis raised his eyes. Porthos gave a start. As for Athos, he remained impassive.

"How much is in that little pouch?" he asked.

"Seven thousand livres in twelve-franc louis."

"Seven thousand livres!" cried Porthos. "That poor little diamond was worth seven thousand livres?"

"It seems so," said Athos, "because here they are. I don't suppose our friend d'Artagnan added any of his own."

"But, gentlemen, in all this," said d'Artagnan, "we're not thinking of the queen. Let us take a little care of her dear Buckingham's health. We owe her that at least."

"Quite so," said Athos, "but that's up to Aramis."

"Well," replied the latter, blushing, "what must I do?"

"Why," replied Athos, "it's quite simple: write a second letter to that clever person who lives in Tours."

Aramis once more took up the pen, began to reflect again, and wrote the following lines, which he submitted that same instant to the approval of his friends:

My dear Cousin,

His Eminence the cardinal, whom God preserve for the good fortune of France and the confounding of the enemies of the realm, is on the point of having done with the rebellious heretics of La Rochelle. It is probable that the help of the English fleet will not even come within sight of the place. I will even venture to say that I am certain M. de Buckingham will be prevented from setting sail by some great event. His Eminence is the most illustrious politician of times past, of the present time, and probably of times to come. He would extinguish the sun, if the sun hindered him. Give this good news to your sister, my dear cousin. I dreamed that that cursed Englishman was dead. I cannot remember whether it was by the sword or by poison; all I am sure of is that I dreamed he was dead, and, you know, my dreams never deceive me. You may be certain, then, of seeing me return very soon.

"Perfect!" cried Athos. "You are the king of poets, my dear Aramis, you speak like the Apocalypse and are as true as the Gospels. It only remains for you to address the letter."

"That's easy enough," said Aramis.

He folded the letter coquettishly, turned it over, and wrote:

To Mademoiselle Marie Michon, seamstress, Tours.

The three friends looked at each other, laughing: they were caught.

"Now," said Aramis, "you understand, gentlemen, that

Bazin alone can carry this letter to Tours. My cousin knows only Bazin and trusts only him. Anyone else would thwart the affair. Besides, Bazin is ambitious and learned; Bazin has read history, gentlemen; he knows that Sixtus the Fifth became pope after tending pigs. Well, and as he counts on placing himself in the Church at the same time I do, he does not despair of becoming pope in his turn, or at least cardinal. You understand that a man with such aims won't let himself be caught, or, if he is caught, will endure martyrdom rather than talk."

"Very well, very well," said d'Artagnan, "I give you Bazin; but you give me Planchet. Milady had him thrown out one day with a good many blows of the stick. Now, Planchet has an excellent memory, and, I guarantee you, if he can imagine for a moment that vengeance is possible, he'll sooner break his back than give it up. If your affairs in Tours are your affairs, Aramis, those in London are mine. I ask therefore that you choose Planchet, who, besides, has already been to London with me and is able to say quite correctly: 'London, sir, if you please,' and 'My master, Lord d'Artagnan.' So you can rest easy, he will make his way there and back."

"In that case," said Athos, "Planchet must receive seven hundred livres for going and seven hundred for coming back; and Bazin three hundred livres for going and three hundred for coming back. That will reduce the sum to five thousand livres. We'll take a thousand each to use as we see fit, and let the abbé keep the remaining thousand for extraordinary cases or common needs. Does that suit you all?"

"My dear Athos," said Aramis, "you speak like Nestor, who, as everyone knows, was the wisest of the Greeks."

"Well, then all's said," Athos continued, "Planchet and Bazin will go. On the whole, I'm not sorry to keep Grimaud: he's used to my ways, and I value that. Yesterday's events must already have shaken him; this journey would do him in."

They sent for Planchet and gave him his instructions. He had already been warned by d'Artagnan, who first announced that it would mean glory, then money, and finally danger.

"I'll carry the letter in the lining of my coat," said Planchet, "and swallow it if they catch me."

"But then you won't be able to carry out your mission," said d'Artagnan.

"Give me a copy of it tonight, and I'll know it by heart tomorrow."

D'Artagnan looked around at his friends as if to say: "Well, what did I promise you?"

"Now," he went on, addressing Planchet, "you have eight days to reach Lord de Winter, you have eight days to come back here, sixteen days in all. If on the sixteenth day after your departure, at eight o'clock in the evening, you have not turned up—no money, even if it's five after eight."

"In that case, Monsieur," said Planchet, "buy me a watch."

"Take this one," said Athos, handing him his own with careless generosity, "and be a brave lad. Know that if you talk, if you blab, if you dawdle, you are cutting the throat of your master, who has such great confidence in your faithfulness that he has vouched for you to us. But know also that if any harm comes to d'Artagnan through some fault of yours, I'll find you wherever you are and will do so in order to slit your belly open."

"Oh, Monsieur!" cried Planchet, humiliated by the suspicion and frightened above all by the musketeer's calm air.

"And as for me," said Porthos, rolling his big eyes, "know that I'll skin you alive!"

"Ah, Monsieur!"

"And as for me," said Aramis, in his soft and melodious voice, "know that I'll roast you over a slow fire like a savage."

"Ah, Monsieur!"

And Planchet burst into tears, we will not venture to say whether from terror, on account of the threats made against him, or from the emotion of seeing four friends so closely united.

D'Artagnan took his hand and embraced him.

"You see, Planchet," he said to him, "these gentlemen are saying this to you out of affection for me, but at bottom they love you."

"Ah, Monsieur!" said Planchet, "I'll either succeed, or

they'll cut me in quarters. If they cut me in quarters, you may be sure that there is not one piece that will talk."

It was decided that Planchet would leave the next day at eight o'clock in the morning, so that during the night, as he had said, he could learn the letter by heart. He gained exactly twelve hours that way, as he was to return on the sixteenth day at eight o'clock in the evening.

The next morning, just as he was going to mount his horse, d'Artagnan, who at the bottom of his heart had a weakness for the duke, took Planchet aside.

"Listen," he said to him, "when you've given the letter to Lord de Winter and he has read it, tell him: 'Watch over His Grace the duke of Buckingham, for they want to assassinate him.' You understand, Planchet, this is so serious and so important that I didn't even want to confess to my friends that I was entrusting you with this secret, and I wouldn't write it down for you even for a captain's commission."

"Don't worry, Monsieur," said Planchet, "you'll see that you can count on me."

And, mounted on an excellent horse, which he would have to abandon twenty leagues from there in order to take the stagecoach, Planchet left at a gallop, his heart slightly wrung by the triple promise the musketeers had made him, but otherwise in the best spirits in the world.

Bazin left the next morning for Tours and had eight days to carry out his mission.

The four friends, for the whole duration of these two absences, as is quite understandable, kept their eyes peeled, their noses to the wind, and their ears pricked up more than ever. They spent their days trying to catch what was being said, keeping watch on the cardinal's attitude, and sniffing out the couriers who arrived. They were seized more than once by an insurmountable trembling, when they were summoned for some unexpected service. They had, besides, to look out for their own safety. Milady was a phantom who, having once appeared to people, never let them sleep peacefully.

On the morning of the eighth day, Bazin, fresh as ever and

smiling his habitual smile, came into the Parpaillot tavern as the four friends were having breakfast, saying, according to the agreed convention:

"M. Aramis, here is your cousin's reply."

The four friends exchanged joyful glances: half the task was done—true, it was the shortest and easiest half.

Blushing in spite of himself, Aramis took the letter, which was written in a crude hand and with very poor spelling.

"Good God!" he exclaimed, laughing. "I decidedly despair of her: this poor Michon will never write like M. de Voiture!"

"Vat doss dat mean, this boor Migeon?" asked the Switzer, who had been chatting with the four friends when the letter came.

"Oh, my God, less than nothing!" said Aramis. "A charming little seamstress I was very much in love with, and whom I asked for a few lines in her own hand by way of a souvenir."

"Dutieu!" said the Switzer, "if she's as pig a leddy as her hentwriting, you're in luck, gomrade!"

Aramis read the letter and handed it to Athos.

"See what she writes to me, Athos," he said.

Athos glanced at the epistle, and, to dispel any suspicions that might have been aroused, read it aloud:

My dear Cousin,

My sister and I are very good at interpreting dreams, and are even awfully afraid of them; but of yours one may say, I hope, that every dream is a delusion. Good-bye! Be well, and let us hear from you now and then.

Aglaé Michon

"And what dream is she talking about?" asked the dragoon, who had come over during the reading.

"Ja, vat tream?" asked the Switzer.

"Eh, pardieu!" said Aramis, "it's quite simple: a dream that I had and that I told to her."

"Oh, ja, partieu! it's to be quite zimple to tell hiss tream; but me, I nefer tream."

"You are very lucky," said Athos, getting up. "I wish I could say the same!"

"Nefer!" repeated the Switzer, delighted that a man like Athos envied him for something, "nefer! nefer!"

Porthos and Aramis stayed to face the gibes of the dragoon and the Switzer.

As for Bazin, he went to sleep on a bundle of hay; and as he had more imagination than the Switzer, he dreamed that M. Aramis, become pope, was placing a cardinal's hat on his head.

But, as we have said, Bazin, by his fortunate return, had taken away only part of the anxiety that goaded the four friends. Days of waiting are long, and d'Artagnan above all would have bet that the days now had forty-eight hours. He forgot the unavoidable delays of sailing. He exaggerated the power of Milady, endowing the woman, who seemed like a demon to him, with supernatural auxiliaries like herself. He imagined, at the least noise, that men were coming to arrest him, and that they were bringing Planchet to confront him and his friends. Moreover, his confidence in the worthy Picard, formerly so great, was diminishing day by day. This anxiety was so intense that it spread to Porthos and Aramis. Only Athos remained impassive, as if there was no danger stirring around him and he was breathing his everyday air.

On the sixteenth day, above all, these signs of agitation were so visible in d'Artagnan and his two friends that they could not stay put, and they wandered like shades along the road by which Planchet was to return.

"Really," Athos said to them, "you're not men but children, if a woman can frighten you so much! And what is it about, after all? Being imprisoned! Well, but they will get us out of prison: they got Mme Bonacieux out well enough. Being decapitated? But every day in the trenches we expose ourselves to worse than that, for a bullet can break your leg, and I'm sure the surgeon will make you suffer more in cutting up your thigh than the executioner in cutting off your head. Keep calm, then. In two hours, in four, in six hours at the latest, Planchet will be here. He promised to be, and I have great faith in the promises of Planchet, who strikes me as a very brave lad."

"But what if he doesn't come?" said d'Artagnan.

"Well, if he doesn't come, it means he was delayed, that's all. He might have fallen off his horse, he might have tumbled over a bridge, he might have ridden so fast that he caught an inflammation of the lungs. Eh, gentlemen, let's make allowance for events! Life is a chaplet of little miseries, and the philosopher tells it over with a laugh. Be philosophers like me, gentlemen. Sit down and let's drink. The future never looks so rosy as when it's viewed through a glass of chambertin."

"That's all very well," said d'Artagnan, "but I'm tired of having to worry, every time I have a cool drink, that the wine may have come from Milady's cellar."

"You're a finicky one," said Athos. "Such a beautiful woman!"

"A branded woman!" said Porthos, with his loud laugh.

Athos shuddered, ran his hand over his forehead to wipe away the sweat, and stood up in his turn with a nervous movement that he could not repress.

The day passed, however, and evening, though it came more slowly, finally came. The pothouses filled up with clients. Athos, who had pocketed his share of the diamond, never left the Parpaillot. In M. de Busigny, who, moreover, had given them a magnificent dinner, he had found a partner worthy of himself. They were playing cards together, as usual, when it struck seven. They heard the patrols pass by, going to reinforce the posts. At half-past seven retreat was sounded.

"We're lost," d'Artagnan said in Athos's ear.

"You mean we've lost," Athos said calmly, taking four pistoles from his pocket and tossing them on the table. "Come, gentlemen, they're sounding retreat, let's go to bed."

And Athos left the Parpaillot, followed by d'Artagnan. Aramis came behind, giving his arm to Porthos. Aramis was mumbling some verses, and Porthos tore a few hairs from his mustache now and then in a sign of despair.

But, lo and behold, all at once a shadow whose form was familiar to d'Artagnan detached itself from the darkness, and a well-known voice said to him:

"Monsieur, I've brought you your cloak, for it's chilly tonight."

"Planchet!" cried d'Artagnan, drunk with joy.

"Planchet!" repeated Porthos and Aramis.

"Well, yes, it's Planchet," said Athos. "What's so surprising about that? He promised to be back by eight o'clock, and here it's just striking eight. Bravo, Planchet! You're a lad of your word, and if you ever leave your master, I'll keep a place for you in my service."

"Oh, no, never!" said Planchet. "I will never leave M. d'Artagnan."

At the same time, d'Artagnan felt Planchet slip a note into his hand.

D'Artagnan had a great desire to embrace Planchet on his return, as he had on his departure; but he was afraid that this token of effusion, given to his lackey in the middle of the street, might seem extraordinary to some passerby, and he restrained himself.

"I've got the letter," he said to Athos and his friends.

"That's good," said Athos. "Let's go home and read it."

The letter burned d'Artagnan's hand. He wanted to quicken the pace, but Athos took his arm and passed it under his own, and the young man was forced to adjust his speed to that of his friend.

At last they went into the tent and lighted a lamp, and while Planchet stood at the door so that the four friends would not be caught by surprise, d'Artagnan, with a trembling hand, broke the seal and opened the long-awaited letter.

It contained half a line, in a very British hand and of a very Spartan brevity:

Thank you, be easy.

Athos took the letter from d'Artagnan's hands, brought it to the lamp, and set fire to it, and did not let go of it until it was reduced to ashes.

Then, calling Planchet, he said to him:

"Now, my lad, you can claim your seven hundred livres, but you weren't running much risk with a note like that."

"Not that I didn't invent lots of ways to keep it hidden," said Planchet.

"Well, now," said d'Artagnan, "tell us about that."

"Oh, it's a long story, Monsieur."

"You're right, Planchet," said Athos. "Besides, they've sounded retreat, and we'll attract notice if we keep the light on longer than the others."

"Very well," said d'Artagnan, "let's go to bed. Sleep well, Planchet!"

"By heaven, Monsieur, it will be the first time in sixteen days!"

"For me, too!" said d'Artagnan.

"For me, too!" repeated Porthos.

"For me, too!" repeated Aramis.

"Well, to tell you the truth—for me, too!" said Athos.

XLIX

Fatality

Meanwhile Milady, drunk with wrath, roaring from the deck of the vessel like a lioness being put aboard ship, had been tempted to throw herself into the sea in order to get back to shore, for she could not accept the idea that she had been insulted by d'Artagnan, threatened by Athos, and was leaving France without having been revenged on them. The idea had soon become so unbearable to her that, at the risk of terrible consequences for herself, she had begged the captain to put her ashore; but the captain, anxious to escape his false position, placed between French and English cruisers like a bat between the rats and the birds, was in great haste to return to England, and stubbornly refused to obey what he took to be a feminine caprice, promising his passenger, who, moreover, had been especially recommended to him by the cardinal, to put her off, if the sea and the French permitted, at one of the ports of Brittany, either Lorient or Brest; but meanwhile the wind was contrary, the sea was rough, they tacked about and ran to windward. It was only nine days after leaving the Charente that Milady, all pale with her afflictions and her rage, saw the bluish coast of Finisterre appear.

She calculated that to cross that corner of France and return to the cardinal would take her at least three days; add one day for the landing and it made four; add those four days to the nine others, that was thirteen days lost, thirteen days during which many important events could take place in London. She reflected that the cardinal would without any doubt be furious at her return, and consequently would be more disposed to listen to the complaints brought against her than to the accusations she brought against others. She therefore let Lorient and Brest go by without insisting with the captain, who, for his part, was careful not to alert her. Milady thus continued on her way, and the same day that Planchet embarked for France at Portsmouth, His Eminence's messenger triumphantly entered port.

The whole town was in an extraordinary commotion: four large ships, recently completed, had just been launched into the sea. Standing on the jetty, glittering with gold, sparkling, as was his habit, with diamonds and precious stones, his hat adorned with a white feather that fell to his shoulder, Buckingham could be seen, surrounded by a staff almost as brilliant as himself.

It was one of those fine and rare winter days when England remembers that there is a sun. The paled but still splendid star was setting on the horizon, empurpling the sky and sea at once with strips of flame, and casting on the towers and old houses of the town a last golden ray, which made the windows glow like the reflection of a fire. Breathing this sea air, more keen and fragrant with the approach of land, contemplating all the power of these preparations that she was ordered to destroy, all the power of this army that she was to combat by herself—she, a woman—with a few bags of gold, Milady mentally compared herself to Judith, the terrible Jewess, when she penetrated the camp of the Assyrians and saw the enormous mass of chariots, horses, men, and weapons that a motion of her hand was to dispel like a cloud of smoke.

They entered the roads; but as they were preparing to drop anchor, a small, heavily armed cutter approached the merchant vessel, claiming to be the coast guard, and lowered its longboat, which headed for the boarding ladder. The longboat contained an officer, a bosun's mate, and eight oarsmen. The officer alone came aboard, where he was received with all the deference a uniform inspires.

The officer conversed for a few moments with the skipper, had him read a paper of which he was the bearer, and, at the order of the merchant captain, the entire crew of the vessel, sailors and passengers, was summoned on deck.

When this sort of summons had been made, the officer inquired in a loud voice about the brig's point of departure, her course, her landfalls, and the captain answered all these questions without hesitation or difficulty. Then the officer began to pass all the people in review one after another, and, stopping at Milady, scrutinized her with great care, but without addressing a single word to her.

Then he went back to the captain and spoke a few more words to him, and, as if it was him that the vessel had henceforth to obey, gave orders for a maneuver that the crew executed at once. Then the vessel started on her way again, still escorted by the little cutter, which sailed alongside her, threatening her flank with the mouths of its six cannons, while the longboat followed in the ship's wake, a feeble speck next to that enormous mass.

During the officer's examination of Milady, Milady, as one might well imagine, had for her part devoured him with her gaze. But, accustomed as this woman with flaming eyes was to reading the hearts of those whose secrets she needed to guess, this time she found a face of such impassivity that her investigation yielded no discoveries. The officer who had stopped in front of her and had silently studied her with such care might have been twenty-five or twenty-six years old; he was white of face, with slightly deep-set light blue eyes; his mouth, thin and well-formed, remained motionless in its pure lines; his chin, vigorously prominent, denoted that force of will which, in the common British type, is ordinarily no more than obstinacy; a slightly receding forehead, as is proper to poets, enthusiasts, and soldiers, was barely shaded by short and sparse hair, which, like the beard that covered the lower part of his face, was of a beautiful deep chestnut color.

It was already night when they entered port. Fog thickened the darkness still more and formed a ring around the beacons and lanterns of the jetties like the ring around the moon when the weather threatens to turn rainy. The air one breathed was sad, damp, and chilly.

Milady, who was such a strong woman, felt herself shivering despite herself.

The officer had Milady's bundles pointed out to him, had her baggage transferred to the longboat, and, once this operation had been carried out, invited her to climb down to it herself by offering her his hand.

Milady looked at the man and hesitated.

"Who are you, Monsieur," she asked, "who are so kind as to pay such particular attention to me?"

"You should be able to see that, Madame, by my uniform. I am an officer in the English navy," replied the young man.

"But, after all, is it customary for officers of the English navy to put themselves at the orders of their lady compatriots when they approach a British port, and push their gallantry so far as to see them ashore?"

"Yes, Milady, it is customary, not out of gallantry, but out of prudence, that in times of war foreigners be taken to a designated hotel, so that, until there is full information about them, they remain under government surveillance."

These words were uttered with the most correct politeness and the most perfect calm. However, they did not have the gift of convincing Milady.

"But I am not a foreigner, Monsieur," she said, with the purest accent that had ever been heard between Portsmouth and Manchester. "I am Lady Clarick, and this precaution . . ."

"This precaution is general, Milady, and it will be useless for you to try to avoid it."

"I shall follow you, then, Monsieur."

And, accepting the officer's hand, she began to go down

the ladder, at the bottom of which the longboat was waiting. The officer followed her. A large cloak was spread out in the stern. The officer seated her on it and sat down beside her.

"Pull away," he said to the sailors.

The eight oars dropped back into the water with the sound of one, made a single stroke, and the longboat seemed to fly over the surface of the water.

Five minutes later they touched land.

The officer jumped onto the quay and offered Milady his hand.

A carriage was waiting.

"This carriage is for us?" asked Milady.

"Yes, Madame," replied the officer.

"So the hôtel is far away?"

"At the other end of town."

"Let us go, then," said Milady.

And she climbed resolutely into the carriage.

The officer saw to it that the bundles were carefully fastened behind the carriage, and when this operation was done, took his place beside Milady and shut the door.

At once, without any order being given and without needing to be told where to go, the coachman set off at a gallop and plunged into the streets of the town.

So strange a reception must have given Milady ample food for thought. And so, seeing that the young officer was apparently in no mood to get into conversation, she leaned back in the corner of the carriage and went over in her mind all the suppositions that occurred to her one after the other.

However, after a quarter of an hour, astonished at the length of the way, she leaned towards the coach door to see where she was being taken. There were no more houses to be seen; trees appeared in the darkness like great black phantoms chasing each other.

Milady shuddered.

"But we are no longer in town, Monsieur," she said.

The young officer remained silent.

"I will not go any further if you do not tell me where you are taking me—that I warn you, Monsieur!"

This threat drew no response.

"Oh, this is too much!" cried Milady. "Help! Help!"

No voice answered hers; the coach continued on its rapid way; the officer seemed like a statue.

Milady looked at him with one of those terrible expressions peculiar to her face, and which so rarely failed of their effect. Anger made her eyes flash in the darkness.

The young man remained impassive.

Milady was about to open the door and throw herself out.

"Take care, Madame," the young man said coldly, "you will kill yourself if you jump."

Milady sat back down, fuming. The officer leaned over, looked at her in his turn, and seemed surprised to see that face, formerly so beautiful, twist with rage and become almost hideous. The cunning creature understood that she was harming herself by letting her soul be seen like that; she calmed her features, and said in a moaning voice:

"In heaven's name, Monsieur, tell me whether it is to you, to your government, or to some enemy that I must attribute the violence that is being done to me?"

"No violence is being done to you, Madame. What is happening to you is the result of a quite simple precaution which we are forced to take with all those who land in England."

"Then you do not know me, Monsieur?"

"This is the first time I have the honor of seeing you."

"And, on your honor, you have no cause to hate me?"

"None, I swear to you."

There was so much serenity, coolness, even gentleness in the young man's voice that Milady was reassured.

Finally, after about an hour's journey, the carriage stopped in front of an iron gate that barred a sunken road leading to a grim-looking castle, massive and isolated. Then, as the wheels rolled through fine sand, Milady heard a vast booming, which she recognized as the sound of the sea breaking on a rocky coast.

The carriage passed under two archways and finally stopped in a dark, square courtyard. The carriage door opened almost at once, the young man jumped down lightly and offered his hand to Milady, who leaned on it and descended in her turn with a certain calm.

"So, all the same," said Milady, looking around her and bringing her eyes back to the young officer with a most gracious smile, "I am a prisoner. But it won't be for long, I'm sure," she added. "My conscience and your politeness, Monsieur, are my guarantees of that."

Flattering as the compliment was, the officer made no reply, but, drawing from his belt a small silver whistle similar to those used by bosun's mates on ships of war, he blew three times, with three different modulations. Several men appeared, unharnessed the steaming horses, and took the carriage to the coach house.

Then, still with the same calm politeness, the officer invited his prisoner to go into the house. The latter, still with her same smiling face, took his arm and went in with him under a low and arched doorway which, through a vault lit only at the back, led to a stone stairway winding around a stone arris. They stopped before a massive door which, after the insertion into the lock of a key that the young man carried with him, swung back heavily on its hinges and opened onto the room destined for Milady.

At a single glance, the prisoner took in the apartment in its minutest details.

It was a room whose furnishings were at the same time rather decent for a prison and rather severe for a free man's habitation. However, the bars on the windows and the bolts on the outside of the door decided the case in favor of a prison.

For an instant, all of this creature's strength of soul, though tempered in the most vigorous springs, abandoned her. She fell into an armchair, crossing her arms, lowering her head, and expecting every moment to see a judge come in to interrogate her.

But no one came in except two or three marines, who brought the bags and boxes, set them down in a corner, and withdrew without saying anything.

The officer presided over all these details with the same calm that Milady had constantly seen in him, not uttering a word himself, and making himself obeyed by a gesture of the hand or a note of his whistle.

One would have said that between this man and his inferiors, spoken language did not exist or had become useless.

Finally, Milady could hold out no longer. She broke the silence.

"In heaven's name, Monsieur," she cried, "what does all this mean? Settle my doubts. I have courage enough for any danger I can foresee, for every misfortune I can understand. Where am I, and what am I here? If I am free, why these bars and these doors? If I am a prisoner, what crime have I committed?"

"You are here in the apartment that was intended for you, Madame. I was ordered to go and take you at sea, and to bring you to this castle. I have carried out that order, I believe, with all the strictness of a soldier, but also with all the courtesy of a gentleman. There ends, at least for the present, the charge I had to fulfill regarding you; the rest is another person's concern."

"And who is this other person?" asked Milady. "Can't you tell me his name? . . ."

At that moment, a great noise of spurs was heard on the stairs. Several voices passed and died away, and the sound of solitary footsteps approached the door.

"Here is that person, Madame," said the officer, moving out of the way, and standing in an attitude of respect and submission.

At the same time, the door opened; a man appeared on the threshold.

He was without hat, wore a sword at his side, and was twisting a handkerchief in his fingers.

Milady thought she recognized this shadow in the shadows. She leaned on the arm of the chair with one hand and thrust her head forward, as if to go to meet a certainty.

Then the stranger slowly advanced. And as he advanced, entering into the circle of light thrown by the lamp, Milady involuntarily backed away.

At last, when there was no more doubt, she cried in utter amazement:

"What? My brother? Is it you?"

"Yes, lovely lady!" replied Lord de Winter, making a half-courteous, half-ironic bow, "in person."

"But this castle, then?"

"Is mine."

"This room?"

"Is yours."

"So I am your prisoner?"

"Nearly."

"But this is a shocking abuse of power!"

"No grand words. Let's sit down and have a quiet chat, as brother and sister ought to do."

Then, turning towards the door, he saw that the young officer was awaiting his final orders.

"Well done," he said, "I thank you. Leave us, now, Mr. Felton."

L

A Brother Chats with His Sister

While Lord de Winter was shutting the door, pushing open a blind, and moving a seat close to his sister-in-law's armchair, Milady, lost in thought, gazed into the depths of possibility and discovered the whole plot that she had not even been able to glimpse as long as she did not know what hands she had fallen into. She knew her brother-in-law for a proper gentleman, an avid hunter, an intrepid gambler, forward with women, but of a strength inferior to hers in regard to intrigue. How had he found out about her arrival? Had her seized? Why was he holding her?

Athos had indeed said a few words to her which proved that the conversation she had had with the cardinal had fallen on other ears; but she could not admit that he had been able to dig a countermine so quickly and so boldly.

She feared rather that her previous operations in England had been discovered. Buckingham might have guessed who it was that had cut off the two pendants, and be revenging himself for that little betrayal. But Buckingham was incapable of committing any violence against a woman, above all if that woman was thought to have acted from a feeling of jealousy.

This supposition seemed to her the most probable. It seemed to her that they wanted to be revenged for the past, and not to forestall the future. However, she congratulated herself in any case on having fallen into the hands of her brother-in-law, with whom she counted on getting off lightly, rather than those of an outright and intelligent enemy.

"Yes, let's chat, brother," she said, with a sort of cheerfulness, resolved as she was to draw from the conversation, despite all the dissimulation Lord de Winter might bring to it, the enlightenment she needed to govern her conduct in the future.

"So you decided to return to England," said Lord de Winter, "despite the determination you so often showed me in Paris never again to set foot on British territory?"

Milady replied to his question with another question.

"First of all," she said, "tell me how you could have had me watched so closely as to be informed in advance not only of my arrival, but also of the day, the hour, and the port I would arrive in?"

Lord de Winter adopted the same tactic as Milady, thinking that, since his sister-in-law was using it, it must be the right one.

"But, you tell me, my dear sister," he picked up, "what you have come to England for."

"Why, I came to see you," replied Milady, not knowing how greatly this answer deepened the suspicions already awakened in her brother-in-law's mind by d'Artagnan's letter, and wishing only to snare her listener's goodwill by means of a lie.

"Ah, to see me?" Lord de Winter said slyly.

"Of course, to see you. What is astonishing in that?"

"And you had no other motive for coming to England than to see me?"

"No."

"And so it was for me alone that you took the trouble of crossing the Channel?"

"For you alone."

"Damn, what affection, sister!"

"But am I not your closest relative?" asked Milady, in a tone of the most touching naïveté.

"And even my sole heir, isn't that so?" Lord de Winter said in his turn, fixing his eyes on Milady's eyes.

However much control she had over herself, Milady could not help giving a start, and as, in uttering these last words, Lord de Winter had placed his hand on his sister's arm, the start did not escape him.

Indeed, the thrust was direct and deep. The first thought that came to Milady's mind was that she had been betrayed by Kitty, and that it was she who had told the baron of that interested aversion, some tokens of which she had imprudently let drop before her maid. She also recalled her furious and imprudent outburst against d'Artagnan, after he had spared her brother-in-law's life.

"I don't understand, Milord," she said, to gain time and make her adversary speak. "What are you trying to say? And is there some unknown meaning hidden in your words?"

"Oh, God, no!" said Lord de Winter, with apparent joviality. "You have the wish to see me, and you come to England. I learn of that wish, or rather I suspect that you feel it, and to spare you all the vexations of a nighttime arrival in port, and all the bother of the landing, I send one of my officers to meet you. I put a carriage at his disposal, and he brings you here to this castle, of which I am the governor, where I come every day, and where, in order to satisfy our mutual desire to see each other, I have prepared a room for you. What is there in all I've just said that is more astonishing than what you have said to me?"

"No, what I find astonishing is that you were informed of my arrival."

"Yet that is the simplest of things, my dear sister. Didn't you notice that the captain of your little vessel, on entering the roads, sent a little boat on ahead carrying his ship's log and the register of his crew, in order to obtain entry into the port? I am the commandant of the port, the book was brought to me, and I recognized your name. My heart told me what your lips have just confided to me, that is, the purpose for which you exposed yourself to the dangers of a sea that is so perilous, or at least so trying, at the moment, and I sent my cutter to meet you. The rest you know."

Milady realized that Lord de Winter was lying, and was all the more frightened by that.

"Brother," she continued, "wasn't it Milord Buckingham that I saw on the jetty as I arrived this evening?"

"Himself. Ah, I can understand that the sight of him struck you!" said Lord de Winter. "You come from a country where they must be much concerned with him, and I know that his preparations against France greatly preoccupy your friend the cardinal."

"My friend the cardinal!" cried Milady, seeing that on this point as on the other Lord de Winter seemed thoroughly informed.

"Is he not your friend, then?" the baron went on casually. "Ah, excuse me, I thought he was! But we'll come back to Milord the duke later. Let us not brush aside the sentimental turn the conversation had taken: you came, you say, to see me?"

"Yes."

"Well, and I replied to you that you would be fully gratified and that we would see each other every day."

"Must I remain here eternally?" asked Milady with a certain fright.

"Might you find yourself poorly housed, sister? Ask for whatever you find wanting, and I will hasten to supply you with it."

"But I have neither my women nor my servants . . ."

"You shall have all that, Madame. Tell me on what footing your first husband set up your household; though I am only your brother-in-law, I will set it up on the same footing."

"My first husband?" cried Milady, looking at Lord de Winter with alarm in her eyes.

"Yes, your French husband; I'm not speaking of my brother. Moreover, if you've forgotten, I could write to him, since he's still alive, and he will send me all the particulars on the subject."

Cold sweat broke out on Milady's forehead.

"You're joking," she said in a hollow voice.

"Do I look it?" asked the baron, standing up and taking a step back.

"Or, rather, you are insulting me," she went on, gripping the arms of the chair with her clenched hands and raising herself on her wrists.

"I, insult you?" Lord de Winter said with contempt. "Truly, Madame, do you believe that's possible?"

"Truly, Monsieur," said Milady, "you are either drunk or insane. Get out, and send me a woman."

"Women are rather indiscreet, sister! May I not serve as your maid? In that way all our secrets will remain in the family."

"Insolent man!" cried Milady, and, as if moved by a spring, she leaped at the baron, who awaited her impassively, though with one hand on the hilt of his sword.

"Ah, yes!" he said, "I know you're in the habit of assassinating people, but I will defend myself, I warn you, even against you."

"Oh, you're right," said Milady, "and you do strike me as being cowardly enough to raise your hand against a woman."

"Perhaps so. Besides, I will have my excuse: I don't imagine that mine would be the first man's hand to be laid upon you."

And with a slow, accusatory gesture, the baron pointed to Milady's left shoulder, which he almost touched with his finger.

Milady let out a low roar and backed away almost into the corner of the room, like a panther at bay and preparing to spring.

"Oh, roar as much as you like!" cried Lord de Winter. "But don't try to bite, for, I warn you, it will turn to your disadvantage. There are no lawyers here to settle inheritances beforehand; there is no knight errant who will come to seek a quarrel with me over the fair lady I hold prisoner. But I have judges here who are ready to dispose of a woman shameless enough to slip bigamously between the sheets of Lord de Winter, my elder brother, and those judges, I warn you, will send you to an executioner who will make your two shoulders match."

Milady's eyes flashed such lightning that, though he was a man and armed facing an unarmed woman, he felt the chill of fear sink to the very bottom of his soul. Nevertheless, he went on, but with increasing fury:

"Yes, I understand, after having my brother's inheritance, it would have been nice for you to have mine. But, know beforehand, you can kill me or have me killed, but my precautions have been taken; not a penny of what I possess will come into your hands. Are you not already rich enough, you who have nearly a million, and can you not stop yourself on your fatal path, if you do not do evil simply for the infinite and supreme enjoyment of doing it? Oh, I tell you, if my brother's memory were not sacred to me, you would go to rot in some state prison or satisfy the curiosity of the sailors at Tyburn. I will keep silent; but you, bear your captivity calmly. In two or three weeks, I leave with the army for La Rochelle. But on the eve of my departure, a ship will come to take you, which I will see depart and which will bring you to our colonies in the South. And, rest assured, I will assign you a companion who will blow your brains out the first time you venture to return to England or the continent."

Milady listened with an attention that dilated her burning eyes.

"Yes, but for now," Lord de Winter continued, "you will remain in this castle. Its walls are thick, its doors are strong, its bars are solid; besides, your window opens on a sheer drop to the sea. The men of my crew, who are devoted to me in life and in death, will mount guard around this apartment, and keep watch on the passageways that lead to the courtyard. Then, once in the courtyard, you would still have three iron gates to get through. My orders are precise: one step, one gesture, one word that suggests escape, and they will open fire on you. If you are killed, English justice will, I hope, be somewhat obliged to me for having spared them the trouble. Ah, your features are recovering their calm, your face is resuming its assurance! Two or three weeks, you say—bah! I have an inventive mind, between now and then some idea will come to me; I have an infernal mind, and I will find some victim. Two weeks from now, you say to yourself, I will be out of here. Ah, just try it!"

Seeing herself found out, Milady dug her nails into her flesh to subdue any movement that might give her physiognomy some significance other than that of anguish.

Lord de Winter went on:

"The officer who has sole command here in my absence—you have seen him, so you are already acquainted with him—knows how to obey orders, as you see, for, knowing you, you did not come here from Portsmouth without trying to make him talk. What do you say? Could a marble statue be more impassive and mute? You have already tried your powers of seduction on many men, and unfortunately you have always succeeded; but try them on him, pardieu! If you get anywhere, I declare you are the devil himself!"

He went to the door and opened it suddenly.

"Send for Mr. Felton," he said. "Wait another moment, and I will recommend you to him."

A strange silence came over these two personages, during which the sound of slow and regular footsteps was heard aproaching. Soon, in the shadows of the corridor, a human form loomed up, and the young lieutenant whose acquaintance we have already made stopped on the threshold, awaiting the baron's orders.

"Come in, my dear John," said Lord de Winter, "come in and close the door."

The young officer came in.

"Now," said the baron, "look at this woman. She is young, she is beautiful, she has every earthly seduction—well! but she is a monster, who, at the age of twenty-five, has been guilty of as many crimes as you could read about for a year in the archives of our courts. Her voice is prepossessing, her beauty serves as bait for her victims, her body even pays what she has promised—we must do her that justice. She will try to seduce you; she may even try to kill you. I brought you out of poverty, Felton, I had you made lieutenant, I saved your life once, you know on which occasion; I am not only a protector for you, but a friend; not only a benefactor, but a father. This woman has come back to England in order to conspire against my life; I have this serpent in my hands. Well, so I have sent for you, and I say to you: Felton, my friend, John, my boy, protect me, and above all protect yourself, from this woman. Swear on your salvation to save her for the punishment she deserves. John Felton, I trust in your word; John Felton, I believe in your loyalty."

"Milord," said the young officer, filling his pure gaze with all the hatred he could find in his heart, "Milord, I swear to you that it will be as you wish."

Milady took this gaze like a resigned victim: it was impossible to see a more submissive and gentle expression than that which then reigned over her beautiful face. Lord de Winter himself could hardly recognize the tigress he had prepared himself to fight a moment before.

"She is never to leave this room, you understand, John," the baron continued, "she is to correspond with no one, she is to speak only with you, if you indeed wish to do her the honor of addressing her."

"Enough, Milord, I have sworn."

"And now, Madame, try to make your peace with God, for you have already been judged by men."

Milady hung her head, as if she felt herself crushed by this judgment. Lord de Winter went out, making a gesture to Felton, who followed him out and closed the door.

A moment later from the corridor came the heavy tread of a marine who was standing watch, his axe in his belt and his musket in his hand.

Milady remained in the same position for a few minutes, for she thought someone might be looking at her through the keyhole. Then she slowly raised her head, which had again taken on a formidable expression of menace and defiance, ran to listen at the door, looked out the window, and going back to bury herself in a vast armchair, fell to thinking.

LI

OFFICER

Meanwhile, the cardinal was awaiting news from England, but the only news that came was either irritating or menacing.

Well invested as La Rochelle was, certain as success might seem, thanks to the precautions taken and above all to the dike, which no longer allowed any ship to get to the besieged town, the blockade might nevertheless go on for a long time yet; and that was a great affront to the king's arms and a great annoyance for M. le cardinal, who, it is true, no longer had to set the king against Anne d'Autriche, for the thing was done, but to reconcile M. de Bassompierre, who had broken with the duc d'Angoulême.

As for Monsieur, who had begun the siege, he left to the cardinal the task of finishing it.

The town, despite the incredible perseverance of its mayor, had attempted a sort of mutiny in order to surrender. The mayor had had the rebels hanged. This execution calmed even the hottest heads, who then resolved to let themselves die of hunger. Such a death at least seemed slower and less certain than to die by strangulation.

On their side, the besiegers from time to time caught messengers that the Rochelois sent to Buckingham, or spies that Buckingham sent to the Rochelois. In both cases the trial was a quick affair. M. le cardinal spoke two simple words: "Hang him!" The king was invited to come and see the hanging. The king came languidly, sat in a good place for watching the operation in all its details: this always distracted him a little and made him less impatient with the siege, but it did not keep him from being terribly bored and from talking all the time about returning to Paris; so that if there had been a lack of messengers and spies, His Eminence, for all his imagination, would have found himself quite at a loss.

Nevertheless, time was passing, and the Rochelois did not surrender. The latest spy to be captured was carrying a letter.

This letter indeed told Buckingham that the town was at the last extremity; but, instead of adding: "If help does not come from you within two weeks, we will surrender," it added quite simply: "If help does not come from you within two weeks, we will all have starved to death before it comes."

The Rochelois thus had no hope except in Buckingham. Buckingham was their messiah. It was evident that if one day they learned for certain that they could no longer count on Buckingham, their courage would collapse along with their hopes.

The cardinal was thus waiting with great impatience for news from England announcing that Buckingham would not come.

The question of taking the town by force, often debated in the king's council, had always been set aside. First of all, La Rochelle seemed impregnable. Then, the cardinal, whatever he might say, knew very well that the horror of the blood spilt in this encounter, where Frenchman would have to fight against Frenchman, would be a retrogression of sixty years stamped upon his policy, and the cardinal was, for his time, what is today known as a man of progress. Indeed, the sack of La Rochelle, the slaughter of three or four thousand Huguenots who would get themselves killed, bore too close a resemblance, in 1628, to the Saint Bartholomew massacre of 1572. And then, beyond all that, this extreme method, which the king, as a good Catholic, found in no way repugnant, always ran aground on this argument of the besieging generals: La Rochelle is impregnable, except by starvation.

The cardinal could not rid his mind of the fear it was thrown into by his terrible emissary, for he, too, had understood the strange dimensions of this woman—now serpent, now lion. Had she betrayed him? Was she dead? He knew her well enough, in any case, to know that, acting for him or against him, enemy or friend, she would not sit still without great impediments. What they were he could not know.

All the same, he was counting on Milady, and with good reason. He had guessed that there were terrible things in this woman's past, which only her red cloak could conceal; and he felt that, for one reason or another, this woman was his, as it was only in him that she could find a support greater than the danger that threatened her.

He decided therefore to make war on his own, and to wait for any foreign success only as one waits for a lucky chance. He went on building the famous dike that was to starve La Rochelle. Meanwhile, he cast his eyes over the unfortunate town, which housed so much deep misery and so many heroic virtues, and, recalling the phrase of Louis XI, his political predecessor, as he himself was the predecessor of Robespierre, he murmured this maxim of Tristan's confederate: "Divide and rule."

Henri IV, besieging Paris, had bread and provisions thrown over the walls. The cardinal had leaflets thrown over in which he pointed out to the Rochelois how unjust, egotistical, and barbaric the conduct of their leaders was. Those leaders had wheat in abundance and did not share it. They adopted the maxim—for they, too, had maxims—that it mattered little if women, children, and old men died, provided the men who had to defend their walls remained strong and fit. Up to then, either from devotion or from powerlessness to react against it, this maxim, without being generally adopted, had nevertheless passed from theory into practice. But the leaflets did it harm. The leaflets reminded the men that those children, those women, those old men who were allowed to die were their sons, their wives, their fathers; that it would be more just if all were reduced to the common misery, so that the sameness of position would lead to making unanimous decisions.

These leaflets had all the effect that could have been looked for by the man who wrote them, in that they induced a great number of the inhabitants to open separate negotiations with the royal army.

But at the moment when the cardinal saw his method already bearing fruit and was applauding himself on having made use of it, an inhabitant of La Rochelle, who had managed to pass through the royal lines—God knows how, so great was the surveillance of Bassompierre, Schomberg, and the duc d'Angoulême, who were themselves under the cardinal's surveillance—an inhabitant of La Rochelle, we say, entered the town, coming from Portsmouth, and said he had seen a magnificent fleet ready to set sail within a week. What was more, Buckingham announced to the mayor that the great league against France was about to be declared, and that the kingdom would be invaded at the same time by the armies of England, the Empire, and Spain. This letter was read publicly on all the squares, copies of it were put up on street corners, and the very same people who had begun to open negotiations broke them off, resolved to wait for the help so majestically announced.

This unexpected occurrence brought back to Richelieu all his original anxieties, and forced him, despite himself, to turn his eyes once again across the sea.

During this time, exempt from the anxieties of its one real chief, the royal army led a merry life. There was no lack of provisions in the camp, or of money either. The corps all rivaled each other in daring and gaiety. Catching spies and hanging them, making hazardous expeditions over the dike or the sea, thinking up mad deeds and coolly bringing them off— such were the pastimes which shortened for the army those days that were so long not only for the Rochelois, gnawed by hunger and anxiety, but also for the cardinal, who blockaded them so vigorously.

Sometimes, when the cardinal, always riding about like the least soldier of the army, ran his thoughtful gaze over these works being built under his command, though much more slowly than he would have liked, by engineers he had brought from all corners of the realm of France, if he met with a musketeer of Tréville's company, he would approach him, look at him in a singular fashion, and, recognizing that he was not one of our four companions, turn his profound gaze and his vast thought elsewhere.

One day when, gnawed by deadly vexation, with no hope of negotiations with the town, with no news from England, the cardinal went out with the sole purpose of going out, accompanied only by Cahusac and La Houdinière, riding along the shore and mingling the immensity of his dreams with the immensity of the ocean, he came, at his horse's easy pace, to the top of a hill, from which he made out seven men reclining on the sand behind a hedge, surrounded by empty bottles, and catching in passage one of those rays of sunlight so rare at that time of year. Four of these men were our musketeers, preparing to listen to the reading of a letter that one of them had just received. This letter was so important that it had left cards and dice abandoned on a drumhead.

The three others were busy uncorking an enormous demijohn of Collioure wine. These were the gentlemen's lackeys.

The cardinal, as we have said, was in a sullen mood, and when he was in that state of mind, nothing increased his grumpiness so much as the gaiety of others. Besides, he had a strange preoccupation, which was to believe that the very causes of his sadness aroused the gaiety of strangers. Making a sign for La Houdinière and Cahusac to stop, he got off his horse and approached these suspicious laughers, hoping that with the aid of the sand, which muffled his footsteps, and of the hedge, which screened his movement, he might overhear a few words of this conversation that he found so interesting. At just ten paces from the hedge, he recognized the Gascon chatter of d'Artagnan, and as he already knew that these men were musketeers, he had no doubt that the three others were the so-called inseparables, that is, Athos, Porthos, and Aramis.

One can imagine how this discovery increased his desire to overhear the conversation. His eyes acquired a strange expression, and with catlike steps he went up to the hedge; but he had managed to catch only a few vague syllables of no definite import, when a brief and ringing cry startled him and drew the attention of the musketeers.

"Officer!" cried Grimaud.

"You spoke, I believe, you rascal," said Athos, propping himself on his elbow and fixing Grimaud with his fiery gaze.

And so Grimaud did not add another word, contenting himself with pointing his finger in the direction of the hedge and by this gesture giving away the cardinal and his escort.

With a single leap, the four musketeers got to their feet and bowed respectfully.

The cardinal looked furious.

"It seems one posts guards among the gentlemen musketeers!" he said. "Is it that the English are coming by land, or might it be that the musketeers regard themselves as superior officers?"

"Monseigneur," replied Athos, for in the midst of the general fright he alone had kept that lordly calm and coolheadedness which never left him. "Monseigneur, the musketeers, when they are not on duty, or their duty is over, drink and throw dice, and for their lackeys they are very superior officers."

"Lackeys?" growled the cardinal. "Lackeys who are under orders to warn their masters when someone passes by are not lackeys, they are sentries."

"His Eminence sees very well, however, that if we had not taken this precaution, we would have exposed ourselves to letting him pass by without paying our respects to him and offering him our thanks for the favor he has done us in uniting us. D'Artagnan," Athos continued, "you were just asking for this chance to express your gratitude to Monseigneur—here it is, take advantage of it."

These words were uttered with that imperturbable phlegm which distinguished Athos in times of danger, and that extreme politeness which made of him at certain moments a king more majestic than those who are born kings.

D'Artagnan approached and stammered a few words of thanks, which soon expired under the cardinal's grim gaze.

"Never mind, gentlemen," the cardinal continued, not seeming deflected in the least from his original intention by the point Athos had just raised, "never mind, gentlemen, I don't like it when simple soldiers, because they have the advantage of serving in a privileged corps, make great lords of themselves like this. Discipline is the same for everybody."

Athos allowed the cardinal to round off his phrase and, bowing in a sign of assent, went on in his turn:

"I hope, Monseigneur, that we have in no way neglected discipline. We are not on duty, and we thought that, not being on duty, we could dispose of our time as we saw fit. If we are so fortunate that His Eminence has some special order to give us, we are ready to obey him. Monseigneur can see," Athos went on, frowning, for this sort of interrogation was beginning to irritate him, "that, in order to be ready for the least alarm, we have brought our weapons with us."

And he pointed out to the cardinal the four muskets stacked together near the drum on which the cards and dice lay.

"Your Eminence may believe," added d'Artagnan, "that we would have gone to meet him, if we had been able to suppose that it was he who was coming towards us in so small a company."

The cardinal chewed his mustaches and even bit his lips slightly.

"Do you know what you look like, always together, as you are now, armed as you are, and guarded by your lackeys?" said the cardinal. "You look like four conspirators."

"Oh, as for that, Monseigneur, it's true," said Athos, "we are in conspiracy, as Your Eminence was able to see the other morning, only it is against the Rochelois."

"Eh, gentlemen politicians!" the cardinal picked up, frowning in his turn. "One might find the secret of many an unknown thing in your brains, if one could read them as you were reading that letter you hid when you saw me coming."

The color rose to Athos's face. He took a step towards His Eminence.

"One would think that you really suspect us, Monseigneur, and that we are undergoing a genuine interrogation. If that is so, let Your Eminence deign to explain himself, and we will at least know what we have to deal with."

"And if it comes to interrogation," replied the cardinal, "others than you have undergone it, M. Athos, and have known how to answer."

"And so, Monseigneur, I have said to Your Eminence that he has only to ask, and we are ready to answer."

"What was that letter you were about to read, M. Aramis, and that you have hidden?"

"A woman's letter, Monseigneur."

"Oh, I conceive you!" said the cardinal. "One must be discreet with those sorts of letters; and yet one can show them to a confessor, and, you know, I have received holy orders."

"Monseigneur," said Athos, with a calm all the more terrible in that he was risking his head in making this reply, "the letter is from a woman, but it is signed neither Marion de Lorme nor Mme d'Aiguillon."

The cardinal turned as pale as death, a wild gleam came from his eyes; he turned as if to give an order to Cahusac and La Houdinière. Athos saw the movement. He took a step towards the muskets, on which the three friends had their eyes fixed like men ill disposed to let themselves be arrested. There were three in the cardinal's party; the musketeers, including their lackeys, were seven. The cardinal judged that the game would be that much less equal if Athos and his friends really were conspirators; and by one of those quick turnabouts that he always kept at his disposal, all his anger melted into a smile.

"Come, come!" he said. "You are brave young men, proud in the sunlight, faithful in the darkness. There's no harm in keeping a watch on oneself, when one watches so well over others. Gentlemen, I have not forgotten the night when you served as my escort on the way to the Red Dovecote. If there were any danger to be feared on the road I am about to take, I would beg you to accompany me. But as there is not, stay where you are, finish your bottles, your game, and your letter. Good-bye, gentlemen."

And, getting back on his horse, which Cahusac had brought for him, he saluted them with his hand and rode off.

The four young men, standing motionless, followed him with their eyes without saying a word until he disappeared.

Then they looked at each other.

They all had dismayed faces, for, despite His Eminence's friendly good-bye, they understood that the cardinal went away with rage in his heart.

Athos alone smiled a strong and scornful smile. When the cardinal was out of hearing and out of sight, Porthos, who had a great desire to unload his bad humor on someone, said:

"Grimaud here cried out rather late!"

Grimaud was about to excuse himself in reply. Athos raised a finger, and he kept silent.

"Would you have surrendered the letter, Aramis?" asked d'Artagnan.

"I?" said Aramis, in his most flutelike voice. "I had made up my mind: if he had demanded that the letter be given to him, I would have handed it to him with one hand, and with the other I would have run him through with my sword."

"I anticipated just that," said Athos, "which is why I threw myself between the two of you. In truth, the man is rather imprudent to speak to other men like that. You'd think he only ever had to do with women and children."

"My dear Athos," said d'Artagnan, "I admire you, but all the same we were in the wrong, after all."

"How, in the wrong!" replied Athos. "Whose, then, is this air we breathe? Whose is this ocean we look out across? Whose is this sand we were lying on? Whose is this letter from your mistress? Are they all the cardinal's? On my honor, this man fancies that the world belongs to him. You were there stammering, stupefied, stunned; one would have thought the Bastille had risen up before you, and the gigantic Medusa had turned you to stone. Come, is it a conspiracy to be in love? You're in love with a woman whom the cardinal has had locked up. You want to get her out of the cardinal's clutches. That's the game you're playing with His Eminence. This letter is your hand. Why would you show your hand to your opponent? It's not done. If he guesses it, fine! We shall certainly guess his!"

"In fact," said d'Artagnan, "what you say makes great sense, Athos."

"In that case, let there be no more question of what just happened, and let Aramis take up his cousin's letter again where M. le cardinal interrupted it."

Aramis took the letter from his pocket, the three friends moved close to him, and the three lackeys once more gathered around the demijohn.

"You had only read a line or two," said d'Artagnan, "so start again from the beginning."

"Gladly," said Aramis.

Dear Cousin,

I believe I shall indeed make up my mind to leave for Stenay, where my sister has put our little servant into a Carmelite convent. The poor child is resigned to it. She knows she cannot live anywhere else without endangering the salvation of her soul. However, if our family affairs get settled as we wish, I believe she will run the risk of damning herself, and will return to those she misses, the more so as she knows that they still think of her. In the meantime, she is not too unhappy. All she desires is a letter from her intended. I know very well that these sorts of commodities are hard to get past the gates; but, after all, as I have proven to you, my dear cousin, I am not too maladroit, and I will take this commission upon myself. My sister thanks you for your kind and eternal remembrance. She had a moment of great concern; but now she is finally somewhat reassured, having sent her agent there so that nothing unforeseen would happen.

Good-bye, my dear cousin, give us your news as often as you can, that is, whenever you think it safe to do so. I embrace you.

Marie Michon

"Oh, what do I not owe you, Aramis?" cried d'Artagnan. "Dear Constance! So I finally have news of her—she's alive, she's safe in a convent, she's in Stenay! Where do you place Stenay, Athos?"

"Why, a few leagues from the border. Once the siege is raised, we can go for a turn out there."

"And that won't be long, it's to be hoped," said Porthos, "for this morning they hanged a spy who declared that the Rochelois were down to their shoe tops. Supposing they eat the soles after eating the tops, I don't see what they'll have left then, unless they start eating each other."

"Poor fools!" said Athos, emptying a glass of excellent Bordeaux, which, though at the time it did not have the reputation it has now, deserved it no less, "poor fools! As if the Catholic religion wasn't the most advantageous and agreeable of religions! All the same," he went on, after smacking his tongue against his palate, "they're brave folk. But what the devil are you doing, Aramis?" Athos went on. "Are you putting that letter in your pocket?"

"Yes," said d'Artagnan, "Athos is right, we must burn it—though who knows if M. le cardinal doesn't have a secret for interrogating ashes?"

"He must have one," said Athos.

"Then what are you going to do with that letter?" asked Porthos.

"Come here, Grimaud," said Athos.

Grimaud stood up and obeyed.

"As punishment for having spoken without permission, my friend, you are going to eat this piece of paper. Then, to reward you for the service rendered, you will drink this glass of wine. Here's the letter first: chew energetically."

Grimaud smiled, and, his eyes fixed on the glass that Athos had just filled to the brim, tore up the paper and swallowed it.

"Bravo, Master Grimaud!" said Athos. "And now, take this. Good, I exempt you from saying thank you."

Grimaud silently swallowed the glass of Bordeaux, but all the while this sweet occupation lasted, his eyes lifted to heaven spoke a language which, though mute, was no less expressive for that.

"And now," said Athos, "unless M. le cardinal has the ingenious idea of having Grimaud's stomach opened, I believe we can be nearly at peace."

During this time, His Eminence continued on his melancholy promenade, muttering between his mustaches:

"Decidedly, those four men must be mine."

LII

FIRST DAY OF CAPTIVITY

Let us go back to Milady, whom a glance at the shores of France has made us lose sight of for a moment.

We shall find her in the same desperate position in which we left her, opening up an abyss of gloomy reflections, a gloomy hell at the gateway to which she has almost abandoned hope: because for the first time she doubts, for the first time she fears.

On two occasions her luck had failed her, on two occasions she had been discovered and betrayed, and, on those two occasions, it was against the fatal genius no doubt sent by the Lord to combat her that she had run aground: d'Artagnan had vanquished her—her, the invincible force of evil.

He had deceived her in her love, humiliated her in her pride, foiled her in her ambition, and now here he was ruining her fortunes, striking at her freedom, even threatening her life. Much more than that, he had lifted a corner of her mask, that aegis with which she shielded herself and which made her so strong.

D'Artagnan had diverted from Buckingham, whom she hated, as she hated all that she had once loved, the storm with which Richelieu threatened him in the person of the queen. D'Artagnan had passed himself off as de Wardes, for whom she had conceived one of those uncontrollable tigress fancies that women of her character have. D'Artagnan knew the terrible secret that she had sworn no one would know and live. Finally, at the very moment when she had obtained a blank permit with the help of which she was going to take revenge on her enemy, the blank permit was snatched away from her, and it is d'Artagnan who holds her prisoner and is going to send her to some foul Botany Bay, to some filthy Tyburn of the Indian Ocean.

For all this undoubtedly comes to her from d'Artagnan. From whom could all these disgraces heaped on her head come, if not from him? He alone could have handed on all those frightful secrets to Lord de Winter, who had revealed them one after another with a sort of fatality. He knew her brother-in-law; he must have written to him.

What hatred she exudes! There, immobile in her empty apartment, her eyes burning and fixed, how well the dull roars that sometimes escape from the depths of her breast as she breathes accompany the noise of the swell rising, rumbling, groaning, and coming to break, like some eternal and impotent despair, on the rocks over which this proud and gloomy castle is built! How well, by the glimmer of the lightning that her stormy wrath sends flashing through her mind, she conceives magnificent plans of revenge against Mme Bonacieux, against Buckingham, and above all against d'Artagnan, lost in the depths of the future!

Yes, but to be revenged, one must be free, and to be free, when one is a prisoner, one must break through a wall, loosen bars, make a hole in the floor—all undertakings that a patient and strong man might carry through, but before which the feverish irritations of a woman must fail. Besides, to do all that one must have time, months, years, while she . . . she had ten or twelve days, according to Lord de Winter, her brotherly and terrible jailer.

And yet, had she been a man, she would have attempted all that, and would perhaps have succeeded. Why, then, had heaven made the mistake of placing this virile soul in this frail and delicate body!

And so, the first moments of captivity were terrible: several convulsions of rage, which she had been unable to master, had paid her debt of feminine weakness to nature. But she gradually overcame the outbursts of her wild anger, the nervous tremblings that shook her body disappeared, and now she was coiled up on herself like a weary serpent resting.

"Come, come, I was mad to get carried away like that," she said, plunging into the mirror that reflected the burning look with which she seemed to question herself. "No violence, violence is a proof of weakness. First of all, I have never succeeded that way. Maybe if I used my strength against women, I might chance to find them still weaker than I, and so might defeat them; but I am fighting against men, and for them I am merely a woman. Let us fight as a woman. My strength is in my weakness."

Then, as if to realize for herself the changes she could impose upon her expressive and mobile physiognomy, she made it take on all its various expressions, from anger, which distorted her features, to the sweetest, most affectionate, and most seductive smile. Then her hair, under her knowing hands, took on successively the waves she believed would contribute to the charms of her face. Finally, she murmured in self-satisfaction:

"Well, so nothing is lost. I'm still beautiful."

It was about eight o'clock in the evening. Milady noticed a bed; she thought a few hours of rest would refresh not only her head and her ideas, but also her complexion. However, before she lay down, a better idea occurred to her. She had heard mention of supper. She had already been in that room for an hour; it could not be long before they brought her meal. The prisoner did not want to waste time, and she decided that, from that very evening, she would make some attempt to test the terrain, by studying the character of the people to whose keeping she had been entrusted.

Light appeared under the door. This light announced the return of her jailers. Milady, who was standing up, quickly flung herself down in her armchair, her head thrown back, her beautiful hair loose and disheveled, her breast half bared under its rumpled lace, one hand on her heart and the other hanging down.

The bolts were slid back, the door creaked on his hinges, there was a sound of approaching footsteps in the room.

"Put it on that table," said a voice that the prisoner recognized as Felton's.

The order was carried out.

"Bring torches and relieve the sentries," Felton continued.

This double order that the young lieutenant gave to the same individuals proved to Milady that her servants were the same men as her guards, that is to say, soldiers.

Moreover, Felton's orders were carried out with a promptness that gave a good idea of the flourishing state in which he maintained discipline.

Finally, Felton, who had not yet looked at Milady, turned towards her.

"Aha!" he said, "she's asleep. That's good. When she wakes up, she'll have supper."

And he started out of the room.

"But, lieutenant," said a soldier who was less stoical than his leader, and who had gone up to Milady, "this woman is not asleep."

"What do you mean, not asleep?" said Felton. "What is she doing, then?"

"She has fainted. Her face is very pale, and, hard as I listened, I couldn't hear her breathing."

"You're right," said Felton, after looking at Milady from where he was, without taking a step towards her. "Go and inform Lord de Winter that his prisoner has fainted, for I don't know what to do, the case was not foreseen."

The soldier went to obey his officer's orders. Felton sat in an armchair that happened to be near the door and waited without saying a word, without making a move. Milady possessed that great art, so well studied by women, of seeing through her long eyelashes without appearing to open her eyes. She made out Felton, who had turned his back to her. She went on looking at him for about ten minutes, and during those ten minutes, the impassive guard never once turned around.

She then reflected that Lord de Winter was going to come and, by his presence, put new strength into her jailer. Her first experiment had failed; she took it as a woman who counts on her own resources. As a result, she raised her head, opened her eyes, and sighed weakly.

At this sigh, Felton finally turned around.

"Ah, so you're awake, Madame!" he said. "Then I have nothing more to do here. If you need anything, you can call."

"Oh, my God, my God, how I've suffered!" murmured Milady, with that harmonious voice which, like the voice of ancient enchantresses, charmed all those she wished to destroy.

And, on sitting up in her armchair, she assumed a more graceful and still more abandoned position than when she was lying back.

Felton stood up.

"You will be served like this three times a day, Madame," he said. "At nine o'clock in the morning, at one o'clock in the afternoon, and at eight o'clock in the evening. If that does not suit you, you may indicate your own hours in place of those I have proposed to you, and on this point your desires will be followed."

"But am I then to remain forever alone in this big, sad room?" asked Milady.

"A woman from the neighborhood has been informed, she will come to the castle tomorrow, and will return anytime you desire her presence."

"I thank you, Monsieur," the prisoner replied humbly.

Felton made a slight bow and headed for the door. Just as he was about to cross the threshold, Lord de Winter appeared in the corridor, followed by the soldier who had gone to bring him the news of Milady's fainting. He was holding a vial of smelling salts.

"Well, what's this? What's going on here?" he asked in a mocking voice, on seeing his prisoner standing and Felton about to leave. "So the dead woman has resurrected? Pardieu, Felton, my boy, don't you see that you are being taken for a novice, and the first act of a comedy is being played for you, of which we will no doubt have the pleasure of following all the developments?"

"That is just what I thought, Milord," said Felton. "But, finally, as the prisoner is a woman, after all, I wanted to show all the consideration that any well-born man owes to a woman, if not for her sake, then at least for his own."

Milady shivered all over. These words of Felton's went like ice through all her veins.

"And so," de Winter picked up, laughing, "that beautiful hair artfully displayed, that white skin, and that languorous look haven't seduced you yet, you heart of stone?"

"No, Milord," replied the impassive young man, "and believe me, it will take more than a woman's wiles and advances to corrupt me."

"In that case, my brave lieutenant, let us leave Milady to think up something else and go to supper. Ah, don't worry, she has a fertile imagination, and the second act of the comedy won't be slow in coming!"

And with these words Lord de Winter put his arm under Felton's and led him off, laughing.

"Oh, I'll surely find what will work on you," Milady murmured between her teeth, "don't worry, poor would-be monk, poor converted soldier, who have had your uniform cut from a cassock."

"By the way," de Winter went on, stopping in the doorway, "don't let this failure take away your appetite. Try the chicken and the fish—on my honor, I haven't had them poisoned. I get on well with my cook, and as he doesn't stand to inherit anything from me, I have full and complete confidence in him. Do as I do. Good-bye, dear sister, until you faint again!"

This was as much as Milady could bear: her hands clenched the chair, her teeth ground secretly, her eyes followed the movement of the door that closed behind Lord de Winter and Felton; and when she saw herself alone, a new crisis of despair came over her. She glanced at the table, saw the gleam of a knife, rushed and seized it; but she was cruelly disappointed: the blade was blunt and of flexible silver.

A burst of laughter rang out behind the half-closed door, and the door opened again.

"Ha, ha!" cried Lord de Winter. "Ha, ha, ha! You see, my brave Felton, you see what I told you? That knife was intended for you, my boy! You see, it's one of her eccentricities to rid herself like this, one way or another, of people who get in her way. If I had listened to you, the knife would have been pointed and of steel: then no more Felton. She'd have cut your throat and, after that, everybody else's. Just look, John, how well she knows how to hold her knife."

Indeed, Milady was still holding the offensive weapon in her clenched fist, but these last words, this supreme insult, slackened her grip, her strength, and even her will.

The knife fell to the floor.

"You're right, Milord," said Felton, with an accent of profound disgust that echoed to the very bottom of Milady's heart, "you're right, and I was wrong."

And the two left again.

But this time, Milady lent a more attentive ear than the first time, and she heard their footsteps going away and dying out at the end of the corridor.

"I'm lost," she murmured. "Here I am in the power of people on whom I have no more hold than on statues of bronze or granite. They know me by heart and are armored against all my weapons. Yet it's impossible that this business will end the way they've decided."

Indeed, as this last reflection, this instinctive return to hope, indicated, fear and weak sentiments did not float for long on the surface of this deep soul. Milady sat at the table, ate several dishes, drank a bit of Spanish wine, and felt all her determination come back.

Before going to bed, she had already commented upon, analyzed, turned over on all sides, examined from every angle the words, steps, gestures, signs, and even the silence of her jailers, and from this profound, skillful, and learned study it resulted that Felton was, all things considered, the more vulnerable of her two persecutors.

One phrase, above all, came back to the prisoner's mind:

"If I had listened to you," Lord de Winter had said to Felton.

So Felton had spoken in her favor, since Lord de Winter had refused to listen to him.

"Weak or strong, then," repeated Milady, "this man has a glimmer of pity in his soul. Of that glimmer I will make a fire that will devour him. As for the other one, he knows me, he fears me, and he knows what to expect of me if I ever escape from his hands. It's therefore useless to try anything on him. But Felton is something else. He's a naive, pure, and seemingly virtuous young man; him there are ways to destroy."

And Milady lay down and slept with a smile on her lips. Someone seeing her asleep would have thought her a young girl dreaming of the garland of flowers she was to put round her forehead on the next feast day.

LIII

SECOND DAY OF CAPTIVITY

Milady was dreaming that she finally got her hands on d'Artagnan, that she was witnessing his execution, and it was the sight of his odious blood streaming from under the headsman's axe that traced that charming smile on her lips.

She slept like a prisoner lulled by his first hope.

When they came into her room the next day, she was still in bed. Felton was in the corridor. He brought the woman he had mentioned the evening before, who had just arrived. This woman came in and went to Milady's bed, offering her services.

Milady was habitually pale. Her color could thus fool someone who was seeing her for the first time.

"I have a fever," she said. "I didn't sleep a single moment all this long night. I am suffering horribly. Will you be more humane than they were with me yesterday? All I ask, besides, is permission to remain in bed."

"Do you want them to call a doctor?" asked the woman.

Felton listened to this dialogue without saying a word.

Milady reflected that the more people there were around her, the more people she would have to move to pity, and the more Lord de Winter would increase his surveillance. Besides, the doctor might declare that the illness was feigned, and Milady, having lost the first hand, did not want to lose the second.

"Why go looking for a doctor?" she asked. "These gentlemen declared yesterday that my illness was a comedy. It will no doubt be the same today, for since yesterday evening they've had enough time to inform the doctor."

"In that case," said Felton, losing patience, "say yourself, Madame, what treatment you would like to follow."

"Ah, how do I know? My God! I feel I'm suffering, that's all. They can give me whatever they like, it matters little to me."

"Send for Lord de Winter," said Felton, weary of these eternal complaints.

"Oh, no, no!" cried Milady. "No, Monsieur, don't call him, I entreat you, I'm well, I don't need anything, don't call him!"

She put such a prodigious vehemence, such a stirring eloquence into this exclamation, that Felton, stirred, came a few steps into the room.

"He's moved," thought Milady.

"However, Madame," said Felton, "if you are *really* suffering, we will send for a doctor, but if you are deceiving us, well, then it will be too bad for you, but at least on our side we will have nothing to reproach ourselves for."

Milady made no response, but, throwing her head back on the pillow, dissolved in tears and burst into sobs.

Felton looked at her for a moment with his usual impassivity; then, seeing that the crisis threatened to be prolonged, he left. The woman followed him out. Lord de Winter did not appear.

"I think I'm beginning to see my way," Milady murmured with a savage joy, burying herself under the covers to hide this fit of inner satisfaction from anyone who might be watching.

Two hours went by.

"Now it's time the illness ended," she said. "Let's get up and achieve some success starting today. I only have ten days, and as of tonight two will have gone by."

On coming into Milady's room that morning, they had brought her breakfast. So she thought that it would not be long before they came to clear the table, and that she would then see Felton again.

Milady was not mistaken. Felton reappeared, and, without paying attention to whether Milady had touched her meal or not, made a sign for the table, which was usually brought already set, to be taken out of the room.

Felton was the last to leave. He was holding a book in his hand.

Milady, reclining in an armchair near the fireplace, beautiful, pale, and resigned, looked like a holy virgin awaiting martyrdom.

Felton went over to her and said:

"Lord de Winter, who is a Catholic like you, Madame, thought that being deprived of the rites and ceremonies of your religion might be painful for you. He consents, therefore, to let you read the order of *your mass* each day, and here is a book containing the ritual."

The air with which Felton placed this book on the little table beside Milady, the tone with which he pronounced the words "your mass," the scornful smile with which he accom-

panied them, made Milady raise her head and look at the officer more attentively.

Then, by the severe cut of his hair, the exaggerated simplicity of his dress, his forehead polished like marble, but also
of a marblelike hardness and impenetrability, she recognized
him as one of those gloomy Puritans that she had so often met
in the court of King James as well as of the king of France,
where, despite the memory of Saint Bartholomew, they sometimes came seeking refuge.

She then had one of those sudden inspirations such as only
people of genius receive in great crises, in those supreme moments which are to decide their fortune or their life.

Those two words, "your mass," and a simple glance at
Felton, had indeed revealed to her all the importance of the reply she was about to make.

But with that quickness of intelligence which was peculiar
to her, the fully formulated reply came to her lips:

"Mine?" she said, with an accent of scorn brought into
unison with that which she had noticed in the young officer's
voice. "*My mass,* Monsieur? Lord de Winter, that depraved
Catholic, knows very well that I am not of his religion, and
this is a trap he means to set for me!"

"And of what religion are you then, Madame?" asked
Felton, with an astonishment which, in spite of his self-control,
he could not conceal entirely.

"I will say," cried Milady, with feigned exaltation, "on the
day when I have suffered enough for my faith."

Felton's look revealed to Milady the whole extent of the
space she had just opened up by this one phrase.

However, the young officer remained mute and immobile;
his look alone had spoken.

"I am in the hands of my enemies," she went on, with that
tone of enthusiasm she knew was habitual to Puritans. "Well,
then, let my God save me, or let me perish for my God! That
is the reply I ask you to give to Lord de Winter. And as for this
book," she added, pointing to the missal with the tip of her finger, but without touching it, as if she would have been soiled
by that contact, "you may bring it back to him and make use

of it yourselves, for no doubt you are the accomplice of Lord de Winter twice over—an accomplice in his persecution, and an accomplice in his heresy."

Felton made no reply, took the book with the same feeling of repugnance he had already shown, and pensively withdrew. Lord de Winter came at around five o'clock in the evening. Milady had had time during that whole day to draw up a plan of conduct. She received him as a woman who has already re-covered all her advantages.

"It seems," said the baron, sitting down in an armchair facing the one occupied by Milady, and casually stretching his feet out towards the fire, "it seems we've made a little apostasy."

"What do you mean, Monsieur?"

"I mean that, since the last time we saw each other, we have changed religion. Might you have married a third husband—a Protestant, by chance?"

"Explain yourself, Milord," the prisoner replied with majesty, "for I declare to you that I hear your words but do not understand them."

"Or else it's that you have no religion at all. I like that better," Lord de Winter said with a snicker.

"It certainly accords better with your principles," Milady replied coldly.

"Oh, I confess to you that it's all quite the same to me!"

"Oh, you may as well confess to this religious indifference, Milord, since your debauches and crimes bear it out!"

"Eh? You speak of debauches, Mme Messalina, you speak of crimes, Lady Macbeth? Either I heard wrongly, or, pardieu, you are quite impudent."

"You speak that way because you know we are being over-heard, Monsieur," Milady answered coldly, "and you want to turn your jailers and hangmen against me."

"My jailers? My hangmen? Oh, yes, Madame, you are adopting a poetic tone, and yesterday's comedy is turning into a tragedy this evening. However, in eight days you will be where you belong, and my task will be finished."

"An infamous task! An impious task!" Milady replied, with the exaltation of the victim provoking the judge.

"On my word of honor," de Winter said, getting up, "I believe the wench is going mad. Come, come, calm yourself, Mme Puritan, or I'll put you in the dungeon. Pardieu! it's my Spanish wine going to your head, isn't it? But don't worry, that sort of drunkenness isn't dangerous and will not have any consequences."

And Lord de Winter went off cursing, which at that time was a perfectly gentlemanly habit.

Milady had guessed right.

"Yes, go! go!" she said to her brother. "The consequences are coming, on the contrary, but you won't see them, imbecile, until it's too late to avoid them."

Silence ensued; two hours went by. Supper was brought, and Milady was found occupied with saying her prayers aloud, prayers she had learned from an old servant of her second husband's, a most austere Puritan. She seemed in ecstasy and appeared to pay no attention to what went on around her. Felton made a sign for her not to be disturbed, and when everything was in order, he left noiselessly with the soldiers.

Milady knew she might be spied on, so she continued her prayers to the end, and it seemed to her that the soldier who was on sentry duty at her door was no longer pacing in the same way and seemed to be listening.

For the moment, she wanted nothing more. She got up, went to the table, ate little, and drank only water.

An hour later they came to remove the table, but Milady noticed that this time Felton did not accompany his soldiers.

He was afraid, then, of seeing her too often.

She turned to the wall in order to smile, for there was in this smile such an expression of triumph that the smile alone would have given her away.

She let another half hour go by, and as at that moment all was silence in the old castle, as one heard only the eternal murmur of the swell, that immense breathing of the ocean, in her pure, harmonious, and vibrant voice she began the first verse of a psalm that was then in great favor among the Puritans:

> If Thou abandon us, O Lord,
> It is to see if we can stand,
> But after that Thou dost award
> The palm to us with Thine own heavenly hand.

These verses were not excellent, even far from it; but, as we know, the Protestants did not pride themselves on poetry.

While she sang, Milady listened. The soldier on guard at her door stopped as if turned to stone. Milady could thus judge the effect she made.

Then she continued her singing with an inexpressible fervor and feeling. It seemed to her that the sounds spread far away under the vaults and went like a magic charm to soften the hearts of her jailers. However, it seemed that the soldier on sentry duty, no doubt a zealous Catholic, shook off the charm, for he said through the door:

"Be quiet now, Madame, your song is as sad as a 'De Profundis,' and if, in addition to the delights of being garrisoned here, one must also listen to such things, it will be unbearable."

"Silence!" said a grave voice, which Milady recognized as Felton's. "What are you interfering for, you rascal? Were you ordered to stop this woman from singing? No. You were told to guard her, and to shoot her if she tries to escape. Guard her, then; and if she escapes, kill her; but do not change anything in the orders."

An expression of unutterable joy lit up Milady's face, but this expression was as fleeting as a flash of lightning, and without seeming to have heard the dialogue, of which she had not missed a single word, she went on, giving her voice all the charm, all the range, and all the seduction the devil had put into it:

> For all my tears and misery,
> For my harsh exile and my chains,
> Youth and prayer are left to me,
> And God, who will make up for all my pains.

This voice, of an unheard-of range and a sublime passion, gave to the crude and uncultivated poetry of these psalms a magic and an expression that the most exalted Puritans rarely found in the songs of their brethren, which they were forced to adorn with all the resources of their imagination. Felton thought he was listening to the singing of the angel who consoled the three Hebrew children in the fiery furnace.

Milady went on:

> But one day we shall be set free,
> For God, our God, is strong and just;
> And if that hope is not to be,
> Death and the martyr's crown still stay for us.

This verse, in which the terrible enchantress tried to put all her soul, ended by bringing disorder to the young officer's heart. He abruptly opened the door, and Milady saw him appear, pale as ever, but with burning and almost wild eyes.

"Why do you sing like that," he said, "and with such a voice?"

"Forgive me, Monsieur," Milady said gently, "I forgot that my songs are not suited to this house. I have undoubtedly offended you in your beliefs, but it was without meaning to, I swear to you. Forgive me, then, for a fault which is great, perhaps, but was certainly unintentional."

Milady was so beautiful at that moment, the religious ecstasy in which she seemed plunged gave such expression to her physiognomy, that Felton, dazzled, believed he was now beholding the angel whom he had only heard before.

"Yes, yes," he replied, "yes, you are troubling, you are disturbing the people who live in this castle."

And the poor madman did not himself perceive the incoherence of his speech, while Milady plunged her lynx eye into the depths of his heart.

"I shall stop singing," said Milady, lowering her eyes, with all the sweetness she could give to her voice, with all the resignation she could impart to her bearing.

"No, no, Madame," said Felton, "only do not sing so loudly, especially at night."

And with these words, Felton, feeling that he could not long maintain his severity towards the prisoner, rushed out of her apartment.

"You did very well, lieutenant," said the soldier. "Those songs upset the soul, yet you end by getting used to them: she has such a beautiful voice!"

LIV

Third Day of Captivity

Felton had come, but there was one more step to be taken: he had to be kept, or rather, he had to stay on his own. And Milady could as yet only dimly discern the means that would lead her to that result.

There had to be still more: he had to be made to speak, so that he could also be spoken to; for Milady knew very well that her greatest seductiveness was in her voice, which ran so skillfully through the whole gamut of tones, from human speech to the language of heaven.

And yet, despite all that seductiveness, Milady might fail, for Felton had been forewarned, and that against the slightest risk. Henceforth, she kept watch over her every action, her every word, down to the simplest look in her eyes, the merest gesture, even her very breathing, which might be interpreted as a sigh. Finally, she studied everything, as a skillful actor does when he has just been given a new role in a line he was not used to taking.

With regard to Lord de Winter, her conduct was easier, and so she had settled on it since the previous evening. To remain silent and dignified in his presence, to irritate him from time to time by an affected disdain, by a contemptuous word, to push him to threats and violence that would contrast with her own resignation—such was her plan. Felton would see: he might not say anything, but he would see.

In the morning, Felton came as usual, but Milady allowed him to preside over all the breakfast preparations without saying a word to him. Then, just as he was about to withdraw, she had a glimmer of hope, for she thought it was he who was about to speak. But his lips moved without any sound coming from his mouth, and, struggling with himself, he locked up in his heart the words that were about to escape his lips, and left.

Towards noon, Lord de Winter came in.

It was a rather fine winter day, and a ray of that pale English sun, which gives light but no warmth, came through the bars of the prison.

Milady was looking out the window, and made as if she did not hear the door opening.

"Aha!" said Lord de Winter, "having done comedy, having done tragedy, now we're doing melancholy."

The prisoner did not respond.

"Yes, yes," Lord de Winter went on, "I understand. You'd like very much to be free on that shore; you'd like to be on a good ship, cleaving the waves of that emerald-green sea; you'd like very much, whether on land or on sea, to set me up one of those nice little ambushes that you know so well how to arrange. Patience! Patience! In four days, the shore will be permitted you, the sea will be open to you, more open than you'd like, for in four days England will be rid of you."

Milady clasped her hands, and raising her beautiful eyes to heaven, said with an angelic sweetness of gesture and intonation:

"Lord! Lord! Forgive this man as I forgive him myself."

"Yes, pray, accursed woman!" cried the baron. "Your prayer is all the more generous in that you are, I swear to you, in the power of a man who will not forgive."

And he left.

Just as he was leaving, a piercing glance slipped through the half-open door, and she glimpsed Felton stepping aside quickly so as not to be seen by her.

Then she threw herself on her knees and began to pray.

"My God! my God!" she said, "you know for what holy cause I suffer! Give me, then, the strength to suffer."

The door opened softly. The beautiful suppliant made as if she had not heard, and in a tearful voice, went on:

"God of vengeance! God of goodness! Will you allow this man's ghastly plans to be accomplished?"

Only then did she pretend to hear the sound of Felton's footsteps, and, getting up quick as thought, she blushed as if she was ashamed to have been caught on her knees.

"I do not like to disturb those who pray, Madame," Felton said gravely. "And therefore, I entreat you, do not be disturbed on my account."

"How do you know I was praying? Monsieur," said Milady, in a voice choking with sobs, "you are mistaken, Monsieur, I was not praying."

"Do you think, then, Madame," Felton replied in the same grave voice, though with a gentler accent, "that I believe I have the right to hinder a creature who is bowing down before her Creator? God forbid! Besides, repentance sits well on the guilty. Whatever the crime committed, a guilty person at the feet of God is sacred to me."

"Guilty? I?" said Milady, with a smile that would have disarmed an angel of the last judgment. "Guilty? My God, thou knowest whether I am or not! Tell me that I am condemned, Monsieur, well and good; but you know that God, who loves martyrs, sometimes allows the innocent to be condemned."

"Were you condemned, were you a martyr," replied Felton, "the more's the reason to pray, and I myself will help you with my prayers."

"Oh, you are a just man!" cried Milady, throwing herself at his feet. "Listen, I cannot hold out any longer, for I am afraid to lack strength at the moment when I must sustain the struggle and confess my faith. Listen, then, to the supplication of a woman in despair. You are being deceived, Monsieur, but it is not a question of that. I am asking you for only one favor, and, if you grant it to me, I will bless you in this world and the next."

"Speak to the master, Madame," said Felton. "I myself, fortunately, am entrusted neither with pardoning nor with punishing, and it is to one higher than me that God has handed over this responsibility."

"To you, no, to you alone. Listen to me, rather than contributing to my destruction, rather than contributing to my ignominy."

"If you have deserved this shame, Madame, if you have
incurred this ignominy, you must endure it while offering it up
to God."

"What are you saying? Oh, you do not understand me!
When I speak of ignominy, you think I am speaking of some
sort of punishment, of prison or death! Please heaven! what
are death and prison to me!"

"It is I who no longer understand you, Madame."

"Or pretend that you no longer understand me, Monsieur,"
the prisoner replied with a doubtful smile.

"No, Madame, on my honor as a soldier, on my faith as a
Christian!"

"What? You are unaware of Lord de Winter's designs
on me?"

"I am."

"You, his confidant? Impossible!"

"I never lie, Madame."

"Oh, he hides himself too little for you not to have
guessed it!"

"I do not try to guess anything, Madame. I wait to be told,
and apart from what he has said to me before you, Lord de
Winter has told me nothing."

"Why," cried Milady, with an incredible accent of truthfulness, "then you're not his accomplice; then you don't know
that he has destined me for a shame that all the punishments
on earth could not equal in horror?"

"You are mistaken, Madame," said Felton, blushing.
"Lord de Winter is incapable of such a crime."

"Good," Milady said to herself. "Without knowing what
it is, he calls it a crime!" Then aloud:

"The friend of the infamous one is capable of anything."

"Whom do you call the infamous one?" asked Felton.

"Are there two men in England for whom such a name is
befitting?"

"You mean George Villiers?" said Felton, and his eyes blazed.

"Whom the pagans, the gentiles, and the infidels call the duke of Buckingham," picked up Milady. "I wouldn't have thought there was a single Englishman in all England who would need such a long explanation to recognize the man I meant!"

"The hand of the Lord is stretched over him," said Felton. "He will not escape the punishment he deserves."

Felton was only expressing the feeling of execration regarding the duke that all the English had vowed to this man whom the Catholics themselves called the exactor, the extortioner, the profligate, and whom the Puritans quite simply called Satan.

"Oh, my God! my God!" cried Milady, "when I beg you to send this man the punishment that is his due, you know I am not pursuing my own vengeance, but am imploring the deliverance of a whole people."

"You know him, then?" asked Felton.

"He finally asks me a question," Milady said to herself, overjoyed at having arrived so quickly at such a great result. "Oh, yes, I know him! Oh, yes, to my misfortune, to my eternal misfortune!"

And Milady twisted her arms as if in a paroxysm of suffering. Felton no doubt sensed that his strength was failing him, and he took several steps towards the door. The prisoner, who never lost sight of him, leaped after him and stopped him.

"Monsieur!" she cried, "be good, be merciful, hear my prayer: that knife which the baron's fatal prudence took from me, because he knew what use I wanted to make of it—oh, hear me out!—give me back that knife for just one minute, out of mercy, out of pity! I embrace your knees! Look, you can close the door, I have nothing against you. God! what could I have against you, the only just, good, and compassionate being I've met! Against you, perhaps my savior! One minute, that knife, one minute, just one, and I'll give it back to you through the peephole in the door. Just one little minute, Mr. Felton, and you will have saved my honor!"

"Kill yourself?" Felton cried in terror, forgetting to withdraw his hands from the prisoner's hands. "Kill yourself?"

"I have spoken, Monsieur," murmured Milady, lowering her voice and letting herself fall limply to the floor, "I have told my secret! He knows everything, my God, I'm lost!"

Felton remained standing, motionless and undecided.

"He's still doubtful," thought Milady. "I haven't been convincing enough."

There was the sound of walking in the corridor. Milady recognized Lord de Winter's footstep. Felton also recognized it and went to the door.

Milady jumped up.

"Oh, not a word!" she said, in a concentrated voice. "Not a word to this man of all I've said to you, or I'm lost, and it is you, you . . ."

Then, as the steps came closer, she fell silent for fear her voice would be heard, pressing her beautiful hand to Felton's mouth in a gesture of infinite terror. Felton gently pushed Milady away, and she collapsed onto a chaise longue.

Lord de Winter passed before the door without stopping, and the sound of his footsteps could be heard going away.

Felton, pale as death, stood for a few moments with his ears strained and listening; then, when the noise died away entirely, he drew his breath like a man coming out of a dream and rushed from the apartment.

"Ah!" said Milady, listening in her turn to the sound of Felton's footsteps, which went away in the opposite direction from those of Lord de Winter, "so you're mine at last!"

Then her brow darkened.

"If he talks to the baron," she said, "I'm lost, for the baron, who knows very well that I won't kill myself, will set me before him with a knife in my hand, and he will see clearly that all this great despair was only playacting."

She went and stood before her mirror, and looked at herself. Never had she been so beautiful.

"Oh, yes!" she said, smiling, "but he won't talk to him!"

That evening, Lord de Winter accompanied the supper.

"Monsieur," Milady said to him, "is your presence an

obligatory accessory of my captivity? Might you not spare me the additional torture caused by your visits?"

"How now, dear sister?" said de Winter. "Did you not announce to me sentimentally, with that pretty mouth so cruel to me today, that you came to England for the sole purpose of seeing me at your ease—a pleasure of which, as you said to me, you felt the privation so sharply that you risked everything for it: seasickness, storms, captivity? Well, here I am, so be satisfied. Besides, this time there's a motive for my visit."

Milady shuddered. She thought that Felton had talked. Never in her life, perhaps, had this woman, who had experienced so many powerful and contrary emotions, felt her heart beat so violently.

She was sitting down. Lord de Winter took an armchair, drew it to her side, and sat down by her. Then, taking a paper from his pocket and slowly unfolding it, he said to her:

"Here, I wanted to show you this sort of passport, which I have drafted myself and which will serve you henceforth as an identification number in the life I consent to leave you with."

Then, shifting his eyes from Milady to the paper, he read:

Order to convey to _____

"The name of the place is left blank," de Winter broke off. "If you have some preference, indicate it to me, and provided it be a thousand leagues from London, your request will be granted. So I begin again:

Order to convey to _____ one Charlotte Backson, branded by the justice of the kingdom of France, but liberated after punishment. She will remain in this place of residence without ever going more than three leagues from it. In case of attempted escape, the death penalty will be applied. She will receive five shillings a day for her room and board.

"This order does not apply to me," Milady replied coldly, "since it bears another name than mine."

"A name? And do you have one?"

"I have your brother's."

"You're mistaken, my brother is only your second husband, and the first is still living. Tell me his name, and I will put it in place of Charlotte Backson. No? . . . You don't want to? . . . You keep silent? Very well, you'll be locked up under the name of Charlotte Backson!"

Milady remained silent, only this time it was not from affectation, but from terror: she believed the order was ready to be carried out; she thought Lord de Winter had moved up his departure; she believed she was condemned to leave that same night. In her mind all was lost for a moment, when all at once she noticed that the order bore no signature.

The joy she felt at this discovery was so great that she was unable to conceal it.

"Yes, yes," said Lord de Winter, who noticed what was going on inside her, "yes, you're looking for the signature, and you're saying to yourself: all is not lost, since this act is unsigned; they're showing it to me in order to frighten me, that's all. You're mistaken: tomorrow this order will be sent to Lord Buckingham; the day after tomorrow it will come back signed by his hand and bearing his seal; and twenty-four hours later, I promise you, it will begin to be carried out. Farewell, Madame, that is all I had to say to you."

"And I will reply to you, Monsieur, that this abuse of power, that this exile under a false name, is an infamy."

"Would you prefer to be hanged under your real name, Milady? You know that English law is inexorable on the abuse of marriage. Explain yourself frankly: though my name, or rather my brother's name, is mixed up in all this, I will risk the scandal of a public trial to be sure of being rid of you at a stroke."

Milady did not reply, but turned pale as a corpse.

"Oh, I see you find peregrination preferable! Splendid, Madame, and there is an old proverb which says that youth is shaped by travel. By heaven, you're not wrong, after all, and life is good! That's why I'm not anxious to have you take it from me. It remains, then, to settle the matter of the five shillings. I'm being a bit parsimonious, am I not? That's because I'm not anxious to have you corrupt your guards. Besides, you will always have your charms to seduce them. Use them, then, if your failure with Felton hasn't disgusted you with attempts of that sort."

"Felton hasn't talked," Milady said to herself, "nothing's lost yet."

"And now, Madame, good-bye to you. Tomorrow I will come to announce to you the departure of my messenger."

Lord de Winter stood up, bowed ironically to Milady, and left.

Milady drew her breath: she still had four days ahead of her; four days were enough for her to finish seducing Felton.

A terrible idea then came to her, that Lord de Winter might send Felton himself to have the order signed by Buckingham. In that way, Felton would escape her, and for the prisoner to succeed, the magic of a continuous seduction was necessary.

Yet, as we have said, one thing reassured her: Felton had not talked.

She had no wish to seem alarmed by Lord de Winter's threats, so she sat down at the table and ate.

Then, as she had done the evening before, she knelt and recited her prayers aloud. As on the evening before, the soldier ceased pacing and stopped to listen.

Soon she heard lighter footsteps than the sentry's, which came from the end of the corridor and stopped outside her door.

"It's he," she said.

And she began the same religious singing which, the evening before, had excited Felton so violently.

But, though her sweet, full, and sonorous voice vibrated more harmoniously and heartbreakingly than ever, the door remained shut. It seemed to Milady, in one of those furtive glances that she cast at the peephole, that she glimpsed the young man's burning eyes through the tight grating; but whether this was a reality or a vision, this time he had enough control over himself not to come in.

Only a few moments after she finished her religious singing, Milady thought she heard a deep sigh; then the same footsteps she had heard approaching went away slowly and as if regretfully.

LV

FOURTH DAY OF CAPTIVITY

The next day, when Felton came into Milady's room, he found her standing on a chair, holding in her hands a rope made from several batiste handkerchiefs torn into strips, braided together, and tied end to end. At the noise Felton made in opening the door, Milady jumped down lightly from her chair and tried to hide this improvised rope behind her.

The young man was still paler than usual, and his eyes, reddened by insomnia, showed that he had spent a feverish night.

Yet his brow was armed with a serenity more austere than ever.

He advanced slowly towards Milady, who had sat down, and taking hold of one end of the deadly braid, which, by inadvertence, or perhaps on purpose, she had left showing, asked coldly:

"What is this, Madame?"

"That? Nothing," said Milady, smiling with that sorrowful expression which she knew so well how to give to her smile. "Boredom is the mortal enemy of prisoners; I'm bored, and I amused myself by braiding this rope."

Felton shifted his eyes to the point on the apartment wall before which he had found Milady standing on the chair she was now sitting in, and above her head he noticed a gilded spike, fixed in the wall, which served for hanging either clothes or arms.

He gave a start, and the prisoner saw this start; for though her eyes were lowered, nothing escaped her.

"And what were you doing standing on that chair?" he asked.

"What is it to you?" replied Milady.

"But," Felton picked up, "I want to know."

"Do not question me," said the prisoner. "You know very well that we true Christians are forbidden to lie."

"Well, then," said Felton, "I shall tell you what you were doing, or rather what you were going to do. You were going to complete that fatal work which you are nurturing in your mind. Consider, Madame, if God forbids lying, how much more strictly he forbids suicide."

"When God sees one of his creatures persecuted, placed between suicide and dishonor, believe me, Monsieur," replied Milady, in a tone of deep conviction, "God forgives the suicide—for then suicide is martyrdom."

"You say either too much or too little. Speak, Madame, in heaven's name, explain yourself."

"I should tell you my misfortunes, so that you may treat them as fables? I should tell you my plans, so that you may go and reveal them to my persecutor? No, Monsieur. Besides, what does the life or death of one wretched condemned woman mean to you? You answer only for my body, isn't that so? And provided you can produce a corpse, and it is recognized as mine, nothing more will be asked of you, and perhaps you will even have twice the reward."

"I, Madame? I?" cried Felton. "To suppose I would ever accept the price of your life? Oh, you're not thinking what you're saying!"

"Let me be, Felton, let me be," said Milady, getting excited. "Every soldier must be ambitious, isn't that so? You're a lieutenant. Well, then you'll follow my funeral procession with the rank of captain."

"But what have I done to you," said Felton, shaken, "that you heap me with such responsibility before men and God? In a few days you will be far away from here, Madame, your life will no longer be under my protection, and," he added with a sigh, "then you can do with it what you like."

"So," cried Milady, as if she could not resist a sense of holy indignation, "you who are a pious man, you who are called a just man, you demand only one thing: not to be blamed or bothered for my death!"

"I must watch over your life, Madame, and I shall watch over it."

"But do you understand the mission you are fulfilling? Cruel enough if I were guilty, what name will you give it, what name will the Lord give it, if I am innocent?"

"I am a soldier, Madame. I obey the orders I have received."

"Do you believe that, on the day of the last judgment, God will separate the blind hangmen from the iniquitous judges? You do not want me to kill my body, yet you make yourself the agent of him who would kill my soul!"

"But, I repeat to you," replied the shaken Felton, "no danger threatens you, and I will answer for Lord de Winter as for myself."

"Madman!" cried Milady. "Poor madman, who dare answer for another man, when the wisest, when the greatest in the eyes of God, hesitate to answer for themselves, and who side with the party of the strongest and most fortunate to crush the weakest and most unfortunate!"

"Impossible, Madame, impossible," murmured Felton, who at the bottom of his heart felt the justice of this argument. "A prisoner, you will not regain your freedom through me; alive, you will not lose your life through me."

"Yes," cried Milady, "but I will lose what is far dearer to me than my life, I will lose my honor, Felton. And it is you, you, whom I will hold responsible before God and men for my shame and my infamy."

This time Felton, impassive as he was, or as he pretended to be, could not resist the secret influence that had already laid hold of him: to see this woman, so beautiful, fair as the most candid vision, to see her tearful and menacing by turns, to undergo the double ascendency of suffering and beauty, was too much for a visionary, too much for a brain sapped by the ardent dreams of ecstatic faith, too much for a heart corroded by a burning love of heaven and a devouring hatred of men.

Milady saw the confusion, she sensed intuitively the flame of the contrary passions that burned with the blood in the young fanatic's veins; and, like a skillful general who, seeing the enemy ready to retreat, marches upon him letting out a cry of victory, she stood up, beautiful as an ancient priestess, inspired as a Christian virgin, and, her arm extended, her neck exposed, her hair disheveled, one hand modestly holding her gown to her breast, her gaze lit up by that fire which brought disorder to the young Puritan's senses, she stepped towards him, crying out to a vehement tune, in her sweet voice, to which, for the occasion, she gave a terrible intonation:

> To Baal his victim surrender,
> To lions the martyr's limbs:
> God will make you repentent . . .
> From the depths I cry to Him!

Felton stopped as if petrified under this strange apostrophe.

"Who are you, who are you?" he cried, clasping his hands. "Are you an envoy from God, are you a minister of hell, are you an angel or a demon, are you called Eloas or Astarte?"

"Don't you recognize me, Felton? I am neither an angel nor a demon, I am a daughter of the earth, I am a sister of your belief, that is all."

"Yes! yes!" said Felton, "I still doubted, but now I believe."

"You believe, and yet you are the accomplice of that son of Belial who is called Lord de Winter! You believe, and yet you leave me in the hands of my enemies, of the enemy of England, of the enemy of God? You believe, and yet you hand me over to him who has filled and filthied the world with his heresies and debauches, to that infamous Sardanapalus whom the blind call the duke of Buckingham and whom the believers call the Antichrist?"

"I, hand you over to Buckingham? I? What are you saying?"

"They have eyes," said Milady, "but see not; they have ears, but hear not."

"Yes, yes," said Felton, passing his hands over his sweat-bathed forehead, as if to tear away his last doubt. "Yes, I recognize the voice that speaks to me in my dreams; yes, I recognize the features of the angel who appears to me each night, crying out to my sleepless soul: 'Strike, save England, save yourself, for you shall die without appeasing God!' Speak, speak!" cried Felton. "I can understand you now."

A flash of terrible joy, quick as thought, sprang up in Milady's eyes.

Fleeting as this homicidal glimmer was, Felton saw it and shuddered, as if it had lit up the abysses of this woman's heart.

All at once Felton recalled Lord de Winter's warnings, Milady's seductions, her first attempts on her arrival. He drew back a step and lowered his head, but without ceasing to look at her, as if, fascinated by this strange creature, his eyes could not detach themselves from hers.

Milady was not a woman to misunderstand the meaning of this hesitation. Beneath her apparent emotions, her icy cold-bloodedness never left her. Before Felton replied to her and forced her to resume this conversation which was so hard to maintain at the same pitch of exaltation, she let her hands fall, and, as if feminine weakness had won out over inspired enthusiasm, said:

"No, it is not for me to be the Judith who will deliver Bethulia from this Holofernes. The sword of the Eternal is too heavy for my arm. Let me then flee dishonor through death, let me take refuge in martyrdom. I ask you neither for freedom, as would a guilty person, nor for vengeance, as would a pagan. Let me die, that is all. I beg you, I implore you on my knees: let me die, and my last sigh will be a blessing on my savior."

At this sweet and supplicating voice, at this timid and downcast look, Felton reproached himself. Little by little, the enchantress had put back on that magic adornment which she took off or on at will, that is to say, the beauty, the gentleness, the tears, and above all the irresistible attraction of mystical voluptuousness, the most devouring voluptuousness of all.

"Alas!" said Felton, "there is only one thing I can do—to pity you if you prove to me that you are a victim! But Lord de Winter has bitter grievances against you. You are a Christian, you are my sister in religion; I feel drawn to you, I who love only my benefactor, I who in life have found only traitors and impious men. But you, Madame, so beautiful in reality, so pure in appearance, for Lord de Winter to pursue you like this, you must have committed iniquities."

"They have eyes," repeated Milady, with an accent of unutterable sorrow, "and see not; they have ears, and hear not."

"But, in that case," cried the young officer, "speak, speak!"

"Confide my shame to you?" cried Milady, with the flush of modesty on her face, "for the crime of one is often the shame of another. Confide my shame to you—you a man, and I a woman? Oh!" she went on, modestly covering her beautiful eyes with her hand, "oh, never, never could I!"

"To me, to a brother!" cried Felton.

Milady looked at him for a long time with an expression which the young officer took for doubt, and which nevertheless was only observation and above all the will to fascinate.

"Well, then," said Milady, "I will trust in my brother, I will dare!"

At that moment, they heard Lord de Winter's footsteps. But this time Milady's terrible brother-in-law did not content himself, as he had the evening before, with passing by the door and going away. He stopped, exchanged two words with the sentry, then the door opened, and he appeared.

During that two-word exchange, Felton had quickly backed away, and when Lord de Winter came in, he was several steps from the prisoner.

The baron came in slowly, and turned his searching gaze from the prisoner to the young officer.

"You've been here quite a long time, John," he said. "Has this woman been recounting her crimes to you? If so, I can understand the length of the conversation."

Felton shuddered, and Milady sensed that she was lost if she did not come to the aid of the abashed Puritan.

"Ah, you're afraid your prisoner may escape you?" she said. "Well, then, ask your worthy jailer what favor I was begging of him just now."

"You were asking a favor?" the suspicious baron inquired.

"Yes, Milord," the confused young man picked up.

"And what favor, if you please?" asked Lord de Winter.

"A knife, which she would hand back to me through the peephole a minute after receiving it," replied Felton.

"Is there someone hidden away here, then, whose throat the gracious lady wants to cut?" Lord de Winter asked in his mocking and contemptuous voice.

"Only myself," replied Milady.

"I gave you a choice between America and Tyburn," said Lord de Winter. "Choose Tyburn, Milady: the rope, believe me, is more certain than the knife."

Felton turned pale and took a step forward, recalling that at the moment when he came in, Milady was holding a rope.

"You're right," she said, "I've already thought of that." Then she added in a hollow voice, "I'm still thinking of it."

Felton shook to the very marrow of his bones. Lord de Winter probably noticed this movement.

"Beware, John," he said. "John, my friend, I am relying on you. Watch out! I warned you! Anyhow, cheer up, my boy, in three days we'll be delivered of this creature, and where I'm sending her, she won't harm anyone else."

"You hear him!" Milady burst out, so that the baron thought she was addressing heaven and Felton understood that it was him.

Felton lowered his head and pondered.

The baron took the officer by the arm, looking over his shoulder so as not to lose sight of Milady until he left.

"Well, well," said the prisoner, when the door was shut again, "I'm not as far along as I thought. Winter has exchanged his usual stupidity for a previously unknown prudence. That's what the desire for vengeance is, and how that desire shapes the man! As for Felton, he's hesitating. Ah, this is no man like that cursed d'Artagnan! A Puritan worships only virgins, and he worships them with clasped hands. A musketeer likes women, and likes taking them in his arms."

Yet Milady waited patiently, for she doubted that the day would pass without her seeing Felton again. Finally, an hour after the scene we have just recounted, she heard low voices talking outside the door; soon afterwards the door opened, and she recognized Felton.

The young man came in quickly, leaving the door open behind him and making a sign for Milady to keep silent. His face was distorted.

"What do you want of me?" she asked.

"Listen," Felton answered in a low voice, "I've just sent the sentry away so as to be able to stay here without anyone knowing I've come, so as to talk to you without anyone being able to hear what I say. The baron has just told me a frightful story."

Milady assumed her smile of the resigned victim and shook her head.

"Either you are a demon," Felton went on, "or the baron, my benefactor, my father, is a monster. I have known you for four days, I have loved him for ten years; thus I may well hesitate between you. Don't be frightened by what I'm saying, I need to be convinced. Tonight, after midnight, I will come to see you, and you will convince me."

"No, Felton, no, my brother," she said, "the sacrifice is too great, and I can feel what it is costing you. No, I am lost, do not be lost with me. My death will be far more eloquent than my life, and the silence of the corpse will convince you far better than the words of the prisoner."

"Be quiet, Madame," cried Felton, "and do not speak to me like that. I have come so that you may promise me on your honor, so that you may swear to me on what you hold most sacred, that you will make no attempt on your life."

"I refuse to promise," said Milady, "for no one respects an oath more than I do, and, if I make a promise, I will have to keep it."

"Well, then," said Felton, "commit yourself only until the moment you see me again. If, once you've seen me again, you still persist—well, then you will be free, and I myself will give you the weapon you have asked me for."

"Well," said Milady, "then I shall wait for you."

"Swear it."

"I swear it by our God. Are you satisfied?"

"Very well," said Felton, "till tonight!"

And he rushed from the apartment, closed the door, and

waited outside, the soldier's half pike in his hand, as if he was mounting guard in his place.

When the soldier returned, Felton gave him back his weapon.

Then, through the peephole, which she had gone up to, Milady saw the young man cross himself with rapturous fervor and go off down the corridor in a transport of joy.

As for her, she went back to her place, a smile of savage scorn on her lips, and repeated, blaspheming, the terrible name of God, by whom she had sworn without ever having learned to know Him.

"My God!" she said, "what a mad fanatic! My God is myself, myself and whoever helps me in my revenge!"

LVI

FIFTH DAY OF CAPTIVITY

Meanwhile, Milady had arrived at a half triumph, and the success doubled her strength.

It was not difficult to conquer, as she had done up to then, men ready to let themselves be seduced, and whom the gallant education of the court led quickly into the trap. Milady was beautiful enough to meet no resistance on the part of the flesh, and she was deft enough to overcome all mental obstacles.

But this time she had to fight against a wild nature, concentrated, insensible by dint of austerity. Religion and penitence had made of Felton a man inaccessible to ordinary seductions. Such vast plans, such tumultuous projects turned over in that exalted head, that there was no room left for any love, capricious or substantial—that emotion which is nursed on leisure and grows in corruption. Milady had thus made a breach, with her false virtue, in the judgment of a man horribly warned against her, and, by her beauty, in the heart and senses of a man who was chaste and pure. Finally, she had taken the measure of her means, unknown to herself till then, by this experiment made upon the most refractory subject that nature and religion could submit to her investigation.

Nevertheless, many times during that evening she had despaired of fate and of herself; she did not invoke God, as we know, but she had faith in the genius of evil, that immense sovereignty that reigns over all the details of human life, and for which, as in the Arabian fable, a pomegranate seed is enough to reconstruct a destroyed world.

Milady, who was well prepared to receive Felton, could set up her artillery for the next day. She knew she had only two days left, that once the order was signed by Buckingham (and Buckingham would sign it the more readily in that this order bore a false name, and he could not recognize the woman it concerned), once this order was signed, we say, the baron would put her aboard ship straight away, and she also knew that women condemned to deportation use much less powerful weapons in their seductions than would-be virtuous women, whose beauty is shone upon by the sun of society, whose wit is vaunted by the voice of fashion, and whom a reflection of aristocracy gilds with its enchanted gleams. To be a woman condemned to a wretched and degrading punishment is no hindrance to being beautiful, but is an obstacle to ever becoming powerful again. Like all people of real merit, Milady knew the milieu that suited her nature and her means. Poverty was repugnant to her; abjection diminished her greatness by two-thirds. Milady was a queen only among queens; the pleasure of satisfied pride was necessary to her domination. To command inferior beings was rather a humiliation than a pleasure for her.

To be sure, she would return from her exile, she did not doubt it for a single moment; but how long would that exile last? For an active and ambitious nature like Milady's, the days when one is not busy rising are ill-starred days; find a word, then, to name the days that one spends falling! To lose a year, two years, three years, meaning an eternity; to come back when d'Artagnan, happy and triumphant, he and his friends, had received from the queen the reward they had well earned for the services they had rendered her—those were devouring thoughts, which a woman like Milady could not endure. Moreover, the storm that was howling in her doubled her strength, and she would have burst the walls of her prison if her body had been able for a single moment to take on the proportions of her mind.

Then, what still goaded her in the midst of all this was the memory of the cardinal. What must the distrustful, worried, suspicious cardinal be thinking, what must he be saying of her silence—the cardinal, not only her sole prop, her sole support, her sole protector for the present, but also the main instrument of her fortune and her revenge to come? She knew him, she knew that on her return after a useless journey, she could argue all she liked about prison, she could make as much as she liked of sufferings endured, the cardinal would respond with that mocking calm of the skeptic who is powerful in both strength and genius: "You should not have let yourself be caught!"

Then Milady gathered all her energy, murmuring at the back of her mind the name of Felton, the sole glimmer of light that penetrated to her in the depths of the hell she had fallen into; and like a serpent coiling and uncoiling its body in order to find out its own strength for itself, she enveloped Felton beforehand in the thousand folds of her inventive imagination.

Yet time went by, the hours seemed to awaken the clock one by one as they passed, and each stroke of the bronze clapper echoed in the prisoner's heart. At nine o'clock, Lord de Winter made his customary visit, checked the window and the bars, tapped the floor and the walls, examined the fireplace and the doors, without a word being spoken between him and Milady during this long and painstaking visit.

Doubtless they both understood that the situation had become too serious for wasting time in useless words and pointless anger.

"Well, well," the baron said on leaving her, "you won't be escaping tonight!"

At ten o'clock, Felton came to place a sentry at the door. Milady recognized his footstep. She could sense it now, the way a mistress senses that of her heart's chosen lover, and yet Milady both detested and despised this feeble fanatic.

This was not the appointed hour; Felton did not come in.

Two hours later, just as it struck midnight, the sentry was relieved.

This time the hour had come. And so, starting from this moment, Milady waited impatiently.

The new sentry began pacing in the corridor.

After ten minutes, Felton came.

Milady pricked up her ears.

"Listen," the young man said to the sentry, "under no pretext are you to leave this door, for you know that last night Milord punished a soldier for having left his post for a moment, and yet it was I who replaced him during his brief absence."

"Yes, I know," said the soldier.

"I enjoin you, then, to the closest surveillance. I myself," he added, "am going to go and inspect this woman's room a second time, for I'm afraid she has sinister designs on herself, and I've been ordered to keep watch on her."

"Good," murmured Milady, "the austere Puritan is telling a lie!"

As for the soldier, he contented himself with smiling.

"Damn, lieutenant," he said, "you're not so bad off to be given commissions like that, especially if Milord authorizes you to look till she's in bed."

Felton blushed. In any other circumstances, he would have reprimanded a soldier who allowed himself such a joke; but his conscience murmured too loudly for his mouth to dare open.

"If I call," he said, "come. And if someone comes, call me."

"Yes, sir," said the soldier.

Felton went into Milady's room. Milady stood up.

"You're here?" she said.

"I promised you I would come," said Felton, "and I have come."

"You promised me something else as well."

"What's that? Oh, my God!" said the young man, who, despite his self-control, felt his knees trembling and sweat breaking out on his forehead.

"You promised to bring me a knife, and to leave me after our talk."

"Don't speak of that, Madame," said Felton. "There is no situation, terrible as it might be, that authorizes a creature of

God to take his own life. I reflected that I must never make myself guilty of such a sin."

"Ah, so you reflected?" said the prisoner, sitting down in her armchair with a scornful smile. "And I have also reflected."

"On what?"

"That I had nothing to say to a man who did not keep his word."

"Oh, my God!" murmured Felton.

"You may leave," said Milady, "I will not speak."

"Here is the knife!" said Felton, taking from his pocket the weapon, which he had brought as promised, but which he had hesitated to give to his prisoner.

"Let's see it," said Milady.

"What for?"

"On my honor, I'll give it back to you at once. You will put it on this table and stand between it and me."

Felton held the weapon out to Milady, who tested its temper attentively and tried the point on the tip of her finger.

"Good," she said, handing the knife back to the young officer, "it's a fine one and of good steel. You are a faithful friend, Felton."

Felton took the weapon back and placed it on the table, as had just been agreed with his prisoner.

Milady followed him with her eyes and made a gesture of satisfaction.

"Now," she said, "listen to me."

The injunction was unnecessary: the young officer was standing before her, waiting to devour her words.

"Felton," said Milady, with a solemnity filled with melancholy, "Felton, if your sister, your father's daughter, said to you: While still young, and unfortunately rather beautiful, I was lured into a trap, but I resisted. Ambushes and assaults were multiplied around me, but I resisted. Blasphemies were uttered against the religion I serve and the God I worship, because I called that God and that religion to my aid. Then outrages were heaped on me, and as they could not destroy my soul, they wanted to taint my body forever. Finally . . ."

Milady paused, and a bitter smile passed over her lips.

"Finally," said Felton, "what did they finally do?"

"Finally, one evening, they decided to paralyze that resistance which they could not conquer. One evening they mixed a strong narcotic in my water. I had barely finished my meal when I felt myself falling gradually into a strange torpor. Though I was unsuspecting, a vague fear seized me, and I tried to struggle against sleep. I got up, I wanted to run to the window, to call for help, but my legs would not support me. It seemed to me that the ceiling was coming down on my head and crushing me under its weight. I stretched out my arms, I tried to speak, I could only produce inarticulate sounds; an irresistible numbness came over me, I held on to a chair, feeling I was about to fall, but soon this support was insufficient for my weakened arms; I fell on one knee, then on both; I wanted to cry out, but my tongue was frozen; doubtless God did not see or hear me, and I slipped to the floor, prey to a deathlike sleep.

"Of all that happened during that sleep, and of how much time passed while it lasted, I have no memory. The only thing I recall is that I woke up lying in a round room, which was sumptuously furnished, and into which daylight penetrated only through an opening in the ceiling. Moreover, there seemed to be no door to it: one would have thought it a magnificent prison.

"It was a long time before I was able to become aware of the place I was in and of all the details I am reporting; my mind seemed to be struggling helplessly to shake off the heavy darkness of that sleep from which I could not tear myself. I had vague images of some distance traveled, of the rolling of a carriage, of a horrible dream in which my strength was exhausted; but it was all so dark and indistinct in my thought that these events seemed to belong to another life than mine, and yet were mixed with mine in a fantastic duality.

"For some time, the state I found myself in seemed so strange to me that I thought I was having a dream. I staggered to my feet. My clothes were near me on a chair. I did not remember either getting undressed or going to bed. Then reality gradually presented itself to me, filled with shameful horrors: I was no longer in the house I lived in; as far as I could tell by the light of the sun, the day was already two-thirds over! It was on the previous evening that I had fallen asleep; my sleep had thus lasted almost twenty-four hours. What had happened during that long sleep?

"I got dressed as quickly as I could. All my numb and sluggish movements testified to the influence of the narcotic, which had still not entirely worn off. Moreover, the room had been furnished to receive a woman, and the most complete coquette could not have formed a desire which, in looking around the room, she did not find already satisfied.

"I was certainly not the first captive to be locked up in that splendid prison; but you understand, Felton, the more beautiful the prison, the more it frightened me.

"Yes, it was a prison, for I tried in vain to get out. I tapped on all the walls to find a door, but everywhere the walls gave back a thick, dead sound.

"I made the rounds of that room maybe twenty times, seeking for some sort of way out. There was none. Overwhelmed by weariness and terror, I collapsed into an armchair.

"During that time, night was falling quickly, and with night my terrors increased. I did not know whether I should stay where I was sitting; it seemed to me that I was surrounded by unknown dangers into which I was going to fall at every step. Though I had eaten nothing since the day before, my fears kept me from feeling hungry.

"No noise from outside reached me, enabling me to measure time; I merely presumed that it might be seven or eight o'clock in the evening, for it was October and pitch dark.

"All at once the creak of a door swinging on its hinges made me start. A globe of fire appeared above the glass opening in the ceiling, casting a bright light into my room, and I perceived with terror that a man was standing a few steps away from me.

"A table set for two, holding a supper all prepared, was standing as if by magic in the middle of the room.

"This man was he who had been pursuing me for a year, who had sworn to dishonor me, and who, at the first words that came from his mouth, made me understand that he had done so the previous night."

"Infamous creature!" murmured Felton.

"Oh, yes, infamous!" cried Milady, seeing the interest that the young officer, whose soul seemed to be hanging on his lips, took in this strange story. "Oh, yes, infamous! He had thought it was enough if he triumphed over me in my sleep for all to be said and done; he came hoping I would accept my shame, since my shame was consummated; he came to offer me his fortune in exchange for my love.

"All that a woman's heart could contain of proud scorn and disdainful words I poured out on this man. No doubt he was used to such reproaches, for he listened to me calmly, smiling, his arms crossed; then, when he thought I had said everything, he came towards me. I leaped for the table, seized a knife, and held it to my breast.

"'Take one more step,' I said to him, 'and besides my honor, you will have my death to reproach yourself with.'

"No doubt there was in my look, in my voice, in my whole person, that truthfulness of gesture, of pose and accent, which carries conviction even for the most perverse hearts, for he stopped.

"'Your death?' he said to me. 'Oh, no, you are too charming a mistress for me to consent to losing you like that, after having had the happiness of possessing you only once. Goodbye, my all-beautiful! I shall wait to visit you until you are in better spirits.'

"With those words, he blew a whistle. The flaming globe that lit up my room rose up and disappeared; I found myself in the dark again. The same noise of a door opening and closing came a moment later, the flaming globe descended again, and I was alone.

"It was a dreadful moment. If I had still had some doubts about my misfortune, those doubts had vanished into a hopeless reality: I was in the power of a man I not only detested, but despised; of a man capable of anything, and who had already given me a fatal proof of how far he might venture to go."

"But who, then, was this man?" asked Felton.

"I spent the night on a chair, jumping at the least sound; for at around midnight the lamp went out, and I found myself in the dark again. But the night passed without any new attempt from my persecutor. Daylight came. The table had disappeared, but I still had the knife in my hand.

"That knife was all my hope.

"I was overwhelmed with weariness; my eyes burned from sleeplessness; I hadn't dared to sleep a single moment. The daylight reassured me. I went to throw myself on my bed, without letting go of the liberating knife, which I hid under my pillow.

"When I woke up, a new table had been served.

"This time, despite my terrors, despite my anguish, a gnawing hunger made itself felt. I hadn't taken any nourishment for forty-eight hours. I ate bread and some fruit; then, recalling the narcotic mixed into the water I had drunk, I did not touch the water on the table, but went to fill my glass at a marble fountain fixed in the wall above my washstand.

"However, despite that precaution, I remained in frightful anguish for some time afterwards. But this time my fears were unfounded: I spent the day without feeling anything like what I was dreading.

"I was careful to empty half of the carafe, so that my mistrust would not be noticed.

"Evening came, and darkness with it. However, deep as it was, my eyes began to get used to it. Amidst the gloom, I saw the table sink into the floor; a quarter of an hour later, it reappeared bearing my supper; a moment later, thanks to the same lamp, my room was lit up again.

"I was determined to eat only things in which it was impossible to mix any sleeping potion: two eggs and some fruit made up my meal. Then I went to draw a glass of water from my protective fountain, and I drank it.

"At the first few sips, it seemed to me that it did not have the same taste as in the morning. A quick suspicion seized me, and I stopped; but I had already drunk half a glass.

"I threw out the rest in fright, and waited, the sweat of terror on my brow.

"No doubt some invisible witness had seen me take water from that fountain, and had profited from my very confidence to better assure my ruin, so coldly resolved upon and so cruelly pursued.

"Half an hour had not gone by when the same symptoms appeared; but as I had only drunk half a glass this time, I struggled longer, and instead of falling asleep completely, I fell into a state of somnolence that left me aware of what was happening around me, while depriving me of the strength either to defend myself or to flee.

"I dragged myself towards my bed, to find there the sole defense that remained to me, my saving knife; but I could not get as far as the bed head: I fell on my knees, my hands clinging to one of the posts of the foot. Then I realized that I was lost."

Felton turned dreadfully pale, and a convulsive shiver ran all through his body.

"And what was most dreadful of all," Milady went on, her voice broken, as if she still felt the same anguish as at that terrible moment, "was that this time I was conscious of the danger that threatened me; it was that my soul, as I may say, remained awake in my sleeping body; it was that I could see, I could hear—true, it was all as if in a dream, but that only made it the more frightening.

"I saw the lamp going up and gradually leaving me in darkness; then I heard the so familiar creak of that door, though the door had only opened twice.

"I felt instinctively that someone was approaching me. They say that the wretch lost in the deserts of America can feel the approach of a snake in the same way.

"I wanted to make an effort, I tried to cry out; with an incredible energy of will I even raised myself, but only to fall again at once . . . into the arms of my persecutor."

"Will you tell me who this man was?" cried the young officer.

Milady saw at a single glance all the suffering she was causing Felton by lingering over each detail of her story, but she did not want to spare him any torture. The more profoundly she wrung his heart, the more surely he would avenge her. She thus went on as if she had not heard his exclamation, or as if she thought the moment had not yet come to reply to it.

"Only this time it was not some sort of inert, unfeeling corpse that the infamous man was dealing with. I've told you: though unable to recover the full use of my faculties, I remained aware of my danger. I thus fought with all my strength, and, weak as I was, I must have put up a long resistance, for I heard him cry out:

"'These wretched Puritans! I knew they wearied their executioners, but I thought them less strong against their seducers.'

"Alas, this desperate resistance could not continue long! I felt my strength failing; and this time it was not my sleep that the coward profited from, but my fainting."

Felton listened without making any other sound than a sort of muffled growl; but the sweat streamed down his marble brow, and his hand, hidden under his clothing, tore his breast.

"My first impulse, on regaining consciousness, was to look under my pillow for the knife I had been unable to reach. If it had not served for defense, it could at least serve for expiation.

"But as I took hold of that knife, Felton, a terrible idea came to me. I've sworn to tell you everything; I've promised you the truth, and I will tell it, though it be my ruin."

"The idea came to you of revenging yourself on this man, is that it?" cried Felton.

"Why, yes!" said Milady. "It was not a Christian idea, I know. No doubt the eternal enemy of our souls, that lion ceaselessly roaring around us, breathed it into my mind. What can I tell you, Felton?" Milady went on in the tone of a woman accusing herself of a crime. "The idea came to me and doubtless never left me again. It is for that homicidal thought that I bear the punishment today."

"Go on, go on," said Felton, "I'm anxious to see you come to your vengeance."

"Oh, I resolved that it would take place as soon as possible!

I had no doubt that he would come back the next night. During the day I had nothing to fear.

"And so, when it came time for lunch, I did not hesitate to eat and drink. I had decided that I would pretend to eat supper, but take nothing. I thus had to use the day's food to combat the evening's fast.

"Only I hid a glass of water from my lunch, thirst having been what I had suffered from most when I went forty-eight hours without eating or drinking.

"The day passed without having any other influence on me than to harden me in the resolve I had taken; only I took care that my face did not betray in any way the thought in my heart, for I had no doubt that I was being observed. Several times I felt a smile on my lips—Felton, I dare not tell you what idea I was smiling at, you would hold me in horror . . ."

"Go on, go on," said Felton, "you see very well I'm listening and am anxious to reach the end."

"Evening came, the customary events took place: in the darkness, as usual, my supper was served, then the lamp was lit, and I sat down at the table.

"All I ate was some fruit. I pretended to pour myself water from the carafe, but only drank what I had set aside in my glass. Moreover, the substitution was done so deftly that my spies, if I had any, would have conceived no suspicions.

"After supper, I gave the same signs of numbness as the evening before, but this time, as if I was succumbing to fatigue or had grown familiar with the danger, I dragged myself to my bed and pretended to fall asleep.

"This time I found my knife under the pillow, and while I feigned sleep, my hand convulsively gripped its handle.

"Two hours went by without anything happening. This time—oh, my God, who would have thought it the day before?—I began to be afraid he wouldn't come.

"At last, I saw the lamp rise quietly and disappear in the depths of the ceiling. My room filled with darkness, but I made an effort to see through the gloom.

"About ten minutes passed. I heard no other noise than the beating of my own heart.

"I begged heaven that he would come.

"At last I heard the well-known sound of the door opening and closing; despite the thickness of the carpet, I heard footsteps that made the floor creak; despite the darkness, I saw a shadow approaching my bed."

"Hurry, hurry!" said Felton. "Don't you see that each of your words burns me like molten lead?"

"Then," Milady went on, "then I gathered all my strength, I reminded myself that the moment of vengeance, or rather of justice, had sounded. I considered myself another Judith. I crouched there, my knife in my hand, and when I saw him close to me, reaching out his arms to search for his victim, then, with a last cry of grief and despair, I stabbed him in the middle of his chest.

"The scoundrel! He had foreseen everything. His chest was covered with a coat of mail. The knife glanced off.

"'Aha!' he cried, seizing my arm and tearing from me the weapon that had served me so ill, 'so you have designs on my life, my beautiful Puritan! But that is something more than hatred, that is ingratitude! Come, come, calm yourself, my beautiful child! I thought you were softening. I'm not one of those tyrants who keep women by force. You don't love me. In my usual self-conceit, I doubted that; now I am convinced. Tomorrow you shall go free.'

"I had only one desire—to kill myself.

"'Beware!' I said to him, 'for my freedom will be your dishonor! Yes, for no sooner will I leave here than I will tell all, I will tell of the violence you have used against me, I will tell of my captivity. I will denounce this palace of infamy. You are highly placed, Milord, but tremble! Above you there is the king, and above the king there is God.'

"Master of himself as he seemed, my persecutor let show an impulse of anger. I could not see the expression of his face, but I felt the arm on which I had placed my hand tremble.

"'Then you will not leave here,' he said.

"'Good, good!' I cried. 'Then the place of my torture will also be my grave. Good! I will die here, and you will see whether an accusing ghost is not more terrible than a threatening person!'

" 'You will be left no weapon.'

" 'There is one that despair puts within reach of every creature who has the courage to use it. I will starve myself to death.' "

" 'Come,' said the scoundrel, 'isn't peace better than a war like this? I will give you back your freedom this instant, I will proclaim you a living virtue, I will call you the English Lucretia.'

" 'And I will declare you the Sextus, I will denounce you to men as I have already denounced you to God; and if, like Lucretia, I must sign my accusation in my own blood, I will sign it.'

" 'Aha!' said my enemy in a mocking tone, 'then that is something else. By heaven, when all is said, you're well off here, you lack for nothing, and if you starve yourself to death, it will be your own fault.'

"At these words, he withdrew, I heard the door open and close, and I was left a wreck—less in my grief, I confess, than in the shame of not having revenged myself.

"He kept his word to me. All the next day, all the next night went by without my seeing him again. But I also kept my word and did not eat or drink. I was determined, as I had told him, to starve myself to death.

"I spent that day and night in prayer, for I hoped that God would forgive me my suicide.

"On the second night, the door opened. I was lying on the floor; my strength was beginning to abandon me.

"At the noise, I raised myself on one hand.

" 'Well?' he said in a voice that vibrated in too terrible a way in my ear for me not to recognize it. 'Well, have we softened a little, and will we buy our freedom with a mere promise of silence? You see, I'm a good prince,' he added, 'and though I don't like the Puritans, I do them justice, as I do their women when they're pretty. Come, make me a little oath on the cross, I don't ask any more of you.'

" 'On the cross!' I cried, getting up, for at that abhorred voice I had recovered all my strength. 'On the cross I swear that no promise, no threat, no torture will shut my mouth; on the cross I swear to denounce you everywhere as a murderer, as a stealer of honor, as a coward; on the cross I swear that, if ever I get out of here, I will demand revenge on you from the whole human race!'

" 'Take care!' said the voice, with a menacing tone that I had not heard before. 'I have a supreme means, which I will use only in the last extremity, of shutting your mouth, or at least of keeping people from believing a single word you say.'

"I gathered all my strength to reply with a burst of laughter.

"He saw that henceforth there was eternal war between us, war to the death.

" 'Listen,' he said, 'I give you the rest of tonight and all day tomorrow. Think it over. Promise to be quiet, and wealth, consideration, honors will surround you; threaten to talk, and I condemn you to infamy.'

" 'You?' I cried. 'You?'

" 'To eternal, ineffaceable infamy!'

" 'You?' I repeated. "Oh, I tell you, Felton, I thought he was mad!

" 'Yes, I!' he replied.

" 'Ah, leave me!' I said to him. 'Go, if you don't want me to smash my head against the wall before your eyes!'

" 'Very well,' he said, 'you want it this way. Till tomorrow evening!'

" 'Till tomorrow evening,' I replied, falling down and chewing the rug with rage."

Felton was leaning on a chair, and Milady saw with devilish joy that he would perhaps lose strength before the end of the story.

LVII

A Means from Classical Tragedy

After a moment's silence, employed by Milady in observing the young man who was listening to her, she went on with her story:

"It was nearly three days since I had drunk or eaten anything. I suffered atrocious tortures. Sometimes it seemed to me as though clouds were encircling my forehead, veiling my eyes. It was delirium.

"Evening came. I was so weak that I kept fainting, and each time I fainted, I thanked God, for I thought I was going to die.

"In the midst of one of these fainting spells, I heard the door open. Terror brought me back to myself.

"My persecutor came in, followed by a masked man. He was also masked himself, but I recognized his footstep, I recognized that imposing air hell had given to his person for the misfortune of mankind.

" 'Well,' he said to me, 'have you decided to make me the oath I asked of you?'

" 'As you said, the Puritans have only one word: you have heard mine, which is to pursue you on earth before the tribunals of men, and in heaven before the tribunal of God!'

" 'So you persist?'

" 'I swear it before God who hears me: I will take the whole world as witness against your crime, and that until I have found my avenger.'

" 'You are a prostitute,' he said in a thundering voice, 'and you will endure the punishment of prostitutes! Branded in the eyes of the world you would call upon, try proving to that world that you are neither guilty nor mad!'

"Then, addressing the man who accompanied him, he said:

" 'Executioner, do your duty.' "

"Oh, his name! his name!" cried Felton. "Tell me his name!"

"Then, despite my cries, despite my resistance, for I was beginning to understand that it was a question of something worse than death for me, the executioner seized me, threw me to the floor, bruised me with his grip, and, choking with sobs, almost unconscious, calling upon God, who did not hear me, I suddenly let out a frightful scream of pain and shame: a burning iron, a red-hot iron, the executioner's iron, had stamped its mark on my shoulder."

Felton let out a roar.

"Here," said Milady, rising with queenly majesty, "here, Felton, see how a new martyrdom was invented for the young girl who was pure and yet was the victim of a villain's brutality. Learn to know the hearts of men, and henceforth do not so easily make yourself the instrument of their unjust vengeance."

With a quick gesture, Milady opened her dress, tore the batiste that covered her breast, and, blushing with feigned anger and mock shame, showed the young man the ineffaceable mark that dishonored so beautiful a shoulder.

"But," cried Felton, "it is a fleur-de-lis I see there!"

"And that is just where the infamy lies," replied Milady. "The brand of England! . . . It would have to be proved which court had imposed it on me, and I could have made public appeal to all the courts in the realm; but the brand of France . . . oh! with that I was really and truly branded!"

This was too much for Felton.

Pale, motionless, crushed by this dreadful revelation, dazzled by the superhuman beauty of this woman, who unveiled herself to him with a shamelessness he found sublime, he ended by falling on his knees before her, as the first Christians did before those pure and holy martyrs whom the persecution of the emperors handed over to the bloody lewdness of the populace in the circus. The brand disappeared, the beauty alone remained.

"Forgive me, forgive me!" cried Felton, "oh, forgive me!"

Milady looked into his eyes and read: "Love, love."

"Forgive you for what?" she asked.

"Forgive me for having joined your persecutors."

Milady held out her hand to him.

"So beautiful, so young!" cried Felton, covering that hand with kisses.

Milady let fall on him one of those looks that turn a slave into a king.

Felton was a Puritan: he let go of the woman's hand in order to kiss her feet.

He no longer simply loved her, he worshipped her.

When this crisis was over, when Milady seemed to have recovered her coolheadedness, which she had never lost, when Felton had seen closed again behind the veil of chastity those treasures of love that were so well hidden from him only to make him desire them more ardently, he said:

"Ah! now I have only one thing to ask you, and that is the name of your true executioner—because for me there is only one; the other was no more than an instrument."

"What, brother?" cried Milady. "Must I still name him for you? Haven't you guessed?"

"What?" replied Felton. "Him! . . . him again! . . . always him! . . . You mean the real guilty one is . . ."

"The real guilty one," said Milady, "is the ravager of England, the persecutor of true believers, the cowardly ravisher of so many women's honor, he who on a whim of his corrupt heart is going to spill so much of the blood of two kingdoms, who protects the Protestants today and will betray them tomorrow . . ."

"Buckingham! So it's Buckingham!" cried the exasperated Felton.

Milady hid her face in her hands, as if she could not bear the shame that his name brought back to her.

"Buckingham, the executioner of this angelic creature!" cried Felton. "And you did not strike him down, my God! And you have left him noble, honored, powerful, for the ruin of us all!"

"God abandons those who abandon themselves," said Milady.

"But he wants, then, to draw down on that head the punishment reserved for the damned!" Felton went on with growing excitement. "He wants, then, that human justice forestall heavenly justice!"

"Men fear him and spare him."

"Oh, but I," said Felton, "I do not fear him, and I will not spare him!"

Milady felt her soul bathed in an infernal joy.

"But how does Lord de Winter, my protector, my father, find himself mixed up in all this?" asked Felton.

"Listen, Felton," Milady picked up, "it's because alongside cowardly and despicable men, there are always great and generous natures. I had a fiancé, a man I loved and who loved me—a heart like yours, Felton, a man like you. I went to him and told him all. The man knew me and didn't doubt me for a moment. He was a great lord, a man equal in every point to Buckingham. He said nothing, he simply buckled on his sword, wrapped himself in his cloak, and went to Buckingham Palace."

"Yes, yes," said Felton, "I understand—though with such men it's not the sword one should use, but the dagger."

"Buckingham had left the previous day, sent as ambassador to Spain, where he went to ask the hand of the infanta for King Charles I, who was then only the Prince of Wales. My fiancé came back.

"'Listen,' he said to me, 'the man has left, and, consequently, for the moment he has escaped my vengeance; but in the meantime let us be united, as we should be; then rely on Lord de Winter to uphold his own honor and that of his wife.'"

"Lord de Winter!" cried Felton.

"Yes," said Milady, "Lord de Winter. And now you surely understand everything, don't you? Buckingham remained absent for more than a year. Eight days before his arrival, Lord de Winter died suddenly, leaving me his sole heir. Where did the blow come from? God, who knows all, must know that; I accuse no one . . ."

"Oh, what an abyss, what an abyss!" cried Felton.

"Lord de Winter died without saying anything to his brother. The terrible secret was to be kept hidden from everyone, until it broke like thunder on the head of the guilty one. Your protector had taken a dim view of his older brother's marriage to a young girl with no fortune. I felt that I could not expect any support from a man disappointed in his hopes of inheritance. I went over to France, resolved to remain there for the rest of my life. But all my fortune is in England; with communications closed by the war, I lacked for everything; I had to come back. Six days ago I landed in Portsmouth."

"Well?" said Felton.

"Well! Buckingham no doubt learned of my return, spoke of it to Lord de Winter, who was already warned against me, and told him that his sister-in-law was a prostitute, a branded woman. The pure and noble voice of my husband was no longer there to defend me. Lord de Winter believed everything he was told, all the more easily in that it was in his interest to believe it. He had me arrested, brought me here, put me under your guard. You know the rest. The day after tomorrow he is banishing me, having me deported; the day after tomorrow he is relegating me to the infamous. Oh, yes, the web is well woven! It's a skillful plot, and my honor will not survive it. You see very well that I must die, Felton. Felton, give me that knife."

And at these words, as if all her strength was exhausted, Milady let herself fall, weak and languishing, into the arms of the young officer, who, drunk with love, with anger, and with unknown delights, caught her rapturously and pressed her to his heart, all ashiver at the breath of that beautiful mouth, all frantic at the contact of that throbbing breast.

"No, no," he said, "no, you shall live honored and pure, you shall live to triumph over your enemies."

Milady slowly pushed him away with her hand, while drawing him to her with her gaze; but Felton, in his turn, seized hold of her, imploring her like a divinity.

"Oh, death, death!" she said, lowering her voice and her eyelids. "Oh, death rather than shame! Felton, my brother, my friend, I beseech you!"

"No," cried Felton, "no, you shall live, and you shall be avenged!"

"Felton, I bring misfortune to everything around me! Felton, abandon me! Felton, let me die!"

"Well, then we shall die together!" he cried, pressing his lips to those of his prisoner.

There was a loud knocking on the door. This time Milady really pushed him away.

"Listen," she said, "we've been overheard; they're coming! That's it, we're lost!"

"No," said Felton, "it's only the sentry letting me know that a patrol is coming."

"Run to the door, then, and open it yourself."

Felton obeyed: this woman was already all his thought, all his soul.

He found himself face to face with a sergeant commanding a patrol of the watch.

"Well, what is it?" asked the young officer.

"You told me to open the door if I heard a cry for help," said the sentry, "but you forgot to give me the key. I heard you cry out, though I did not understand what you said. I went to open the door, it was locked from inside, and so I sent for the sergeant."

"And here I am," said the sergeant.

Felton, bewildered, nearly mad, was left speechless.

Milady realized that it was for her to take over the situation. She ran to the table and took the knife that Felton had set down there.

"And by what right do you wish to keep me from dying?" she said.

"Good God!" cried Felton, seeing the knife gleaming in her hand.

At that moment, a burst of ironic laughter echoed in the corridor.

The baron, attracted by the noise, in his dressing gown, his sword under his arm, was standing in the doorway.

"Aha!" he said, "now we've come to the last act of the tragedy. You see, Felton, the drama has followed all the phases I indicated. But don't worry, no blood will flow."

Milady realized that she was lost if she did not give Felton an immediate and terrible proof of her courage.

"You're mistaken, Milord, blood will flow, and may this blood fall back upon those who made it flow!"

Felton cried out and rushed to her. It was too late: Milady had stabbed herself.

But the knife had fortunately, or we ought to say skillfully, encountered the metal busk which in those days protected ladies' bosoms like a cuirass. It had glanced off, tearing her dress, and had penetrated at an angle between the flesh and the ribs.

Milady's dress was nevertheless stained with blood in a second.

Milady fell backwards and seemed to faint.

Felton snatched the knife away.

"You see, Milord," he said with a gloomy air, "here is a woman who was under my guard, and she has killed herself!"

"Don't worry, Felton," said Lord de Winter, "she's not dead. Demons don't die so easily. Don't worry. Go and wait for me in my room."

"But, Milord . . ."

"Go, I order you."

At this command from his superior, Felton obeyed; but as he left, he slipped the knife into his shirt front.

As for Lord de Winter, he contented himself with sending for the woman who served Milady. When she came, he entrusted the still unconscious prisoner to her and left them alone together.

However, since the wound might, after all, be serious, despite his suspicions, he sent a man on horseback that same moment to fetch a doctor.

LVIII

ESCAPE

As Lord de Winter had thought, Milady's wound was not dangerous. And so, once she found herself alone with the woman whom the baron had sent for and who was hurriedly undressing her, she reopened her eyes.

However, it was necessary to feign weakness and pain. This was not a difficult thing for an actress like Milady, and the poor woman was so completely fooled by her prisoner that, despite her entreaties, she insisted on watching over her all night.

But the presence of this woman did not keep Milady from reflecting.

There was no longer any doubt; Felton was convinced; Felton was hers. If an angel should appear to the young man and accuse Milady, he would certainly take it, in the state of mind in which he found himself, for an emissary of the devil.

Milady smiled at this thought, for Felton was henceforth her only hope, her only means of salvation.

But Lord de Winter might have suspected that, and Felton might now be under surveillance himself.

Towards four o'clock in the morning, the doctor arrived.

But since the time when Milady had stabbed herself, the wound had already closed. The doctor was thus unable to measure either its direction or its depth; he could only tell from the patient's pulse that the case was not serious.

In the morning, under the pretext that she had not slept at night and needed rest, Milady sent away the woman who was watching over her.

She had one hope, which was that Felton would come at breakfast time, but Felton did not come.

Had her fears been realized? Was Felton, suspected by the baron, going to fail her at the decisive moment? She had only one day left: Lord de Winter had announced that she would be embarking on the twenty-third, and they had just reached the morning of the twenty-second.

Nevertheless, she waited rather patiently until dinner time.

Though she had not eaten in the morning, dinner was brought at the usual hour. Milady noticed then with fright that the uniforms of the soldiers guarding her had changed.

Then she ventured to ask what had become of Felton. She was told that Felton had mounted a horse an hour ago and ridden off.

She inquired whether the baron was still in the castle. The soldier replied that he was, and that he had orders to inform him if the prisoner wished to speak with him.

Milady replied that she was too weak at the moment, and that her only wish was to be left alone.

The soldier went out, leaving dinner on the table.

Felton had been sent away, the marines had been changed, Felton was thus distrusted.

This was the last blow to the prisoner.

Left alone, she got up. This bed, which she kept to out of prudence and to make them believe she was seriously wounded, burned her like a bed of coals. She cast a glance at the door. The baron had had a board nailed over the peephole. He no doubt feared that through this opening she might still manage, by some diabolical means, to seduce the guards.

Milady smiled for joy. She could thus give way to her passions without being observed. She paced the room with the exaltation of a raving madwoman or a tigress locked in an iron cage. To be sure, if she still had the knife, she would have considered killing, not herself this time, but the baron.

At six o'clock, Lord de Winter came in. He was armed to the teeth. This man, in whom till then Milady had seen only a rather foolish gentleman, had become an admirable jailer. He seemed to foresee everything, guess everything, forestall everything.

One glance at Milady told him what was going on in her soul.

"Very well," he said, "but today again you will not kill me; you have no weapons left, and besides I'm on my guard. You had begun to pervert my poor Felton; he was already falling under your infernal influence, but I intend to save him. He will not see you again. It's all over. Gather up your rags, you're leaving tomorrow. I had fixed the embarkation for the twenty-fourth, but I thought that the sooner it happened, the surer it would be. By noon tomorrow I will have the order for your exile, signed by Buckingham. If you say a single word to anyone at all before getting on the ship, my sergeant will blow your brains out—he has orders to do so. If, on the ship, you say a word to anyone at all without the captain's permission, the captain will have you thrown into the sea—that is agreed. Good-bye. I have nothing more to say to you today. Tomorrow I will see you again to give you my farewells!"

Milady had listened to this whole threatening tirade with a scornful smile on her lips but rage in her heart.

Supper was served. Milady felt she had need of strength; she did not know what might happen during that night, which approached menacingly, for big clouds were rolling across the sky, and distant lightning heralded a storm.

The storm broke towards ten o'clock in the evening. Milady felt consoled to see nature share the disorder of her heart. Thunder rumbled in the air like the anger in her mind; it seemed that the squall, in passing, disheveled her hair as it did the trees whose branches it bent, stripping away their leaves; she howled like the storm, and her voice was lost in the great voice of nature, which also seemed to wail and despair.

Suddenly she heard a tapping on the windowpane, and, in a flash of lightning, she saw a man's face appear beyond the bars.

She ran to the window and opened it.

"Felton!" she cried. "I'm saved!"

"Yes," said Felton, "but silence, silence! I need time to cut through your bars. Only be careful they don't see you through the peephole."

"Oh, that is a proof that the Lord is with us, Felton," replied Milady. "They've boarded up the peephole."

"That's good. God has deprived them of reason!" said Felton.

"But what am I to do?" asked Milady.

"Nothing, nothing; just close the window. Go to bed, or at least get into bed fully dressed. When I'm finished, I'll tap on the windowpane. But will you be able to go with me?"

"Oh, yes!"

"Your wound?"

"It hurts, but it doesn't prevent me from walking."

"Be ready, then, for the first signal."

Milady closed the window again, put out the lamp, and went, as Felton had recommended, to huddle in her bed. Amidst the howling of the storm, she heard the grating of the file on the bars, and, with each flash of lightning, she made out Felton's shadow outside the window.

She spent an hour breathless, panting, sweat on her brow, and her heart gripped by dreadful anguish at each movement she heard in the corridor.

There are hours that last a year.

At the end of an hour, Felton tapped again.

Milady leaped out of bed and went to open the window. Two bars less made an opening a man could pass through.

"Are you ready?" asked Felton.

"Yes. Must I bring anything?"

"Gold, if you have any."

"Yes, luckily they left me what I had."

"So much the better, for I used all mine to charter a boat."

"Take it," said Milady, putting a pouch full of gold into Felton's hand.

Felton took the pouch and dropped it to the foot of the wall.

"Now," he said, "will you come?"

"Here I am."

Milady climbed onto a chair and passed the upper part of her body through the window. She saw the young officer hanging above the abyss on a rope ladder.

For the first time, a fit of terror reminded her that she was a woman.

The void appalled her.

"I was afraid of that," said Felton.

"It's nothing, it's nothing," said Milady. "I'll go down with my eyes shut."

"Do you trust me?" asked Felton.

"Need you ask?"

"Bring your hands together. Cross them. That's good."

Felton tied her wrists with his handkerchief, then, over the handkerchief, with a rope.

"What are you doing?" Milady asked in surprise.

"Put your arms around my neck, and don't be afraid of anything."

"But I'll make you lose your balance, and we'll both be dashed on the rocks."

"Don't worry, I'm a sailor."

There was not a second to lose. Milady put her arms around Felton's neck and let herself slide out the window.

Felton started to go down the ladder slowly, rung by rung. Despite the weight of the two bodies, the blast of the storm swung them in the air.

All at once Felton stopped.

"What is it?" asked Milady.

"Silence," said Felton, "I hear footsteps."

"We've been found out!"

There were several moments of silence.

"No," said Felton, "it's nothing."

"But what is that noise then?"

"The noise of the patrol just coming along the circuit path."

"Where is the circuit path?"

"Just below us."

"They'll see us."

"Not if there's no lightning."

"They'll run into the foot of the ladder."

"Luckily it's six feet short."

"There they are, my God!"

"Silence!"

They both remained suspended, motionless and breathless, eleven feet from the ground, while the soldiers passed under them laughing and talking.

It was a terrible moment for the fugitives.

The patrol passed on. They heard the sound of footsteps going away and the murmur of voices growing fainter.

"Now," said Felton, "we're safe."

Milady heaved a sigh and fainted.

Felton continued to go down. Coming to the end of the ladder and feeling no support for his feet, he let himself down hand over hand; finally, reaching the last rung, he stretched out his legs and touched the ground. He bent down, picked up the pouch of gold, and took it in his teeth.

Then he picked Milady up in his arms and went off quickly in the opposite direction from that taken by the patrol. Soon he left the circuit path, went down over the rocks, and, coming to the shore of the sea, let out a whistle.

A similar signal answered him, and five minutes later a skiff appeared with four men aboard.

The boat came as close to land as it could, but there was not enough depth for it to touch the shore. Felton waded into the water up to his waist, not wishing to entrust his precious cargo to anyone.

Fortunately, the storm had begun to abate, though the sea was still rough. The little skiff bobbed up and down on the waves like a nutshell.

"To the sloop," said Felton, "and row quickly."

The four men bent their backs to the oars, but the sea was too heavy for the blades to get much of a grip on it.

Nevertheless, they moved away from the castle, which was the main thing. The night was pitch dark, and it was already almost impossible to make out the shore from the skiff; still less would anyone be able to make out the skiff from the shore.

A black speck was rocking on the waves.

It was the sloop.

While the skiff advanced with all the strength of its four rowers, Felton untied the rope and then the handkerchief that bound Milady's hands.

Milady heaved a sigh and opened her eyes.

"Where am I?" she asked.

"Safe," replied the young officer.

"Oh, safe, safe!" she cried. "Yes, here is the sky, here is the sea! This air I'm breathing is the air of freedom. Ah! . . . Thank you, Felton, thank you!"

The young man pressed her to his heart.

"But what's wrong with my hands?" asked Milady. "It feels as though my wrists have been crushed in a vice."

Milady raised her arms: her wrists were indeed bruised.

"Alas!" said Felton, looking at those beautiful hands and slowly shaking his head.

"Oh, it's nothing, it's nothing!" cried Milady. "Now I remember!"

Milady looked around for something.

"It's here," said Felton, nudging the pouch of gold with his foot.

They approached the sloop. The sailor on watch hailed the skiff, and the skiff answered.

"What is that vessel?" asked Milady.

"The one I've chartered for you."

"Where will it take me?"

"Wherever you like, provided you put me ashore at Portsmouth."

"What are you going to do in Portsmouth?" asked Milady.

"Carry out Lord de Winter's orders," said Felton with a gloomy smile.

"What orders?" asked Milady.

"So you don't understand?" asked Felton.

"No, explain yourself, I beg you."

"As he distrusted me, he wanted to guard you himself, and sent me in his place to have Buckingham sign the order for your deportation."

"But if he distrusted you, how did he entrust you with this order?"

"Was I supposed to know what I was carrying?"

"That's true. And you're going to Portsmouth?"

"I have no time to waste: tomorrow is the twenty-third, and Buckingham is leaving tomorrow with the fleet."

"He's leaving tomorrow? Where for?"

"For La Rochelle."

"He mustn't leave!" cried Milady, forgetting her accustomed presence of mind.

"Don't worry," replied Felton, "he won't leave."

Milady jumped for joy. She had just read to the bottom of the young man's heart: the death of Buckingham was clearly spelled out there.

"Felton . . ." she said, "you are as great as Judas Maccabaeus! If you die, I will die with you—that is all that I can say."

"Silence!" said Felton. "We're here."

Indeed, they touched the sloop.

Felton climbed up the ladder first and gave his hand to Milady, while the sailors supported her, for the sea was still quite choppy.

A moment later they were on deck.

"Captain," said Felton, "here is the person I spoke to you about, who is to be taken to France safe and sound."

"For a thousand pistoles," said the captain.

"I've already given you five hundred."

"That's so," said the captain.

"And here are the other five hundred," picked up Milady, placing her hand on the pouch of gold.

"No," said the captain, "I have only one word, and I have given it to this young man. The other five hundred pistoles are due me on reaching Boulogne."

"And we will reach it?"

"Safe and sound," said the captain, "or my name's not Jack Butler."

"Well," said Milady, "if you keep your word, I'll give you not five hundred but a thousand pistoles."

"Hurrah for you, then, my lovely lady," cried the captain, "and may God keep sending me customers like Your Ladyship!"

"In the meantime," said Felton, "take us to the little bay of Chichester, before Portsmouth. You know you've agreed to take us there."

The captain replied by ordering the necessary maneuver, and towards seven o'clock in the morning, the little vessel dropped anchor in the said harbor.

During this passage, Felton told Milady everything: how, instead of going to London, he had chartered this little vessel; how he had come back; how he had climbed the wall by placing crampons in the gaps between the stones to rest his feet on; and how finally, on reaching the bars, he had attached the ladder. Milady knew the rest.

It was agreed that Milady would wait for Felton until ten o'clock. If he had not come back by ten o'clock, she would leave.

In that case, supposing he was at liberty, he would rejoin her in France, at the convent of the Carmelites in Béthune.

LIX

What Happened in Portsmouth on the Twenty-third of August 1628

Felton took leave of Milady as a brother going for a simple walk takes leave of his sister, by kissing her hand.

Generally, he seemed to be in his usual state of calm, only an unaccustomed light shone in his eyes, like the glitter of a fever. His brow was still paler than usual, his teeth were clenched, and his speech had a curt and abrupt accent which indicated that something dark was stirring in him.

As long as he was in the skiff that brought him to land, he sat with his face turned towards Milady, who, standing on deck, followed him with her eyes. They were both rather reassured about the fear of being pursued: no one ever entered Milady's room before nine o'clock, and it took nine hours to get from the castle to London.

Felton stepped ashore, climbed the little crest that led to the top of the cliff, saluted Milady a last time, and set out for the town.

After about a hundred paces, as the terrain sloped downwards, he could no longer see more than the mast of the sloop.

He raced off at once in the direction of Portsmouth, whose towers and buildings he saw before him, about a half mile away, emerging from the morning mist.

The sea beyond Portsmouth was covered with ships, whose masts, like a forest of poplars stripped bare by winter, swayed to the blowing of the wind.

Felton, during his rapid march, went back over what ten years of ascetic meditations and a long stay in the milieu of the Puritans had furnished him by way of true or false accusations against the favorite of James VI and Charles I.

When he compared the public crimes of this minister—glaring crimes, European crimes, if one may say so—with the private and unknown crimes Milady had charged him with, Felton found that the more guilty of the two men contained in Buckingham was the one whose life was unknown to the public. His love, so strange, so new, so ardent, made him look at the infamous and imaginary accusations of Milady as through a magnifying glass, where one sees frightful monsters that in reality are atoms barely visible next to an ant.

The speed of his running inflamed his blood still more: the idea that he was leaving behind him the woman he loved, or rather adored like a saint, exposed to a dreadful vengeance, the emotion he had been through, and his present fatigue, all exalted his soul still further above human feelings.

He entered Portsmouth towards eight o'clock in the morning. The entire population was afoot; drums were beating in the streets and at the port; the troops of the embarkation were moving down to the sea.

Felton arrived at the Admiralty covered with dust and streaming with sweat. His face, ordinarily so pale, was purple with heat and anger. The sentry was going to chase him away, but Felton sent for the head of the guard post, and taking from his pocket the letter of which he was the bearer, said:

"An urgent message from Lord de Winter."

At the name of Lord de Winter, who was known as one of His Grace's closest intimates, the head of the post gave the order to admit Felton, who, moreover, was himself wearing the uniform of a naval officer.

Felton rushed into the palace.

Just as he entered the vestibule, another man also entered, dusty, out of breath, leaving at the door a post-horse which, on arriving, fell to its knees.

He and Felton addressed themselves at the same time to Patrick, the duke's confidential valet. Felton named the baron de Winter, the unknown man would name no one, and declared that he would make himself known to the duke alone. They each insisted on going ahead of the other.

Patrick, who knew that Lord de Winter had both official and friendly relations with the duke, gave preference to the one who came in his name. The other was forced to wait, and it was easy to see how he cursed this delay.

The valet led Felton across a large hall in which the deputies of La Rochelle, headed by the prince de Soubise, were waiting, and ushered him into a dressing room where Buckingham, just out of the bath, was finishing his toilet, to which, this time as always, he paid extraordinary attention.

"Lieutenant Felton," said Patrick, "on the part of Lord de Winter."

"On the part of Lord de Winter?" repeated Buckingham. "Show him in."

Felton came in. At that moment, Buckingham threw a rich, gold-brocaded dressing gown onto a couch, in order to put on a blue velvet doublet all embroidered with pearls.

"Why didn't the baron come himself?" asked Buckingham. "I was expecting him this morning."

"He asked me to tell Your Grace," replied Felton, "that he deeply regrets not having that honor, but that he was prevented by the guard he is obliged to mount at the castle."

"Yes, yes," said Buckingham, "I know, he has a prisoner."

"It is precisely of that prisoner that I wished to speak with Your Grace," Felton picked up.

"Well, speak then!"

"What I have to say can be heard only by you, Milord."

"Leave us, Patrick," said Buckingham, "but stay within earshot of the bell. I shall summon you presently."

Patrick left.

"We are alone, Monsieur," said Buckingham. "Speak."

"Milord," said Felton, "the baron de Winter wrote to you the other day asking you to sign an order of transportation concerning a young woman named Charlotte Backson."

"Yes, Monsieur, and I replied that he should bring me or send me the order, and I would sign it."

"Here it is, Milord."

"Give it to me," said the duke.

And, taking the paper from Felton's hand, he quickly glanced over it. Then, seeing that it was indeed the one that had been announced to him, he placed it on the table, took a pen, and prepared to sign it.

"Excuse me, Milord," said Felton, stopping the duke, "but does Your Grace know that Charlotte Backson is not the real name of this young woman?"

"Yes, Monsieur, I know that," replied the duke, dipping his pen into the inkwell.

"Then Your Grace knows her real name?" asked Felton in a curt voice.

"I do."

The duke brought the pen to the paper.

"And, knowing her real name," Felton went on, "Monseigneur will sign all the same?"

"Of course," said Buckingham, "and twice over."

"I cannot believe," continued Felton, in a voice that was becoming more and more curt and abrupt, "that His Grace knows it is a question of Lady de Winter . . ."

"I know it perfectly well, though I'm surprised that you know it!"

"And Your Grace will sign this order without remorse?"

Buckingham gave the young man a haughty look.

"Are you at all aware, Monsieur," he said to him, "that you are asking me strange questions, and that I am quite foolish to answer them?"

"Answer, Monseigneur," said Felton. "The situation is more serious than you may think."

Buckingham thought that the young man, coming on the part of Lord de Winter, was probably speaking in his name, and he calmed himself.

"Without any remorse," he said, "and the baron knows that Milady de Winter is a great offender, and that it is almost doing her a favor to limit her punishment to deportation."

The duke put his pen to the paper.

"You shall not sign that order, Milord!" said Felton, taking a step towards the duke.

"I shall not sign this order?" said Buckingham. "And why not?"

"Because you will look into your own heart, and you will do justice to Milady."

"It would be doing her justice to send her to Tyburn," said Buckingham. "Milady is an infamous creature."

"Monseigneur, Milady is an angel, you know it very well, and I demand that you set her free."

"Are you mad," said Buckingham, "that you speak to me in this way?"

"Milord, forgive me, I speak as I can! I will restrain myself. Nevertheless, Milord, think of what you are about to do, and beware of going beyond the measure!"

"I beg your pardon? . . . God help me," cried Buckingham, "but I believe he's threatening me!"

"No, Milord, I am still entreating, and I tell you: one drop of water is enough to make the full cup run over; one slight fault can draw down punishment on a head that has been spared despite so many crimes."

"Monsieur Felton," said Buckingham, "you will leave here and place yourself under arrest at once."

"You are going to hear me out, Milord. You have seduced this young girl, you have outraged her, sullied her. Make good your crimes against her, let her leave freely, and I will demand nothing more of you."

"Demand nothing more?" said Buckingham, looking at Felton in astonishment and stressing each syllable of the three words as he spoke them.

"Milord," Felton went on, becoming more excited as he spoke, "Milord, take care, all England is weary of your iniquities. Milord, you have abused the royal power that you have almost usurped. Milord, you are held in horror by men and by God. God will punish you later, but I—I will punish you today."

"Ah, this is too much!" cried Buckingham, taking a step towards the door.

Felton barred his way.

"I ask you humbly," he said, "to sign the order setting Milady free. Consider that she is the woman you have dishonored."

"Withdraw, Monsieur," said Buckingham, "or I shall call and have you put in irons."

"You will not call," said Felton, thrusting himself between the duke and the bell sitting on a silver-inlaid stand. "Take care, Milord, for now you are in God's hands."

"In the devil's hands, you mean!" cried Buckingham, raising his voice to attract people, though without calling out directly.

"Sign, Milord, sign the freedom of Lady de Winter," said Felton, pushing a paper towards the duke.

"By force? Are you joking? Ho, there, Patrick!"

"Sign, Milord!"

"Never!"

"Never?"

"Help, ho!" cried the duke, and at the same time he leaped for his sword.

But Felton gave him no time to draw it. He had the knife with which Milady had stabbed herself unsheathed and hidden in his doublet. At one bound he was upon the duke.

Just then, Patrick came into the room, crying: "Milord, a letter from France!"

"From France?" cried Buckingham, forgetting all except the thought of whom this letter might be from.

Felton seized the moment and plunged the knife into his side up to the hilt.

"Ah, traitor!" cried Buckingham, "you've killed me . . ."

"Murder!" shouted Patrick.

Felton looked around for a way to escape and, seeing the door free, rushed into the neighboring room, which, as we have said, was where the deputies from La Rochelle were waiting, crossed it at a run, and raced for the stairs. But on the top step he ran into Lord de Winter, who, seeing him pale, wild, livid, stained with blood on his hand and face, threw himself on his neck, crying:

"I knew it, I guessed it, and I came a minute too late! Oh, wretch that I am!"

Felton offered no resistance. Lord de Winter handed him over to the guards, who, while awaiting further orders, led him to a small terrace overlooking the sea, and himself hurried to Buckingham's dressing room.

At the duke's cry, at Patrick's shout, the man whom Felton had met in the antechamber rushed into the room.

He found the duke lying on a sofa, his clenched hand pressed to his wound.

"La Porte," said the duke in a dying voice, "La Porte, do you come from her?"

"Yes, Monseigneur," replied the faithful servant of Anne d'Autriche, "but too late, perhaps."

"Silence, La Porte, you might be overheard! Patrick, let no one in. Oh, I will never know what she wanted to tell me! My God, I'm dying!"

And the duke fainted.

Meanwhile, Lord de Winter, the deputies, the leaders of the expedition, the officers of Buckingham's household had burst into his room. Everywhere cries of despair rang out. The news that filled the palace with groans and laments soon overflowed everywhere and spread through the town.

A cannon shot announced that something new and unexpected had just happened.

Lord de Winter tore his hair.

"A minute too late!" he cried, "a minute too late! Oh, my God, my God, how terrible!"

Indeed, they had come at seven o'clock in the morning to tell him that a rope ladder was swinging from one of the castle windows. He had run at once to Milady's room, had found the room empty, the window open, and the bars cut through. He had recalled the verbal instructions d'Artagnan had sent him by his messenger; he had trembled for the duke, and, running to the stable, without taking time to saddle his horse, had leaped upon the first he came to, had raced flat-out, and, jumping down in the courtyard, had gone rushing up the stairs, and on the top step, as we have said, had run into Felton.

However, the duke was not dead. He came to, reopened his eyes, and hope returned to all their hearts.

"Gentlemen," he said, "leave me alone with Patrick and La Porte. Ah, it's you, de Winter! You sent me an odd sort of madman this morning; look what state he's left me in!"

"Oh, Milord!" cried the baron, "I'll never forgive myself!"

"And that will be wrong of you, my dear de Winter," said Buckingham, holding out his hand to him. "I know of no man who deserves to be mourned throughout another man's life—but leave us, I beg you."

The baron went out sobbing.

In the dressing room there remained only the wounded duke, La Porte, and Patrick.

The doctor had been sent for, but he could not be found.

"You will live, Milord, you will live," repeated Anne d'Autriche's messenger, kneeling beside the duke's sofa.

"What does she write to me?" Buckingham said weakly, streaming with blood and overcoming immense pain in order to speak of her he loved. "What does she write to me? Read me her letter."

"Oh, Milord!" said La Porte.

"Obey, La Porte. Don't you see I have no time to lose?"

La Porte broke the seal and placed the parchment under the duke's eyes; but Buckingham tried in vain to make out the handwriting.

"Read it, then," he said, "read it. I can't see anymore. Read it! For soon I may not be able to hear anymore, and I'll die without knowing what she has written to me."

La Porte made no more difficulties, and read:

Milord,

By all that I have suffered through you and for you, since I have known you, I entreat you, if you have any care for my peace, to break off the great armament you are preparing against France, and to stop a war of which it is said aloud that religion is the visible cause and said softly that your love for me is the hidden cause. This war may lead not only to great catastrophes for France and England, but also to misfortunes for you, Milord, which would leave me inconsolable.

Watch out for your life, which is threatened, and which will be dear to me the moment I am no longer obliged to look upon you as an enemy.

Your affectionate

Anne

Buckingham summoned up all the life that remained in him to listen to this reading. When it was finished, he asked, as if he had found the letter bitterly disappointing:

"Have you nothing else to tell me by word of mouth, La Porte?"

"I have, Monseigneur. The queen told me to tell you to watch out for yourself, for she had been warned that they wanted to assassinate you."

"And is that all, is that all?" Buckingham went on impatiently.

"She also told me to tell you that she always loved you."

"Ah!" said Buckingham, "God be praised! My death will not, then, be the death of a stranger for her!"

La Porte burst into tears.

"Patrick," said the duke, "bring me the box where the diamond pendants were."

Patrick brought the object he asked for, which La Porte recognized as having belonged to the queen.

"Now the white satin bag with her monogram embroidered on it in pearls."

Patrick obeyed again.

"Here, La Porte," said Buckingham, "these are the only tokens I had from her, this silver box and these two letters. Give them back to Her Majesty. And as a last souvenir . . ." (he looked around him for some precious object) ". . . add this . . ."

He went on looking, but his gaze, darkened by death, met only with the knife that had fallen from Felton's hand, still steaming with the crimson blood smeared on its blade.

"And add this knife," said the duke, pressing La Porte's hand.

He was still able to put the bag into the bottom of the silver box and drop the knife in, making a sign to La Porte that he could no longer speak. Then, with a last convulsion, which this time he had no more strength to combat, he slid from the sofa onto the floor.

Patrick uttered a great cry.

Buckingham wanted to smile a last time, but death arrested his thought, which remained graven on his forehead like a last kiss of love.

At that moment the duke's doctor arrived in a great flurry. He had been aboard the admiral's ship already; they had been obliged to go and fetch him there.

He went up to the duke, took his hand, held it for a moment in his own, and let it fall again.

"There's no use," he said, "he's dead."

"Dead! Dead!" cried Patrick.

At that cry, a whole throng came into the room, and everywhere there was only dismay and disorder.

As soon as Lord de Winter saw Buckingham expired, he ran to Felton, whom the soldiers were still guarding on the palace terrace.

"Wretch!" he said to the young man, who, since Buckingham's death, had recovered that calm and coolheadedness that would not abandon him again. "Wretch! What have you done?"

"I have taken my revenge," he said.

"You?" said the baron. "Say rather that you served as an instrument of that cursed woman. But, I swear to you, this crime will be her last."

"I do not know what you mean to say," Felton replied calmly. "I killed M. de Buckingham because he twice refused your own request to make me a captain. I have punished him for his injustice, that is all."

De Winter, stupefied, watched the people who were binding Felton, and did not know what to think of such insensibility.

One thing, however, clouded Felton's pure brow. At each sound he heard, the naive Puritan thought he recognized the footsteps and voice of Milady, coming to throw herself into his arms, to accuse herself and perish with him.

All at once he gave a start. His gaze was fixed on a certain point on the sea, which lay wholly open to view from the terrace where he stood. With the eagle eye of a sailor, he had recognized, where anyone else would have seen only a seagull rocking on the waves, the sail of a sloop that was heading for the shores of France.

He paled, brought his hand to his heart, which was breaking, and understood the whole betrayal.

"One last favor, Milord!" he said to the baron.

"Well?" the latter asked.

"What time is it?"

The baron took out his watch.

"Ten minutes to nine," he said.

Milady had moved up the time of her departure by an hour and a half. Once she had heard the cannon shot that announced the fatal event, she had given the order to raise anchor.

The boat was sailing under a blue sky far away from the coast.

"It was God's will," said Felton, with a fanatic's resignation, and yet without being able to tear his eyes from that ship, on board which he undoubtedly believed he could make out the white phantom of her to whom his life had been sacrificed.

De Winter followed his gaze, wondered at his suffering, and guessed everything.

"Be punished *alone* first of all, wretch," Lord de Winter said to Felton, who let himself be dragged away with his eyes still turned to the sea. "But I swear to you by the memory of my brother, whom I loved so much, that your accomplice will not get away."

Felton lowered his head without uttering a single syllable.

As for de Winter, he quickly went down the stairs and made his way to the port.

LX

In France

The first fear of the king of England, Charles I, on learning of this death, was that such terrible news might discourage the Rochelois. He tried, says Richelieu in his memoirs, to keep it from them for as long as possible, closing the ports throughout the kingdom, and being very careful that no vessel should leave until Buckingham's army was ready to depart, taking it upon himself, for want of Buckingham, to oversee the departure.

He even pushed the strictness of this order so far as to detain in England the ambassador of Denmark, who had taken leave, and the ambassador ordinary of Holland, who was to bring back to the port of Flushing the ships from the Indies that Charles I had restored to the United Provinces.

But as he had not thought of giving this order until five hours after the event, that is to say, at two o'clock in the afternoon, two ships had already left port: one, as we know, carrying Milady, who, already suspecting what had happened, was confirmed in that belief on seeing the black flag unfurl from the mast of the admiral's ship.

As for the second ship, we will say later whom it bore and how it left.

During this time, moreover, all was quiet in the La Rochelle camp. Only the king, who was terribly bored, as always, but perhaps still a bit more in camp than elsewhere, decided to go incognito to spend the feast of Saint Louis at Saint-Germain, and asked the cardinal to prepare him an escort of only twenty musketeers. The cardinal, who was sometimes infected by the king's boredom, was very pleased to grant this leave to his royal lieutenant, who promised to come back around the fifteenth of September.

M. de Tréville, informed by His Eminence, packed his bags, and as he knew, though without knowing the cause of it, the intense desire and even imperious need his friends had to return to Paris, it goes without saying that he picked them as part of the escort.

The four young men learned the news a quarter of an hour after M. de Tréville, for they were the first to whom he communicated it. It was then that d'Artagnan appreciated the favor the cardinal had granted him in finally moving him to the musketeers. Without that circumstance, he would have been forced to remain in camp when his companions left.

It will be seen later that the cause of this impatience to return to Paris was the danger Mme Bonacieux would be running if she met with Milady, her mortal enemy, in the convent of Béthune. And so, as we have said, Aramis had written immediately to Marie Michon, the seamstress of Tours who had such fine acquaintances, so that she might get the queen to give her authorization for Mme Bonacieux to leave the convent and retire either to Lorraine or to Belgium. The reply was not long in coming, and, eight or ten days later, Aramis received this letter:

Dear Cousin,

Here is my sister's authorization for my sister to take our little servant from the convent in Béthune, where you think the air is bad for her. My sister sends you this authorization with great pleasure, for she loves the little girl very much and intends to be useful to her later on.

I embrace you.

Marie Michon

To this letter was attached an authorization drawn up in these terms:

The mother superior of the convent of Béthune will put into the hands of the person who gives her this note the novice who entered her convent with my recommendation and under my patronage.

At the Louvre, 10 August 1628.

Anne

We can imagine how these family relations between Aramis and a seamstress who called the queen her sister lifted the young men's spirits. But Aramis, after blushing to the roots of his hair two or three times at Porthos's gross pleasantries, had begged his friends not to return to the subject, declaring that if another word was said to him about it, he would no longer employ his cousin as an intermediary in these sorts of affairs.

There was thus no further question of Marie Michon among the four musketeers, who anyhow had what they wanted: the order to take Mme Bonacieux from the convent of the Carmelites in Béthune. It is true that this order would not be of much use to them so long as they were in the camp at La Rochelle, that is, at the other end of France. And so d'Artagnan was going to ask M. de Tréville for leave, confessing to him quite openly the importance of his departure, when the news was passed on to him, as well as to his three companions, that the king was going to Paris with an escort of twenty musketeers, and that they would make part of that escort.

They were overjoyed. The valets were sent ahead with the baggage, and they set out on the morning of the sixteenth.

The cardinal accompanied His Majesty from Surgères to

Mauzé, and there the king and his minister took leave of each other with great shows of friendship.

However, the king, who sought distraction even while traveling as fast as he possibly could, for he wished to reach Paris by the twenty-third, stopped from time to time to hawk for magpies, a pastime he had once acquired a taste for from de Luynes, and for which he had always kept a great predilection. Of the twenty musketeers, sixteen rejoiced greatly for the good sport whenever this happened, but four grumbled loudly. D'Artagnan, in particular, had a constant buzzing in his ears, which Porthos explained as follows:

"A very grand lady taught me that that means someone is talking about you somewhere."

At last the escort traversed Paris on the night of the twenty-third. The king thanked M. de Tréville, and allowed him to hand out four-day leaves, on condition that none of those so favored should appear in any public place, on pain of the Bastille.

The first leaves granted, as we might well imagine, were to our four friends. What's more, Athos managed to get six days instead of four from M. de Tréville, and added two more nights, for they set off on the twenty-fourth at five in the afternoon, and M. de Tréville obligingly postdated the leave to the morning of the twenty-fifth.

"Ah, my God," said d'Artagnan, who, as we know, never suspected anything, "it seems to me that we're making a lot of fuss over a rather simple thing: in two days, at the risk of foundering two or three horses (I don't care, I have money), I'm in Béthune, I hand the queen's letter to the mother superior, and I go off with the dear treasure I'm seeking, not to Lorraine, not to Belgium, but to Paris, where it will be better hidden, above all as long as M. le cardinal is in La Rochelle. Then, once we're back from the campaign, half through the protection of her cousin, half owing to what we've done for her personally, we will get what we want from the queen. Stay here, then, don't wear yourselves out uselessly; Planchet and I are enough for such a simple expedition."

To this Athos calmly replied:

"We also have money, for I haven't quite drunk up the remains of the diamond, and Porthos and Aramis haven't quite eaten them up. So we can just as well founder four horses as one. But consider, d'Artagnan," he added, in a voice so grim that his accent gave the young man chills, "consider that Béthune is a town where the cardinal gave a rendezvous to a woman who brings misfortune with her wherever she goes. If you had only four men to deal with, d'Artagnan, I'd let you go alone; but you have this woman to deal with, so the four of us will go, and God grant that, with our four valets, there will be enough of us!"

"You frighten me, Athos," cried d'Artagnan. "My God, what is it you fear?"

"Everything," replied Athos.

D'Artagnan studied the faces of his companions, which, like that of Athos, bore the marks of deep anxiety, and they continued on their way as fast as their horses would carry them, without adding a single word.

On the evening of the twenty-fifth, they entered Arras, and just as d'Artagnan alighted at the Inn of the Golden Harrow to drink a glass of wine, a horseman came out of the posting yard, where he had just changed horses, and went galloping down the road to Paris. As he came through the main gate to the street, the wind blew open the cloak he was wrapped in, though it was the month of August, and tore at his hat, which the traveler grasped with his hand just as it was about to leave his head and pulled down sharply over his eyes.

D'Artagnan, who had his eyes fixed on this man, became extremely pale and dropped his glass.

"What's wrong, Monsieur?" asked Planchet . . . "Oh, come running, gentlemen, my master is unwell!"

The three friends came running and found d'Artagnan, not unwell, but dashing for his horse. They stopped him in the gateway.

"Well, where the devil are you off to like this?" Athos cried to him.

"It's he!" cried d'Artagnan, pale with wrath and sweat on his brow. "It's he! Let me catch him!"

"But he who?" asked Athos.

"He, that man!"

"Which man?"

"That cursed man, my evil genius, whom I always see when I'm threatened with some misfortune: the one who accompanied the horrible woman when I met her for the first time, the one I was looking for when I provoked Athos, the one I saw the morning of the day when Mme Bonacieux was abducted! I mean the man from Meung! I saw him, it's he! I recognized him when the wind blew his cloak open."

"Devil take it!" said Athos, pondering.

"To horse, gentlemen, to horse! Let's go after him and catch him!"

"My dear," said Aramis, "consider that he is going in the opposite direction from the one in which we are going; that he has a fresh horse, while ours are tired; that consequently we will do in our horses without even having a chance of catching him. Let's let the man go, d'Artagnan, and save the woman."

"Hey, Monsieur!" cried a stable boy, running after the unknown man, "hey, Monsieur, this paper fell out of your hat! Hey, Monsieur!"

"My friend," said d'Artagnan, "a half-pistole for that paper!"

"By heaven, Monsieur, with great pleasure! Here it is!"

The stable boy, delighted with the good day's wages he had made, went back into the hotel courtyard. D'Artagnan unfolded the paper.

"Well?" asked his friends, gathering around him.

"Only one word!" said d'Artagnan.

"Yes," said Aramis, "but it's the name of a town or a village."

"'Armentiers,'" read Porthos. "Armentiers—never heard of it!"

"And this name of a town or a village is written in her hand!" cried Athos.

"Well, well, let's take good care of this paper," said d'Artagnan. "Maybe I haven't wasted my last pistole. To horse, my friends, to horse!"

And the four companions set off at a gallop on the road to Béthune.

LXI

THE CONVENT OF THE CARMELITES IN BÉTHUNE

Great criminals bear a sort of predestination with them that enables them to surmount all obstacles and to escape all dangers until that moment which Providence, grown weary, has marked as the shoal on which their impious fortune will founder.

It was so with Milady. She passed between the cruisers of two nations and arrived at Boulogne without mishap.

On landing at Portsmouth, Milady was an Englishwoman driven from La Rochelle by French persecution; on landing at Boulogne, after a two-day crossing, she passed for a Frenchwoman whom the English harassed in Portsmouth, in the hatred they had conceived against France.

Milady had, besides, the most effective of passports: her beauty, her noble bearing, and the generosity with which she scattered pistoles. Exempted from the usual formalities by the affable smile and gallant manners of an old port governor, who kissed her hand, she stayed in Boulogne only long enough to post a letter worded thus:

> To His Eminence Monseigneur le Cardinal de Richelieu, in his
>   camp before La Rochelle.
> Monseigneur,
>   Your Eminence may rest assured: His Grace the duke of Buckingham will *never leave* for France.
>   Boulogne, the evening of the 25th.
>
>   Milady de———

P.S. As Your Eminence wished, I am going to the convent of the Carmelites in Béthune, where I shall await your orders.

Indeed, that same evening Milady set out on her way. Night overtook her; she stopped and slept in an inn; then, the next day, at five o'clock in the morning, she left, and three hours later she came to Béthune.

The Carmelite convent was pointed out to her, and she went in at once.

The mother superior came to meet her. Milady showed her the cardinal's order, and the abbess had her given a room and served breakfast.

The whole of the past was already effaced in this woman's eyes, and, her gaze fixed on the future, she saw only the high fortune reserved for her by the cardinal, whom she had served so successfully, without having her name mixed up in any way with that bloody business. The ever new passions that consumed her gave her life the appearance of those clouds that move across the sky, reflecting now azure, now fire, now the opaque black of the storm, and that leave no other traces on earth than devastation and death.

After breakfast, the abbess came to visit her. There was little distraction in the cloister, and the good mother superior was anxious to make her new pensioner's acquaintance.

Milady wanted to please the abbess, which was an easy thing for this truly superior woman to do. She tried to be amiable: she was charming, and seduced the good mother superior by the variety of her conversation and by the graces diffused throughout her person.

The abbess, who was a daughter of the nobility, was most fond of stories about the court, which rarely reached the far corners of the realm and had special difficulty passing through the walls of convents, on the thresholds of which the noises of the world expired.

Milady, on the other hand, was quite up-to-date on all the aristocratic intrigues, which she had been living in the midst of constantly for the past five or six years, and thus set about to converse with the good abbess on the worldly practices of the court of France, mixed with the extravagant devotions of the king; she recited the scandalous chronicle of the lords and ladies of the court, whom the abbess knew perfectly well by name, and touched lightly on the amours of the queen and Buckingham, speaking much in order to be little spoken to.

But the abbess contented herself with listening and smiling, all without any reply. However, as Milady saw that this sort of story amused her greatly, she went on; only she turned the conversation to the cardinal.

But she was rather perplexed: she did not know whether the abbess was a royalist or a cardinalist. She kept to a prudent middle line; but the abbess, for her part, kept to a still more prudent reserve, contenting herself with making a deep bow of the head each time the traveler uttered His Eminence's name.

Milady began to think that she was going to be extremely bored in the convent. She thus resolved to risk something in order to find out at once which side to take. Wishing to see how far the good abbess's discretion would go, she began to speak ill of the cardinal, very covertly at first, then in great detail, telling about the minister's amours with Mme d'Aiguillon, Marion de Lorme, and several other gallant ladies.

The abbess listened more attentively, gradually became animated, and smiled.

"Good," Milady said to herself, "she's getting a taste for my twaddle. If she's a cardinalist, at least she's not a fanatical one."

Then she went on to the cardinal's persecution of his enemies. The abbess merely crossed herself, without approving or disapproving.

This confirmed Milady in her opinion that the nun was more royalist than cardinalist. She went on, raising the price more and more.

"I am very ignorant of all these matters," the abbess finally said, "but, far as we are from the court, quite outside all worldly interests as we find ourselves here, we have very sad examples of what you have just been recounting, and one of our pensioners has suffered much from the vengeance and persecution of M. le cardinal."

"One of your pensioners?" said Milady. "Oh, my God, the poor woman, in that case I pity her!"

"And right you are, for she is greatly to be pitied: prison, threats, ill treatment—she has suffered everything. But, after all," the abbess went on, "M. le cardinal may have had plausible motives for acting in that way, and though she seems an angel, one must not always judge people by their looks."

"Good!" Milady said to herself. "Who knows, maybe I'll discover something here. I'm in luck!"

And she applied herself to giving her face an expression of perfect candor.

"Alas!" said Milady. "I know that. They say one must not believe in physiognomies; but in what are we to believe, then, if not in the most beautiful handiwork of the Lord? As for me, perhaps I shall be deceived all my life, but I shall always trust a person whose face inspires sympathy in me."

"You would be tempted to believe, then," said the abbess, "that this young woman is innocent?"

"M. le cardinal does not only punish crimes," she said. "There are certain virtues that he prosecutes more severely than certain wrongdoings."

"Allow me, Madame, to express to you my surprise," said the abbess.

"At what?" Milady asked naively.

"Why, at the language you use."

"What do you find astonishing in this language?" asked Milady, smiling.

"You are the cardinal's friend, since he sent you here, and yet . . ."

"And yet I speak ill of him," Milady picked up, completing the mother superior's thought.

"At least you do not speak well."

"The fact is that I am not his friend," she said, sighing, "I am his victim."

"And yet this letter in which he recommends you to me? . . ."

"Is an order to me to keep myself in a sort of prison, from which he will have me taken by some of his henchmen."

"But why haven't you run away?"

"Where would I go? Do you think there's a place on earth that the cardinal cannot touch, if he wishes to take the trouble of reaching out his hand? If I were a man, it would still be faintly possible; but a woman—what do you want a woman to do? This young pensioner you have here—has she tried to run away?"

"No, it's true. But she is something else. I think it's some love that keeps her in France."

"Well, then," said Milady with a sigh, "if she's in love, she's not altogether unfortunate."

"And so," said the abbess, looking at Milady with increasing interest, "it's another poor persecuted woman that I see?"

"Alas, yes," said Milady.

The abbess looked at Milady uneasily for a moment, as if a new thought had just occurred to her.

"You are not an enemy of our holy faith?" she stammered.

"I?" cried Milady. "I, a Protestant? Oh, no! I call God who hears us as my witness that I am, on the contrary, a fervent Catholic."

"Well, then, Madame," said the abbess, smiling, "rest assured, the house you are in will be no harsh prison, and we will do everything necessary to make you cherish your captivity. What's more, you will find here that young woman, persecuted, no doubt, as the result of some court intrigue. She is kindly, gracious."

"What do you call her?"

"She was recommended to me by someone very highly placed under the name of Kitty. I have not tried to find out her other name."

"Kitty!" cried Milady. "What? Are you sure? . . ."

"That she calls herself that? Yes, Madame. Do you know her?"

Milady smiled at herself and at the idea that had come to her, that this young woman might be her former chambermaid. Mixed with the memory of that young girl was the memory of wrath, and a desire for vengeance had distorted Milady's features, which, however, recovered almost at once the calm and benevolent expression that this woman of a hundred faces had momentarily lost.

"And when might I see this young woman, for whom I already feel so great a sympathy?" asked Milady.

"Why, this evening," said the abbess, "or even this afternoon. But you have been traveling for four days, you told me so yourself. This morning you got up at five o'clock. You must need rest. Lie down and sleep; we will wake you at dinner time."

Though Milady could very well have done without sleep, sustained as she was by all the excitement that a new adventure aroused in her intrigue-loving heart, she nonetheless accepted the mother superior's offer: in the past twelve or fifteen days she had lived through so many different emotions that, if her iron body could still sustain fatigue, her soul had need of rest.

She thus took leave of the abbess and went to bed, gently lulled by the ideas of vengeance to which the name of Kitty had quite naturally led her. She recalled the almost unlimited promise that the cardinal had made her, if she succeeded in her undertaking. She had succeeded; she could thus be revenged on d'Artagnan.

Only one thing frightened Milady: the memory of her husband, the comte de La Fère, whom she had thought dead or at least out of the country, and whom she had found again in Athos, d'Artagnan's best friend.

But, if he was d'Artagnan's friend, then he must also have assisted him in all the maneuvers by means of which the queen had foiled His Eminence's plans. If he was d'Artagnan's friend, he was the cardinal's enemy, and she would no doubt manage to wrap him in the folds of that vengeance in which she intended to smother the young musketeer.

All these hopes were sweet thoughts for Milady, and, lulled by them, she fell asleep at once.

She was awakened by a gentle voice that came from the foot of her bed. She opened her eyes and saw the abbess, accompanied by a young woman with blond hair and a delicate complexion, who fixed upon her a gaze filled with benevolent curiosity.

The face of this young woman was completely unknown to her. The two studied each other with scrupulous attention, all the while exchanging the usual compliments: they were both very beautiful, but their beauty was of entirely different sorts. However, Milady smiled on recognizing that she outshone the young woman considerably in her noble air and aristocratic ways. It is true that the novice's habit which the young woman was wearing was not very advantageous for sustaining a contest of that kind.

The abbess introduced them to each other; then, once this formality had been performed, as her duties called her to the church, she left the two young women alone.

The novice, seeing Milady lying down, was about to follow the mother superior, but Milady held her back.

"What, Madame," she said to her, "I have barely glimpsed you, and you already want to deprive me of your presence, which I was somewhat counting on, I confess to you, for the time I am to spend here?"

"No, Madame," replied the novice, "only I was afraid I had chosen the wrong moment: you were sleeping, you must be tired."

"Well," said Milady, "what more can sleepers ask for than a good awakening? You have granted me that awakening; let me enjoy it at my ease."

And, taking her hand, she drew her to an armchair that was next to her bed.

The novice sat down.

"My God," she said, "how unlucky I am! For six months now I've been here without the shadow of a distraction, then you come, your presence would be charming company for me, and here, in all probability, I'll be leaving the convent any moment!"

"What?" said Milady. "You're leaving soon?"

"At least I hope so," said the novice, with an expression of joy that she did not try to disguise in the least.

"I believe I understood that you have suffered at the hands of the cardinal," Milady went on. "That would have been one more reason for sympathy between us."

"So what our good mother told me is true, that you were also a victim of this wicked cardinal?"

"Hush!" said Milady. "Even here we must not speak of him like that. All my misfortunes come of having said more or less what you have just said before a woman who I believed was my friend and who betrayed me. And are you also the victim of a betrayal?"

"No," said the novice, "but of my devotion to a woman I loved, for whom I would have given my life, and for whom I would still give it."

"And who abandoned you, is that it?"

"I was unjust enough to believe so, but two or three days ago I received proof to the contrary, and I thank God for that—it would have cost me dearly to think she had forgotten me. But you, Madame," the novice went on, "it seems to me that you are free, and that if you wanted to run away, it would depend only on you."

"Where do you want me to go, with no friends, no money, in a part of France I don't know at all, where I have never been? . . ."

"Oh," cried the novice, "as for friends, you will have them wherever you show yourself, you seem so good and are so beautiful!"

"That does not change the fact," Milady picked up, sweetening her smile in a way that gave her an angelic expression, "that I am alone and persecuted."

"Listen," said the novice, "one must have firm hope in heaven, you see; a moment always comes when the good one has done pleads one's case before God, and, you know, perhaps it's fortunate for you that you should have met me, humble and powerless as I am, for if I leave here, well, then I will have some powerful friends who, after working on my behalf, may also work on yours."

"Oh, when I said I was alone," said Milady, hoping to make the novice speak by speaking of herself, "it did not mean that I don't also have highly placed acquaintances; but these acquaintances themselves tremble before the cardinal. The queen herself dares not stand up to the terrible minister. I have proof that Her Majesty, in spite of her excellent heart, has been obliged more than once to abandon people who have served her to the wrath of His Eminence."

"Believe me, Madame, the queen may seem to have abandoned those people, but one mustn't believe appearances: the more persecuted they are, the more she thinks of them, and often, at the moment when they're least expecting it, they have proof that they are well remembered."

"Alas!" said Milady, "I believe it: the queen is so good."

"Oh, you know her, then, this beautiful and noble queen, if you speak of her like that!" the novice cried with enthusiasm.

"That is to say," Milady picked up, driven into a corner, "I do not have the honor of knowing her personally, but I know a good number of her most intimate friends: I know M. de Putange; I knew M. Dujart in England; I know M. de Tréville."

"M. de Tréville!" cried the novice. "You know M. de Tréville?"

"Yes, indeed, even quite well."

"The captain of the king's musketeers?"

"The captain of the king's musketeers."

"Oh, but you shall see," cried the novice, "that very soon we shall be perfect acquaintances, almost friends. If you know M. de Tréville, you must have been to his house?"

"Often!" said Milady, who, having started on this path, and perceiving that the lie was working, wanted to push it to the end.

"In his house you must have seen some of his musketeers?"

"All those that he is accustomed to receive!" replied Milady, for whom this conversation was beginning to take on a real interest.

"Name some of those you know for me, and you'll see that they turn out to be my friends."

"Why," said Milady, embarrassed, "I know M. de Louvigny, M. de Courtivron, M. de Férussac . . ."

The novice let her speak; then, seeing that she had stopped, said: "You don't know a gentleman by the name of Athos?"

Milady turned as white as the sheets she was lying on, and, for all her self-control, could not help letting out a cry, seizing the novice's hand, and devouring her with her gaze.

"Oh, my God, what's the matter with you?" asked the poor woman. "Have I said something that has offended you?"

"No, but the name struck me, because I also knew this gentleman, and it seemed strange to me to find someone who knows him well."

"Oh, yes, very well, very well! Not only him, but also his friends MM. Porthos and Aramis!"

"Indeed, I know them, too!" cried Milady, who felt a chill penetrating her heart.

"Well, then, if you know them, you must know that they are good and openhearted companions. Why don't you turn to them, if you need support?"

"That is to say," stammered Milady, "I have no real ties to any of them. I know them from having heard them much spoken of by one of their friends, M. d'Artagnan."

"You know M. d'Artagnan?" the novice cried in her turn, seizing Milady's hand and devouring her with her eyes.

Then, noticing the strange expression on Milady's face, she said: "Excuse me, Madame, but in what sense do you know him?"

"Why," Milady picked up, embarrassed, "as a friend."

"You are deceiving me, Madame," said the novice. "You were his mistress."

"It is you who were, Madame," Milady cried in her turn.

"I?" said the novice.

"Yes, you. I know you now: you are Mme Bonacieux."

The young woman drew back, filled with surprise and terror.

"Oh, don't deny it! Answer!" said Milady.

"Well, then—yes, Madame, I love him!" said the novice. "Are we rivals?"

Milady's face lit up with such a savage fire that, in any other circumstances, Mme Bonacieux would have fled in fright; but she was entirely in the grip of her jealousy.

"Come, tell me, Madame," said Mme Bonacieux, with an energy one would have believed her incapable of, "were you or are you his mistress?"

"Oh, no!" cried Milady, with an accent that admitted no doubt of its truthfulness. "Never! never!"

"I believe you," said Mme Bonacieux. "But why, then, did you cry out like that?"

"What, you don't understand?" said Milady, who had gotten over her confusion and recovered all her presence of mind.

"How do you expect me to understand? I don't know anything."

"You don't understand that, being my friend, M. d'Artagnan should take me as a confidante?"

"Really?"

"You don't understand that I know everything, your abduction from the little house in Saint-Germain, his and his friends' despair, their useless searching since that moment? And how do you not want me to be astonished when, without suspecting it, I find myself face to face with you, with you about whom we have spoken so often together, with you whom he loves with all the strength of his soul, with you whom he has made me love before I ever saw you? Ah, dear Constance, so I've found you, I've found you at last!"

And Milady held out her arms to Mme Bonacieux, who, convinced by what she had just said, no longer saw in this woman, whom a moment before she had thought her rival, anything but a sincere and devoted friend.

"Oh, forgive me, forgive me!" she cried, letting herself fall on Milady's shoulder. "I love him so much!"

The two women embraced each other for a moment. To be sure, if Milady's strength had been equal to her hatred, Mme Bonacieux would never have left that embrace alive. But, not being able to smother her, she smiled at her.

"Oh, my dear, beautiful little thing!" said Milady, "how happy I am to see you! Let me look at you." And, as she said these words, she actually devoured her with her gaze. "Yes, it's really you. Ah, I recognize you now from what he told me, I recognize you perfectly."

The poor woman could in no way suspect the dreadful cruelty that was going on behind the rampart of that pure brow, behind those shining eyes in which she read only concern and compassion.

"Then you know what I've suffered," said Mme Bonacieux, "since he has told you what he suffered. But to suffer for him is happiness."

Milady replied mechanically: "Yes, it is happiness."

She was thinking of something else.

"And then," Mme Bonacieux went on, "my torment is reaching its end. Tomorrow, or tonight perhaps, I will see him again, and then the past will no longer exist."

"This evening? Tomorrow?" cried Milady, drawn from her musing by these words. "What do you mean? Are you expecting some news from him?"

"I'm expecting him himself."

"Himself? D'Artagnan here?"

"Himself."

"But that's impossible! He's at the siege of La Rochelle with the cardinal. He won't come back to Paris until the city is taken."

"So you think, but is anything impossible for my d'Artagnan, that noble and loyal gentleman?"

"Oh, I can't believe you!"

"Well, then read this!" said the unfortunate young woman, in the excess of her pride and her joy, handing Milady a letter.

"Mme de Chevreuse's handwriting!" Milady said to herself. "Ah, I was quite sure they had intelligence from that quarter!"

And she avidly read the following few lines:

My dear child,

Keep yourself ready. *Our friend* will see you soon, and he will see you only to wrest you from the prison where your safety demanded that you be hidden. So prepare yourself for departure and never despair of us.

Our charming Gascon has just shown himself as brave and faithful as ever. Tell him they are quite grateful to him somewhere for the warning he gave.

"Yes, yes," said Milady, "yes, the letter is precise. Do you know what the warning was?"

"No. I only suspect that he informed the queen of some new machination of the cardinal's."

"Yes, that's undoubtedly it!" said Milady, handing the

letter back to Mme Bonacieux and bowing her pensive head again.

At that moment they heard the galloping of a horse.

"Oh!" cried Mme Bonacieux, rushing to the window. "Can it be he already?"

Milady stayed in bed, petrified by the surprise. So many unexpected things had happened to her all at once that, for the first time, her head failed her.

"Is it he?" she murmured. "Can it be he?"

And she remained in bed, her eyes staring.

"Alas, no!" said Mme Bonacieux, "it's some man I don't know, and yet he seems to be coming here. Yes, he's slowing down, he's stopping at the gate, he's ringing."

Milady jumped out of bed.

"You're quite sure it's not he?" she asked.

"Oh, yes, quite sure!"

"Maybe you didn't see clearly?"

"Oh, I'd recognize him just by the feather in his hat or the tip of his cloak!"

Milady was still dressing.

"Never mind! The man is coming here, you say?"

"Yes, he has come in."

"It's either for you or for me."

"Oh, my God, how agitated you seem!"

"Yes, I admit, I don't have your confidence. I fear everything from the cardinal."

"Hush!" said Mme Bonacieux, "someone's coming!"

Indeed, the door opened, and the mother superior came in.

"Is it you who came from Boulogne?" she asked Milady.

"Yes, it is I," the latter replied, trying to recover her coolheadedness. "Who is asking for me?"

"A man who does not want to give his name, but who comes on the part of the cardinal."

"And who wants to speak with me?" asked Milady.

"Who wants to speak with a lady coming from Boulogne."

"Please show him in, then, Madame."

"Oh, my God! my God!" cried Mme Bonacieux, "can it be some sort of bad news?"

"I'm afraid so."

"I will leave you with this stranger, but as soon as he goes, if you will permit me, I will come back."

"Oh, please do, of course!"

The mother superior and Mme Bonacieux left.

Milady remained alone, her eyes fixed on the door. A moment later, the jingling of spurs came from the stairway, then footsteps approached, then the door opened, and a man appeared.

Milady let out a cry of joy: the man was the comte de Rochefort, His Eminence's tool.

LXII

TWO SORTS OF DEMONS

"Ah!" Rochefort and Milady cried out together, "it's you!"

"Yes, it's I."

"And you're coming? . . ." asked Milady.

"From La Rochelle, and you?"

"From England."

"Buckingham?"

"Dead, or dangerously wounded. As I was leaving without having been able to get anything from him, a fanatic had just assassinated him."

"Ah!" said Rochefort with a smile, "there's a lucky chance for you! And one that will greatly please His Eminence! Have you informed him?"

"I wrote to him from Boulogne. But what brings you here?"

"His Eminence was worried and sent me to look for you."

"I arrived only yesterday."

"And what have you done since yesterday?"

"I haven't wasted my time."

"Oh, I'm quite sure of that!"

"Do you know who I've met here?"

"No."

"Guess."

"How can I?"

"That young woman the queen took from prison."

"Little d'Artagnan's mistress?"

"Yes, Mme Bonacieux, whose hiding place the cardinal didn't know."

"Well, now," said Rochefort, "there's another chance that makes a good pair with the first. M. le cardinal is truly a privileged man!"

"Can you understand my astonishment," Milady went on, "when I found myself face to face with that woman?"

"Does she know you?"

"No."

"So she looks upon you as a stranger?"

Milady smiled.

"I'm her best friend."

"On my honor," said Rochefort, "only you, my dear countess, can perform such miracles!"

"And much good it does me, chevalier," said Milady, "for do you know what's happening?"

"No."

"They're coming to fetch her tomorrow or the day after with an order from the queen."

"Really? And who is coming?"

"D'Artagnan and his friends."

"Truly, they'll go so far that we'll be obliged to send them to the Bastille."

"Why hasn't it been done already?"

"What do you want! Because M. le cardinal has a weakness for these men that I cannot understand."

"Really?"

"Yes."

"Well, then, tell him this, Rochefort: tell him that our conversation in the inn of the Red Dovecote was overheard by these four men; tell him that after he left, one of them came upstairs and tore from me by violence the safe conduct he had given me; tell him that they warned Lord de Winter of my crossing to England; that, this time again, they almost caused the failure of my mission, as they caused the failure of the one with the pendants;

tell him that, of these four men, only two are to be feared—
d'Artagnan and Athos; tell him that the third, Aramis, is Mme
de Chevreuse's lover: he must be left alive, we know his secret,
he may be useful; as for the fourth, Porthos, he's a fool, a fop,
and a ninny, and not even worth bothering with."

"But these four men should be at the siege of La Rochelle
right now."

"I thought the same as you, but a letter which Mme
Bonacieux received from Mme de Chevreuse, and which she
had the imprudence to communicate to me, leads me to believe
that these four men, on the contrary, are on their way here to
abduct her."

"Devil take it! What are we to do?"

"What did the cardinal say to you about me?"

"To take your written or verbal dispatches, to return by
post, and, when he knows what you have done, he will see
about what you should do."

"I must remain here, then?" asked Milady.

"Here or hereabouts."

"You can't take me with you?"

"No, the order is explicit: in the neighborhood of the
camp, you might be recognized, and you understand that your
presence would compromise His Eminence, above all after
what has just happened over there. Only tell me beforehand
where you will await news from the cardinal, so that I always
know where to find you."

"Listen, I probably won't be able to stay here."

"Why?"

"You forget that my enemies may arrive at any moment."

"That's true. But is this little woman then going to escape
His Eminence?"

"Bah!" said Milady, with a smile that belonged only to her,
"you forget that I'm her best friend."

"Ah, that's true! So, then, with regard to this woman, I can
tell the cardinal . . ."

"That he can rest easy."

"That's all?"

"He'll know what it means."

"He'll guess it. Now, what must I do?"

"Leave again this very moment. It seems to me that the news you're bringing is worth the trouble of making haste."

"My post chaise broke down on entering Lillers."

"Perfect!"

"Perfect, you say?"

"Yes, I happen to have need of your post chaise," said the countess.

"And how will I go, then?"

"On a fast horse."

"That's easy for you to say—it's a hundred and eighty leagues."

"What's that to you?"

"Nothing. What else?"

"On passing through Lillers, you will send me your post chaise with orders for your servant to put himself at my disposal."

"Very well."

"You no doubt have some order from the cardinal?"

"I have my full authorization."

"You will show it to the abbess and say that someone will come for me, either today or tomorrow, and that I will have to go with the person who presents himself in your name."

"Very good!"

"Don't forget to speak harshly of me when you talk to the abbess about me."

"What for?"

"I am a victim of the cardinal. I must inspire confidence in this poor little Mme Bonacieux."

"That's so. Now, will you make me a report of all that has happened?"

"But I've told you all the events, you have a good memory, repeat the things as I told them to you. Papers get lost."

"You're right. Only let me know where to find you again, so that I don't go running around the neighborhood in vain."

"That's so. Wait a minute."

"Would you like a map?"

"Oh, I know this country perfectly!"

"You do? When did you ever come here?"

"I was raised here."

"Really?"

"It's good for something, you see, to have been raised somewhere."

"So you'll wait for me . . ."

"Let me think for a moment. Ah, that's it, at Armentières."

"What's Armentières?"

"A little town on the Lys. I have only to cross the river, and I'll be in a foreign country."

"Perfect! But it's understood that you'll only cross the river in case of danger."

"It's understood."

"And in that case how will I know where you are?"

"You don't need your lackey?"

"No."

"Is he reliable?"

"Completely."

"Give him to me. No one knows him. He'll stay behind when I leave and lead you to where I am."

"And you say you'll wait for me in Argentières?"

"In Armentières," replied Milady.

"Write the name down on a slip of paper, lest I forget it. The name of a town isn't compromising, is it?"

"Ah, who knows? Never mind," said Milady, writing the name on a half sheet of paper, "I'll compromise myself."

"Good!" said Rochefort, taking the paper from Milady, folding it, and sticking it into the lining of his hat. "Anyhow, don't worry, I'm going to do as children do and repeat the name all along the way, in case I lose the paper. Is that all, now?"

"I think so."

"Let's check carefully: Buckingham dead or gravely wounded; your talk with the cardinal overheard by the four musketeers; Lord de Winter warned of your arrival in Portsmouth; d'Artagnan and Athos to the Bastille; Aramis the lover of Mme de Chevreuse; Porthos a fop; Mme Bonacieux found again; send you the post chaise as soon as possible; put my lackey at your disposal; make you a victim of the cardinal, so that the abbess has no suspicions; Armentières on the banks of the Lys. Is that it?"

"Truly, my dear chevalier, you are a miracle of memory. Incidentally, add one thing . . ."

"Which?"

"I saw a very pretty wood that must border on the convent garden. Say that I am permitted to stroll in that wood. Who knows, I may need to leave by a back door."

"You think of everything."

"And you are forgetting one thing . . ."

"What's that?"

"To ask me if I need money."

"That's right, how much do you want?"

"All the gold you have."

"I have about five hundred pistoles."

"I have as much again. With a thousand pistoles, one can face anything: empty your pockets."

"There you are, Countess."

"Good, my dear Count! And you're leaving? . . ."

"In an hour. Time enough for a bite to eat while I send for a post-horse."

"Perfect! Good-bye, Chevalier!"

"Good-bye, Countess!"

"Commend me to the cardinal," said Milady.

"Commend me to Satan," replied Rochefort.

Milady and Rochefort exchanged smiles and parted.

An hour later, Rochefort galloped off on his horse; five hours later, he passed through Arras.

Our readers already know how he was recognized by d'Artagnan, and how this recognition, arousing fears in the four musketeers, lent a new impetus to their journey.

LXIII

A Drop of Water

Rochefort had only just left when Mme Bonacieux came back in. She found Milady with a smiling face.

"Well," said the young woman, "so what you were afraid of has happened; tonight or tomorrow the cardinal will send someone to take you?"

"Who told you that, my child?" asked Milady.

"I heard it from the mouth of the messenger himself."

"Come and sit beside me," said Milady.

"Here I am."

"Wait till I make sure nobody's listening to us."

"Why all these precautions?"

"You'll soon know."

Milady got up and went to the door, opened it, looked into the corridor, and came back to sit down again beside Mme Bonacieux.

"So," she said, "he played his role well."

"Who did?"

"The man who introduced himself to the abbess as the cardinal's envoy."

"You mean he was playing a role?"

"Yes, my child."

"Then that man is not . . ."

"That man," said Milady, lowering her voice, "is my brother."

"Your brother?" cried Mme Bonacieux.

"Well, you are the only one who knows that secret, my child. If you tell it to anyone in the world, I will be lost, and you will be, too, perhaps."

"Oh, my God!"

"Listen, here's what is happening: my brother, who was coming to my aid in order to take me away from here by force, if necessary, ran into the cardinal's emissary, who was on his way to fetch me. He followed him. Coming to a solitary and secluded place on the road, he drew his sword and called on the messenger to hand over the papers he was carrying. The messenger tried to defend himself. My brother killed him."

"Oh!" cried Mme Bonacieux, shuddering.

"It was the only way, you realize. Then my brother decided to use guile in place of force: he took the papers, introduced himself here as the cardinal's emissary, and in an hour or two a carriage is to come to take me away on the part of His Eminence."

"I understand: it's your brother who will send the carriage."

"Exactly. But that's not all. This letter that you received, and that you think is from Mme de Chevreuse . . ."

"Well?"

"It's a forgery."

"What?"

"Yes, a forgery. It's a trap to keep you from resisting when they come to fetch you."

"But it's d'Artagnan who will come."

"Don't believe it. D'Artagnan and his friends are detained at the siege of La Rochelle."

"How do you know that?"

"My brother met emissaries from the cardinal dressed as musketeers. They would have called you to the door, you would have thought they were with your friends, they would have abducted you and taken you to Paris."

"Oh, my God! I lose my head amidst all this chaos of iniquities. If this goes on," Mme Bonacieux continued, burying her face in her hands, "I feel I shall go mad!"

"Wait . . ."

"What is it?"

"I hear the hoofbeats of a horse. It's my brother setting out again. I want to say a last good-bye to him. Come."

Milady opened the window and made a sign to Mme Bonacieux to join her. The young woman went over.

Rochefort galloped past.

"Good-bye, brother!" cried Milady.

The chevalier raised his head, saw the two young women, and, without slackening his pace, gave Milady a friendly wave of the hand.

"Good old Georges!" she said, closing the window with an expression on her face that was filled with affection and melancholy.

And she went to sit down in her place again, as if she had been plunged into the most personal reflections.

"Dear lady," said Mme Bonacieux, "forgive me for interrupting you, but what do you advise me to do? My God! You have more experience than I. Speak, I'm listening."

"First of all," said Milady, "it may be that I'm mistaken and that d'Artagnan and his friends really are coming to your rescue."

"Oh, that would be too wonderful!" cried Mme Bonacieux. "So much happiness is not meant for me!"

"So, you understand, it's quite simply a question of time, a sort of race to see who comes first. If it's your friends who win, you are saved; if it's the cardinal's henchmen, you are lost."

"Oh, yes, yes, lost without mercy! What to do, then? What to do?"

"There would be one quite simple, quite natural way . . ."

"What is it, tell me?"

"It would be to wait, hidden in the neighborhood, and thus make sure which men come asking for you."

"But wait where?"

"Oh, that's hardly a problem. I myself am going to stop and hide a few leagues from here, waiting for my brother to come and join me. I'll just take you with me, we'll hide and wait together."

"But they won't let me leave. I'm almost a prisoner here."

"As they think I'm leaving on an order from the cardinal, they will not think you are in much of a hurry to follow me."

"Well?"

"Well, so the carriage is at the gate, you say good-bye to me, you stand on the footboard to hug me one last time; my brother's servant, who has come to take me, is forewarned, he gives the postilion a sign, and off we gallop."

"But d'Artagnan, what if d'Artagnan comes?"

"Won't we know it?"

"How?"

"Nothing could be simpler. We send my brother's servant back to Béthune. As I've told you, we can trust him. He puts on a disguise and takes lodgings facing the convent. If the cardinal's emissaries come, he doesn't stir; if it's M. d'Artagnan and his friends, he takes them to us."

"He knows them, then?"

"Of course! As if he hasn't seen M. d'Artagnan in my house!"

"Oh, yes, yes, you're right! And so, all is well, all is for the best; but let's not go far from here."

"Seven or eight leagues at the most. We'll keep close to the border, for example, and at the first alert, we can leave France."

"And what to do between now and then?"

"Wait."

"But if they come?"

"My brother's carriage will come before them."

"What if I'm far away from you when they come to take you—at dinner or supper, for instance?"

"Do this one thing."

"What?"

"Tell your good mother superior that, in order for us to be apart as little as possible, you ask her permission to share my meals."

"Will she permit it?"

"What objection can there be?"

"Oh, very good! In this way we won't be apart for a moment!"

"Well, go down to her, then, and make your request. My head feels heavy, I'm going to take a turn in the garden."

"Yes, do. And where shall I find you?"

"Here, an hour from now."

"Here, an hour from now. Oh, you're so good! Thank you, thank you!"

"How should I not take an interest in you? You're not only beautiful and charming, but also the friend of one of my best friends!"

"Dear d'Artagnan! Oh, how he'll thank you!"

"I hope so. Come, it's all agreed. Let's go down."

"You're going to the garden?"

"Yes."

"Follow this corridor, a little stairway will take you to it."

"Perfect! Thank you."

And the two women parted, exchanging charming smiles.

Milady had told the truth, her head was heavy, for her ill-assorted plans were colliding there as if in chaos. She needed to be alone so as to bring a little order to her thoughts. She had a vague view of the future, but she needed a little peace and quiet to give to all her still confused ideas a distinct form, a finished plan.

Besides, she sensed, as one senses an approaching storm, that the outcome was near and could not fail to be terrible.

The main thing for her, as we have said, was thus to keep Mme Bonacieux in her hands. Mme Bonacieux was d'Artagnan's life; she was more than his life, she was the life of the woman he loved; in case of bad luck, she was a means of negotiating and of securing good conditions.

Now, this point was settled: Mme Bonacieux would follow her unsuspectingly. Once hidden with her in Armentières, it would be easy to make her believe that d'Artagnan had not come to Béthune. In two weeks at the most, Rochefort would be back. During those two weeks, moreover, she would see about what to do in order to be revenged on the four friends. She would not be bored, thank God, for she would have the sweetest pastime that events could grant to a woman of her character: the perfecting of a nice vengeance.

While she mused, she glanced around her and arranged in her head the topography of the garden. Milady was like a good general, who at the same time foresees both victory and defeat, and who is quite ready, according to the chances of battle, to go forward or beat a retreat.

At the end of an hour, she heard a sweet voice calling her: it was Mme Bonacieux. The good abbess had naturally agreed to everything, and, to begin with, they would have supper together.

As they came into the courtyard, they heard the sound of a carriage stopping at the gate.

"Do you hear?" she said.

"Yes, the rolling of a carriage."

"It's the one my brother is sending us."

"Oh, my God!"

"Come, come, have courage!"

Milady was not mistaken: someone rang at the convent gate.

"Go up to your room," she said to Mme Bonacieux. "You must have some jewelry you wish to bring with you."

"I have letters," she said.

"Well, go and fetch them, and come to join me in my room. We'll have a quick supper. We may be traveling for part of the night; we'll need to fortify ourselves."

"Good God!" said Mme Bonacieux, putting her hand to her breast, "my heart is failing me, I can't walk."

"Courage, now, courage! Just think that in a quarter of an hour you'll be safe, and consider that what you're about to do, you are doing for him."

"Oh, yes, all for him! You've given me back my courage with a single word. Go on, I'll join you."

Milady quickly went up to her room, found Rochefort's lackey there, and gave him his instructions.

He was to wait at the gate. If by chance the musketeers should appear, the carriage would set off at a gallop, circle around the convent, and go to wait for Milady in a small village located on the other side of the wood. In that case, Milady would go across the garden and reach the village on foot. As we have already said, Milady knew that part of France perfectly.

If the musketeers should not appear, things would go as agreed: Mme Bonacieux would get into the carriage on the pretext of saying good-bye to her, and Milady would carry her off.

Mme Bonacieux came in, and to remove her last suspicions, if she had any, Milady repeated before her the entire last part of her instructions to the lackey.

Milady asked a few questions about the carriage. It was a post chaise harnessed to three horses, driven by a postilion. Rochefort's lackey was to precede them as a courier.

Milady was wrong to fear that Mme Bonacieux might have suspicions: the poor young woman was too pure to suspect such perfidy in another woman. Besides, the name of the countess de Winter, which she had heard spoken by the abbess, was perfectly unknown to her, and she was even unaware that a woman had played such a great and fatal part in the misfortunes of her life.

"You see," said Milady, when the lackey had left, "everything's ready. The abbess suspects nothing and believes they have come for me from the cardinal. This man is going to give the last orders. Eat a little something, drink a sip of wine, and let's be off."

"Yes," Mme Bonacieux said mechanically, "yes, let's be off."

Milady made a sign for her to sit down opposite her, poured her a small glass of Spanish wine, and served her a chicken breast.

"See," she said to her, "how everything assists us: night is falling; by daybreak we will have reached our refuge, and no one will suspect where we are. Come, have courage, eat something."

Mme Bonacieux mechanically ate a few mouthfuls and dipped her lips into her glass.

"Come, come," said Milady, bringing hers to her lips, "do as I do."

But as she brought the glass to her mouth, her hand stopped suspended: she had just heard what sounded like the distant drumroll of hoofbeats approaching along the road; then, at almost the same time, she seemed to hear the whinnying of horses.

This noise roused her from her joy, as the sound of a storm awakens one in the middle of a pleasant dream. She turned pale and ran to the window, while Mme Bonacieux, getting up all atremble, supported herself on a chair so as not to fall.

Nothing could be seen yet, only the hoofbeats could be heard coming closer and closer.

"Oh, my God!" said Mme Bonacieux, "what is that noise?"

"Our friends, or our enemies," said Milady, with terrible coolness. "Stay where you are, I'll go and see."

Mme Bonacieux remained standing, mute, motionless, and pale as a statue.

The noise grew louder, the horses could not have been more than a hundred and fifty paces away; if they still could not be seen, it was because of a bend in the road. However, the noise became so distinct that one could have counted the number of horses by the staccato beating of their iron shoes.

Milady looked with all the power of her attention. It was just light enough for her to recognize those who were coming.

All at once, around the turning of the road, she saw the gleam of gold-trimmed hats and the flutter of feathers. She counted two, then five, then eight horsemen. One of them rode two lengths ahead of all the others.

Milady let out a muffled roar. She recognized the one in the lead as d'Artagnan.

"Oh, my God! my God!" cried Mme Bonacieux, "who is it?"

"It's the uniform of the cardinal's guards; there's not an moment to lose!" cried Milady. "We must flee, we must flee!"

"Yes, yes, we must flee," Mme Bonacieux repeated, but without being able to take a step: terror nailed her to the spot.

They heard the horsemen passing under the windows.

"Come on! Come on!" cried Milady, trying to drag the young woman by the arm. "Thanks to the garden, we can still get away. I have the key. But we must hurry, in five minutes it will be too late."

Mme Bonacieux tried to walk, took two steps, and fell to her knees.

Milady tried to pick her up and carry her, but she could not manage it.

Just then they heard the rolling of the carriage, which at the sight of the musketeers set off at a gallop. Then three or four shots rang out.

"For the last time, will you come?" cried Milady.

"Oh, my God! my God! you can see I have no strength left; you can see I can't walk: flee by yourself!"

"Flee by myself and leave you here? No, no, never!" cried Milady.

All at once, a livid light flashed from her eyes. With a bound, frantic, she rushed to the table, poured into Mme Bonacieux's wine glass the contents of the gem of her ring, which she had opened with a singular promptness.

It was a reddish grain that dissolved at once.

Then, taking the glass in one hand, she said:

"Drink, drink—this wine will give you strength."

And she brought the glass to the lips of the young woman, who drank mechanically.

"Ah, this is not how I wanted to be revenged!" said Milady, setting the glass on the table with an infernal smile, "but, by heaven, one does what one can!"

And she rushed from the apartment.

Mme Bonacieux watched her flee, without being able to follow her. She was like those people who dream they are being pursued and try in vain to move.

Some minutes passed. There was a terrible noise by the gate. Mme Bonacieux expected to see Milady reappear any moment, but she did not reappear.

Several times—from terror, no doubt—cold sweat broke out on her burning forehead.

Finally she heard the creak of the gates being opened. The sound of boots and spurs rang out on the stairs. There was a loud murmur of voices coming nearer, in the midst of which she seemed to hear her name spoken.

All at once she let out a great cry of joy and rushed for the door. She had recognized d'Artagnan's voice.

"D'Artagnan! d'Artagnan!" she cried, "is it you? This way, this way!"

"Constance! Constance!" replied the young man. "My God, where are you?"

Just then the door to the cell did not open but yielded to impact. Several men burst into the room. Mme Bonacieux had fallen into an armchair without being able to move.

D'Artagnan cast aside the still-smoking pistol he was holding in his hand and fell on his knees before his mistress; Athos thrust his pistol back into his belt; Porthos and Aramis, who were holding bare swords, sheathed them again.

"Oh, d'Artagnan! my beloved d'Artagnan! so you've finally come, you didn't deceive me, it's really you!"

"Yes, yes, Constance, we're together again!"

"Oh, *she* could talk all she liked about how you wouldn't

come, but I secretly hoped. I didn't want to flee. Oh, how right I was, how happy I am!"

At the word *she,* Athos, who had calmly sat down, stood up all at once.

"*She? She* who?" asked d'Artagnan.

"Why, my companion; the one who, out of friendship for me, wanted to get me away from my persecutors; the one who just fled, taking you for the cardinal's guards."

"Your companion?" cried d'Artagnan, turning paler than his mistress's white veil. "What companion do you mean?"

"The one whose carriage was at the gate, a woman who said she was your friend, d'Artagnan, a woman to whom you had told everything."

"Her name, her name!" cried d'Artagnan. "My God, don't you know her name?"

"Yes, I do; it was spoken in my presence. Wait . . . but that's strange . . . Oh, my God, my head is confused, I can't see anymore."

"Help me, friends, help me! Her hands are ice cold," cried d'Artagnan. "She's ill! Good God, she's lost consciousness!"

While Porthos was calling for help at the top of his voice, Aramis ran to the table for a glass of water; but he stopped on seeing the terrible alteration in the face of Athos, who, standing by the table, his hair on end, his eyes glazed with stupor, was looking at one of the glasses and seemed a prey to the most horrible suspicion.

"Oh, no!" said Athos. "Oh, no, it's not possible! God would not permit such a crime!"

"Water, water!" cried d'Artagnan. "Bring water!"

"Oh, poor woman, poor woman," murmured Athos in a broken voice.

Mme Bonacieux opened her eyes again under d'Artagnan's kisses.

"She's reviving!" cried the young man. "Oh, my God, my God, I thank you!"

"Madame," said Athos, "Madame, in the name of heaven, whose is this empty glass?"

"Mine, Monsieur . . ." the young woman replied in a dying voice.

"But who poured you the wine that was in this glass?"

"*She* did."

"But who is this *she*?"

"Ah, I remember," said Mme Bonacieux, "the countess de Winter . . ."

The four friends cried out with one voice, but Athos's dominated the others.

Just then Mme Bonacieux's face became livid, a dull pain overwhelmed her, she fell gasping into the arms of Porthos and Aramis.

D'Artagnan seized Athos's hands with an anguish difficult to describe.

"And what," he said, "you think . . ."

His voice died out in a sob.

"I think everything," said Athos, biting his lips till they bled.

"D'Artagnan, d'Artagnan!" cried Mme Bonacieux. "Where are you? Don't leave me, you can see I'm going to die."

D'Artagnan let go of Athos's hands, which he was still holding clenched in his own, and ran to her.

His handsome face was all distorted, his glassy eyes no longer saw anything, a convulsive trembling shook his body, sweat streamed from his brow.

"In the name of heaven, run for someone! Porthos, Aramis, call for help!"

"No use," said Athos, "no use. To the poison she pours out, there is no antidote."

"Yes," murmured Mme Bonacieux, "help, help!"

Then, gathering all her strength, she took the young man's head in her hands, looked at him for a moment as if all her soul were in that look, and, with a sobbing cry, pressed her lips to his.

"Constance! Constance!" cried d'Artagnan.

A sigh escaped from Mme Bonacieux's mouth as it brushed against d'Artagnan's; that sigh was her chaste and loving soul ascending to heaven.

D'Artagnan held only a lifeless body in his arms.

The young man cried out and fell down beside his mistress, as pale and chill as she was.

Porthos wept, Aramis raised his fist to heaven, Athos made the sign of the cross.

At that moment a young man appeared in the doorway, almost as pale as those who were in the room, looked all around him, and saw Mme Bonacieux dead and d'Artagnan unconscious.

He appeared just at that moment of stupor that follows great catastrophes.

"I was not mistaken," he said. "Here is M. d'Artagnan, and you are his three friends, MM. Athos, Porthos, and Aramis."

Those whose names had just been spoken looked at the stranger in astonishment. All three seemed to recognize him.

"Gentlemen," the newcomer went on, "you, like me, are searching for a woman. She must have passed this way," he added with a terrible smile, "for I see a dead body!"

The three friends remained mute; only the voice, like the face, reminded them of a man they had already seen, though they could not remember in what circumstances.

"Gentlemen," the stranger continued, "since you do not wish to recognize a man who probably owes you his life twice over, I shall have to name myself: I am Lord de Winter, that woman's brother-in-law."

The three friends cried out in surprise.

Athos stood up and held out his hand to him.

"Welcome, Milord," he said, "you are one of us."

"I left Portsmouth five hours after her," said Lord de Winter, "I reached Boulogne three hours after her, I missed her by twenty minutes at Saint-Omer; finally, at Lillers, I lost her trail. I was going around at random, questioning everybody, when I saw you gallop by. I recognized M. d'Artagnan. I called out to you, but you didn't answer me. I wanted to follow you, but my horse was too tired to keep pace with yours. And yet it seems that, despite all your speed, you still came too late!"

"As you see," said Athos, indicating to Lord de Winter the dead Mme Bonacieux, and d'Artagnan, whom Porthos and Aramis were trying to revive.

"Are they both dead, then?" Lord de Winter asked coldly.

"No, fortunately," replied Athos, "M. d'Artagnan has simply fainted."

"Ah, so much the better!" said Lord de Winter.

Indeed, at that moment d'Artagnan opened his eyes again.

He tore himself from the arms of Porthos and Aramis and threw himself like a madman on the body of his mistress.

Athos got up, went to his friend with a slow and solemn step, embraced him tenderly, and, as he burst into sobs, said to him in his noble and impressive voice:

"Be a man, my friend: women weep for the dead, men avenge them!"

"Oh, yes!" said d'Artagnan, "yes, if it's to avenge her, I'm ready to follow you!"

Athos profited from this moment of strength, which the hope of vengeance had restored to his unfortunate friend, to make a sign for Porthos and Aramis to go and fetch the mother superior.

The two friends met her in the corridor, still all upset and distraught from so many events. She summoned several nuns, who, against all monastic custom, found themselves in the presence of five men.

"Madame," said Athos, taking d'Artagnan's arm under his own, "we leave to your pious care the body of this unfortunate woman. She was an angel on earth before being an angel in heaven. Treat her as one of your sisters; we shall come back one day to pray on her grave."

D'Artagnan hid his face on Athos's chest and burst into sobs.

"Weep," said Athos, "weep, heart filled with love, youth, and life! Alas, I wish I could weep like you!"

And, affectionate as a father, comforting as a priest, great as a man who has suffered much, he led his friend away.

All five, followed by their valets who led their horses by the bridle, went towards the town of Béthune, whose outskirts they could see, and stopped at the first inn they came to.

"But," said d'Artagnan, "aren't we going to go after that woman?"

"Later," said Athos. "There are measures I must take."

"She'll escape us," said the young man, "she'll escape us, and it will be your fault."

"I'll answer for her," said Athos.

D'Artagnan had such confidence in his friend's word that he bowed his head and went into the inn without any reply.

Porthos and Aramis looked at each other, not understanding Athos's assurance at all.

Lord de Winter thought he spoke that way to soften d'Artagnan's grief.

"Now, gentlemen," said Athos, when he had made sure that there were five vacant rooms in the hotel, "let us each retire to his own room. D'Artagnan needs to be alone to weep, and you to sleep. Don't worry, I take everything upon myself."

"It seems to me, however," said Lord de Winter, "that if there are measures to be taken against the countess, that is my concern: she is my sister-in-law."

"Yes," said Athos, "but she is my wife."

D'Artagnan shuddered, for he understood that Athos was certain of his vengeance, since he had given away such a secret. Porthos and Aramis looked at each other and turned pale. Lord de Winter thought Athos was mad.

"Retire, then," said Athos, "and leave it to me. You see very well that, in my quality as husband, it is my concern. Only, d'Artagnan, if you haven't lost it, give me back the paper which fell from that man's hat and had the name of a town written on it."

"Ah!" said d'Artagnan, "I understand, the name was written in her hand . . ."

"So you see," said Athos, "there is a God in heaven!"

LXIV

THE MAN IN THE RED CLOAK

Athos's despair had given way to a concentrated grief, which made the man's brilliant mental faculties still more lucid.

Given entirely to one thought, that of the promise he had made and the responsibility he had taken on, he was the last to retire to his room. He asked the host to bring him a map of the province, bent over it, studied the lines traced out, discovered that four different roads went from Béthune to Armentières, and had the valets summoned.

Planchet, Grimaud, Mousqueton, and Bazin presented themselves and received clear, precise, and stern orders from Athos.

They were to leave at daybreak the next morning and go to Armentières, each by a different route. Planchet, the most intelligent of the four, was to follow the one down which the carriage that the four friends had fired upon had disappeared, accompanied, it will be remembered, by Rochefort's servant.

Athos put the valets in the field, first of all, because, since these men had been in his and his friends' service, he had discerned different and essential qualities in each of them.

Then, valets who question passersby arouse less suspicion than their masters, and find more sympathy among those they approach.

Finally, Milady knew the masters, while she did not know the valets. On the other hand, the valets knew Milady perfectly well.

All four were to meet together the next day, at eleven o'clock, in the appointed place. If they had discovered Milady's retreat, three would remain to keep watch, the fourth would return to Béthune to inform Athos and serve as guide for the four friends.

Once these dispositions were made, the four valets retired in their turn.

Athos then got up from his chair, buckled on his sword, wrapped himself in his cloak, and left the hotel. It was around ten o'clock. At ten o'clock, as is known, provincial streets are nearly deserted. Yet Athos was obviously looking for someone to whom he could put a question. At last he met a belated passerby, went up to him, and said a few words. The man he addressed drew back in horror, but answered the musketeer's words by pointing his finger. Athos offered the man a half pistole to accompany him, but the man refused.

Athos went down the street that the pointer had indicated

to him with his finger; but, coming to an intersection, he stopped again, obviously perplexed. However, as one has more chance of meeting someone at a crossroads than anywhere else, he stood there. Indeed, after a moment a night watchman passed by. Athos repeated to him the question he had already put to the first person he had met. The night watchman evinced the same terror, refused in his turn to accompany Athos, and showed with his hand the road he should follow.

Athos walked off in the direction indicated and reached the outskirts at the opposite end of town from the one by which he and his friends had entered. There he again seemed worried and perplexed, and he stopped for the third time.

Fortunately, a beggar came along, who went up to Athos to ask for alms. Athos offered him an écu to accompany him where he was going. The beggar hesitated for a moment, but on seeing the silver piece shining in the darkness, he made up his mind and went ahead of Athos.

Coming to the corner of a street, he showed him from afar an isolated, solitary, sad little house. Athos went up to it, while the beggar, who had received his salary, made off as fast as his legs would carry him.

Athos circled around the house before making out the door amidst the reddish color with which the house was painted. No light appeared through the chinks in the blinds, no sound led one to suppose it was inhabited, the place was as dark and silent as a tomb.

Three times Athos knocked without any response. At the third knock, however, footsteps approached from inside. Finally, the door half opened, and a tall, pale-faced man with black hair and beard looked out.

He and Athos exchanged a few words in low voices, then the tall man made a sign that the musketeer could come in. Athos profited from the permission at once, and the door closed again behind him.

The man whom Athos had come so far to seek, and whom he had had so much trouble finding, ushered him into his laboratory, where he was busy wiring together the rattling bones of a skeleton. The whole body was already reassembled: the head alone was sitting on the table.

All the rest of the furnishings indicated that the owner of the house was occupied with the natural sciences: there were bottles filled with snakes, labeled according to species; dried lizards gleamed like cut emeralds in big frames of black wood; finally, bunches of wild herbs, fragrant and no doubt endowed with virtues unknown to the common run of men, were tied to the ceiling and hung down in the corners of the room.

Moreover, no family, no servants; the tall man lived alone in this house.

Athos cast a cold and indifferent eye on all these objects we have just described, and, at the invitation of the man he had come to seek, sat down near him.

Then he explained to him the reason for his visit and the service he required of him. But he had hardly stated his request when the unknown man, who had remained standing in front of the musketeer, drew back in terror and refused. Then Athos took from his pocket a small paper on which two lines were written, accompanied by a signature and a seal, and presented it to the man, who had shown signs of repugnance too prematurely. The tall man had hardly read those two lines, seen the signature, and recognized the seal, when he nodded as a sign that he had no further objections and was ready to obey.

Athos asked for nothing more. He got up, bowed, left, took the same road back that he had taken in coming, returned to the hôtel, and shut himself up in his room.

At daybreak, d'Artagnan came in and asked what he was going to do.

"Wait," replied Athos.

A few moments later, the mother superior sent to inform the musketeers that the burial of Milady's victim would take place at noon. As for the poisoner, there was no news of her; only she must have escaped through the garden: her footprints had been recognized in the sandy path, and the gate was found locked again. As for the key, it had disappeared.

At the appointed hour, Lord de Winter and the four friends

went to the convent. The bells were ringing loudly, the chapel was open, the grille of the choir was closed. In the middle of the choir, the body of the victim, dressed in her novice's habit, was on view. On either side of the choir and behind the gates opening onto the convent, the entire community of the Carmelites was gathered, listening to the divine service and mingling their own singing with the chanting of the priests, without seeing the laymen or being seen by them.

At the door to the chapel, d'Artagnan felt his courage abandoning him again. He turned to look for Athos, but Athos had disappeared.

Faithful to his mission of vengeance, Athos had asked to be taken to the garden, and there, in the sand, following the light steps of this woman who had left a bloody trail wherever she had passed, he advanced as far as the gate that gave onto the wood, and penetrated into the forest.

Then all his suspicions were confirmed. The road down which the carriage had disappeared skirted the forest. Athos followed the road for a while, his eyes fixed on the ground; slight stains of blood, which came from a wound inflicted either on the man who accompanied the carriage or on one of the horses, marked out the way. After about three-quarters of a league, fifty paces from Festubert, a larger bloodstain appeared. The ground was trampled by horses. Between the forest and this telltale place, a little beyond the churned-up ground, he found again the same small footprints as in the garden. The carriage had stopped.

Here Milady had left the wood and climbed into the carriage.

Satisfied with this discovery, which confirmed all his suspicions, Athos went back to the hôtel and found Planchet there, waiting impatiently.

Everything was as Athos had foreseen.

Planchet had followed that road. Like Athos, he had noticed the bloodstains; like Athos, he had recognized the place where the horses had stopped; but he had pushed on further than Athos, and in the village of Festubert, while drinking in a tavern, had learned, without needing to ask questions, that the night before, at half-past eight, a wounded man, who was accompanying a lady traveling in a post chaise, had been obliged to stop, unable to go further. The incident had been blamed on thieves, who had supposedly stopped the carriage in the wood. The man had remained in the village; the woman had changed horses and continued on her way.

Planchet went in search of the postilion who had driven the post chaise, and found him. He had driven the lady as far as Fromelles, and from Fromelles she had set out for Armentières. Planchet went across country, and by seven in the morning was in Armentières.

There was only one hôtel, the Hôtel de la Poste. Planchet went to introduce himself as an unemployed lackey who was looking for a position. Before he had spoken ten minutes with the folk of the inn, he knew that a woman had arrived alone at eleven o'clock in the evening, had taken a room, had sent for the maître d'hôtel, and had told him that she wished to stay for a time in the neighborhood.

Planchet had no need to know more. He ran to the rendezvous, found the three punctual lackeys at their post, placed them as sentries at all the exits of the hotel, and went to find Athos, who had just finished receiving Planchet's information when his friends came in.

All their faces were gloomy and tense, even the gentle face of Aramis.

"What must we do?" asked d'Artagnan.

"Wait," replied Athos.

Each of them retired to his own room.

At eight o'clock in the evening, Athos gave orders to saddle the horses, and informed Lord de Winter and his friends that they should make ready for the expedition.

In an instant all five were ready. Each of them saw to his weapons and put them in good order. Athos went down first and found d'Artagnan already mounted and growing impatient.

"Patience," said Athos, "we're still missing someone."

The four horsemen looked around them in astonishment, uselessly racking their brains for who this missing someone might be.

At that moment, Planchet brought Athos's horse, and the musketeer leaped lightly into the saddle.

"Wait for me," he said. "I'll be right back."

And he set off at a gallop.

A quarter of an hour later, he indeed came back, accompanied by a masked man wrapped in a large red cloak.

Lord de Winter and the three musketeers looked questioningly at each other. None of them could enlighten the others, for none of them knew who this man was. However, they thought that it ought to be so, since the thing had been done on Athos's orders.

At nine o'clock, guided by Planchet, the little cavalcade set off, taking the route that the carriage had followed.

It was a sorry sight to see these six men riding along in silence, each sunk in his own thoughts, dismal as despair, grim as retribution.

LXV

The Judgment

It was a dark and stormy night. Big clouds raced across the sky, veiling the brightness of the stars. The moon would not rise before midnight.

Sometimes, by a flash of lightning that gleamed on the horizon, the road could be seen stretching away white and solitary; then, when the lightning died out, everything fell back into darkness.

Athos kept asking d'Artagnan, who always rode at the head of the little troop, to fall back into line, but after a moment he would abandon it again. His only thought was to go on, and on he went.

They passed silently through the village of Festubert, where the wounded servant had stayed, then followed along the wood of Richebourg. On reaching Herlies, Planchet, who was still guiding the column, turned left.

Several times, Lord de Winter, or Porthos, or Aramis had tried to address a word to the man in the red cloak; but to each question put to him, he had nodded without replying. The travelers had understood then that there was some reason for the unknown man to keep silent, and they had stopped speaking to him.

Besides, the storm was building up, flashes of lightning came in rapid succession, thunder began to rumble, and the wind, precursor of the tempest, whistled across the plain, ruffling the horsemen's plumes.

The cavalcade went into a fast trot. Cloaks were unfurled. There were still three leagues to go: they made them under torrents of rain.

D'Artagnan had taken off his hat and had not put on his cloak; he found pleasure in letting the water stream down his burning brow and over his body, shaken with a feverish trembling.

Just as the little troop passed Goskal and was coming to the posting station, a man, sheltered under a tree, detached himself from the trunk with which he had blended in the darkness, and stepped into the middle of the road, putting his finger to his lips.

Athos recognized Grimaud.

"What is it?" cried d'Artagnan. "Has she left Armentières?"

Grimaud nodded his head affirmatively. D'Artagnan ground his teeth.

"Silence, d'Artagnan!" said Athos. "It is I who have taken charge of everything, so it is for me to question Grimaud.

"Where is she?" asked Athos.

Grimaud stretched out his hand in the direction of the Lys.

"Far from here?" asked Athos.

Grimaud held up a bent index finger.

"Alone?" asked Athos.

Grimaud nodded yes.

"Gentlemen," said Athos, "she is alone, a half league from here, in the direction of the river."

"Very good," said d'Artagnan. "Lead us, Grimaud."

Grimaud set off across country and served as the cavalcade's guide.

After some five hundred paces, they came to a stream, which they forded.

In a flash of lightning, they made out the village of Erquinghem.

"Is it here?" asked d'Artagnan.

Grimaud shook his head negatively.

"Silence!" said Athos.

And the troop continued on its way.

There was another flash of lightning. Grimaud stretched out his arm, and in the bluish light of the fiery serpent they made out an isolated little house on the bank of the river, a hundred paces from a ferry. There was light in one window.

"Here we are," said Athos.

At that moment, a man lying in a ditch stood up. It was Mousqueton. He pointed to the lighted window.

"She's there," he said.

"And Bazin?" asked Athos.

"While I was watching the window, he's been watching the door."

"Good," said Athos, "you are all faithful servants."

Athos jumped down from his horse, gave the bridle to Grimaud, and went towards the window, after making a sign for the rest of the troop to circle around to the side where the door was.

The little house was surrounded by a quickset hedge two or three feet high. Athos went through the hedge and came to the window, which was shutterless but had its half curtains carefully drawn.

He climbed on the stone windowsill, so that he could look over the curtains.

By the light of a lamp, he saw a woman wrapped in a dark-colored mantle sitting on a stool near a dying fire. Her elbows were resting on a shabby table, and her head was propped in her ivory white hands.

Her face could not be seen, but a sinister smile passed over Athos's lips: there was no mistake, she was indeed the woman he was looking for.

Just then a horse whinnied. Milady raised her head, saw the pale face of Athos pressed to the window, and uttered a cry.

Athos realized that he had been recognized, shoved against the window with his knee and hand, the window yielded, the glass broke.

And Athos, like the spectre of vengeance, leaped into the room.

Milady ran to the door and opened it: paler and still more threatening than Athos, d'Artagnan stood on the threshold.

Milady backed away with a cry. D'Artagnan, believing she had some means of escape and fearing she would elude them, drew a pistol from his belt, but Athos raised his hand.

"Put up your weapon, d'Artagnan," he said. "It is important that this woman be judged and not simply killed. Wait a moment longer, d'Artagnan, and you will be satisfied. Come in, gentlemen."

D'Artagnan obeyed, for Athos had the solemn voice and the powerful gesture of a judge sent by the Lord himself. And so, after d'Artagnan, Porthos came in, followed by Aramis, Lord de Winter, and the man in the red cloak.

The four valets guarded the door and the window.

Milady had fallen into her chair with her arms stretched out, as if to ward off this terrible apparition. On glimpsing her brother-in-law, she uttered a terrible cry.

"What do you want?" exclaimed Milady.

"We want Charlotte Backson," said Athos, "who was first called the comtesse de La Fère, then Lady de Winter, Baroness Sheffield."

"That's me, that's me!" she murmured, at the height of terror. "What do you want of me?"

"We want to judge you according to your crimes," said Athos. "You will be free to defend yourself. Justify yourself, if you can. M. d'Artagnan, it is for you to make the first accusation."

D'Artagnan stepped forward.

"Before God and men," he said, "I accuse this woman of poisoning Constance Bonacieux, who died yesterday evening."

He turned to Porthos and Aramis.

"We testify to it," the two musketeers said with one impulse.

D'Artagnan continued.

"Before God and men, I accuse this woman of having wished to poison me by means of wine she had sent to me from Villeroy with a false letter, as if the wine came from my friends. God saved me, but a man whose name was Brisemont is dead in my place."

"We testify to it," Porthos and Aramis said with one voice.

"Before God and men, I accuse this woman of having urged me to murder the baron de Wardes, "and, as no one is here to testify to the truth of this accusation, I testify to it myself. I have spoken."

And d'Artagnan crossed to the other side of the room with Porthos and Aramis.

"It is your turn, Milord!" said Athos.

The baron stepped forward.

"Before God and men," he said, "I accuse this woman of having the duke of Buckingham assassinated."

"The duke of Buckingham assassinated?" those present all cried out as one.

"Yes," said the baron, "assassinated! On receiving your letter of warning, I had this woman arrested, and I placed her in the custody of a loyal servant. She corrupted the man, she put the dagger in his hand, she had him kill the duke, and at this very moment, perhaps, Felton is paying for this fury's crime with his head."

A shudder ran through the judges at the revealing of these previously unknown crimes.

"That is not all," Lord de Winter went on. "My brother, who had made you his heir, died in three hours of a strange illness which left livid spots all over his body. My sister, how did your husband die?"

"What horror!" cried Porthos and Aramis.

"Assassin of Buckingham, assassin of Felton, assassin of my brother, I demand justice against you, and I declare that if it is not done me, I will do it myself."

And Lord de Winter went to stand beside d'Artagnan, leaving his place open for another accuser.

Milady buried her face in her hands and tried to collect her wits, caught up in a deadly whirl.

"It is my turn," said Athos, trembling as a lion trembles at the sight of a snake, "it is my turn. I married this woman when she was a young girl; I married her in spite of all my family; I gave her my property, I gave her my name; and one day I discovered that this woman was branded: this woman was marked with a fleur-de-lis on her left shoulder."

"Oh!" said Milady, rising, "I defy you to find the tribunal that pronounced that infamous sentence against me. I defy you to find the one who carried it out."

"Silence," said a voice. "That is for me to answer!"

And the man in the red cloak stepped forward in his turn.

"Who is this man, who is this man?" cried Milady, choking with terror, her hair undone and standing up on her livid head as if alive.

All eyes turned to this man, for he was unknown to all of them except Athos.

But Athos, too, looked at him with as much stupefaction as the others, for he did not know how he could turn out to be involved somehow in the horrible drama that was unfolding at that moment.

After approaching Milady with a slow and solemn step, so that only the table separated him from her, the unknown man took off his mask.

With ever increasing terror, Milady gazed for a long time at that pale face framed by black hair and side-whiskers, whose only expression was an icy impassivity. All at once she said, "Oh, no, no!"—getting up and backing towards the wall. "Help me! help me!" she cried in a hoarse voice, turning to the wall, as if she could open a way through it with her hands.

"But who are you, then?" cried all the witnesses to this scene.

"Ask this woman," said the man in the red cloak, "for you can see very well that she has recognized me."

"The executioner of Lille, the executioner of Lille!" cried

Milady, prey to a mad terror and clinging to the wall with her hands so as not to fall.

Everyone stepped back, and the man in the red cloak was left standing alone in the middle of the room.

"Oh, mercy! mercy! forgive me!" the wretched woman cried, falling to her knees.

The unknown man let silence be restored.

"I told you she had recognized me. Yes, I am the executioner of the town of Lille, and here is my story."

All eyes were fixed on this man, whose words were awaited with an avid anxiousness.

"This young woman was once a young girl, just as beautiful as she is today. She was a nun in the Benedictine convent of Templemar. A young priest of a simple and believing heart served in the church of this convent. She set about to seduce him, and she succeeded—she could have seduced a saint.

"The vows they had both taken were sacred, irrevocable; their liaison could not last long without ruining them both. She got him to agree that they should leave that part of the country. But to leave there, to run off together, to go to another part of France, where they could live peacefully because they would not be known, required money. Neither of them had any. The priest stole the sacred vessels and sold them; but as they were getting ready to leave together, they were both arrested.

"Eight days later, she had seduced the jailer's son and escaped. The young priest was sentenced to branding and ten years in irons. I was the executioner of the town of Lille, as this woman said. I was obliged to brand the guilty man, and the guilty man, gentlemen, was my own brother!

"I swore then that this woman who had ruined him, who was more than his accomplice, since it was she who had driven him to crime, would at least share the punishment. I guessed where she was hiding, pursued her, found her, bound her, and printed upon her the same brand I had printed upon my brother.

"The day after my return to Lille, my brother managed to escape in his turn. I was accused of complicity and was sentenced to sit in prison in his place for as long as he did not give himself up. My poor brother knew nothing of this verdict. He had rejoined this woman, and they had fled together to Berry. There he obtained a small parish. This woman passed for his sister.

"The lord of the land on which the curate's church was located saw this supposed sister and fell in love with her, so much in love that he proposed marriage to her. Then she left the man she had ruined for the one she would ruin, and became the comtesse de La Fère . . ."

All eyes turned to Athos, whose real name this was, and he nodded as a sign that everything the executioner had said was true.

"Then," the latter went on, "mad, desperate, resolved to rid himself of an existence from which she had taken all honor and happiness, my poor brother returned to Lille, and learning of the decree that had condemned me in his place, gave himself up and hanged himself that same night from the bars of his prison window.

"Moreover, to do them justice, those who had sentenced me kept their word. The identity of the body had scarcely been established before they restored me to liberty.

"That is the crime I accuse her of, that is the reason why I branded her."

"Monsieur d'Artagnan," said Athos, "what penalty do you call for against this woman?"

"The penalty of death," replied d'Artagnan.

"Milord de Winter," Athos continued, "what penalty do you call for against this woman?"

"The penalty of death," answered Lord de Winter.

"MM. Porthos and Aramis," Athos went on, "you who are her judges, what penalty do you bring against this woman?"

"The penalty of death," the two musketeers replied in the same hollow voice.

Milady uttered a dreadful cry and moved several paces towards her judges, dragging herself on her knees.

Athos held his hand out towards her.

"Anne de Breuil, Comtesse de La Fère, Milady de Winter," he said, "your crimes have wearied men on earth and God in heaven. If you know any prayer, say it, for you are condemned, and you shall die."

At these words, which left her no hope, Milady raised herself to her full height and was about to speak, but her strength failed her. She felt a powerful and implacable hand seize her by the hair and drag her away as irrevocably as fate drags man. Thus, without even trying to offer resistance, she left the cottage.

Lord de Winter, d'Artagnan, Athos, Porthos, and Aramis left after her. The valets followed their masters, and the room remained deserted, with its broken window, its open door, and its smoky lamp burning sadly on the table.

LXVI

The Execution

It was approaching midnight. The moon, cut away by its waning and bloodied by the last traces of the storm, rose behind the little village of Armentières, which stood out against its pale light with the dark silhouette of its houses and the skeleton of its tall openwork belfry. Opposite, the Lys rolled its waters like a river of molten pewter, while on the far bank one could see the black mass of trees profiled against a stormy sky invaded by dense, coppery clouds that made a sort of twilight in the middle of the night. To the left rose an old abandoned mill with motionless sails, in the ruins of which a screech owl uttered its sharp, recurrent, and monotonous cry. Here and there on the plain, to right and left of the path followed by the lugubrious procession, a few low and thickset trees appeared, looking like misshapen dwarfs crouching in wait for men at that sinister hour.

From time to time a big flash of lightning opened the horizon out in all its breadth, snaked over the black mass of trees, and came like a frightful scimitar to cut the sky and water in two. Not a breath of wind stirred in the heavy atmosphere. A deathly silence weighed upon all of nature. The ground was wet and slippery from the recent rain, and the revived grasses gave off their scent more energetically.

Two valets dragged Milady, each holding her by an arm. The executioner walked behind them, and Lord de Winter, d'Artagnan, Athos, Porthos, and Aramis walked behind the executioner.

Planchet and Bazin brought up the rear.

The two valets brought Milady to the riverside. Her mouth was mute, but her eyes spoke with inexpressible eloquence, pleading by turns with each person she looked at.

As she found herself a few paces ahead, she said to the valets:

"A thousand pistoles for each of you if you cover my flight; but if you hand me over to your masters, I have avengers nearby who will make you pay dearly for my death."

Grimaud hesitated. Mousqueton trembled all over.

Athos, who had heard Milady's voice, came up quickly, as did Lord de Winter.

"Send these valets away," he said. "She has spoken to them; they are no longer trustworthy."

They called Planchet and Bazin, who replaced Grimaud and Mousqueton.

When they reached the water's edge, the executioner went up to Milady and bound her hands and feet.

Then she broke her silence to cry out:

"You are cowards, you are wretched assassins, it takes ten of you to cut one woman's throat! Watch out, for if I'm not rescued, I will be avenged."

"You are not a woman," Athos said coldly, "you do not belong to humankind, you are a demon escaped from hell, and we are going to send you back there."

"Ah, the gentlemen are men of virtue!" said Milady. "Mind you that he who touches a hair of my head is an assassin in his turn."

"An executioner may kill without for all that being an assassin, Madame," said the man in the red cloak, tapping his broad sword. "He is the last judge, that is all—*Nachrichter,** as our German neighbors say."

*Literally, "he who comes after the judge."

And as he was binding her while saying these words, Milady uttered two or three wild cries, which made a gloomy and strange effect as they flew off into the night and lost themselves in the depths of the wood.

"But if I am guilty, if I have committed the crimes you accuse me of," shouted Milady, "bring me before a tribunal. You are no judges to condemn me!"

"I offered you Tyburn," said Lord de Winter. "Why didn't you want it?"

"Because I don't want to die!" Milady cried, struggling. "Because I'm too young to die!"

"The woman you poisoned in Béthune was even younger than you, Madame, and yet she is dead," said d'Artagnan.

"I'll enter a convent, I'll become a nun," said Milady.

"You were in a convent," said the executioner, "and you left it to ruin my brother."

Milady uttered a terror-stricken cry and fell to her knees.

The executioner picked her up in his arms and was about to carry her to the boat.

"Oh, my God!" she cried, "my God! are you going to drown me?"

There was something so heartrending in these cries that d'Artagnan, who at first had been the most relentless in his pursuit of Milady, sank down on a stump and hung his head, stopping his ears with the palms of his hands. And yet, despite that, he still heard her threatening and crying out.

D'Artagnan was the youngest of all these men, and his heart failed him.

"Oh, I can't bear to see this frightful spectacle! I can't consent that the woman should die like this!"

Milady heard these few words and recovered a glimmer of hope.

"D'Artagnan! d'Artagnan!" she cried, "remember that I loved you!"

The young man got up and took a step towards her.

But Athos suddenly drew his sword and barred his way.

"If you take one more step, d'Artagnan," he said, "we will cross swords."

D'Artagnan fell to his knees and prayed.

"Come, executioner," Athos continued, "do your duty."

"Gladly, Monseigneur," said the executioner, "for as truly as I am a good Catholic, I firmly believe I am being just in carrying out my function on this woman."

"Very well."

Athos took a step towards Milady.

"I forgive you," he said, "the evil you have done me; I forgive you my future shattered, my honor lost, my love tainted, and my salvation forever compromised by the despair into which you have thrown me. Die in peace."

Lord de Winter came forward in his turn.

"I forgive you," he said, "the poisoning of my brother, the assassination of His Grace the duke of Buckingham; I forgive you the death of poor Felton, and I forgive you your attempts on my person. Die in peace."

"And I," said d'Artagnan, "ask you to forgive me, Madame, for having provoked your anger by a deception unworthy of a gentleman; and, in return, I forgive you the murder of my poor love and your cruel vengeance upon me. I forgive you and I weep for you. Die in peace."

"I am lost!" Milady murmured in English. "I must die."

Then she stood up by herself and cast around her one of those bright glances that seemed to spring from a blazing eye.

She saw nothing.

She listened and heard nothing.

She had only enemies around her.

"Where am I to die?" she asked.

"On the other bank," replied the executioner.

Then he put her in the boat, and, as he was about to step into it, Athos handed him a sum of money.

"Here," he said, "this is the price of the execution. Let it be plainly seen that we are acting as judges."

"Very well," said the executioner. "And now let this woman know, in her turn, that I am not carrying out my profession, but my duty."

And he threw the money into the river.

The boat moved off towards the left bank of the Lys, bearing the guilty woman and the executioner. The others all stayed on the right bank, where they had fallen to their knees.

The boat glided slowly along the rope of the ferry, under the reflection of a pale cloud that hung over the water at that moment.

They saw it land on the other bank. The figures stood out black against the reddish horizon.

During the crossing, Milady had managed to untie the rope that bound her feet. On reaching the shore, she jumped out lightly and started running.

But the ground was wet; on reaching the top of the embankment, she slipped and fell to her knees.

A superstitious idea must have struck her. She understood that heaven was refusing her its aid, and she remained in the attitude in which she found herself, her head bowed and her hands joined.

Then, from the other bank, they saw the executioner slowly raise both arms, a ray of moonlight gleamed on the blade of his broad sword, both arms fell again, they heard the hiss of the scimitar and the cry of the victim, and a truncated mass sank under the blow.

Then the executioner unclasped his red cloak, spread it on the ground, laid the body on it, threw in the head, tied it by its four corners, loaded it on his shoulder, and got back into the boat.

Coming to the middle of the Lys, he stopped the boat, and holding his burden up over the river, cried in a loud voice:

"Let God's justice be done!"

And he dropped the dead body into the deepest part of the water, which closed over it.

Three days later, the four musketeers reentered Paris. They had kept within the limits of their leave, and that same evening they went to pay their accustomed visit to M. de Tréville.

"Well, gentlemen," the brave captain asked them, "did you amuse yourselves well on your excursion?"

"Prodigiously," said Athos, clenching his teeth.

LXVII

CONCLUSION

On the sixth of the following month, the king, keeping the promise he had made the cardinal to quit Paris and return to La Rochelle, left his capital still stunned by the news just spreading there that Buckingham had been assassinated.

The queen, though warned that the man she had loved so was in danger, refused to believe it when his death was announced to her. She even went so far as to cry out imprudently:

"It's not true! He has just written to me!"

But the next day she was forced to believe this fatal news. La Porte, detained in England like everyone else by the orders of King Charles I, arrived bearing the last doleful present that Buckingham had sent to the queen.

The king's joy was very keen. He did not bother to disguise it, and even showed it blatantly before the queen. Louis XIII, like all weak hearts, lacked generosity.

But the king soon became gloomy and ill-humored again: his brow was not the sort that clears for long. He felt that in returning to the camp he was going back into slavery, and yet he returned.

The cardinal was the fascinating serpent for him, and he was the bird that flits from branch to branch without being able to escape him.

And so the return to La Rochelle was profoundly sad. Our four friends especially aroused the astonishment of their comrades. They traveled together, side by side, their eyes grim and their heads bowed. Athos alone raised his broad brow from time to time; his eyes flashed, a bitter smile passed over his lips; then, like his comrades, he let himself lapse again into his ruminations.

As soon as the escort arrived in a town, once they had taken the king to his lodgings, the four friends withdrew either to their own quarters or to some out-of-the-way tavern, where they neither gambled nor drank; they only spoke in low voices, looking around carefully to see that no one was listening to them.

One day when the king had made a halt en route in order to hawk for magpies, and the four friends, as was their habit, instead of following the hunt, had stopped off in a tavern on the main road, a man who came galloping from La Rochelle stopped at the door to have a glass of wine and glanced into the room where the four musketeers were sitting at a table.

"Ho, there! M. d'Artagnan!" he said. "Is that you?"

D'Artagnan raised his head and uttered a cry of joy. This man, whom he called his phantom, was the unknown man of Meung, the rue des Fossoyeurs, and Arras.

D'Artagnan drew his sword and rushed for the door.

But this time, instead of fleeing, the unknown man leaped from his horse, and advanced to meet d'Artagnan.

"Ah, Monsieur!" said the young man, "so I've found you at last! This time you won't escape me."

"Nor is that my intention, Monsieur, for this time I am seeking you. In the name of the king, I arrest you and declare that you must surrender your sword to me, Monsieur, and that without any resistance. Your life depends on it, I warn you."

"Who are you, then?" asked d'Artagnan, lowering his sword, but without surrendering it yet.

"I am the chevalier de Rochefort," replied the unknown man, "equerry to M. le cardinal de Richelieu, and I have orders to bring you to His Eminence."

"We are returning to His Eminence, Monsieur le chevalier," said Athos, stepping forward, "and you will certainly accept M. d'Artagnan's word that he is going directly to La Rochelle."

"I must place him in the hands of guards, who will take him back to the camp."

"We will serve him for that, Monsieur, on our word as gentlemen. But, also on our word as gentlemen," Athos added, frowning, "M. d'Artagnan will not part from us."

The chevalier de Rochefort cast a glance behind him and saw that Porthos and Aramis had placed themselves between him and the door. He understood that he was entirely at the mercy of these four men.

"Gentlemen," he said, "if M. d'Artagnan will surrender his sword to me and join his word to yours, I will content

myself with your promise to bring him to the quarters of
Monseigneur le cardinal."

"You have my word, Monsieur," said d'Artagnan, "and
here is my sword."

"That is all the better for me," added Rochefort, "for I
must continue my journey."

"If it's to rejoin Milady," Athos said coldly, "there's no use,
you won't find her."

"What's become of her?" Rochefort asked sharply.

"Go back to camp and you'll find out."

Rochefort stood in thought for a moment, then, as it was
no more than a day's journey to Surgères, where the cardinal
was to come to meet the king, he decided to follow Athos's advice and go back with them.

Besides, this return offered him an advantage, which was
to keep watch on his prisoner himself.

They set out again.

The next day, at three o'clock in the afternoon, they came to
Surgères. The cardinal was there waiting for Louis XIII. The
minister and the king exchanged many flatteries, and congratulated each other on the stroke of luck that had rid France of the
relentless enemy who had been stirring up Europe against her.
After which, the cardinal, who had been informed by Rochefort
that d'Artagnan had been arrested, and who was anxious to see
him, took leave of the king, inviting him to come the next day to
see the work on the dike, which had been completed.

On returning in the evening to his quarters at the pont de
La Pierre, the cardinal found, standing before the door of the
house he lived in, d'Artagnan without a sword and the three
musketeers armed.

This time, as he was in force, he looked at them sternly
and made a sign with his eye and hand for d'Artagnan to follow him.

D'Artagnan obeyed.

"We'll be waiting for you, d'Artagnan," said Athos, loudly
enough for the cardinal to hear it.

His Eminence frowned, stopped for a moment, then continued on his way without saying a single word.

D'Artagnan went in after the cardinal, and Rochefort after d'Artagnan. The door was guarded.

His Eminence went to the room that served as his study and made a sign for Rochefort to usher in the young musketeer.

Rochefort obeyed and withdrew.

D'Artagnan remained alone facing the cardinal. It was his second interview with Richelieu, and he confessed afterwards that he had been convinced it would be his last.

Richelieu remained standing, leaning against the fireplace. A table stood between him and d'Artagnan.

"Monsieur," said the cardinal, "you have been arrested on my orders."

"I was told that, Monseigneur."

"Do you know why?"

"No, Monseigneur, for the one thing I could be arrested for is not yet known to His Eminence."

Richelieu looked fixedly at the young man.

"Oho!" he said, "what does that mean?"

"If Monseigneur will first tell me the crimes I am accused of, I will then tell him the deeds I have done."

"You are accused of crimes which have made heads higher than yours roll, Monsieur!" said the cardinal.

"What are they, Monseigneur?" asked d'Artagnan, with a calm that astounded the cardinal himself.

"You are accused of having corresponded with the enemies of the realm, you are accused of having betrayed state secrets, you are accused of having tried to make your general's plans miscarry."

"And who accuses me of that, Monseigneur?" asked d'Artagnan, who suspected that the imputations came from Milady. "A woman branded by the justice of the land, a woman who married one man in France and another in England, a woman who poisoned her second husband and who tried to poison me!"

"What are you saying, Monsieur?" cried the astonished cardinal. "Of what woman are you speaking in this way?"

"Of Milady de Winter," replied d'Artagnan. "Yes, of Milady

de Winter, of whose many crimes Your Eminence was no doubt unaware when you honored her with your trust."

"Monsieur," said the cardinal, "if Milady de Winter has committed the crimes you say, she will be punished."

"She has been, Monseigneur."

"And who punished her?"

"We did."

"She is in prison?"

"She is dead."

"Dead?" repeated the cardinal, who could not believe his ears. "Dead? Did you say she was dead?"

"Three times she tried to kill me, and I forgave her. But she killed the woman I loved. Then my friends and I caught her, tried her, and condemned her."

And D'Artagnan recounted the poisoning of Mme Bonacieux in the convent of the Carmelites in Béthune, the trial in the isolated house, the execution on the banks of the Lys.

A shudder ran through the cardinal's body, though he did not shudder easily.

But all at once, as if under the influence of some mute thought, the cardinal's physiognomy, sombre up to then, began to brighten little by little until it reached the most perfect serenity.

"And so," he said, in a voice whose gentleness contrasted with the severity of his words, "you set yourselves up as judges, without considering that those who have no mission to punish and who punish anyway are murderers!"

"Monseigneur, I swear to you that I have never for a moment had the intention of defending my head against you. I will submit to the punishment that Your Eminence wishes to inflict on me. I am not so attached to life as to fear death."

"Yes, I know, you are a man of courage, Monsieur," said the cardinal, in an almost affectionate voice. "I can therefore tell you in advance that you will be tried, and even condemned."

"Another might reply to Your Eminence that he has his pardon in his pocket. As for me, I will content myself with saying to you: give your order, Monseigneur, I am ready."

"Your pardon?" Richelieu asked in surprise.

"Yes, Monseigneur," said d'Artagnan.

"And signed by whom? By the king?"

And the cardinal uttered these words with a singular expression of contempt.

"No, by Your Eminence."

"By me? Are you mad, Monsieur?"

"Monseigneur will undoubtedly recognize his own handwriting."

And d'Artagnan presented to the cardinal the precious paper that Athos had wrested from Milady, and which he had given to d'Artagnan to serve him as a safeguard.

His Eminence took the paper and read in a slow voice, stressing each syllable:

It is by my orders and for the good of the State that the bearer of this present has done what he has done.

In the camp before La Rochelle, this 5 August 1628.

Richelieu

After reading these two lines, the cardinal fell to pondering deeply, but he did not give the paper back to d'Artagnan.

"He's considering by what sort of execution he'll have me die," d'Artagnan said to himself. "Well, by heaven, he'll see how a gentleman dies!"

The young musketeer was perfectly well disposed for a heroic passing.

Richelieu went on thinking, rolling and unrolling the paper in his hands. Finally he raised his head, fixed his eagle eye on that loyal, open, intelligent physiognomy, read on that tear-furrowed face all the sufferings he had endured over the past month, and reflected for the third or fourth time on how much future this boy of twenty-one had before him, and what resources his activity, courage, and spirit could offer to a good master.

On the other hand, the crimes, the power, the infernal genius of Milady had appalled him more than once. He felt a sort of secret joy at being rid forever of this dangerous accomplice.

He slowly tore up the paper that d'Artagnan had so generously given back to him.

"I'm lost," d'Artagnan said to himself.

And he bowed deeply before the cardinal, as one who says: "Lord, thy will be done!"

The cardinal went to the table, and, without sitting down, wrote a few lines on a parchment that was already two-thirds filled and set his seal to it.

"That is my condemnation," thought d'Artagnan. "He's sparing me the boredom of the Bastille and the delays of a trial. That's really quite nice of him."

"Here, Monsieur," the cardinal said to the young man, "I gave you one blank permit, and I am giving you another. The name is missing on this brevet: you will fill it in yourself."

D'Artagnan hesitantly took the paper and ran his eyes over it.

It was a lieutenancy in the musketeers.

D'Artagnan fell at the cardinal's feet.

"Monseigneur," he said, "my life is yours, dispose of it as you will; but this favor which you are granting me I do not deserve: I have three friends who are more deserving and more worthy . . ."

"You're a brave lad, d'Artagnan," the cardinal interrupted, patting him familiarly on the shoulder, delighted as he was to have conquered this rebellious nature. "Do as you please with this brevet. Only remember that, though the name is blank, it is to you that I am giving it."

"I will never forget that," replied d'Artagnan. "Your Eminence may be certain of it."

The cardinal turned and said in a loud voice: "Rochefort!"

The chevalier, who had no doubt been just outside the door, came in at once.

"Rochefort," said the cardinal, "here you see M. d'Artagnan. I am receiving him into the number of my friends. Kiss each other, then, and be sensible, if you care to keep your heads."

Rochefort and d'Artagnan barely brushed each other with their lips, but the cardinal was there, observing them with his watchful eye.

They left the room at the same time.

"We shall meet again, shall we not, Monsieur?"

"Whenever you like," said d'Artagnan.

"The chance will come," replied Rochefort.

"Eh?" said Richelieu, opening the door.

The two men smiled, shook hands, and bowed to His Eminence.

"We were beginning to get impatient," said Athos.

"Here I am, my friends," replied d'Artagnan, "not only free, but in favor."

"You'll tell us about it?"

"This very evening."

Indeed, that same evening d'Artagnan went to Athos's lodgings, where he found him in the process of emptying his bottle of Spanish wine, a task he performed religiously every evening.

He told him what had gone on between the cardinal and himself, and, taking the brevet from his pocket, said:

"Here, my dear Athos, this belongs quite naturally to you."

Athos smiled his gentle and charming smile.

"My friend," he said, "for Athos it is too much; for the comte de La Fère it is too little. Keep the brevet; it's yours. Alas, you've paid quite dearly for it!"

D'Artagnan left Athos's room and went into Porthos's.

He found him dressed in a magnificent outfit, covered with splendid embroidery, and looking at himself in the mirror.

"Aha!" said Porthos, "it's you, dear friend! How do you think this costume suits me?"

"Perfectly," said d'Artagnan, "but I've come to offer you an even more suitable outfit."

"Which?" asked Porthos.

"That of a lieutenant in the musketeers."

D'Artagnan told Porthos about his interview with the cardinal, and, taking the brevet from his pocket, said:

"Here, my dear, write your name on it, and be a good leader for me."

Porthos ran his eyes over the brevet and handed it back to d'Artagnan, to the young man's great astonishment.

"Yes," he said, "that would be quite flattering for me, but I wouldn't have long enough to enjoy the favor. During our expedition to Béthune, my duchess's husband died, my dear, so that, with the deceased's coffer holding its arms out to me, I'm marrying the widow. You see, I'm trying on my wedding outfit. Keep the lieutenancy, my dear, keep it."

And he returned the brevet to d'Artagnan.

The young man went into Aramis's room.

He found him kneeling before a prie-dieu, his forehead resting on his open book of hours.

He told him about his interview with the cardinal, and, taking the brevet from his pocket for the third time, said:

"You, our friend, our light, our invisible protector, accept this brevet. You have deserved it more than anyone, by your wisdom and your advice, which always brought such good results."

"Alas, dear friend!" said Aramis, "our latest adventures have disgusted me entirely with the life of a man of the sword. This time my choice is made irrevocably: after the siege, I am entering the Lazarists. Keep this brevet, d'Artagnan, the profession of arms suits you; you will be a brave and adventurous captain."

D'Artagnan, his eye moist with gratitude and shining with joy, went back to Athos, whom he found still at table and holding his last glass of Malaga up to the light of the lamp.

"Well," he said, "they also refused me."

"That is because no one, my dear friend, is more worthy of it than you."

He took a pen, wrote d'Artagnan's name on the brevet, and handed it back to him.

"So I'll have no more friends," said the young man. "Alas! nothing but bitter memories . . ."

And he let his head drop into his hands, while two tears rolled down his cheeks.

"You are young," replied Athos, "and your bitter memories have time to turn into sweet ones."

Epilogue

La Rochelle, deprived of the help of the English fleet and the division promised by Buckingham, surrendered after a year of siege. On the twenty-eighth of October 1628, the capitulation was signed.

The king made his entry into Paris on the twenty-third of December of the same year. He was given a triumph, as if he was coming back from defeating an enemy and not fellow Frenchmen. He entered by the faubourg Saint-Jacques under archways of greenery.

D'Artagnan took over his rank. Porthos left the service and, in the course of the following year, married Mme Coquenard. The so-coveted coffer contained eight hundred thousand livres.

Mousqueton got a magnificent livery, and on top of that the satisfaction, which he had sought all his life, of mounting behind a gilded carriage.

Aramis, after a trip to Lorraine, disappeared all at once and stopped writing to his friends. It was learned later, through Mme de Chevreuse, who told it to two or three of her lovers, that he had taken holy orders in a monastery in Nancy.

Bazin became a lay brother.

Athos remained a musketeer under d'Artagnan's command until 1633, at which time, following a trip to the Touraine, he also left the service, under the pretext that he had just come into a small inheritance in Rousillon.

Grimaud followed Athos.

D'Artagnan fought three times with Rochefort and wounded him three times.

"I'll probably kill you the fourth time," he said to him, as he offered a hand to get him to his feet.

"It would be better, then, for you and for me, if we stopped here," replied the wounded man. "Corbleu! I'm more of a friend to you than you think, for from our first meeting on, with one word to the cardinal, I could have had your throat cut."

This time they kissed each other good-heartedly and with no second thoughts.

Planchet obtained from Rochefort the rank of sergeant in the guards.

M. Bonacieux lived on quite peacefully, perfectly unaware of what had become of his wife and hardly worrying about it. One day he had the imprudence to remind the cardinal of his existence. In response, the cardinal said he would see to it that henceforth he lacked for nothing.

Indeed, the next day M. Bonacieux, having left his house at seven o'clock in the evening to go to the Louvre, never reappeared again on the rue des Fossoyeurs. The opinion of those who seemed best informed was that he was being housed and fed in some royal castle at the expense of His Generous Eminence.